By Desperate Appliance

By Desperate Appliance

R. M. Catton

Three Springs Book Company

This is a work of fiction. Any similarity
between the characters appearing here
and any real persons, living or dead, is purely coincidental.

FIRST EDITION

Published by Three Springs Book Company
45 Ridge Road Phoenixville, PA 19460

Transcribed and formatted by M-K Computing Services, Collegeville, PA

Manufactured in the United States of America
ISBN: 0-9762084-1-5

This book is dedicated to my friends and co-workers at the State Hospital

“ . . . diseases, desperate grown,
By desperate appliance are relieved,
Or not at all.”

— *Hamlet*, act 4, sc. 3

One

Carefully he looked up from the open page before him, squinting to focus on the distant, hazy thought called forth by the text. He adjusted the squint as he scanned the outer reaches of his consciousness, trying thus to hold open the boundaries of his peruse so that he might perceive what he felt, more than espied, was out there awaiting his retrieval. But the more he concentrated, the more the quarry seemed to recede. So he had the task of maintaining an oblique attentiveness necessary for luring closer the chimeric, unseen thought while carefully avoiding a direct pursuit that would assuredly close the border to its passage. Nothing new, really. He had been at this peculiar point countless times before, feeling each and every time that he was on the verge of some piercing insight or revelation, only to have the concentrated moment dissolve into vapors as though nothing of real substance had ever neared his grasp. Not unlike the ghost in Hamlet, he usually considered at such moments, savoring the Gothic murk of that thought. He tried to linger in this mental stance, hoping that a new wave of its press would move him closer to the nearly-perceived, almost-retrieved cognizance just beyond his shadow. But the dispelling glare of clarity was rising and he felt himself being moved farther and farther away from what he once again almost glimpsed into recognition. Now, as with each time before, it was swiftly becoming a matter of his awareness working against him, like turning on a light to get a better look at the dark.

He held his pose for a few more moments—elbows on the desk, hands closed and resting against his temples to steady his head—and once again experienced the decay of the verge as the sharpness of the immediate surround began to crowd his mind. In a minute or less, the transformation would be done, and the feeling of vexing incompleteness would close in. Then, to add to the nettling distraction of it all, there was no handy name or phrase for the experience itself. Years earlier as an adolescent he came across, or *thought* he came across, a French term similar to *déjà vu*, the more familiar expression of something having been experienced or seen before, and had since gone through dozens of books on foreign phrases, most medical dictionaries, plus every French dictionary he could lay his hands on in an effort to retrieve that lost, elusive term but with no more success than he had in capturing what he "almost saw" of the larger matter, that taunting "something" just beyond his view. Dutifully, he wondered often enough if his sense of once having actually come across that perfect term was itself merely a disconnected part of the larger, phantom-like phenomenon, which essentially was the ineffable feeling of his being on the verge of perceiving something penetrating, even cosmic, but never being any closer to grasping some part of it than in capturing the whole. The epistemology of it was daunting. There he was, the forever-aspirant knower, halted at the border of the transcendent knowable and left to grope for that tranformational generative password which, possessed, just might, Sesame-like, open to him the frontier of supereminent knowing. Surely, just having the password at hand would likely put him one up in getting well beyond the border into an Elysium of pure knowledge, as he suspected actually awaited. But he just couldn't recall that cursed password, though his search efforts predictably yielded degraded by-products to serve as work-a-day compensation, such as the term "lethologica," the inability to recall words, or "loganamnosis," an obsession for trying to recall forgotten words. Just wonderful. Worse, there it was once again: if you couldn't solve a problem just assign it a nifty new name and proclaim it work well done. Accordingly, he'd settled on naming his quirky presentiment—the feeling of almost seeing, or just about to see—as "being on the verge," or simply "the verge," since the French phrase *presque vu*—"almost seen"—he'd contrived and tried to apply simply did not sing. So by default it had become "the verge." Moreover, he never, ever mentioned any of it to anyone.

"Missed out, again," he mumbled, officially bringing the moment to a close. With the slightest of sighs he reached for his mug and sipped the now barely tepid coffee, feeling himself successful at least in that modest retrieval. His elbows still in place, he began to examine the mug abstractedly. Several hairline cracks laced its surface like wrinkles, prompting him to reflect on the many years he and his coffee mug had been meeting unfailingly at five o'clock each morning and sharing that quiet hour in a dedicated tryst that left each drained of what had been brimming. It was his way of ordering the elements of the waiting day. It was also the last remaining installment of a precious solitude, which he sorely coveted even as a boy but which he'd come to forfeit piece by piece as he acquired the bonding accoutrements of growth and maturity, this hour or so of early morning being the surviving principal in his privacy account that had suffered repeated draughts over the years in payment for that very growth. Hence, it was now rare indeed that any call on this time was allowed to invade the principal or to garnish its yield.

He took another sip of coffee and in doing so caught a fillip of movement on the right. It was the digital clock on his desk, flicking a new minute into position.

"Almost six o'clock," he noted as he scanned the clock-calculator-pen desk set positioned next to the lamp at the corner of his desk. He then looked up and matched the now graying window of his study with the numbers on the clock, 5:56, and found the two in suitable concordance, though again too soon in coming. "Where did the morning go?" he chuckled to himself as he returned his gaze to the clock. But this dollop of levity abruptly shifted to the wistful as his gaze acknowledged the small, engraved plaque affixed to the desk set beginning to show the patina of advanced age:

Frank A. Cantrelle, M.D.
From the Class of 1991
Moreland State Hospital

"Where did the *years* go?" he corrected himself in sober enlargement of his lament. He quickly regretted that query because he had now opened himself to a swell of poignancies—and rosy delights as well—that larded his reverie to overflow. Especially about his residents. All one hundred-odd of them. Eighteen year's worth of teaching, and each graduating class distinct in its own right, the last twelve under his directorship though he couldn't offhand remember that many separate groupings of graduates even if he were rash enough to try. But he did have a mental file card on each former resident, and with a little urging could resurrect any given graduate to open recall: moods, speech, mannerisms, needs, hurts—all the points of humanness which mark each of us to the other's ken. He often compared the bond he had to all of them to the bond we hold for the childhood of our children. The children grow, up and away, and the bond changes apace, but in our very richest memories of them our children are preserved as children, the tenderness of that wondrous time seeming to achieve fuller vintage in us with each passing year, ultimately becoming almost too tender to recall. And so it was with the residents, but to a lesser, more manageable degree and mercifully not while they were still in training, for feeling so then would put exactly the wrong accent on that strict, tutorial enterprise. Their task of learning and growing and becoming a psychiatrist was hard enough as it was, especially in these parlous times, and the keenness of tutorial focus needed no blunting come of paternalistic sentimentalism. And particularly so with him, given his position.

"Ho-hum," he sighed in mock tedium, "so very heavy a burden, this thing called responsibility. Rather makes one pause, doesn't it now?" he continued in playful banter with himself.

"Sure does," he replied from the alter position which usually could be counted on to play the part of the straight man, and just now a simpleton adroitly capable of naked truth. "And they say," his familiar continued, "the more lead in the ass, the heavier the responsibility seems."

"True, true, old rugger," he conceded, now shorn of pretense to tedium for his being called to accountability, "but since you're so damned watchful, where the hell were you when I was groping for that idea I almost thought?" he fired back, Parthian-like.

No answer. There never was when he called upon his other to explain itself. He had long ago learned that the best and only way to come to terms with his alter self and its pronouncements was simply to listen to it. Period. Any attempt to challenge it stilled it abruptly as though it abhorred any questioning of its proper dominion. Compliant banter it permitted, even encouraged, though never at the expense of its full ascendancy in the matter of overdue dialectic.

"All right, all right! You win," he affirmed in apology, hoping to court some residual contact.

Silence.

"Hamlet's ghost at least offered suggestions," he chided in a last effort to evoke some response.

But it was over. The silence now hung even heavier.

"Everything's slipping away from me this morning," he groused as he leaned back in his chair. The window had now brightened noticeably and he felt the beginning of the day's crowding presence. Soon noises of arousal would rise up within the house and he would take his place in their busy flow as they acquired human form.

He returned to the text lying open before him which now seemed more kindred to his mordant drift. He had been reviewing a section on toxic organic mental states; more specifically, mental disturbances, "syndromes," caused by different chemical substances. The list of culpable agents ranged from Alcohol to Zinc, with new ones being identified almost daily as industry and human inventiveness seemed to vie with each other in the production of new toxins to tilt the mental apparatus this way or that. The general effect of most of the agents—marijuana, LSD, cocaine, lead, thallium, PCP, as he recited a few to himself—tended to be similar in the overall, but specific differences in presenting symptoms often identified the responsible agent even before the lab results were in. And just keeping up with the growing list, plus identifying the quirks of each agent, drove him to the texts and journals often enough, this morning being a case in point. The environment had become so toxic, it seemed, and in more ways than just drug abuse. In fact, he ruefully observed often enough of late, the seeming ubiquity of toxins come of pesticides, industrial effluence, even atomic wastes was nothing more than the physic-chemical extension of a more general cultural toxicity which seemed to be eroding the foundations of the nation's social and moral weal. And not only in this country, though America, as usual, seemed to be leading the world in this grim derby as well as in everything else. And, just a few months back, the exposé about corruption in the Supreme Court. He figured that he worried about these times pretty much as other Americans did, and wondered, as he suspected they did, if America had had its run and that these signs of spoilage were actually the symptoms of an impending demise, or at least the demise of our present conception of government and its relationship to the individual citizen and his society. When he read the crime and drug abuse statistics which arrived almost daily of late and which seemed to be exceeding by far all efforts at rehabilitative address, not to mention their battering effect on the nation's volatile economy, he feared that the country had exhausted its application of democratic principles as understood and formulated some two centuries earlier and was now caught in the inevitable and irrevocable decay phase of the growth-maturity-decline curve which applied to everything else in the universe. An example of just such a phenomenon was offered to the world just a few years back when the Soviet Union, meteoric in its seventy-five year rise to super-power status, burned out in economic collapse over the course of just a few years, returning Russia to its traditionally quite modest position in the line-up of industrially and culturally advanced nations. Was it now America's turn, the counter-posing and goading exactions of Cold War priorities no longer in force? He wondered and fearfully suspected that America would demonstrate its impending collapse by way of the behavior of the individual citizen, since it was inherently a nation of individuals—each proclaimed as being at least as important as the whole—and not by way of a central debacle, as with the Soviets. Yes, America would do it via the individual, and only at some later time would the whole convey the collective state of the individual parts and hence the state of the nation. Yes, it would be done American style. Already the process seemed to be seeping upward to municipal and state level as more and more cities and states were experiencing not only budgetary failure, but decay of function in even basic civic services such as education and law enforcement. The SAT scores were again lower this year than last, he sighed, feeling a personal affront in that sad telling, and the crime rate in the nation's cities was soaring such that there seemed to be a macabre competition for being designated the murder capital of the land. And, most appalling, the nation's executive, legislative, and judicial capital, Washington, DC, was also far and away the murder capital as well. In other nations of different political pitch, it seemed that crime was primarily the province of the governing body while the citizens were splendidly law-abiding. No individual crime; only national crime, as in Nazi Germany, or more recently Soviet Russia. In America, crime was primarily an individual enterprise while the government usually made sincere effort to pursue a common weal. At least, until late. Now it seemed one government agency after another was being overhauled because of entrenched corruption. Worse, the criminal was still being accorded more and more rights and protection, as though the nation tacitly had targeted him as the test case for the preservation of every individual's constitutional protectives, prompting some genuine concern on the part of many as to the wisdom in selecting so questionable a commodity as the common felon to be representative of the quintessential American, at least from the statutory standpoint. Maybe such activist thinking, he again wondered, was rooted in the fact that the criminal element still constituted a minority—thank God—and that minorities in America had in recent years been granted a compensatory leeway exempting them, by and large, of the laws governing the majority, and hence were obliquely favored by a code, mostly unwritten, which nourished their droit as well as their durance, especially since they now voted. Plus, as Wilde noted, we Americans did seem to draw our folk heroes from the criminal class. It also seemed that any majority wore a collective guilt for minorities being what they were: groupings avowedly and numerically other than the majority and yet somehow unfairly deprived of majority influence, hence deserving of privilege not otherwise accorded them in the standard construction of the law, even if discrimination or abuse were not in any way at actual issue. In effect, a collective societal horror of any underdog's having to live a dog's life, even if deserved, seemed to cast the legal system, especially the criminal justice system, adrift in a Sargasso of social rescue. And discrimination, that misconstrued and misused notion! Well . . . .

"Whoa, Buddy!" he called to himself as he reined in over a grumble, "Let's get on with what you just might know something about!" He didn't mind reflecting on what he observed as political and social trends, but it would upset him whenever he became categorical about such things in the manner of any run-of-the-mill, irate citizen on the march. He saw himself as being more even-handed than that, and he well realized that issues, particularly political or social ones, were never as simple or as clear-cut as he, the isolated, removed individual, saw them. Also, he felt it prudent to be the more careful in any of his thinking if it happened to have a lot of heat behind it. He had no hesitance in likening his take on such national themes to that of the lay public's on Psychiatry—naive, usually misinformed, and all too often distorted along the lines of personal need and bias. Moreover, he also considered that he himself was certainly subject to the same influences he accused every other American of being subject to, singly and collectively. For example, he had too often said that while America stood uniquely capable of correcting its excesses, it stood just as uniquely incapable of preventing them. He had read that dictum somewhere long ago when he wasn't yet up to grasping its significance, which came later, like right now. And he often worried about personally being victim to, or at least respondent to, that very quirk just as were all Americans collectively. So best leave politics to the mercies of the professionals, he grumped, and get on with the task for which he was more genuinely accountable, that of putting himself in the right frame of mind for the A.M. Diagnostic Staff Conference, or, as everybody more simply knew it, the A.M. Staff Conference, or even just A.M. Staff.

Upon regaining that focus he felt the comfort of easy familiarity return to his thinking. Here, on his own ground, he knew what he was talking about, much of the time, anyway. Moreover, he had been presiding over the A.M. Staff Conference for so many years it was now also referred to as "Cantrelle's Conference," that appellation no doubt being helped along by its alliterative ring. The conference, one of the Residency Training Program's key teaching exercises, had been established well over sixty years earlier by the renowned psychiatrist and then superintendent, Dr. William J. Palmer, whose writings and teachings set the standard not only for psychiatric diagnosis and treatment, but for psychiatric education as well, and many an aspiring young psychiatric resident who was fortunate enough to study under him went on to make singular contributions of his own to the field as well as to his own personal recognition. And as well then as now, the A.M. Staff Conference was the premier conference of the clinical and teaching mission of the hospital. Initially it was held daily, and every staff psychiatrist and resident physician attended, including the hospital pathologist. The structure of the conference then was simplicity itself in that just about every new admission was presented to Dr. Palmer for interview. The interview was followed by collective discussion in which a diagnosis was made and a course of treatment defined. It was in the format of this morning conference that most of the didactic teaching of the resident physicians was offered, and the offering usually devoured the entire morning.

But gradually the conference format changed, right along with the times. With the advent of more and more information as to the contributing factors comprising the etiology, symptomatology, and therapy of mental disorders, more and more disciplines were added to the membership of the conference. Interpersonal, family, social, and even cultural contributors to the overall psychopathology of the given case now saw participation of psychologists, social workers, attendants, vocational therapists, recreational therapists, even music therapists in a correspondingly more comprehensive assessment of a patient's malady, thus significantly enlarging the scope and focus of any decided-upon treatment. Formerly the elite preserve of the psychiatrist and his junior counterpart, the resident physician, the conference was now, in varied weave, as democratic a display of the American way as anything the federal judiciary might ordain.

Accordingly, the more materia medica to be covered, the fewer the patients reviewed or interviewed during the conference. Far from every admission, the number of patients seen in conference was gradually reduced right along with the number of conferences held. For years it hung at two or, at the most, three patients per conference with only two conferences per week what with the various participants being pulled more and more to other clinical and administrative responsibilities throughout the hospital complex. By the time he was appointed Director of Residency Training the conference was built around the presentation of one case per meeting, and one meeting a week. Thus, the patient presented was now a most carefully selected one such that the former elitism of conference constituency had now become an elitism of the presented case. He had tried to sustain the conference much as he had received it, but in time its frequency had to be reduced farther to bi-weekly with the task of case presentation delegated solely to the resident physicians on a rotating basis. The cases selected for presentation were still drawn from the most recent admissions and hence yet in the process of initial evaluation but already seen as presenting some special challenge in diagnosis or management, or both. The general attendance was constituted of a nucleus of hard-core devotees supplemented by a variable and shifting periphery drawn by particular case interest. And, mercifully, the conference was held on Friday mornings, as today.

The window was now resplendent in the morning's exuberant gush. Motes of silvery dust floated languidly across the rays shafting through gaps in the curtains. Everything in the room seemed now to have moved closer to him as light moved the contents of his study along that magical orbit which at deepest night placed everything at its dark-most and farthest reach, and, by day, in closest conjunction with his positioned self. Now with everything once again back in its sidereal place it was time to go and fix her coffee.

It was one of his happier rituals, fixing her coffee. He had been doing it for most of their twenty-odd years of marriage and it was offered as an enduring statement of his devotion to her and his cherishment of all that she did for him, which was just about everything. Comparatively, a mere gesture, the coffee, but it was one of the few opportunities open to him on a daily basis for making some kind of a reciprocal contribution to the well-being of their primal and native intimacy which over the years had suffered the usual encroachments incident to their joint success on the broader front of having a life together. Their intimacy, which he hailed salaciously as their "touch," a reference which never failed to bring the tint of embarrassment to her cheeks, remained remarkably undiluted by all that had come into their lives. If anything, it had become all the more preciously their private preserve and thus the more fulfilling for its being sequestered, like an intimate and exclusive vacation spot. He had long ago pronounced that everything they did together—*everything*—was for them some form of foreplay. Even the rare arguments. If they painted a room together he would come to panting awareness of the way she stretched on tip-toe. Or, if they worked together in the garden, the flare of her hips when she kneeled before the flower beds. Or of the proud taper of her breasts when she straightened up, trowel in hand, to sweep her brow with a pass of her forearm. And that was just in routine things. If they had a night out for dinner or for some other gathering, it was then a case of out and out seduction, her lissome grace receiving fuller play in that more enabling milieu. He used to wonder what it was that kept his awareness of her at least on low smolder at all times, but soon enough concluded that it was simply the special way she moved. True, she had ultimate legs—absolutely perfect of line and proportion, with smooth and coyly dainty feet which he regularly kissed, toe by toe. Her legs offered a composite of charms he had never encountered before, anywhere, much less ever touched or kissed. And he knew what he was talking about because ever since his earliest juvenile years he knew himself to be—he sighed at the thought—first and always a leg man with consummate skill in sizing up at a glance any woman's givens. True, other body parts received their due attention, but for him the legs were everything, and the merest flaw in that quarter rendered all else manqué. And to this day he held her legs to be nonpareil, and also held it a fact that with year after year of younger women falling within his casual survey none had yet come anywhere near producing a contender suitable to his notice. And loyal he had been; absolutely, except during his mid-teens when he had that lengthy fling with Marlene Dietrich, and then later a steamy affair with Juliet Prowse just before he began medical school. But that was long before he and Laura had met, and once having found her legs he felt no need whatever to plight his troth to any other legs in his prowling survey. And he found her at a CPR class, of all places.

The memory of that meeting brought him back to the premise about the way she moved. He would never forget how she carnally yet modestly curled her legs under her when the class was instructed to sit down on the large floor mat in readiness for practicing resuscitation. That was before manikins had been developed as CPR training aids, and people paired off by gender to practice on each other. He and some fellow, probably Tom Wilson, huffed and puffed away for over an hour that long ago morning to secure experience in the mechanics of sustaining a tidal flow of breathing, thumping the heart back into action, clearing the mouth of obstructing food or dentures, finding the right rhythm to maintain. The rhythm. That was the key element in his and her transcendent moment of encounter in the CPR class, and it was specifically *her* rhythm which he found. The movement and motions of the others seemed an awkward enactment of new and unskilled approximations of what was to be the art of snatching desperate persons from the brink of death. But her movement was something else—graceful, unhurried, fluid, caressive. It riveted his attention and he knew he was making her uncomfortable by keeping her in the corner of his eye as they all went through the motions, quite literally, of what they might actually have to do some day in a restaurant, or at a staff meeting, or somewhere. He often made adolescent reference during their later playful reveries how her movements in that class certainly had picked up his breathing and heart rate. By the time the training class had ended it was all settled, at least in his own mind. She was the natural successor to Juliet Prowse, and a lot more available, too, if he could swing it. And so it began, with their marriage taking place eighteen spectacular months later, midway through his last year of residency training. That was in Washington, DC, a most vibrant place to be back then. Too bad it had become what it was today. Back then one could get around easily enough and wouldn't be afraid to do so. Friends who still lived there told him that the old downtown haunts were now a municipal No Man's Land, especially after dark, and, hence, all the more a relic of the irretrievable past. More the pity. She continued her work as a medical statistician after they moved to this area upon his completion of residency training. He developed a busy private practice fairly quickly, and she, almost as quickly became pregnant with their first child. As his practice firmed up and income became steady she resigned her post as statistician and spent the last two months of her pregnancy at home, nesting. He joined the teaching staff of the State Hospital on a part-time basis a couple of years after their son was born and thereafter divided his time between his family, his practice, and his teaching the resident physicians at Moreland. Over the years they added two more children, and in time he was appointed Director of Residency Training, a position he managed ever since on a half-time basis, the other half of the working day given over to his private practice. He liked the balance, and he also liked to think the tri-partite arrangement—family, teaching, practice—offered a stern dialectic whereby either pursuit would be kept sensible by the other two; a sort of personal and individualized balancing of powers.

He got up from his chair, stretched away sedentary stiffness, and walked across the study to the door opening into the foyer. He crossed into the living room, noting enroute that the light coming through the French doors was now sufficient to suffuse the room almost to the level of breakfast brightness. Continuing, he entered the dining room which was brighter still for the several windows and the double doors leading to the patio. By the time he entered the kitchen several paces farther on the house seemed completely reclaimed by daylight. He now registered fully the battering effect of the kitchen's buoyant sunshine on the hushed penumbra of his study he still carried within himself, once again sensing in its lingering shadow an oblique wish to avoid the arrival of the day and all its glaring responsibilities. And it was not a particularly new thought to him.

"Damn it," he grumped as he filled the kettle with water, "I'm always running behind, no matter what the hell time I get up." He smiled indulgently as he followed up with the corollary thought that he was always complaining about it, too, and often to just about anybody who would listen, though not in such a manner as to imply he expected anyone to do anything about it, or, heaven forbid, to offer suggestions as to how he might better deploy his time. People generally indulged his complaining, but if the question arose as to why he did complain if not really expecting any help to come of it he would explain that the Lord did not detract from one's allotted time those moments spent in complaining, a gramercy which did not extend to persons under age eighteen, he consistently reminded his children. After adjusting a filter in its holder and spooning out the grinds, more than necessary by his reckoning but suitable to her preference that the coffee be hostilely strong, he put the kettle on the stove burner to heat up while he retraced his steps through the house to the front door. It was now six thirty and the morning paper would be waiting. He made his way to the front door, unlatched it, and stepped out onto the landing of the front walk. He was immediately greeted by the singing of the birds. So abashingly pleasant to have the first sounds of the day a happy avian chorus which begins on cue with one's opening the door to the outlying world.

"Thank you, one and all," he offered, gesturing grandly to the trees lining the street. A few birds flitted about upon his approach. "And please don't let me interrupt."

He moved up the walk toward the curb, spying enroute the paper lying in wait on the edge of the lawn, the blue of the protective plastic wrapper contrasting starkly with the grass. He always felt a bit like a bird dog as he neared the paper, yielding to the mounting excitement of retrieval as he approached it. By the time he reached the paper there would be the expectation, or at least the emotional underpinning of such, that he was about to receive momentous news upon contact with that particular edition. But the news was pretty much always the same, give or take a few variations for season, and the letdown come of that rueful confirmation would constitute the first installment in the day's ration of obligatory disappointments. Still and all, there was a tingle of anticipation, he delighted as he paced along in a noticeable gradient of intent. He took a moment to note also that as usual he was the only soul out. However, he knew he was probably being observed by someone because a few neighbors had commented about his consistency in retrieving the morning paper precisely at the stroke of the half hour. One neighbor had joked that the paper boy lived in mortal dread of being late and arriving to find him standing on the edge of the curb, arms folded, grim set to the jaw, and tapping a foot in imperial impatience. That would be about right, he had conceded. So, as he reached the paper, he took a moment to scan the neighboring houses in a congenial half smile as a good morning gesture to anyone who might be looking his way. That done, he picked up the paper, the plastic sheath damp with the morning's dew, and started back to the house, fortified with American journalism's gift of the daily word which he regarded more as entertainment than exposition. He retraced his way to the house brisker of step—he truly didn't like the vulnerability of being *al fresco* in pajamas and robe no matter the domestic gentility it bespoke—and he entered the house to hear the kettle whistling its merry summons. He extracted the paper from its plastic sheath as he approached the kitchen and opened it enough to scan the headlines.

ECONOMIC SUMMIT BEGINS

The story went on to convey the optimism congressional leaders shared with leaders of the Central and South American countries in furthering preliminary accords for developing an equivalent of the European Common Market, which, since the collapse of the Soviet Union, had grown into a mercantile force so globally influential that its member nations were now doing, perhaps only for the while, what previously had been thought forever impossible, that of subordinating local nationalism to a collective common good. The net result was that political control of the world was slowly returning to Western Europe, its traditional seat. America and Japan were struggling to remain competitive—and credible—in a world which now combined the uncontested cultural superiority of Europe with its newly-found collective economic ascendancy which perhaps for the first time in history was not likely to be squandered in internecine wars. Hobbled by their separate brands of isolationism, America and Japan were now trying desperately to establish an economic trim which would allow each to cruise along with the accelerating Common Market, and the acquisition of alliances was the means being sought. Japan was courting its dowager mother, China, who was still proving unnegotiable on the issue of recognizing a brazenly successful Taiwan which would command an unpalatable parity in the Greater Asia Economic Consortium sponsored by Japan. Sovereignties from the Pescadores down to Indonesia were clustering around Japan's leadership, and even Australia felt strong attractions to the new alignment, finding herself in totally unforeseen sympathy with Russian Siberia in needing to straddle both European as well as Asiatic options. Canada full well appreciated such checkered horizons, seeing herself in an equivalent position vis-a vis the Pan American Trade Forum and her European ties. The economic map was being re-drawn everywhere and the hectic gerrymandering of traditional accords and alliances into new configurations played hob not only with time-honored political ententes but with ethnic and racial kinships as well. The very idea of Australia's constituting the southern flank of a Greater Asia Economic Consortium to defend against European hegemony! And, sooner or later even against the Pan American Trade Forum! It was all too much for the loyalists of the *règime ancienne* to endure, and not for the first time in history did there arise a grim wish for another little Balkan war to restore things to their natural order. Unfortunately, because of recent unpleasantness in that region, it had become apparent that the world could no longer afford little Balkan wars, or any other kind, for that matter. Economic might had now become the ultimate instrument of diplomacy, and it was at last generally accepted by all genuine contenders that traditional war, while capable of certain astringent short-term benefits, provided nothing by way of durable long-term gain, as the crowded events of the past one hundred years attested.

"But if Plato is right that all wars are made for money," he snickered as he poured the steaming water over the grinds, "they'll somehow find a way to work good old fashioned blood-letting into their blueprint." He set the kettle down and pondered on that point for a moment. If war ultimately is made for money, then what, ultimately, is money made for? To make war? That surely couldn't be, for even though there had been too many times over the centuries that means and ends were hopelessly confused, the overall course of human endeavor, admittedly just as often inscrutable, subtended a certain hard logic despite its spasmodic lurches and twists. But only in the large retroview did it appear that the human predicament had evolved by dint of a measured and progressive cadence. Dead ends, violent twists, lost purposes, and much of the mortal mischief of the past tended to be smoothed out or even expunged in the distilling and cleansing perspective of the long view, much the same as one sees in looking over the Darwinian tree of amphibian to primate evolution. There, short shrift is given to models that didn't get very far. And thus it was with human history as well, the recording of which demanded first and foremost demonstrable causality for a seamless flow. Presentism in its noblest form, but so comfortably pragmatic, he sighed.

The pungent smell of the tinkling coffee brought him back to immediate focus. He watched the coffee rise in the carafe as he added more water to the grinds in the filter cone. Slowly the level rose to the unofficial Plimsoll line that would signal enough to yield a heaping mug for her plus a refill for himself. He needed at least two mugs before seven A.M. to bring him to usable wakefulness, which in effect was the task of transition from pre-dawn nether thinking to everyday common sense. And he was almost there because he now felt the first tremors of the urge to look at the automobile classified section of the paper to see if any bargains had surfaced on some car he knew in time would become a classic. He was nothing if not diligent in his vigil for that dented treasure, now held in the contempt of familiarity but destined in time to be pricelessly vintage and available to him this day for a song, provided he had the courage to act. Here again and every so often he would find himself on a different kind of "verge," ready to take the plunge on this or that model, only to pull away at the last moment, a victim of unnegotiable doubt. Enthusiasm and conviction would wane but doubt somehow never did. So he tended to credit doubt as being more substantial. No matter how wrong he knew that notion to be, it brought little change to the issue. Like the time he almost—*almost*—got the 1967 Mercedes. The last of the great finds, and just a few small rust spots here and there. Everything original and working, even the clock. But he hesitated, having to pay obligatory homage to his doubt, and then when he was finally ready to act, the treasure was gone. He was the first to check it out, and had requested a day to think about it. Worry, rather. But less than an hour later someone came by and snapped it up in a trice. He still groaned when he thought about it, so best return to kinder currents, as he often counseled himself when cruel recall humbled his hopes.

"There, that's about right," he pronounced as the carafe level reached sufficiency. He quickly rinsed out his cup and placed it next to hers for charging. His was given to him by the kids on some Father's Day some years ago and was done up in bold reds and blues; hers, just about as old, was in the more traditional gray and indigo of the old-time China trade. Too somber for her, he always held, though she seemed to like it as much as he liked his own. He filled both and then fished the cream out of the refrigerator, noting the parsley in the glass of water, the heads of lettuce in cellophane wrap, the shallots bundled together by rubber bands, alfalfa shoots in plastic boxes, and generally enough greenery to merit his recurring comment that their refrigerator was little more than a polar greenhouse. Freshness was her fetish, and one he happily indulged. Kept him rabbit frisky, she would remind him in their playful moments. She had such definite needs—and expectations—when it came to such matters, he smiled wistfully as he poured the cream. He then returned it to its leafy keep. Hoisting a mug with each hand, he left the kitchen and balanced a path down the hallway to the stairs, mounted the treads gingerly, and leveled off at the upstairs hallway as he proceeded to their room at the corner of the house. He hipped the door open and then toed it close behind him. Just now the sunlight was displaying her slumbering form exactly as he needed to see it every morning. As was her wont, she was lying on her side, thus granting all the more flare to her hips. One leg was partially drawn up while the one below was outstretched, the thin blanket limning the lines of a fluid grace stilled by repose. Her hands were together next to her cheek on the pillow and her lips were barely open as though waiting but too modest to ask. Tousled blond hair nested her head on the pillow in a billowy fluff of curls which never fully submitted to discipline. He stood before her, mugs in hand, and traced her form tenderly with captured eyes that saw in her beauty, even after twenty-plus years, the makings of every torrid and riotously erotic interlude in which they'd swept each other away. He also knew that if he stood before her a moment too long he would assuredly see the next instant as their undeniable, immediate new installment in a perfect passion.

"Why not?" he queried himself teasingly as he looked at her for that decisive extra moment. That did it. The issue was joined and decided. He was now well into the mood, he fast discovered, the mugs now incongruous in his encumbered hands as he stood before the languid sheer of her body. There was nothing to do but set the mugs down and find out if she would receive his suit. He carefully placed the cups on the bedside table next to her book dealing with cluster analysis in utilization review programs. He then sat on the edge of the bed next to her and looked at her glorious profile, set like a slumbering cameo on the pillow, and wondered how, even in sleep, she could still seem as pert and quick as she was when about. He heard her slow breathing, almost like a sigh, and he instinctively altered his to couple with hers. He passed his hand lightly over her hair, taking care not to have her curls ensnare his fingers. Not yet, anyway. The touch of her hair brought him to a sharpened awareness of her scent, the scent that wafted him restfully along during the night as he slept next to her, the scent that identified her as his mate forevermore, the scent that was also present in their children even from the day of their birth, the scent he sought with every kiss he gave her, no matter how fleeting, and which touched the wellsprings of his desire, never failing to stoke his throb when he savored it for more than the safely allowable second or so, as now. He straddled her with his arms and leaned down to kiss her gently on the cheek, making sure his nose rested against her temple where the scent always seemed strongest and purest, undiluted by the smell of perfume, powder, or other well-intended additives. He sighed his warmth upon her, his lips still on her cheeks, and moved his hand to her head to cradle it as he lingered in his kiss. His fullness was now forming into a throbbing search, and her return sigh as she eased her body into a hint of supine assent stoked a richer, more succulent kiss on her cheek and closer to her mouth. As he tasted her cheek he felt it crinkle under his lips in a smile of endorsement, the beacon he had heeded all their married years in reading her readiness, whether in the darkness of the night or in the dimness of half-consciousness, and it never misled him. Only once in their years together had she ever refused him, and that was after a particularly painful argument. Because of its uniqueness, that one-time refusal quickly assumed an endearing quality, and he gave her a silver bracelet to commemorate the occasion, suitably engraved as to the date. They called it the "no-nookie" bracelet and she usually wore it to signal the onset of her periods and hardly ever anytime else, except when she felt like teasing him into competitive pursuit. Her smiling cheek under his lips now keyed that pursuit as she lay before him, eyes still closed, her breathing now measured to his mounting passion. He stood up to undo his robe which he dropped to the floor, and as he crossed to the other side of the bed he shed his pajama top, and stepped out of the bottoms as he eased under the blanket to her side. As he did so, she turned toward him and placed her arms open on her pillow in readiness to be taken. He gathered her in his arms, at first gently as though to ease his presence on to her, and then held her more tightly as his lips commanded hers. He kissed her deeply as her smell, huddled under the covers, now found its release to swirl around his reeling head. He stroked her cheek as he kissed her, and then let his fingertips glide down her neck now arched in offering. Her breathing sharpened as he unbuttoned her filmy nightgown to cup the yielding softness of her breast. The nipple was already drawn into a firmness that beckoned him the more. His pounding firmness rested against her thigh which she moved in a stroking caress. He moved his lips to her neck and licked its throbbing pulse as he urged her breast closer. She sighed sharply as his lips touched her nipple, and his tongue began to swirl around its erect readiness. She caressed his head as he hungered at her breast, and his hand, now freed, searched out her body. It glided over the curve of her belly, girlishly trim and firm as ever, and he massaged it slowly through the satiny slickness of her nightgown as she pulled him to her to deepen their kiss. He moved her nightgown upwards and placed his hand on her warm belly, his finger finding its fit in the dimple of her navel. Her belly quivered at his touch as her hips began to rise in search of union with his. His finger trailed down until his hand rested on her mons and she groaned as he began to caress the splay of her thighs which now trembled in readiness while his hand moved on to her moist warmth. In frenzy she bit at his lip, and he moved his hand to hold her chin in assent as he mounted her open form to achieve possession. After the briefest of confirming touch he thrust deep and they sighed together in the capture of full union. They lay for a moment to allow the flow of pulsing readiness guide their rush to oneness and then, gently at first, they wove their movement into rhythmic massage of each other's hunger. Their tongues swirled a duet of play as his muscles tensed in tempo with the rhythmic sway of her hips. They wanted it to be so forever, to hold always to this moment of their merge, their passion freed and joined, but the intensity of their union compelled its own purpose and their undulations, at first slowly like a primal dance to thralldom, heightened as they began to lose themselves to the beat of a pulsing crescendo now inexorable in its control of their bodies. Their breathing sharpened into pants and groans as his thrusting sought its release, and she clutched at his back to pull him closer to that very moment. Then, suddenly, she arched forward as a bolt of ecstasy streaked through her, and between gasps she cried, "Now! Now! Now!" to drive his violent thrusts ever deeper. He clutched her as his thrusting became a spasmic pounding. He bit her neck and she dug her nails into his back as they fused together in a shattering implosion of ecstasy. Their cries of blinding release broke the stillness of the morning and for that consummate moment of joined and total abandon they were timeless in their union. They tried to sustain the moment, but it retreated as though frightened by itself, and they became conscious of clutching each other's now sweating and sweetly exhausted bodies. Their breathing lengthened into a steady tidal flow, and they became aware of each other's sighs savoring the warm and restful afterglow. They held each other several moments longer as she lightly stroked his back while he kissed her tenderly on her cheek.

"Good morning, Sweet," he whispered into her ear.

She opened her eyes immediately, widening them in mock surprise.

"Oh! Frank! It's you!" she blurted.

"Who the hell did you think it was?" he shot back, quickly picking up on the theme of her antic and looking at her face on.

"Well, I . . . I . . . you see, it was so very wonderful, I . . . I mean . . ." she stammered in broad embarrassment.

"I bet you thought it was that son-of-a-bitch, Art, didn't you? Every god-damned time I turn around he's there, somewhere. I don't know why the hell he doesn't just move right in," he flailed in comic indignation.

"Now, dear, it's not as bad as you think. If you weren't so terribly jealous there really wouldn't be a problem at all. And besides, no one could ever really take your place," she patronized soothingly.

"Well," he grumbled, relenting against his will, "It's just that when we're making love I'd like to think that I'm the one you . . . well, you know . . . ," he trailed off.

She gave him a quick peck on the cheek as their signal to disengage their bodies. He then withdrew gingerly as both quivered in one last spasm of excitement. He took a deep breath as he steadied himself on his knees before her, her legs still splayed open before him. Almost idly he stroked her knees as he surveyed her beauty, now glistening in the filmy sweat of love fulfilled. Fixing the image in his mind for reverie later in the day he returned to the banter.

"It's just that he could never love you as much as I do—or deserve you as much," he groused.

She pulled him down beside her as they cuddled up in their official afterglow position.

"He does write nice poetry, though, you've got to admit," she pointed out delicately.

"Maybe from a woman's standpoint, I guess," he allowed, granting a reluctant and grudging harrumph in partial concession.

"Is there really any other when it comes to poetry?" she persisted brightly.

"I just don't know what the hell you see in that reprobate," he griped.

"All the other things I need," she announced simply as she snuggled up a little closer for the mandatory dozy interlude that was now beginning to settle upon them. They then became silent as their breathing subsided into the deep and oozy waft of their afterglow.

Art—Art Moody—was his nemesis and her true love. He had no known gainful employment but rather traced his way through the accidences of life much as a troubadour philosopher-poet might who saw only questionable merit in the workaday world. Yet, he always seemed to feel he was in touch with the cosmic significance of any earthly matter he chose to put his hand to. He saw nullity, portent, truth, bathos, purpose, chaos, destiny, futility, humility, glory, and just about every other quality of human existence in anything he surveyed. Also, he went on about it by way of poems, pontificating expostulations, and droll practical jokes on himself as well as on everybody else, and he did so with a matter-of-fact hedonism she found wondrously irresistible. And he did it all with a style built on his speaking always to far more than the apparent matter at hand. In his good-natured raillery of life he was five years old and five thousand years old, and from that point of address he was party to just about everyone and everything, yet ever alone. And she knew it all totalled up to an ordained and vital demand for her complete love which she gave to him with the same natural ease as she knew in drawing her daily breath, or as in telling the white lies she now felt were called for by the jealous arms of her husband. Art Moody took her love with the blameless entitlement of a newborn and she exulted in the thrill of his egregious need of her. And he said as much often enough in his poems to her. And that thrilled her all the more. And he knew it. Moreover, he was totally content in his quirky waywardness, holding the quixotic view as the surest path to the quintessentially real. He had the indomitable hope of the romantic, the irrepressible zest of the innocent, and the felicitous wisdom of the delivered, and he blended it all together in a grand and lofty sense of personal noblesse. In a word, he was anointed. He believed that everyone would benefit by seeing what he saw, and that everybody actually could see it if only they would allow it of themselves. And he would gladly lead them in that venture of liberation, but only on the condition that honest questions, those natural enemies of evil, be ever regarded as more important than the ready answers. To her he was gentle but untamed, generous but totally himself, masterful but needy, noble but simple. He was, in a word, her poet.

And he was entirely imaginary.

Well, almost. He was the innermost part of her husband, his alter self, who lived merrily in the safe confines of the murky dawn, or in the breakaway freedom of family vacation; in midnight drives to the lake, and certainly with every first snowfall; in each and every Christmas and Easter, and in those occasional inexplicable flights of *joie de vivre* that would arise of no known cause other than to have their moment. Art Moody was the creature Dr. Frank Cantrelle could rarely afford to be but nonetheless always was. He was the one who was closest to his wife's heart and the one to whom she gave herself totally and unconditionally, and in doing so savored fully the wondrous wickedness of serving herself up to two contending men in a duty beyond challenge.

And they both loyally nourished the fantasy; she for the perpetuation of the unique song which only they, her two men, could play on her heart strings, he for the rousing spirit of tournament he needed to mount from time to time to freshen his possession of her, and both for the endless supply of non sequiturs such a spectral *mènage a trois* offered to daily conversation. It constituted a kind of cornerstone to their privacy and it also embodied the singular modus they employed in loving and enjoying each other. Just the three of them.

As they savored their swoon he felt the day's schedule begin to materialize in his mind. He pretended not to notice it as he adjusted his embrace to insert himself deeper into his wife's aroma. The ploy was beginning to work and he was settling into his dreamy repose when the spell was shattered by the flushing of the hallway toilet.

"Do you think they heard us?" she worried aloud, now also shaken out of her reverie. Ever since the children were old enough to know the meaning of such bedroom commotions hardly a conjugal episode passed without her concern that they had been heard by their young. That was probably the main reason why they now preferred the early morning for their trysting, the kids long since beyond observance of a nine o'clock bedtime. It also accounted for their infrequent weekend retreat, just the two of them, to the Ralston Hotel for special occasions such as anniversaries, or simply when helpful family members could be mustered to mount guard over the home and progeny. The Ralston was and ever would be their Helikon, its service to their cause having begun with their courtship. And for all the times they went there, they knew only one room, Room 111, which they had adopted as their own from the beginning as their private bower away from home. They referred not to the Ralston, but to "the room" when they spoke of their need for a visit or made plans for such, and they took a quiet comfort in knowing that their room always lay in wait.

But the sounds of arousal were crowding in. An alarm clock was jangling in Ellie's room. Ellie, their second born, was pushing eighteen. She was also in her last year of high school, blessed with her mother's figure, mathematically gifted, and well on her way to Topology, but totally committed to the conquest of her swirling blond hair every morning in preparation for her arrival at school where she held court among her devoted following. She had about her a hale self-satisfaction and inner poise which all who knew her found reassuring and comforting. The upshot was that Ellie was foreverlastingly in the throes of office—chairman of this, president of that—which she discharged indefatigably and with the uncomplaining dignity of the born-to-rule. Several of her friends held her in absolute worship, and she reciprocated by being at once their protector, confidant, advocate, and ideal. The volume of daily phone calls attested to the workability of the arrangement, for hardly anything happened in her life or in the life of any of her following without first the collective clearance of all concerned, and a running phone conference was the only feasible means of addressing that necessity. Her boyfriends, those of ardent intent, anyway, numbered in the dozen and could be grouped under two distinct headings: those who were happily enterprising and assertive, given to public demonstration of their mettle and unabashedly responsive to the approbation of the electorate; and those who were more brooding, fiercely individualistic, and tender. She, for her part, felt no special commitment to either, though each provided an acceptable and interim arrangement for her current venue. If anything, she gave the sense of a young lady abiding, not quite knowing that she was so, but nonetheless thoroughly committed to her yet unmet choice, and confident that he would appear precisely when she was ready. Her mother pronounced the outlook to be most felicitous and estimated the unknown suitor likely to be, in the best classic tradition, as adept with the Homeric sword as with the Byronic pen. Rather like her own true love, Art, as a matter of fact. Richard, their eldest, had just started his last year of pre-med at Norton, his father's Alma Mater. Richard was the family Conservative—family Fascist, Ellie would often suggest—who for awhile considered the service academies and a military career, preferably as a pilot, but demurred in favor of the rigors of medicine. He was Olympian in his manner and outlook. Commandingly tall, broad-shouldered, and lithe, he moved among his friends with the ease of the admired but seemed always to be judiciously restrained by a self-imposed ascetism which was generally regarded as a predilection for recognizing the needs of others first. His thick, wavy, and dazzlingly blond hair marked him as the traditional hero, and his penchant for the epic saw elaborate display in his high school years when he quarterbacked his team to regional championship. Seen as a tough and canny contender, he was exquisitely fair and demanded the same of his opponent at the threat of a merciless drubbing, if it could be delivered. Lessons needed to be taught, it seemed. And for it all he was seen as selfless. If his team won by twenty points, he would have scored none; if the team won by one point, he would have scored twenty. He would even call hand-off plays to let linemen score, especially when they had heavy family representation in the stands. He led, and did so pretty much his own way. He declined, much to his mother's relief, the dozen or so football scholarships urged upon him by every major university, though his father would have enjoyed seeing his son perform agonistic magic on the college gridiron. Instead, disapproving of the college professional farm system mentality, he opted for the track team at Norton which readily came to scholarship terms to have someone so distinguished in the javelin and middle distances join their traditionally world-class track squad. Beset by female admirers who were constantly contriving to loom into his notice, he concerned himself with only one, Meredith. Meredith had been his companion and female Boswell for several years now. Their relationship evolved gradually without the driven intensity of a love-at-first-sight discovery as so often was the case among their friends. Rather, they just seemed to move ever more together since their stint as lab partners in their Earth Science class when high school juniors. Meredith perceived her life as having two callings, the one forlorn, the other expectant, and each busily at peace with the other. She had the heart and soul and grace of a dancer—the one—but was distinctly too tall for it ever to happen as she dreamed. The other was to be Richard's wife, companion, helpmeet; and for this she felt she was destined, also body and soul, her height now a decided boon to pair with his in a fitting cameo of regal portraiture. Laura sometimes worried aloud to her husband about the unconflicted ease of their closeness and what might be the resulting intensity of their intimacy when marriage did not seem very close at hand what with both still in college, but he would blithely remind her that whatever might be their private life together they were managing it tastefully, discreetly, and clearly without burden to others. He did not disguise the fact that he was delighted with his son's choice, seeing Meredith's willowy vitality all the more resplendent in the service of his son's needs, and he kept a not-too-secret collection of newspaper and magazine clippings of her modelings, for which she was in considerable demand by several major agencies and which she did only as often as was necessary to help with tuition. She and Ellie were fast friends, though Ellie felt that Meredith might be just a bit too selfless in this matter of love, even with her excellent brother, because, after all, how could one ever be sure that, etc. , etc. Todd, their youngest, saw her as simply super. Period.

Most likely it was he, Todd, who was just now using the bathroom, typical as it was of him ever since childhood to be the last to bed and the earliest to rise. Now sixteen and framed out massively with the assistance of a weightlifting regimen he followed more or less faithfully, Todd Cantrelle was cut from an entirely different cloth. Unlike his brother and sister, he was not given to tactically spaced retreats for brooding reflection on the meaning and purpose of things. Nor did he seem to concern himself with questions as to larger purpose, be they personal, national, or global. Moreover, he appeared to be distinctly uncomfortable when on hand for family discussions on such traditional topics as differences in generations, life's work, or heritage. While his siblings seemed to have from early on a sense of their personal calling, Todd exercised the right of abstention whenever it came time to declare. He saw himself as a free spirit who was not yet ready to join the ranks of the committed, and his theme of personal independence was the one consistent motif in his manner. Todd knew he was different from his brother and sister in large and irreconcilable ways, and all knew that the differences were drawn more from accident and circumstance than from what he would rather regard as his preference and strategy. As a child he was marked with the blemish of hyperactivity which inclined him to a collision course with everybody and everything in his life, to which Richard and Ellie could now more playfully attest. Moreover the problem was compounded by the two other components of the baleful triad, bedwetting and dyslexia. The bedwetting had ended some years ago and there had been no need for medication since, but the memory of that hateful experience and its debilitating effect on his self-regard lingered. The family tried to make light of the problem then as now whenever reference to it came up, but it could never be seen as other than a mark of difference, and a difference unpreferred. The dyslexia had begun to yield to the combined salutary effects of time and assiduous tutoring. But here, too, traces lingered, and to this day be rarely ever picked up a book voluntarily, unless it was heavy with illustrations. But movement on these two fronts had not carried over to the problem of his dogged restlessness. He still tended to flit from one enterprise to another, and often enough from one group of friends to another. There was recurrent concern that some of those friends were similarly marked outsiders also disadvantaged socially, or academically, or both; but from Todd's point of view, with its empathically less stringent standards of acceptance, they were seen as simply kindred souls.

"I think Todd is up and around," she mumbled to his neck.

"Did sound like his distinctive tinkle," he quipped in acknowledgement that it was now time for them to be up and around as well. "Do we have anything on for this weekend," he queried idly in an effort to draw out their repose a moment longer.

"Nothing this week, but you said you wanted to go to that symposium next weekend, didn't you?" she reminded him.

"Oh, yes! Just couldn't forget that, could we?" he winced. "Lately I look forward to something light and easy on weekends."

He wasn't sure he really wanted to go, but he felt he should, as he did with so many meetings, seminars, symposia, and their ilk. It usually took some effort for him to attend them, but once there he would get caught up in the gathering, frequently to become a spirited participant, and then be reluctant to see the meeting end. Just as he was now reluctant to see their morning together end. But there was nothing to be done about it. Also, thoughts of the symposium brought to mind his A.M. Staff Conference held every other Friday morning promptly at nine-thirty in the Admissions Unit and, hence, now less than three hours away. And there were still scads of things he had to take care of before then. But at least he—and she—had started the day right.

"Well, you have your teaching conference this morning, haven't you? Think maybe you get a headstart by going light and easy on the resident this one time?" she cooed playfully.

"Never," he insisted in mock resolution. "They need to know the bracing and purifying effect of pointedly applied tutorial terror. And history does not record that Venus was better at the medical arts than Aesculapius was. Harrumph."

"She could treat some things," she purred, undaunted.

"That does it!" he announced with indignant finality. "Up we go!" He threw aside the blankets and bounded out of bed, pulling her up to a sitting position as he did so. She reluctantly got out of bed as he stood before her to force her into respectable verticality as punishment for her rank venery.

"The very idea! Aesculapius must be blushing," he continued.

"I speak only the truth," she offered in defense as she drew herself to him for another embrace. "And besides," she continued, "who wants to be cured of this fever anyway?"

He growled and squeezed her with delight.

"I proposed to a sweet and wholesome girl and liberated a wanton hussy," he spoke in dour declamation.

"Your favorite secret and you know it," she teased.

"All right, you win," he conceded as he gathered her in for the deep kiss she had been jockeying for and which always served as official temporary closure for each consummated embrace. She groaned softly as their lips met again. And again he felt the sinuous caress of her body against his nakedness. In a moment the bonding settled into a stable and conjoint equipoise, ready to meet the distractions of the day.

"I love you so much, my lady," he whispered as their lips parted.

She squeezed him in response.

"Now that your values are suitably in place, the day may begin," she announced.

His girl! Always the right touch, the right word. And never, ever a complaint.

"I hope Todd isn't too balky about getting off to school this morning. I have to get going early today," she observed as she considered the next moment.

Well, almost never a complaint. Todd's revulsion of school as the primary locus of demeaning confrontation with his reading problem nourished a never-ending test of wills between his power of avoidance and the persistence of parental coercion, the latter task delegated almost solely to Laura. The plan, and hope, was for him to persevere for the breakthrough his teachers and tutors confidently predicted would happen at some approaching time. Todd ran hot and cold in his readiness to credit their efforts, but there was always a smoldering resistance to the entire matter of remediation, and, coupled with the ordinary ebb and flow of adolescent moods, that resistance too often flared up as hard defiance disguised as forgetfulness, slowness, haplessness, helplessness, punctilio, or disinterest. And, just as often the net result was that Laura would have to drive him to school, the schedule-bound bus driver having expended his reservoir of patience waiting for the dilatory Todd. Ellie openly sided with the driver, herself long past the point of silently enduring the embarrassment of being the sister of the provocatively tardy boy for whom the laden school bus sat and waited. In the tense silence of those waits she heard every snicker, giggle, sigh, and pencil tap. She would pray aloud that he would emerge from the house before the driver closed the bus door in exasperation, threw the bus into gear, and pulled away a bit too forcefully. Over the past few years the driver didn't even bother to wait for more than a curt moment, so she and the other kids were now spared the duty of forbearing Todd's irksome balk. On such days, Laura would drive him to school, even if a bellyache, a headache, a sore throat, or some other undiagnosable ailment seemed to urge otherwise. But despite his trying manner, he was generally well-liked by just about everybody. People felt instinctively protective of him in spite of his titanic proportions. Plus, the underdog, no matter who, never had a fiercer champion than Todd. His smile, which would probably never change, compelled a reciprocal warmth and acceptance, and it disarmed his exasperated victims out of hand. All in all, just about everybody warmed up to him, albeit against their better judgment, and especially so every maternally inclined female in his age group who felt called to the task of looking after this big, lovable lout. But most especially his mother who, because of his flaw, saw him as her eternal charge, her child who needed more than the others, and thus the one to whom she gave the most, the one to whom she was perhaps the closest because he had been the less able to separate toward independence. Todd was the child he himself was least comfortable with, or, said better, was closest to in a way he did not prefer. He was tortured by his son's pitiful efforts to keep up with Richard and Ellie, as well as by the frequent reckonings of those efforts, such as a report card, or even a birthday card which Todd could read only with some effort and which lay bare the unbridgeable gap separating this child from the many and laudable accomplishments of the other two. Or, conversely, by Todd's pretense of insouciance to deaden an anguish come of having to labor at tasks he would probably never master. In short, of seeing his son wrestle with an invalidism wretchedly and specifically matched to the family's several strong suits. The crushing poignancy of it all was too much for him to accept and so he chose to delegate most of the day-to-day struggle of it to his wife whose unqualified solicitude seemed to insulate her from the anguish he unfailingly felt on contact with his son's distress. Plus the guilt of it, because, after all was said and done, Todd was their very own flesh and blood. Many times he thought of sitting down with Todd and confronting together in the most loving, consoling, and comradely manner feasible the unalloyed and simple basics of the matter in the hope of establishing a neat, practical, and collaborative agreement to serve as a "new and promising point of departure for achieving a happier and more congenial path to life's promises," or so the phrase might run. After all, he was quite good at just that in his daily clinical work. He was known for his deft in making interpretive comments to his patients such that they felt more the lift of insight rather than the wrench of exposure when he brought their conflicts, anxieties, or hidden impulses to interpretive disclosure. It was simply the right and necessary thing to do, and he had no problem either with the timing of his interventions or in preserving the humanity of their purpose. But that was there. Here, with his son, he felt nothing but dread at the prospect of talking to him in a similar way and had earlier deferred to a succession of counselors and therapists Todd never managed to attach himself to for the understanding to happen as it should. He had even rehearsed different approaches: "Todd, I think it's time we talked about why it is you seem to have so much trouble in . . . ." Or, "Todd, I think we have to come to grips with something we've perhaps avoided acknowledging . . . ." Or, "Todd, I think we can agree that the best way to confront a problem or issue is first to frame its dimensions, and maybe we can do that with . . . ." Or, "Todd, the time has come, the Walrus said, to talk . . . ." And no approach seemed right. So he waited, and avoided, and estimated that he felt as remiss about the whole thing as did his son, and hoped that at least in their joint sense of dereliction he and Todd shared a special entente.

Now, fully returned to the tonus of the workaday world, both he and she set about the business of preparing for the day.

"Me first," she smiled as she slid away from him and disappeared into the bathroom.

As he waited he shifted his thinking to the overall good fortune he knew. All in all he had it pretty good. So good, in fact, by comparison his troubles seemed to shrink to minor account. So good, he was given to pricks of conscience goading him toward a redeeming philanthropy. And it all seemed more evident in early Autumn, his favorite time of the year. He long ago concluded that it was primal in all of us to like the Autumn. It was the time of reward for one's work. Harvest time in the fullest sense, and rich with bounty. To him it included back-to-school in its strictest sense and also the exhilaration of new challenge. For him it was likewise the beginning of his professional year. He had begun his private practice as well as his teaching some twenty-odd years ago at just about this time of the year, not to mention the many preceding returns-to-school he had savored prior to that time. He had always loved school, and saw its spiritual power rooted in challenge, adventure, and reward. Whether it was football, English drama, gross anatomy, or psychopharmacology, it was all the same to him in its fundamental offering. And he was ever grateful of the gift. He was never heard to complain about being in school; to him such would be tantamount to sacrilege, such as complaining about one's church or, worse, one's faith. School was his church, and learning was his faith. So Autumn and its theme of return to school had the sanctity of a pilgrimage, even resurrection, but he rarely ever said so to anyone. But Laura knew, and that helped. It was not lost on him that his credo smacked too much of naivete and juvenile excess, but . . . .

She emerged from the bathroom brushing her naughty hair into obedience. He patted her on the behind as she passed by and then took his turn at the morning ablutions.

About a half hour later—showered, shaved, and suited up for the day—he re-joined Laura in the kitchen as she was getting the toast and juice together. With a mug of fresh coffee cradled in his hands and leaning against the door jamb of the kitchen's entrance he watched her flit through the breakfast preparation routine. He watched her do so most mornings, and though he would help in small things needing to be done, generally he would stay out of her way. She was swift at such things and he wasn't, and for the most part she made better time if all he gave her was company. And, besides, today she had already pretty much gotten things in place by the time he reached the fresh coffee.

"There. This'll do it," she announced as she carried a platter of toast to the dining room.

"We made good time this morning," he quipped as he followed her into the dining room.

"Couldn't have made it any better," she smiled over her shoulder as she set the platter down on the table. "Children! Breakfast is ready!" she announced to the other regions of the house.

He grunted with the satisfaction of a man about to be gratified anew as he sat down to the gay array of jams, the mound of toast, the beaded pitcher of chilled orange juice, and lo, a small centerpiece of flowers. Zinnias, he guessed. And the sunlight bursting in from the patio sliding door set it all a-tingle with readiness.

They then began their breakfast. It was standard during the week that Ellie and Todd might or might not join them, depending on whether some last minute homework or class project would demand higher priority. But on weekends, especially Sundays, breakfast was communal. And for most holidays, too.

"Are you ready for Clay this morning?" Laura twitted over a bolus of toast.

He rolled his eyes in mock forbearance before replying.

"I'm never ready for that smart-ass SOB. It would ruin his day if I were," he grumped.

She wrinkled her nose in glee at her husband's display of sportive truculence. The thought of his girding himself for some contest of arms stirred her to rapt expectancy: she delighted at the thought of her man snaring victory on the field of scholastic tourney.

Clay Moyer was one of his dearest friends. He was also his most loyal intellectual foil. Seemingly alone among the many, Moyer applied his own considerable intelligence, cast in a restless interrogative mold, to the rightful rehabilitation of soft and flabby thinking wherever he might find it—and wherever his stalwart dialectic could be tolerated. In the name of truth and training he hustled the residents into a critical and disciplined approach to the rigorous duty of clinical observation, and every case formulation had to pass the keen muster of his drumbeat review. He was the attending psychologist on the Intensive Treatment Unit and one of the charter members of the Cantrelle edition of the residency training curriculum at Moreland State Hospital. He was also the unit's cynic in residence, ever ready to season the day's work with dollops of his wry wit. It was one of Moyer's tasks to teach the residents the use of diagnostic nomenclature, and many an hour in their first year of training was given over to his tutorial zeal whereby the residents were driven along in an uncompromising pursuit of disciplined observation and diagnostic precision. The residents referred to it as being "Moyerized," and Moyer himself found no reason to question that appellation. It was also his duty to select some suitable case, usually in collaboration with the unit's attending psychiatrists who might wish to have a particular clinical issue addressed, and assist the resident to whom the case was assigned in organizing a multi-discipline presentation of the case at the Morning Conference. In effect, the resident had to bring together the findings of Social Work, Psychology, Nursing, Occupational Therapy, and often others as well, blend them with his own clinical findings, and come up with an overall case formulation that yielded a diagnosis, a specification of etiology, and some rational plan of treatment, plus, under the watchful eye of Clay Moyer, manage the presentation in such a way as to extract the nugget of psychological truth from the cache of clinical ore brought to bear, thereby enriching all in attendance, even the patient who was dutifully on hand to assist in the process by way of interview for additional exploration as discretion and need dictated. All in all, a formidable exercise for everybody concerned, and it marked the bi-weekly academic high point for the ITU staff as well as for the first year residents who were then able to glide through the remainder of the day in earned diminuendo, satisfied that good and right work had been done now that the training week was officially brought to crest by the A.M. Staff Conference.

"I'm sure the conference will go as triumphantly as ever," she announced confidently as she handed him the toast, recalling enroute the times she attended the conference when she worked at the hospital years ago. She had often reminded him that her first impression of his conference manner, and little changed since, was that of someone oddly blended of arrogance with kindness, youth with wisdom, gentility with excitement, tenderness with strength. From time to time she would threaten him with the notion that it wasn't his interview skill, the march of his dialectic, or the grace of his logic that carried the conference but the peculiar blend of his personal traits which others embraced as easily as she and succumbed to just as readily. He would pshaw that notion out of hand to hide his chagrin at the likely accuracy of the charge.

"We'll have to have Clay and Helen and a few other couples over for dinner sometime next month," she added, now dismissing the conference to Old Business status. She and Helen, Moyer's wife, got along swimmingly. Moyer had quipped that the reason the two wives did so was because each secretly thought herself slightly superior to the other and hence free to be selfless in a shared affection. He gave due credit to Moyer's notion but preferred to think that what made them click was more their being such frank opposites and hence of little threat to each other, and maybe a little of each other's alter ego, a circumstance he could readily appreciate. Laura was blonde, brisk, open, and efficient; Helen was raven, casual, reserved. He was about to second Laura's motion for dinner when Ellie entered the room in her usual manner which was not unlike that of Loretta Young in the old television series. Without really intending it she immediately commanded one's attention, he delighted as he obediently beheld her willowy grace and radiance. Arresting, he'd often said. Today she was in a blouse and pleated skirt, seeming more destined for a lawn party than a high school classroom. Usually the rest of the week was done in simpler fare, mostly blue jeans and chambray skirts and such, but Fridays called for more. Indeed, the whole family did up Fridays. He always saw to it that he was a little bit better turned out for his Friday conferences, and somehow the accent had become something of a family mark.

"Good morning, you early risers," she chirped as she sat down at the table. She beamed a teasing smile and then took a sip of juice.

"Is Todd getting ready?" inquired Laura to slide past any hint of salacious play contained in the reference to early rising.

"Hi, Sweet," he said simply, suppressing a grin and shifting his attention to the sheen of her iridescent hair in the morning sunlight shimmering among her springy locks. All three of his children had golden hair much like their mother's and unquestionably authored by her. Of the three, Todd's was the darkest, and it thus hinted at some credit due paternal contribution in his construction. For his part, when he was Todd's age his hair was similarly caramel blond; since his mid-thirties it had slowly darkened into its present extinguished brown.

"I heard him up and about. At least, I heard some of his music," she offered. It took years to get Todd to play his music at a volume compatible with the family's ecosystem, and the happy result was that conversation became possible though his chords be aloft and racing.

"Good," Laura pronounced in obvious relief. No struggle this morning in arousing him and pointing him in the general direction of school. Too often her efforts and his resistance verged on the wretched in what amounted to out and out coercion to get him to do what Ellie and his brother did effortlessly. Here again, Fridays were usually easier on that score. It was as though he would acquiesce because of the prospect of a liberating Saturday to follow and could thus tough it out one more time since it would be only for a day. So school day mornings preceding holidays and weekends were usually spared his guerrilla tactics, thus providing enough time in the overall for by-gones to become by-gones. For a while, anyway, but never to carry over into the next school day, for sure.

"Settling in pretty well?" he inquired of Ellie off-handedly, referring to the semester which had begun just two weeks earlier.

"Yeah, Dad," she returned, "Looks as though it's gonna work out pretty well. They're already talking about senior projects and the SAT's. Oh, that reminds me, Mom. We have to go to Latimer's. Maybe tomorrow? I need to pick out a dress for the Great Big Bash." She and her mother reveled in shopping together.

The school bore the name of Christopher Columbus, and every Columbus Day was the occasion of a dance called traditionally the Great Big Bash. In its size and social importance it was second only to the senior prom, for though the prom identified who was leaving, it was the Bash which announced who was arriving. And, of course, all had pretensions to being among those having achieved arrival. It was also the opportunity to display sartorial wealth come of summer jobs recently relinquished though now collectively regarded as first entries in the evolving resumès of personal accomplishment.

Ellie was about to clinch the agreement for shopping when Todd drowsily entered the dining room. Though likely to rise earlier, he took longer to recover from the torpor of sleep than did the others, and this morning saw no change in format. He moved to his place at the table as though in a trance, his bulk conferring an added thickness to the motion. He seemed not to notice the others present as he settled into his chair.

"Hi, Champ," Cantrelle greeted cheerily as a supplementary dash of cold water to Todd's sleepy visage.

"'Morning, Dad . . . everybody," he returned, managing a sheepish, self-conscious smile as he took in his family with a sidelong glance more impish than furtive. He then set about filling his bowl with cereal.

"I hear that the team tryouts are still on, Todd," continued Cantrelle in veiled plea which he hoped Todd would not hear as coercion. This year, as well as last, Todd had gone out for Spring training, only to lose interest after a couple of weeks. His size and power had just about guaranteed him a place on the squad. Plus, there was the certifying influence come of his brother's now legendary leadership of the championship team several years earlier. A burden for Todd, to be sure, but also, coupled with the right attitude, a ready benefice.

"Yeah," Todd minimized, his attention now ostensibly directed at the manifestly more important matter of adding a sufficient amount of milk to his cereal.

Cantrelle felt an immediate flush of anger at being put off so. Dismissed, really. Nothing new about that, though. It was Todd's way with everyone and everything that didn't suit his preference. Agreed, his attitude was his attitude, and he had a right to it even if he exercised no conscious choice in the play of it, but it was the galling display of a companioned expectation that others were to oblige what was most congenial to his interests alone, unmindful of others' preferences or feelings. Now, grousing inwardly, he reminded himself how truly hard it was to talk to Todd. To ward off the blast of guilt he knew would soon follow on the heels of that assessment he amended his resentment to include the exculpating prospect that his son would soon be his usual puckish self after he had awakened fully, as was indeed typically the case. But, damn it, even so, Todd probably wouldn't follow-up on trying out for the team, and he was a born linebacker if there ever was one, as everybody knew, except perhaps Todd himself.

"I see that the morning paper has an article about the symposium next weekend on the drug problem," Laura offered in rescue directed primarily at her husband. She could always be counted on to guide the family over the rough spots.

"Yeah, Dad. Even our science teacher mentioned it," added Ellie in concert. "He said that the panel would be made up of some of the biggest thinkers in the country. He named them and one of them was that fellow Burleson you bring up a lot."

He was already much too aware of the symposium. In fact, he had encouraged the residents to attend it and had given each a confirmatory letter to qualify them for a reduced admission fee. Indeed, he had assured them that the symposium would be worthwhile specifically by dint of Burleson's participation in it. Burleson was the country's, and the world's, leading expert in neurotransmitters. It was his work which had proven the thesis that any exogenous chemical used by man to achieve a desired subjective state had its endogenous and naturally occurring counterpart in the body's chemical network along with a specific receptor site, typically in the central nervous system for the psychotropics. His work on the intermediary metabolism of neuro-transmitters and their receptor sites in relationship to the chemistry of addiction pretty much clinched that hypothesis beyond dispute. Addicting agents, he contended, had a naturally occurring endogenous counterpart in the human metabolic sequence and thus secured their addictive properties by having agonist activity sufficiently similar to that of the endogenous agent though possessing even greater metabolic affinity for the particular receptor. The example of heroin and the prototypic endorphins was a simple example of the process, as was ethyl alcohol and the many prototypic alcohols seen in the normal metabolic chain. But Burleson had taken his work beyond the level of basic discovery and clinical observation. He had catapulted his findings to the level of theory, particularly social theory. His contention, hortatory in its ring, was that modern technology had placed in man's hands not only the means of discovering the secrets of his mental life but also the means of dilapidating both his mind as well as his society. He likened the dilemma to the liberation of atomic energy with its potential for both good and bad. The nation's rampaging drug problem coupled with the advent of seemingly endless additions to the array of available street drugs lent grim testimony to his gospel. But there was concern that Burleson, like many a fine investigator before him, had parlayed his splendid scientific accomplishments right along with his personal renown to mount a social, even political, commentary which, for all its humanitarian reach, wasn't as well grounded or as carefully objective as was his basic research. Nevertheless, his was a voice to be heard. He had been nominated for the Nobel Prize shortly after his work broke upon the scene—the only psychiatrist to be so honored in almost a hundred years—only to be edged out by that Stanford team which demonstrated the subviral infectious basis for diseases collectively considered auto-immune in their pathogenesis, diseases as varied as multiple sclerosis, rheumatoid arthritis, regional ileitis, and the like. Many thought he might still be awarded the prize at a future time, perhaps some year when the crop of epic new discoveries was lean. But it was also true that research moved on, and with it the fashions to which the scientific community was subject, much like any other human gathering.

He had met Burleson about ten years earlier when both sat on a panel formed to explore the prospects of moving psychiatric nosology—the classification of the various psychiatric disorders into discrete diagnostic categories—away from the traditional behavior basis and on toward a neurochemical basis more in keeping with modern medicine. It happened that he, the psychoanalyst, and Burleson, the neurochemist, found themselves to be remarkably at one in their general thinking on the issue but with important differences on the matter of timing. He himself felt that the moment was long overdue for the adoption of at least a trial nosology built on what was currently known about the neurochemistry of the various psychiatric disorders, accepting temporarily the many large blank spots such a system would presently carry. Burleson, however, urged patience and especially caution, contending that even highly validated, internally consistent nosologic systems, by their very structure, contain certain biases which so determine and shape subsequent observation they tend to generate the very referents of the system itself—cast in its own image, so to speak—thus leading to yet another edition of restrictive reductionism. When Burleson began to quote from Russell's *Theory of Sets* to demonstrate his point the rest of the panel, one training director in particular, subsided into humble acquiescence. It was as though Burleson had been making a collegial effort not to streak on ahead of the panel to reach what was already well understood by himself yet still beyond the reach of the panel's collective membership and so was settling for simply nourishing the discussion along, Socratic-like, to serve the disquisitional needs of the panel's modest grasp. But when the question of how and when to implement change arose, Burleson asserted his fundamental ascendancy and therewith significantly deepened the colloquium waters, and the other panelists, himself included, suddenly had enough to do just to keep afloat in the now unfamiliar depths. He remembered it as quite an experience, and a most chastening one to boot. He often spoke of it as the only time in his life he literally sat next to greatness. He just as often wondered how he had been chosen to sit on that panel in the first place. And he feared the others wondered the same about his being there. But, in truth, it was more a matter of how it happened that Burleson was chosen to sit with *them*. Or had agreed to do so. Someone on the program committee had erred, all later agreed, and that Burleson hadn't the heart to decline. After the panel discussion ended Burleson sought him out ostensibly to follow through on a few points that had been raised in their discussion, but more likely to get a closer look at this young fellow who had thrown in with him on the panel. Undoubtedly, Burleson had some question as to the sincerity of the demonstrated affinity, not being a stranger to gestures of doctrinal sympathy based more on an effort to acquire a reflected lustre from his established fame. "Darshan," it was called by the Hindus who made no bones about getting it. Burleson suggested that they continue the discussion, just the two of them, over a cup of coffee. The klatch only took about fifteen minutes but in that brief time Burleson was able to dissect the thinking of his would-be cohort sufficiently to conclude that this unknown quantity in the form of one Frank A. Cantrelle, M.D., was indeed for real, or enough so to encourage Burleson to pronounce their tete-a-tete as most enjoyable and pleasantly informative. For his part, Cantrelle's participation in the conversation was more like a suppliant under gentle interrogation which he found to be as revealing to himself as it was informative to Burleson. There was something about the way Burleson posed his questions. Moreover, throughout the interview Cantrelle had that peculiar sense of almost seeing, of once again being on the verge. It was the same uncanny feeling which would occasionally descend upon him when he was quietly alone and pondering at full tilt. But that time was the first time ever he experienced it while talking with someone. They agreed to look forward to their next meeting, each attesting to the hope that it would be soon enough in the coming. But, except for a few salutations of recognition at chance encounters over the subsequent ten years, the return meeting never occurred.

Now he doubted that it ever would happen. But then again, since he would attend the symposium next weekend, maybe . . . .

"Ma," Todd interposed, now considerably more focused, "when can we go for my driver's test? If you can't take me I can go with Eddie." Eddie was in Ellie's class and had pretensions to Ellie's affections, though never seriously considered by her. In fact Ellie and most other members of her group had little encouragement for Eddie whose main interests seemed to be cars, part-time jobs, and week-end parties. Moreover, as far as anyone could tell he never held academics to be anything more than a tariff to be paid for access to the social and economic scene of his preference which openly featured a pleasure-bent pragmatism just too bold to suit Ellie's militant idealism. Plus, it was no secret that he befriended Todd, most of whose friends were a year or two older than he, so that he might gain favor not otherwise forthcoming from Ellie. Todd seemed not only oblivious to the tactic but quite satisfied with the conveniences returned by the friendship. "I asked him yesterday and he said O.K. Maybe one day next week after school if you can't make it," Todd continued.

Now it was his mother's turn to be miffed with him. Firstly, the family didn't particularly approve of his association with Eddie, the difference in their age being the more assailable point. Secondly, she didn't like being placed, fait accompli, in the position of having to choose between imposed compliance and pyrrhic resistance when a little preliminary discussion of the matter might easily have yielded a more cooperative arrangement. And here it was again, his taking steps without checking ahead, and doing so in such a way as to force upon her the very same onus he self-righteously resented as his own unfair lot, and his alone, to hear him tell it.

A moment of silence hung over the table, challenged only by the scraping of Todd's spoon in his bowl. The others pointedly ignored looking at each other in shared recognition of the issue now broached, though Todd seemed oblivious to what had now become a hovering discomfort. Cantrelle and Ellie knew that Laura was using the moment to compose herself before responding to Todd's levy. For his part, Cantrelle was applying no small amount of self-control himself in deferring to his wife for the next move; it had been resolved many times afore that it was better policy to let the one to whom the problem was directed field it rather than to have others rush in unsolicited. Yet, he still felt he should assert his authority on such occasions so that his silence might not be heard as acquiescence. The question, again, was more of timing.

"Todd," she answered in steadied tones and without looking at him, "I don't object to taking you—I would be pleased to take you to your driving test—but I do object to being told that I have only one chance to do so, take it or leave it. *When*, not *if*, I take you is more properly the issue to be worked out between us. And besides, isn't it required that a parent or guardian accompany a minor applicant?"

"Ma, I didn't mean it that way," Todd replied, looking up from his bowl with a stricken expression. "I just didn't want to have to wait. That's all. And no, it doesn't have to be a parent or guardian because I called them and they said it just had to be a responsible adult," he added testily.

A responsible adult? Eddie Shanks! Didn't he see he was pushing it a bit far to offer Eddie as a responsible adult? Did he really regard Eddie so? Or likewise his way of going about getting to the driving test? Here again the frightening difference between Todd's way of thinking and that of the family was beginning to yawn before them, evoked even by such a simple, commonplace matter as arranging for a driving test. With Richard and Ellie it was more a shared adventure and challenge, everybody's pitching in with enough preparation and humor to go around.

"I was only trying to be helpful if you couldn't make it," Todd added, wounded by his mother's implication of manipulation.

He probably did see his effort as being helpful, Cantrelle mused ruefully. It was just that Todd didn't see things the same way the rest of the family did. Granting that as a valid starting point, miscues and misadventures logically followed, plus the need for an occasional cunning or a certain obliquity in his moving things along. The upshot was that the family felt it couldn't reach Todd, that despite their efforts and partly because of them they were alienated from him. In the heat of exasperation it was too easily forgotten that Todd assuredly felt likewise about the family in addition to an uncomprehending sense of isolation which was his alone to bear but perhaps softened by people like Eddie. Whenever Cantrelle's thinking came around to this point in pondering the problem with Todd, an indelible and crushing guilt, coupled with anguished compassion, would cause him to break off the train of thought before dole took too firm a hold. He would then lighten the moment.

"Take it easy, Champ," he quipped in his best affability as he reached over and jostled Todd's shoulder in the right comradely manner, "we know you were just trying to help. Sometimes, let us in on it and give us a chance to help, too. Right?" It was lame, but it eased the moment.

"I guess I could have," relented Todd in concession, giving his father that puckish smile to signal his gratitude for the effort made.

They all then settled into an easier silence over the ensuing minutes as restoration of family amity was allowed its due. Some minutes later breakfast quietly achieved a mutually agreeable windup.

"O.K., Todd, I guess it's time for us to hit the pavement and wait for the yellow phoenix to shuttle us off to misery," announced Ellie as she planted her napkin on the table with resolute finality.

"Sure, Sis. One more mouthful," returned Todd, smiling at the aptness of her metaphor. He then daubed his mouth with his napkin, got up, and joined his waiting sister.

"Let's let those two linger over their coffee. Every little bit helps when you've reached parenthood, I guess," Ellie tossed.

She and Todd chuckled together over that fillip as they disappeared into the interior of the house.

When they were safely out of earshot, Laura spoke.

"I'm sorry I came down so hard on him, but sometimes he really gets to me. It seems uncanny how he knows exactly which buttons to push. But that's no excuse; I should be better about it," she glummed.

"I felt pretty much as you did, Laura; it was just your turn at bat. I hope he hears the purpose of what we say to him. He must," he averred, "but I just worry that he'll burn too many bridges before that damned problem lets up."

"His reading has gotten a lot better," she was pleased to report, "but writing a theme is still more of an agony for him than anybody deserves. Shouldn't he be on his way out of this thing? In eight months he'll be seventeen."

His wife's impatience was no less pressing than his own, but his clinical experience with the problem tempered his brighter expectations.

"He'll probably need another year or so before we can expect any real big gains. For the time being it's still a matter of perseverance and support. And hope, I guess," he sighed.

"I know," she agreed as she lifted her cup with both hands. She stared at it for a moment, and then continued. "Is there anything else we should be doing?"

"I don't know what," he despaired, "Some of it is up to him, I'm afraid."

They had reached this point many times before in commiseration over their son's handicap, and it always ended up the same way—in a joint endorsement of hope. He was about to remind himself once again that he just had to talk to his son one of these days, but he brought that reproof to a halt with the reminder that he would better get cracking if he expected to be on time for the conference. Punctuality was the courtesy of kings, he'd let drop much too often. He straightened up in his chair as he took one last gulp of coffee.

"Have to get on your way, huh?" she assessed, reading the shift. It was always harder to see him off in the morning after a conjugal triumph.

"Yup," he sighed as he yielded a wan smile of resignation.

"Well, don't forget today is Friday," she reminded, placing her elbows on the table and cupping her chin in her palms, "and the evening has its joys as well." She now wore a bold smile of entrenched naughtiness.

They often went out to dinner Friday evening, just the two of them, and particularly if the kids obliged by having events of their own scheduled and hence likely to settle for an extempore dinner snack that wouldn't delay the launch of the evening. Also, he and she usually rounded out their dinner evening with a shared nightcap which always heralded yet another conjugal enterprise.

"You never get enough," he charged in mock indignation.

"Never enough of you, lover mine," she retorted, unphased.

He snorted appreciatively, got up from his chair, and crossed over to her and positioned himself beside her. She rested her head against his chest as he caressed her hair gently. Taking her face into his hands he bent down, kissed her gently.

"And don't you ever, my dear!" he breathed.

"No chance," she promised.

He brought the interlude to an end with a quick peck on the tip of her nose.

"Gotta get rolling—now or never," he announced firmly.

"I'll walk you to the door," she added helpfully.

They left the dining room, traversed the living room, and entered the foyer. He picked up his briefcase enroute. They stood before the door for the standard good-bye kiss and the concluding pat on the behind he unfailingly gave her.

"I'll try to buzz you later today and check with you," he promised.

"Uh-huh," she acknowledged, flicking a piece of lint off his lapel.

"Good-bye, kids," he yelled along the foyer and up the stairs.

Return good-byes were offered from afar.

One more peck on her cheek and he opened the door and stepped out into the now blazing sunshine. He moved briskly down the walk and turned to the garage. She watched him walk away, his vigorous gait reminding her of their morning together.

Two

One of his unrepentant indulgences was his cars. Three, as a matter of fact. He had a simple compact for economy and everyday use, but the other two were something else. One was a Jaguar coupe "black as sin," and the other a Corvette in adolescent red. He had bought them used after careful and meticulous search for the right vintage, the right mileage, plus the right initial depreciation, and time had pretty much proven his selections correct. He kept them carefully garaged while his utilitarian car and the two family cars, Laura's station wagon and the family sedan, had to contend with the elements from berths in the driveway. His thoroughbreds, as he called them, were used only on special occasions such as glorious Autumn Sundays, rejuvenating Spring mornings, and the woefully infrequent getaway weekends he and Laura cherished.

Today it was the compact, though the morning's events thus far seemed to designate the Corvette. He was of a mind to follow through on that notion, but driving to the hospital, though only fifteen miles away, traversed two rivers, three small towns, and parts of two counties with their serried traffic lights, congested intersections, and inevitable shopping centers that seemed to trail, like camp followers, every new housing development in urbia's inexorable march across the land. Hardly grand. Over the years he had watched his route to the hospital transform from open countryside and neatly tilled farmland to rectilinear clusters of even neater housing developments standing nakedly arriviste against the backdrop of the offended land. He wasn't a rabid environmentalist but he did rail against the resulting increase in traffic over his route, for what used to be a fairly wholesome excursion to be enjoyed daily had lately become something of a logistic ordeal. So, of late not only was there definite challenge to it, but there wasn't much left that was restful to see. Most of the farms along the route were gone, and so there were no languid, placid cows around anymore to dapple the pastures with bucolic tranquility. And the forests, with their occasional flashes of bounding white tails, had retreated to distant horizons. So the more logistically practical compact would suit better.

"Too many people and their asphalt," he often grumbled, and especially when tied up at a slow intersection.

However, this morning the traffic moved along tolerably well and he was thus able to attend to the welcomed nip in the air—minimal, but still discernible as it can refreshingly be in the earliest hints of Autumn—and also to the particularly bright and golden sunshine of this quite pretty morning. He felt he was almost at peace with the world of today, at least as much as any reasonably informed citizen could be.

As he neared the hospital the ambience became notably more urban. The yellow bulk of school buses figured more prominently in the traffic as well as the consequent slows and halts in the traffic surge. But this was more than adequately compensated by the refreshing sight of cute and bouncy elementary school children filing aboard with their burdens of text books and colorful lunch boxes. Soon the first of the double houses began to appear along his route. Beyond the hospital and toward the center of town the double houses would coalesce into row houses to serve as front line sentinel domiciles whose duty was to invest and contain the commercial district of the community which ever and always assaulted the boundaries separating the worlds of where people lived and where people worked.

As he neared the hospital he was able to use side streets to avoid the mainstream traffic. Here again things had changed. As much a short-cut as a means of avoiding the heavy traffic on the main arteries he'd years earlier adopted an offbeat route in the last leg of his approach to the hospital. He recalled that earlier, driving through the quiet and orderly neighborhoods removed from the seethe of traffic, he felt he was intruding upon the privacy of others, like an uninvited and unwanted presence at a not so public gathering. With time he began to feel like a regular of the neighborhoods and was soon enough on fairly intimate terms with the residents' lawn care, the snow removal habits, the holiday display style, and sundry other of the visible indicators of family fancy and fortune. It had gotten so that some of the homeowners would wave to him as he drove through, his having become as reliably familiar to them as they to him. And he would wave back, grateful of the acceptance and forgiveness. But over the past few years his transit of these neighborhoods had become less exclusively his. More and more cars seemed to be tracing the same route, and undoubtedly for the same reason. He felt offended by their invasion of his private corridor, much the same, he figured, as the homeowners felt about him years earlier and maybe still did deep in their hearts. Moreover, he felt guilty that maybe he had served as bellwether for what was beginning to look like the rolling spoliation of the happy neighborhoods. At times he felt like seeking out another route to absolve himself of complicity in any further damage to the homesteads of those unnamed residents with whose community interests he had gradually become identified. But he never did, because that would just add to the burdens of another place. So here he was, making his checkered and daily way through the backstreets of the gentler path to his teaching job.

Soon enough he reached the hospital. Like most hoary psychiatric hospitals, Moreland State Hospital was surrounded by a barrier. Its barrier wasn't the usual neolithic stone wall but an eight-foot-high black iron fence formed of halberd-shaped pikes. The menacing authority of the fence laid bare with awful clarity the formidable determination of society to sequester and cloister the violators of its fragile sanity, and whenever he drove through the massive front gate, as he now did and which was no longer guarded as in years past, he felt that he was indeed crossing the frontier of the collective societal mind and entering a realm of exile, a realm to which he had been granted privileged access and right of free passage much like that of a diplomat to a hermit nation. No matter how many times he entered the hospital's grounds he was still greeted by that sense of favored and select status, though along with it a heavy regret no less weighty for the almost total failure of his specialty in the area of disease prevention. Unlike the other fields of medicine, Psychiatry was still essentially a palliative art, not a preventive one as so much of the rest of Medicine had been for the past hundred or so years. But it wasn't for lack of effort or purpose that his field had such a humble status among its sister specialties; it was just that the human brain—and mind—remained everybody's frontier, and its secrets seemed always to be just beyond the reach of every new and promising technology. True, a great deal had been learned over the past fifty years, thus forcing the retirement of several of the more dramaturgical theories on the genesis of human behavior, which theories in fact were derivatives reflecting more the social and political assumptions of their time rather than the science of the day. Those theories spoke more of sin than they did of science. The more colorful of the theories were inadvertent contributors to the traditional bugaboo of blurred distinction between form and content with the result that the more easily observed behavioral and interpersonal consequences of a given disorder were assigned causative status in the genesis of the disorder itself. As a result, and for the better part of four decades, American psychiatry took itself down a tautologic cul-de-sac in which the gains, though considerable by any means, were primarily in the humane treatment of the mentally ill, and quite determinedly so because the theories of the day defined mental illness as a product of personal mistreatment in the formative years of life. Every patient was thus a victim, entitled to the redress of the interpersonal crimes perpetrated on him as a child when he was unable to defend himself. Child abuse was the cause, and every patient's family was thus an etiologic culprit of sorts deserving corrective rehabilitation, or more. Cantrelle had often wondered just how much American psychiatry had contributed to the victim mentality that had now become so pervasive in American society and, conversely, how much his field was itself a victim of its own regrettable and essentially pathologic distortion. Probably more the latter, he hoped, because he could not countenance the idea that American psychiatry, too often skewed by certain activist elements in its ranks, had in its missionary zeal of the past several decades succeeded primarily in cultivating a collective confabulation of the nation's populist identity. European psychiatry to this day remained discreetly quiet on the matter. Though his training had been fairly classical—he was both a psychiatrist and a psychoanalyst—he had always been something of a maverick but never to the point of alienating the heuristic benefits of his larger professional milieu. Thus he remained on fairly good terms with the more responsible representatives of the contending schools of thought, both in and out of vogue, and was at least on better terms with those representatives who were routinely available to him. However, he managed the entente with an agreed-upon premise that no basic assumption, his or theirs, likewise in or out of vogue, was excused the cold stare of critical review, ever. It was a tacit compact that enabled him to avoid the charge of mere mischievous apostasy as might be levied by the more cultish of his field.

The broad main gate yawned open before him. He drove through and dropped his speed to what the signs bade. As always, the sweeping and well-tended greensward gave more the impression of an expansive estate, and the older buildings, bearing the then trendy and heavy hand of Victorian Neo-Gothic stamp, gave a feudal ambience to the grounds. He was ever thankful that the original architect had laid out the hospital complex such that the roads connecting the buildings curved and meandered a bit to suggest an inherent placidity and even casualness to the siting of the buildings. The hospital complex was indeed that, a complex. It was composed of approximately fifty buildings laid out over some one thousand acres of lawn, fields, roadways, recreation areas, parking lots, and even a working farm. Also, there was a good-sized creek that burbled through the grounds. The trees, in their variety and extent, plus the literally thousands of plants and shrubs composing dozens of gardens, kept the grounds crew, complete with a full-time horticulturist, more than adequately occupied in meeting the seasons. But the results were well worth it, for in former times, when doors were locked and gates guarded, there was little to distinguish the hospital from a state prison, save for the lovely and mannered grounds. And even today, the grounds played no less a role in conveying the humane and salutary intent of the hospital's brute existence. Sunday afternoons still found families of townspeople strolling the grounds as though the hospital were a community park like any other, but more exclusive and better tended. Or like some former ducal estate, still tenanted, but now open to the public.

His office was located in one of the newer buildings. The successive stages of the hospital's construction could be traced by its growth rings, much as with a tree. The oldest buildings were in the center of the grounds. Later construction surrounded those buildings in widening concentric rings. And the effect was also conical, for the original buildings were also the tallest with lofting ceilings to the several floors, bell towers and spires on the facades, and pinnacles set at strategic points along the cornices and eaves. The newest buildings were of lighter hue, two stories at most, and rambling in their lines of Spartan simplicity. The older buildings were trimmed in cast iron filigree; the newer ones looked neatly aeronautic in their extensive glass and brushed stainless steel treatment. There had been three distinct construction periods: the mid-Victorian, the art deco, and the post-war. The color ranged from brooding umber for the oldest to can-do khaki for the newest. And none were centrally air-conditioned, except the newest building of all called the Community Center, which was actually a six-hundred seat auditorium where only the most important events were staged. For years he had tried to mount an annual symposium that would be held in that impressive building. The symposium would serve as an update on the latest developments in the field, a kind of a briefing to be given by the noted thinkers and researchers who collectively set the tone for American psychiatry. Like Burleson, for instance. But he had never been able to sell the idea to enough people to get the project off the ground. The hospital did, indeed, host an annual symposium, appropriately called the Moreland Conference, but in a frank effort to stimulate interest as well as attendance its program was not allowed to stray from the immediately and agreeably popular or the faintly sensational. As a result, there was little theme continuity from year to year and thus there was the sense that the symposium had to be resurrected annually, phoenix-like, to address whatever new fad might have arisen in the field of human striving during the intervening year. He had openly stated more often than was necessary that the conference made no effort to rise above the crowd-pleasing level of fads and fancies which represented little more than surface eddies stirred by the deeper currents of materia medica. Moreover, those eddies were often pseudo-issues, spun off by the workings of more seminal movements, and thus evanescent at best. At the worst, they were the stuff of professional gossip dressed up in the trappings of sober debate. Even so, that's what the people seemed to like, for the conference was generally well attended. And it certainly had acquired a regrettable activist, even political, cast in its recent years, all the more to further its alliance with the glitzy and faddish. He had merrily said to his residents once or twice that the conference more and more demonstrated the fundamental difference between the politician and the scientist: the politician offered popular solutions to eternal problems while the scientist sought eternal solutions to popular problems. Yet he encouraged his residents to attend the conference for the purpose of bemusement if nothing else, and they usually did. He himself hadn't been to the conference for years and saw his disaffection more as entitlement than dereliction. The administration of the hospital wasn't so sure, but never made an issue of it.

His relationship with the hospital administration was overall splendid. He had been through four superintendents and as many assistant superintendents over the years, and in every instance he and his training program were accorded privileged status in the hospital muster, much the same as when a family member joins the clergy and thereafter enjoys a relative absolution in the family's ordering. He had been recruited for the job of Training Director partly because he had studied elsewhere and thereby had not acquired his professional vetting within the political and personal cross-currents typical of any operation the size of Moreland's, a practice too often dysgenic to the scholarly intent of classical psychiatric education. Also, his earlier work at Moreland as a junior member of the teaching staff had identified him as an uncompromisingly fair, gracefully irreverent, compulsively historical, and boyishly enthusiastic mentor. One of the former superintendents had said that the reason Cantrelle fit the job so well was because he was actually a Childe Harold and thus as comfortable with the past as with the future, though rarely with the present. It was thought an added plus that the residents and teaching staff all knew it. Also, it was a tacit and honored understanding between him and the administration that if he protected the training program from the political winds that howled up and down the corridors of the state capital, usually originating in the high pressure systems of nepotism and cronyism, the administration would protect the program from the local fiscal winds which blew just as fitfully. And each had kept the faith these many years; he because he would not have been able to find it within himself to do otherwise, and the superintendents because they themselves had been residents of the program during its glory years when the legendary Dr. William J. Palmer—author, teacher, administrator, and unquestioned leader of American psychiatry—was Moreland's superintendent. Many of the senior staff, not just the subsequent superintendents, were former students of Palmer's, and the training program was thus seen as the spiritual tie to that cherished heritage. Hence, there was a hierarchical grading of the psychiatric staff along a scale of academic heritage which loftily transcended all civil service status. Those who had actually studied under Palmer were far and away the anointed ones. Next, there were those who trained in the program, though after Palmer had passed on. Proper descendants once removed, so to speak. Then, came the residents currently in training, heirs apparent being taught the manner and scope of their regal duties. It went without saying that those of the lineage, Palmer and post-Palmer, thus merited preferred access to teaching staff membership since their training was in large part a preparation for subsequent teaching in satisfaction of the collegiate obligations of the profession. This arrangement accounted for the inordinately high proportion of Moreland graduates in the ranks of the residents' teachers.

Rounding out the lower levels in this pedagogic layering were the members of the teaching staff who had studied elsewhere. Chosen people, to be sure, but certainly not of the truest blood. And lastly, there were the general staff psychiatrists, non-teaching staff, who bore up under the misfortune of having trained elsewhere at a time in their youths when they didn't know any better and who, worse, had never acquired a knack for teaching.

Cantrelle himself was outside of the lineage and initially had been brought in on the lowest rung of the teaching staff. But the circumstances of the times, with the program distinctly down at the heel, plus his refreshing academic style and sense of pedagogic purpose, had combined to identify him as something of a puerile knight errant come to do some good. After all, he did drive a white Volkswagen at the time, modest conveyance indeed for an up-dated Lohengrin, but certainly a circumstance exceeding mere coincidence. The honor of appointment to the program's directorship followed after a discreet and prudent period of watchful assessment by those in charge and during which he demonstrated enough of the right stuff to assure all that he could never have truck with the likes of some scheming civil service Cromwell.

He drove past the looming and ancient administration building that always looked incomplete for the lack of bats flying in and out of its bell tower, and turned down the long quadrangle to the parking area fronting the low, glass-fronted structure that served as the Medical Office Building. It was of early post-war vintage, and its interior, especially the corridors, displayed the advent of bare cinderblock as the new medium of architectural expression. He had dubbed the style Contemporary Bunker, which he thought particularly suitable whenever a budget cut imposed an embattled stance on his operation. But despite its Spartan texture the building performed its job suitably well, housing the majority of the psychiatric staff in accessory offices away from the work site offices on the wards which usually carried enough of the din of daily activity to discount that precinct as a place of contemplation or repose. So when the staff members came to the MOB it was usually for a moment of respite and sanctuary. Also, various staff conferences and meetings were held in the building, an arrangement that usually struck a collegial note as seasoning to its milieu. All in all, the MOB was a pleasant place to be and it was where most of the didactic teaching of the residents took place.

He pulled into his unofficial parking slot—only the Superintendent and Assistant Superintendent had reserved parking spaces—and fished his briefcase from the back seat of the car. Thus fortified he strode across the roadway and mounted the steps of the building, two at a time as per usual, and tugged at the massive and reluctant plate glass double door of the entrance. He entered the lobby and then swung down the left corridor.

"And a good morning, Dr. Cantrelle," came the greeting. It was from Dr. Brossort. Jean-Pierre Brossort, M.D., one of the staff psychiatrists who regularly attended the Individual Case Review Conference Cantrelle conducted for and limited to the psychiatric staff of the hospital. This conference was held bi-weekly on Friday mornings, alternating with the A.M. Staff Conference, and was given to the focused review of a chosen case identified as particularly vexing diagnostically, therapeutically, or both. The case was presented by the attending psychiatrist, and most of the psychiatric staff came to join in on the brain-storming that the conference unfailingly engendered. Cantrelle liked this gathering almost as much as he did the A.M. Staff Conference.

"Bon jour, Dr. Brossort," returned Cantrelle with a twinkle. "How's the old lady? Holding up O.K.?" he inquired pleasantly, referring not to Brossort's wife but to the vintage Mercedes-Benz he drove to work only in pleasant weather.

"This morning she does my every wish," Brossort returned with a scabrous leer in the purse-lipped accent reserved exclusively for the French.

The memory of his morning with Laura danced before his mind as he offered an appreciative chortle ostensibly in credit solely of Brossort's quip. Brossort then smiled charitably, satisfied that his select wave length with Cantrelle—cars in an erotic frame of reference—was as clear and as operant as ever. Brossort was from Quebec, and from the there's-only-one-language-worth-speaking secessionist class of that province. His upbringing was such that English was carefully cultivated as a foreign language to be spoken only with the correct accent and inflections suitable for an unadulterated Frenchman. As an extra guarantee of purity, Brossort received much of his medical training in France where, oddly, he felt more at liberty to practice his English on typically baffled American tourists. It was there that he developed an interest in helping the needy American, an interest which subsequently hardened into a decision to emigrate to America as a cultivated missionary for his ministry to shape itself along the lines of psychiatric practice. After residency training in New England, he joined the Moreland staff, and soon afterward, upon learning that Cantrelle also was of French extraction, adopted him as a fellow evangelist in the call to apostolic ministry for the enculturation of rustic America. Cantrelle took a mischievous delight in Brossort's presumption of mission, perhaps ultimately a brasher form of his very own, and savored the irony of present-day Americans being cast in the role of indigenes needy of salvation. Others on the staff weren't always so amused.

"Your conference, Dr. Cantrelle; we begin again next week, no?" he inquired, shifting to their other conjoint interest. Unfailing in his attendance of the gathering, Brossort was also one of its most animated participants.

"That's right, Dr. Brossort. Starts the new year," he replied. The academic year, he meant. The conference, like so many other educational rigors, was, if not suspended, at least attenuated over the summer months, especially during August when so many of the staff were on vacation. "Did you make it back to Quebec this summer?" he added in polite solicitude.

"Certainement! Where else could I go?" returned Brossort in pretended astonishment at so inane a question. And then, more warmly. "And you, too, must go there some time. Your ancestors would approve." Brossort persisted in the belief that Cantrelle's predecessors had migrated from Canada a few hundred years earlier, as was the case with so many Americans of French nationality. At the outset of their friendship, which coincided with Brossort's discovery of Cantrelle's pedigree, it was clearly stated by Cantrelle that his family had emigrated from France directly to Louisiana just after Jefferson bought it and not by way of Canada, or so his grandmother had said. This fact seemingly did not jibe with Brossort's preferred construction, and hence was ignored ever since. Cantrelle acquiesced to the illusion as part of his contribution to the bright folly he enjoyed with Brossort.

"I'm sure they would," Cantrelle offered in concession as he began to shift his weight in the direction of his office, "but don't distract me just now with visions of Paradise. This morning"—he pronounced the words with a hint of Gallic accent—"I must grapple with the sheer hell of the A.M. Staff Conference, and in fact I could use a little spiritual help from those ancestors just now."

"Dr. Cantrelle," he said as he shook his head sadly, "they will not come to help you, for like all beings who have found a better world, they will not leave Quebec."

After the briefest moment in mock gravity they broke into laughter come of an exchange of wit brought to a mutually agreeable point of conclusion.

"See you at the conference next week," Cantrelle smiled, gesturing a comradely farewell as he started to turn toward his office.

"I think so," agreed Brossort with a hint of a bow before he walked away.

Cantrelle bounded up the hallway to make up for the time spent with Brossort in banter but came to a halt before the open door of his secretary's office. His office was an inner one and entered only through his secretary's, which also served as a waiting area for his callers.

His secretary was already watching the doorway to greet him, having recognized his footfalls in the hallway. Here again he had the best of all possible worlds. Everybody at Moreland agreed that Georgia Andretti—late thirties, chestnut hair, hazel eyes, and tall—was the unquestioned best secretary the hospital had ever seen. Smart, efficient, canny, loyal, and ever a lady to her very fingertips, Cantrelle had often chided her that she had all the wily virtues to be the power behind any throne, anywhere. And she was a knock-out dresser too. Predictably, lots of people came to her with lots of things in need of her deft attention. She, too, had a hard time saying no.

"Good morning, Mrs. Andretti," he announced to her welcoming smile. "Today's pay day, isn't it?" he observed looking at the stack of window envelopes before her on the desk. He tended to lose track of the bi-weekly pay schedule.

"Good morning, Dr. Cantrelle. Yes, it is," she replied with cheery anticipation. "Yours is on your desk."

"Thank you," he returned, having begun his transit of her office to reach his own now that the formality of arrival and morning greetings had been settled. It was one of his quirks that every morning he would come to a complete halt to greet his secretary before proceeding to his office. He felt that doing so affirmed the proper pitch of office formality he insisted upon. To him it was unthinkable that the business day might begin with his walking past his secretary without the tender of a proper greeting. He usually lathered over the Victorian bulkiness of this ritual with a spot of light chatter. In the first few weeks when she started to work for him years earlier, Mrs. Andretti betrayed a mild discomfort with this unwonted display of attention which may also have seemed too formal in its tenor. He sensed her uncertainty and explained one day when the opportunity arose that his mother had "brung him up good" and that there was no getting around her lasting influence on him and that he and certain others, like Mrs. Andretti herself, would have to make the best of what another notable behind-the-throne power had wrought. Since that explanation the matter had settled into a jointly observed recognition of proper office protocol which also demanded that he never address her by her first name.

"You have a call from Dr. Weaver. He wants to talk to you before your conference this morning," she added as he was entering his office.

"O.K.," he acknowledged over his shoulder as he approached his desk.

His office conveyed more a sense of debris than decor. The furniture was the usual institutional mix of completely styleless pieces spanning decades of Accounting Office purchases. The carpet was a vertiginous pattern of green and black and a salvagee from a local motel in the throes of decorative upgrading, but it did match the civil service green of the walls. The walls themselves were marked with a riot of hangings, each a contribution from residents over the years, and included a large, scowling ceremonial mask from Haiti, a wood inlay portrait of a Latvian church, a cloth picture of a bare-breasted Mogul dancing girl, a framed bullfight billboard which carried his name for the main corrida of the afternoon, and a Currier and Ives print depicting a New England Autumn. His contribution was two alpine scenes lifted from a pharmaceutical calendar of forgotten vintage. One wall was completely taken up by a large, framed felt blackboard on which he had the names of all the residents affixed under headings to signify their current study blocks and locations.

And the state of the book shelves on the window wall was little better. He kept his important books at home—all four hundred plus of them—and allowed his Moreland office to acquire whatever happened by. This resulted in a disparate gathering of pamphlets, old medical school books, out of print syllabi, soft cover editions of conference abstracts, a few up-to-date periodicals, and several victims of the hospital library purges he felt were too good to throw away. Of the latter, he even had a book on "rational hydrotherapy" published in 1903. He said the illustrative pictures were just too precious to be without in their stark, self-conscious rectitude, as only medical pictures of that era could be. Thus, the bookshelves were more for storage than for access. If he had to look up anything he did so at home or at the hospital's library where he enjoyed a certain accommodation, being Chairman of the Library Committee in perpetuity for the yet unforgiven deed of having consolidated some years earlier the nine separate libraries of the hospital's constituent departments into one inconveniently located athenaeum grandly called the Central Library.

He propped his briefcase on the windowsill where he poured himself a cup of coffee from the ever-waiting carafe. He then returned to his desk and settled into his chair. Resting in it limply, he sipped from his cup and stared blankly at the wall fronting his desk as he allowed speculation to catch up with him. He was now once again alone and he sighed in savor of its restfulness. Heavy fatigue was catching up with him as happened daily at this time after the busy ordeal of getting the work day moving along its proper course, the additional vigor lately come of a promised Autumn notwithstanding. He rested for a moment as the aroma of the coffee gently wafted his thoughts, its liquor just beginning to course through his sagging veins. In a few minutes his caffeine level would be back to rights and he'd be ready to shove off again. In the meantime, he rested.

"I wonder what Jess wants?" he asked idly, elbows planted on the arms of his chair as he held his coffee in both hands to savor its nose.

Jesse Weaver, M.D., was one of the grand older men of psychiatry. Tall, burly, and Falstaffian of wit, he was also the compleat scholar and gentleman. Moreover, he was the canny Assistant Superintendent of the hospital. But, more importantly, he had studied under Palmer and, hence, was one of the more devoted supporters of the training program, and now of Frank Cantrelle as well. Never openly stated, their mutual respect and affection was a given which was never questioned. He had risen to Commissioner level years earlier and had restored genuine distinction to that pork-ridden office. Later he left the state system for awhile, but upon the unexpected advent of a vacancy in the hospital assistant superintendency several years later was asked to return in that lesser office as a civic gesture for which he was paid "slightly more than a dollar a year," he explained. Because he transcended the usual ambition-driven clamber up the state mental health ladder he was able to bring to the assistant superintendency a selfless and compassionate administrative style more typically seen of the British aristocracy in their noblesse oblige approach to public service.

He sipped at his coffee, lingering over its bracing finish as he continued to stare blankly at the wall before his desk. A serviceable reverie couldn't quite get started because of the hovering uncertainty over the purpose of Jess' call. He could find out what it was about easily enough by just picking up that damned phone, but right now he'd rather try to preserve a few moments of restful remove over his coffee before slipping into the current of the day's events. However, it was becoming apparent to him that his willful delay in returning the call, though intended to protect a contemplative warm-up period of wall staring, was now beginning to work the opposite effect by tightening his focus on just what in the world would soon be dropped into his lap on this heretofore lovely morning.

"It had better be good," he grunted in submission as he leaned forward to reach for the phone, the creaking of his swivel chair echoing the groanings of his not yet limber joints. He punched in the numbers with a retaliatory briskness, smiling slightly at his peevishness as he did so. He knew that as soon as Jess answered, his mood would change instantly. It always did, and for the better. It rang only twice.

"Dr. Weaver," came the reply.

"Jess, It's me, Frank. Good morning. You called?" he greeted.

"Yes, I did. Can you come over? I need to talk to you about something," Weaver explained.

"Jess, you know I have the A.M. Staff Conference with the residents in a little while," he objected.

"Yes, I know. It has to do with that, as a matter of fact. Something has come up and I have to talk to you about it before you get to the conference," Weaver explained.

"All right. I'll be over in a few minutes. Give me a moment to take care of a few things here first," he relented.

"Right. See you then," Weaver agreed.

He returned the phone to its cradle and wondered what pain in the ass proposal, or program, or general purpose vaudeville act had arrived from the Department of Mental Health requiring his devout participation for the purpose of pulling someone's political chestnuts from the Commonwealth fire. That sort of thing didn't happen very often, but he was eternally vigilant for it and he perhaps often sniffed the spoor of political encroachment where none was actually intended, thus certifying him in certain quarters as being a touchy, suspicious, and unrelentingly cynical prick who believed he owned the training program and all its contents. And to a certain extent the charge was valid, though his own point was that he was merely seeing things as they truly were. But Jess Weaver didn't at all mind such outrageous presumption; he was reassured by it, as a matter of fact, and he often confided certain prospective policies and plans up for action in the DMH long before their formal introduction so that their implications could be perused and any points of infringement, inevitable or potential, of Moreland's sacerdotal teaching effort be ferreted out and thus girded for well in advance. Actually, such was seldom necessary, but when it did happen there was no question that being ready to offer "corrective reaction" was priceless, such as the time a blanket hiring freeze was mounted by the governor's office in an effort to limit expenditures throughout the civil service system. Commendable enough, but no one from the DMH had been intrepid enough to mention that state-based training programs, of which Moreland's was only one, graduated a portion of its student body every year and received an approximately equal number just as annually in replenishment of the beginner class for the coming year's training, the overall number of trainees remaining about the same. The hiring freeze, in its blanket application, would certainly have allowed for graduation but would have forbidden an incoming class, and if allowed to stand as pronounced would have suspended just about every accredited state-based training endeavor in the system, which certainly was never intended. It was like a college being encouraged to graduate annually and forever, but forbidden to bring in any new freshman classes. When recognition of this most infelicitous consequence was urged upon the DMH, it then became a matter of short-strawing one of its members to approach the throne and, in effect, have the wretched messenger report that, as magnificent as they were, the emperor's new clothes were regrettably unsuitable.

It was an incredible oversight that seemed to fuel his abiding displeasure with the state's higher administrative chambers, ruled as they were by political accommodations not easily brought to accountability. He also knew that his general attitude toward the DMH, even in the absence of legislative or administrative misadventure, was categorical, tendentious, and unfair. He was as aware as the next that the vast majority of the people in the state system, even in the capital, were dedicated, honest, and hard-working, as the phrase usually ran. However, for him such awareness bore no conciliatory fruit in what he considered to be a famine of integrity in so many of the political appointees in any given gubernatorial administration, the DMH having its fair share of such genre. It was also the case of so many of the enduring rank and file civil servants working too close to the flagpole for so long that they became lost in the dark of its penumbra. In effect, they were removed from the harsh, direct light of the real world and lived in the slant light of a virtual world. Yet, they were given the task of leading the way to a brighter land. So the basis of his thinly veiled contempt wasn't even personal, though from time to time particular appointees, local as well as regional, made it almost irresistible to avoid being so. Actually, his contempt was decidedly more doctrinal in nature. He loathed any system that failed to identify its basic assumptions, much less failed to put those basic assumptions, openly identified, up for periodic testing. Any system, such as a gubernatorial administration, which avoided doing so was, he contended, inherently totalitarian and restrictive, regardless of its sweet name, gentle purpose, or tender hopes. The so-called notorious "total institution," he would rant. He also knew that this conviction was the puerile part of himself speaking, an aspect of unreconstructed adolescence and the product of a credo unleavened by the sobering effect of maturity. But he knew of no way around the matter for he truly and sincerely believed he was right. In application of his belief he would gleefully point out to his residents the carefully unstated basic assumptions hidden in reputable, even exalted, laboratory or clinical work. The naughty consequence was that while the work's discoveries might not be wholly vitiated thereby, such open disclosure of underlying, unproven basic assumptions specifically generative of the work often rendered its discoveries a lot less absolute, the merry result of which was an obligatory enlargement of the field of critical inquiry to include the very work itself in an even more impartial review. Science, he taught, was founded upon the mandate to test basic assumptions, its own as well as all others, and it labored mightily to protect and sustain that precept, though history abounded with examples of unintentional misfeasances by many of its most dedicated sons and daughters. Yet, in the overall, the integrity was usually there to acknowledge error and to move on to better effort. And it was on this point he assailed the other systems of man, particularly the political. Too often the political scene, particularly the American one, he insisted, was ruled by whim and fad without the slightest interest by party or personnel in questioning the nature of its givens. In fact, quite the contrary; its givens were more to be confirmed as absolute, to be sustained by the unquestioned faith of its adherents. Actually, quite religious in its manner, its members subject to being shunned as apostate upon the breathing of any doubt as to the validity of the party's premises. He saw the same in the less scientific side of medicine with certain groups, particularly the specialty of Psychiatry because of its soft and not too scientifically solid grounding, organizing themselves into cultish enclaves bent more on self-protection than on the self-examination they professed, with the result that at times he was for shame hard put to direct his criticisms beyond the ranks of his very own legion. But he did, with his belabored residents and too many of his totally innocent friends becoming the weary beneficiaries of his sallies into censure. And his enemies—he had a few, he boasted, "because something would have to be wrong with me and my principles to have a person like *that* guy as a friend"—waited for their moment. He knew as much, and knew that a few of them lived in the DMH, his having more than once accused that office of selling old snake oil in brand new bottles to the state mental health system by way of self-serving and thoroughly suspect programs of mental health deliverance that came and went with the various reformers, visionaries, and medical messiahs swept into the DMH by the tidal spoils of various state administrations. Such DMH appointees often saw themselves as enlightened missionaries bringing The Word to the unwashed civil servant savages of an evil state mental health system jointly seen as the wicked instrument of the very diseases the system publicly purported to treat. Indeed, more than one Secretary of the DMH over the preceding twenty years had proclaimed the state mental health workers and their system to be the very cause of the mental diseases in their keep, extolling the patients as pathetic, undeserving, even noble victims—that term again—of an evil design perhaps innocently perpetrated but which nevertheless yielded outrageous benefit to the workers at the cruel cost of the patient's immortal mind. There was no way to talk to such people because they were certain they already knew everything worth knowing about the matter. And their zeal, often fortified by vigorous Cabinet support, made the defense of their basic assumptions, often long-standing private and frequently quite peculiar convictions now energized to the level of personal apotheosis by the happy advent of some social or political fad, well nigh impregnable. And then the more responsible workers, among which he counted himself—a basic assumption in its own right and about which he chided himself for its being insufficiently examined—waited for their moment which invariably came as the new order fragmented into contradictions, regresses, and iterating epicycles of program adjustments taken to mask the surfacing folly of the fraying crusade. Fanaticism, so to speak. And then the old standby, good-guy state mental health workers would step forward and redouble their efforts to sustain the system's better purpose until the misbegotten and faltering crusade faded into an oblivion of embarrassment, the exit route often pointed out by a chagrined administration finally up to realizing that it was time for a different kind of panacea. But America was ever a crusading nation, and evermore would there be movements of emancipation, led by impassioned carriers of some current Word, the bearer only later to be seen as another false prophet, and then banished as required. And yet, some good often came of it all. Some aspect of treatment or patient management would be called into question, subjected to remediation, and then adopted as the expectable standard of care, sometimes significantly elevating the system's sensitivity to the wounded humanity present in all mental illness. But such movements and programs almost never contributed to a better understanding of the *cause* of mental illness itself because, after all, the crusading messiahs already knew what needed to be known on that score. And in view of that certitude their mandate was graciously excused the devoir of closer scrutiny, at least in the thinking of the faithful.

But one thing he noticed in the succession of reformers. Even though they and their hangers-on were often little more than well-intentioned purveyors in snake oil done up in the colors of humanistic rectitude, they themselves bought the stuff just as readily as they sold it, and artlessly at that. Moreover, the annunciation of mission by such an appointee to the DMH leadership would usually call forth fringe elements of the mental health movement to make their overdue mark, and much too often they were accorded instant recognition in exchange for their support of the New Word. Frequently that recognition translated into jobs, which, in turn, often led to infusions of yet other brands of snake oil readily accessed by the leadership. Very miscible, it usually turned out, and too quickly spooned out.

"Blah, blah, blah," he intoned to himself as he pushed away from his desk, got up, and walked over to the window. "Lately, it doesn't take much to get me going," he mumbled in reference to his litany of discontent with the political side of the system. "I hope to Christ the day will come when someone from the front office can call me up without being obliged to witness my virtuosity at variations on a theme of distressed self-righteousness. I must be a colossal pain in the ass to those people," he rued, donating a moment of charitable pause to that notion as he gazed out upon the greensward. "But they deserve it!" he affirmed. He shook his head in consternation at his own unnegotiable obduracy. "You would think I was some kind of a reformer or something," he added, laughing out loud at the irony of seeing himself the existential counterpart of the very arrogance he railed against.

"Did you say something, Dr. Cantrelle?" Mrs. Andretti inquired. The door between their offices was usually kept open; it was closed only when some matter of high sensitivity or confidentiality was at hand, such as chastising a resident or interviewing a candidate. It was never closed during his pontifications beamed at the front office.

"Well, yeah," he shifted. "I have to see Dr. Weaver before the conference this morning and I want to get that letter off to the Directors of Training association before I go. Can you get it out this morning?" he inquired as he rose and walked toward her.

"It's already done. It's on your desk. Just needs your signature," she informed him evenly.

He retraced his steps and approached his desk, scanning it enroute. Sure enough, there it was, exactly in place where all the completed correspondence was always placed to await his signature. He had missed noting its presence while caught up in his soliloquy on righteous indignation.

"Good," he chipped briskly to override his chagrin. "What on earth would I do without that woman?" he wondered discreetly to himself as he gingerly reached for the waiting letter. All of her typing was so resplendently neat that he signed what he had to with fingertip care so as not to leave the slightest smudge anywhere on the perfect pages. Moreover, she cranked out that immaculate work with ferocious efficiency and unerring accuracy. Everybody knew that she was destined to be the Superintendent's Executive Assistant some day, but for the present she belonged to him, Frank Cantrelle, for better or for worse.

He signed the letter, a questionnaire actually, soliciting his suggestions for the program format being developed for the annual mid-winter meeting. He then took it to her for mailing.

"Thanks," he offered in acknowledgment of her aptness, adding, "I'll go directly from Dr. Weaver's office to the ITU, so if you need me for anything I'll be at either of the two places." He always told her exactly where he would be when away from his office so that she would not ever be placed in the demeaning position of having to hunt him down when he was called. He bridled at the thought of secretaries having to say they didn't know where their bosses were when the phone summoned. And, in turn, she, spared that indignity, never failed him.

"O.K.," she returned, smiling him on his way.

"Great gal," he thought to himself for the ten thousandth time as he re-entered the hallway.

The hallway was empty and so his march to the door was unhampered by any additional greetings. He pushed his way through the doors and hopped down the steps to make up the time he would spend in Weaver's office on God knows what. He quickly traversed the parking area, got into his car and revved up. It was less than a block away to Weaver's office, but driving would save him the walk back to his car for the spin to the ITU which was on the far side of the campus and a quarter of a mile into the greensward. He pulled away and was only in second gear when he slid into a slot in front of the Administration Building. Already the asphalt was beginning to collect its annual leafy dappling of russets and gold.

"They're falling early this year. Must be the dry summer," he mused as he eased his car to a halt next to Weaver's, determined not to have a bothersome call to administrative attention override his awareness of a nicer world. He locked up and then mounted the steep steps of the narrow entrance, one at a time now, and squeezed through the balky and incongruously modern front doors that had levers rather than door knobs. The Administration Building was the oldest on campus, built in the late 1870's and at the epitome of its genre. Exquisitely parqueted tile floors, head-high paneled wainscoting, exposed-beam ceilings celestial in reach, bay windows in every room, and, in an alcove off the hallway, a stately oil portrait of kindly William D. Palmer, M.D. reverently in view under the eternal light of a frame fixture. He offered a respectful nod to the great man as he strode past the portrait onto the door that opened into Weaver's office complex. And it was, indeed, a complex because the outer office which berthed three secretaries in its capacious reach served as a waiting area not only for his office but also for yet another office adjacent to his but separated by a room which housed an enormous walk-in safe, storage files, and copying machines. Also the coffee pot.

He swung open the large, rattly door and entered. Weaver's secretary motioned him forth. He walked to the open doorway of Weaver's office, drew to a halt, and knocked politely on the jamb. Weaver immediately looked up from his desk.

"Frank! Come on in," he greeted, eagerly consigning him to a chair beside the desk.

"'Morning, Jess. How you doing?" he returned with genuine bonhomie, his wariness set aside for the time being.

"Fine," Weaver assured, "And yourself?"

"Pretty good. Hard to be otherwise on a morning like this," he recommended, looking past Weaver at the idyllic landscape framed by the huge bay window on the far wall. The arrangement of the trees was superlative.

"Yeah" concurred Weaver with a nod in the direction of the view, "That's my tranquilizer. One prolonged gaze four times a day pleasantly carries me through."

They both chuckled lightly in a shared commiseration over the regrettable thorniness of their otherwise cherished jobs. He also noted, though not for the first time in Weaver's case, that someone else was given to the equivalent of wall gazing. He had often said that any one who took any time to gaze at a wall in abject thoughtfulness had to be basically decent. The introspection encumbent upon that enterprise simply was incompatible with personal dishonesty, as he definitely knew to be the case with one Jesse Weaver.

"Frank, I want to mention something to you about the case this morning before you leave for the conference," he broached carefully. "Might help you in sizing up the issues."

Cantrelle's eyes automatically narrowed as his wariness returned with the shift in conversation. Any suggestion, ever, that the conference, *his* conference, be used for purposes other than education had always met with immediate, unnegotiable, indignation-drenched refusal. There was another conference for reviewing cases cursed with administrative sensitivity—political, personal, litigious, or whatever—and that was the Individual Case Review Conference, the one anticipated by Brossort. And Weaver knew that. Thus the earlier qualms about the purpose of this meeting.

"Go on," Cantrelle urged cooly.

Weaver knew he was being watched, and heard, keenly. So he proceeded with elaborate good will.

"The case you're going to see this morning, Winston Jordan, is the son of an old college buddy of mine. He called me at home a few days ago to let me know that his son had been admitted to the unit. Of course, he was pretty upset about it, but he wanted to fill me in on some things that might be of help and I could pass on," Weaver explained.

So that was it, Cantrelle snickered inwardly. A personal friend probably wanting some kind of accommodation.

"The father and I were in the same fraternity. Really a nice guy. He went on into the ministry. Hadn't heard from him in years until this came up. They live outside Akron. His son is a third year Business major at Franklinton. Just started the semester a few weeks ago," Weaver added.

"What did his father want you to know?" Cantrelle asked with rising impatience.

"He wanted us to know," Weaver continued patiently, emphasizing the word 'us,' "that over the summer his son had begun to dabble in street drugs, or so the family suspected. The boy had never been a problem before, except for always being a bit high strung and, for a brief period as a very young boy, doing a stint of fire setting. Only two times they know of and really minor, like trash in garbage cans. But that was when he was a kid. Good student in high school; active, steady girl friend, the works, so his father says."

By now Cantrelle had begun to nod in sympathy with the unfolding elements of the story, but also because of weariness at the familiarity of it. The anguish of the family was not to be denied, and that in itself was an ordeal to apprehend what with the devastation of the family's high hopes and simple happiness being displayed in their desperate efforts to help in the treatment. But it had become so familiar a story that there was little of positive value in its usefulness. Almost universally the family initially portrayed their affected child as an all-around good and promising kid somehow mysteriously gone wrong with the advent of dread symptoms from out of the blue. It would be later, deeper into the investigation of those symptoms, that a different kind of story would unfold to reveal that there had been ample warning of trouble in the making, and that the family, being all too human, either tended to deny the evolving issue or had inadvertently abetted its growth, and often both. The initial consternation adequately substantiated the family's innocence of any contributory dysgenic intent or complicity, but it also served the family's natural need to distance itself from the uncanniness of mental disease. In time, this stance would change into one of mutual fault finding, often and regrettably urged along by mental health workers themselves. It was then that the concepts of etiology and blame, cause and guilt, would be meshed to define the patient as a sad victim. He had heard it all too often.

"The only thing his father is requesting, 'cause he knows we'll certainly do the best job we can in helping his boy," Weaver continued, "is that we shoot straight with him, tell it like it is so that he and the rest of the family can do what they have to—if there's anything at all they can do. And unless his father has changed a lot since I last saw him, he means it."

"They always mean it in the beginning," Cantrelle mused to himself ungraciously as he listened to his colleague. It would be later that the family line would harden, generally when the patient, also all too human, began to exploit the treatment setting in the service of settling scores over family grievances, real or fancied, but now being able to do so from the protected position of entitled victim endorsed by the minions of American mental health advocacy. The sense of compensable injustice would then prevail and the taking of sides would assume paramount importance. That's the way it was done in this country, democratic and freedom-loving as it was.

"So the request I would like to make, Frank, is that after the conference today you let me know how you see the case so that I can pass it on to his Dad. That's all," Weaver concluded with too easily detectable innocence.

Cantrelle looked at him impassively for a moment and then drew in his breath to position himself for the question they both knew he had to ask.

"Who chose the case for presentation this morning?" he exhaled with a weary wheeze.

For a moment Weaver looked down at the opposed fingertips of his hands resting on the desk before him, and then returned Cantrelle's gaze face on. After just the right amount of time in rapt silence he answered through a smile of triumphant vindication.

"Clay did," he said simply.

Cantrelle absorbed the stroke, and smiled.

"Honest Injun?" he asked for surety.

"Honest Injun," Weaver replied, decently suppressing a gloat, but not completely. "Right after I spoke with the father I called the unit to find out how things were going with the boy and Clay told me he had been selected for presentation to you today. Morello is going to do it," he offered with casual finality.

Cantrelle stared at him for a moment, measuring Weaver's smile of placid supremacy. They had been through this before. The selection of cases for the A.M. Staff Conference was to be driven by academic necessity and nothing else. Cases requiring his special attention for other reasons, he had pronounced often enough before, would be seen in the other forum and so forth. The A.M. Staff Conference was to remain a colloquium inviolate, and so it would remain this day if the incorruptible Clay Moyer had indeed selected this case for its format.

Just as Weaver's smile began to cure into a self-satisfied snicker, Cantrelle struck back.

"Jess, you son of a bitch, why didn't you tell me that from the very beginning? I could have sat here in congenial comfort rather than having to watch you like a god-damned hawk," Cantrelle flashed.

At the first temblors of Cantrelle's eruption Weaver placed his hands flat on the desk and broke into a well-deserved guffaw. He continued in rollicking, red-faced laughter as Cantrelle railed on, and Cantrelle, unable to resist, joined in the hilarity of the fustian scene, shaking his head as though to push aside the foolish smile that now overrode his earlier vigilant glower.

After sharing a moment of the absurd, they reclaimed a measure of composure.

"You did it again, didn't you? Why do you put me through this? Pregnant pause and all," Cantrelle added through a few after-tremor giggles.

"Because, my dear Frank," Weaver explained in good will and with discernible affection, "we all benefit when we dismount from our high horse, even if only occasionally, and especially so with a little help from waggish friends." As he spoke his finger tapped the air in tutorial emphasis.

Cantrelle chuckled abashedly and, after a moment of appreciative receipt, nodded in acknowledgment.

"Got to admit that you're right, Jess. Damn it. And I guess you know you're the only one around who knows how to set me up in just the right way, I'm relieved to say!" he added.

"Well, I'm not so sure about that," Weaver returned as he fidgeted, now his turn to be abashed.

Their conversation had reached its end point. Cantrelle took the initiative by thumping the arms of his chair with a brisk readiness to move on.

"O.K.!" he announced, "As soon as I wrap up the conference I'll call you and let you know what we come up with."

"Fine," Weaver agreed.

"All right. Now let me get going so I can do something to earn my pay around here," he tossed in sounding the appropriately trivial note for departure.

"Right," echoed Weaver with a satisfied smile.

He rose from his chair and gave a perfunctory wave as he retraced his steps out of the office. He moved past the pool of secretaries and soon was beyond the observant portrait. Pushing his way through the balky entrance doors he re-entered the Estival brightness now rapidly warming the ambience. He broke into a trot to cover the short distance to his car because he was now running a few minutes late and his people would be waiting. In a moment he was working through the gears and discreetly exceeding the fifteen-mile-per-hour speed limit of the hospital grounds enroute to the ITU on the far side of the campus. A few of the strolling patients waved to him as he passed, some out of recognition, some just in hope of making contact with another living soul. As he waved back it again occurred to him that it seemed axiomatic the patients never walked briskly or resolutely; rather, they moved along in the manner of grazing cattle. For the most part, it was their medication that slowed them to a near halt, imposing upon them what amounted to a chemical strait jacket. But it was the diseases, too, particularly in their chronic and advanced forms, which often left their sufferers burned out wrecks that drifted purposelessly in their closed and empty world. The harsh conclusion that these sad people wandered so purposelessly because they had long lost knowing how to have a where to go was forced upon him once again as he scanned their vacant faces and felt anew the guilty helplessness known to all mental health workers. As usual he resisted that debilitating feeling—the bane of every sensible mental health program and the graveyard of all idealistic dedication for working with the mentally ill—and redoubled his effort to look beyond the immediate despair of these lost people. But even so, that effort often failed in the face of the stark statement presented by their appearance. The drabness and often disarray of their clothing spoke the pathos of personal neglect that could never adequately be corrected by solicitous attendants. Moreover, that was only the *exterior* dilapidation befalling their indented capacity for sustaining a sense of self. It seemed that not only had they lost the ability to conceive of a where to go, they had also lost knowing who and what they were, their very own *being*. And one of the great injustices of the larger *mise en scène* was that recurrently the populace at large, usually led by the blustery clamor of a reformer, would hold hospitals and their staffs responsible for the inexorable march of those baleful stigmata of severe, chronic mental illness even though so much effort to prevent exactly such deterioration was the anguished centerpiece of the hospitals' and the staffs' ceaseless but only modestly successful labor. Often it was obvious to everybody, save the clamorers themselves, that much of the criticism hurled at the hospital was little more than the desperately displaced guilt the families, which could not manage having the ill member around, demanded the hospital feel in their stead as they went on and on about their need to protect the member from the *hospital's* neglect, a pure projection and a kind of bribery to their own conscience—and so often in the name of reform! And everybody was required to play the rôle carefully, especially the DMH. Moreover, there were some, too often former patients, who had a stake in vengefully proving the hospital flat out sick and evil. But all this the profession accepted as its grim lot, and seldom breathed a word of demur. Indeed, it would have been unethical, in a way, to challenge such charges on the basis of their alter and less than healthy motivation. It was very much like the professional restraint practiced by the individual psychiatrist in his work with any patient. Though he might be accused by his patient of all manner of sin and wrong, he was bound to regard such accusations as just more clinical data to be analyzed objectively and to be understood much as any other clinical offering, even the laudatory kind. Certainly, patients often traded on this sober restraint honored by all responsible therapists, and even consciously exploited it for less than therapeutic purposes. But the therapist was still ethically bound more to understand than to refute, much less to pursue a counter-defense. To do so would be like rubbing the patient's nose in his illness. And so with the families, too. Thus it was as well on the scale of large institutions where it generally was *de rigueur* to grin and bear it in the face of groundless or, even worse, malevolent affronts which might at the moment offer social or political balm to the more credulous part of society. It was simply the tradition, enervating as it was.

"God damn it," he yelped to himself as he rounded a curve in the road, "why can't I just get the hell off this carousel of self-pity? I'm a pain in the ass even to myself today. Maybe I should just retire," he pronounced as he pulled himself away from what he dubbed the whining wheel which delivered prematurely the assorted regrets of advanced age. But lately he didn't say it so jokingly. He had noted over the past few years that he had become much less accommodating to what at an earlier time he regarded as the vigorous activism of American society. Of late he had come more and more to see that very activism as being at least as flawed as the problems it purported to correct. He had begun to fear that no matter what part of its visage our society attempted to correct or improve, the approach to doing so was still framed in its very own image and, hence, no less needy of improvement or correction. At times it all seemed so futile. Worse, maybe it was just that his slant on such matters correspondingly had the wrong tilt so that he and his attitude were merely part of even a larger, fatally flawed piece. Maybe it was actually his own personal futility in his own personal world which was at issue and thus, as he accused everything and everyone else around him, was merely reading the rest of the world through his very own maculate image. Or maybe it was just that he was getting tired. He considered that possibility more often of late, and it was Clay who just as often reassured him that weariness was the unavoidable handmaiden of wisdom, and that fretting about it was distinctly unwise. That lovable son of a bitch seemed to have a smart-ass answer for every doubt and quandary, which answers he distributed with a sense of privilege come of the conviction that he had successfully breasted every conceivable assault that human uncertainty could mount, thus earning him, he boasted, his own distinct brand of fatigue. Moreover, Clay highly recommended it to all who stood in genuine danger of falling victim to the twin treacheries of zeal and hope.

He had begun to giggle inwardly at Clay's irreverent cynicism when the ITU came into view directly ahead. The circular drive in front of the building had a nicely enclosed garden sporting a variety of early chrysanthemums. Those hefty blooms always reminded him of All Saints Day and its analogue, Halloween, which were still a ways off.

He pulled into his usual slot on the periphery of the parking lot, locked up, and was soon hurrying up the several steps to the front door which was usually kept open wide during obliging weather in a compensatory contrast to every other door in the building kept fast shut. "Locked Unit" was the term, and necessary to prevent patient elopement, or, in the case of the more confused patients, simply to guard against their wandering off. The building was one of those from the post-war phase of the hospital's construction and had as part of its facade a center tower that reached one full story above the wings that housed the patient wards. The third and topmost floor, his destination this morning, consisted of three wards, one in each wing of the T-shaped building; one male, one female, and a coed unit for patients farther along in their treatment and nearing discharge home or transfer to an extended treatment unit on campus. At one time the building also housed an excellent research facility on its second floor where good work was being done in the investigation of monoamine oxidase activity in blood platelets, an accessible source of that enzyme which was known to be one of the more important factors in the neurotransmitter function of norepinephrine, a major player in the neurochemistry of the central nervous system. For a while some years back he had been the "pro tem" director of the research staff in its effort to generate an applied research format which would extend the investigative skills and scientific perspective of the research staff to the various treatment units of the hospital, a kind of shift from an *in vitro* to an *in vivo* mode of investigation. The move, intended to energize research within the treatment setting so as to harvest the morale and milieu benefits which naturally derived of such union, was welcomed and supported by all, with the notable exception of the DMH which unilaterally later determined in a budget caucus some smoky afternoon that state hospital-generated basic research would no longer be permitted in the system, though research generated elsewhere, such as at the medical school teaching centers, might be supported for extension to the state facilities whose staffs could then serve as ancillaries in any such investigative projects. The DMH funding of state hospital research was then axed and Moreland's research scientists "furloughed," as was the euphemism of the day. Research well along in its clinical application came to a halt despite local protests which offered solid evidence that research activity in the treatment units themselves yielded benefits far beyond the mere acquisition of scientific data. But to no avail, and seemingly overnight the hospital was without its research team. For several years thereafter, research at Moreland went underground to skirt the proscription enforced by the DMH. But more recently a DMH administration more congenial to the heuristic benefits of an investigative milieu had lifted the research ban, though for awhile afterward the hospital's resurrected research committee out of caution shaped its function more along the lines of wary risk management than of ranging and vigorous inquiry. But all of that was now in the past and a sense of scientific curiosity was no longer regarded as seditious, reckless, or wasteful. And it was to that hallowed and now empty second floor he set his present course, to use its neglected conference room where, in oblique memorium, the A.M. Staff Conference did its tutorial business.

He threaded his way through the busy lobby of the building, past some milling patients being escorted by their attendants to sundry clinics and clinical labs for various medical attentions, and drew up to the elevator doors against the far inner wall. By the time he reached the button panel he had already fished his ring of institution keys from his coat pocket and had begun ferreting through the collection for the one which would activate the button panel. Dickering with the numbered keys was always a noisome task; finding the right key for a particular door or, at the present moment, elevator, and again he wondered why after all these years he hadn't color coded the keys to save the time of putting on his glasses to read the identifying numbers on the almost identically shaped set, picking through them one at a time for the needed key. Colors would certainly make it easier since the keys were distinguished by aggregate function. One key opened inside doors, such as wards. Another, elevators. Yet another opened building entrances. And then another opened administrative offices, or physicians' offices, and so forth. The more peripatetic the staff member in his work, the more keys he carried. Large, jingly rings of keys abounded, often anchored to hips and belts by chains, the attendants usually being most demonstrative of the identifying authority the keys conferred. He used to think that such a vaunt could not be other than an affront to patients, but over the years he had learned that many patients, if not most, also saw in such custodial display a protective security since it was not only a matter of their being locked in but, perhaps more importantly, what was being locked out. However, the patients, like so many civil service workers, all military careerists, and most spouses, publicly lamented their indenture all the while they obediently sustained it.

He worked the key into the elevator lock, activating the circuit, and then pushed the button. He then began to hum a few passages of Boccherini in preparing himself for the usual extended wait, which was generally preferable to using the stairwell because of the several locked doors which would have to be traversed along that route. But, uncharacteristically, the elevator rumbled into bay soon enough, prompting him to cut short his private musicale. He wondered idly if today even the elevator was in a hurry, though ordinarily it was the most forbiddingly casual entity in the entire Moreland world. Its doors then yawned open in its more familiar meter, and as he stepped inside he wrote off the unwonted convenience of the moment as just one of those things. He then repeated the key procedure for activating the floor button and punched in for the second floor where the conference was held because of the relative quiet on that level for its being free of the clinical din which permeated all space on the third floor housing the patients. The elevator groped to a halt and the doors labored open. He stepped out into the empty lobby and turned up the left hallway that would take him to the conference room at the far end. His stride, already quick, was picking up in goal gradient fashion as he neared the conference room door. In passing he reached out to the button of the water fountain stationed against the wall and bent down for a last minute sip as he drew in his stride a tad to pivot around the stream's contact with his lips as he continued his motion in the general direction of the conference room. Momentum unbroken, he returned to the upright and resumed his forward trot, wiping his mouth with the back of his hand to tidy up his entrance.

Upon nearing the door he brought himself to a more stately gait to suit the mannered scholarship sought by the conference, and the Boccherini quintet popped into mind again as he began to hear the light chatter of the waiting group within, which he immediately likened to an orchestra's tuning up before a different kind of concert. Pleased that he had acquired the right set, he pulled the door open.

The chatter subsided as he entered. He scanned the gathering with a smile of greeting as he walked toward his waiting chair at the large conference table at the front of the room. The table's size suitably matched the room's expanse. Chairs for perhaps forty or fifty attendees filled much of the room, and the conference table, set classroom fashion before them, had its own line-up of chairs for those who would participate in the case presentation. The chair placed at one end of the table, the one next to his and the only chair with arms, was for the patient when the time for interview came.

All eyes followed him as he approached the table, its gathered panel already settled in place and waiting. He took in the waiting panel with a beam of humble satisfaction, touched, as always, by their faith in him as leader and teacher, or so their presence seemed to declare. In fact, he regarded the conference with its entire extended membership as constituting a most generous and even affectionate endorsement of his efforts, and its members included not only those in training status such as residents, medical students, nursing students, and psychology interns, but also various social work, occupational therapy, recreational therapy, and even music therapy externs, plus any member of the general hospital staff who chose to attend. The attendance varied from session to session, but there was a nucleus of regulars which sustained much of the dialectic momentum while the periphery changed according to circumstance. Particularly challenging cases or particularly pleasant weather usually saw a large turnout, and the size of today's gathering seemed to mark a synergism of the two. Except in unusual circumstances, such as today's, he never knew beforehand what kind of a case was to be presented—a preference he himself registered and encouraged as desired format in an effort to minimize the likelihood of distortions or bias coming of any unintended pre-judgment. So, coming to the conference even ideally cold, he usually could tell how much work had been cut out for him any given conference morning just by the size of the attendance. Today's attendance said that it was a lot. Also, it suggested that word may have gotten out that the case was special, the son of a friend of a friend. That thought annoyed him for it reinstated the pique which had accompanied him to Jess' office earlier, and now was just not the time to have that thought cluttering his thinking.

"Good morning, Frank," Moyer greeted with an energetic smile as he adjusted some papers before him.

"Morning, Clay. Great day for biking, huh?" he offered.

Moyer was an avid bicyclist and often pedaled to work, trussed up in the svelte accoutrements associated with that exertion. Of modest height and with a mane of thick, black hair cropped for speed, he presented an image of youthful trimness which strikingly set him apart from others of his age group. People automatically regarded his sinewy regimen and his dedication to its rigors as the cause of that youthfulness. But Cantrelle wasn't so sure; he considered and fairly well believed that it was the other way around: it was Clay's innate vitality that kept his bike moving so well, right along with his dark, restless eyes. Cantrelle, also looking brashly younger than his years, felt a visceral kinship with his psychologist friend of long standing, and even though Moyer, older by a few years and at Moreland considerably longer, had followed a substantially different route in his professional upbringing—graduate school as opposed to medical school—the two of them meshed just as congenially in their clinical stripings as could have been wished. As a consequence, there was so much that didn't need to be said. Thus, their collaboration proceeded from an advanced point not ordinarily embraced elsewhere in their work with others.

"Yeah, and we're planning on its holding for the weekend," Moyer replied. "Helen and I are going to hit the countryside tomorrow and Sunday, weather permitting. Only treatment for the Moreland staggers," he quipped to the appreciative chuckles of the attentive residents and several others.

"Well, for the time being," Cantrelle continued with a smile, "let's stagger forward with what we have this morning. I understand you have an unusual case lined up," he added, hinting at the administrative background music.

"We'll let you decide," Moyer followed with a puckish grin, an infallible sign that a diagnostic problem was afoot. "Ready Dr. Morello?" he inquired of the waiting resident.

"Ready!" replied the resident with the patient's clinical chart held at the ready.

John Morello, M.D., was like so many residents he had taught over the years, and yet he was one of a kind. Much too tall—six feet plus—for his big baby blues and blond ringlets, he had the usual youthful zeal inclined to impose a sometimes regrettable excess on many of his efforts. He was also redoubtedly idealistic and, hence, unassailably righteous in the application of those efforts just as he was woefully inexperienced in recognizing the sobering limitations of energy and good intentions alone. But like all such residents he was accordingly precious, refreshing, exasperating, and, when allowed his own run, tedious. In a word, he was like a child, as they all were, and thus one looked after them, taught them, disciplined them, encouraged them, consoled them, berated them, cherished them, and too soon graduated them. Then, one prayed for them, for, like all children, the power of their youth was matched amply by its vulnerability. He often saw little to choose from in comparing the worries he had for his own children and those he had for his residents. In turn, like his children, they adored him, feared him, tolerated him, mimicked him, thwarted him, followed him, but soon enough left him. Then they revered him, for as with all mentors his meaning to them grew as did their learning. And on that score John Morello might have been a bit ahead of his peers, for early in his training at Moreland he had developed a keen attachment to Cantrelle but, to his credit, only rarely allowed its filial, affectionate character intrude openly upon the more mannered cast of tutorial accord. Now in his last year of training he was serving a wind-up elective on the Admissions Unit as Chief Resident to assist in the teaching of the junior residents assigned there. Blessed with encyclopedic knowledge —"Do you know the name of the highest active volcano in the world?"—and cursed by the remorseless passion to acquire it, he inflicted his trivia questions on everyone in earshot, and he did so with an outrageous and disarming mischief that made his victims laugh as they winced.

"Let's start," directed Cantrelle.

"O.K.," replied Morello, "Buckle your seat belts! Here we go! The patient's name is Jordan, Winston Jordan. He is a twenty-year-old single caucasian male in his Junior year at Franklinton University. He was transferred to us two weeks ago from the psychiatric unit of the medical school hospital for continued evaluation and extended treatment, if necessary. The transfer diagnosis was Organic Mental Disorder, secondary to drug abuse. They included a rule-out of an underlying schizophrenic process."

"Let's stop there for a moment," interrupted Cantrelle. "What does that suggest, the inclusion of that rule-out with what is primarily regarded thus far to be a drug-induced organic psychosis, at least in their reckoning?" he queried of the five junior residents sitting at the table. After a moment of hesitant silence he added, "Anybody? I don't expect you to have a framed answer after just a couple of sentences of identifying information, but what you've heard so far should be generating some broad and unpolished hunches about the case, or about the diagnostic problem it might offer. Don't be afraid. You have to learn to work with the uncertain as well as the incomplete in this business of formulating a testable hypothesis. Remember?"

They had better remember, he pondered menacingly as he waited, for he'd preached that missive to them and to all their predecessors so often he was sore put to tolerate a hint of its infraction. Morello smirked knowingly, restrained from answering for the question's having been directed to his juniors.

"Could it be that the patient had shown earlier aberrant behavior," one resident raised hesitantly, "and that's why the case wasn't seen as just a drug-related psychosis?"

"Good!" Cantrelle pounced, "That's a distinct possibility and we'll find out more about that as we get to the History of the Present Illness and then into the Background History. That's one hypothesis, but is there anything else suggested?" he urged.

"I don't know about this," another resident volunteered, "but maybe the history of taking drugs, if there really is one, has nothing etiologically to do with the patient's current behavior, psychotic though it may well be."

"*Very* good!" Cantrelle underscored. "That's really keeping your options open, and I would expect no less from you, Dr. Brewer." A ripple of laughter followed. The punctilious Dr. Brewer was long regarded as the unit's full-time skeptic judged to be well on his way to an astringent and disavowing nihilism. Thus his suggestion was most fitting. "But more seriously," Cantrelle continued, "it's quite correct to regard the transfer diagnosis as a logically arrived-at conclusion based upon certain preliminary observations. However, what the previous evaluator regarded as the basic data of observation—in other words, the clinical signs which tallied with certain basic assumptions of his own—is what's at issue here. And we all know the treachery that lurks in basic assumptions, don't we, gang?"

It was an everlasting *cri de coeur*, his admonition concerning unspecified and questionably warranted basic assumptions. He would have his residents believe that such unspecified basic assumptions were much like the unseen bacteria around us—ubiquitous, frequently helpful, often innocuous, but sometimes quite pernicious, and occasionally pathogenic in epidemic proportions. He held that most if not all of the major political, military, religious and even scientific movements of history were ideologically funded by the confluence of a populace's, or a group's, basic assumptions having come to flash point on some cause or purpose at its ordained moment, the leader of the movement being the agent of ignition in liberation of the moment's divine fire. Nazi Germany was a more recent example of his point, that baleful period in history come of the Teuton innate in all Germans having reached a militant unity in their unquestioned assumption of a destiny, and fitness, to rule all others.

"Right," Morello vowed for all. "The patient," he then continued after a pause to ascertain whether or not Cantrelle had anything else to say on the matter, "gave a chief complaint of 'It's funny. You can't see how funny. I can.'"

"That's an unusual one," mused Cantrelle aloud. Morello nodded in agreement from his position of senior resident and its credited experience. The junior residents abstained. "Does it suggest anything?" Cantrelle posed. "Don't forget now, the chief complaint—and especially one bearing the stamp of psychosis as this one does—is usually the patient's condensation of his subjective experience of the entire problem, and it frequently contains symbolization and displacement, just as in dreams."

They remembered, having heard it often enough, that a good understanding of a given case should result in an elucidation of the uniquely compacted meaning contained in the chief complaint, much as a dream may be interpreted and reconstituted into a more comprehensible, logical form.

"I don't know what the chief complaint means; I don't think any of us can say with certainty at this point," pert and pretty Gloria Sumner, M.D., opined with her usual whiff of cheekiness, "but I wonder about the possibility of a strong affective component being present."

Cantrelle smiled indulgently at her comment. Despite her junior status he saw her as one of the more talented and promising of the entire resident group but feared that she organized far too much of her science around a need to suppress a determined and solicitous femininity she ostensibly regarded as decidedly too tender for her own good. Only later in her training and professional growth would she, he hoped, come to regard her natural warmth and sensitivity as a treasure to enrich her professional identity as well. But right now it seemed she felt it more politic, and sober, to be a canny competitor, though the intensity of her clinical work betrayed her exquisite sensitivity to the painful needs and sad hopes of her patients, sometimes to her own great personal distress.

"Correct," Cantrelle allowed. "But even though he refers to a feeling—something is 'funny'—we can't, as you suggest, know at this time how large a component that feeling plays in his overall mental status, such as whether there is a basic feeling of mirth conferring a sense of merriment on any and everything he apprehends, or whether he has concluded something—an ideational act—which identifies the world around him as amusing, or even 'funny' in the sense of being odd. That's what we'll have to explore. Please go on, Dr. Morello," he added after a pointed pause to allow his comment to register.

Morello then detailed the chronology of events leading up to the hospitalization, and he did so in the ordained manner demanded by Cantrelle of all his aspiring charges. That manner featured a strict survey of the critical interplay of events and symptoms across the fabric of the patient's existence, the unique pattern of which traced the personal warp of the five fundamental pursuits in the human predicament—the Fabulous Five, the residents twitted: Work, Play, Eat, Sleep, and Love. Then, there were the Subsidiary Six: the Who, What, Where, When, How, and Why within the context of each of the Five. The weft, so to speak. They knew that no History of the Present Illness was considered adequate by their mentor unless it gave full and fair representation to each of those Five plus their qualifying Six which together were held to be the sum and substance of all human endeavor according to Cantrelle, the particular balance and blend of those Five cardinals and their Six ordinals serving as a personal signature for each individual's effort called his Adaptive Life Style, a notion vaguely reminiscent of Adler's pronouncements almost a century earlier. A mere recitation of the symptoms and their progression was scorned as trivial, but any accounting of the symptoms vis-a-vis *each* and *of* the five basic pursuits and their six particulars was held basic to the discipline of competent assessment which allowed no compromise this side of the main gate of Moreland. He was never certain which of his residents, if any, followed the format out of genuine conviction and which did so out of mere compliance. Hence, the need to remind them from time to time of the seminal difference between discipline and obedience.

But he had no doubts about Morello, who now proceeded with the story of the patient's descent into psychosis.

"There is little history of truly unusual or symptomatic behavior prior to three weeks ago," Morello began. "Approximately one month ago the patient returned to college after the summer vacation at his home in Ohio. He was entering his junior year at Franklinton, majoring in Business Administration in the Horton School. His grades were low average and he'd been quite active, according to his family, in his fraternity during his Freshman year. Maybe too active, they felt, especially his father who had hoped, we're told, that the patient would have taken his studies more seriously and persisted in Engineering, which is what the patient had started out in. The story is that he found Engineering difficult and demanding, and that it cut into his social life too much. So after his first semester he shifted to the Horton School, with a major in Marketing—and partying."

A ripple of knowing laughter passed through the group. Cantrelle felt a more somber chord begin to take form in him. He had heard so many similar stories over the years, especially in the sixties and seventies, and they seldom were pretty or had nice endings.

"Apparently, during his first week back to school he settled in as usual. The family said they noted nothing unusual. He always groused about going back to school and would make mild threats of dropping out, but he always registered on time, they say, and usually with the help of their urging, but he would soon get into the swing of it which usually took about a week or so, his father said. But this time he made more than his usual number of return-to-school fraternity parties. His friends said that almost every night he was with some group of revelers, even people he had not previously socialized with. And apparently it was at one of those parties that something happened."

By now the group had settled into an alert silence. Cantrelle had levered himself a little lower in his chair and was squinting over the tips of steepled fingers arched over his nose, his chin resting on his thumbs. The case presentation always acquired a sober and intent tone after the first few moments of welcoming levity, and this case saw that transition occur on time, maybe a bit sooner, given the patient's youth and his collegiate identity, elements which put him existentially closer to the residents and to the other young trainees present. This patient's evaluation and care would not be neglected, not by these young compatriots, Cantrelle mused.

Morello went on to recount that it was at a fraternity party the patient experienced the acute onset of odd and disordered behavior. Allegedly his friends present thought little of it at first and assumed that he had combined some street drug with his beer and that the effect would pass in the course of the evening. However, as the evening wore on, Morello detailed, the patient's behavior did not abate. Friends watched over him during the night but by next morning, when he continued to be as disturbed as he was the evening before, he was taken to the Student Health Service Dispensary. From there he was admitted to the psychiatric unit of the University Hospital. Morello concluded the accounting with the pointed mention that a drug screen run at that hospital was negative for the known street drugs and the usual proprietary ones as well.

"Any history of prior drug use?" Cantrelle queried in puzzlement.

"We'll get to that later in the background history," Morello deferred. He then reviewed the patient's hospital course at the University Hospital, giving particular attention to the ineffectiveness of the various medications used in an effort to bring the patient back to some state of emotional and mental equipoise. "Gradually over the course of two weeks his behavior subsided a bit, but when it became apparent that he'd have to be hospitalized for some time, he was transferred here," Morello explained. "They didn't come up with anything other than a drug psychosis, agent unknown. The blood tests, electroencephalogram, and CT scan of the head were all pretty negative. The only medication he came here on was Lorazepam and only one half milligram three times a day. They felt it reduced his restlessness and enabled him to sleep better at night, but it didn't improve his mental status in any way," he summarized.

"What about the mental status?" Cantrelle inquired, a bit impatient that it hadn't been included earlier. He was beginning to feel that Morello, long come to understand his boss and his predilections, was delivering the case in measured servings more to whet the appetite than to satisfy, the better to tantalize the very inductive bent he labored so hard to cultivate in his charges, though now being tweaked for it by one of his leading apprentices. Fair enough, Cantrelle conceded on a note of paternal tolerance mixed with satisfaction; he laid large store in their knowing that he never asked of them what he himself wouldn't do, or attempt. Now, and not for the first time, that policy was being brought to issue in taking him to turnabout task on a matter where it expressly applied. He thus adjusted upward the setting on his usually too sensitive impatience monitor to allow for the leeway today's carefully confected presentation required. Morello noticed the cagey smile of recognition and offered one of his own in return as he continued.

"We'll also get to that in a minute," Morello teased, "but first I'd like to bring out something about the early onset symptoms noticed by his fraternity buddies, as we have it from the transfer records."

"You will have your way, won't you? You may fire at anything you wish, Gridley," Cantrelle yielded.

Morello chortled an acknowledgment and then resumed.

"The thing that tipped off his friends at the party that something was wrong with him was his giggling. It's said that after about fifteen minutes to a half hour of brooding and apparent puzzlement, which they also thought odd for him but didn't then think that much of, he began to giggle uncontrollably. Along with it he behaved as though he were unbearably embarrassed, hiding his face in his hands as he giggled. They noticed also that his face was flushed bright red, and it was that which convinced them that he had taken something, though he hadn't confided it to anyone there like people do, you know, with marijuana and other recreation drugs."

"I know," Cantrelle sighed.

"Anyway," Morello continued, "his friends tried to talk him down but couldn't. They say, or the record says, that he would just sit there, giggling to himself as though he were enjoying some huge private joke, and feeling embarrassed in the face of his own glee. And when people tried to talk to him he wouldn't face them, as though he were too embarrassed to do so. He wasn't violent or disruptive, and apparently he didn't show increased motor activity. They didn't report anything to suggest that his perception or motor coordination were disturbed in any way. He just sat there and giggled. Also, he was pretty cooperative when they could get through to him, past his giggling, for urging him to lie down or to drink some coffee or such. That's why they decided to keep him at the frat house overnight and give him a chance to come around rather than take him to the dispensary right then and there."

"What about drooling or bowel and bladder control?" Cantrelle probed, clearly perplexed by what he was hearing.

"Nothing mentioned either way," Morello responded.

"What about what he was saying while he was going through this? There must be something there," Cantrelle urged.

"He did keep saying things between runs of giggling. Things like . . ." Morello quickly fumbled through his notes to find the quotes. "Yeah, here they are. He'd say 'Funny, funny, funny,' or something like 'God, it's too funny,' and at least once he said, 'It's so funny it'll never go away.'"

"Did he say anything about God, or anything to suggest thought control or insertion, like some power was making him laugh?" Cantrelle fished.

"They wondered the same thing at the Psych Unit at the University Hospital. They checked out that point every time they interviewed him but couldn't come up with anything remotely like formal delusions. In fact, they couldn't document hallucinations either," Morello replied.

"Hmmm," Cantrelle groaned as he twisted his face into a grimace. He saw that he hadn't set his impatience monitor quite high enough for this case. "Oh," he remembered with a glint of hope, "what about tremors, tics, or twitches?"

"Nothing reported," Morello shrugged.

Cantrelle returned to his grimace which Morello read as a sign to proceed.

"That takes us to his admission to the hospital Psych Unit," Morello cited. "As I said, his friends sat up with him all night but his giggling continued pretty much unchanged—maybe a little less, they thought—but the flushing pretty much all went away. When it got to be daylight and he hadn't come out of it yet they felt they had no choice but to take him to the dispensary. None of his friends had seen anything like it before."

"I know how they felt," Cantrelle added drolly. Morello seemed to relish it.

"Anyway," Morello continued, "he was admitted to the Psych Unit at Franklinton where they did the drug screen. They also did the basic lab studies plus a CT scan of the head—all within normal limits. The admission diagnosis was Organic Mental State—Toxic Psychosis, agent unknown. Mental Status on admission to their unit was not much different from what it is now, except for being more acute then. He seemed to be oriented when he could focus long enough to respond to questions about date and location, but they couldn't detect any real misperceptions—no delusions, no hallucinations, no illusions. Maybe some referential thinking since he seemed to think that everything he perceived related to some fundamental hilarity which only he comprehended, a kind of a delusion but not formed in the usual sense, they felt. They couldn't test him on serial 7's or on the other standard cognitive checks because either they couldn't reach him or he couldn't focus his attention long enough to see the tests through. He'd break off into giggling even if he made a stab at the questions."

"Sounds a little like hebephrenia, doesn't it?" Cantrelle managed tentatively.

"I think they thought so, too; at least from the descriptive standpoint, and that's probably why their final diagnosis included reference to a possible underlying schizophrenic process," Morello suggested.

They hadn't seen a genuine case of hebephrenia at Moreland for quite a few years, and it was usually at the State Hospital level that such a rare form of Schizophrenia was encountered. It was usually in that setting the more distinguishing and debilitative elements of the general disorder evolved into their characteristic and all too often chronic form. Each sub-type of Schizophrenia had a prevailing tone to its psychosis, at least in the acute phase, and the prevailing tone for hebephrenia was that of silliness and crass giddiness, just as the prevailing tone for the paranoid type was persecution or grandiosity, while mute immobility was that for the catatonic. He had taught that the paranoid type accounted for the thinking form of schizophrenic psychosis, while catatonia comprised the motoric form, and hebephrenia the feeling form. Not exactly accurate on every account, but enough so to be handy reference during preliminary clinical assessment.

"With that possibility in mind let's now go to the Background History," Morello continued, making no effort to disguise his intent to ply Cantrelle's confoundment. "What we have is what the social worker and psych resident at Franklinton got from the parents when they came during the first week of his hospitalization, plus what Mrs. Rolf and I were able to get from the parents personally when they came back to assist in his transfer here. They plan to visit weekly as long as he's here."

"Since then," interjected the slightly plump and pleasantly stylish Elaine Rolf, chief of the unit's social work team for the past ten years or so, "I've had several follow-up phone interviews with the parents. So we're pretty much up to date."

Ever efficient, she was.

"Is the family fairly cooperative?" Cantrelle queried in an oblique reference to the validity of the information gathered.

"Very much so," Rolf returned. "What we have is fairly reliable, as far as they're able to make it so," she explained, sensing his concern.

"Good, and since you've hit your cue just right, maybe we can get on with the Social History right now, unless Dr. Morello has something more to add," he advised.

"No," Morello said, "That about does it for the Present Illness."

"O.K. We'll give you a rest and then return for the current Mental Status soon as Mrs. Rolf takes us through the Background History," Cantrelle added, motioning with a nod in her direction and eager to move the conference along. This damned waiting for the clarifying data, he groused inwardly, but he knew that Elaine Rolf with a good fifteen years of experience in the field would get to the hard data in jig time and make it loads easier for him to pull the case together, for in such matters she was literally worth her weight in gold, including those extra fifteen pounds which bedeviled her beyond the exorcistic potency of her devotional diets. She foreswore those fifteen pounds as not of her true essence but more the stigmata of an impious spell cast upon her by some sardonic force ever in league with calories.

"Winston Jordan, our patient, is the only child of The Reverend and Mrs. Frederick Jordan who describe their marriage as happy and stable," she began in the stylized presentation form of her craft," and the information given by them is considered reliable and accurate," she reaffirmed. She then recounted the circumstances of her meeting with the parents and endorsed their conjoint as well as separate responsiveness to the interview and its purpose. Declaring all to be in good order, she proceeded with a summary of the patient's developmental history, beginning with the mother's several miscarriages before and after the successful gestation of the patient, though delivery was complicated by a prolonged labor requiring induction. There followed a colicky but fairly healthy infancy with developmental milestones generally falling in line as expected, though an erratic sleep pattern persisted well into the fourth year. The spectre of hyperactivity had hovered over the patient's childhood years, she reported, and his school performance was undermined by an awkward eagerness which teachers saw as his excessive need to please, compounded by poor impulse control. His grades began to reflect his behavioral unevenness, and it was necessary for him to have tutoring in the fourth and fifth grades to prevent his falling behind his peers. It was during this time that the early signs of a tendency to brood appeared and was read by his teachers and parents alike as his discouragement over not being able to excel despite his ardent efforts to do so while those around him seemed to do so much better with half the effort. The parents were not insensitive to the patient's distress, Rolf emphasized, and they endeavored to be supportive without conveying inordinate expectation. Plus, they cooperated readily with the school's efforts to help their son manage his onus.

"It was at this time a few fire-setting incidents occurred, one in an open field, and the other in a trash can in school," Rolf detailed. "They never determined that he set them, but he was the one associated with both locations. He denied responsibility. There were no other incidents, so nothing more was made of it."

"In Junior High he seemed to have an easier time of it. Friendships became foremost in importance and he played on the school soccer team and even developed into one of the better players, we're told. The parents even began to feel that at last he was over the worst of his growing pains. His grades improved as well. The only concern the parents had was that he tended to draw his friends, some of them anyway, from the lower end of the class, some of whom were thought to be trouble makers. But he presented no special behavior problems. His family knew he took some teasing as a preacher's son and understood that he had to do a bit more to prove himself one of the boys.

"That takes us to High School. The first year went O.K., but in the tenth grade—he had reached sixteen—he tied in with a group of fellow students regarded as a bit wild and certainly not the academic leaders of the school. Now, friendships and fitting in became a passion with him, and his parents believe he went along with the group's behavior as the price he had to pay for acceptance. As you would expect, his grades dropped and his parents became concerned not only about that part of it but also about the beer drinking everybody knew was going on in his group. He denied it, they say, and insisted upon his friends' innocence though the friends would openly brag about it. The parents say that for a while battle lines were drawn—he and his friends against them—though open confrontations were rare. He finished the tenth grade with barely passing grades and spent the summer working as a bus boy and staying out too late after work with those friends. He was hoping to save money to buy a car. A few of his friends had cars, and cruising around was the prevailing social activity when they were together. His parents were opposed to his having a car, and he responded to their opposition with a more determined alliance with his friends. They say he even threatened to drop out of school, as a few of the friends were considering doing. However, by the end of the summer vacation the worst of the confrontation had blown over and he returned to school for the eleventh grade.

"Not greatly different from a lot of teenagers," Cantrelle observed off-handedly.

"But again, his studies were given short shrift in favor of his social pursuits, at least in the beginning," Rolf continued. "Near Thanksgiving time an event occurred that brought a marked change in Winston. His friends had scheduled a party for one of the school's football games. By this time his parents were sure that the friends were well into drinking and probably also drug experimentation, though Winston hotly denied any participation of his own, and he continued to defend his friends. In any event, the parents forbade his going to the party. A row developed over it and Winston threatened to go anyway and even talked of running away from home to boot.

It ended up that he didn't go to the party, but later in the evening several of his friends at the party went driving around on something of a spree. They were speeding and ran into another car head on. The other car was driven by an elderly couple and the wife was killed instantly. One of Winston's friends was killed also and another sustained brain damage. The police report and subsequent investigation showed the cause of the accident to be reckless driving, speeding, and drug and alcohol intoxication on the part of Winston's friends. Following this terrible development, Winston withdrew from that group and pretty much stayed close to home for a few months. The experience seemed to shock him into a sober awareness, his parents said. For a while he became something of a loner; he avoided his former friends and he had no others to turn to for having earlier alienated most of the other kids in his class. His parents saw his withdrawal as a brooding, painful reassessment of himself and they tried to be as supportive and encouraging as they could. For a while he turned to the Bible, and his father hoped that his son would secure the guidance and inspiration a renewed faith could bring. But Winston never sought his father's counsel in his search and apparently side-stepped the father's efforts to help. After a few months he lost interest in religion and settled for a subdued and uneventful address to his school work with minimal social life. He had become quieter and more cooperative. And pensive.

"The next summer he worked as a bus boy again and he did so uneventfully. In September he returned without demur to school for his senior year. This time there was no talk of getting a car. His parents felt he never really got over the shock of the accident, but they allowed that in the overall his behavior had changed for the better. He had become amenable to the idea of college and he genuinely worked at preparing himself for such during his senior year. He also re-established himself in the mainstream group of classmates though his parents suspected he probably never felt fully comfortable with them. He made his best grades since elementary school and was able to get accepted at Franklinton, a little family influence helping, the father admitted.

"All in all, his senior year in high school was by far his best in all ways, and his parents believed that he had turned a point and had begun to settle down to a more serious view of life and also to prepare himself for it. He even acquired a steady girl friend in his senior year; and that development pretty much accounted for his social life. The parents approved of the girl who had already decided on going to nursing school after graduation. He continued to see her even during his freshman year at Franklinton, though only on holidays and between semesters."

"Anything to suggest drug use during the summer after graduation?" Cantrelle asked, eager to elicit more definitive data.

"Nothing," Rolf returned. "He drove a delivery truck as a summer job and there was nothing to suggest any troubles. He dated his girl friend and pretty much got ready to enter Franklinton, according to his parents."

Rolf sensed that before she proceeded everybody could use a moment to register what she thus far had related. She gave that moment by offering the parenthetical comment that the history so far didn't offer much significantly different from what might be found in the background of any number of American adolescents, the same point that Cantrelle had made earlier.

"In fact," she expanded, "there was a hint in the parents' accounting that they covertly approved of some of his behavior—not the drinking, though, or any of the drug use, but as being individualistic, searching, and redeemable. A kind of prodigal son foredestined to return."

There were no comments from the others, so she continued.

"As we know, he started Franklinton in Engineering. Apparently it became obvious in the first month or so that he was having trouble keeping up, despite good effort at his studies. He confided in his parents over a series of calls home that he was considering switching his curriculum or even dropping out of school. They suggested he speak with his student advisor first, and he did. Apparently his grades improved slightly for a while but the parents said it was clear he was not enjoying his studies and probably was more lovesick over his girlfriend than he wanted to admit. They hoped the problem would subside as he settled down and made new friendships. But at the Thanksgiving break he informed his parents that he didn't want to continue in Engineering. It was agreed that he finish the semester with a genuine effort to make the best grades he could and then switch to something else for the Spring semester. By the time the Christmas break arrived it was all settled. He had passed three courses and failed one. Christmas time was strained for the family in view of his and also their disappointment, and it was at that time they noted the return of his brooding. Also, while home on the break he and his girl friend decided not to continue seeing each other and the family thinks it was more his decision than hers. The family recalls the time as being somber at best. After the holidays he returned to Franklinton and switched his curriculum to Political Science. It soon appeared he had done the right thing because he called home several times early in the second semester to tell his parents that he was pleased with his new major and that he was making a new set of friends he felt he fit with better. And his social life improved considerably, they concluded. All in all, the parents felt relieved that perhaps their son was beginning to find his niche in the college scene."

"None of which is particularly remarkable," Cantrelle summed up. "Anything available to link with drug usage?"

"Nothing directly," Rolf replied. "I asked his parents just that and they said that if he did tap into drugs they saw no effects from it. He finished the Spring semester without incident, had a pretty good summer, and worked in the stock room of a department store. He picked up on a few of his old friends and looked forward to getting back to Franklinton for his sophomore year. The only thing the parents noticed was that he confided in them much less than usual and seemed more inclined to avoid them altogether, but they saw that as his growing up and growing away."

"It was well into his sophomore year," Rolf continued, but now with a slight shift in her tone, "that the family noticed something they in retrospect feel should have alerted them. Since he hadn't called home in some time they called him. It was a Sunday afternoon. They remember his speech was slurred and they had to encourage him to pay attention to their phone conversation because he seemed to be drifting off and not answering. He said he had been to a big party the night before and hadn't gotten much sleep. They doubted that fatigue alone was the reason for his vagueness, but didn't pursue it."

"Do you think there might have been indications of drug usage even earlier which they chose to ignore?" Sumner queried impatiently.

"Hard to say," Rolf returned, "but it is clear that the parents were trying mightily to maintain their optimism over his improved school performance. But during the second semester of his sophomore year his grades began to drop again and they received a letter from the Dean explaining that their son had been counseled for missing class and for poor academic performance and that he had been put on probation for the remainder of the semester. His parents were so upset they visited him at school to urge him to pull himself together and to get some therapy, if necessary. So I guess you're right, Dr. Sumner; maybe they had been trying to look the other way, because their reaction to the Dean's letter seems to imply an inner awareness of a problem brought rather abruptly to full light. In any event, the patient explained to his parents that he was losing interest in his studies and was thinking of changing his major to something like Environmental Sciences. Apparently this led to a heated exchange between him and his father about wasting his college years, not shouldering his responsibilities, and needing to shape up. The father urged prayer and counseling. The parents recall that the visit ended on a note of weary impasse with the patient's vague agreement to see the semester through in better form, which he did with barely passing grades in all of his courses. The patient's excessive involvement in fraternity activities plus an all around academic waywardness were seen as the basis of the poor school performance."

"I'm not so sure," Cantrelle doubted cryptically. "It might be the other way around. We'll see. Please go on, Mrs. Rolf," he urged.

Rolf smiled conspiratorially as she resumed her narrative.

"Odd you should say that, Dr. Cantrelle," she teased in confirmation. "It just so happened," she continued, "that right before the end of the Spring semester last year his fraternity put him on some kind of probation as well. It didn't come out till later that the probation was not only for using drugs but also for selling drugs to his fraternity brothers on the premises."

Cantrelle only nodded. His suspicion was being borne out that perhaps it wasn't so much a matter of the patient's being a victim of fraternity waywardness as much as it was the fraternity's feeling itself at risk from his excesses. Too often fraternities were given the blame for what was distinctly individual behavior. He had often considered that perhaps one of the covert inducements of membership was the opportunity to shift responsibility, and, when necessary, dilute blame. He decided to pose the question which was on everyone's mind.

"Do we know what drugs?" he asked.

"Amphetamines, mostly," Rolf revealed. "Occasionally some cocaine, but generally it was amphetamines. And he didn't sell them for profit, they say," Rolf added in his defense, "but just to get his money back. His friends said that he felt he was just doing them a comradely service by making the stuff available. Sort of his contribution to the scene."

It figured; amphetamines, that is, Cantrelle reckoned. What with this young man's childhood history of a likely learning disability, the hint of hyperactivity and attention difficulties, plus his more recent moodiness and academic shortcomings, street amphetamines would be a natural: close enough to the methylphenidate he possibly could have benefitted from in childhood but sufficiently divorced from the legitimate formulary of the medical establishment to spare him the abashment of clinical identification. Contrary to their effect upon the general populace, amphetamines usually gave a calming effect to those adults with the maladaptive residuals of the attention disorder complex, very much as methylphenidate did for children with the more typical form of that problem. While on amphetamines the patient probably felt, Cantrelle estimated, more in control of himself, more self-assured, more focused, and maybe even a bit euphoric—all likely vast improvements over his usual fragile sense of well-being. Included, however, was the inevitable problem of drug tolerance with the need to sustain the drug's desired effect by escalating the dosage. Plus, there was the problem of side effects—insomnia and anorexia—which moved right along *pari passu* with the drug dosage. Here it was again, a too prevalent and distressingly unremitting element in the milieu of current-day young Americans being played out in the person of one college student who had taken it one dose too far. He chose not to reiterate once again what he had already expounded too many times in the conference setting as well as in assorted classrooms that "recreational drug" usage so common nowadays was not as innocently "recreational" as it was purported to be. Rather it was, in large part, a folk medicine attempt at treating defects and deficiencies in many of society's membership. The historical abuse and popularity of alcohol in the management of anxiety was a compelling example. Though street drugs and alcohol were folk medicine in their own way, they did not have the stamp of hoary respectability traditional folk medicine carried; they were not born of an attempt to discover simples that could be used, frontier fashion, to compensate for the regrettable lack of proven and professional care; more, they were too often an attempt to avoid the clinical reality professional medicine would lay bare in people who worked at not seeing themselves neurochemically deficient. The businessman who drank too much might mischievously admit to the practice if granted the standard exculpation summed up in bland rationalizations such as pressure at the job, or a jolly weakness for high-spirited bon homie, or merely the vexatious persistence of a tendency toward bad habits "like in all of us." Almost endearing, such blandishments, and definitely popular, but pretty much debunked by the findings of recent medical research which might not be so congenial to that businessman's preference in as much as he would be loathe to see his tippling as rooted in an inherited and transmissible deficiency in his gamma amino butyric acid neurotransmitter system, the result of which was the pathologic anxiety he attempted to control with alcohol. The upshot would thus be that he drank more because he was flawed, rather than that he was flawed because he drank. Most people, he had learned, and Americans in particular, would much prefer to have their behavior regarded as defiant rather than defective. Not to regard it as defiance would take a fair portion of their behavior right out of their autonomous hands. It would also take it right out of the hands of certain dedicated reformers. He decided to tuck that particular infelicity away for future reference, if needed. For the moment he sighed at the magnitude of this huge natural experiment in diagnostic psycho-pharmacology being played out across the nation, feeling just as helpless as anyone else to influence it, even in the singular application of one college student's case being presented to him in the climate-controlled comfort of a proper clinical conference. But better to let those thoughts rest for today; everybody had heard them before, anyway.

Rolf resumed her narrative after reading his silence as acquiescence to the details yet to come.

"That brings us to this semester. His parents say that the summer again passed uneventfully with his spending more time with a small group of friends and at a job, sort of an internship, in the office of one of the county commissioners. His parents saw nothing unusual in his behavior other than that he confided in them less and less, a trend they equated with his becoming older and more independent. Plus, he returned to school without complaint. And there had been no recurrence of anything to suggest that he was drinking excessively or taking anything, and therefore the matter did not come up. So he returned to school several weeks ago to begin the semester, and that takes us to the evening preceding his admission to the hospital. After he was put on probation by his fraternity last semester he withdrew from his standard friends at the frat house and spent most of his time in his dorm brooding. A few of those friends said that it seemed he felt betrayed by being put on probation. But now, with the new semester, they encouraged him to put the incident behind him and to pitch in with the preparations for a pre-Rush Week party. However, he still remained pretty scarce and on the night of the party he showed up fairly late, after the party was well along. As soon as they saw him they knew he was on something. They recall he had a silly grin on his face and he behaved in a giddy, detached way which had nothing to do with what was going on around him. They say he was in a world of his own and that when anyone tried to talk to him he would begin to giggle. At first they thought maybe it was more alcohol than drug but there was no smell of booze and his coordination was perfectly O.K. Later in the evening he began to giggle even when he wasn't spoken to. Before long he was sitting alone in a corner, blushing and laughing uncontrollably. It was then that his friends began their vigil over him. You know the rest."

"Was there loss of consciousness at any time? Sleep, or even stupor?" Cantrelle queried.

"No report of such. They say he was fully awake the entire time but completely out of it. Wouldn't even drink anything. They tried to give him some coffee, hoping it might help," Rolf added.

"What about any left-over drugs. They didn't find any on him, did they?" he guessed.

"I'm afraid not," Rolf returned. "Later, after he was admitted and his parents were on hand, they searched his room. The only thing they came up with was an empty plastic vial. They analyzed washings from it and it apparently had contained methamphetamine at some earlier time."

"Methamphetamine couldn't cause all this," Cantrelle pronounced unnecessarily, "And the drug screen—both serum and urine—was negative?" he persisted with mounting vexation.

"Right," Morello resumed, feeling the question more his to pursue. "The lab said their screen was set up to detect the standard street and proprietary drugs, plus their metabolites. When a new drug appears on the scene they have to alter the screen. Apparently it takes a while to make that adjustment and they need some of the free drug to work with in setting up the new screen," he continued in his usual encyclopedic manner.

Young Dr. Morello's declarative largesse prompted a cautionary hesitance in Cantrelle. So far, everybody present seemed to have settled on drugs as the cause of the patient's psychosis. Was that really warranted? Other possible etiologies—granted, long shots—should be considered, he reminded himself. Maybe viral encephalitis. Some strange symptoms have often been generated by that disease. Sometimes few of the typical findings of a CNS infection are in evidence. Or a metabolic problem, like porphyria, that rarely diagnosed and remarkably protean clinical entity. Even an accidental intoxication, like thallium or mercury, though he couldn't imagine how that could occur in this case. Still, he reminded himself sententiously, one shouldn't become too settled on any one basic assumption. With that brooding admonition now registered he leaned forward in readiness.

"What about the other lab work? Blood count, electrolytes, heavy metals?" he asked.

"Negative for metals, and the rest perfectly within normal limits," Morello supplied.

"Sed rate, too?" Cantrelle persisted.

"We didn't do that one," Morello admitted through a show of chagrin.

Cantrelle really didn't expect that particular lab test to reveal much, even if positive; it was much too non-specific. Yet . . . .

"In the name of thoroughness we should include that one, too," Cantrelle recommended gently. "Also, check for porphyria if you haven't already done so."

"Right, Chief," Morello snapped adroitly. He typically addressed Cantrelle as "Chief" whenever he set about to make amends for some shortcoming or oversight. His cooperative obedience was not to be doubted.

"I know there's no recent history of his having flu or a URI," Cantrelle explained, "but we have to consider encephalitis along with those other possibilities. Frequently the EEG is normal early in the course of that disorder, especially if the affected brain structures are the deeper ones. Repeat EEG's, taken serially, might show something. Also, there's the option of a spinal tap. That might even show evidence of an early degenerative disorder too punctate to show up yet on the MRI. Let's not close our minds to these other possibilities, no matter how ominous."

"Dr. Cantrelle, in that regard," inquired John Feldman, M.D., second year resident fresh out of his internship and eager to establish himself in the resident group, "could we also consider carbon monoxide poisoning?"

"You're thinking of the flushed facies—cherry red, as the text books say—aren't you?" Cantrelle added in endorsement. "Good. That also might not show up on the EEG, and it would be too late now to pick it up through the blood gases and hemoglobin. How carbon monoxide poisoning could have come about would be a big question. Like nodding off in a car, engine running? His subsequent clinical course could be informative on that point. Good thought, Dr. Feldman; we'll definitely keep it in mind." After a scanning pause he added, "Any more thoughts? If not, I'd like to get on with his Mental Status upon admission here."

"O.K.," replied Morello, harkening to his cue. "The patient presented as a nineteen-year-old single caucasian male who appeared his stated age and who was in no acute distress," he began in formal tones. "He entered into the interview cooperatively but with an air of distraction as though his attention were elsewhere though he made no effort to avoid any aspect of the Mental Status exam itself. He was generally neatly dressed in street clothes though small signs of neglect were present, such as some shirt buttons being unbuttoned and one shoe string untied, and so forth. Frequently during the interview he would twirl his high school ring on his ring finger with his free hand, first one way and then the other. He volunteered nothing and made no attempt to engage in any form of conversation. He answered the questions, interrogation fashion, and otherwise simply sat in his chair restlessly. He scanned his surroundings from time to time as though trying to figure out where he was, and while doing so he seemed to regard the interviewer as being just another part of the scenery, like a chair or door. It was as though he didn't have the urge for human contact, or had lost that channel. Most of the time he had a vacuous smile on his face and it didn't seem to be connected to anything going on around him. Yet, he didn't seem settled, either. Frequently he'd break into giggling and would bend forward to cover his face with his hands as he laughed. That's when he'd speak spontaneously, but only to say such things as 'Funny . . . funny done . . . I can't tell . . . too funny, right?' And the spell, if you could call it that, would pass and he'd become quietly distracted again.

"That's how he looked in general," Morello continued. "He was completely disoriented—time, person, place. Or, at least, I couldn't get him to reveal that he was oriented. He would answer my questions—when he did—with something nonsensical or too distantly related, such as 'snow coming' when I asked if he knew where he was. He couldn't get past 93 on the serial seven's even though he seemed to understand what I was asking and made a real effort to concentrate on the task. Similarities he didn't attempt, or didn't seem either to understand what I asked or just wasn't able to keep the idea in his head long enough to follow through on it. The same with spelling 'WORLD' backwards. Simple motor commands, like telling him to touch his left ear with his right hand, he could do, but only with effort and with the help of my repeating the command. I saw no evidence of formed misperceptions—such as illusion or delusions. Couldn't say about hallucinations. Sometimes when he would break into that giggling I wondered if he was hearing voices, but nothing else suggested that he was. And, also, he didn't seem to get tired in the interview, though it wore me out. And that's it."

It wore Cantrelle out, too, just listening to it. There was a general rule of thumb in the business that the more intact and healthy a patient was, the easier and even enjoyable the Mental Status exam was likely to be. This case, by dint of Morello's labored effort, boded large ill. But not to pre-judge, he reminded himself, for the interview today could just possibly yield large gains, gains not only prognostically vital, but perhaps diagnostically so as well.

"And your impression?" Cantrelle requested.

"Organic Mental Disorder, with psychosis, probably toxic, agent unknown," Morello supplied in telegraph fashion.

"Acute or chronic?" Cantrelle persisted in an effort to draw Morello into less charted waters for sounding out his acumen.

Morello hesitated, glanced at his papers a moment to consider, and then looked up at Cantrelle as though he were placing himself in harm's way.

"Dr. Cantrelle, I think this is chronic," he replied in the tone of coerced resolve.

Cantrelle smiled benevolently at Morello who now sat fully upright with an expression of frozen trepidation. If Morello was right, this morning's story would not have a happy ending because the notion of acute versus chronic spoke loads about probable outcome. In the diagnostic nomenclature of Psychiatry acute and chronic had nothing to do with the character or speed of onset of a disorder, or even its duration, but rather its reversibility. Put simply, to say that a disorder was chronic was to imply that its symptoms were not reversible; controllable, perhaps, but not reversible. Hence, any expectation of clinical improvement would be straitened.

"You do, huh?" Cantrelle stalked. "What makes you think so?" He suspected that Morello was right but he felt it proper still to cultivate more hopeful possibilities.

"Well," Morello began, "it's been over two weeks since his psychosis started and there hasn't been much improvement except in the blushing and the giggling, as you'll see when we get to the hospital course. But more than that, in my interviews with him I haven't been able to detect anything in his mental functioning that was solid and stable enough for him to start rebuilding on. Everything is superficial and peripheral. It's as though the central structures of his mind, his sense of self, or his core identity, are all gone, or almost. I don't see any sustained personality from interview to interview. It's almost as though he's now all sensory-motor with no intervening variable we can call an organized self."

"The behaviorists would love you for that comment," Cantrelle quipped in an effort to lighten the gloomy portent of Morello's assessment. "What you've described," he continued "pretty much matches what we used to see years ago in burned-out hebephrenics. But those poor souls were long-standing schizophrenics with years of hospitalization behind them. That's not the case here. We have to be careful to avoid being categorical in our thinking so that we don't end up diagnosing by association," Cantrelle continued in a hortatory display directed at no one in particular but designed to reaffirm the commendable virtue of looking before leaping. Labels had a way of sticking, even when grossly inaccurate, he had often warned, adding that the chore of reversing earlier diagnostic wrongs could be a pitiless task, particularly if disease chronicity had exhausted prognostic hope.

"Not all behaviorists are as soulless as you suggest," Moyer retaliated playfully. Thus far in the case presentation Moyer had been reviewing his write-up on the psychological tests administered, making notes here and there as aspects of the case unfolded. He rarely intervened during a presentation to correct or elaborate on some point or other, but typically held his peace until the moment came to report on the psychological testing. Ever committed to moving the case presentation along with a minimum of digression he usually confined his discussion to a humbling question or two he typically offered at each conference as a means of clarifying and centralizing the unknowns. Cantrelle suspected he would do about the same today, for this case certainly granted him larger range for disquieting questions he no doubt was tallying right along with each presenter's flow of details. Or so Cantrelle wearily supposed. "In fact, you might say that today could find us a-going soul searching," he added in sly innuendo. "How would you feel about psychs like that?"

He was teasing. Their recurrent colloquy on consciousness and its generative substrate was an academic repertory from which each drew nourishment. One of the polemics listed in the play bill was Cantrelle's complaint that Psychology lacked a good, standardized test for measuring the depth and scope of consciousness in individuals. He held that because we all normally had the gift of speech we tended to regard each other as about equally conscious though in all likelihood consciousness followed the same normal distribution as any other human trait, such as height or intelligence, with some people being exceptionally high in the trait and some exceptionally low, with most people clustering around an average. Certainly people felt that there was such a difference, commonly portrayed anecdotally and often derisively in the form of the ethnic joke. And the difference was not seen as always correlating directly with differences in intelligence which, of course, very much followed a Gaussian distribution. The entire issue ultimately devolved into two contending premises, one for Cantrelle and one for Moyer, and each tapping into separate academic and professional heritages. The fundamental question, always at hand, was whether consciousness, like speech or mathematical ability, was a specific agency of the human brain, driven by the neurochemical substrate of specific anatomic structures, or whether it was more an epiphenomenon, the collective, derivative superation of many separate structures driving the intellectual and sensori-motor functions of the human central nervous system. Moyer, the strict reductionist, endorsed the latter. Thus, to him, consciousness and its relationship to brain structure and function was nothing more than "the hum of its parts," as had been amply stated in other fields, especially in computer engineering. Cantrelle, on the other hand, believed that consciousness was a distinct, recent phylogenetic development serving as an extension of the sensory system but in a higher octave, a genuine sixth sense that functioned as the medium for the deployment of the more basic mental faculties which traditionally were always more formally and readily testable. He felt it would be fundamentally informative to develop tests to measure the medium and not prolong a psychometric emphasis upon the message. So it went without saying that Cantrelle held, as his position required, that consciousness was thus the product of specific anatomic structures whose proper devoir was not only to keep us aware, but to keep us self-aware as well. A self-consciousness center, so to speak.

Already this morning he could hear this theme as background music to the case presentation. And, as so often before, he began to wonder if the dialectic bother was worth all the pedagogic trouble in the absence of determinative data. But you had to maintain polemic contact with your adversary, as any responsible tactician knew. Damn that Hegel!

"Clay, I think you're going to lay something on me today," he ruefully acknowledged to Moyer's sardonic grin. "So, I would like first to enjoy a moment of something more amicable, like OT. Later we'll go on to Nursing. What's OT got to say this morning, Miss Saylor?" he directed.

It was largely known that he had a soft spot in his heart for that much under-appreciated discipline. He believed if ever a field of study stood capable of translating clinical description, such as "flattened affect," into measurable behavior, it was Occupational Therapy. Their Sensory Integration Assessment battery was a sophisticated behavioral scaling of the more abstract, often unwieldy complexities of Psychology's richly elegant neuropsychological test scale. The OT people frequently were in the best position to speak when it came time to provide specifics for mounting a treatment plan with defined goals and measurable indicators. But, characteristically, they usually took a back seat to the traditional top players of the treatment team, thus extending their role as the unappreciated. Cantrelle figured the reason for their umbral status was part the nature of their work and part their particular style. Their work focused on the wellsprings of human enterprise, quite simply, and addressed the interplay of right and left-brain function in general, and in symptomatic behavior in particular. Thus their work required a bit more than the conventional understanding of human mental functioning, and it correspondingly obliged the scientific community to see Arts and Crafts as a legitimate arena for disciplined data gathering. Thus, a certain expansion in perspective was required, plus a handiness in working with *right-brain* phenomena, a knack not readily available in people who tended to be preferentially *left-brain* in their particular discipline, the much more common arrangement. Moreover, it seemed also to be a matter of the kind of people who went into Occupational Therapy. They were all winsomely bright and, hence, often regarded as rivals by other team members quite happy with the traditional hierarchy. Plus, they were almost always uncomplicatedly feminine—he didn't recall ever seeing a male OT worker though he was sure some existed, somewhere—and thus set apart by an odd purity of cast which conferred on them a kind of Edenic wholesomeness. Hence, he never met an OT worker he didn't like, and he had long ago concluded that every OT worker he ever knew was a closet poetess who had to work for a living. He had often wondered what his life would have become if he had thrown in with one of those right-brain sprites, and there had been a few he felt to whom he could happily have given suit were it not for his apotheosis with that smartass, long-legged left-brain statistician who cozily slept with him every night. Heidi Saylor—bright, pretty, and single—fit the OT genre most agreeably.

"Dr. Cantrelle," she began with a sweeping gesture of her hand as she shook her head fretfully over her notes, "I don't have very much to add to what's already been said, but maybe" she continued tentatively "that in itself might be helpful."

"I've often had the same fear, but never had the courage to admit it," Cantrelle teased.

"I don't mean it that way," she retorted coyly. "I mean that what we couldn't test might say more than what was tested."

"Roger," Cantrelle replied, returning to the straight format.

"We started out with the tile task," she continued, "but we didn't get very far with it. He would start on it but not until after he thought about it for a while, and then only when he could keep his attention on it. Even when he could, it seemed he had to figure out all over again every time he resumed the task just what the object of the task was, sometimes even that it was a task at all and that he was supposed to figure it out. So, right off, there was a very spotty and inconsistent performance and it seemed that impairment was showing up on at least three disconnected levels of function. Shall I mention them now or wait?" she requested.

His chickens were coming home to roost, and for the moment this pretty little thing was their cautious keeper. Long he had schooled his residents, and anybody else in earshot, to hold off on conclusions, otherwise known as diagnoses, until all the data were in. Yielding to the naughty and often compromising impulse to display the virtuosity of the snap diagnosis was sometimes O.K., *if* offered with caveat. Then, if the snap diagnosis later turned out to be correct, one could lay claim to follow-through caution and discipline for validating objectively what was intuitively fathomed at the very outset. If, however, the snap diagnosis proved to be erroneous, a certain personal exoneration was available by way of the professional rectitude displayed in the compensatory caution and discipline employed in the pursuit of the more methodical diagnosis. And now here he was, an ostensible spokesman for discipline, eager to hear what he perhaps had correctly concluded snap diagnosis fashion much earlier in the conference before a defensible amount of data was in, now being constrained by his own dictum to bide his time and bear up while duty was being done.

"Let's work up to it gradually, as God intended, shall we?" he sighed.

"All right," she beamed, amused by the slightly scabrous tilt of their interchange. A few in the group tittered as Cantrelle smiled in mock innocence at Moyer who merely raised his eyebrows, his unfailing sign of disapproval.

"Pain in the ass," Cantrelle grumped inwardly as he adjusted his attentiveness. But he knew Moyer was right. Cantrelle had a tendency to become playful, even trivial, whenever cramped by procedure or delay. Granted, he simultaneously recognized the need to guard against taking diagnostic action then and there on bald speculation alone. Thus, his banter and drollery were to be seen more correctly as the civil flip side of a restrained impatience and intolerance. Moyer knew this, and, moreover, didn't particularly care to have either part of it in the disciplined confines of the A.M. Staff Conference. "Sometimes he really is a sour pain in the ass," Cantrelle reaffirmed to himself, "and sometimes I wonder if he thinks this conference is really more his than mine," he snipped as balm to the sting of Moyer's reproof.

But it was all over in a flash, and Heidi Saylor continued her report as Cantrelle allowed his thinking to return to a more sober cast.

"After the tile task we gave him the Draw-A-Person test. Here it is," she offered, motioning for it to be passed around at the table. "Note that the drawing is not a continuous person but pieces of a person loosely connected. The parts are approximately in correct relationship to each other, but you'll see that the left arm and left leg might have been interchanged. Hard to say, they look so alike. The eyes are just blank circles, the mouth is a hint of a line, and there is no nose or ears. You couldn't call the drawing child-like because children tend to emphasize the sense organs, and especially the mouth. This drawing is more disorganized than immature, more a fragmentation than a regression."

Cantrelle had been handed the drawing and was now examining it intently as Saylor spoke. He had never seen so dilapidated a drawing, even from the back-ward schizophrenics who, despite the severity of their illness, were still able to confer some organization on their notably weird tracings. In theirs, the organization of the drawing was relatively intact and was often the vehicle for strange, Boesch-like themes. Here, there was no message of weirdness; its very disorganization was what was so bizarre about it. Again, the medium, not the message; the form, not the content.

"So we thought we would try him on the Sensory Integration schedule to see if we could get more on his ability to organize and process sensory input," she continued. "Well, this is where we didn't get very far, but we had the feeling that this was the key assessment to be made. Sort of like the one test we felt would be the most informative was precisely the one he couldn't handle."

"Couldn't hold his attention?" Cantrelle queried.

"Partly," she expanded. "At times it *was* a problem with attention, but at other times something would get through and he would really go at it. Or at least he would seem to be tuned in. But then he either couldn't make sense out of what he was doing—even though another part of his mind seemed able to grasp the task—or he just didn't know *how* to respond to satisfy what he understood was a test. All very strange and like nothing I've ever seen before in someone so young and previously pretty healthy."

Cantrelle was perplexed, too, and likewise by the apparent lack of a discernible pattern to the deficits described. Only the extensively brain damaged or the severe hebephrenic displayed as much cognitive disorganization, and they usually had the right kind of history, quality and quantity, to go with it. But such wasn't the case here.

"So we settled for the Sensory Integration screening test hoping to get an idea of general areas of impairment, like maybe tactile-spatial-temporal, as an example," she continued. "Well, we tried all the subtests, and over and above his problem of understanding and attending to the tasks he seemed to be impaired in all modalities, but not specifically from the receptive side. He usually could perceive the task, whether it was visual or auditory, for example, but he couldn't organize it. But sometimes he even seemed to have trouble perceiving it, too, like his categories of perception would unexpectedly shut off. And then at other times he would just go blank when he was attempting a task, like his expressive functions would shut off. All in all we couldn't make much sense of it except to say that the problem seemed global. And that's it."

"That's it?" reiterated Cantrelle in frank disappointment. Usually OT gave him more to go on. "But," he offered, "I suspect you're right on in your suggestion that what *isn't* there might be more instructive than what *is* there, because there's certainly a lot missing; a lot of what you would expect typically to be present, if we can say it that way."

"Yes, that's what we mean," she agreed. "It's like the figure is almost there but the ground is totally missing."

Cantrelle thought on that for a moment.

"Miss Saylor, he then said slowly as in a dawning, "you might be most excellently right. Most excellently." He then let it rest as he prepared to call on Moyer, shifting his approach accordingly. "Any other comments or questions?" He didn't expect any because the conference was already running longer than anticipated. "If not," he continued, "we'll just move on. I guess it's time for the validating information. Right, Clay?" he joshed.

"Sure," Moyer complied tolerantly.

Arching his head back a bit to look through his half glasses perched on the tip of his nose, shopkeeper fashion, he arranged his papers one last time as he scanned the data. Then, settled, he began.

"The patient entered into the testing willingly and complied with the instructions as best he could, and the test results are considered valid approximations of his current cognitive functioning," Clay intoned in the standard pro forma overview to set the assessment frame. That done he then proceeded with the specifics. “We attempted the WAIS but weren’t very successful in getting a solid reading because of his extreme variability in attention to the task. He couldn’t sustain an effort; but worse, he couldn’t even sustain an understanding of the task. And the giggling would often pull him away from his effort. The test scores are probably a valid assessment of his current level of overall function but are not valid readings of his basic ability. Or, certainly, what his basic ability used to be. On the verbal scale he scored a 68, and on the performance scale a 52, for a full scale score of 58, placing him in the moderately retarded range. But there was extreme scatter in the subtests, and his overall score obviously represents a severe decrement from his previous level of function. That, of course, comes as no surprise to us, but the numbers give an idea of how large a decrement it is. Probably about fifty percent or better.”

So now the boy was about half as smart as he used to be, Cantrelle sighed.

“His scatter on the subtests was extreme, as I’ve said,” Moyer continued. “For example, on one or two items of the Information subtest he scored near the top, but missed most of the simpler ones, bringing his score down overall, while on the digit span he didn’t get beyond three forward, and he did none backwards correctly. I had expected rote memory to fare better, but it didn’t, and mostly, I believe, because he couldn’t sustain continued function of that particular faculty. It’s more than just an attention deficit; that’s too simple. It’s more that he can’t sustain the structure of his own mental functioning. It’s as though his thinking becomes like static, then becomes a little clearer, then becomes like static again and so forth. For example on the block design he would try to duplicate the design but whenever he added a new block he would apparently disrupt the gestalt he had managed to erect in his thinking and he would become confused by what he had done, at least until he reoriented himself to the altered design he himself had constructed. It was as though slight increases in the level of complexity of the task, his efforts included, overloaded his circuits temporarily, and that’s when the static would come in. We tried him on the Halstead-Reitan hoping to get a better reading on the memory component of the problem, but we just didn’t get enough to work with. His performance was too meager, too erratic for valid data. But, being good soldiers, we plodded on. We made a stab at the neuropsych screening battery, but here again there wasn’t enough data forthcoming to do a specific assessment. Like

Heidi described and like what we found on the WAIS his performance was more erratic and scattered than focused and revealing. One thing we can say is that his perception of the stimulus is apparently unimpaired suggesting that on a cortical level he manages the input reasonably well. It seems that the problem is that he doesn't process the correctly perceived stimuli with the result that he's recurrently confounded by any change in the stimulus field. If the field remains the same he seems to settle down with it, perhaps manage some kind of simple adaptation to it even though he may not understand it."

"That's right," Mary Samuels, a veteran aide and member of the nursing staff, seconded. "Soon as you give him something different to do he falls apart."

Cantrelle smiled at her steady eagerness. She was one of the units most involved and caring aides. When she said something it was usually worth listening to, as was so often the case with all of the seasoned aides on the unit. They lived with the patients eight hours a day and came by their knowledge of a case most honestly, and with little in the way of frills.

"I guess that's your way of telling us we're finally getting around to the real substance of the case, huh, Mrs. Samuels?" Cantrelle coaxed.

"Well, I wouldn't put it exactly that way, Doctor," she hedged politely.

"Let's finish up on the psychs first and then we'll get back to Nursing. O.K.?" he suggested as she nodded agreement.

"Not much else to add," Moyer continued. "The overall impression is that of an Organic Psychosis, severe, with a degree of disorganization that prevents even primitive attempts at restitution. Not a hint of a delusion, for example, as an attempt to make some sense out of his chaotic environment. It doesn't look good, Frank," he averred in conclusion.

Cantrelle just nodded. He needed time to think, and he needed help with it. Now would be a good time to hear more from nursing, he figured. Other members of the group were getting restless in overdue anticipation of some declarative statement or clarifying commentary from him, but he needed more to hook on to.

"You were saying, Mrs. Samuels?" he pursued.

"Yes," she resumed, "as long as you lead him along in a way that's familiar to him, he's O.K.; but soon as you do something new or something he's not familiar with he comes apart. Gets a dazed look and then breaks out in that giggling. And sometimes he cries while he's giggling."

He sensed that the group was a bit distressed hearing the patient discussed this way. It was too human, too real. Mrs. Samuels didn't use insulating abstractions when she spoke of her charges. He thought it best to re-inject a note of clinical inquiry.

"How do you know when he's familiar with something?" he asked.

"Why, he smiles!" she announced with indignant surprise that such a superfluous question should come from Cantrelle. "And he has such a sweet smile, too," she added more gently.

God! She was only making it worse. She, like most of the aides, revealed the patients to be so human; so achingly, excruciatingly human. He had wondered too many times over the years how the aides managed to work with so much living and breathing heartache and misery every blessed day without succumbing to the very sensible temptation to become cold and distant. Some did, but they were the few, and they usually didn't stick around very long anyway. If ever people were underpaid for their work surely they were, these totally genuine people, he once again proclaimed forthrightly to the sympathetic population of his inner world.

"Yes," Mrs. Wotjek, the doughty and unsinkable chief nurse of the unit added. "If we take our time with him, explain things slowly he generally tries to help himself, in his pathetic way. Like even going to lunch. If we talk to him about lunch on the way there, how he's going to eat it and like it, he's O.K. and manages the meal without much confusion, such as forgetting what he's supposed to do with the food. If we don't guide him like I just said he just sits at the table and giggles. I think he has a kind of Alzheimer's disease because he's a lot like what you see in those cases that are pretty advanced. And in someone so young," she added sadly.

"Sure sounds similar to it in some ways, doesn't it?" Cantrelle allowed. "Does he ever show any signs of snapping out of it, let's say, for even a brief moment? Say, when he's not trying so hard, or when he's not being watched carefully?"

"No, not now," she pointed out. "When he first came here two weeks ago I think there were moments when his mind would clear a little bit, or at least it would look as though something was getting through and he realized it, but lately I don't see any of that."

The implication of her observation jolted him into quickened heed, and he knew he'd better check it out fast.

"Mrs. Wotjek," he pursued pointedly, "are you suggesting that perhaps he's getting *worse*, from what you've seen?" The automatic expectation, he was now abruptly called to consider, was that when patients came into the treatment unit, especially those patients with a drug-induced psychosis, their clinical course would be one of slow, even agonizingly slow, improvement, but improvement nonetheless now that they were removed from the inciting agent and were in a structured and therapeutic environment. And that was fairly typical of just about all of them, except for the first few days in some cases when separation from the agent might spawn a short-lived heightening of symptoms. The withdrawal. But, for the most part, a general and progressive improvement in clinical status was the normal, expectable course as the toxic effects of the offending agent wore off and the agent's last traces cleared the patient's system. But now the suggestion was being made by this steady nurse that such was not the case with this patient. No one earlier in the conference had openly suggested that the patient's condition was *worsening*, so it came to Cantrelle as something unexpected when Mrs. Wotjek corrected that critical oversight. He felt a stab of annoyance with himself for feeling unprepared for her surprise enjoinder, and he was just too aware the upshot was that he had unwittingly allowed his mind to swing shut on an option he should have kept receptively open—the very thing he forbade in his residents and excoriated in all others in his best declamatory rant! Over and above his personal pique, he noted that it was the same old story once again and one whose lessons he should not have forgotten; namely, that Psychology and OT, and especially the attending Psychiatrist, spent a comparatively brief time with the patient compared to Nursing, and while the former could eloquently detail the patient's status at a given moment and offer some rather general assessment as to his course, it was Nursing who invariably had the most valid picture as to how the patient was responding to treatment and to his disease, and it was this oft-documented truth which he'd let slip from his reckoning in his approach to the case. And even beyond that, he suspected everybody in the conference noted his lapse just by the tone of dismay in his questions. So, he quickly resolved, he might as well own up to it, real hero fashion, and maybe even retrieve some small grace. "Mrs. Wotjek," he breasted, "I've got to say I'm just a bit surprised to hear that he's not doing well, or at least not showing some convincing signs of improvement. I guess I had assumed that he was settling in and had begun some kind of recovery." He knew he spoke for more than just a few at the conference, but especially for Morello who now had a startled look on his face not yet formed into structured chagrin. "What you say," he continued, "sort of sets my teeth on edge, that maybe I've been missing the point here. Maybe we're dealing with an *active* process still on the up side, though no toxic agents can be implicated at this point in his clinical course. Right?"

"Dr. Cantrelle," she reassured, "everything said so far is as right as rain, and all the points that were made we, too, see in his behavior, just like the others described it. It's just that we see it getting worse since the time he was admitted."

That was only two weeks ago, Cantrelle mulled anxiously as he listened. If she was right about his condition's worsening, then there had to be more going on than just a straightforward drug psychosis, he parlayed. But what else could be going on?

"At first he would do for himself; at least, as much as he could, which wasn't much. But he would try," Mrs. Samuels added, rejoining the flow of discussion. "Lately he doesn't even try, and I think it's because his understanding is leaving him," she pronounced.

"Do you think maybe he's just getting used to the ward and might be taking advantage of people's eagerness to help him. Like slacking off?" queried Morello in an effort to salvage some personal exoneration by displacing on to the patient a portion of his own culpability for not being alert to this unexpected turn, a traditional device waggishly known as Risk Management, which states that if you don't know what's going on, blame the patient.

"I don't think so," Mrs. Samuels fielded. "When the young ones get used to the ward, as you say, they *do* try to shine up to the staff in order to get things, like more privileges, but mostly to be permitted to do more things for themselves, not for you to do more things for them. The older patients and the chronic ones might try to get you to do everything for them, but not the younger ones; that is, not unless they're getting worse. He's different from the other younger ones, but it's not because he's slacking off," she sniffed.

"That's why I think he's like an Alzheimer's, as I said," Mrs. Wotjek added.

A silence hung in the air as tautness returned to the session. In the usual case presentation the recitations of the several participants, one after another, tended to lull everybody into a light torpor as the information unfolded, point after frequently repetitious point, and it was his job as presiding psychiatrist to fend off that torpor by pointing out interesting and provocative implications of the raw, unrendered, frequently duplicated information. He sensed some minutes earlier that the torpor had begun to settle in and thus had moved himself to a higher level of alert for hidden points of interest to be offered as a tonic to any creeping tedium stalking the group. But today it was unnecessary for him to sound reveille because Nursing, ever vigilant as mothers in the care of children, had done it for him, and alerted him to where he hadn't been looking. As the meaning of Nursing's observations sank in he tried to re-group his thinking as fast as he could to address the silence that now demanded an answer. His concentration was distracted by a few murmurs in the back of the room where some members were testing out on each other new ideas and hunches evoked by the case's unexpected turn. He decided to regard the murmurs more as a cue than a distraction.

"Sort of opens the field beyond what we had expected, doesn't it? You can always count on Nursing to keep you to your task. Right, ladies?" he directed lightly and left-handedly to Mrs. Samuels and Mrs Wotjek who were now sitting resolutely with chins ever so slightly raised in proud satisfaction. "Let's assume that what we've just been told is exactly correct, that the patient's decrease in agitation and his apparent adaptation to the unit are not what we would like to think they are; namely, not that he's getting over the worst of his toxic psychosis, but rather that he's showing a worsening of his condition because his progressive loss of cognizance is making him less and less aware even of what to be upset about. Is that the essence of it, ladies?"

"That's right, Dr. Cantrelle," Mrs. Wotjek replied.

Now the silence was even worse. No helpful murmurs were being offered about. He didn't know why he was so reluctant to take the next logical step. Maybe it was because he intuitively sensed that to do so would take him well beyond his familiar boundaries. That would be reason enough, for such would undoubtedly aggravate his own distress beyond what he already felt for desperately inventorying his mind in search of a familiar and congenial answer to the evolving enigma and yet still coming up quite dry. In short order the negative yield of his failed inventory forced his hand as time glaringly ran out.

"If Nursing is right," he reiterated guardedly, "we have to consider at least two other possibilities. Number one, that the offending agent is still present, but exerting its effect in some form which escapes detection by our standard screening methods—and that's a good possibility since the usual methods didn't pick it up in the first place—or, number two, that what we're dealing with is not primarily a drug psychosis but an organic psychosis of another etiology with his alleged drug use being only an incidental contributor."

"Like what, Dr. Cantrelle?" Morello challenged. "We've checked him out for infections, for metabolic, vascular, and even trauma possibilities, and we've come up with nothing. Neurology saw him at the Psychiatric Unit at Franklinton and they couldn't suggest any possibilities beyond those."

"Not at that time," returned Cantrelle as he began to warm up to the chase. "What I have in mind, if this isn't caused by some yet undetectable drug, perhaps it's one of those acute, idiopathic, degenerative diseases of the central nervous system. Something like multiple sclerosis, but of course more in the way of dementia. And fulminant, too. Like the old Dementia Praecox, but rapid-fire."

"It would be hard to imagine a degenerative process so acute and so fulminant sparing the sensory and motor systems," Morello added skeptically.

"I know," Cantrelle conceded, aware that it wasn't only Morello who had misgivings about so questionable a likelihood, "but when the familiar doesn't help you, then you're justified in reaching for the unusual. In this case, I grant you, we feel more like we're reaching for the unknown. Well," he added with a sigh, "they say that when everything else fails, you ask the patient. I guess it's about that time, would you say? Is he waiting?"

"Yes, he is, Dr. Cantrelle," Mrs. Wotjek affirmed.

"Then let's bring him in and see if young Mr. Jordan can help us figure out what's wrong with him," he directed.

As Mrs. Wotjek left to retrieve the patient from the waiting room up the hallway he became aware of his dread in meeting this young man. He knew such dread arose of not having a sufficient grasp of the case to allow him to conduct a neatly tactical interview to demonstrate salient or particular features he wanted the residents to see in vivo, as was the ideal in psychiatric teaching. Today it would be a matter of groping, even fumbling, about in an effort to get a rudimentary sense of what was assailing this young man. At best, he suspected, he might demonstrate the form such inquiry took in the face of obdurate unknowns, but as yet he had little hope for coming up with anything in the way of conclusive content to give today's conference that audible click which came of a solid diagnosis being achieved. Today's conference wouldn't end on that triumphant note, he could predict, and the sense of feeling helpless in the face of the patient's need would linger.

He was about to sigh again when the door was opened slowly by Mrs. Wotjek to admit a female aide leading the patient into the room. Being led by the hand, the patient was not quite shuffling, though he was stooped forward a bit. He followed the aide without resistance and was directed to the vacant chair at the end of the conference table.

"Yes. Up this way, please," assisted Cantrelle as he rose from his chair to indicate location.

The patient looked at Cantrelle vacuously and slowly scanned all the faces directed at him. He immediately began to giggle and managed to cover his face with his free hand as he moved along to the chair awaiting him. There was no change in his halting gait as this occurred, suggesting the basic startle reaction, preparation for fight or flight, had been obliterated. The result was an impression of profound helplessness. And dementia. The others were right. He did look like a case of Alzheimer's in its advanced stages where so much is lost that the patient sinks into an empty indifference. He fought back the surge of despair carried along by the pity and perplexity welling up in himself with the patient's approach. As the patient neared, the giggling stopped, and in its place a boyish smile came forth along with an extended arm for a handshake. Cantrelle took the proffered hand and shook gently.

"Please sit down, Winston," Cantrelle directed as the aide withdrew to a chair off to the side.

The patient blinked a few times and slowly settled into his seat. He then sat motionless with his arms hanging at his sides as the expression took on an interrogative cast directed at all present.

"Good morning, Winston. I'm Dr. Cantrelle. We wanted to meet with you this morning to talk about your reason for being here. We have some questions as to how best we may be of help and we thought you might assist us with those questions," Cantrelle began carefully.

The patient listened to Cantrelle as he spoke, pondered, and then nodded.

Encouraged, Cantrelle continued.

"I understand you've had trouble keeping your thoughts together and . . . ."

The patient began to giggle and then swept the audience with a broad grin. Cantrelle waited a moment until the giggling subsided before resuming.

". . . and that maybe it hasn't been clear to you what's been going on." Generally, Cantrelle preferred not to lead so directly in interview, but he sensed that in this case it was necessary to provide a measure of structure by which the patient might orient a response. It was so much more preferable for teaching purposes to allow the patient to supply, unbidden, the determinative data for a given diagnosis. But in some cases, such as this one, he rued, that luxury was not at hand.

The patient stared at him and began to knit his brow in apparent effort.

"What are you thinking, Winston?" Cantrelle pursued.

"School is out," the patient stammered haltingly while making a gesture of finality with his right hand.

Cantrelle quickly wondered if he meant that school was now out of the question or whether he thought he was still on summer vacation.

"Do you know where you are?" Cantrelle asked in followup.

The patient nodded.

"Where are you?" Cantrelle repeated.

"Akron?" the patient asked, arching his eyebrows.

"Do you know what this place is? The place we're in—you and me—right now?" Cantrelle attempted.

"You a teacher?" the patient asked.

"In a way," Cantrelle allowed.

"This is a school," the patient answered rapidly with a smile of triumph. "School is out," the patient added as perplexity slowly replaced his grin. "Can I go home . . . do my homework?" the patient began as a plea but ended with a burst of giggling.

Cantrelle was trying to total up the implications of those associations when the patient suddenly pulled himself into a more erect sitting position and began a series of calisthenics with his arms.

"Gym time!" the patient announced through the rapid cadence of folding and extending his arms before him, above his head, and sideways. "Work out . . . then go home. Right, teacher?" he bargained.

Cantrelle concluded that the patient knew in some vague way that he was in a hospital and that he had to show improvement before being allowed to go home. Calling it a school could have been a compromise of convenience; or, perhaps just an out and out distortion, though probably not quite all happenstance. He decided to trace it out, if he could.

"Are you getting better now?" Cantrelle asked with an emphasis to override the distraction of the patient's exercising.

The patient stopped immediately and placed his hands in his lap. He looked at Cantrelle with a wavering focus for a prolonged moment.

"I don't know," he said.

The clarity of the statement startled Cantrelle, who quickly scanned some of the others present to see if they shared his surprise. Most did. He noted that Nursing didn't. Eager to enlarge upon what seemed to be an open channel, Cantrelle continued.

"Are you feeling better?"

"I don't know," the patient repeated in the tone of blank abstraction.

Cantrelle decided to take a chance at reaching the patient's sense of his own thinking.

"Are your thoughts feeling any better?" he attempted.

The patient didn't answer at first but stared at Cantrelle as though becoming aware of something.

"Are you a doctor?" he asked.

"Yes," Cantrelle answered, "I'm a doctor."

"Headache number seven," the patient announced and then briskly resumed the giggling along with the calisthenics. "Headache number seven," he repeated playfully as he burst into giggling which quickly shaded into an acceleration of the calisthenics.

It was gone. Cantrelle grimaced at his having overloaded the circuit, shutting the channel down. He scored himself for being too aggressive and losing the only open channel the patient had offered.

"Winston," Cantrelle said more firmly in an effort to interrupt the calisthenics, "Do your thoughts hurt too much?"

"One, two, three, four" the patient counted as he picked up the cadence of the calisthenics and stared fixedly ahead.

"Your thoughts scare you, don't they?" Cantrelle persisted.

The patient began to count louder as he continued the calisthenics determinedly. Then his eyes began to moisten rapidly and within a few moments the movement of his exercising spilled the puddled tears down along his cheeks. Cantrelle felt the collective pang of the group adding to his own. Mrs. Wotjek gave an audible mutter which was unmistakably a cease and desist order in defense of her helpless charge. Cantrelle knew it wise to concur.

"We won't ask you any more questions, Winston." Cantrelle relented. "You can settle down now. Thank you for coming in this morning. You may go back to the unit now," Cantrelle soothed as he nodded to the aide sitting at the ready who then came forward to take the patient by the hand again. As soon as the aide approached the patient stopped his calisthenics, but not the counting. He rose obediently at the aide's urging and followed her out of the room, again being led by the hand. He continued to count and he mimicked a march step as he left the room. Then his counting stopped.

The conference room was now excruciatingly silent. Ordinarily at the conclusion of his interview Cantrelle would invite the participants at the table and all others in the gathering to ask the patient any questions suitable for clarifying particular points. But not today. Mrs. Wotjek had made that clear, and he had agreed. He was certain continued interrogation—and that's what it would have had to be; interrogation—would see only more regressive deterioration in the patient's behavior plus a significant amplification of the anguish, neither for any useful purpose.

Within a few moments sound began to return in the form of people shifting uncomfortably in their chairs. All awaited Cantrelle's next word while he searched his mind in pursuit of the right note for restoring the conference to a more balanced clinical stance. Gloom hung in the air like a miasma which he knew he was expected to dispel. But the gloom was valid, even if it wasn't the total say for the case.

He took a deep breath, followed by a quick that-does-it nod.

"I agree with Nursing;" he announced. "He's gotten worse, and rapidly, too. And why do I say that?" he added pointedly as he surveyed the panel at the table. "Because the way he is right now Psychology and OT would not be able to get the test results they got not very long ago. How long ago was it?" he asked.

"September twentieth. Twelve days ago," Saylor calculated as she riffled through her notes.

"I tested him eleven days ago," Clay added.

"That's not very long. And I don't think you would find him testable now, would you?"

"Probably not," Clay conceded.

Heidi Saylor just shook her lowered head.

"So, whatever it is, it's still happening and at a pace we're not used to seeing. Right?" Cantrelle continued in a step-wise, syllogistic manner he hoped would take him somewhere more familiar. But he knew he needed a few moments to gather his thoughts, plus a few more bits of data, if possible. "First let's check out some other impressions before we move on. Let's sample the residents, shall we?" he proposed.

The residents had to be brought into the discussion. It all too often happened that when a given case such as this one moved on to murkier precincts the residents, feeling their novice status, would tend to fade into the background in deference to those staff members of fuller credentials. Cantrelle fought against that regrettable forfeiture, for, after all, the conference was geared primarily for resident teaching. Hence, his press gang tactics in keeping the residents aboard. Also, the residents, in their innocence, usually came up with novel notions which could not spring forth from the over-ploughed, over-cultivated thought beds of the standard, well-credentialed staff. And to boot, the polling gave him the additional time to inventory his own thinking. He waited.

"I can see that he's taken a downturn," Morello volunteered in the direction of Nursing who nodded in concurrence, "and so I have to go with the idea that the agent is still working its effect, and the sooner we identify it the better. Then we might be able to do something."

"I don't know that it'll be so easy," Dr. Sumner was quick to challenge. "I think we have to give more weight to an acute degenerative disorder, maybe unrelated to his drug usage. And I think we should ask Neurology to take another look at him. This is an emergency situation."

"An MRI," Dr. Brewer pronounced.

"Right," Cantrelle underscored. "Since he's apparently worsened, the process and location might now be demonstrable radiographically."

The Magnetic Resonance Imager was the nearest thing available to taking a high-resolution snapshot of the *in vivo* body organs and any part thereof, brain or otherwise, and had wondrously expanded medicine's knowledge of organ pathophysiology and its clinico-anatomic correlates. It constituted a significant gain over the earlier CT—Computerized Tomography—scan which did essentially the same thing but in a less refined way. Only the PET—Positron Emission Tomography—scan was more sophisticated from the standpoint of visualized organ function.

"And possibly a PET scan," Brewer added in concluding the technology line-up.

"Quite possibly," Cantrelle agreed, "but I suspect the MRI, coupled with clinical correlation, might be enough. Any other thoughts?"

There were none from the residents, and that served as a signal to the floor.

"Dr. Cantrelle," one of the social work interns asked, "are there any street drugs we know of that cause behavior similar to this?"

"Not any I know of," Cantrelle replied. "What about you, Clay?"

"If it is drug caused, it certainly isn't a hallucinogen," Moyer averred. "Nor a stimulant, either. There's nothing to suggest it's a narcotic. It doesn't seem anything like LSD or PCP, and we've certainly seen our share of those. I don't know."

"If it is a drug," Cantrelle continued to the intern but actually to all present, "the desired, initial effect is lost to us. We're seeing the progressive, untoward sequelae. Reports from others tell us that at the outset he was red-faced and very giggly, like he was embarrassed. I can't imagine anyone taking a drug just for those effects. There must have been some other subjective effect sought which could have been fleeting, or which, though sought, may never have happened."

"It couldn't be carbon monoxide poisoning like we mentioned earlier, could it?" Dr. Feldman posed.

"The effect of carbon monoxide poisoning would be diffuse enough to account for a lot of the clinical picture, but not for the progressive severity. Also, as I recall, the test for carboxyhemoglobin was negative, wasn't it? Or was it done?" Cantrelle posed.

"It was done, and it was negative," Morello confirmed.

"But it does bring up the question of tissue vulnerability. A mind drug, if we can call it that, pretty much gets to all brain structures, and some of these structures are specifically reactive to the drug to yield the effect the user desires. But by the same token, some structures of the brain may be specifically vulnerable to the drug from the standpoint of toxicity. I think that's the situation here," Cantrelle reached. "What he shows is certainly not the desired effect."

"A new drug, you think?" Saylor suggested.

"That's exactly what I'm thinking, Miss Saylor," he replied. "In fact, we have little option to suspect otherwise. It's definitely an organic psychosis," he began to review, "and other organic causes have so far been ruled out. Moreover, its like nothing we've ever seen before. Plus, it's apparently progressive. Yes, I would say the best bet is a new drug on the street. Or was, because we may never see another case like this. To push it one additional step I would say it was a designer drug and maybe a one-time thing from some basement chemistry lab trying to crank out new models. You all remember the MPTP episode in California? That drug produced the rigidity of advanced Parkinson's disease in its young victims. It came from one of those basement operations. Thank God it turned out to be a one-time thing. But they were able to pick up on that one's chemistry because its metabolites lingered in the bloodstream for a while. Plus, the drug screen used was apparently sensitive enough. In this case maybe the drug was metabolized so rapidly there was nothing left to detect. Or that the breakdown products of the drug didn't differ enough from normal blood components to be detectable. I don't know, but I'm fairly certain we're dealing with a new drug. A very toxic one, certainly."

"Dr. Cantrelle," one of the male attendants near the back of the room asked with hand raised, "do you think he might have taken something in a suicide attempt?"

The thought had flitted across his mind earlier in the conference but had not attached itself to any of the case information offered.

"You mean," he expanded, "that he might have gotten his hands on some chemicals somewhere and used them in an effort to do himself in?"

“Yes,” the attendant replied, “and if so, we probably won’t see any more like it. But if it’s a designer drug that went wrong, like those you say in California, then there could be some others like him out there who took some of the same batch.”

As he listened he found himself nodding in aroused agreement. He hadn’t considered the possibility of other patients hospitalized elsewhere with the same perplexing clinical picture, perhaps being presented at conferences just like this one with everybody arriving at the same point in case formulation as was this group just now.

“Then you’re suggesting, I take it,” Cantrelle continued, “that we check with other treatment centers to see if there are any others like him, and maybe benefit from their work-ups. Is that it?”

“Yes,” the attendant agreed, “and if there’s another one then we know it’s a street drug of some sort. If not, then maybe it was just a suicide attempt with God knows what.”

“An excellent point,” Cantrelle cited as several murmurs from the group joined in approval. “We can have Social Work canvas the other hospitals,” he continued, though in his heart he felt the distinction between a failed drug trip and a blundered suicide attempt was of little import at this point, except from the epidemiologic standpoint. Regardless of motive, the case as it now stood was the same. Moreover, he suspected that the notion of a suicide attempt was engendered more by the pathos of the patient’s present state rather than by anything very substantial in the history preceding hospitalization. Cantrelle nodded to the attendant in endorsement of the suggestion.

A fatigued silence then settled on the gathering. Cantrelle recognized it as the infallible sign that the conference had reached an end point. It was the group’s usual way of saying that it had had its fill, that the morning’s work had been done, that enough of a future course in the case had been defined, and that it was time for him to summarize. So he began.

“Let’s tie some pieces together and map out our plan. Since the case is still ‘acute’ only in the sense that the pathophysiology is progressing, we’ll get an MRI as soon as we can schedule one. Also, repeat the EEG so that we’ll also have that in hand when we get another Neurology consult. In the meantime, go easy on the medications so as not to mask any important findings, though he might need a mild sedative for sleep, given his degree of confusion and its potential for agitation. Also, Nursing can give him the structure and support he needs—simple, even repetitious reassurance and guidance—until we know better if there's anything else we can do. You might also repeat the drug screen on the outside chance a metabolite might show up. And the blood chemistries, too. Anything else?" he asked in appeal.

"What about contacting his friends about his drug use before all this happened? Might turn up something about the drug that did this," urged Mrs. Wotjek.

"Yes. Maybe now someone will come forth with something. Another task for Social Work," he directed as he nodded toward Mrs. Rolf.

"Anything else?" he asked. The silence was now complete, his cue to bring the conference to a close in the traditional manner. "Final diagnosis, Dr. Morello?" he bade.

"Organic Brain Syndrome, severe, probably chronic, most likely toxic, agent undetermined," Morello levied.

At a glance he quickly polled the agreement in the silent faces of the gathering and then officially closed the conference with his usual "Thank you very much" directed at all present.

After a slight pause in which all seemed to acknowledge the very large period punctuating his closing tribute the gathering stirred and rose to the accompaniment of screeching chairs and renewed conversation as it re-formed itself into small groups to depart the conference room in continued discussion of the case. Generally, the residents and the presenting staff lingered awhile at the conference table for whatever last minute commentary, often pithy, which might arise in the more private and more exclusive post-conference round.

"Bad case," Cantrelle moaned. "You all did as good a job as could be expected given the limitations imposed," he continued in a sweeping acknowledgment to all the participants, "but one can't help but leave with the feeling of incompleteness and futility. I hate the thought of meeting with Dr. Weaver to pass on our glum tidings. He knows the boy's father, you know," Cantrelle shared. "At least we can say the boy is receiving the best work-up possible anywhere and probably the most complete one he'll ever have from here on in. But that'll be small consolation, I fear."

"Yeah," seconded Moyer. "His deterioration really caught me flat-footed. I knew from seeing him on the unit now and again that he wasn't showing great gains, but it didn't occur to me that he had slipped so much since the testing," he added in apology.

"Dr. Cantrelle," Morello interjected, "the idea of a designer drug really seems to click. If its O.K. with you I'd like to work along with Social Work to see if we can come up with anything. As you know, I start my elective next week in Forensic and maybe I can follow this case along and do a little double-dipping. How about it?"

While Dr. Sumner was sometimes cheeky, Dr. Morello was often outright brash. "*How about it?*" Cantrelle repeated the cocky proposal to himself in measuring the degree of unintended effrontery it contained, chuckling as he did so. Morello was like that; often abrasive in his boyish zeal but always ready to go that extra mile to do the better thing. Thus, he really couldn't fault him for his manner, though others frequently did. But nor could he fault them for doing so.

"Sure, Dr. Morello," he agreed. "Check it out first with Dr. Sorenson to make sure it doesn't conflict with what she's planned for you on the Forensic Unit."

"Right, Chief," Morello retorted.

"Well . . ." Cantrelle sighed as he made a motion to rise from his chair for departure.

"One more question, Dr. Cantrelle!" Dr. Sumner announced with index finger raised.

"Yes, Dr. Sumner?" he yielded, not surprised that she might deliver a Parthian question at adjournment.

"Do you think his history of a learning disability and probable attention deficit disorder could in any way have something to do with his susceptibility to whatever he took?"

He was ready for most questions from the irrepressibly pert Dr. Sumner, but he wasn't ready for that one.

"Hadn't considered that, Dr. Sumner. Assuming he did take something and that it accounts for his clinical findings, I guess I would have to say yes," he granted, "but only in the sense that any organ or organ system that starts out impaired is likely to be preferentially vulnerable to any insult. I know that's pretty general, but it's the best I can do."

With that, all agreed that the post-conference wrap-up had indeed come to an end. Papers were now gathered together and people began to move about and stretch.

"Oh, Clay," Cantrelle mentioned brightly as he rose from his chair, "I have to warn you that Laura told me this morning that it's time we four got together again for dinner. I expect she's on the phone right now with Helen deciding when. Thought I would prepare you for it for when you got home tonight. Also, ready for that symposium next week?"

"Thanks for the tip, Frank, Yes, I am," he smiled back.

With that Cantrelle gave a collective "See y'all" to the group as he made for the door, being granted the privilege of first in train from the conference table. As he trotted on ahead down the hallway on his way to the hallowed privacy of his car he noted that he felt especially drained this morning despite the deceptive quickness of his gait. Moreover, the effect was worsened by the prospect of having to meet with Jess to pass on the bad news. He knew Jess wanted so much to reassure his old friend and help the boy, for it didn't happen too often in life that seldom-seen friends could be of such vital assistance to each other in honor of old ties, as it was hoped this occasion offered. And now he had to discount that hope. But if nothing else, he reassured himself, Jess Weaver was a stalwart scholar who saw benefit in all learning, no matter how infelicitous. And hence their friendship.

By now he had reached the building entrance. He pulled open the door resolutely and stepped out to be temporarily blinded by the waiting sun.

THREE

The applause was subsiding and the overhead lights were turned on as the symposium was brought to a triumphant conclusion. Dr. Paul Weinroth, the panel's moderator, Chairman of Biology at Columbia Tech and probably the world's leading authority on gene mapping for which he had received a Nobel prize, had moments earlier delivered the concluding remarks which united the presentations of the several panelists into the forward-thrusting prediction that within ten years the majority of genetically transmitted diseases, psychiatric diseases in particular, would be identified not only as to chromosome number but also to gene location. His comments on the consequent impact this would have on psychiatric nosology—the definition and classification of clinical disorders—was particularly well received by Cantrelle whose exhortational efforts in that direction over the years were too well known by the staff at Moreland. In fact, during Weinroth's wrap-up Cantrelle leaned forward and caught Moyer's eye to make the thumb's up sign of approval. The wives were maternally tolerant of the dumbshow communication that usually occurred between Cantrelle and Moyer during such conferences as their husbands seemed bound to demonstrate that they were sustaining a joint wavelength and also achieving the proper pitch on major points. To minimize this practice to a socially allowable level, the women usually sat together between their husbands, as they did today. Thus, Laura and Helen years ago had agreed that in the name of civic duty they would accompany their husbands and serve as monitoring buffers whenever their spouses attended the same conference, for it went without saying that if not restrained the two men would sit together and establish themselves as reciprocal running commentary on the proceedings at hand, straining mightily the tolerance of all within earshot. One wife apparently was not proof enough to the task, and parity in numbers was a bare sufficiency. Some cross-commentary still managed to get through, but because of the distance imposed by the wives it was usually reduced to semaphore, as now. The restraint always generated a reservoir of unresolved issues that demanded follow-through address, thus unfailingly guaranteeing a joint post-conference luncheon in which those impatient arrears were made up. And that was the plan for today.

As unruly as their husbands tended to be during the conference, Laura and Helen were models of scholarly propriety. Both would sit with seeming total absorption in the presenter's words, as though unmindful of their guardianship function vis-a-vis their husbands, and each, equipped with pencil and pad, would dutifully take notes throughout. Cantrelle and Moyer eschewed such practice as slavish and bothersome, and much too distracting. Yet, often enough it was the merciful availability of those very notes which would set to rights important points in the luncheon follow-up parleys when discussion became polemic. Also, the wives had their own post-conference points to pursue; Laura was ever alert to new clinical developments that might translate into statistical tools for extending the efficiency and efficacy of health care, while Helen, a Masters level social worker, was a busy family and marital counselor at a private clinic and was particularly attuned to new medical findings that could clarify presenting issues for the families and couples, particularly in the area of genetic counseling, of late an increasingly important field of reference.

The four arose from their seats as the attendance began to collect into streams seeking the exits. A general din filled the auditorium as though to help move the streams along. Released from silence, Cantrelle offered a collective generalization.

"It looks like the genes have it for a while. I hope they don't bury dynamics prematurely," he sighed.

"Your buddy Burleson certainly made his position clear on that point, wouldn't you say?" Moyer added.

His "buddy"—the chummy appellation derived of his happenstance meeting with Burleson almost ten years ago and proudly referred to often enough by Cantrelle to merit Moyer's mild jibe—had indeed cautioned vigorously against the probably inevitable excessive emphasis on genetic determinants at the expense of a more balanced, molar conception of human behavior. "Don't lose sight of the person as you look at his cells," Burleson had charged at one point in his presentation. Here, today, he again played something of the devil's advocate on the panel, a role most congenial to the omnium-gatherum character of his interests and talents. Cantrelle noted that over the past year or so Burleson had lost a few pounds, leaving him to appear more ascetic than his protean tastes would suggest. If anything, and especially today, Burleson seemed to be insatiable in his enjoyment of the intellectual buffet offered by the singularly distinguished panel. In addition to himself and Weinroth, there was Willard Anderson, Ph.D., a leading sociologist who spoke on the societal implications of genetic research, especially in regard to family planning, transmissible disorders, and eugenics. The newly-evolved National Health Plan connected to the issue in no uncertain way, he saw fit to warn. The other two members of the five man panel were commensurate luminaries who balanced out the representation agreeably. Jeremy Markman, philosopher, author, university dean, and frequent member of Oval Office ad hoc think tanks, spoke on the broader issue of ethics, research, and political determinism, his point being that, of itself, knowledge was amoral, simplistic, and pure, and that man's relationship to his knowledge constituted a realm beyond the scope of the scientific method and thus demanded a review discipline offered thus far only by the field of ethics. The final panelist was Edwin Malloy, Ph.D., the mathematician, who as a boy prodigy achieved international fame with the space program years earlier and who more recently added to his credits as the key contributor in working out the probability sets for the newly enacted National Health Plan, a monumental piece of work understood by probably no one on Capitol hill but sufficiently validating in its scope and meaning to enlist legislative approval of the health plan proposed and subsequently adopted. Almost a year earlier Ellie had talked about Malloy's work while it was in progress and nearing completion and deemed it the most sterling example of mathematics as an applied tool for creative social engineering, an application she foresaw as finally at hand and awaiting her participation. He also was a Nobel laureate.

A few of the panelists had dismounted the stage and were standing together at the front of the center isle chatting with a few members of the audience who had gone forward to greet and to congratulate. The relaxed and casual interchange carried hand shakes, elaborate gestures of surprise and delight, and broad laughter—all signs of a job well done and thoroughly appreciated. As he was sure everyone else present did, Cantrelle savored how the panelists, in a mere three-quarter hour's time allotted to each, had covered the breadth and depth of the material addressed, and had somehow rendered it clear, focused, and expository. A major feat in conference craft, but perhaps a feat more rooted in panel selection than in topic structuring. The theme of this conference, "American Society and Horizons of Change," probably could not have been addressed by a panel of lesser figures, so daunting and inclusive the challenge presented by so grand a palette. But these panelists, in their limited presentation time, had identified the seminal points so precisely and had applied them so cogently and with such a convergent focus it seemed that they had rehearsed the symposium well in advance to achieve such a union of theses. That degree of integration of discussion was a rarity in conferences, as they ran, and to see it happen on a topic whose dimensions traditionally defied definition was an event to be cherished. The points registered and vistas framed took everybody in attendance beyond their usual limits, he guessed, and he knew this to be a valid notion because throughout the conference he had that nagging, hovering, elusive sense of being on the verge, just like at home when at his desk or when staring at his office wall. Plus, as the speakers came and went the feeling swelled or subsided accordingly; but, as usual, it did not achieve ultimate fulfillment come of some blinding insight.

As they stood at the edge of their row waiting to slip into the stream of audience flowing up the aisle he watched Burleson, Weinroth, and Markman chat with friends and well-wishers clustered around them at the front of the auditorium. How magnificently superior those thinkers were, he marveled as he again felt the enormous gulf that separated people like himself from any one of the panelists, perhaps from Burleson in particular since that splendid man was a psychiatrist as well, and hence more comparable. It was expectable to consider oneself greatly different and removed from a given famous figure whose work was totally in another field, but he and Burleson were both psychiatrists, sharing the kinship come of that calling. Yet, the sense of his being in a much lesser world than Burleson's realm was so ruefully distinct. The automatic deference such recognition compelled ran roughly counter to his usual populist sentiments. Thus the twinge of poignant and wistful regret in being witness to what he knew his own life and efforts would never achieve.

Just as Moyer was ready to wedge an entry into the aisle flow leading out, Cantrelle caught Burleson's eye as Burleson looked up from his small gathering in front of the stage to scan idly the ebb of the audience. Burleson returned the glance with a half-smile and brow knitted in tentative recognition. He then gave an uncertain wave to Cantrelle who returned the gesture in confirmation. Cantrelle then immediately decided to act on it.

"Clay," he hurriedly instructed, "don't go up the aisle; go down to the front."

"What?" Moyer hesitated.

"Go down to the front; to where the speakers are. I want to say hello," he explained.

All three looked at him in surprise.

"Burleson just waved to me. I want to introduce you all to him," he continued.

"As you say," submitted Moyer doubtfully.

"Think he remembers?" Laura questioned.

"Apparently he does," Cantrelle replied.

Moyer caught an opening in the now thinning flow and pulled Helen along with him. Laura followed with Cantrelle as they wended their way against the current toward the base of the stage. As they neared, Cantrelle took the lead and headed toward Burleson who was watching his approach from the corner of his eye as he chatted with the two colleagues. When Cantrelle neared handshake distance, Burleson shifted from his conferees and greeted Cantrelle brightly.

"Hello! How are you? Dr. Cantrelle, as I remember. Right? It must be six or seven years."

"Almost ten, Dr. Burleson," Cantrelle corrected politely.

"That long? Goodness, how time gets away from us," he continued busily. "I've often remembered our morning together at that symposium. Enjoyed it very much."

"Not quite as cosmic as today's agenda, though," Cantrelle offered.

"You're very kind to suggest so, but back then maybe things were a bit simpler, or so it might now seem. I hazard we didn't think so back then, though, would you say?" Burleson offered.

"I know I felt very amply employed that morning," Cantrelle demurred.

"I did too," Burleson dissembled graciously. "Isn't it awful how we seem always to be just shy of what's before us, never quite fully up to the task, always hovering on the verge, and furiously worrying about it?"

"My God," Cantrelle thought, *"not him, too!"* He felt a rush to commiserate but quelled it quickly out of fear of presuming. As the moment passed he posed the doubt that Burleson was actually sincere in his complaint, or that "the verge" he made reference to was in any way similar to the misty experience Cantrelle suffered now and again, even just moments before and during the presentations. Burleson noted Cantrelle's hesitance and picked up the missed beat.

"Are you still at . . . Moreland, I think?" Burleson inquired tentatively.

The man had a remarkable memory, Cantrelle thought as he nodded affirmation.

"Yes, still there. Some things never change," he added gratuitously, feeling vaguely remiss at the disclosure.

Burleson returned the nod and them smiled at the three standing with Cantrelle as though to inform him that introductions were now in order.

"Oh, yes," responded Cantrelle, reclaiming his social responsibility, "Dr. Burleson, I'd like you to meet my wife Laura, and Mr. and Mrs. Moyer. Clay is the psychologist on the Intensive Treatment Unit at Moreland and we unite to wrestle the residents into professional respectability before graduating them upon an unsuspecting public," he quipped in an effort to recoup.

"I'm most pleased to meet you, Mrs. Cantrelle, Mrs. Moyer," he charmed in his courtly manner reserved for ladies, and then, shifting, "Mr. Moyer, I knew that Dr. Cantrelle could not in good conscience take full credit for the excellent young psychiatrists produced by Moreland, and I'm happy to see that he is equal to making public attribution where appropriate." He extended his hand to an impressed Moyer, who responded to the duty of return.

"I'm pleased to meet you, Dr. Burleson. In our conferences Frank often refers to your work. In fact, he's made it clear to the residents that they won't be allowed to become those excellent young psychiatrists until they can recite your papers backwards and forwards," Moyer contributed.

Burleson threw his head back in a good-natured guffaw at the bold flattery. As they smiled at his generous acknowledgment he returned his attention to Helen and Laura.

"Are you ladies full-time managers of your husbands' better destinies, or do you find time for pursuits of your own as well?" he lavished.

"Helen manages a busy family as well as a marital counseling practice, and I do medical statistics for a QA/UR service," Laura contributed brightly. "And, yes, we do look after these two from time to time."

"Time is your eternal adversary, isn't it, with all that finds its way to your care, no?" he observed sympathetically.

"That's the truth!" confirmed Helen readily as she eyed her husband in cool vindication.

"But I assure you, Mrs. Moyer, though time is merciless, it really does try to be impartial. Wouldn't you say, gentlemen?" he added wryly.

At that moment the group took notice of Jeremy Markman's presence on the distant periphery of the foursome. He was now making a gesture to Burleson by holding his wrist forward and pointing to his wristwatch.

"See what I mean!" Burleson burst forth in a chuckle. "It appears that my timekeeper is summoning me. And go I must," he added heroically. He then continued more seriously, "The panel has a luncheon critique session scheduled and I suppose we have to get moving, I'm being reminded."

"We're up to the sacrifice, Dr. Burleson," Moyer volunteered, "and dasn't keep you. Thanks again for such a pleasant conference, and please convey our deep gratitude to the other members of the panel."

The others seconded the sentiment effusively.

"It has been indeed a pleasure to meet you, Mrs. Cantrelle and you, Mr. and Mrs. Moyer," Burleson returned. "Perhaps again soon. Oh! That reminds me, Dr. Cantrelle. At that conference ten years ago I think we agreed to get together at a later time for lunch and conversation. Never got around to it, did we? Let's see if we can do better this time, shall we?"

"I would be delighted, Dr. Burleson," Cantrelle gushed.

"Good. Now I must be off to my keeper who just now seems to have expended his limited store of patience. Good morning," he nodded, and was off with a quickened pace that jostled the air of casual discourse still enveloping the four of them. They watched him join Markman who fell in step with him as the two talked hurriedly along toward the side exit.

"Some teamwork, huh?" Moyer observed.

"How do you mean?" Cantrelle queried as he watched Burleson and Markman leave the auditorium.

"I mean the signal he gave Markman about the time and how Markman moved right on it," Moyer explained.

Cantrelle looked at him in puzzlement. After a moment his face opened in disbelief.

"You mean to say you think that when he was talking to Laura and Helen, Burleson made the comments about time as a signal to Markman to make use of it, like calling time to give Burleson an out! And make it seem that it wasn't his doing?"

"I think so. They're certainly clever enough," Moyer insisted.

Cantrelle stared at Moyer in exasperation. Helen just rolled her eyes in the forbearance of having been there with her husband many times before.

"Clay," resumed Cantrelle with a definite edge to his voice, "they may be clever, but not nearly enough to match your cynicism. Christ! Can't you take anything as offered?" he volleyed, offended that Moyer's petulance was tarnishing the idyllic glow of the morning's windup.

Moyer just raised his eyebrows in his characteristic register of lofty disdain he reserved for those moments when he felt that any additional corrective advice on the matter would be wasted. Cantrelle was about to call him on it when Laura interceded.

"Wait, wait! Never start a serious discussion immediately before lunch or dinner. Remember?" Laura reminded her ruffled husband. Over the years he had held that particular admonition to be a basic tenet in program arrangement and had always advised accordingly whenever he was called upon to serve on a conference or symposium planning committee. He maintained that free-ranging discussions mounted on an empty stomach too often had an unpleasant tendency to become snarling and inconclusive. "Hold on to your friendship for a few more minutes. Lunch is almost ready," she soothed.

He smiled sheepishly as he pulled in his horns.

"Right. One thing I guess we can agree on: those guys really can stir up controversy," he displaced as he assumed an apologetic amiability.

"We're all starving, your mention of food prompts me to announce," Moyer supplied in deflection. "I suggest we hit the vittles, fast."

It was standard for them that morning conferences held in the city be followed by lunch at Manney's which was the quintessential out-of-the-way-family-restaurant-with-high-cuisine-at-low-price-and-hope-it-never-gets-discovered-by-the-pricey-crowd place. They had been doing lunch there for years and had come to regard the post-conference meals as a passage ceremony reversing the soma-to-psyche exaction fostered by the conference. The repast usually included the exercise of recalling to view for discriminatory savoring at the dining table any and all ideas served up earlier at the conference table. So it was typically a lively lunch with more than just comestibles being digested.

That much assumed, they moved with measured pace up the now noisy aisle and soon reached the crowded foyer where groups had coalesced to vent pent-up energies called into resonance by the speakers. Predictably the din was deafening and seemed to be on its way to declamatory heights, a compelling measure of the success of the conference.

"We'll meet you there," Cantrelle shouted to Moyer and Helen above the din as they picked their way through the congestion. In doing so they were released from united effort in favor of a more serviceable every-man-for-himself means of making it to the parking lot, and away.

In short order they were out of the building and descending its broad steps. It had turned cloudy and the wind had picked up, hurrying the Autumn's first drizzle of leaves across the greensward of the campus. There was now a nip in the air which seemed to liven the pace of the students moving about in their gathering pre-game bustle. He always felt a certain exhilaration when on a college campus in the Autumn; or at *any* time, for that matter. But mostly Autumn. And just about any college campus would do, though his own alma mater did it best. But Franklinton was quite good, too, steeped in all the right traditions, as it was. He knew that it was his youth calling him back to its glories and he treasured his unwavering responsiveness to its call. It rarely took much at homecomings, his or Richard's and presumably soon enough Ellie's and Todd's, for him to start singing those ageless drinking and fight songs and their ilk at the off-campus pubs done up in college decor. It was all part and parcel of his belonging rightfully to the college life in keeping with his dearest fantasy of being a college professor at some pure and peaceful college where he would teach what he knew in his heart and soul was his true calling, Philosophy. In his undergraduate days he had almost taken that plunge as he idealized his acclaimed Philosophy teacher as the one he would follow and whose life style offered all he could want for the cultivation of those amenities the scholarly life granted. After about a year and a half of loading his pre-med schedule with philosophy courses wherever he could fit them in he learned quite inadvertently from a gabby instructor that his ideal, the renowned professor of Philosophy and celebrated author who seemingly had gathered about himself all the gracious emoluments of the scholarly life, was also the fabulously wealthy heir of a huge retail store chain and as such had never ever needed to work for any part of the living he enjoyed. The happy illusion that pure knowledge would tend to the creature comfort of its seekers was laid bare and found wanting. His ideal, though still estimable, became rather less credible once he was seen as being fiscally buoyed up by the efforts of others. And that ended his approach to the academic orders; he would stay with science for the everyday business of making a living. Yet, whenever he was on campus the siren call would return, and he loved the temptation.

"It wouldn't be enough for you," Laura interrupted as they walked hand in hand across the campus toward the parking lot.

"What do you mean?" he asked, pulled away from his reverie.

"You had that far away look as though you were seeing a beckoning glory. You know, the look you get every time you set foot on a college campus," she explained.

"Oh," he acknowledged with a smile of chagrin.

"It wouldn't be enough for you to be a full-time teacher. Too confining and you know it," she reminded him in the manner of a light splash of cool water. She then squeezed his hand consolingly. "You're already a half-time teacher; a director of training, in fact. And besides, you need your private practice. Keeps you sober and honest, neither of which is required or fostered by the academic life, you've often said. Remember?"

"Yeah, I know," he yielded in a balky chuckle. "But after a conference like today's, and walking among the ivy in Autumn, it's a pretty heady temptation. Just think, you could be the wife of a college professor, wear tweed skirts and sensible Margaret Mead shoes, and swig the vitriol of distaff academia."

"Hard to resist, I admit, but I think I'll make do with the ordinary joys of freedom and sincerity. And also with the fruits of my man's successful private practice," she pronounced with a more resolute squeeze of his hand. "By the way, you're on call this weekend, aren't you?" she mentioned pragmatically.

"Yeah," he sighed. "I'll check in with the answering service when we get to the restaurant." He had earlier done so at breaktime during the conference and was free of calls then.

They were now on the asphalt of the parking lot and trooping the serried ranks of waiting cars. They spotted Moyer and Helen several ranks off to their right, homing in similarly.

"There they are," he indicated. "This is working out pretty well this morning," he preened.

"You shouldn't be so quick to jump on Clay when he doesn't agree with you," she advised gently as their car loomed ahead in its slot.

Again, he felt that flash of anger. He granted it a moment to have its flare, and then acknowledged her admonition, almost as gently.

"I know. But that son-of-a-bitch, as lovable as he is, can be a pain in the ass at exactly the wrong time," he grumped.

"But, my love, you've praised him for just that; relied upon him for it in the teaching program. Certainly you've used him to demonstrate to the residents the stance of independent objectivity. You've even protected him from the Administration on the basis that what he does is good for them, too. So, my dear," she twitted, "I think you ought to own up to its being good for you, also. You know, fair play, integrity, and all that sort of thing. And besides, he never jumps on you, does he?"

She was right, as usual, and this time he didn't have to acknowledge it. So, better simply to brazen it out.

"Just because you're right doesn't mean I have to agree with you. Perversity has it points too," he pouted playfully.

"It's amazing you two get along at all. You think he's supercilious; I think he's very forgiving, and probably that accounts for it," she concluded, shaking her head in mystification.

"Speaking of being forgiving," he shifted, "do we let Todd use the car tonight after skipping school yesterday?"

"Whatever you say, but I don't think we should," Laura advised. "But, worse, if we don't he'll probably end up cruising around with that Eddie Shanks tonight. And I certainly don't want to encourage that; I know you don't. Yet, we can't make him stay home as though he were a twelve-year-old. Also, I worry that if we make too much of an issue of his skipping school he'll drop out entirely. What do you think?"

"Pretty much the same," he glummed. "But we can't pussy-foot around his limit testing. It's just not right. Sooner or later its going to come either to his knuckling down and preparing himself for some decent kind of work or to just forgetting about the whole thing and getting some job somewhere to enable him to move out on his own. After days like yesterday I fear it'll likely be the latter," he dreaded.

They had been through similar discussions before whenever Todd skipped school or had perpetrated some other dereliction, and they were about equally weary of reciting their resolve to maintain standards and bring him to heel—all for Todd's own good, of course. But yesterday's peccadillo enlarged significantly the bill of particulars in Todd's misbehavior, they feared. Always before, he would acknowledge his misfeasances when they were brought to his attention. If he skipped school, he would admit to it almost good-heartedly with a self-conscious smile and some show of remorse. But yesterday he had initially lied about it when Laura brought the question up. Only when confronted with the conclusive fact that the teacher had called out of concern for his whereabouts did he submit to the truth of the matter, and even then with a surliness that arose more out of defiance than acquiescence. And there were no offers of atonement as always before. Nor was there any conciliatory explanations as to where he had been and why. Laura sensed a fundamental shift in his attitude, a change from an appreciation of the wrongness of his dereliction and of the need for some remediation to a satisfied defiance not inclined to brook any challenge of his preferences. She had tried to reassure herself that it probably was only a transient thing, just a particularly bad day for him, and that he would bounce back to a frame of mind more in keeping with his usual lovable nature, but now she knew better. Something in him had changed. That evening she reported the incident to Cantrelle who then spoke to Todd about it, but by that time the heat of the moment had long subsided and the interchange between him and Todd became something less than pointed for having been diluted in the return of more familiar and gentler family currents. But she knew a change had occurred. Todd knew it, too. Even Cantrelle in his efforts ever to ameliorate family turbulence knew that things were somehow different now in the unsettled matter of his son's need for direction.

"I'll have to talk to that boy," he offered resignedly. But he had said that many times before and had never followed through. Laura knew that the promise was more his way of bringing the discussion to a close for the time being. She wasn't sure whether he simply didn't want to confront Todd outright and run the risk of rupturing forever the gentle and caring tie he had with his troubled son, or whether he was prudently waiting for the right moment and right issue to give the confrontation the best chance for achieving effect. Either way, Laura worried that time was running out, especially after yesterday.

"Frank, please don't wait too long," she pleaded.

"I won't, hon. I just want to do it right," he deferred.

She kept her sigh to herself.

"All right! Here we are. Hop in, my lady," he announced with elaborate gallantry upon reaching the car at precisely the right moment.

"Where are they?" Laura scanned as he unlocked and swung the door open. "Oh, there they are," she signaled with her finger, then waving.

As she slid into the car and nestled into the seat he noted the sheer of her legs, extended as they were to brace her as she settled into the seat's contour. Those legs! Her skirt had slid up to mid thigh and, as always, at the sight of her beauty his heart began the tom-tom of anticipation. And, as always, good thoughts rushed forth, such as how much better just now would be a picnic in their woods where they spent many a Saturday afternoon in torrid courtship rather than in a crowded public restaurant with friends, even best friends. How much better a splash of their pre-nuptial chablis *al fresco* than a doughty lunch deductible as a business expense. Well, at least a wonderful evening was not too far away, he consoled himself. And he conveyed as much through gleeful eyes set above a leering smile as he swung her door shut much too slowly. She returned his proposition with a coquettish pursing of her lips to signal her acceptance of what she exactly knew was in his head and for when. He gave his usual snort of wavering control as he clicked the door shut. He then eased away with a knowing smile that sealed the understanding, and the quick little nod she gave in return settled the matter fetchingly. As he circled the rear of the car enroute to his seat the usual commentary assailed him: that this woman of his really had his number; that a mere glimpse of her thigh was all it took; or even just a sly smile; that they had made love in literally every room in the house, including the attic as well as on the kitchen floor; that according to his last estimate they had made love together well over four thousand times. Four thousand times! It was amazing how durable a person's sexuality was. And there was no let-up in sight, he chortled to himself as he savored the anticipation of the coming evening.

He opened his door vigorously and mounted his seat at the wheel. He then fired up the engine and backed out of the slot and swung into the exit path. While doing so they sustained their joint smile of resolved expectation, lingering that extra moment over their accomplished dalliance. As they exited the lot and settled into traffic he placed his hand on her thigh, caressing its girth at just that height compatible with delight, safe driving, and the inconvenience of public visibility. It was their traditional and official arrangement when driving alone together anywhere, and in the beginning it had created a modest dilemma in travel style since he was a purist in the matter of automobile transmissions and would have nothing but a standard gear box on anything he drove. But the unquestioned convenience of an automatic when Laura was literally at hand was not to be ignored. He ended up holding on to both in greedy compromise which he regarded as the key factor for confirming every opportune moment in their lives as beckoning consummation. Even that antic moment on the kitchen floor. They openly shared the conviction that their love life verged on merry and riotous nonsense, just exactly as they wished. And they just couldn't imagine having it any other way.

"Oh," Laura recalled, "I forgot to tell you. Richard phoned and said he would be in next weekend. He and Meredith have to go to a wedding. A childhood friend of hers. He said to tell you he would be in Friday night and if you could squeeze it in you and he might be able to do joint slaughter on the local pheasant population Saturday morning. He really loves being with you, Frank," she added with beaming maternal satisfaction.

Now he felt the warmth of fatherly pride well up in him and along with it the sharp regret that Todd had never moved into the easy and invigorating comradeship he shared with his older son. Both he and Richard had tried to initiate Todd at every turn in the earlier years, but Todd, despite what for him was commendable effort, simply did not share with his father the same sense of purpose and pleasure as was the case with his brother, Richard. As a result, and in deference to what was perceived by them as Todd's regrettable loss, Cantrelle and Richard mounted their pleasant moments together with a certain mindful discretion bordering on the covert so as not to cast Todd openly in the role of outsider. Thus, too often, as now, the prospect of a joint undertaking carried with it the regret of its being exclusionary as well. The overall effect was that of a dampening restraint being imposed by their concern for Todd's injured sense of belonging, plus their own muted resentment for having to observe restraint at the expense of what the rightness of their relationship promised. Their effort to average out the situation to minimize a gross and culpable imbalance resulted in something less than full satisfaction for all concerned.

"That's right! Next Saturday is the first day of the season. Good! I'll oil up the old fowling pieces," he delighted. "And I'll tell Todd to keep the day open to make it a threesome," he added in exoneration. Also, it was so much more salubrious to shift the venue's emphasis from what was being denied to what was being offered in his upcoming talk with Todd over the use of the car, missing school, lying about it, and the virtues of personal responsibility, if it came to all that. It would just be so much better if all three of them could join together in honored comradeship. So much better.

They shared a moment of silence for fear that any additional discussion of the matter would damage his tender hope. Anyway, they were nearing Manney's—just a few blocks more—and it was time to shift conversation to suit their approach.

"What do you have planned this afternoon, Sweet?" he blandished.

"First, Ellie and I have to go food shopping. Then it's off to the Kimberville Antique Show," she supplied.

"There goes the budget," he groaned.

"It's time to start on Christmas presents, is what it is," she corrected.

"I'll stay close to the house, since I'm on call," he sighed, "and burn a candle in hope that I'll be able to make it through the game without interruption. Penn State's playing Syracuse, probably for the Lambert trophy, as usual," he continued.

"It's not too crowded. Good," she observed as they turned into the restaurant's parking lot.

Both hands now on the wheel he jockeyed the car into a convenient slot near the entrance. They were just locking up when Moyer and Helen pulled into the lot and found a slot a short distance away. In a few moments the four of them were walking along in chatty amiability toward the restaurant entrance, all agreeing enroute that there was no appetite like the appetite stirred by a zesty conference. They entered and were greeted by Fritz, the maitre d', who never failed to acknowledge them with some pleasantry to reveal that he remembered them by name, profession, and preferred apèritif.

"Good afternoon, ladies and gentlemen," he beamed through huckleberry freckles and unruly red hair under temporary pomade arrest, "it must be conference time again for all four of you to drop in for lunch."

"You've got it, Fritz," Cantrelle confirmed, "and now we're ready to taste of a more basic kind of wisdom."

"And so it shall be!" Fritz retorted in appreciation. "Your usual?"

"You bet," Cantrelle urged, "but make mine dry sherry," he added.

"Then you must be on call, Dr. Cantrelle," Fritz mused aloud with arms folded and index finger on chin to affect a pose of sober discernment.

"Right again, my clever friend," Cantrelle complimented.

"The usual" meant their traditional corner table and their inveterate pre-dinner drinks—martini for Cantrelle, chablis for Laura, and screwdrivers for Clay and Helen.

"Tsk, tsk," Fritz commiserated, "no rest for the wicked," he tossed playfully as he led them to their table and alerted the waitress. He then took leave of their jovial gratitude for his hearty welcome. The drinks would be immediately forthcoming, he assured as they took their seats.

"Oh! What a morning!" Cantrelle exhaled as he leaned back and stretched his arms. It was nice to settle into a restful lunch.

"I'm sure you're aware of the implications, Frank," Moyer began.

Cantrelle had a pretty good idea of what Moyer, in his non-sequitur style, was introducing, but pretended uncertainty.

"Like what, Clay?" he asked.

"The genetic mapping. If they can do what they say, then there won't be much room left for dynamics, will there be?" he proposed like a good behaviorist.

"I think that's what Burleson was cautioning against, just as you said; playing too hard with a new toy, however promising, and doing so at the expense of what's for years been useful and instructive. And productive, I might add," Cantrelle cited. "I think his point that as long as people use their minds to understand their brains, the mind simply has to have a pre-eminent place in our general psychology, and I think that that sobering notion was the best observation of the morning. I know that's just the sort of thing test-tube behaviorists like yourself hoot at, though it happens to be the way we live as people, not as scientists," he added.

"Sure, but it's not the way we do research, and I don't have to tell you that the farther our practice is from our research methodology the closer we are to shamanism, magic, and religion, like you yourself never tire of accusing us of practicing," Moyer retorted.

"Here we go again! Content without form!" Cantrelle countered with rising intensity. "Don't ever let our research be contaminated by a sense of direction or purpose," he smirked.

"Or without privileged basic assumptions," Moyer carped with a merry twinkle.

"Ho, ho, ho!" Cantrelle derided. "What we don't need is more damned reductionistic research and publications that don't amount to anything more than finding the umpteenth way of pronouncing shibboleth. Don't you get tired of reading the same dreary paper over and over again, the only difference one from another is the author, and too often that's the same, also? You've got to have noticed that our journals are like the menus of those Russian cruise ships: the menu changes every day but the food remains the same. C'mon!" he gibed enroute to his high horse where he was ever invulnerable to compromise.

"*You* c'mon, Frank! You're being categorical. Not all publications are resumè padding and you know it. Some of it, yes. And the editors go along with it, true. Because they need copy, absolutely. But you can't just write it all off—if you'll forgive the metaphor—as nothing more than choir practice, as you already have the residents believing. Some of the publications are obviously really good stuff—innovative, crisp, truly informative. You certainly quote them often enough in your lectures," Moyer reminded him.

"Sure, Clay," Cantrelle allowed, "but how many are really worth quoting? One in a hundred? Or a thousand? It's just the fast food mentality of American research that's so appalling. Find out what the funding people like and crank it out as fast as you can, but please don't look at the basic assumption behind any of it. The funding committees wouldn't cotton to that."

"Speaking of fast food," Laura interceded, "ours is anything but. I wonder what's taking so long with the drinks?"

Cantrelle looked at his wife and smiled appreciatively.

"Yeah," he agreed, accepting her deflection, "We've earned a soothing sip, I'd say. Which in some strange way reminds me, Clay; how is that young fellow doing? The one we saw a week ago in conference. The college kid. What was his name? Johnson?"

"Jordan," Moyer corrected. "He's not doing well at all. We had to transfer him to Building Nine for extended care."

"Building Nine? That's for bedridden cases!" Cantrelle started.

"That's pretty much what he's become, and rapidly, right before our very eyes. Every day he became a little more demented—incoherent, unconnected, and finally mute. But still smiling. When he became incontinent—or at least began not caring about his toilet habits—we had to transfer him to Building Nine," Moyer explained. "They're working on arrangements now to transport him back to a long-term care facility in his home state. The family visits weekly, usually on Wednesdays because of the father's church duties back home. They called in a couple of consultants. They looked him over and agreed with what we're doing. They were just as perplexed as we as to what was going on. One suggested sending him to Bethesda, but the family voted that down; said it sounded a little too much like research. The family preferred to start making arrangements to have him transferred to a facility closer to home. Social Work is helping with the contacts."

"He's declined that fast?" Cantrelle asked, incredulous.

"Like nothing we've ever seen before," Moyer glummed. "Nor has Neurology, either. They said whatever the drug was—we never did find out—it seems to have set up an auto-immune reaction with progressive destruction of the mid-brain structures. The EEG remained pretty normal, but the MRI showed destruction of all the medial nuclei of the thalami and also punctate lesions of the hypothalamus. They said they'd never seen anything like it, either.

They also said that maybe, ipso facto, the lesions had identified the consciousness center—or at least the self-consciousness center of the brain. The thalamic nuclei. We got a repeat MRI just yesterday and it showed progressive loss of thalamic and hypothalamic tissue. That, coupled with his worsening clinical course, convinced everybody it was probably an ongoing auto-immune process. They had tried to stop it with steroids, but at best that only slowed it down a bit . . . maybe. It all happened so fast. They're following him in Building Nine and he's still on the steroids," Moyer detailed as he stared at his folded hands before him on the table.

A somber silence followed Moyer's grim accounting. Cantrelle felt it his duty to shift the tone of the moment.

"These damned kids don't realize what the hell they're getting into when they start larking around with drugs," he grumbled. "Some chemistry major somewhere in his basement laboratory concocted this 'designer drug,' as they call them, and this poor kid took it, probably as a volunteer guinea pig. And now he's going to die an incontinent, demented heap of flesh. And maybe pretty soon, too, at the rate he's going, because it likely won't be long before the reaction spreads to the vital centers," he railed.

"That's what Neurology fears," Moyer confirmed.

"Oh! Here come the drinks!" Helen announced with relief as she spotted the waiter enroute.

"Great! Nothing like an ancient, conventional, proven, and storied substance to soothe us in our distress over the ravages caused by those young and irresponsible substances desecrating the sanctity of a more cultivated intemperance," Cantrelle quipped in mock sententiousness.

The drinks, served amidst an intent and patient silence, were then sipped to liberate a collective sigh of delight. The tenor of the moment thus adjusted, Cantrelle continued.

"Well, so far we can be thankful that this Jordan boy is one of a kind. A designer drug experiment gone wrong. A pathetic object lesson, but one which will be quickly forgotten by his friends, probably," he gloomed.

"Never by the family, though," Helen sighed.

"Those poor people," Laura sorrowed.

"I guess Jess has been kept up to date on the case," Cantrelle queried as he took another sip.

"Sure, and you can imagine how it must be for him to carry such news to the boy's father," Moyer replied.

"I'd rather not, thank you," Cantrelle declined as they all toasted in a gesture of closure on that plaintive subject.

An extended moment of silence followed in which all took a turn staring at the drink in hand in search of a brighter topic.

"The salads will probably be here in a few minutes," Laura then observed. "Helen, my nose needs attention. Let's make a quick circuit of the ladies' room while we're waiting."

"Super! You'll excuse us, gentlemen?" Helen chirped. And they were off.

"Frank," Moyer resumed solicitously after the women left, "are you sure you're not alienating yourself by being so . . . so . . . ."

"Intolerant?" Cantrelle supplied.

"No," Moyer declined, "Your flippant intolerance is one of the things I enjoy about you. A jollier W. C. Fields. I was going to say 'unforgiving.' You really come down hard on people who truly don't intend to do harm, or, heaven forbid, contrive to waste your time. People—people who happen to like you and who want to work with you—might get to be a little reluctant if they feel they have to watch themselves so carefully when all they're trying to do is help out a bit. We don't have to go on about it again, but, as you know, there are several people at Moreland who will probably never forgive you for denying their requests to join the teaching staff. Not that you were wrong to do so, because I agree with your decision in every case, but in their resentment they grab on to your impatience and well-known intolerance and package it as your particular blend of contempt. And arrogance. Worse, some of the other staff members are inclined to go along with it, especially if you step on their toes, even if ever so gently, like in the Individual Case Review Conference."

"Maybe their accusations are right," Cantrelle said coolly as he lifted his drink casually to effect the very disdain Moyer was addressing.

"Now don't be a piss-ant," Moyer snapped. "I only bring this up because I think you might be causing yourself some unnecessary trouble at just those times when you don't need it. Like not very long ago when you tried to get more applied research going on the units. Some of the staff—the touchy ones, I mean—saw that as your way of trying to correct their deficiencies. A few even said that it was your attempt to re-train the entire psychiatric staff into being the kind of psychiatrists you thought they should be, and not at all a sincere plug for research itself. How's that for contempt? Just like your own words coming right back at you, huh?"

It wasn't the first time he was being told that he tended to treat everybody like residents, a bias by which he set the standards for clinical, ethical, and academic acceptability. Nor was it the first time he felt miffed at the suggestion, though he would concede that perhaps there was a measure of truth in it. But that's what he did best, with the residents, at least: setting standards and applying them impartially. So what if a little spilled over on to innocent bystanders? Wasn't the greater good it provided more than enough to offset any collateral damage from muzzle-blast? He thought so. And besides, what kind of a person was it who put his personal sensitivities and comfort above the pursuit of high standards in education or in anything else, he adroitly asked himself whenever necessary.

"And don't hide behind the happy illusion that these people are simply putting their personal sensitivities before the pursuit of majesty, because that just unfairly demeans them as well as the issue," Moyer cautioned.

"*Jesus Christ,*" Cantrelle thought with amused alarm, "*he's reading my god-damned mind.*"

"You think you're pretty good, don't you?" he said in reluctant admiration of Moyer's deft tactic.

"Cut you off at the pass, didn't I?" Moyer relished.

"Sort of," Cantrelle chuckled.

"Seriously, Frank, you do hurt people without meaning to do so. They think you intend it because of a personal dissatisfaction with them. *Personal*, mind you. Look, I've told you this before and I'll try not to belabor it, but you're the most competent and most articulate man I know, but you, dear friend, just don't seem to grasp it, or at least not in a way that enables you to be realistic and patient with people not so well off, You seem to think that what you expect is a wholly impersonal standard applicable to everybody. Like the Frenchman who just automatically expects everybody to be able to speak French and there's something wrong with them if they don't, but, of course, nothing very personal intended. I can tell you they straight out see your expectation as coming solely from your advantage, and then they see you as being very self-serving about it at their *very* personal expense. That's why they think you're so arrogant, especially when you get upset with them."

"Does it upset you?" Cantrelle probed with concern.

"You mean *personally*? No, not anymore. In the beginning, yes," Moyer admitted. "But then I realized that hidden in your apparent arrogance was a kind of left-handed generosity and—God forbid!—a simplistic egalitarianism. I realized that far from being arrogant you were sincerely treating everybody as equal and truly believed them to be innately just as empowered as yourself but perhaps lacking a bit of drive or direction which you, again quite sincerely, would readily help with since you had been fortunate enough, you seemed to say, to have stumbled upon the groundswell of certain enabling habits enroute to your present work. When I finally caught on, I quickly stopped being pissed off with you and began to feel, fool that I am, protective of you, like I do today. The residents think its great that their leader is seen as imperial because they make no bones about being your charges, there to learn—and imitate. So it works well with them, but, other than with them, it works only with the people close enough to you to sense what I've just said. I know my telling you this isn't going to make you change one whit, but it might help you to tone down some of your . . . ."

"Muzzle-blast?" Cantrelle offered.

"Right," Moyer agreed. He then waited.

Cantrelle looked down at his almost depleted sherry and pondered for a moment before answering.

"Now let me say something about you, O.K.?" Cantrelle bade. "You're the most honest, incorruptible, penetrating, courageous, and accurate son-of-a-bitch I've ever known, and therefore the most dangerous man I've ever met—and also the dearest friend I've ever had. So, you can take it from there, which should lead us directly to another drink, if I may," he recommended as he motioned for a repeat to the waiter alertly standing by. "And also, Clay," he continued as he paced himself, "thanks for bringing me up to date on what I never seem to be able to keep in touch with. I know you're right—again. Do you think there's any hope at all for the Triage Unit, or do you think I've bolloxed it up enough to keep it from ever happening? The muzzle-blast factor?" he groped, knowing that this issue, the setting up of a separate, rapid assessment, rapid disposition Triage Unit at Moreland in relief of the over-burdened ITU, which presently undertook acute management of all new admissions, was the critical issue to which Moyer had oblique reference.

"I don't know, Frank," Moyer replied, "but I know the talk is that you're cooking up more work for people, and *some*—you know who—would prefer to labor at their customary pace rather than dance to the tune a Triage Unit would call. I think they're telling administration—in fact, I know they are—that you're trying to change the hospital to suit yourself and Residency Training, and they're reminding everybody that it should be the other way around."

"Again, huh?" he grimaced.

"Yeah, again," Moyer replied.

From time to time complaint would arise that Residency Training put itself above the overall welfare of the hospital. Such complaint would usually come forth at those times when Cantrelle was moving along some policy or procedure which, granted, had its primary focus in the training program but which also urged a valid developmental move for the hospital. At those times the training program would be offered by Cantrelle as the best tool for implementing such change, not in the expectation of acquiring hegemony but in the nature of assuming some operational responsibility for the work involved. So, from his view, it was more a charitable thing and less an initiative requiring the work of others for the selfish benefit of residency training and its Director. But try as he might, the accusations came anyway. The Triage Unit proposal was a case in point. The major clinical work involved would be managed by the residents assigned to that unit, and all concerned knew it. Yet, the fear persisted—on the lower levels, anyway—that the change, admittedly a departure from the traditional admission procedure of the hospital and from that of probably every other state hospital, would orient the entire clinical staff in obligatory follow-through on the treatment decisions of an elite few at the front end of the hospital—the Triage Unit—with the result that the pace and scope of the clinical work distributed to the interior of the hospital would then become little more than conformity to delegated task. Indeed, the interior psychiatrist might well fear encroachment upon his already reduced clinical autonomy, limited as it currently was in consequence of existing hospital accreditation requirement that there be multi-discipline treatment planning on every patient. Already reproachful, the interior psychiatrist would thus be inclined to credit any new charge that someone, this time Residency Training, was trying to gain power at the expense of his embattled plight.

"I hope Jess knows better," Cantrelle groaned.

"Oh, you don't have to worry about him," Moyer assured. "He and I have had more than a few conversations about you and the trouble you bring, and he's even more protective of you than I am. He also knows you through and through, but, as you know, he's got to be totally even-handed in his reign, so at the least he has to acknowledge the concerns of the other members of the staff, even if only to reassure them that the sky isn't really falling, much less that it's being brought down by you. He's got his hands full, Jess has."

He felt a rising heat generated of embarrassment combined with gratitude, and with it a need to make it up to the good buddies who fronted for him, unbidden, to take the flak not only caused by him but also directed at him.

"I guess I'll . . ." he began contritely, but his reply was cut short by the simultaneous arrival of the drinks, the salads, and their returning wives.

"Played that just right, didn't we?" Helen applauded for herself and Laura as they settled into their chairs in readiness for the salads being served.

"Hmmm. Second drinks. And at lunch time, too," Laura noted. "Must have been some heavy disquisition going on in our absence. Isn't that just the way it is?" appealing to Helen for effecting a carping liaison. "Every time we turn our backs they fall into neediness."

"It was the salads we yearned for," Moyer retorted, "and the drinks to brace us till they arrived."

"I'll remind you of that, my intemperate rabbit, at some important moment later this evening," Helen teased a she lifted her salad fork.

They all laughed lightly and began their lunch.

The food had its usual comforting and restorative effect, and the conversation settled into a more casual exchange of newsy bits for updating each other on general doings. While this was happening to the accompanying tinkle of china, the shift in conversation tone reminded Cantrelle of his contention that just about any discourse mounted immediately before lunch became too fangy simply because that's they way people were in the face of hunger. Glands were everything, it seemed.

The salads were dispatched with swift efficiency, and the adept removal of the spent china left the table open for the next topic of pursuit. Cantrelle traced a circle along the rim of his sherry and then lifted his finger for attention.

"This morning I think we saw a preview of the new training curriculum in Psychiatry, probably still fifteen years off, but coming, and I'd like to take this opportunity to register that I'm telling you so," he announced.

The others just looked at him with uncertainty and waited. It was well known that a glass of sherry made Frank Cantrelle more fluent on just about everything, and, like a frisky pony released from his stall, he would gambol about exuberantly in any field at hand until the intoxication of release wore off, at which time he'd trudge back into his stall, tired and even meek.

"Clay, remember when we made inquiry through the Accreditation Council and the Boards about developing a combined four year Psychiatry-Neurology training curriculum? I think that was about fifteen years ago. Remember?" he posed.

"Yes, I do, Frank. It didn't work out," Moyer supplied.

"That's right, it didn't," Cantrelle agreed. "We maintained that the time had come and that technology had ordained that Psychiatry and Neurology be reunited into one comprehensive field like it used to be years ago—the old Neuro-Psychiatry—before the separatists in each persuasion had their tea party and dumped integration overboard back in the late thirties and throughout the forties. By the time the fifties rolled in, Psychiatry was so loftily dynamic it was hardly on speaking terms with Neurology, which was just fine with the neurologists who were pleased enough to become better strangers to a prodigal sibling that had abandoned its fastidious medical heritage and had become ambitiously sociologic in seeking the fast company of those noisy parvenus, Community Mental Health and Social Reform, both now long past their boom days and distinctly down at the heel in funding as well as credibility. Well," he continued, "I think today's symposium is a harbinger of a long overdue and necessary—shall I say 'reconciliation'—between Psychiatry and Neurology with a temporary nod being given to Neurology. I suspect that's what Burleson had in mind when he cautioned everybody not to lose sight of the mind while we go after the brain because sooner or later we'll have to put the two together in some better way than we've done thus far. And, hence, I would like so very much to point out to you with all the emphasis allowable of one and a half glasses of sherry that every psychiatric residency training program which hopes to get its bills paid through the lordly offices of the NIH will be called upon to show its integrational heart, and to place it front and center for the review committee to endorse as the shiny new benchmark of tutorial health. Those fellows up on the panel this morning carry awesome weight—probably more so than any other five people in the bio-research world—in determining the direction of NIH education funding and hence the ultimate shape of accredited residency training curricula. So I suspect that before very long we'll hear the Accreditation Council and the Boards begin to make resonant sounds about combined curriculum options for the implementation of integrated study, as I'm sure the phrase will run. And then the scrambling for alliances will begin, whereupon the cookie-cutter will leap into action. Mark my words."

"You're probably right," Moyer nodded in the direction of his glass, not wishing to pursue the matter all over again.

"But you make it sound so banal, as though you were opposed to it all. I thought you supported the unification," Laura urged, preferring that her husband downplay his cynicism in deference to the natural buoyancy of the meal.

"Oh, I do," Cantrelle hastened to explain, "I'm very much in favor of where we're going doctrinally. It's how it probably will be done administratively that gets to me."

"He calls it the Detroit mentality," Moyer supplied.

"Thanks, comrade," Cantrelle smirked. "What usually happens, and what will probably happen here as well, is that when a new perspective arrives the different training programs quickly insert a few courses here and there to satisfy a revised accreditation checklist. The program reviewers, using the checklist, find the program precisely in order. And development is proclaimed. Nothing has changed, actually, other than the addition of a few courses. But specifications have been met. Therefore, quality has been achieved. That's what I mean by the Detroit mentality—achievement of specifications being equated with quality. In another country it might be called merely achieving standards. Here, we call it quality. And it sells. Thus, in our way of thinking, all credos, manifestos, doctrines, perspectives, and other such enabling constructions which supposedly orient and direct our training strategies amount to little more than a listing of very transient details known as courses, clinical rotations, electives, and selected journal articles, the work of their integration for the realization of the grand strategy being left to the component parts themselves for finding their way to the right alignment with each other, very much like free and enfranchised individuals finding their way to a voluntary cooperation. Just like everything else in this country, like a Detroit production line. For all the energy, production, great good will, and enormous financial expenditure in this country there is very little to show in the way of substantive change, at least in our approach to our problems, anyway. I think it's because we stay doggedly with the particulars, brazen out the charge of being superficial, busy ourselves into believing we're making headway, and await new directives on how to re-arrange the deck chairs while the Ship of State sails on to God knows where. So to get back to this notion about integrating a training program, all accredited accreditors will be pleased if the almighty list is in order when in actuality the program is no more integrated in its function than it is integrated in the head of its Director. I have spoken!"

"All that from gene mapping?" Helen oohed in classic ingenue, to which they all responded in a burst of laughter.

Just as they were surfacing for air, the waiter arrived juggling an outsized tray laden with their entrees. The steamy redolence of the food captured their attention and they now shifted into drooling anticipation as the waiter distributed the plates to the accompaniment of the now sincere oohs. In a moment they were united in absorption with their meals, and only after several undeflected moments in address of their hunger did they resume the sharing of thoughts and feelings.

"I don't know why we don't come here more often!" Helen sighed with eyes closed in ecstasy over a particularly delicious morsel.

"Because if we did our wardrobes would abandon us to fig leaves, our bicycles would lie fallow, and we'd lose our memberships in the Ponce de Leon Society of Concerned Quatrogenarians. That's why," Moyer remonstrated as he sampled his way along the topography of his meal. He and Helen were unremitting devotees of physical fitness, and for years their family vacations were organized around bicycles, touring, light-weight clothing, high energy expenditure, and low cholesterol foods. And their trimness fully attested to it. He and Helen maintained their bicycling as a daily devotional, weather permitting, and would no more forego its observance than they would neglect brushing their teeth. Often enough Moyer would breast weekday commuter exhaust fumes and pedal his way to work at the hospital and arrive, helmet-clad and ready to join battle. His reference to their wardrobes was not entirely a casual one, for Moyer, foremost among several at Moreland, was a conspicuous down-dresser, and for years his wardrobe followed the style of measured insouciance. Cantrelle had observed some time back during Moyer's Open Shirt period that in one year Moyer had done more to set back the cause of the necktie than Fidel Castro had done in twenty. But over the past few years he had gradually returned to the more conventional sartorial line with hardly a sign of his former reprobation in evidence.

"Still and all," Helen persisted, "it wouldn't hurt to get together like this more often than just two or three times a year dictated by conference scheduling. There's something particularly invigorating about Saturday luncheon, I think."

Cantrelle agreed. He felt that it probably bore on the fact that, unlike dinner, lunch did not indenture the remaining hours of the day. Luncheon was closer to the day's opening than to its closing, such as was dinner, and his claustrophobic touchiness found merit in that. Saturday morning, of course, was portal to the blessed expanse of the weekend where openness and choice reigned. Except today, he reminded himself. He was on call this weekend—he had let that fact slip his mind for the past half-hour or so—and when he had that binding duty his movements were suitably circumscribed to enhance his availability for psychiatric emergencies at the general hospital where he was department chairman. The general hospital was in the town where he had his private practice, and he lived almost within walking distance of the hospital as well as his office. Ordinarily he had office hours on Saturday morning, and thus closing his office at about noon on that day was the *de facto* beginning of his weekend. And of freedom. But for the moment he acknowledged the need to check with the answering service to see if there were any calls waiting.

Laura noticed the frown move across his face as he recalled himself to duty.

"Something?" she solicited.

"Oh, nothing. I just remembered that I have to check in with the answering service, that's all. And of course my cell phone is in the glove compartment where it belongs," he tossed. "I'll give them a buzz when we get to the coffee," he resolved.

She knew he wouldn't rest until he had taken care of that chore. Plus, it worried her that he would be preoccupied for the rest of the meal. Ordinarily, when he was on call he would take care of reporting in before sitting down at the table; she figured that he had forgotten to do so upon their arrival at the restaurant because of still being caught up in the conference. She accepted some of the blame for not reminding him, but for sure the lion's share belonged to him for refusing to carry his cell phone; said it didn't go with anything he wore. Actually, he routinely objected to throwing in with what he considered faddish, glitzy technology. It had to prove itself first.

"If you want to," she assisted, "you could call right now and get it out of the way while we're still so crazed by hunger we wouldn't notice your absence for those few moments."

"I guess you're right," he said with relief. "If you all will excuse me I'll be back in a few minutes to rejoin this feeding frenzy."

"Chop, chop," Moyer taunted.

He was off at a half-trot across the dining room and quickly pulled up to the phone in the lobby. Providentially, he had enough change at hand and he quickly dialed the call number. The ring was answered soon enough.

"This is Dr. Cantrelle. Are there any messages?" he asked in standard form.

"Let's see," the service operator crackled. "Dr. Cantrelle . . . yes, there is one here. It's from a Dr. Morello; he says he's one of your residents and that something has come up he thinks you should know about. That's what he said. He says you can reach him at 883-2000. You're to page him. He's on call."

"That's Moreland's number," he recognized immediately as he listened. "So he's also on call this weekend," he concluded as the operator completed the message. "Thank you, operator," he said, releasing her to the jangle of incoming calls in the background.

As he returned the receiver to its cradle he wondered why the hell Morello was calling him. Problems which called for senior assistance were supposed to be directed to the Administrator on Call, a staff psychiatrist in charge of the hospital after normal working hours and on weekends. The only time he ever got an after-hours call from a resident was when the resident was having some particular problem with the Administrator himself. Rare, but it did occasionally happen. He wondered who the Administrator was today; knowing so might offer an estimate as to the cast of the probable flint-to-steel collision between Morello's cockiness and the particular sensitivities of the Administrator. His mind drew a blank, nettling him all the more.

"Well," he mused as he readied another coin, "when everything else fails, ask the patient, they say." He inserted the coin and dialed.

"Moreland State Hospital," came the reply.

"This is Dr. Cantrelle. Dr. Morello is trying to reach me," he explained. "Would you page him, please?"

"Yes, Doctor. Thank you, doctor. Please hold," the switchboard replied dutifully. During the ensuing silence he wondered about how cold his food was getting, suspecting that the high point of the meal had by now slipped away. He noticed that he was actually drumming his finger tips on the booth counter when Morello came on the line.

"Guess what, Chief?" Morello challenged in his irrepressible and just now insufferable manner.

"I haven't the slightest, Dr. Morello, but it had better be damned good," warned Cantrelle, secretly relieved by Morello's clearly playful tone, which would not likely preamble a truly dire issue.

"Remember that Jordan case and the designer drug, or what we figured was a once only designer drug?" Morello reviewed.

"Yes, I do," he replied, noting it odd that he had just been talking to Clay about it a few minutes back.

"Well, it looks like the design is catching on. We just admitted another one," Morello announced triumphantly.

"Another one? Another patient with the same symptoms? Drug induced?" Cantrelle rattled off in a rush of galvanized interest.

"You bet," persisted Morello, gloating over his stroke.

"Are you sure? I mean, it's not just another drug psychosis in a jubilant adolescent and just superficially similar," Cantrelle challenged as he parried with a foreboding now gathering in the wake of his initial jolt.

"Hardly," Morello continued with a hint of pique in not being praised out of hand for so bright a discovery. "This is a forty-seven-year-old dedicated junkie from Commerce Street, on welfare, long history of heroin addiction, needle tracks everywhere, a few visits to detox centers but no psychiatric hospitalizations before. Somewhat different walk of life, you might say."

"I would say," Cantrelle yielded as puzzlement now entered his thinking. "It doesn't fit. I mean, what's it doing in him? Are you sure it's the same symptom picture? All the more reason to double check," he implored.

"I'm telling you Chief, it's the same. In fact, he's sitting on the other side of the room right now with an attendant, and he's giggling away trying to cover his blushing face," Morello emphasized in driving home the point. "Just like Jordan did when he came here."

Cantrelle bit his lip in ranging thought. Commerce Street was the urban center for the drug subculture—pushers, flophouses, rampant crime, sudden death, and just about all-around degeneracy of every shade. But the addicts who lived there generally were not inclined to experiment with the newer drugs. Usually they had long found their addiction niche, their specific agent, and would stay with it and work out the life style—dealing, prostitution, theft, whatever—favored by the alliance. If that were the case with this new admission, and most likely was, how could it happen that . . . . His thinking was short-circuited by a decision.

"Dr. Morello, I'll be over in a little while. Watch him carefully," Cantrelle ordered.

"Right, chief. Be waiting for you," Morello clicked, delighted to be off on a sally with his leader.

Cantrelle hung up the phone slowly as he pondered what was happening. Questions raced about as he tried to latch on to an answer—any answer—that would bring the swirl of perplexity under some control; specifically, some control over the vague, shapeless dread he sensed forming on the boundary of his thinking. He then started back to the dining room, at first with hesitant, barely intentional steps as he squinted at some distant notion dancing just beyond his reach, and then, giving up on its retrieval just now, with a burst of hurried strides as he approached the waiting table.

As soon as she saw him hurrying back Laura knew something was wrong. Her eyes watched him in readiness as he came up to the table. She waited until he was back in place, napkin in lap.

"What's up, Frank?" she asked.

After a compensatory forkful of his almost cool food and a sip of almost warm water he took a deep breath and leaned back. They were all waiting.

"I think we've got trouble. I don't know why I'm making so much of it, but I think we're on to something we—or at least I—don't understand," he sighed. He didn't want to keep them waiting longer for some explanation, but he didn't particularly feel like talking about it, either. At least, not just yet. "Clay," he yielded, "Morello just admitted another one."

"Another one what? Patient?" Moyer queried.

"Another one just like the Jordan kid," Cantrelle clarified.

Moyer just looked at Cantrelle in silence and nodded his head slowly.

"Something bad?" Helen asked.

"Very possibly very bad," Moyer rued.

The women glanced at each other in shared consternation.

"The case Clay and I were talking about a little while ago," Cantrelle began, "you know, the college kid who took some strange drug and who's now undergoing a progressive dementia? Well, the drug was never isolated or identified, and we figured—or hoped—that it was a one-time thing. Now, just a few minutes ago, I talked to one of our residents at Moreland—there was a waiting call at the answering service—and he says he just admitted another patient with the same symptoms of toxicity. That's the second one, in just over a week. So it's not a one-time thing—*if* it's the same thing. That's a big 'if.'"

"Let's hope it's not the same thing," Helen ventured. "Maybe the resident is wrong. You know, eager to see the unusual."

"I hope you're right, Helen, but I fear he knows exactly what he's talking about. He usually does," Cantrelle gloomed. "But let's put that aside for the moment and do honor to this good food—and the good company," he urged.

"Right," Moyer seconded.

The remainder of the meal was passed in light chatter, though nothing spoken bore on what was unquestionably on everybody's mind. The phone call and its implications hovered over the table like a storm cloud ready to break forth at any moment. It was thus pointedly ignored for the remainder of the meal.

When the coffee arrived it did so amidst a sense of duty smartly done that the phone call had not been mentioned again. And now, with the restriction relaxed, Laura broached the unspoken.

"I guess you're worried about that new case," she posed.

"Sort of," Cantrelle minimized as he brought the steaming cup to his lips.

His reluctance to pursue the topic convinced her that he was wrestling with himself about what he should do. She had learned over the years that when he was in doubt about anything he usually pulled into himself to narrow the field of deliberation, and of decision.

Moyer listened intently to the interchange, and did so more from Cantrelle's position of defensible preoccupation. He, too, had shown signs of drifting away, fugue-like, from the usual coffee chatter, with the result that the women began to feel they were holding their men to a conjugal task contrary to their wishes.

"I guess you're worried right along with him, aren't you?" Helen teased her husband.

Moyer knew it was coming but hadn't insulated himself fully from the chagrin of disclosure. He now smiled as though he had been caught at mischief.

"Well, hon, we never really figured out the other case and here we have a second one. I can only imagine what's going to be waiting for me when I walk in on the unit Monday morning," he confessed in tones of self-pity leavened with right duty.

"Well," Helen continued with the inflection of broad irony, "it simply won't do for you to wait around that long, worrying yourself into a frazzle, now would it? I think you'll just have to put your pleasures aside for the moment and tend to duty's call, burdensome though it be," she sighed heavily. "Right, Laura?"

"You're so right, Helen," Laura played along, "In fact, I think Frank ought to help Clay with the task and give him some company. Lighten the burden, you know. You'll be kind enough to help Clay with the task, won't you, dear? It probably won't take very long and you both would probably feel better for it later. Inconveniences like this do come up, don't they? We understand."

By now both men were smiling in embarrassment as their wives made sport of the tacit conspiracy being laid bare by their sarcasm. The women had done this often enough before, usually when neither Cantrelle nor Moyer had the courage to own up to a due inevitability which they feared would disgruntle their wives who, seeing right through their husbands, would then trippingly mount an affectionate raillery cast in tones of the broadly disingenuous.

"Well, if you two *insist*," Cantrelle burbled in his best aw-shucks manner.

"Oh, but we *do*," Helen rejoined with a conclusive flick of her wrist coupled with a collaborative nod to Laura.

Cantrelle knew that Laura and Helen were justifiably a little miffed at the prospect of the luncheon's abbreviation so that he and Moyer could dash off to the hospital on another clinical chase, but he also knew that they secretly delighted in presiding maternally over what they regarded as the boyish zeal in their husbands. It probably was just that, by and large; but when it really came down to it he and Moyer collaborated in allowing their spouses to play their maternal solicitude any way they wished for enlisting indulgence in what he as much as Moyer saw as business much too serious ever to be subordinated to the punctilio of matrimonial decorum. If anything was truly an operant conspiracy between him and Moyer, it was that given.

"Frank," Laura offered more definitively, "why don't you and Clay use our car and I'll go with Helen. She can drop me off at the house. It's on the way for her."

"O.K. That sounds pretty good," he concurred with a tentative glance at the others.

"Laura, maybe you could stop over for a minute. There are some patterns I'd like to show you. I'm thinking of re-doing the living room," Helen volunteered in support of their return to the distaff, doing so in a manner awash in largesse.

"You two are being great sports about this, and we'll make it up to you, won't we, Clay?" Cantrelle promised.

Moyer had kept his silence while the negotiations were in process.

"Or else," Moyer now added gravely.

"Tush, tush," Helen blandished. "You two get going before that resident calls again."

Cantrelle was already signaling for the check. He and Moyer alternated in paying for their joint outings at dining, and Moyer had paid the last time. Cantrelle motioned to the waiter who, sensing their haste, soon appeared with the check, the maitre d' in accompaniment.

"Ladies and gentlemen," the maitre d' beseeched, "you're dashing off before your second cup of coffee. And no dessert! Has everything been O.K.?"

"You're right, Fritz; we are zipping off a bit early, and with very deep regret. Everything was just fine. It's just that I got a hospital call," Cantrelle explained as he paid the check, "and now we have to go take care of it."

"Perhaps you and Mr. Moyer will consider bringing the ladies back soon to make up today's losses," the maitre d' continued merrily.

Cantrelle guffawed at such bold pandering while Moyer just rolled his eyes.

"Oh, Fritz," gushed Helen, "you're an absolute dear! Isn't he, Laura? I think that's a splendid idea. How about next Saturday night, Laura? Suitable?" Helen pressed, fully aware of her and Laura's advantage.

"I think we're free that night, aren't we dear?" Laura suggested sweetly.

Cantrelle and Moyer were now chuckling at the power bargaining going on and in the most dulcet of accents.

"Well, then, gentlemen, shall I put you and the ladies down for next Saturday? The usual eight o'clock?" Fritz inquired helpfully.

"I think that goes without saying," Cantrelle acknowledged. "Right, Clay?"

Moyer smiled in resignation.

Actually both he and Cantrelle were pleased with the playful intervention of the maitre d'. It had helped to give the meal an upbeat ending that otherwise might have gone tiresomely flat. Also, the prescribed dinner date now freed the men of obligatory remorse come of putting business before the company of their wives, a chancy step even under the most compelling circumstances. Plus, the prospect of an evening out together was pleasant in its own right. And all of it neatly wrapped up by the maitre d's deft intercession. He was good at his job.

They all rose, the men elaborately eager to help their wives, and the maitre d' beaming his benediction on their departure.

"Thanks again, Fritz," Cantrelle offered.

"My pleasure, ladies and gentlemen," the maitre d' demurred. "See you next Saturday. Eight o'clock."

"Sure thing," Cantrelle confirmed as they all turned toward the lobby.

Just then the sense of the verge swept over him, startling him with its intensity. "What the hell . . . ." he thought to himself in perplexity over the cause of its arrival at this particular moment, and in this particular place. His thoughts raced ahead to the hospital and the matter waiting there for him and Moyer. That ready association didn't clarify anything for him, so he put the entire matter aside as best he could and returned to the business of accompanying his wife and friends out of the restaurant.

As they stepped outside, the brilliant mid-day light re-imposed its control over his focus. Now it was perfectly O.K. to walk resolutely to the cars and get things moving. And they did. After settling their wives in one car and planting departure kisses Cantrelle and Moyer hurried to the other car and pulled out of their slot to follow their wives out the parking lot exit. After several blocks of convoy, the wives turned off on their route and the men, signaling safe voyage by a toot of the horn, continued on to the artery that would take them to the hospital. It wasn't until their wives were out of sight that they began to talk of the destination and what it held.

Not knowing quite where to start, Cantrelle deferred to doubt.

"Sure as hell I hope Helen is right that Morello is over-reading something and that we're off on a wild goose chase," he opened.

"Could be, but I doubt that as much as you do. Once you've seen that syndrome—if I can call it that—you're not likely to mistake it for something else, or vice versa," Moyer held.

"Yeah," Cantrelle agreed, "but how in the hell can it happen that a dilapidated druggie from right around here," Cantrelle motioned with his hand in the general direction of the blighted section of the city not very far from their present position on the main artery, "end up with some strange new agent not seen previously except for the case of the college kid from Franklinton? Really worlds apart."

"At least, not previously seen by us," Moyer corrected.

"That's true, but eventually all the tough ones come to us, and these two cases certainly qualify," Cantrelle deemed.

"I mean, not seen by us here but maybe seen in other cities or other sections of the country," Moyer explained.

"I had forgotten about that!" Cantrelle exclaimed. "Maybe you're right, but there hasn't been a hint of a report or article about it, not even in the newspapers like there was with the MPTP episode a few years back. Or even like it was with LSD way back," Cantrelle cited.

"Yeah, that's true, but others might be fumbling around with it just like we're doing, not knowing what to think, much less what to say in print. I think we have the tendency to look upon these problems first as being local because we're caught up in trying to comprehend them within the context of our familiar locale. Maybe we're just not yet ready to broaden the scope of the issue for fear of increasing our perplexity right along with it," Moyer proposed.

"Sure, and that's not a bad way to proceed; initially, at any rate," Cantrelle agreed. "First a few trees before taking on the entire forest, as I'm sure some trenchant person would say."

"I just have a bad feeling about this. Just like with LSD when we first started out. Like when those trees became a national overgrowth. Remember?" Moyer added.

Cantrelle did remember. He had just begun teaching at Moreland and was in charge of the weekly New Case Conference. There, too, Moyer was instrumental in structuring the didactic cast of the conference, and new-admission cases were selected for their challenge as well as heuristic value. Cantrelle recalled that back in the very beginning an LSD psychosis was an uncommon event. Generally, those patients admitted to the hospital were the ones who didn't rebound from the "trip" in the standard period of time allotted for the experience by groupie practices of the day. Psychoses secondary to street hallucinogens were a new phenomenon then, and though only a small percentage of all the users were ever admitted to a psychiatric unit, Moreland, being the final common pathway for recalcitrant cases, received all the area's cases which did not reconstitute quickly enough to be discharged from the various acute treatment centers back to everyday society. Hence, Moreland received a culled, concentrated sample which displayed the destructive potential of repeated hallucinogen usage in those having some idiosyncratic vulnerability. Not only did a fair number of these cases remain hospitalized for years, but most of them subsequently required repeat hospitalization in treatment of psychoses apparently spontaneous in their recurrence. These were the cases rarely seen in the acute treatment centers, and certainly never over a protracted period of time. Cantrelle remembered that these cases began as a trickle—true oddities, like the recent case, and now possibly the new case awaiting—but they soon grew into a flood as more and more outlying hospitals and acute treatment centers added to the flow, tributary fashion, such that within the space of two years the hospital became sorely stretched to provide facilities for so many adolescents and young adults who were refractory to standard treatment. It happened that while the tributary hospitals saw maybe one or two cases a week, Moreland would receive as many as ten or fifteen weekly, and generally only the sicker ones. Hence, Moreland was in a questionably preferred position to know the enormity of the problem. Newer medications, plus the natural healing process, were able to return a fair number of these cases to the community in some condition of improvement, but re-admissions continued to occur and many of the patients eventually managed on an out-patient basis remained indefinitely on the rolls of the mentally disabled. It had been considered then, and still so, that in those particular cases LSD did little more than prematurely activate congenital neurochemical deficiencies which in all likelihood would have shown up at some later time in life. But the question which remained unanswered was whether or not such an artificial activation had aggravated the disease beyond what would have been its more spontaneous intensity, accordingly making it significantly less treatable. Also, there was still the lingering suspicion that many of the patients, though inherently at risk because of the congenital neurochemical imbalance, might have escaped entirely any clinical experience of that vulnerability had it not been ignited by the LSD experience in the first place. Sort of like people genetically inclined to diabetes but never developing the disease by keeping trim and holding to a disciplined diet. Yes, Cantrelle remembered only too well. He would have preferred to forget. The memory of it was made more indelible by a piece of survey work he and Moyer had done together on the relationship of the number of LSD exposures—"trips"—and the reversibility of the induced psychosis. It appeared to them that those patients who, by their own accounting, had had upwards of a hundred to one hundred fifty "trips" never made it back anywhere near to full restitution, even if their premorbid state had been ostensibly healthy. So he and Moyer decided to check out that observation in a more disciplined and objective fashion. Interviews and a standard battery of psychological tests were employed in assessing the personality and psychometric configuration of an extended series of LSD admissions to Moreland. The standard interviews and the test battery were given to each case approximately six weeks after admission to the unit when the patient was generally less acute and more amenable to the testing procedure. The results demonstrated what had been suspected and clinically well noted, that the fewer the "trips" per patient the more likely the sample to show a return to a fairly typical distribution of personality types and psychometric function, while the more "trips"—generally one hundred or so being the cut-off point—the more likely the patients were to show a similar profile in affective and cognitive impairment. In other words, the more "trips," the more likely they were to resemble each other despite their premorbid personality configurations. The observed drift toward a personality and behavioral uniformity was seen as the coordinates of a chronicity deriving of the induced psychoses. The typical picture of the observed residual impairment in high-exposure cases was one featuring vagueness, weakness of attention, internal preoccupation in the direction of "primary process"—that dreamy part of mental functioning—a loss of empathic capacity, grossly impaired reality testing under even minor stress, a reduction of initiative in just about all interpersonal areas, and a general overall dulling of affect. It was noted that this symptom mosaic very closely approximated that which was attributed to the diagnostic group called Simple Schizophrenia in the older texts but which was now carried by the term Chronic, Undifferentiated Schizophrenia. All evaluators who participated in the survey agreed that whatever the essential action of LSD and its effect upon the neurochemistry of the central nervous system in repeated dosages, the result approximated the evolution of chronic symptoms closely resembling those of the old time Simple Schizophrenia, or, perhaps more accurately still, the even older Dementia Praecox. Cantrelle had made much of the survey's suggestion that an exogenous agent could actually achieve a change in the *form* of the user's thinking and, with repeated exposure, do so in a progressively identifiable way over time. He had proposed the notion that the civic nightmare generated by the LSD phenomenon was correspondingly also a large, natural experiment in the toxin theory of Schizophrenia at a time when social and interpersonal factors were still considered to be etiologically paramount. And it all seemed so long ago. Their sense of futility in the face of that clinical onslaught was best forgotten, but never would be. The people at Moreland still remembered because many of the reminders were still there.

"Yeah, I remember. We never did write that paper on the survey, did we?" Cantrelle winced. He had never gotten over that dereliction.

"No, we didn't," Moyer returned with a sigh of shared default.

They remained silent for a few moments in their separate reveries about what could have been done, should have been done those years ago when they labored in the forefront of that unique social and clinical phenomenon. It was a silence of regret, jointly appreciated. Those years were also a time in their lives when many other things pulled at them—family growth, making a living, laying out one's professional course, paying off loans, and so forth. Moreover, their backgrounds in research notwithstanding, they were being paid at Moreland to be clinicians—to diagnose, treat, and discharge back to the community—not to collect, measure, and report. Yet, *not* to do so would have been a rank nonfeasance. But, were they really able to . . . .

"Aw, Christ!" Cantrelle groaned.

"You, too, huh?" Moyer sympathized.

"I just feel the whole god-damned thing is starting up all over again! We weren't equal to it then and we probably won't be now, either. It's been twenty years and now our arteries are the hardest thing about us," Cantrelle railed.

"You do have a way with medical metaphor, Frank," Moyer quipped.

"I guess so," Cantrelle smiled in mollification. "Look," he cited, resolution returning, "let's not just sit here on our self-pitying asses. Let's brainstorm this thing and see if we can come up with some hunches we might be able to work on when we get there. Right?"

"I'll be careful not to let us fall afoul any unwarranted basic assumptions," Moyer joshed.

"Kiss my now determined ass," Cantrelle returned in kind. Then, after a moment for shift in tone, he continued. "What do we have to go on? First, a college student several weeks ago with a toxic psychosis, agent undetermined. Characteristic flushing and giggling, and progressive dementia. Basement, do-it-yourself designer drug chemistry gone wrong? In the absence of additional and subsequent cases, probably so. Case closed. Now, a supposedly similar case, from an entirely different world. Designer drug? Not likely. Case re-opened. But what's the link between the two cases? First, is it the same agent? Or is it by some wild coincidence a different drug entirely, sprung of totally different origins but producing a similar clinical effect. Possibly. Notice, my punctilious friend, the skillful avoidance of unwarranted basic assumption of identity of agents. It's only *likely* that the agent is the same in each case inasmuch the observable *clinical* effects are very similar, which happens to be another assumption we have to watch out for since we might see the clinical signs as very different from what Morello perceives them to be. But even granting that the agents are the same, where does that take us? It could still be the case of a one-time drug misadventure being disseminated like pollen in the wind, couldn't it, crossing all social and geographic boundaries with little likelihood of there being any more to come of it now that the entire crop has been spent."

"I like that one," Moyer registered.

"I do too, but I'm afraid it's too hopeful. And besides, there's an inconsistency," Cantrelle added.

"Which is?" Moyer asked.

"The time. The time element," Cantrelle stated.

"How so?" Moyer puzzled.

"Well, the Jordan case began about six weeks ago. He took the drug, was admitted to the university hospital, treated there for a couple of weeks, then transferred to us a little over two weeks ago. Then I saw him, and that was one week ago. Right?" Cantrelle reviewed.

"Yeah, that's about right. What are you leading up to?" Moyer queried.

"This," Cantrelle explained. "The present case awaiting us probably comes directly from a base unit emergency service since he's a long-time druggie. Base units usually send their Commerce street medical assistance psychotics like this one directly to us rather than to some other in-patient treatment center first. Right?"

"True enough," Moyer agreed.

"Then, in all likelihood, this fellow took the drug no longer than a few days ago at most, and that makes a time gap of about five weeks between cases from the standpoint of time of drug ingestion. Four weeks minimum. Right?" Cantrelle detailed.

"Probably. I think I'm beginning to see where you're going," Moyer stated.

"Sure. If we're talking about two cases separated over that much time and over that much demography we've got to be talking, I think, of two different times of drug procurement and probably two different places where it was gotten. If it had been some chemistry students fiddling around in the basement in search of a new kick, I can't imagine their not being concerned about the drug's effect and not finding out about Jordan's reaction to it—or the reaction of some other sleepers in the area we're yet to receive. Even so, those sleepers would still be from *their* side of the tracks, not from Commerce Street. In any event, those chemistry kids would not likely regard the drug as one of their better efforts to be passed on to their frat brothers and friends. So, I think the time gap—the drug shows up again five weeks later in a different kind of world—as well as the social gap pretty much discounts the designer drug theory."

"Can't argue with that, Frank, but so what?" Moyer questioned.

"So this. If it bridges time and class, it probably was geared for street distribution. That likely means the Jordan kid got his hands on it through some *standard* channel—a friend pusher or street vendor—just as the present case most likely did," Cantrelle added.

"And so they . . ." Moyer pursued.

"And so they probably believed they were getting something *else*, some other drug. I don't think they would go searching on the street for some untried drug to get some new, unknown kind of buzz no one could vouch for; certainly not the druggie, because the long-time user tends to settle down with the tried and true, his particular chemical companion that suits him best, and he generally sticks to it. The Jordan kid? Well, maybe adventure and daring did race too far ahead of discretion. But not likely the veteran druggie. So, dear fellow sleuth, conclusion—or should I say hunch—number one is that both of these patients thought they were taking something else, had intended to take something else, but were given this new item instead. With the Jordan kid, new to the drug scene and maybe only his first or second time around on this particular distribution circuit, probably was given the straight, unadulterated agent since he wasn't experienced enough to know if an item was the genuine article or not. Duped, sort of. But with the hardened druggie, his item was probably his usual but laced with the new agent and he none the wiser for it. Duped, too, but more planfully. If that's the case, then it would explain why the boy's drug screen was negative for known agents," Cantrelle resolved.

"But that would mean we can expect this new case to have a drug screen positive for some known agent," Moyer added with mounting anticipation.

"And that, my friend, is conclusion—or hunch—number two. Daring, don't you think?" Cantrelle exulted. He was now in his syllogistic frame of mind and was clicking off premises right along with street intersections as though riding to the hounds. The sense of chase was thoroughly upon both of them and thoughts of the abandoned luncheon and unrequited wives were nowhere in reach. It was just like old times and the tenor of frenetic mission was forming up rapidly. Also, Cantrelle had just turned on to Stanhope Avenue, the street that led to Moreland's main gate now only a few blocks away.

"So, are you ready for conclusion number three, old buddy?" Cantrelle teased.

"I think I'm already there, comrade," Moyer affected. "Whoever made it available to Jordan five weeks ago made it available again a few days back, but this time for a seasoned addict and with *full knowledge of what the effect would be*, though disguising the drug this second time by mixing it with a standard street number."

"Bingo, my sharpshooting companion," Cantrelle congratulated, "but I think we can extend that thought a bit farther."

"I'm all ears," Moyer assured.

Moreland's main gate now hove into view. Cantrelle aimed for the familiar entrance.

"And it sounds something like this," Cantrelle continued. "Remember some years back when we had a rash of shelf poisonings? Someone doctoring up the acetaminophen tablets on the drug store shelves with cyanide and several people dying from it because some crazy out there was intent on hurting someone, just anybody, and perhaps the designated pharmaceutical company in particular. Well, if what we've constructed of this mess holds any water at all, we have to suspect that there is some kind of a super crazy out there who has it in for the druggies and intends to get at them wholesale through the street drug network.

"If that's true, Frank," Moyer added soberly, "then more are coming."

"I fear so, Clay," Cantrelle agreed. "And that's conclusion number four."

They entered the front gate and headed directly for the ITU.

FOUR

Thank God for walls, he thought as he stared ahead, elbows on his desk and chin resting on the crest of his folded hands. He had held that position for almost half an hour and, miraculously, the phone had not rung. Nor had anyone knocked on his door. No inquiries as to why this resident wasn't present for such-and-such a conference, or why Dr. So-and-So had changed which classroom for what course, or why weren't the reading lists for next week's course distributed yet, or anything else of the administrative grit that constituted fully half his job as Training Director. Not only miraculous but also merciful that the time for his wall staring was so providentially unencumbered this morning. A large part of that gramercy undoubtedly emanated from Mrs. Andretti who sensed he needed the time for some thinking in view of the hastily called meeting of the Executive Council to be held a little later this morning and at which he was requested to appear. She was probably fending off foragers left and right to protect his sanctum, a duty which at times undoubtedly constituted fully half *her* job as Residency Training Executive Assistant, and maybe especially so this morning.

The meeting of the Executive Council was called by Martha Corley, M.D., the quietly dignified Superintendent of Moreland. He had known her since he began at Moreland at the inception of his teaching as a junior member of the teaching staff when she was a staff psychiatrist on the old Admissions Unit. Since he did most of his teaching at that time with the residents on her unit their paths, his and hers, crossed early in his tenure, and it was a good fit from the beginning. She had studied under Palmer and carried in her gentle and composed manner a large share of that same Darshan which had come to be associated with all who had studied under that renowned teacher. Over the years she had unflinchingly supported Cantrelle's effort to sustain the teaching mission of the hospital in tenor and in tempo with the changing times, and had, like most Superintendents at Moreland, also actively participated in the teaching of the residents. Martha Corley, in addition to her innumerable administrative duties come of being the boss of a good-sized community consisting of five hundred patients attended by eight hundred employees in accordance with all the policies and procedures appertaining thereto, also precepted at least one resident weekly during any given training period. She also taught the annual basic course on Addiction and Substance Abuse to the beginning residents. Cantrelle never questioned that in her he had a stalwart ally. Just a few years after he became Training Director and she had been elevated to the assistant superintendency he submitted a proposal that the Admissions Unit of the hospital be relocated to a more compact area and serve as the designated primary teaching center for all the hospital's accredited clinical training—psychiatry, psychology, social work, nursing, and the various other disciplines sponsoring students, externs, interns, and the like. The training would be concentrated there under the tutelage of a totally volunteer, handpicked staff representing a cross section of the teaching and service disciplines of the mental health field. In effect, an elite teaching and treatment effort as only a special kind of state hospital could mount; specifically, an Admissions Unit where focused treatment would be brought to bear with an intensity not feasible elsewhere in the hospital complex, and perhaps not often anywhere else beyond. In a word, an Intensive Treatment Unit, as it was now named. She studied the proposal, ironed out several wrinkles, made some important suggestions, and then approved it. But not only that, she then single-handedly undertook its implementation, first securing its endorsement up and down the administrative chain, then meeting as necessary with carpenters, electricians, bricklayers, and plumbers to see to it that the architect's blueprints were followed to the letter, blueprints she herself helped draw up in translating the proposal into a procedural flow, a gift she had as in no other person he knew. He also knew that in her heart of hearts she just had to take care of the needy—patients, staff, residents, and, when he wanted something, himself as well—while her own needs never seemed to be in evidence. Thus there was something finely patrician and private about Martha Corley, and her superintendency gave the hospital some of its very best days.

Without breaking the set of his wall staring position, he glanced sidelong at the clock on his desk. Quarter of nine. The meeting was scheduled to start at nine. He didn't yet know who else would be there. He knew Jess would be, of course. In fact, he was pretty sure Jess was the one who had urged the meeting. He had met with Jess the Monday after that Saturday afternoon when he and Clay had dashed over to the hospital to see that second case. God, that seemed so long ago in view of all that had happened since, though actually it was only two weeks past. Only two weeks, and since then twelve more admissions, at last count, of the same kind of case. When he met with Jess and told him of the concerns he and Clay had, Jess concurred in the overall, especially when the report of the drug screen on that second case turned up positive for heroin and nothing else. However, Jess was still focused on the initial case, his friend's son, and was grappling with the anguish of that grim scene without needing to be apprised of yet larger dimensions of futility to be met. But undoubtedly, subsequent events had crowded in on him rudely enough to generate this meeting, announced late last week. Since they wanted him, one Frank Cantrelle, M.D., present, there was a pretty good chance that Residency Training would be called upon to contribute something, but probably nothing more than its complete all.

Then the phone rang.

"I knew it was too god-damned good to last," he grumped as his yoga-like musing was shattered by the electronic jingle. He loved his wool-gathering and did not easily suffer its loss, especially when work was waiting for him. "Maybe the meeting is canceled" he flashed as he picked up the phone. "Dr. Cantrelle," he grumped into the receiver.

"Dr. Cantrelle, I'm sorry to interrupt you," Mrs. Andretti apologized, suggesting awareness of what he was about, "but Dr. Morello is here and says he would like to talk to you about something."

"About what?" he snarled.

"He didn't say," she said simply, her way of conveying that she thought he meant it was to be a private matter.

"Oh, O.K., tell him to come in," Cantrelle submitted with a sigh of resignation carrying the lament that Morello was always into something, the more conspiratorial the better. "That boy can really be an itch," he mumbled as he returned the phone to its cradle.

The knock on the door was simultaneous with his hanging up the phone.

"Come in," Cantrelle shouted.

Morello entered done up in a tropical-colored tie and equally bright smile.

"Good morning, Chief," he let fly.

"Good morning, Dr. Morello. What's up? Night call schedule again?" Cantrelle asked, hoping the matter would be something as customary as that perennial problem. He had already agreed with his cranky side that he didn't have time for some novel pain in the ass this morning.

"Nah! Nothing like that. Something much better. You'll like this," Morello taunted, pausing for effect before plopping into the chair beside the desk.

"You *are* going to tell me, aren't you?" Cantrelle groused, rapidly approaching the limits of his tolerance.

"Ready?" Morello asked in the tone of a drum roll. "Gloria—Dr. Sumner—has an almost ran."

Cantrelle waited for more, but nothing came as Morello again paused for effect. He figured that since he was being called upon to be the straight man, it was his turn to speak.

"All right, I give up. What kind of 'almost ran' are we talking about, Dr. Morello?" he obliged with a heavy sigh.

"She has a patient who almost took that new street drug," Morello announced. "At least he says so. It's probably not part of the delusions that brought him here because how would he know about it in the first place if he hadn't heard something about it on the street. And he doesn't mind talking about it, either," Morello explained proudly.

Cantrelle, now totally alert and dutifully upright, felt his weariness with Morello's playfulness change quickly into frank impatience.

"The patient knows something about the drug? He knew what he wasn't taking? That is, he didn't take it himself?" Cantrelle raced on.

"Right to all those, Chief," Morello agreed cheerfully. "I think you should talk to him. No telling what little tidbit he might drop," Morello advised in sustained, self-indulgent delight. "I told her that you would be interested and that you'd probably want to come over and interview him this morning, and so by all means not to let him off the unit. Couldn't have him elope just yet, now could we?" he continued breezily.

That cautionary measure reminded Cantrelle that Morello was ever a careful and competent resident who enjoyed the affectation of whimsy but in reality was a cool and cunning performer capable of being as steady as the situation required. For example, Cantrelle knew that one of Morello's hobbies was tying his own fishing flies.

"Good," Cantrelle replied. "I can't go over there now because I have a meeting with Dr. Corley in . . ." he glanced at the clock ". . . in just five minutes. As soon as it's over I'll hop over to the Unit. Tell Dr. Sumner to get all the material together and tell Mr. Moyer to be on hand . . . ."

"I've already done that," Morello preened.

"Good," Cantrelle repeated, smiling in acknowledgment of being impressed. "We'll have an impromptu A.M. Conference. And tell Social Work it would be nice if they could be on hand, too. Also, if there's any lab work pending maybe Dr. Sumner can call ahead to see if it's ready but hasn't been sent yet. Oh, yes," Cantrelle remembered, "tell her to hold off on any morning meds, if she can, so that he's not too sedated for the interview. Anything else? Can't think of anything now."

"If anything else pops up I'll take care of it, Chief," Morello assured.

"Thanks. Now I have to get over to that meeting," Cantrelle announced in gentle dismissal.

Now energized, he rose from his chair, and Morello, following suit, clapped his hands once sharply as though he were breaking from a huddle and ready for the next play.

"O.K., Chief. Meet you at the Unit," he promised as he left the office and closed the door behind him.

Cantrelle stood there for a moment and pondered this new development. He then slowly settled back into his chair to take one last look at his wall before moving on to the meeting.

"What a windfall!" he exulted. "But maybe nothing'll come of it. I wish to Christ I didn't have to go to that meeting right now. But for all I know . . . oh, never mind. Piss and moan; wind and rain, stress and strain, because, after all, Cantrelle, everyone knows that absolutely nothing can go right in this goddamned world unless you and only you do it. Right? Right!."

Self-ridicule was the smelling salts he applied when he felt himself slipping into the coma of dogged ambivalence. It was his way of reminding himself that there really was enough time to get around to what was waiting if he just didn't permit himself to stray into the short circuitry of endless thought as a deceptive equivalent of action.

"So let's act!" be resolved as he sprang from his chair and made for the office door. He picked up a notepad enroute and swung the door wide in a sweeping display of vigor and settled resolve.

"I'm going over now. If there are any calls, you know where I am. When the meeting is over I'm going directly to the ITU. I should be back just before lunch," he detailed to his secretary.

"O.K.," she acknowledged with a cheery wave.

He then entered the hallway and walked quickly to the front door and out, where he found it to be gray and cold and windy.

"I was right—wind, and probably rain," he tittered in relief at being out of doors and somehow farther from the confinement of his duties.

The raw north wind buffeted his face as he trudged the seventy-five yards to the administration building. A few shriveled leaves left over from the now nearly forgotten colors of Autumn scudded along the ground in lowly accompaniment to the gray wrack gurging by overhead. The flag on the magnificently bold pole in the center of the hospital's approach greensward flapped frantically, adding its snapping and ruffling to the rushing sound of the wind. It was too soon for snow but it seemed to be what the weather had in mind.

He reached the double door of the administration building, swung it open, and then pushed through the second inner door to mount the several steps to the elevated hallway leading past the Superintendent's office to the Board Room, named so as the meeting room for the hospital's Board of Trustees but actually the main conference room for all the hospital's top level meetings. A private passageway from the Board Room to the Superintendent's office identified the room as the special province of the Superintendent and quite literally an extension of that office. But, over the years, exclusivity of use had been relaxed such that the room was available to all departments for any meeting or gathering that needed an August setting to give the special stamp of ceremony to its proceedings. He used the room twice a week year-round for one of the courses he taught, having stated at the outset years earlier that the dark paneling, the yawning bay window, the elegantly Victorian lighting fixtures, and the huge red mahogany conference table all lent just the right touch of classic scholarship his course was designed to pursue. Perfect staging, he felt. To him the room meant congenial diggings because for him it carried the intended accent of his delivery whenever he was in it, whatever he said or to whom, regardless of the nature of the meeting or occasion. Today the room might not so readily lend itself to such indulgence, he thought as he neared its door. He grasped the ornate, marquis-shaped door knob, gave it a good turn, and pushed the heavy door open.

He scanned the gathering as he entered. Everybody was in place, quietly waiting. That alone gave him pause, for usually there was a buzzing chatter toiling the air before the meeting was called to order, which apparently hadn't yet been done. Secondly, the chair left vacant and intended for him was opposite Weaver's and next to that of Corley's at the head of the table. He knew immediately that this arrangement signaled some central role he would be called upon to play in the forthcoming proceedings. But even more than that, when he entered everybody noted his arrival but said nothing to him in greeting, ostensibly in deference to Corley for this particular occasion, suggesting that something was in the air that should come from her alone. Had they had a meeting prior to his arrival with something already settled and merely to be announced to him now that he was there, he wondered? As he took a hesitant step toward his place at the table Corley spoke.

"Good morning, Frank. I'm glad you could make it," she greeted warmly, gentling the severity of her salt and pepper bun and blue serge business suit. She rarely wore make-up; her smile was usually enough to highlight her finely handsome features, as it did now with his arrival.

"I hope I didn't keep you all waiting," he grinned, suggesting his awareness of their readiness, plus his interest in some explanation of it.

"Not at all. We just settled in and were getting ready to start," she offered simply, and then paused.

He scanned the table. Indeed they were ready to start, pencil in hand almost to the man: Charlie Riegel of Administration, Ruth Fawcett of Nursing, Saul Klein of Support Services, John Wingate of Maintenance, and Mildred Simpson of Social Work. Weaver sat with his hands folded before him.

"Let's begin," she resumed as he settled himself into his chair. "Most of you know that over the past few weeks we've had an increase in admissions from our catchment area. You also know that the increase comes from a particular kind of case," she continued, giving Weaver a passing glance of acknowledgment. "These cases place an extra demand on our resources because they're quite different from the usual admissions. The reason I've called this meeting is because we have reason to believe that the increase in these cases will probably not be transient."

Several began to look at each other in a display of innocent perplexity.

"Frank, I know that you and your residents are working to keep up with the influx," she allowed, "but the Admissions Unit is beginning to feel the pressure of the added numbers. Jess has met with the staff of the unit several times over the past two weeks," she added, "and the upshot is the same each time. With this new type of patient adding to the admission rate, the staff of the unit are having increasing difficulty keeping up with the treatment demands, the crowding, plus the transfer planning, not to mention the paper work. We're rapidly approaching overload, and that's just at the front end of the hospital. It's beginning to look like this new type of patient isn't likely to leave the hospital as readily as some of the more typical admissions, so we can therefore expect a declining availability of beds. Isn't that correct, Jess?" she asked.

"Seems that way," Weaver replied. "We haven't been able to discharge one of them yet, and so far their hospital course suggests we might never be able to discharge any of them."

"I don't get it," Riegel challenged. "What's so special about these patients? I heard that the Admissions Unit was being hit with a new kind of drug case, but what's the problem? We've had things like that happen before."

"Nothing like this, Charlie," Weaver corrected. "This one's not like anything else we've ever seen, and we don't seem to be able to do much about it. Right, Frank?"

"So far, Jess," Cantrelle agreed tentatively. Other clinical service members of the group mumbled their concurrence. "But as far as the need for beds goes," he continued, "we might have to use other facilities temporarily until the source of the problem is rooted out. All—well, almost all—of these new patients have come from the Commerce Street section of the city, so it's likely just a matter of time before the supplier of the drug is nailed. In fact," he added encouragingly, "that point may be closer than we think because Dr. Morello called me just before I came here to tell me they have a patient on the unit who knows something about the drug. He was offered it and didn't take it, so he probably knows something about the source. But in the meantime we'll need more beds."

"I'm sure he'll give helpful information, and that you'll make full use of it, Frank," Corley granted, "but it appears that the problem is bigger than we earlier realized. Those other beds might already be spoken for."

Jess nodded at his folded hands. The others, Cantrelle included, became alert with misgiving at the dread tone of her reply. She noted the concern on their faces before continuing.

"The reason I called this meeting is because yesterday I received a call from Pittsfield state hospital," she began. "The Superintendent, Dr. Polaski, wanted to know if we'd been receiving any unusual cases lately. He explained that he was inquiring about it because over the previous three weeks they admitted eight cases of a kind of psychosis they'd never seen before, all of the cases known drug abusers but with a clinical picture they couldn't ascribe to any known agent. Frank," she directed, "he described pretty much what we've been getting on our ITU lately. Seems his cases are identical to ours."

Her words numbed him. He sat transfixed as they sank in. His thoughts tumbled about haphazardly at the implications of her disclosure and he felt unable to bring them to order. He heard himself exhale "Jesus Christ!" but it went unnoticed among the position shifting and the worried mumblings of the others.

She continued.

"I explained to Dr. Polaski that we had admitted fourteen similar cases in about the same period of time but had no better idea as to what the agent was. We had nothing else to say about the situation other than that the DMH should be brought into it as soon as possible."

"Are we certain they're the same kind of case?" Saul Klein asked in search of hope-sustaining error.

"He described psychosis with blushing, giggling, and dementia," Corley replied.

"That's it, I'm afraid," Klein conceded. "What do you think, Dr. Cantrelle?"

The question recalled him to the meeting. He had drifted away to an inner maelstrom of angered turbulence. He had blundered! He had assumed—there was that fucking word again!—assumed that their own cases were the product of some local nut and hadn't seriously considered or suspected anything beyond that. And because of that he was totally unprepared for Corley's disclosure. Plus he knew that confusion was written all over his face. Damn it, he always preached to others to keep their options open when sizing up a problem, and here he was looking like somebody's fool for failing to do precisely that. And Jess—and probably Martha, too—knew of his blunder. He had let Jess down because Jess probably had been caught flat-footed also, right now just as he himself was; Jess should have been prepared for such a turn, prepared for it by one Frank Cantrelle. It was his job to keep Jess informed; *fully* informed. This time Jess was absolutely nowhere near being fully informed. The checking in with other facilities in the state system should have been started by the ITU to work its way up to Jess, and then to Martha, so that Pittsfield's phone call would not have been unexpected. Martha then would at least have been ready to discourse on the problem's broader scope. He and the residents had been so wrapped up in themselves and fussing over the cases, they—at least he—had neglected a larger responsibility to the front office. And Jess and Martha were being so damned nice about it, as usual.

"Yeah," he groaned, "it sounds like the same thing. Not likely to mistake something like that. We should have . . . *I* should have . . . about the number of cases . . . ." he blurted, ". . . aw, never mind . . . I'm sure they're the same kind of case."

"So I made calls to the other hospitals in the system," continued Corley as she passed over his display. "Most of the other facilities have either not received any such cases, or no more than one or two and so do not see it as a looming problem or trend—yet. Of course, they all were thankful for the warning. Dr. Weaver helped me make the calls. Afterwards, on the basis of our findings, we agreed on certain points. It appears that those state hospitals directly serving the large urban centers—mainly ourselves and Pittsfield—are the ones receiving the bulk of the new cases. Thus, the problem so far seems to be centered in the heavily urban catchment areas."

"Where it can grow rapidly, like typhoid," added the ascetic Mrs. Simpson.

"We fear so," Corley agreed. "Whatever is moving this pestilence along—maybe you'll be able to come up with something on that after you talk to that patient, Frank—is moving it along at a good clip if the past two weeks are any indication, now that we know it's statewide. Also, the DMH will check it out with the neighboring states, I'm sure; get some idea how regional it is. But in any event, we've got to consider that we might be in for a heavy run of these cases, and the way we're set up right now we won't be able to handle a significant increase over what we've been receiving. And an increase seems likely. Do you agree, Jess?"

"Yes," Weaver returned, now sitting fully upright and gesturing with his hand as he scanned the group. "There's simply too large a vulnerable population around for there *not* to be an increase. I even wonder if most of our former patients now in the community only because medication is able to keep them out of the hospital might be coming back to us immeasurably worse. Remember, we used to have nearly five thousand patients here not too very long ago. Think of that!" he posed.

"But so far the cases I've heard about are limited to drug users," the fastidious Mrs. Fawcett pointed out in a veiled call for restraint.

"So far," Weaver allowed, "but there's too much about this we don't know to allow us to be complacent. Who knows what direction this thing will take?"

"I wasn't recommending complacency, Dr. Weaver," Fawcett replied icily. "Just common sense. I mean," she hurriedly amended, "the patients should have enough sense not to take street drugs."

"On that score I'm not at all optimistic," Weaver sighed.

"Well, our preliminary task this morning is to plan for some immediate response to the problem," Corley intervened gently, "and that's why I need all of you to consider a proposal that has come up before. In fact, Frank, you were the one who first brought it up," she directed.

He had continued to work on his private trove of *mea maxima culpa* during the discussion and had paid only nodding attention to the points being made. Now, hearing his name mentioned, his attention was once again brought front and center, along with a look of perplexed arousal.

"Perhaps when you first brought it up," she reviewed to allow him time to catch up, "it was not yet it's time, and, like a good wine, had to be put on its side a bit longer."

Several of the committee smiled at her kind teasing. He strained at her allusion, trying to anticipate what was coming, but didn't get very far. This just wasn't one of his better days.

"Frank," she relented mercifully, "I mean the Triage Unit."

"Of course!" he bellowed in recognition. "Now would be the time—the perfect time—to get it going, if what we fear will come our way actually does!" his thoughts echoed. But he also realized that again he had been asleep at the switch. The Triage Unit was something he'd been urging for two years, and now, when the perfect time arrives for him to make a telling and unassailable case for its establishment, he's cast adrift among the very clinical matters the Triage Unit would address. So, of course, Martha has to bring up his own proposal for him! At the rate things were going, this was indeed going to be a very long day, he feared. Forestalling that thought, he made a stab at a consoling cynicism by reminding himself that, try as he may, he could be truly incompetent at only one thing at a time and that no mortal, no matter how accomplished, could hope to have his fundamental incompetence in all things come together all in one place at the same time. Along with that oblique reassurance he felt a glimmer of hope rise right along with the triage proposal from the ashes of its earlier shelving, and it was from that feeling he mustered his reply. "Yes. Now that you mention it, that would seem to be a first step," he agreed with limp modesty. "But," he continued as he recovered himself, "we'll have to get a move on, because you know we'll still need a separate ITU, distinct from the Triage Unit. Plus all the staffing."

"Yes, I know. Last night I reviewed the updated proposal you submitted last year. In fact," Corley added as she reached for a stack of paper on a small table off to her left, "I've made copies of the proposal and I'd like each of you to look it over from the standpoint of staffing and mission as they pertain to your departments." She then passed the stack to Jess who took his copy and passed the others along. After everybody had received a copy, she resumed. "Ladies and gentlemen, first we should give credit where due. Our Training Director here, Dr. Cantrelle, has been trying to impose this Triage Unit on us for over two years. Isn't that so, Frank? And each time it's come up we've been able to temporize in favor of some other priority. As I was reading it last night, the thought came to me that we're indeed very fortunate to have such a proposal ready at hand at a time like this, and I know I speak for the group when I take this moment to thank him for his persistence."

He was becoming visibly embarrassed by her encomium, and so he had to dilute it.

"You might have some other feelings later on when we get into the rigors of setting up a unit like this, if we decide to do so," he paltered. "In fact, we've been through something very much like this once before, I don't need to remind Dr. Corley," he recalled to the group.

She led the group in good-hearted laughter at the memory of her working right along with the plumbers and electricians in the construction of the ITU years ago.

"The experience did me well, and this one will do the same for all of us, I think. Please look it over and I'll get back to each of you individually over the next week to hear your ideas. Any questions?" she asked.

There were several.

"Will all admissions, even the returned elopements, be processed through the Triage Unit?" asked Mrs. Fawcett as she leafed through the proposal.

Corley deferred to Cantrelle.

"Yes," he affirmed. "Frequently, if not usually, when elopers return they're a lot worse off than when they left and so need a round of more intensive treatment before returning to their primary units. Triage would identify those requiring some time on the ITU before their being assigned to another building. Couldn't have them go directly to their primary unit first; they would strain the usual operations of that unit, as you know."

Fawcett nodded, satisfied.

"Does anyone have any idea what this drug is or where it comes from?" demanded Riegel, indignant that the hospital was being coerced into herculean effort by external forces. "Seems to me the chemistry boys ought to be on top of it by now."

Weaver picked up that point.

"It hasn't been isolated or identified yet," he volunteered. "So far, the thinking is that either it's so powerful or so specific it's able to achieve its effect even in trace amounts well beyond the sensitivity of the current assay equipment, or that it's metabolized completely and immediately after ingestion and hence not present for assay, but, remarkably, not before achieving its effect. The upshot there is that by the time the symptoms appear to alert anyone to draw a blood sample, the drug is already broken down to normal components of the serum. They're working on it, I assure you."

"Where?" Riegel persisted.

"The private clinical pathology labs," Weaver replied, "the ones we and most other hospitals contract out to. The state lab hasn't gotten into it and probably won't have to."

"I see here the unit would be co-ed," Wingate observed as he perused the proposal. "The question becomes," he continued as he looked at Corley, "where around here will we find a twenty-eight bed unit that can be set up as co-ed? That's a lot of plumbing work in a short while since I expect you would like to have this unit on line *tout suite*."

"We thought you could help us narrow the field of possible choices since you know the physical layouts already in place and which one or ones could be more readily adapted," Corley explained.

"It might be easier to go with a larger unit, say forty beds. Would give us more to work with," he posed.

"Quite possibly. When I meet with you we can pursue it further," Corley concurred.

"What about staffing? Will it be volunteer like the Admissions Unit?" Fawcett asked.

"We don't know yet," Weaver responded. "I think we'll have to see first how much we're getting into by way of physical plant size before we get down to staff selection,"

"According to this" Fawcett continued in referring to the proposal she was now waving in front of her, "the length of stay in this unit is to be a maximum of one week before transfer to some other unit. That's moving pretty fast for diagnostic work-up and assessment of response to initial treatment. You'll have to have our most—can I say?—efficient and competent people on board in order to pull it off. But would our best people go for it? The work would demand a pretty hectic pace. I think I could get the nurses, but what about the others?" she questioned, again flinging her recurring gauntlet that her nurses were unflinching in their duties while others tended to be significantly less so and, worse, inclined to depend on the nurses to carry them.

Corley fielded that one.

"It would not be a full diagnostic work-up," she explained. "That would be done later at the receiving unit after Triage had performed the initial assessment to determine which unit that would appropriately be, such as Geriatric, Long-Term Care, Forensic, Intensive Treatment, or the like. The time period, a ten-day maximum length of stay, is thought to be sufficient for that initial assessment. Correct, Dr. Cantrelle?"

Cantrelle nodded in agreement.

"The Emergency Mental Health centers have been doing essentially the same thing for years," he added, "but we would be doing it on a higher level of differentiation. They do it to determine which ones require in-patient treatment and which ones don't. We would be taking those already selected for in-patient treatment and then determining which kind of treatment for each, and then sending them to the appropriate unit."

"I think you can see," Corley continued, "that the purpose here would be to identify as early as we can just who should be where so that we can free up our diagnostic operations and streamline our treatment capacities to absorb the increased number of admissions we expect."

It all seemed clear enough, and a moment of settled silence united the gathering in that assessment.

"I know this is pretty far down the line," Klein conceded, "but has there been any thought about setting up a separate unit for the drug cases themselves?"

"That's the big one," Weaver acknowledged. "And it's not knowing what we might be getting into and what's coming our way that makes it so. On the basis of our experience with these patients thus far, there's very little we can offer except custodial care, like it was for all hospitalized psychiatric patients seventy-five years ago. Psychiatric hospitals have changed a lot since then, but these patients are like throwbacks to the old days because we're no better off with them now than we were with any of the general patients back then. So the big question is whether or not they belong here at all, or whether they should be in some other type hospital or setting where they can get as much, or as little, as anybody can offer them. As long as there's no specific treatment available—and we certainly don't know of any just now—they could do just as well in a nursing home, or if we had any left, a good old-fashioned State Hospital vintage 1930. It may come to that."

The silence was too grim to last.

"Well, let's hope it blows over, like other drug fads have," Simpson blandished. "Sometimes just preparing for them seems to make them go away."

Corley allowed a moment for that frail hope to sink in.

"If there are no other questions," she then announced, "we can adjourn till further notice. None? O.K. Thank you very much."

The meeting broke up into private interchanges as the members rose and paired off in leaving the board room.

He continued to sit at the table, reviewing events and pondering his next move, and would have done so a bit longer had he not been aroused by Corley's voice.

"Frank, could you stay a bit longer so that Jess and I can have a moment with you?" she asked.

"Of course, Martha," he replied as he switched focus.

"Good. Let's go into my office. I've got some fresh coffee there," she coaxed.

She didn't have to coax him because he would go anywhere fresh coffee was offered, and since he'd had only three cups so far this morning, his caffeine titre was nowhere near optimum.

"Lead on," he sprung, knowing full well that the coffee and confidentiality were likely to be vehicles for some appeal to his volunteerism.

They traced their way single file, Corley leading and Jess in tow, through the passageway to her office which was stately, large, and seasoned with heritage in the form of various plaques, faded portraits, and heavy-cut vases. But, happily, the furnishings were comfortable and restful. The waiting coffee cups were centered on a low circular table with a hammered copper surface. Several flanking arm chairs clustered around it. She led the way to the table and motioned them to their seats. As she began to pour she opened the discussion with the comment that it had come to her that the residents were quite animated in their interest in this new type of patient, the agent of their present administrative exertions. Somehow the way she said it told him immediately what the purpose of this meeting was and what he could expect to hear. So he settled back in his chair, sipped his coffee, and waited.

"Ruth Fawcett's concerns about staffing the Triage Unit were certainly in line with getting down to business, weren't they? In fact, that's the reason Jess and I wanted to talk to you this morning, as I suspect you already know," she continued.

He grinned, Cheshire-like.

She smiled, relieved that his response was thus far playful and collaborative.

"To get down to it," she proceeded more boldly, "we wondered how you felt about the possibility of putting some residents on the Triage Unit to help out. The staff psychiatrists working there, whoever they turn out to be, will probably be some of our better ones who could help in the teaching and, in turn, get a little help from the residents. At least, in the start-up phase. Once the unit is working smoothly you might prefer to have the residents there as one of their standard rotations. I don't know. What do you think, Frank?"

The air developed a tense anticipation as she spoke. Over the years it had become too well known that Residency Training at Moreland was never to be regarded as an available and handy resource for pulling someone's clinical, political, administrative, or economic chestnuts out of the fire, and he had on several notable occasions stood his ground, jawbone in hand, ready to defend the inviolate sanctity of his priestly orders and the purity of his mission. All in all, there had been no serious challenges, ever, but all knew that when issues concerning the structure and mission of Residency Training arose, Frank Cantrelle could be expected to shoot first and ask questions later. Hence, Corley's light tread and the tightened air.

He took a dramatic sip of coffee as Corley and Weaver waited.

"I think that would be the right thing all around," Cantrelle began, eying the rim of his cup, "and it certainly would be right for the patients to have such concentrated attention in their assessment stage. It would be right for the resident to work with the patients, especially this new variety, immediately upon their admission. And certainly it would be right for Residency Training to help in the follow-through on the staffing of one of its very own recommendations. And, of course, it would be right for the hospital to bring all its resources to bear on this terrible problem coming at us. So, sure; just tell me when," he consented.

"Good," Corley said as she nodded her gratitude.

Weaver leaned back in his chair and beamed his satisfaction that his friend had come through again in fine form.

"But there's also a selfish side," he continued, "though I'm sure you're fully aware that my cooperative spirit is driven so much more by scholarly magnanimity." He paused a moment to collect their snickers, and then proceeded. "You remember back in the Seventies and Eighties when we had that rush of LSD cases—kinda similar to this present problem—and Clay and I started collecting data for a paper we intended to write about the number of LSD trips and its relationship to the chronicity of impairment? And we never got around to finishing it up and publishing it? Well, I figure this is a chance to make amends for that. There's a good paper in this present situation, especially since we'll have the largest sample of these new and quite mysterious cases of all other facilities around, and undoubtedly for the longest period of time. So bringing the residents in to help with data gathering would be another right thing."

"I agree," Weaver seconded, ever committed to the research effort of the hospital.

The mention of the residents and Moyer brought back to mind the ITU and Dr. Sumner's patient awaiting him there. He had almost forgotten, with all the business of the Council meeting boiling over. Again he felt the goad to make up arrears.

"But this time I'm sure we'll follow through," he vowed, "that is, if I can pull myself away from this pleasant company and get myself over to the Unit and talk to that 'almost ran,' as Morello calls him. Before the Council meeting I had hoped that we might find out from the patient something about the main source of the drug, but now I guess we'll have to settle for something less; maybe just something about local distribution. I've been living in a fool's paradise thinking that the problem was only local," he felt compelled to admit.

"Move over, Frank. You've got company," Weaver consoled with a guffaw.

"O.K. Time to go," he whooped as he bounded out of his chair. "If I turn up anything, I'll call and let you know," he added as he made for the door.

"Thanks, Frank," Corley bade warmly.

"Right, Frank," Weaver added.

A dozen or so loping steps and he was through the building entrance and back on the drive. It was just beginning to drizzle lightly, somehow making the wind more personal, as though it were working harder at seeking him out. He didn't need much help in feeling more of that after such a meeting, he reflected as he leaned into the chill. He now began to register the let-down feeling come of learning that the problem was no longer his unique challenge, though he had never consciously acknowledged to himself that he thought it was. He did feel, he could admit, that as long as the problem was regarded as local he felt central to the challenge of dealing with it, maybe even to solving it somehow. Now, he found himself to be one of God knows how many teacher-administrators confronted with the task of extracting good learning from an evolving human tragedy, as though there were really any other kind, he harrumphed. His zeal for interviewing the waiting case had flagged significantly and he now felt that gripey sense of needing to see one's wearying commitments through begin to rise within him as he approached his car.

"There's no such thing as useless knowledge," he reaffirmed to himself with mock sincerity. "Only failures in wisdom. And besides, the gang's waiting for me and I have to bring them up to date, something they thought they would be doing for *me* this morning."

That particular irony carried him to his car which he was now happy to enter as the drizzle picked up. He started the engine and was quickly on his way along the familiar drive to the ITU.

In no more than two minutes he was pulling into a parking slot near the ITU's entrance. By now the rain was arriving in gusts, hurricane fashion. He sprinted the distance to the building's door and once inside daubed his face with his handkerchief and stamped his shoes more or less dry. He then wound his way to the stairwell and up its steps, not inclined this time to check to see if the elevator might be waiting for him. Not enough time even for that just now.

He reached the top floor landing in commendably good time and unlocked the door to the unit, entered, and then locked the door behind him.

The unit and the building's floor plan, being cruciate with its two lateral wings joining the third central wing, defined a lobby at their junction which held offices for secretaries and nurses, plus a lounge for visitors. The elevator debouched into this lobby. The layout was the one settled upon several years earlier when the unit was restructured along lines more compact than the cavernous dimensions of the former admissions building. The arrangement served to concentrate the treatment and teaching effort more effectively than was workable in the former Admissions Unit. And it served well. Such is the power of our milieu upon our function, as he had held forth on so often.

But one of the few drawbacks in the new rearrangement was the noise. It, too, had been concentrated, and he would automatically recoil from its blare whenever he entered the unit, and on this morning in particular it was a lot easier to disapprove of the clangor.

Because of the peculiar acoustics of the place, the noise had a sharper, penetrating quality which likely resulted, he often suggested, in the need to dispense larger dosages of psychotropic medication than would otherwise have been the case. Plus, there was also its effect on the staff.

He made for the nurse's station on the open ward, passing a cluster of three patients who were intently doling out cigarettes to each other from a shared pack. Their driven pursuit of nicotine was always something of a mystery to him as well as to others, and it was also something of a truism that the more chronic and severe the schizophrenia, the deeper the cigarette stains on the fingers. There had been much talk of the oral regression inherent in the disease as accounting for the passion for smoking, but the patients didn't show as much a passion for eating, and he wondered if rather the disease in some way affected the metabolism of nicotine with a resulting need to hoard it in its most available form, cigarette nicotine. Or perhaps, alternatively, the pursuit of nicotine came partly as a consequence of the use of neuroleptics in the treatment of the primary disorder itself. In any event, the severely impaired schizophrenic's pursuit of tobacco could not simply be seen as a bad habit. It was much too characteristic.

He walked into the station where a nurse was charting in a patient's record. She looked up as he entered.

"Oh, good morning, Dr. Cantrelle," she greeted pleasantly.

"Good morning," he returned, "are Mr. Moyer and Dr. Morello around?"

"Yes. I think they're in the side conference room right now. In fact, I think they're waiting for you because they told me to keep John Frieden available for interview. He's the new patient I think they want you to see," she detailed.

"Good. I'd better hurry then. Thanks a lot," he returned with an approving smile. It was gratifying when things were laid on with such efficiency.

He walked to the far end of the open wing where the unit conference room formed the terminus. The door was half open in expectation and he entered to find Clay and several residents gathered around the long conference table. They all turned to him as he entered the room.

"Good morning everybody; Clay," he greeted.

"Good morning, Frank," Moyer returned. "I trust Dr. Morello gave you enough basics to goad you into a good frenzy of anticipation. The patient is pretty conversant and generally cooperative, wouldn't you say, Dr. Sumner? We've been pumping him, and bits and pieces are coming forth, but I'm sure its one of those situations where he doesn't realize how much he knows, so he has to be helped along. I'm sure there's more to come. I think if we work at it we might come up with a pretty good lead or two. And it sure comes at a good time the way the cases have been coming in. Some enterprising pusher out there has been pretty busy," he recapped in briefing Cantrelle for the approaching interview.

On the way over to the unit he had worked peripherally at steeling himself for disclosing to Clay and the group Martha's announcement which he knew could only result in a pall of disappointment being draped over their zeal. Yet, he was still taken aback by the starkness of the contrast between their confident innocence and his lowering regret. The gap between the two now demanded bridging, yawning before him as it did, and their simple eagerness carried a poignancy he would just have to bear as he did so. Moreover, he felt himself largely responsible for this moment because he had enlisted them in this enterprise much like a voluptuary recruiting for a crusade, and now he had to tell them that the promised glory had been nothing more than an illusion. The sting of his own disappointment come of the Council meeting lingered as a reference point for estimating what he would bring down upon these innocents, multiplied many times over to cover all others who had heeded his call. The prospect of opening a Triage Unit might offset some of the loss, as it did for him, and maybe even serve as a balm for their wounded zeal, but he cringed at the thought of being heard as trying to sell them on a lesser item for having failed to deliver on what initially had been promised. And he knew that his mind was overworking the issue because, in truth, he had been just as innocent as they at the outset of this misadventure. But the larger truth, he reminded himself, was that as Training Director he wasn't permitted the luxury of such innocence. It wasn't in his job description, he'd said too many times.

He surveyed their eager, ready faces, and decided to take his medicine straight.

"Before we get on with the interview, I want to bring all of you up to date on some developments. I just left a Council meeting called by Dr. Corley specifically because of these new cases and the effect they'll likely have on the admission rate and hospital census. The Council is very aware that if these cases continue to come to us in the numbers of the past two weeks we'll soon be desperate for beds, and services will be spread pretty thin. Some things have recently come forth to indicate that we can expect exactly that. The admission rate on these new patients will likely not only continue, but worsen."

He could see their expressions transform into concern as he brought their thoughts to this different focus.

"What's up, Frank?" Moyer reached in visibly mounting alarm. He knew Cantrelle's tone signaled trouble.

"Simply this, Clay," he directed to all present. "This is not just our problem. Dr. Corley has learned that other hospitals in the system have received similar cases."

"Other hospitals like where?" Moyer persisted.

"Like Pittsfield," Cantrelle supplied.

"Jesus Christ!" Morello blurted.

"Are they sure it's the same kind of case?" Moyer challenged.

"I asked the same question, Clay. Not only Pittsfield, but a couple of other places too. In fact, they didn't know of our cases and yet described exactly what we've been seeing. They're the same, Clay, I'm sure," he sighed.

The group retracted into a glum silence and the air in the room became heavy with the expirant of deflated buoyancy.

"Well," Morello resumed after a moment, "it looks as though we now won't be able to save the world from the plague because the world has already gone ahead and gotten it. What now, Chief?" he asked in search of new purpose.

"We can try to save ourselves, and if we manage to do so and do it well enough, maybe we can still offer something to the other hospitals facing the same mess. I can tell you they're even less set up to handle all this than we are, especially the smaller hospitals," he pointed out in recalling them to their responsibilities. "And that brings me to the next thing I wanted to pass on to you," he added.

"Before you go on, Frank," Moyer interjected, "are they sure that their cases—Pittsfield and the others—aren't just drifters from our catchment area? Imports and not domestic? Our people really get around, you know, and we're always making arrangements for their transfer back here for their treatment. Maybe their cases will end up here too," he reached.

"Clay, I'm sure if any of those patients had been from our catchment area they would have been hand-delivered back to us long before now. I see your point and I agree we shouldn't jump to conclusions and make the problem bigger than it has to be, but it really does seem that this new drug is being unloaded across the state. Also, Dr. Corley will ask DMH to check with neighboring states to get a handle on how widespread this 'plague' is, Dr. Morello," he specified in attribution, "but we won't know much on that score for maybe a couple of days. If it's truly that widespread, you can imagine hospitals in other states groping around just as we're doing right now trying to get a fix on this thing and feeling pretty lonely in the process. They're probably ready enough to learn that there are fellow sufferers out there beyond their own borders. So I think the larger demographics of this thing will begin to take shape over the next few days. Right now it's just like when a tornado hits and people come out after it passes and count the casualties and damage and then check with neighboring communities to see how others fared to find out if help is needed, or available.

"I'll stick with the plague metaphor since I know more about disease than I do about meteorology, Chief," Morello quipped, his irrepressibility returning. The other residents pitched in and laughed in relief.

Cantrelle saw the reaction as a sign that the numbing effect of their disappointment was fading and that perhaps a sense of the enlarged importance of the challenge was beginning to register. So he proceeded.

"I think we can appreciate the implications of some of this," he began. "The investigative part of the problem is obviously no longer our private preserve, though our feeling that we were in the forefront of the problem did get the pioneering juices going. Well, I can assure you we're still just as much in the forefront, but it does appear that before long we may have a lot of company right up there with us. So, I suggest we be magnanimous about it as our colleagues share the doubt, the fear, the disillusionment, and the exhaustion come of that pioneering spirit as we tighten our ranks to face whatever the hell this enemy turns out to be."

Everybody tittered, even Moyer. The group now seemed restored.

"Morale, isn't it wonderful?" Cantrelle continued. "But I'd like to bring up something else, something very much in line with what we've been talking about. Then, we'll get on with the patient. Remember the Triage proposal, Clay?" he urged. "Well, Dr. Corley and the Council want to get it going as soon as possible. Jess in particular. They think—they know—its time has come, as the phrase runs, and that the time is right now."

"Overdue," Moyer corrected, "but until now it lacked an enabling crisis."

"Of course. But don't forget, we're going to be magnanimous," Cantrelle teased.

Morello beamed in satisfaction. The proposal had been pushed when he was a beginning resident and he was thus familiar with it. In fact, as was his usual, he had taken a proprietary interest in it as though it would be his to implement since it depended so heavily on resident participation. He had long seen himself as the resident of the hour to take the Triage Unit through a successful inception. But the shelving of it forced him to settle for significantly lesser glories. While he beamed in anticipation of reclaiming his crusade the junior residents at the table registered little more than curiosity, their tenure having begun only recently and thus a few years after the initial push for the unit.

Cantrelle noticed the disparity.

"Dr. Morello, this morning after we finish interviewing the patient will you please meet with the junior residents—all of them—and give them a briefing on what the Triage Unit proposal is all about," he urged. "The residents in your class probably remember enough about it but you can review it with them also if they need it and if you have the time. I think you probably remember most of the particulars, but if you need a refresher Mrs. Andretti will give you a copy of the original proposal. Clay," he shifted, "whether or not we activate the unit depends on what Martha and Jess come up with in their canvassing, but I think it's a pretty sure bet we're going to have a Triage Unit. And that's where we'll start the process of taking a methodical and very searching look at this crazy mess."

"Right, Chief!" Morello seconded, aloft in the restored buoyancy of the room.

Moyer smiled a nodding satisfaction. He had pushed hard for the unit.

"All right, Dr. Sumner, you're on," he directed as he briskly changed course. "Let's hear about the 'almost ran,' as I understand he's called."

Morello led the residents in mischievous snickers.

"By the way, Dr. Sumner, what's the reason for the patient's admission?" Cantrelle asked.

"Suicide gesture. We'll get to that," she assured, adjusting her notes one final time. "The patient's name is John Frieden. He's a thirty-eight-year-old single, unemployed, caucasian male," she began, "with a known history of heroin addiction of at least fifteen years duration. He is considered to be an adequate historian. He has had multiple hospital admissions for detoxification and at least two extended admissions to drug rehab centers, the more recent being about eight years ago. His legal history includes a six-month jail sentence for breaking and entering, burglary, receiving stolen goods, and conspiracy."

"Perhaps the only period in his life over the past fifteen years he was drug free," Cantrelle estimated.

"Not according to him," Dr. Sumner corrected. "Also, he's had two, maybe three—he's not sure—brief psychiatric hospitalizations at city hospitals, each time apparently for psychosis secondary to drug overdosage. Those hospitalizations occurred in his early and mid-twenties, and there have been no subsequent ones till now."

"Fairly typical, so far," Cantrelle observed. "In the early stages of their disorder, addicts might experiment with various drugs kindred to the prime agent—heroin in this case—before settling down to their one and only. The experimentation frequently gets them into trouble and into hospitals. Please continue, Dr. Sumner," he urged.

"So much for the identifying data. Now for the History of the Present Illness. The patient states that he was in his usual state of health until two weeks ago," she continued in the prescribed manner, "when the precipitating event arose. 'Usual state of health' for him means that he was using his customary five to seven bags of heroin a day and doing enough dealing to keep himself comfortably supplied. He said he would sell two to pay for one and he would use his public assistance check for rent and food. He felt he had things worked out pretty well. He would spend time with his drug culture friends, and they would 'nod off' together almost daily. In that regard he says his sleep had been pretty good, his appetite fair with weight remaining stable. No real sex life except occasional masturbation when he would do what he calls a 'double dip,' meaning he would combine marijuana with the heroin, or, in his words, 'shoot up and then suck weed.' He hasn't worked in over ten years. He was fired from his last job as a dispatcher because of being suspected of stealing. No contact with his family in well over five years and he's not even sure if his parents are living."

"So, in a way, he'd found his place as well as his Grail, and was quite content to continue this way indefinitely, I suspect," Cantrelle summed up.

"Apparently so," Dr. Sumner agreed, now settling into a more relaxed delivery.

"But something upset the balance," Cantrelle anticipated. "Always, always," he emphasized once again, "seek the patient's last steady state—the last time the patient felt things were going reasonably well—to establish a point of departure for defining the precipitating event of the Present Illness, just as Dr. Sumner is doing. And don't look just for the most dramatic event or the most abrupt change. Frequently the more colorful events are secondary ones, already well along the causal chain and often little more than the patient's belated recognition that something has gone wrong. Usually, the initial precipitating event is more subtle, or, at least at the time of its onset, not recognized for its importance. Let's see what Dr. Sumner has come up with."

"Well, as far as I can tell," she hedged slightly, "the change began when his sales began to drop off." She waited a moment for challenge. Receiving none, she judged the coast clear and so continued. "He said that most of his usual customers continued to buy from him, but the week-enders, he calls them, began to come around less often. People like college kids, yuppies, and others he says dabble in drugs for a change in scenery, not as a daily staple. He said word had gotten around that the market had become contaminated with a 'louse,' which he says is a bad batch of something, anything, that gets mixed with the standard article and 'can put you away,' which means anything from transient malaise to death," she detailed, gesturing quotes with her fingers where necessary. "The reputable dealers, like himself, he insists, are careful about their suppliers, but the 'whores,' the ones who don't care where they get their merchandise or to whom they sell it, are the ones who were passing around the loused up heroin."

"So far, only the heroin," Cantrelle noted, betraying more focus on the agent than on the patient.

"That's all he mentioned," Dr. Sumner replied. "He says that dealing got so bad so fast that only his hard core regulars came around, and that was only half of his usual turnover, and he began to have trouble making ends meet for his own habit. He says he began to dip into his 'egg money'—the rent and food money—to buy his bags. He says he even considered going back to burglary but lived in terror of being locked up again. A friend of his, one of the ones he often nodded off with, said he knew where they could get some heroin fairly cheap from a new supplier trying to get established and selling below the usual market price even though the heroin wasn't too 'trimmed,' meaning diluted. He says he at first kinda liked the idea because he had gone through something like this a couple of times before when supply became contaminated because of sloppy production. He had then changed suppliers, but this time he wasn't so sure. They got a sample of the new supplier's heroin and were just about ready to nod off together. But at the last minute he decided to play it safe and let his buddy do it first since the buddy apparently had no qualms at all about it. Well, to bring the story to a point, the buddy is now one of those fourteen recent admissions."

"So this patient pretty much witnessed the whole thing," Cantrelle reached quickly.

"So it seems," Dr. Sumner concurred.

"Go on," Cantrelle urged, knowing that he spoke for the entire group who were now sitting a bit more upright in their chairs.

"He says that after his buddy was hospitalized he himself became reluctant to take anything, even from his steady supplier. He decided, as he had done before in similar supply crises, that it was time for him to undergo detox to keep him away from his drug, lower the overall cost of his habit, and give enough time to let the 'louse' clear the system. In the meantime he didn't want to have to worry about room and board. So he presented himself to first one and then a second detox center where he had been treated before, and was turned down both places. Apparently they remembered him only too well from his previous admissions and didn't want to waste time and resources on such a poor candidate. He states that over the next few days he became increasingly desperate as withdrawal symptoms, coming on the heels of his dwindling, safe drug supply, began to circle ever closer, 'like hyenas waiting for me to stumble,' he said.

It was then that he decided to cut his wrist and force a hospital admission. And that's what he did. The city hospital wanted to discharge him the next day on some tranquilizers but he threatened to cut himself again if they did. So they transferred him here."

Cantrelle sat in thoughtful silence for a long moment. That verge feeling was beginning to surface again, and, as always, was tempting him to regions beyond the immediate. He side-stepped the drift, but wondered why it was happening just now.

"I don't think it will be necessary to go through a formal background history," he suggested on his return to focus, "but if there's anything there to sharpen our grasp of this case, we'll use it. Anything?"

"Well," Dr. Sumner sighed in her uniquely pert way, "I guess I should mention that there's a history of bed wetting and behavior problems in school. But he was able to finish high school and even put in a year at a community college. After that, its all drug history. Apparently his family tried everything to help, even family therapy—but he didn't seem to benefit. He has two brothers—he's the middle one—and both are married and doing well. The record says that when he was a boy he showed artistic ability and had wanted to be a commercial artist. That's what he studied at the community college."

"I suspect it was that particular talent various counselors along the way tried to salvage to get him back on his feet again," Cantrelle estimated. "What about the mental status? Anything special there?"

"Not much, really. He's still showing withdrawal signs, but otherwise nothing very remarkable. He's alert and oriented times three. I don't see any delusions or hallucinations, but like so many who have been heroin addicts for so long he tends to be vague, drifty, and introverted. He's evasive and yet he isn't; it's more like he takes his time and responds only as much as he wants, when he wants. He's not too easy to interview," she warned.

"I'm sure," Cantrelle allowed. "Unless there are any questions just now, we'll bring him in and see what we can get."

There were no questions. Morello rose to go forth and retrieve the patient. As he left, the others settled in their chairs more comfortably to await the patient's arrival. Stretches and grunts abounded.

"Frank, where will the Triage Unit be?" Moyer asked, returning to prospects. "Any idea yet?"

"Martha is going to meet with Wingate after he's checked out the proposal. He's already suggested enlarging the bed capacity to forty to make it easier to accommodate co-ed facilities. They'll probably consult with us before any final decision is made," Cantrelle said.

"That's bigger than we had anticipated when you wrote up the original proposal, but I guess that was for another time and certainly not for this present admission rate," Moyer observed.

"Which may get significantly worse, they fear. Yeah, I think forty beds might be a better figure all around," Cantrelle averred.

The sound of footsteps in the hallway brought to the group to silence.

The door opened and the patient entered, followed by Morello. Cantrelle rose in greeting.

"Please come in and have a seat, Mr. Frieden," he bade, motioning to the chair adjacent to his at one end of the table.

After a moment of hesitance the patient impassively shuffled up to the chair and sat down to settle into languid repose. As he did so he yawned fulsomely. Somehow that gesture added to the impression that what he needed most was a good scrubbing. His dark hair was long, matted, and in defiant disarray; and his bleary eyes, still watering in withdrawal, sleepily took in the waiting group. His notice of Dr. Sumner included no sign of acknowledgment. His ill-fitting state clothes added to the impression of slumping as he sat. He folded his hands in his lap as he silently awaited what he obviously regarded as a pointless and wearying obligation in the service of routine. After a moment he looked up at Cantrelle.

"Man, you got a cigarette?" he asked.

"I'm sorry, Mr. Frieden but I don't smoke," Cantrelle explained.

"Anybody got a cigarette?" he implored the group.

The collective silence answered in the negative as a few heads shook.

"Jeez," he exhaled as he leaned forward to place his face in his hands. Cantrelle noticed that his fingers were finely tapered, almost feminine, though the dirty and uneven fingernails challenged that impression. The skin of his hands was almost a translucent white suggesting a smooth softness that didn't connect easily with his blotchy and stubbly face sprinkled with the squalor of blackheads. As he cradled his head in his hands a drop of rheum formed at the tip of his nose. Cantrelle winced in dread that it might at any moment fall on the conference table. The patient then swept it away with his sleeve and sniffled.

Bracing himself, Cantrelle continued.

"Mr. Frieden, Dr. Sumner has filled us in on the basics leading to your hospitalization here," he proceeded in his standard fashion, "but there are some additional points we would like to pursue and which we thought you might be able to help us with."

"Like what, man?" the patient groaned in the general direction of the table, head in hands.

"We understand you came to the hospital to get away from heroin for awhile," Cantrelle posed.

"No, man, you got it wrong," he replied impatiently. "You sure you ain't got a cigarette?"

"No. I mean it. I don't smoke," Cantrelle reaffirmed. "Then why did you come to the hospital, Mr. Frieden?" he pursued.

"To get away from the louse," he groused irritably. "I told them that," he added peevishly, "so why d'ya ask?"

"To get to the point, Mr. Frieden. If you were willing to cut your wrist to get away from the louse, as you call it, knowing that you would have to leave your heroin behind for a while, you must be pretty concerned about that louse," Cantrelle suggested.

"I've put my snow behind me before when I had to," the patient bristled, lifting his head from his hands to glare at Cantrelle. The suggestion of fear had touched a nerve.

"Sure," Cantrelle allowed, "But this time the louse was the problem, as I understand it."

"I don't give a fuck what you understand, man," the patient snapped.

"O.K., we're square on that score. Mr. Frieden, I'm not trying to talk you *into* anything or *out* of anything," Cantrelle leveled. "What you do or don't do in your private life is *your* business, but while you're here in this hospital your reason for being here is *our* business. I know you've been through detox and rehab enough to know the routine and all of the questions, so I know there's nothing I can come up with this morning you haven't heard more than a few times before."

"That's right," he concurred with sly pride.

"But this time around it's a little different, isn't it?" Cantrelle proceeded.

"Maybe," he begrudged.

"And why here, a hospital, when a small felony with no blood loss could have given you the security of jail?" Cantrelle probed.

"Man, you're fucking with me now," the patient spat in a flash of open anger. "There ain't no way they'll get me inside those walls. You or nobody else."

The open and animated defiance confirmed what Cantrelle had suspected.

"No windows, huh?" Cantrelle mentioned.

The patient again looked at Cantrelle, but this time with an expression of puzzled interest. The play of surprise across his face held contact with Cantrelle's settled and reassuring fix.

"Yeah . . . yeah," the patient considered, as though he were hearing himself for the first time.

"There doesn't have to be any such problem here, Mr. Frieden, and I'm sure it will never happen that you'll ever require any time in seclusion," Cantrelle registered darkly. "We'll help you with what you need . . . and maybe you can help us, too."

The patient turned away from Cantrelle and stared at his hands now folded on the table before him. He was also visibly more alert. The evasive languor had now diminished. He wiped his nose and sniffled.

"What's on your mind, man?" he yielded.

"How bad is your withdrawal right now?" Cantrelle asked.

"Almost on the other side. Cramps gone, shivers gone; ripped-out feeling about over. Just dripping a lot." he droned.

"Need a little more Valium?" Cantrelle tendered.

"Could always use a little more when I'm like this. But rather have a cigarette. Nobody around here with the habit?" the patient ragged.

"Soon as you get back to the ward," Cantrelle assured over a reluctant smile. "What's the talk about this louse?" he resumed.

"There ain't much; just that it's out there and moving," the patient yawned.

"Any lowdown on who's moving it?" Cantrelle persisted.

"There's some new dealers around. Maybe they're moving it. That's where we got it. Say, how's my buddy doing? He still here?" he switched.

"He's in another building. I'm sure he's settled down by now. He might be here a while," Cantrelle evaded.

"I hear they don't leave," the patient grunted.

"So far, none has," Cantrelle admitted. "And you say no one has any dope—oops! That's a poor word—*information* on the louse?"

The patient as well as some others chuckled at Cantrelle's gaffe.

"No one, man. But they say whoever's moving it is trying to get all of us, like they got my buddy," the patient glowered.

"How do you mean that?" Cantrelle pursued, alert to any projective or paranoid aspects of the patient's thinking.

"Just that, man, trying to *get* us," the patient repeated.

"But why would that be? What reason?" Cantrelle continued.

"Who knows? There's some crazy people out there, man," the patient explained.

Now, everybody laughed, Cantrelle included. The patient seemed pleased with his quip and blew his nose loudly in a yellowed handkerchief he dug out of his pocket.

Cantrelle decided on another tack.

"I hear that everybody is getting pretty skittish about the louse," he posed.

"You bet. Some not enough, though," the patient rued.

"Any word on how to spot it?" Cantrelle continued.

"New dealers and neat bags. That's all they say. Neat bags," the patient grumbled. "Man, how much longer with this? I'm getting tired," he groaned.

"Just a minute or so more, Mr. Frieden, and then you're on your way back to the ward. How long does it usually take for a louse to get out of the distribution system?" Cantrelle queried, mostly as informational for the junior residents.

"If it's like before, maybe a month or two," the patient estimated.

"You'll be out of here before then. What do you think?" Cantrelle posed.

The patient was silent for a while. He then looked at Cantrelle.

"Doc, you know I've got to have my snow, sooner or later. So I guess I'll take my chances—but if I don't need it so bad maybe I can play it smarter on what I use. So if the louse is still out there when I leave here, I'll play Russian roulette," he explained in even tones.

"But what'll be your chances Mr. Frieden?" Cantrelle persisted. "Not so good, eh?"

The patient looked away.

"If it's still out there, it'll get me; sooner or later," he said quietly.

The ensuing silence announced the end of the interview.

"Thank you, Mr. Frieden," Cantrelle said with genuine compassion.

The patient just nodded.

Cantrelle rose and extended his hand. "Thank you for joining us this morning. I hope you enjoy your cigarette back on the ward," he offered in an effort to lighten the departure.

"Sure, man," the patient acknowledged as he took the handshake, using it to lever himself upright.

As the patient turned to leave Cantrelle was reminded of one last question.

"Oh, Mr. Frieden. Before you go . . . I forgot to bring it up earlier. Is there a name for the louse yet?" he asked.

The patient smiled at Cantrelle as he moved toward the door.

"They call it 'Blush,' man," he said as he walked away, Morello in tow.

The group now settled back in their chairs as Morello accompanied the patient back to the ward. The silence was as much a courtesy to Morello in wait of his return as it was a moment of observance for what had been witnessed, and a kind of requiem solemnity held the group members to their separate doles for the while. A wave of sadness had swept over Cantrelle, too, as he watched the patient leave the conference room. He had a momentary flash of meeting the patient again soon enough, a victim of his own obligatory roulette, giggling and blushing. He had earlier suppressed that grisly image only to have its affects bind him now to a somber hush.

He noted that Moyer, staring at the edge of the conference table on which he rested his hands, had his eyebrows raised in his characteristic what-can-you-do expression. A few residents glanced sidelong at each other uneasily. One even whispered something to another, a sign that the silence was becoming unmanageable. Cantrelle sensed that it was high time either to say something or to hear Morello's returning footsteps, one or the other. To his relief he then heard Morello's approach, as did the others, and the effect was tantamount to the lifting of a spell. A few residents shifted in their chairs in anticipation of resumed discussion. Moyer broke his stare and scanned the contents of the room as though preparing to re-enter a less clement world. He then looked at Cantrelle.

"Well?" he sighed.

"Yeah," Cantrelle concurred, "it really gets across, doesn't it?"

With that, the residents began to mumble among themselves as Dr. Sumner adjusted herself to a ready alertness for the discussion that was to come.

Just then Morello burst in and made for his chair.

"He said he liked talking to you, Chief. Said you were up front with him, but that you ought to carry cigarettes," he sprinkled enroute.

Cantrelle and Moyer smiled, and a few residents cackled in release.

"I think we felt worse than he did," Moyer sighed.

"Probably. Every once in a while we're reminded that we should get around to feeling some of what they're feeling. Not pleasant, but that's the job, isn't it?" Cantrelle philosophized as he maneuvered the analytic mode back into gear. "Now where shall we take this?" he continued. "First, let's touch on some individual issues, and then afterwards we'll move on to the epidemiologic stuff. Dr. Sumner, for starters give us a few of your thoughts about his overall diagnosis and the motives behind the hospitalization," he began as he smiled encouragement to her waiting prettiness.

"Well, he's certainly passive-aggressive," she declared as she picked her way along carefully, "and his way of getting himself hospitalized says a lot about that. And the dependency on drugs and hospitals, even cigarettes," she added lightly. "Also," she continued, "his detached and distant manner suggest he tried to isolate his affect, his feelings; or at least suppress them. I think that's where the drugs come in. The heroin keeps him away from his feelings probably better than his own psychic defenses can. Plus, there's now the learned pattern over many years of shifting away from the anxiety-binding use of his own defenses to a reliance on heroin for doing so. Add to that the physiology of addiction which keeps the whole pathologic process going and I think you have enough to account for a lot of his behavior, I think," she dotted with a crinkle of her nose.

"Any other thoughts?" Cantrelle directed to the others.

"I think the oral factors are definitely important," the frenetic Dr. John Feldman insisted. "True, he has anal-obstructionistic traits out the gazoo, but I think what he's looking for is an oral Nirvana. You know, Lewin's triad to eat, be eaten, and to go to sleep. Or, to put it another way, to consume his drug, then have it consume him, and then to nod off. Add to that an ersatz Isakower effect and I think we have an idea of how he experiences his world from the position of his regression. Also, I think that his thoughts about falling victim to the louse—'Blush,'I guess we should say—are in keeping with a sense of just nodding off in a more cosmic and complete way. While we regard that prospect with horror it wouldn't surprise me if he actually anticipated it, as though it were The Big Nod Off he's been trying to achieve all along but is hesitant to try just now. I agree the whole thing is pitiful and tragic," he reaffirmed to dispel any gathering charges of insensitivity, "but we have to try and see it from his standpoint to know how to reach him. If we can," he added.

Cantrelle was always pleased with Feldman's surgically precise, though sometimes coldly ruthless approach to clinical analysis. This promising charge had comfort with depth analysis which seemed to place the wellsprings of human behavior closer to his clever grasp, though sometimes at a loss of his sense of the patient's self. The latter was more an issue of maturity and thus remediable by time alone, as he had contended of him in the resident evaluation meetings. And besides, he hadn't heard mention of the Isakower effect since his training days. His mind flashed quick recall of the phenomenon as one of those almost ineffable phenomenon so basic and so universal as to have gone unnoticed for millennia. It consisted of a sensation of turning the head inward as to the breast upon falling asleep to achieve reunion. It was described by its remarkably perceptive namesake back in the Fifties.

"I see you've been reading again, Dr. Feldman," he chided. "I'll overlook it this time but the point you make is a very good one, that the likelihood of his falling victim to this 'Blush' thing would not be merely a matter of statistical circumstance. Were it only that, the sense of it would be only sporting, like gambling. Roulette, as he tried to make it. What we responded to in him was more agonal, more tragic than that, something more akin to his destiny coming to collect its due, something more like the predator coming in to claim its rightful prey. Plus, the pitiless inevitability of it. Hence, the tragedy of it. Yes, I think he feels not only drawn to it, but a genuine part of it as well. And I suppose that's what you had in mind when you dropped the Isakower effect upon us, that ill-gotten gain of renegade reading."

Dr. Feldman smiled his pinched grin of abashed satisfaction as Cantrelle offered a nod of approval before continuing.

"Any other thoughts? . . . Why a hospital rather than jail? He gave us a lead," Cantrelle prompted in the direction of the other residents.

"I guess he feels safer here," one of the residents volunteered carefully.

"I'm sure that's so. But why does he feel so safe here?" Cantrelle urged.

"Because he's less likely to have access to heroin—and 'Blush'?" another resident guessed.

"I'm sure that's correct, too, up to a point," Cantrelle agreed. "But I'm also sure that once he has ground privileges he'll be able to find a way to get heroin, if he chooses. So I think the safety factor applies, but only partially because soon enough it will be much easier for him to get his hands on heroin around here—just walk off the grounds for an hour or so—than it would be if he were in jail. I think there's more to it than just safety. Some other ideas, maybe?" he persisted.

"Do you think he's afraid of jail?" Dr. Sumner posed as she rejoined the discussion.

"I do," Cantrelle declared. "Everybody is, that's why it's held up as punishment, of course. But I think his fear of jail is a bit more than the normal or average, but probably drawn from the same root fear we all share . . . . Anyone want to hazard a guess?"

"You mentioned windows and he agreed," Dr. Feldman recalled. "You're not thinking along the lines of a claustrophobia, are you?" he tested.

"I sure am," Cantrelle revealed at last. "Let's look at it; try to get a picture of his defense make-up that goes beyond heroin addiction, but includes it. His history suggests problems with attention and impulse control as a kid. I think we can presume that restrictions didn't sit well with him even then. My hunch is that he really wanted to be a commercial artist, hence the semester of college. That's another tragic point, because I suspect he began to use drugs as a way of controlling the anxiety come of what he felt were restraints and enclosures—classrooms, assignments, schedules, rules—and all the other regulatory matters we chafe at but usually find a way to manage individually as well as socially. But not he. I think his degree of discomfort set him apart and he knew it. Dr. Sumner didn't get a history of panic attacks during late adolescence or in his twenties but I wouldn't at all be surprised if he had more than just a couple back then. And if he did, then it probably would have been the push for him to increase his drug use. We know his drug use in college increased to the point of his dropping out, and I would guess that it was coincident with the time he experienced a marked increase in his anxiety. I also expect it was related to the classroom setting—crowded classes, long sketching sessions, lots of homework, and the like. So I think he increased his drug use initially to help him through the confining work. But as you know a point is reached where the drug use defeats its initial purpose, and by that time he was probably already addicted. But why heroin? We can speculate that some subtle genetic defect in endorphin metabolism renders him specifically susceptible to narcotic addiction and also generally more sensitive in the overall. The latter, coupled with some talent, perhaps inclined him in the direction of artistic ambition in the first place. But that would be a very ranging speculation indeed. Suffice it to say, my young colleagues," he continued, "we have enough straws in the wind to suspect that Mr. Frieden has determined that if he has to shun his drug for a while and undergo the agony of withdrawal he would rather do it in the relative airy openness of an insane asylum where his misery would less likely be complicated by the terror of panic than it would be in the hermetic confines of prison where panic would be more likely and which would make withdrawal unbearable."

"But what about the people here being nicer than the people in the penal system?" another resident asked in unintended self-service.

"Dr. Hardy, I assume your question applies to staff as well as patients," Cantrelle specified to the resident's chagrin. "It's easy to think of the penal system as brutal and inhuman, but let's not forget that their clientele are not innocent of the need for controls. That's why they're there in the first place," he reminded the group. He paused for a moment and gazed wistfully beyond the far window. Residents were forever falling into a pathologic identification with the patients as fellow victims thrown together by a cruel and uncaring system perpetrated by fiendish others bent on persecution. Thus, who could be a better rescuer than the resident himself? He knew his cautious reminders were heard as tedious, platitudinous irrelevancies, at least until the resident discovered himself unwittingly caught up in some egregious interpersonal warp with a manipulative patient. "The prison staff," he continued, "are constantly being drawn into the cruelty and ferity of the inmates' world even while they work at the task of sustaining rules of reason and humanity in the correctional system, very much the same way we here, constantly at the mercy of our deranged patients, have to bust our behinds daily to foster a sane and compassionate milieu. So, Dr. Hardy, if you mean nicer staff, then in either setting it's a giant step up for the patient, considering what he's been used to living with. If you mean nicer inmates, I don't know that there's much to choose from, though you and I certainly prefer psychiatric patients, don't we? No," he rounded out, "I think its more the windows, and the presence or absence thereof."

He had the sense that he had talked everyone into submission and thus felt the need to volunteer a caveat.

"Of course, all of this is an hypothesis. Dr. Sumner's continued work with him," he nodded in her direction, "will provide the additional findings which will either substantiate the hypothesis or invalidate it. If the latter, then we have to come up with another hypothesis that fits the data. For the time being, though, I think we're doing just about what we can for him therapeutically, and in a week or so he'll be able to go to a sub-acute unit. He'll feel a lot better then, but, as you know, the extended phase of the withdrawal remains in force a minimum of six months after the acute withdrawal is completed. That's when the arguments begin between what he feels and what you know: he feels he's over the worst of it and you know better. But in the meantime, Dr. Sumner," he asked as he returned to a more Socratic style, "what should be included in the priorities in his management, if we go with this hypothesis?"

She bit her lip thoughtfully before answering.

"Going with this hypothesis, we would have to be on the lookout for panic attacks, or at least his mounting anxiety over being confined," she chanced.

"Exactly," he exclaimed, delighted with her deductive stroke. "More the latter because sometimes a panic attack may come without warning, whether he's confined or not, I suspect. Being confined, though, generates its own anxiety which could then trigger a panic attack. So the mounting anxiety would be the symptom to watch for.

It's also the one that could easily be mistaken for some aspect of the withdrawal experience. It would be important to keep the distinction in mind because the management of each is quite different. Also, when he gets on the sub-acute unit the staff there will have to be alert to the difference if the addiction is not to be rekindled by an unattended anxiety. Make sure they know. But even if we do everything right he still may prefer to pick up on old friends, as we know the clinical odds favor. Our job, of course, is to make it as easy as we can for him not to do so. Still, is there something else we might do?" he asked.

"I guess we should keep him busy so that he doesn't feel immobilized," she added.

"That's a good thought," he allowed, "and I'm sure OT and activities will do just that. You should bear in mind the ordinary things that promote a sense of confinement in anxiety, like rainy weather, physical illnesses, crowding on the ward, high levels of noise on the unit, dull routine—all the things that might make any one of us just want to get away for a breather would drive him to elopement or recidivism. But I had in mind something simpler and even more basic than that," he urged.

He waited, but there were no takers.

"Maybe it's too obvious, or too simplistic and really not necessary to mention at all," he allowed, "but at the outset I would sit with him and explain to him in direct and uncomplicated terms what the thinking was about his situation—the hypothesis—and lay it out to him what we propose to do and why. The technical term is clarification, remember?" Their nods said they did. "I would tell him," he continued, "the diagnosis, our understanding of his stresses and his symptoms, and the rationale for the medication and other therapies ordered. Of course he might not be able to grasp very much of it right off, but I think he's accessible enough to recognize its relevance—*if* it's a reasonably correct hypothesis. We keep coming back to that, don't we? Maybe, just maybe—ready for this?—it might enlist a certain cooperation from him, also known as motivation. Supportive sessions with him could use the clarification as a frame of reference as well as a point of departure. And watch out for saying too much and taking too long to say it. We wouldn't want him to feel too confined by your liberating therapy, now would we? But first you have to be pretty clear in your own thinking as to issues and goals; otherwise treatment might become a variation on a snipe hunt, as unfocused psychotherapy too often becomes. Any other thoughts?" he added after a pause. "If not, I think we can call it a morning. If any of you are curious about the Isakower effect, I'm sure Dr. Feldman will be glad to conduct a brief tour." He liked to encourage the residents to teach each other.

The gathering broke up with chairs being pushed from the table and side conversations begun in pursuit of particular points. Cantrelle then spoke above the noise in summon.

"Clay, and you, too, Dr. Morello; I'd like to talk to both of you for a minute. Clay, can we use your office?" he posed.

"Sure," Moyer replied, sensing something afoot in Cantrelle's tone.

Morello, feeling about to be taken to task, donned his characteristic what-did-I-do-wrong-now look.

They moved ahead of the milling residents and up the hallway to Clay's office. After entering they selected chairs and quietly settled to attention. Cantrelle stretched as be began.

"Christ, I think it's really going to hit the fan before this is all over," he groaned as an opening. Moyer raised his eyebrows in concurrence. "I wanted to meet with both of you first off on a matter separate from the administrative changes coming our way. I know that in short order we're going to have more damned planning meetings than Carter has you know what and I don't want this matter to get lost in the shuffle. I'm pretty sure that Martha and Jess are going to find out that this thing is more than just regional, so we'll have to get moving fast on the Triage Unit. But I think we'll also have to set up an entirely separate treatment unit for the 'Blush' patients. Or *management* unit, I should say, since we have no real treatment to offer as yet. God knows how big a unit that may have to be, and that's what I wanted to talk to you two about. Martha and the Council haven't yet gotten that far in their thinking—or planning—to foresee the need of a special unit in addition to the Triage Unit for the management of the cases in the numbers I fear will materialize. Right now the Neurology building is handling the dozen or so cases we've admitted so far, but their bed capacity is already about exhausted. Building Four, the old urban catchment unit we closed about five years ago, may be a good candidate for re-opening. What I need—and this is my point—is a fairly detailed proposal for the establishment of a Management Unit—or building—for holding all these 'Blush' cases. A Blush Unit. The proposal would be a format for the who, what, when, where, how, and why that the Council will have to address when it becomes apparent the Triage Unit will be overwhelmed if it can't move the new cases on in jig time."

"You really think it's going to get that big," Moyer worried.

"I do, Clay," Cantrelle replied. "Even if this new agent takes only a month or two to clear the system, as Frieden said is usually the case, the number of heroin addicts out there who need their 'snow,' as he reminds us, makes for a huge attack rate which will sooner or later descend upon all the area hospitals. And I can assure you, any 'Blush' case admitted in our catchment region, given the course of the dementia as we've seen it, will end up right here on the Triage Unit of good old Moreland State. So, my dear colleagues, what I'd like from you two is some help in working up that format so that we can have it ready for Council when the time comes. Actually, I expect it to be about three weeks after the Triage Unit gets going, and, giving that unit about two weeks from now to start up, I would say a month or six weeks at the latest. Clay, I would like you to map out the staffing for the Blush Unit—which disciplines, how many slots, and so forth. Count on about one hundred beds. Don't forget, all these patients will be maximum care brain cases. Dr. Morello," he shifted, "this is all very new to you and you may not be sure you should be included in this part of the problem, but I think the Chief Resident has to be in on it somewhere. For example, I think it would be appropriate for you to work on resident assignment for both the Triage and the Blush Management Units. I don't believe we can work those units in just yet as standard clinical rotations—we simply don't know just where we're going with this entire matter or for how long—so, for the time being, resident assignment would best be on a volunteer basis drawn from elective time. Also, at some point soon I would like you to meet with all the residents, lay out the overall problem we'll have in staffing both units, and then see if there are any volunteers. Make sure they know we think there should be residents on both units and that ideally each resident would spend some time on each unit to get a glimpse of this new species in all stages of its hospital course."

"Gotcha, Chief," he reported, ready to move at full tilt.

Cantrelle then took a deep breath and sighed in respite from his labors. After a moment of recovery he continued.

"And there's something else."

Moyer looked at him and smiled slyly.

"You smell a rat, don't you, Clay?" he returned.

"A louse," Moyer corrected.

Now it was Cantrelle's turn to smile. Morello giggled.

"You're right, Clay," Cantrelle confirmed through his smile. "Remember 'way back about twenty years ago when we had that run of LSD cases," he explained, "and the paper we set out to write and never did?"

"Oh, yeah!" Moyer acknowledged ruefully.

"Remember how we talked ourselves out of it? There we were, awash in the most complete sample of LSD psychoses available anywhere—all varieties of acuteness, chronicity, and dual diagnoses, each case complete with performance data from the test battery—and we, in our meekness, didn't follow through on the project because we figured the medical school training centers with all their staff power to bring to bear were more on top of it than we were and that our humble offering would probably, we thought, reveal nothing more than our embarrassing meagerness. Remember? So we let our project wither only to find out later that those teaching centers, cranking out their papers, were doing an awful lot with what was by our standards a very limited sample, with the result that their findings were in the main limited to the acute process and wholly bereft of any address of the phenomenon we observed farther down the evaluation and treatment chain—that means us and this state hospital. Here we were, the real experts on the fuller size of the problem and we didn't know it! I'm sure you would prefer to forget, as I would, that it was only some time later we realized that not only did we have a treasure of clinical data but we also had the staff talent all across the board to put us right up front with the best though we didn't see ourselves that way because, after all, we were always the poor country cousins—state hospital employees—much too far removed from the lustrous altars of academia. It was a wretched, telling example of victimist thinking whereby we, teaching our residents the pathology of that attitude in the patients, lived it out in our own attitude about ourselves and in our relationship to the medical school training centers. I saw it as an example of our holding in reverence, at the expense of more realistic reckoning, those institutions where we receive our early training, ennobling them grandly through a primitive kind of idealization right along with the special sense of belonging they impart to us during our classroom years, thus casting much of our experience following those tender years as somehow less authentic even though one's richer learning certainly arrives later, well into one's maturity. A fixation of a sort, but no doubt the essence of Alma Mater. Also, a prolonged adolescence, I suspect. Anyway, we suffered through an abashing second childhood here twenty years ago and I don't want us to do it again. Hear me, Dr. Morello?"

Morello nodded.

"So, Clay, what could be the rat—louse—that you smell?" Cantrelle continued. "Just this! Clay, I want you to resurrect the research format we mounted back then on that LSD study, check it over to see how it would have to be modified to fit this new wrinkle, and then submit the proposal to the Research Committee. Then, I'll help move it along pronto. Once again we'll be sitting on a vast trove of clinical data while other places are seeing only a fraction of the phenomenon. I don't want it to happen all over again that some enterprising academician with limited data leaps into the breach caused by information dearth and fires off some paper to become, for awhile anyway, the bellwether of cloistered thinking which others would likely follow as doctrine, at least until time and experience corrected the skew."

"Aren't you being a little tough on the academicians?" Moyer teased, knowing that his fellow aspirant would have trouble resisting the bait.

"Not at all, Clay. I'm simply holding them responsible for our own shortcomings, that's all," he breezed flippantly. "But you're right," he added, softening a bit. "It's just that in their life or death struggle to publish I think they sometimes forget the responsibilities of majesty. Add to that my festering wound come of our not having published when we should have and you've got the ingredients of the temperament of a bear with hemorrhoids."

All three welcomed the reference.

"Dr. Morello," he resumed, "make sure the residents know that those opting for the Triage Unit and the Blush Management Unit will have the opportunity to be part of the research team, taste and time permitting. They might want to section off a piece of the overall protocol as their own for more individual pursuit. We can help with the format."

"But what about me, Chief," Morello pleaded.

"What do you mean?" Cantrelle asked.

"I mean, would I be able to get in on the research part of it, too?" Morello asked.

"I don't see why not. Why do you ask?" Cantrelle pursued.

"Because, as Chief Resident I'll be tied down overseeing the other residents. I might not have much time for doing my own thing if there's some research I'd like to do," Morello explained.

Cantrelle saw Morello's point. Being Chief Resident was already an added duty, above and beyond the usual training schedule. If a research project were added to his chores he would be hard put to manage any separate posting. Cantrelle mulled it over for a moment. Certainly Morello was not to be penalized for being Chief Resident and deprived of the very opportunity now being extolled and available to the other residents. Yet, scheduled training was not to be abridged. As he pondered the point an idea hove into view.

"You're scheduled to begin the Neurology block in a couple of weeks, aren't you?" Cantrelle queried in search of a means.

"Right," Morello affirmed.

"How was your Neurology in your internship at the medical school?" he posed tentatively.

"Had two months, full-time. It was a good block, Chief," Morello supplied in an effort to help Cantrelle over the hurdle.

Cantrelle usually required his residents to have several additional months of Neurology in their senior year to offset any deficiencies in that required study as might linger from an internship served in another training program. Morello had stayed at his medical school for his internship year and had demonstrated a fairly solid grasp of Neurology's essentials in his subsequent years at Moreland. Occasionally Cantrelle excused a resident of the senior Neurology block when it seemed justifiable on the basis of the resident's skill and aptness. Clearly, that's what Morello was angling for, and Cantrelle had to agree that present particulars, plus unique opportunity, made a strong case for just such a dispensation. Cantrelle stretched out the silence a little longer to punish any presumption lurking in Morello's petition, and then answered.

"O.K., you win," Cantrelle conceded. "You'll be excused of the standard senior Neurology rotation, but make it clear to the Neurology Department that you're using the time to do research in the field and that you'll work in a kind of liaison for us when we need them in a consulting capacity for their help in the Neuro part of what we're doing. O.K.?" Cantrelle instructed.

"Thanks, Chief. It'll work out, I'm sure. Also, I might be able to get some leads from my old college fraternity brother. He's a neurochemist at NIH," Morello exulted.

"Sure, every little bit helps," Cantrelle blandished. "And that takes me to my next point," he continued. "Clay, I remember the LSD protocol made a point of doing the standard psychometric battery on all identified cases as soon after admission as possible to serve as a baseline for comparison with the results of the re-testing at intervals along the way. Right? Also, with our new protocol the earlier the testing the better, I would think, because these cases become worse and progressively less testable as they go along, just the exact opposite to what we saw with the LSD cases. Here, the test results will be documenting the cognitive decay, not recovery like before."

"That's right, Frank. What's the point?" Moyer wondered.

"Well, by the time we'll get them they'll already present a problem in testing. Some of the decay will have already taken place for them to merit transfer here in the first place. Some, if not most, might be too damaged to get a valid baseline on. Right?" Cantrelle pointed out.

"That's true. We might not be able to do even basic neuropsych screening, something we didn't have available back in the LSD study. But in this study it would be the thing to do for the most definitive measure of cognitive decay. Yeah, it doesn't look too promising, I'm afraid. So?" Moyer appealed.

"So why wait?" Cantrelle chirped, as he lifted his palms.

It was the gesture that did it, for Moyer immediately eureked.

"Of course! Test them before Blush gets them!" he exulted.

"Right, and I think Mr. Frieden will be reasonably compliant, if you keep him supplied with cigarettes. Not that we need to heap cynicism on top of fatalism, but I think we all expect Mr. Frieden to return to us sooner or later, as he says. So why not test him now while we can get the baseline, and also take our cue from what he offers to teach us?" Cantrelle added as he trotted his dialectic along.

"Like what, Chief?" Morello beseeched as he raced to catch up.

Clay was now shaking his lowered head in amused dismay. It was just like twenty years ago when the two of them hammered out the original research design in a similar skull session; the design evolved almost parenthetically, as though part of a larger quizzical romp. That's the way this nut Frank Cantrelle did things, Moyer chuckled under his breath.

"Dr. Morello, I'm sure you've noticed that the training curriculum includes a two-month study block in Alcohol and Substance Abuse," Cantrelle twirped with a sarcastic nip, "and that each of our residents spends that amount of time at an excellent rehab facility, Valley Medical Center, just up the road a bit, to work with a very representative cross section of drug and alcohol abusers, as our curriculum brochure proclaims. Thus one could expect that . . . ."

". . . that some of those druggies are going to end up here as Blush patients, like Frieden probably will, and so why not test them while they're in drug rehab and still testable!" Morello filled in excitedly. "*Before* they bump into Blush! Right?"

"That's it," Cantrelle acknowledged, returning to a more correct demeanor. "And, Clay," he extended, "remember in the LSD study we didn't have a pre-drug baseline reading because we never knew who would take the LSD and so we couldn't test every pre-trip adolescent in the region so as to have a baseline on those who eventually did take the stuff? Well, here we have a situation where we know exactly who is likely to take the offending agent—Blush, the remorseless, uncontrolled variable—and we know exactly where a certain number of likely victims presently are. Plus—and get this—the same resident who'll see those likely victims in the pre-ingestion phase will see them also in the post-ingestion phase. Maybe we can even tag those patients early on in drug rehab for rapid transfer here to Moreland if or when they succumb to Blush so that we can get the follow-up testing done sooner. In any event, the whole pathologic sequence—before, during, and after—of this pestilence will be contained within the purview of one residency training program and its research arm. *One*, mind you! No other program could cover it! How do you like those apples, amigo?" he finished in crescendo.

Morello actually applauded.

"With that, young man, you're excused," Cantrelle reprimanded playfully through a whiff of embarrassment. "Seriously," he continued, "the earlier you meet with the residents on all of this, the better. And please don't oversell it. This is still just tentative, merely the outline of a proposal still subject to an awful lot of change, even if it's ever adopted. Also, tell them that it would be better to keep it mum for a while; I would prefer that Administration hear it from me and Mr. Moyer first. Now off with you," Cantrelle motioned cheerily.

"Gotcha, Chief," Morello snapped as he rose from his chair, his head obviously soaring with anticipation. As he opened the door on his way out of the office, he turned and offered with brazen ease, "I'll just casually mention to them that the Glory Road awaits." He then closed the door behind him.

"That kid!" Moyer groaned.

Cantrelle smiled proudly and then drifted into musing as his gaze lingered on the door.

"Clay, remember the doubts we had about him when he started here?" Cantrelle recalled. "That he was too silly? He's really come along, hasn't he? Moyerized, I'd say."

"He's just grown up some, that's all," Moyer deferred in abashment.

Cantrelle allowed the moment to subside.

"Clay," he continued, "there's one other thing I wanted to bring up but thought it better to keep just between us for the time being. I don't trust my thinking on this point so I thought I'd fly it by you first. And it has to do with Frieden's comment that the louse meant that someone was trying to get him and his fellow addicts. I didn't hear that as delusional but more as a fear, and a realistic one as far as he's concerned. When he said it I felt a cold dread go through me—probably the counterpart of what he was feeling—but also a realistic reaction and certainly an appropriate one, *if* what he says is right. It didn't sound like the usual worry about hot shots that dealers occasionally dole out to discredit each other or for retaliation against a customer who doesn't pay up. No, this sounded different; something I've never heard an addict say before. I hope it's just the subtle beginning of some outlandish delusional system soon to emerge, but I doubt it."

"Well, Frank," Moyer responded, "I agree with you that he's not delusional, but as far as his being right in his fears . . . . Well, that's something else. He could just simply be mistaken. Addicts," he reminded Cantrelle, "are always seeing themselves as victims of somebody—the drug, their dealers, the police, their family, us—and there's a certain measure of truth in it. Maybe that's all he meant. If he meant more, he could just flat out be wrong. Mistaken. Nothing more."

"But suppose he isn't? That's what's gnawing at me," Cantrelle persisted. "True, if its just a batch of bad heroin—the result of some goof-up in its production—then it'll run its course until the supply is exhausted and we'll have a certain fixed number of cases. Right? The people producing the stuff will mend their ways soon enough when they find out what their product is doing to their customers. Can't put your own customers out of commission and expect to prosper. Right? As Frieden said, it'll take a month or two, the length of time he expects to be here with us. Actually, only about one month because Blush has already been upon us a good month. So if it's just a production error we should expect the attack rate after this initial rise to diminish sometime within a month or so, wouldn't you guess?" Cantrelle urged as he traced out his reasoning.

"I'm following," Moyer assured.

"But let's suppose this louse—Blush—is no accident," Cantrelle continued darkly, "then the attack rate should increase progressively, *despite* the common knowledge that the heroin market is contaminated. Certainly the producers would know it. Also, as Frieden says, the addict has to have his 'snow' and sooner or later will take his chances, and, I think we all can agree, sooner or later will lose. The result: another case for us."

Moyer knitted his brow in critique. He felt a natural reluctance to credit Cantrelle's grim forecast, built as it was on unfettered speculation, but he also had to allow for the very possibilities Cantrelle posed.

"Christ, you make it sound Doomsday, Frank. I like the way you frolic about in your decision tree, but you'll excuse my reluctance to monkey around with you since I prefer to keep my feet flat-ass on the ground, to use a well-mixed metaphor," Moyer chided pointedly. "If what you say is true then that stirring proposal you just sold to Morello—and to me—would be a trivial irrelevance in view of the scope of this thing as you see it."

"I don't think it would be trivial, my earth-bound hominid friend," Cantrelle continued to frolic, undeterred. "It would just mean that we would have to look a bit beyond our immediate tactic. By the way, the proposal we just cooked up a few moments ago *is* our immediate tactic," he underlined in elaborate condescension.

"Kiss my ass," Moyer retaliated. "And look for what?" he asked, unable to resist.

"For a 'neat bag,' you monkey," Cantrelle burbled.

Moyer had that old feeling of being hooked again. This was vintage Frank Cantrelle. Right or wrong, you felt it was right to go along with him because some kind of discovery hovered in the offing. It really was just like twenty years ago when he felt an identical reluctance to get too far into the LSD study Cantrelle proposed. But he threw in with Cantrelle back then, heart and soul, and enjoyed every damned minute of the sally.

Cantrelle sensed his acquiescence.

"Someone should try to get a hold of some of that Blush," Cantrelle continued. "Most especially someone who has to deal with it's consequences. That means us, doesn't it? If we get some soon enough we can be in on its analysis. Maybe we'll be able to tell from the analysis—those biochemists are bright chaps—whether the contamination is from sloppy production or whether it's something specifically *added* to otherwise good heroin. If it's the former, case closed. If it's the latter, then it's just the beginning. And the reason why I say that, Clay," he knitted his brow in a shift to the sober, "is because whoever is adding it to heroin could just as well add it to crack, methamphetamine, cocaine; even LSD."

Moyer sat quietly, eyebrows raised, and pondered the prospect as he stared blankly at the floor beneath his feet. After a moment he looked up at Cantrelle.

"Well, Frank, I guess we go looking for a neat packet. Any ideas?" he asked.

"I think so," Cantrelle replied. "Where do we always go when we want something beyond the perimeter of this hospital? We go to Social Service, of course."

Five

"Happy Halloween," he whispered into the hollow of her neck now that their breathing had returned almost to normal. Their hearts still raced on, chasing the departing frenzy that had fused them together a few moments earlier, but their trailing pulses were falling far behind the spent eruption which, like a swift summer storm, had showered its wondrous violence upon them only to fade just as rapidly over the horizon and leave a stunned fulfillment in its wake. It was now the beginning of their glow time—the heady savoring of that fulfillment—and he gathered her to him more fully as she adjusted her softness beneath his bulk. His guttural sighs sounded the perfection of their fit as they settled into their moment of timelessness. A few after-shocks brought flash spasms, like distantly receding lightning, but soon all was still. He breathed deeply as he took in her oestrual warmth, while with one hand she lightly played her fingers through the hair above his neck and slowly caressed the small of his back with the other. Their basic position, they had long ago pronounced, and the phrase "getting down to basics" was to them their inside reference to just such rendezvous. She loved him completely and he adored her without stint, and their glow time was the seal they placed on their holy testament of love.

"Boo?" she replied after a few moments of gentling repose.

The labial puff tickled his ear, and he nuzzled into her the more to dampen the arousal. In a minute or so the ripples passed and all was peaceful again.

"Boo?" she asked again.

"No," he muttered after a pause.

More silence followed, sculpted by the rhythmic sibilance of their breathing.

"Boo hoo," she whimpered after a drawn minute.

"That does it!" he exclaimed. "You never get enough, even when you're not in heat!" he chided. "What you need is a tireless incubus, like that son-of-a-bitch Art, and especially on Halloween, too," he railed.

"My love, I need something more substantial than an incubus. Something I can sink my teeth into," she explained as she lunged at his neck, vampire-like.

He pulled in his neck to ward off the tickle and wrestled her back into obedience.

"Listen, my naughty nympho vampire," he pleaded, "I have a meeting this morning and I haven't done a thing to prepare for it 'cuz I've spent all my time since the crack of dawn riding the whirlwind with you. It would be jolly scandalous if I showed up rankly stupefied *and* bedraggled. I already show enough of that as a rule, your rampant lechery being what it is. No, we'll continue this convulsion tonight when the moon is high and our virtue is low. Besides, my batteries need recharging. I promise."

"All right," she groaned petulantly. "But don't forget. Tonight's Halloween and I don't go to all the trouble of being wicked for nothing. I worry that you just take it for granted."

"Hon," he hastened to reassure, "you're absolutely the only witch in my life. I wouldn't think of being under any other spell . . . ."

"All right," she drew out slowly in reluctant mollification. "But if I see any other puncture marks on your neck—or anywhere else . . . ."

He winced at the thought.

". . . watch out!" she bade.

She then began to giggle her satisfaction with their antics and he gave her a rollicking hug in return. This was followed by a deep and concluding kiss which, like returning through the looking glass, brought them back to their surroundings. After a moment of quivering withdrawal and grunting adjustment they were sitting up together, their backs against the headboard. He reached over to the night table and retrieved his coffee. The cup was now less than tepid.

As he took a measured sip he managed a sidelong glance at the clock on the bedside table. Six forty-five. Hearing their cue, his thoughts on all the gearing up which awaited him, along with the logistics to follow, plus the meeting to be attended this morning, began to race about mischievously in his head. He let them run their frenetic course as he stared at the mound in the blankets caused by his feet.

She reached for his hand and entwined her fingers in his as she wedged their clasp between their touching thighs. Resting her head on his shoulder she gazed wistfully into the room's silence.

"Want some cold-sober coffee, sweet?" he asked.

"Uh-uh," she declined, holding to her gaze.

He had to get going, but he knew she didn't want him to move. Hell, he didn't want to move either, but that god-damned mess at the hospital wasn't going to wait for anybody, and already he felt he'd fallen irrevocably behind in its crush.

She sensed he was thinking ahead to the day before him and felt herself being pulled along into that dimension where sharp edges abounded and nothing flowed as smoothly as it did in their love bower. Though she felt it wise to resist departing from their Eden, she was first and last his helpmeet wherever he was. So she cinched up and got in step.

"Big meeting, huh?" she commiserated.

"Not so big as it is futile, or so I think," he bemoaned, revealing just how far he had now drifted from their leafy glade. "It's going to be one of those catch-up meetings where we detail our helpless passivity but do so in the obliquity of defining brisk new means of dealing with its consequences. You know, like welfare recipients becoming more active to demand increases in the subsidy of their helplessness, and doing it as a noble exercise of civil liberties. Except that *we* don't have any votes to sell to the highest bidder."

She knew that when he talked like this it was usually because he had collided with the unmovable mass of the State Mental Health System. Over the years on such occasions he had recited his lament that the State Hospital System shared too much of a common passivity with the Public Assistance division of the parent Office of Public Welfare. In fact, it had been demonstrated time and again, he seldom failed to point out, that officials in the one division could transfer to the other with little change in tread or rhetoric. The more he saw, the more he came to see that public service at its best, and seemingly by design, was indistinguishable from pandering to the weaknesses of the general constituency, and that only a vigilant and courageous electorate could keep it from breeding the very ills it purported to correct. However, such an electorate thus far was, likewise, indistinguishable from fantasy. Plus, he tended to write off career legislators as pimps of one shade or another. Moreover, she now sensed a sullen pugnacity being mobilized in him just at his mention of the meeting, no doubt to have that sentiment ready at hand if and when needed. All in all, their morning tryst was over, and too abruptly to suit her. That's why their evening love was so much better; the only thing then to follow their unioned moment was a conjoining sleep. Her thoughts, too, had begun to take an anticipatory turn for she now remembered that she wanted to talk to him about Todd—she had tactically avoided the issue the night before because of the several successive phone calls he had received from the hospital about some shake-down problems encountered in the transfer of patients from the new Triage Unit—and had decided to pursue the matter today when perhaps he would be more receptive. Or maybe she meant attentive. Todd's avoidance of school, episodic in the long view, was beginning to flare up again. That in itself was not greatly urgent because they had all been through successive cycles of that struggle often enough, but it was more the matter that his dereliction was beginning to take on more the character of frank truancy. Over the years he had enlisted bellyaches, headaches, fatigue, phantom fevers and chills, and various other undiagnosable maladies to underwrite his misfeasance at those times his standard barricade of dawdling failed to stay the advent of deliverance as might take the form of some class outing, a final exam, a class project, or any such enterprise that called upon his open participation. But it had happened several times that Todd had willingly enough left the house in the morning for the school bus only to slip away from school shortly after arrival, and it was only the phone calls from the principal's office in follow-up of his truancy that alerted her to the matter, though she could not pretend surprise in the discovery. Her confrontations with Todd on the matter—two thus far in as many weeks—usually brought forth his winsome, sheepish smile along with a bland explanation that he and a few friends had taken "a mental health day" and had gone to a movie. It was only when she probed about the effect his absences might have on his class work that the wall of silence would go up. It was his shutting her out that frustrated her so much and moved her to set the problem before her husband who claimed a favored channel of access to their son. Never mind that the channel seemed tuned to the protection of a special comity each hoped to preserve with the other, she knew that the problem of his truancy threatened to become, if ignored and unchecked, the means available to Todd for ruining his already indented chances for a reasonably successful transit of adolescence.

Thus, the matter qualified as a top item in their parental agenda. However, she now felt that this wasn't the best moment to bring it up. Also, if Todd breasted school adequately today, she could bring it up tonight as an issue not out of control but one deserving sustained and progressive intervention more supportive than retributive. It was important to keep things, even problems, as positive as possible, the better to reach the equally positive solutions sought. Also, by tonight her husband's meeting would be behind him and hopefully less distracting. Moreover, she considered, by electing the pixie she just might bring it up as the trick warranting their promised treat. She regarded the matter as settled.

As though on cue he let out an extended groan as he stretched.

"Time to get moving," he exhaled as he completed his stretch. With that, he gave her a quick peck on the cheek and resolutely bounded out of bed. As he was working his way into his robe he made a reluctant decision. "Hon, the meeting starts at eight. I want to be at the office early to get together some things I need to present if I'm going to try to make a convincing case. So I'll skip breakfast this morning and get going early. O.K.?" he beseeched under arched eyebrows.

She had expected it because he usually skipped breakfast when he was girding himself for battle, early meeting or no. He was convinced he fought better on an empty stomach.

"Sure," she agreed. "How about a glass of juice on the way out?"

"I'd love it," he beamed as he departed for the bathroom.

She sat in bed a moment longer to tuck away remembrance of the morning's success thus far. That done, she thought ahead to breakfast alone with Todd and Ellie and felt a wave of regret sweep over her that the family wasn't as young as it once was when he would make it a point to start Halloween with a bang by showing up at breakfast in costume to send the kids into peals of laughter. Or putting rubber spiders in their cereal, or a set of false teeth clenched on the toast. Or some such antic to send the kids off to school laden with anticipation for the nether mysteries of Allhallows Eve. Today, she rued, he'll be on his way to the hospital by the time the kids come to breakfast, which they most likely would rush through as well. She wondered if in our daily dash to get quickly to what awaits us somewhere else are we leaving far too much behind? Of course we are, but that was the way of Time, wasn't it? Still and all, there seemed to be a basic flaw to it, no matter what the office of its issue, she sighed. Further, she wondered, was it truly the future's potential that pulled us on so hurriedly, the promise of what yet needed to be; or was it more simply the push come of the failure of total satisfaction at any and every prior instance, the accumulated and pressing disappointments of all earlier moments driving the system forward with our sense of future being no more than our hectic effort to fashion a more promising footing in unmet uncertainty? Probably the latter, she suspected. If so, then vaunted Future, seen so meretricious and insincere, was the absolute and ultimate prostitute: forever beckoning, forever desirable, forever available, forever costly, and forever false. Thus, we all are destined to be deceived and exploited by her promises, but subject ever to her waiting arms. Such was Time's embrace.

"How about that, Mr. Plato!" she harrumphed. "I can do thoughts like that, too."

At that moment she heard the shower start. Something inside her quipped that the shower was mocking her soliloquy on the natural flow of things, whereupon she laughed aloud in good-natured delight.

"Trick or treat!" she yelped, arms extended in a worldly embrace. Then, all caution dispelled, she picked up his cup and took a bracing swig of his cold and rancid coffee. She weathered a grimace, and then decided aloud, "I'd better go start squeezing some oranges."

In a flurry of bedclothes, slippers, and robe she was on her way to the kitchen. Other than the hiss of the shower the house was still silent. Ellie and Todd had not yet stirred.

In a moment she was rinsing out the coffee percolator and charging it with fresh grinds. Soon the water would be bubbling along in its transubstantion into her own reveille draught. She then fished six oranges, enough for all, out of the red net bag in the bin next to the refrigerator and placed them on the work surface next to the sink. A quick probe into one of the lower cabinets produced the juicer which she then plugged in next to the as yet uncalled toaster. A quick dousing to remove unseen contaminants and the oranges were ready to be rendered. As she carefully placed a paper towel in position next to the oranges she began to think of what to have for dinner. Nothing elaborate, certainly, because at about dinner time children would be showing up at the door for Trick or Treat, and some of the more recognizable youngsters of the neighborhood would of course be invited in with their accompanying parents for appropriate comments on the skill, cuteness, or frightfulness of their costumes. So it would best be something simple and quick. Besides, Ellie and Todd would probably have their own activities scheduled for the evening, this being a Friday as well. It occurred to her as she pursued these thoughts that she did so as if she were humming them to a background rhythm. Certainly not to the sound of the shower or the bubbling percolator water, but something rhythmic, almost melodic in her. Their earlier love-making probably had something to do with it, if not a lot. But knowing herself as she did it was probably more her feeding instinct being given its play. Preparing food for her family, even orange juice and coffee, touched something unfathomably basic and vital in her, and if she did it when things were quiet enough and her mood just right she could count on hearing that inner hum, or almost. She smiled at her musings and began to slice the oranges in half neatly on the paper towel. Just as men needed to provide, she continued, women needed to feed, and each apparently took an irresistible pride and satisfaction in doing it well. She knew their love-making somehow captured both and, as with this morning, she saw her work in the other rooms of the house as either fore or after-play depending on the temporal location of their bedroom work in the diurnal schedule. She wondered if that harmonic hum she felt rather than heard within herself was the very substrate of happiness, a special toning that lent the sense of satisfaction and fulfillment to feelings and thoughts applied to one's sense of self. Wasn't it the oriental who said that harmony was everything? Also, she wondered, why was it that people were reluctant to admit to satisfaction or fulfillment, and even happiness? Guilt was the reason usually offered. Yet, she suspected that while guilt could apply in any number of cases, the more basic reason might be simpler. She suspected that happiness, like most all instinctually driven things, probably worked so much better if you weren't consciously caught up in it, like the act of breathing, and that the chagrin and embarrassment at being faced with the fact of being happy were natural devices for keeping the condition subliminal and hence more true. Later, when the toils of happiness were successfully completed, or nearly so, it was more allowable to acknowledge that secret state with the recognition "we were so happy then" along with the obligatory lament "but we didn't know it." So the happy life could be something of a trick in a bigger treat, she congratulated herself for perceiving as she applied the orange halves to the whirling cone of the juicer, and she thought it right to have it all total up to a reminder of the evening's promise, but with care not to think too keenly on it. Then, after peering off for a moment into the distance, she shrugged.

"What do you think of those oranges, Mr. Plato?" she chirped.

Just as the last orange was being squeezed the phone rang.

Beyond the annoyance of the rude interruption she wondered who could be calling at ten after seven in the morning. She had spoken to Ellie before about such early calls from her friends. As she reached for the phone she flash-alerted herself to the possibility of a Halloween prank, and with that expectation in mind she picked up the receiver.

"Hello?" she inquired.

"Good morning, Mrs. Cantrelle," the other end replied. "This is Dr. Feldman. I'm sorry to call so early, but I was hoping to speak with Dr. Cantrelle. Is he available?"

"Yes he is. Just a minute, please," she returned.

As she placed the receiver down she noted that it was rare for a resident to call, and especially in the early morning. She puzzled over the reason as she set out for the bedroom to fetch her husband.

The shower had stopped and so he must be dressing or shaving, she surmised as she approached the bedroom. As she entered he was pulling on a shirt.

"For me?" he anticipated by virtue of her approach.

"Yes, it's Dr. Feldman and he wants to talk to you," she said.

An immediate frown of concern covered his face. As he pondered the possible nature of the problem coming his way he moved to the phone on the bedside table and picked it up while silently acknowledging his perplexity to his wife.

"Yes, Dr. Feldman," he answered tentatively.

"Good morning, Dr. Cantrelle, I'm sorry to bother you so early, but something's come up I thought you would like to know about right away," the resident explained with some hesitance.

"Yes, go on," Cantrelle replied more affirmatively.

"Remember that patient, Winston Jordan, the college student from Franklinton? Admitted a little over two months ago? Our first Blush case?" the resident described.

"Yes, I do," Cantrelle affirmed. Of course he remembered the case. How could he ever forget it? He wanted the resident to get to the point which he now sensed might be dire.

"Well, he died some time during the night," the resident announced.

"Died! From what?" Cantrelle demanded in alarm.

"We don't know," Feldman explained. "According to Nursing he was O.K. last night, about the same as he had been for the past month or so. They put him to bed at the usual time last night, and when they made bed checks later he was sleeping soundly. About an hour ago when they made morning checks they found him peacefully dead in bed. No sign of struggle or distress. His vital signs at bedtime last night were normal."

"An embolus?" Cantrelle offered through his dismay.

"I asked about that" Feldman replied, "particularly if they heard any heavy breathing or anything to suggest acute discomfort. They said not. And his bed clothes weren't disturbed especially. They were sure he didn't have any swelling of his legs or feet yesterday because they would have noticed that. They think he just stopped breathing in his sleep."

"He didn't receive any new medications yesterday, did he?" Cantrelle searched.

"No, none at all," Feldman replied.

"No resuscitation attempt, I guess," Cantrelle asked, his shock now evolving into a more controlled search.

"No. When they discovered him he was already cold. They figure he died sometime in the middle of the night," Feldman explained.

Cantrelle had now regained some composure and his thoughts began to project ahead of the present moment. After a brief silence he returned to the waiting resident.

"Thank you for calling and letting me know, Dr. Feldman. When you make out your report make sure you mention what you've described to me. I'll check with you later in the day if I need your help. How did the rest of the night go?" Cantrelle asked solicitously.

"Not too bad. Only one admission. A few nuisance calls for aspirin. Got about four hours of sleep," Feldman reviewed.

"Good," Cantrelle consoled. "Thanks again for calling." He then slowly returned the phone to its cradle. As he did so he looked up at Laura who was standing by waiting to be relieved of the awful dread come of hearing only his half of the call.

"Who's dead?" she demanded, suspecting it was most likely a patient but fearing other possibilities.

"You might remember our talking about that college boy patient at lunch after the symposium? The time I got a call and Clay and I went on to the hospital? The son of one of Jess' friends? Well, he died last night in his sleep," Cantrelle transmitted, his mind noticeably far ahead of those fey particulars.

"Oh," emitted Laura as compromise between general human compassion at such a tragedy and her relief that it wasn't a lot closer.

"He was our first Blush patient. You know, that new street drug," Cantrelle noted in an effort to help her focus her response.

She only vaguely remembered that part of it and thought it just as well.

He continued to ponder this stark turn of events as he resumed tucking in his shirt. His mind was already at Moreland.

"Your juice will be ready in a jiffy," she assured as she left to return to the kitchen. She knew he would need a few undistracted moments to review any change in plans incident to the call and she also knew that when he left the house he would now do so with even more push than usual and certainly with heightened preoccupation. God, how the morning had changed, she lamented as she moved toward the kitchen. She passed the kids' rooms enroute and heard their earliest stirrings. Muted music was coming from Todd's room.

"Dead," he repeated to himself as he yanked impatiently at his tie. The thought sent a shiver through the tentative agenda he had formed in his own mind for the meeting this morning. He quickly estimated which of the points he had planned to make were now diminished and which ones were sharpened by this awful event. *All* were diminished, he saw in a flush of shame at the thought of using the death of a twenty-one-year-old boy to extend his own program, and yet all were strengthened by the now escalated gravity of this Blush thing and its relation, if any, to the boy's death. All of the points he had intended to make dealt with the prospect of locally-based research on the prevailingly enlarged problem of Blush victims, now arriving in ascending numbers. The tawdry thought came into view that it would be most infelicitous for the boy's death to be in some way linked to hospital negligence, actual or imagined. A shift of focus from the disease to the constant issue of staff performance, which so often served as a crafty displacement from more challenging issues, now needed to be avoided as never before. Staff performance was a time-honored red herring readily enlisted as quarry for reformers who could not accept the natural frailties of the system or the formidability of the diseases themselves, and it was similar to the high priest proclaiming the typhoon to have been caused by the sins of the villagers and seeing penitential human sacrifice as a more valid approach to salvation than would ever be the study of meteorology. He hoped he would not have to sit through another one of those primitive lynch exercises this morning, now that the issue of mortality was imposed upon the Blush problem. His cynicism led him directly to a pinch of guilt over having already established himself as the primary respondent in this tragedy. What about poor Jess, who was probably on the phone this very moment notifying the family? And what a hell of a way for the pained family to begin their day. He put on his jacket, checked himself in the mirror, and hoped that his selfishness was now suitably contained for him to go forth and endorse the essential but injured humanity of the work ahead. He truly hoped so.

He strode out of the bedroom and made his way up the hallway towards the kitchen. As he passed the kids' rooms he could hear their bustling about inside, and so decided on at least an acknowledgment.

"Hey, kids," he shouted. "I have to leave early, so Happy Halloween! I'll catch you all later tonight."

Ellie and Todd shouted back their recommendations for tricks and treats, Todd over the now louder strains of his music.

It was good to hear the fresh and busy sounds of their privileged youth. The contrast to his earlier thoughts helped him enter the kitchen in a more accessible frame of mind. Laura noted it immediately and applied herself to him as she circled his neck with her arms.

"I know the people at the hospital need you, too," she allowed as she sustained the embrace, "but I'm not going to forfeit all my selfishness so early in the day. Give me a call later and let me know how things are going, O.K.?" she entreated. She knew it was not going to be an easy morning for him and she had already begun to mount the vigil of worry. "And now for the magic potion that will confer invincibility," she da-dahhed as she released him to reach for the glass of orange juice. She handed his to him and held up hers in toast. They clicked glasses and drank as they tucked away the vision of each other for later use.

He drained his glass and then held it chest high as he cocked his head back in a pensive tilt. He twisted his mouth slightly, the better to savor some elusive notion, and then returned the glass to the counter,

"If God didn't want us to have a good time he never would have created confetti," he declared.

She broke out into a relieved giggle.

"Where did that come from?" she puzzled in mock concern.

"Heard it years ago on a TV comedy show," he confessed as he scooped her up in a hug that lifted her off her feet. As he held her aloft he gave her a kiss more athletic than tender, and then returned her to her feet. "Gotta get going," he announced.

As she walked him to the door she took relief in his apparent return to a grittier frame of mind. The orange juice, no doubt, she quipped to herself. He picked up his briefcase waiting for him in the foyer, grabbed his coat from the closet, and opened the door. He leaned back to give the farewell kiss on the cheek.

"I'll call later, and maybe even remind you we have a date tonight," he affirmed.

He pulled away from her smile and trotted to his car in the parking bay. A quick assessment of the weather enroute—a brilliantly crisp autumn day just right for apple dunking—and he was in his car and maneuvering it down the driveway to the street. Then, a final quick exchange of waves with Laura lingering in the doorway and he was on his way.

In a minute or so he was again on the main thoroughfare which would take him to Moreland, and as his home and family receded behind him he could feel that odd metamorphosis come upon him whereby he shaded from the force field of his family and home on to that of his work and Moreland as he transited some imaginary point of equipotentiality about five minutes into his trip, much as though he were moving out of range of one radio station into that of another. In that regard, he noted, the music this morning was mercifully not something from that muse of gloom, Mahler, but more acceptably the elegantly evil "Mephisto Waltz." He seldom strayed from the classical music station, and especially so when driving, except in early afternoon when he checked in with BBC for the news, American newscasts being thoroughly avoidable as productions bearing the show biz stamp of Radio City entertainment. He needed music this morning to keep him from sinking deeper into the morass of anticipatory angst pulsing him forward to the meeting just moments ahead. He wanted to escape into triviality for a few minutes, and his car and its radio constituted his special sensory control chamber where conative input could be managed better than anywhere else in his world.

The absence of a desk phone went a long way in conferring that special state. Certainly, being alone was basic to the arrangement. Also, the frequent whimsy of the radio station's programming definitely contributed. It was not unlike the station to play Handel's "Water Music" during a downpour, or the Bacchanal from "Samson and Delilah" after a news brief about some public figure caught at some saucy indiscretion. Once when an international panel judged an American car all around better than an equivalent Japanese model, the station followed up the announcement with the playing of Haydn's "Surprise" symphony. And that was followed by Mozart's "Exultate Jubilate." Over the years he had developed an intimate fondness for the station and its clever people and drew upon their offerings daily in sustaining that small segment of his life still privately his. In view of what he suspected was ahead for today's venue, that small piece of him was, for the moment, all the more important, and he wished to indulge it for the while.

As he drove East the blazing sunlight diffused through his windshield, almost blinding him with the overwhelming newness of the day. He loved the sensation of it as he squinted his way along, adjusting the visor as necessary. Thus far, the balance of affects was upbeat despite the calamitous phone call earlier, and the consoling life-goes-on platitude was played out along his route by swirls of toilet paper draping hedges, mailboxes knocked over here and there, some soaped up car windows now and again—all leftovers from the previous night's mischief. When he was a boy, he recalled, it was mostly trick and very little treat, and all was accomplished on Halloween night. Now, tricks were discreetly separated from the treats by a twenty-four-hour interim, the better to give each fuller play, perhaps. In his day, things were not so orderly or contrived. But nor was there a problem with drugs.

He quickly returned his attention to the music which had now become the sardonic "Danse Macabre," and the jerky, sonorous chords of the violin lead made imps and skeletons cavort hellishly before his mind's eye. It was impossible *not* to be fascinated by the horrible, he conceded. The essential ambivalence in everything human decreed it to be so, despite civilized preferences; and efforts to package neatly our less noble urges failed to alter a basic, and perhaps quite base, truth: we were all good, we were all evil, and we all enjoyed it each way. The issue, more correctly, was one of being honest about it, and *that* we all weren't. And, as a group probably couldn't be, because the loss of illusion would be much too disruptive socially, at least as long as we lived in a world in which our guiding notables were sprung more from passion than from reason. And thus far, only Athena could lay claim to the latter, and she certainly wasn't the vogue these days. "Martha sprung from the head of Palmer?" he dangled wickedly in his now impious mind. That sportive blasphemy was followed by a bolt of bell-ringing curiosity as to what William J. Palmer, M.D., would think and do in the situation now facing the hospital. Or more precisely, how would he direct the meeting this morning? Interesting questions, he mused. From what he had learned of the esteemed Dr. Palmer's style, he could imagine the meeting's hosting a think-tank perspective authored by undisputed scholarly privilege. According to all, Palmer wore that mantle consummately well. Nowadays, the haute couture of administrative style was cast in shades of fiscal green, not academic ivy. He wondered how Palmer would manage that arrangement. Or would he even be permitted to? He was now less than a mile away from the hospital and the malevolent opening bars of "A Night on Bald Mountain" jolted his anticipation into affrighted vigilance. God, the programmer was going ape this morning, he blinked. How about a little Boccherini for relief, he pleaded. But, given the cast of the morning thus far, sweetness and light would in itself be profane. He abruptly remembered that Boccherini as well had composed a piece that could fit the day—his "Casa diDiablo." It seemed there was room enough for everybody on a morning like this.

The hospital's towers were now in view, and the gothic peaks of the older buildings rose above the cumulus trees now just about a week or so beyond full color, but glorious yet. As he neared the grounds' entrance the closer trees filled up the view as they seemed to rise up with his approach and swallow the turreted towers of the looming buildings. Entering the grounds gave the impression of setting out in a forest that contained the greensward on which the buildings were clustered. The effect was most pronounced in the summer when the trees were densely verdant.

He drove on and wound his way to the MOB and to his waiting parking slot. Soon enough in place he flicked off the ignition and sat staring ahead for the moment it took the engine to shudder to a halt. His arrival was now official, and the momentary stillness served as an administrative point of origin for the course he would follow today and which would take him God knows where. The death of a young patient was not, mercifully, a frequent enough event to confer familiarity on what lay ahead. Moreover, several very restive notions playing on the periphery of his mind—and now ominously so, given the morning's affliction—were beginning to coalesce into a solid dread approaching presentiment. Maybe—just *maybe*—the meeting would provide the right medium for drawing those notions forth in a context which didn't cast them as out and out alarmist. Maybe, maybe, always maybe, he shook his head as he opened the car door and got out.

Playful gusts and their gamboling leaves seemed to accompany him to the entrance of the MOB. He pushed through the building's double doors to enter the relative silence of the main hallway. Too silent, he observed. A little bustle would have been welcome this morning. As he walked down the empty hallway to his office he was nagged by a mounting sense of loneliness, maybe even abandonment. He was becoming more aware of his dread of the morning's meeting, probably in large part because of feeling unprepared for it though he couldn't imagine what more he could do to achieve a sense of readiness. Maybe it was just because he might have to admit to helplessness, especially in view of the morning's baleful turn, and the prospect of submitting to helplessness in the face of challenge just happened to be his most private nightmare.

As he strode up the hallway he could hear bits of conversation coming from his office. He estimated that someone was chatting with Mrs. Andretti in the outer office, perhaps waiting for him. As he neared the office doorway he made out the voice of Elaine Rolf. Since it was so rare of her to come to his office he was well on to doubting that she was waiting for him, but their abrupt silence upon his entering the room bode otherwise. The expression on their faces not only told him both were aware of the morning's event but that Elaine Rolf was indeed here to see him.

"Good morning, Mrs. Rolf. It's seldom I have the pleasure of your visit," he greeted in general invitation.

"Good morning, Dr. Cantrelle," she replied simply.

"Mrs. Rolf wondered if she could talk with you for few minutes before you go to the meeting with Administration this morning," Mrs. Andretti interceded in explanation.

"Good morning, Mrs. Andretti," he mentioned belatedly, as much out of their standard courtesy as to give himself an extra moment to think. He sensed that Mrs. Andretti strongly endorsed Mrs. Rolf's petition for an audience. No need to think beyond that, he concluded. "Of course. Please come in, Mrs. Rolf," he complied, wondering at the nature of her surprise visit. As he puzzled over it he had the vagrant thought that he now wouldn't have time this morning for a moment of wall staring to prepare him for the meeting.

He led the way into his office and directed her to the chair beside his desk. As he docked his briefcase and shed his hat and coat in the direction of the hall tree he opened conversation with an idle allusion at having to wake up the office. He then sat down at his desk.

"Something important, eh?" he asked.

"I think so," she nodded, setting her blond curls in motion over the turtleneck of her bulky sweater. "When I got in this morning the whole place was abuzz about Winston Jordan's death. Everybody liked him and felt so sorry for him, you know."

"I do know," he assured.

"I was talking to Dr. Morello about it when the phone rang," she continued. "It was the nurse, Mrs. Perry, in Building Twelve. She said that a patient, John Frieden, wanted to see me right away. You remember him, don't you? You interviewed him that time."

"Yes, I remember him very well. The residents called him the 'almost ran,' didn't they?" he replied.

"Right. I worked with him while he was on the ITU and he really tried to help himself along. Said it was his last chance. A couple of times he mentioned he liked your being straight with him and not talking to him like he was some kind of a specimen," she added.

Cantrelle felt a whiff of embarrassment at her comment and thought it better to say nothing.

"So I went to Building Twelve right away because I figured that something important came up and he wanted me to know about it," she continued. "We had agreed that if he felt himself slipping as he got nearer to discharge he was to contact me or the social worker in his building before it got too far. So I got over there—it couldn't have been later than eight fifteen—and he was waiting at the nurses station. He said he wanted to talk to me, privately. So we went into one of the offices. And then he handed me this," She extended to Cantrelle a neatly folded translucent paper packet. "He said to give this to you; that you'd be interested in it and would know what to do with it."

Cantrelle trembled as he reached for the packet. He knew what it was, or what it was purported to be, and he hesitated for the briefest instant before accepting it because of the inane thought that he shouldn't let his fingerprints get on it. He held it gingerly by its edge between thumb and forefinger and stared at it in controlled dread as she continued.

"I knew what it was, but I asked him anyway," she explained. "He said it was some of what his friend took. I said that if it was Blush, where did he get it? He said that I was asking too much and that I should give it to you. And that's all he was going to say about it. But I asked him how he knew it was Blush. He said the packet was too neatly folded, just like the other one. And besides, he recognized the particular tint of the paper."

Cantrelle continued to examine the packet as she spoke and was now turning it over from hand to hand as fear yielded to curiosity. It was, indeed, neatly folded as though the contents were packaged by a machine. Also, the translucent paper carried a beige tint he would not have noted if his attention hadn't been called to it, though it was the sort of thing an addict or dealer might. Or an artist. He could just make out the powdered contents through the hazy paper as he held the packet against the light to peer at the "neat bag" more closely as he spoke.

"Who else knows about this?" he asked.

"Only Dr. Morello, because I went back to the ITU right away and called to see if you had come in yet. He was waiting for me to get back because he knew where I had gone. I showed him the packet," she said.

There were unnegotiably strict rules and directives regarding the confiscation and disposition of contraband drugs brought on campus by patients, visitors, or anyone else, and security spent no small part of its time monitoring the milieu to prevent drug trafficking in the highly vulnerable and highly available patient population of the hospital. He would, of course, later turn the packet over to Security, but for the moment Mrs. Rolf and Dr. Morello had already violated the spirit of the rule by transmitting the drug in accordance with the patient's wishes rather than abiding by the procedures in the regulations.

He placed the packet on the desk before him and watched it for an odd moment, and then he turned to Mrs. Rolf.

"Did Dr. Morello open it?" he asked.

"Yes, he did," she supplied. "He looked at it and pushed the powder around a little bit with a pencil tip. He said he couldn't be certain, but it looked just like ordinary heroin and not different in any way he could tell."

Cantrelle figured that Morello, who was destined for Forensic Psychiatry, would not have been capable of resisting the opportunity to examine the packets' contents, but he needed to have that fact verified in case any questions came up later at Council, or more immediately at this morning's meeting where he would present the packet to highlight the ominous point he intended to make. He didn't want to appear unknowing or uninformed of its particulars when display of the packet ignited salvoes of frantic questioning.

Mrs. Rolf was becoming notably uncomfortable with his line of questioning. Being aware of her discomfort and not wishing to appear unappreciative of her generous deed, he decided to deflect the focus a bit.

"I guess we could call this 'gift horse'," he quipped.

"That's awful!" she chortled in relief as she joined him in naughty disport.

"I suppose I should take a peek at this stuff myself. It simply won't do to have the residents know more about these things than their Director does," he continued more brightly.

He proceeded to open the crisply folded packet, and he did so with surgical precision, careful not to have any of the powder flick out on his desk. When the contents were bared, the small amount of fine white powder about the size of a fingernail seemed anticlimactic to the heavy dread its aura carried. He stared carefully at its pure and snowy whiteness which belied any tint of evil, not sure of what he was looking for, and noted that it looked all the world like ordinary powdered sugar. For something so wickedly destructive it should be gray, or sooty, or grimy in hue, he mused as he continued to stare into the small patch of deceptively blameless white powder.

"Doesn't look like much, does it?" he mentioned to include the patiently attentive Mrs. Rolf in his musings.

"That's the same thing I said to Dr. Morello," she agreed, "and he said there was only one way to check out its authenticity."

"Right," Cantrelle concurred as he began to re-fold the packet "and that's to ship it to the state lab and let them do their analytic magic. Find out what the louse is, by God. And maybe come up with some hint on how to counteract its effects. You know, it could turn out that in our treatment of the psychosis caused by the louse the medications we're using might be making it more destructive," he shared with her to convey the degree of importance he attached to her feat of acquisition. "You know, like PCP and Chlorpromazine. Wouldn't that be something?"

She smiled modestly at his oblique plaudit.

He sensed that enough had been said for the moment.

"Again, thanks for waiting for me this morning," he shifted. "Please tell Dr. Morello I'll be in touch with him later today after the meeting. Oh, also tell him to keep quiet about your meeting with the patient. Got to protect confidences all around, right?" he added as a measure of reassurance to her.

They rose simultaneously and he accompanied her to the door. He opened it for her and she left. He watched her wave a farewell to Mrs. Andretti as she passed on toward the hallway. He lingered at the door to listen as her footsteps diminished in the distance.

"A real trooper," he smiled to himself. He had always liked her and often teased her about her Pennsylvania Dutch background—good, solid, dependable stock, he covertly approved—and she, just as covertly proud of it, responded with mock indignation at the liberties he took. As he turned to regain his desk he estimated that her husband had to be aware of his grand good fortune. A steady player, she was, and great legs, too.

He playfully chided himself for his momentary lapse in professional rectitude, but as he reached his desk the sight of the packet abruptly brought him back to the grim store of this morning's events. He stood before his desk and stared at the packet, almost visualizing a nimbal question mark hovering over it. He didn't want to be pulled back into mincing dread. So, half aloud and to himself he breezed, "Now this is carrying Trick or Treat much too far."

Satisfied with that fillip he sat down in his chair and assumed the necessary set for a dash of wall staring to prepare himself for the meeting.

He wasn't a full minute into it when the office intercom buzzed.

He groaned as he reached for the speaker button and worked at shaping a cordial response as he pressed it.

"Yes, Mrs. Andretti?"

"Dr. Cantrelle, I hate to interrupt, but it's just a few minutes before nine and they specifically asked that you be present. Dr. Weaver especially."

"Thank you, Mrs. Andretti, I'm on my way," he relented.

"Might as well stop futtzing around and get over there and get it over with," he groused to himself as he sprang from his chair and swung into his coat. He then carefully picked up the packet and put it in his coat pocket where he cradled it protectively in his hand. He then strode out, waved his way past Mrs. Andretti with his free hand and trotted down the hallway, marshalling enroute a delinquent concern about being late for the meeting.

Once outside and pointed in the direction of the Administrative building he felt the preparatory and necessary mind-shift begin to take form in him. Going from the clinical-investigative to the administrative-operational was to him the equivalent of moving from Athens to Sparta with all the implied differences in values, purposes, and even dialect. In his reckoning, it was the happy emissary indeed who could unite the two in congenial venture, and he tried to do just that in his administration of the training program, once even video-taping a training series on administrative style as a function of group process and its principles. But all too often he found such an alliance to be a shaky one because of a fundamental difference in interests and priorities, which difference, while often forgiving and accommodating in halcyon times, would tend to foster divisive partisanship in the face of knottier problems. The regrettable splitting process, he held. In that regard, he now worried that the all too often polarization of issues he saw in his own office and even in his very own person might play itself out this very morning in the membership of the meeting awaiting him up the street. If it did, it wouldn't be the first time he would end up holding forth in high fustian for education and research in an effort to shame the godless Philistines of bureaucratic tyranny into right contrition. But today the stakes were too high for such theatrics, however satisfying. Yet, his wishing it all to be sensibly amicable and mature would not necessarily make it so, even if he carefully avoided adding to even basic Council friction. So, damn it, just to be safe and ready he would keep a direct line open to his store of canny truculence.

Now set, he picked up his step as he made for the Board Room. The chill was fading from the air as the cloudless sun soon made rapid inroads into the night's carry-over pall. It was going to be one of those brilliantly fair days.

He walked up to the double doors of the building, tugged one open, entered the vestibule, then squeezed through the second door and bounded up the several steps to reach the tiled hallway. Dr. Palmer's shrine glowed as always, and as he walked by he again wondered as he gave a quick search of the portrait's expression what this noble forbearer would do at a time like this. No answer came, so he continued up the hallway to the Board Room to see if there might be an answer there.

Not hesitating long enough to allow uncertainty to catch up with him he pushed the paneled oak door open and entered. The Council was at full attendance and in place at the conference table, he noted in a quick glance, but again a taut silence recorded the absence of the usual roundelay of the group's preliminary banter. Nor was there the normal ripple of greetings that confirmed group complementarity. Already he was sorry he had come as he silently made his way to his seat, shedding his coat enroute. He settled into his chair and took quick stock of the gathering. Martha was intently tidying up an arrangement of several papers before her. Jess was sitting deep in his chair as though gravity were pulling more heavily upon him while he stared beyond the table at some distant point underneath. Ruth Fawcett, the Chief Nurse, already looked tired as she rested her hands in her lap and kept watch over a clinical chart directly in front of her on the table. Dr. Lyle Benson, Head of Psychology and subbing for Saul Klein, was gazing through the large bay window in survey of the grounds colorful ambience, while Harriet Simpson of Social Work and Charlie Riegel of Administration seemed perplexed by the group's silence though compliant with it. John Wingate of Maintenance diligently worked at his fingernails with a pen knife.

"I think we can get started now," Corley announced benignly as she adjusted her height in her chair. "I initially called this meeting for follow-up on our previous one and to give you a progress report on how we were doing with the Triage Unit in particular and the admission rate in general. I also had a few announcements to make from the DMH—and I'll get around to them later—but last night something happened that I think we ought to bring up first."

He could tell who hadn't yet learned of the boy's death by whose ears perked up at her remark. It seemed that only he, Jess, and Ruth Fawcett were thus far in on the know.

"Last night," she continued, "the patient, Winston Jordan, died in his sleep. He was our first Blush patient, you might recall."

The unknowers now searched each other's faces for an explanation while the knowers waited.

"So far," she resumed, "all indications are that he died peacefully as he slept with no sign of trauma, intercurrent illness, or negligence," tactically adding the last word in address of the inveterate question cast up by the dread of clinical misadventure.

As she took a moment to read the group's reaction she noted that Cantrelle didn't signal his usual call to arms when presented with a damaging surprise. She arched her eyebrows at him in request of an explanation.

"The resident on call notified me a few hours ago," he complied as he offered a sympathetic glance in the direction of Weaver.

She nodded and returned to her remarks.

"The family has been notified and we're doing everything we can to help those poor people through this ordeal," she continued. "Dr. Weaver has been in touch with them and they'll be arriving sometime later today. In the meantime I want all of you who've had anything to do with the case to be discreet in your discussion of it and to caution your people to be likewise. Distortions and rumors always brew up around an event like this and we don't want the patient's family to be subjected to any thoughtless or insensitive talk about their son's death. He was liked by the staff and everybody pitied him so much that there's bound to be a lot of talk going around once his death becomes generally known."

"Don't we have any idea as to what caused it?" Harriet Simpson appealed with urgency.

"Yeah, there's got to be some idea as to why it happened," Benson seconded. "I know that you can't be definite just yet, but there's got to be something to go on."

"This morning as the charge nurse was making her six-thirty rounds she found him dead in bed," Corley replied evenly. "He had apparently died sometime during the night. Nothing unusual was noted during the night, and when he went to bed at the usual time he seemed to be clinically no different from earlier in the day. Vital signs were normal then. And he offered no complaints."

"I heard that he had become pretty much uncommunicative," Benson pursued.

"That's true," Weaver agreed, now joining the interchange. "He had just about reached the point of total care, and, because of that, nursing was watching him all the more carefully. Incontinence was beginning and he also had to be helped with his food. So, if anything, he was under increased scrutiny more recently, especially so since we had no idea how far his dementia would go," he detailed.

"Now we know," Riegel snapped.

"Nursing checked with the attendants and even with other patients to find out if anybody had noticed anything during the day or early evening to suggest that he was in any kind of discomfort or distress, or if there was anything different about him. Nobody observed anything of the sort," Corley continued in an effort to smooth the discussion along.

"The family has agreed to an autopsy," Weaver added disconsolately, "and maybe we'll get the answer there." A moment of silence hung.

"But don't we have any hunches to go on?" Benson persisted, unable to wait.

There was a palpable reluctance to pursue the particulars, and Cantrelle could feel the weight of doing just that devolve upon Martha and Jess. Yet, their positions did not allow them the pleasure of parley in the hypothetic or conjectural. They could not stray far from the known, however meager, because any and everything they said, no matter how casually, had an *ex cathedra* ring to it. And especially so in a situation such as this one where even a considered speculation could become, within the hour and after a few embellished transmissions, a traveling fiction preferred by all to the temporary vacuum imposed by more deliberate investigation.

"He was a college kid, wasn't he? Here because of that strange, new, street drug?" Wingate groped.

"Yes. He was our first contact with Blush," Fawcett explained.

"Think maybe somehow he got some more of it? What do you think?" Wingate posed.

"We're considering all possibilities in our review of the matter," Corley said carefully, "and we won't be able to have a complete report until probably next week."

"His parents will certainly ask. I think we should have something ready, even if it's tentative," Benson suggested.

Cantrelle estimated that Jess might regard that comment as gratuitous, even egregious, though he detected nothing in his demeanor to indicate so, for he merely nodded. Perhaps the comment was akin to what Jess himself felt and thus likely heard as an offer of support.

"What part of the state are the parents from?" Benson continued.

"They're from Ohio," Weaver intoned.

The moment of silence that followed announced that those who hadn't been aware of the residence issue were framing problems now likely to arise in the inquiry.

"You mean he's not a state resident?" Benson asked incredulously.

"No, he isn't. He was a student at Franklinton when he was admitted," Corley supplied.

"Well, then, how did he qualify for treatment here? We usually transfer non-residents to facilities in their home states after emergency treatment. Was he being prepared for transfer?" Benson queried for those who shared his surprise.

"We'd just reached the point in his treatment to firm up transfer arrangements. In fact, his transfer was scheduled for next Tuesday. He was to go to a Skilled Nursing Facility near his home," Corley offered.

"But if he had reached the point of total care, what took us so long? Seems to me we should have acted sooner," Benson persisted, now doing so with focused intent. Not only was he now speaking for the other members of the group who had not been aware of this administrative culpability, but he was also, in the style of Devil's Advocate, rehearsing for Corley and Weaver the line of interrogation they most likely would receive from the DMH when the problem became known there. This preparatory ordeal, a dry run among friends and supporters, was one of the sinister benefits of Council function. At least, this Council, anyway. Thus, often in the face of special necessity the Council meeting took on the flavor of an administrative psychodrama with its membership playing the sundry roles of the extra-mural agencies and interests to which the hospital was respondent. But, as with all effective psychodrama, a real play often arose within the staged one, in the fashion of *Pagliacci*. That very phenomenon was now at hand and evolving right along with Benson's questioning, each level being jockeyed forth by the more personal sentiments moving into focus.

"The family felt our facilities were perfectly adequate to their son's need and we felt that if his evaluation and treatment were conducted closer to the circumstances of onset of his disorder more could be learned directly about the problem, and that maybe we could use that information in arriving at a more definitive treatment," Corley explained tactically. "Plus, he was the first of a kind and we felt obligated to do as complete an evaluation as we could before acting on a transfer," she added in palpably strained justification.

Benson hesitated for a moment to rein in his impulse to go for the jugular and hold more to a mock inquisitional tone in the matter. Benson, like Clay Moyer, was a devoted and uncompromising member of the hospital family. Younger than Moyer, he had risen in the departmental ranks by dint of pure professional ability plus a touch for administrative precision that seemed to switch on, like a beam, immediately upon contact with any issue smudged by managerial murkiness.

"I'm sure all of that applies, Dr. Corley," he resumed as he adjusted his tone, "but the fact that he is—was—a non-resident and died in patient status is enough to raise questions about the wisdom of his being kept here at all. The hospital, the DMH, and now even the Commonwealth are party to his death when it all could have been avoided. If his family decides to question our treatment of his illness, or if anything suggests the hospital was negligent in any way, or if—God forbid—his death turns out to be a result of mismanagement on our part then our ass is Mudd, and I'm sure you know it."

"I do know it," Corley replied tolerantly, seemingly resolved to accept full blame. "I expect that some questions will arise."

"The family won't cause any trouble," Weaver interceded protectively. "I've kept in touch with them almost daily and they're grateful for all that we've done. They know they couldn't have gotten anything better anywhere else, and they know we took a special interest in their son."

"But how do we know that?" Benson persisted as he properly traced out the inveterate worst possible scenario. "How do we know that if even a small discrepancy in his treatment pops up they won't see their grief in another light, say more like injury demanding compensation any number of legal jackals out there would be delighted to take to litigation for them? In fact, they'll probably start getting calls today from bottom-feeding lawyers announcing their sympathy, and availability."

"The family is not like that," Weaver insisted.

"But how can you be so sure?" Benson challenged.

"Because the parents are personal friends of mine," Weaver revealed.

The silence that followed said it all. No more questions were necessary, and the delicacy of Weaver's—and Corley's—positions was now perfectly clear. Weaver had acted out of compassion and personal kindness in securing the patient's stay at Moreland, skirting the soulless rules and regulations governing the system, and Corley had permitted it. An act of humanity, indeed, but completely indefensible when mischance invited a return of lynch law as the system's alter method of dealing with its violators. The group pondered on the vulnerability of both their Superintendent and their Assistant Superintendent, and in the silence Cantrelle could almost hear the gears of predation shift so as to reconnoiter another flank. Over the years he had come to know how the Council thought.

As if on cue, Riegel resumed.

"Even if the family is cooperative, we still have the problem of the DMH when it finds out we harbored a non-resident. Will our justifications wash with them? I'm not so sure. They've always thought that we're a little too hotsy-totsy for our own good, thanks to Palmer, and they never pass up an opportunity to rub our noses in it. So I don't think they'll back off from this one. I think they'll try to burn our asses," he warned.

"I agree," Benson concurred, "and I think we'd better get our story straight for when they come knocking. They're already all worked up about the admission rates getting out of hand, and when they hear of our keeping a non-resident—and then one who dies!—well, I kinda think it's gonna hit the fan."

Several of the other members nodded sententiously. Corley looked at her Council in silence and held back a wave of dread which was barely visible in the momentary widening of her eyes. He wondered if she felt she was losing the support of her own people and that the lynching was already beginning. Probably. Moreover, his annoyance titre had been rising as the group dwelled on shoring up administrative defenses and identifying suitable sacrifices while failing to address what he felt was the more urgent and valid issue of how to combat an evolving medical catastrophe. He saw the group's focus on itself—wrapped in the mantle of protecting Dr. Corley, Jess, and the hospital at large—as a self-serving regression designed to defend against a small-minded assault expected from the DMH. He allowed that, individually, the membership probably hadn't lost sight of its nobler purpose—to lead, not to cower—but groups, any group, being what they are, tended otherwise in concert with the membership's apparent need to play on each other's fears, with the result that too often an us-against-them mentality was called forth to shape group strategy and tactic. For the Council to slide into that mordant cast this morning was something he could not countenance, not while he held in his hand a neat packet to keep him, talisman-like, free of that curse. He decided that it all now totaled up to his cue, and he was careful not to look at anyone in particular when he spoke.

"Ladies and gentlemen, I think we're missing the point a bit," he began. "I agree that we should be mindful of our position—and our culpability. That goes without saying and it applies at all times, not just when we hit a rough spot. And I agree that we should keep clear our options right along with our concerns. Again, something that goes without saying. But I don't think we should spend all our time," he could hear his voice rise as he felt control slip away—"assigning blame and measuring fault, and doing so to generate cover for our tender asses." The pugnacious edge to his voice was now in place. "It should be clear to anybody who has the slightest inclination to see it that Dr. Weaver and Dr. Corley did a humane thing by allowing that boy to stay here for treatment, and, I might add, for probably the most complete evaluation he could get this side of NIH. You all understand, of course," he added with a bite, "this boy's disease is something no one has ever seen before. So, from a medical standpoint, there is no, quote, proper or customary, unquote, treatment center where he should otherwise have been. Any place where good care and a keen diagnostic effort were available was a right place for him, state residency requirements notwithstanding. And as Martha said, his problem began in our neighborhood so perhaps we had a certain moral responsibility to take care of him as best we could and use the resources we had, as well as those of the larger neighborhood, to piece together the bits of the puzzle surrounding the onset of his disorder. On top of that, Jess tried to help a friend in time of anguished need. For shame, huh? Not only that, if you, as a group, are having a little trouble seeing this tragedy from a humanitarian standpoint you might note that it now sorely behooves this Council to know as much as it can about this plague which lately is descending upon us in earnest. Even though we didn't in the beginning know he was going to be the first of many, we still had an ethical responsibility to do what we could to learn as much about this awful disease as we could so that not only might we do our best for him, but as it turns out, also for the many others like him we soon learned would follow. Those *bona fide* state residents! O.K.? So I would regard his staying here for evaluation and treatment as being very much in keeping with our mandate as a hospital, but which, I agree, may not be in total keeping with our personal identity as a collection of timid civil servants dedicated to keeping our asses safe. Also, there was perhaps something providential in his coming to us, and I'll say as much to his parents, because his receiving treatment here, in our catchment, where this plague was introduced to the nation, maybe even to the entire world, put us in the forefront of meeting the challenge this pestilence begs for understanding it and, if we're lucky, arresting it. Instead of rehearsing our fright, we should be commending Martha and Jess for managing to do the sane and human thing in what too often is a cruelly mindless system. And—I wish to emphasize—we should, as a group, be resolving to stand by what they, and we, have done as something we had the opportunity and great good fortune to offer in one of the kinder and better efforts the mental health system of this state was fundamentally designed to provide, even if occasionally to a *non-resident*!" He paused to catch his breath as the others looked at him dumbstruck. Every once in a while he would go on a tirade like this, but neither he nor the others had expected it this morning. But it had now begun, and it would have to run its course, as all present had long come to know. So they listened as he was carried away. "And I, too, don't for one minute think that the DMH is primed to see the issue so charitably, certainly not as I would like to think they should, but I also don't think we should forfeit our own decency because of it," he held. "The DMH is too far from the bedside and too close to the flagpole to judge of the humane—that's *our* task—but if we give them no clear signal as to what we believe to be *medically* important they'll be just too damned happy to tell us what their cushy caucus determines to be *politically* important. And at their remove, you can bet it'll be something closer to the needs of the DMH than it will be to the needs of that under-represented, functionally disenfranchised portion of the electorate we call state hospital patients. So, ladies and gentlemen, I don't think we should busy ourselves with plans for abandoning the high road just because we fear that the DMH may fail to rise above the level of chicken shit. I think it befits us to walk tall rather than try to agree on how low to stoop to make a smaller target. I have spoken."

And he knew that he had spoken too much. His eruptions of moral indignation were ever a source of embarrassment to all around, but to him only after the fact. During such paroxysms he soared above his maculate adversaries who would stare agape at the frenzied tumult his Gallic blood lust stoked. It was only after the seizure was over that he was able to listen to what he had said, and it was then that regrets, his as well as those of people singed by the heat of his rhetoric, would pour in. This morning, however, he was resolved not to dwell on regrets. And he waited for takers as he looked up and down the table. Corley and Weaver seemed more reassured than embarrassed, while Riegel just smiled and shook his head resignedly. Several of the others shifted in their chairs. John Wingate looked up from his pen knife and spoke.

"Don't forget, they pay our salaries," he pointed out.

It was exactly what he needed to hear to introduce the second act of his passion play. He even wondered if Wingate had said it to provide a cue.

"In a pig's ass they pay our salaries!" he roared. "You think just like *they* do, because they truly *do* think they pay our salaries. The *people* pay our salaries! The same people who pay *their* salaries, though you'd be hard put to get some of those petty little shits in the DMH to admit to it. *That's* what I'm saying. Those clerks in Harrisburg tend to forget that *we* run the hospital and do it to serve the *people*, not to serve the DMH. When you tell 'em that they respond with all the grace and dignity of an unveiled, self-serving middleman whose actual usefulness was now being called into question. Let's remember that no matter what the political or social fad of the day might be, it's the hundreds of daily human dramas that go on in the wards of the hospital that make up the important work of the state mental health system, not the mincing dither over yesterday's memo or tomorrow's directive, as some people around here would like to think."

He saw that a few of the members were now trying to suppress smiles and he felt rising alarm that his behavior was beginning to spill over into the ludic. The thought of being seen as some kind of blustering clown sobered him swiftly. He continued, slower and in several octaves lower.

"And something else I'd like to mention," he added. "We've been going on about who might be blamed for what. I think it's significant that we haven't even begun to consider what may be the authentic mischief in all of this. Suppose it turns out that his death is not just incidental? Suppose his death turns out to be, not somebody else's fault, but the inevitable outcome of dementia from this thing, 'Blush.' Suppose his death becomes just one of many, that in due time *all* of our Blush patients are destined to die suddenly, and that he died first only because he was our *first* patient with the problem? If we can ever get around to considering that appalling possibility, then maybe we can get around to thinking more about patient care and less about our naked asses."

Now it was their turn to feel sobered. Apparently, no one else had considered that possibility and the cited prospect quickly brought them to heel. He had now regained the ascendancy, and he sensed that Corley and Weaver, their chins now chucked up a little higher, were for the moment deferring to his estimate of the issue.

"I fear," he resumed in a gentler tone, "that what happened last night may be telling us what lies ahead for—how many now, Jess?" he queried.

"Forty-seven," Weaver replied.

"For the forty-seven Blush patients we already have on hand, and God knows how many more on the way! That's the kind of thing we should be talking to DMH about, and not the administrative quiddities and quillets of one case because it was a *non-resident*," he scored.

"But we can't be sure that's what killed him," challenged Benson. "If it turns out that it was caused by a piece of food getting stuck in this throat, or aspiration of vomit in his sleep—the usual kind of thing—we would look pretty damned silly after telling DMH that the sky was about to fall," he warned, restored of composure and ready to resume the debate.

"True," Cantrelle agreed. "But asphyxiating on food or vomitus, when it does occur, does so almost exclusively in the elderly or in patients pretty heavily sedated. He was neither. I'm worried that it's just as I fear."

"I guess there's just one way to find out," Benson relented.

"I'm afraid so," Cantrelle agreed. "We wait for the next one."

"But if what you say is right," Ruth Simpson protested, "can't we do something to prevent it? We can't just sit by and wait for someone to die in order to prove a point. That's murder, or something like it."

The word offended everybody present, but Simpson's egalitarian brand of humanism, now fully aroused, would not retreat from it, and she swept the gathering with a look of primed defiance.

"Mrs. Simpson," Weaver soothed, "If Dr. Cantrelle's fear is borne out, there is little we can do to protect those patients. If the degenerative process does spread to include the vital centers—and I guess you meant respiratory arrest from destruction of the respiratory center?" he inquired of Cantrelle.

"That would be my guess," Cantrelle replied.

"If it did spread to the respiratory center in the brain stem," Weaver continued, "there would be little we could do short of putting every Blush patient on a ventilator as assurance to keep their breathing going, even when their breathing was *normal*, because you couldn't wait until they stopped breathing; that would be too late. They certainly would have to be restrained. Jordan showed no preliminary signs of distress, we're told. Also, we don't have the equipment, the facilities, or the personnel to do it. And we don't know how long the patients would last on it, anyway. And even if we could arrange it, can you imagine having untold numbers of ventilator patients here, each one sooner or later posing the question of when to pull the plug? The ventilator cases that made headlines several years back were relatively isolated ones. Here, we're talking about—I can't even imagine how many," he gestured in dismay.

Cantrelle looked around the table to watch Weaver's words sink in. He thought he saw each member shudder in his or her own way. Certainly the pitch of the conference had shifted noticeably; its members were beginning to sense what might be the true enormity of Winston Jordan's death. And what lay ahead for Moreland."

"But there's got to be something we could do for those people. They're doomed if we don't. My God, Dr. Cantrelle, I hope you're wrong," Simpson pleaded, now speaking for everyone.

"If I'm right they're doomed in any event, regardless of what we do for them," he replied, "and because of that our best effort probably shouldn't be directed at them at all, but at *this*!"

He tossed the packet on the table. It came to rest about where a centerpiece would be.

Everybody stared at it for a moment and then turned to him for explanation, just as he had planned. It was important to keep their thinking pointed in the right direction.

"Is that the stuff?" Riegel asked almost flippantly in a play at bravado. He had to show that he wasn't afraid of the big, bad wolf.

"I think so. It was given to me as being the stuff," Cantrelle explained.

"But how did you get it?" Benson asked, speaking the question on everybody's face.

"It was passed along to me by someone who knew that we were interested in analyzing some of it. He had almost taken it himself earlier, so apparently he was able to get his hands on some more," Cantrelle explained carefully.

Several of the members continued to stare at the packet, deceptively simple in its thin, neat angularity. No one reached to touch it, and, noting that, he was recalled to his own initial dread upon being presented with the packet.

"So I think it probably is what we've been looking for," he continued, urging them beyond their reluctance. "The white powder you can barely make out in the packet is probably heroin because the 'bag', as they call it, was sold as just heroin. But it's probably been laced, or 'loused' as they say, with Blush, which you can't distinguish visually from the heroin, or so I'm told. This," he pointed to the packet, "is a set-up to enlist another victim, and if we make an effort anywhere it should be to find out what the hell this Blush is, maybe come up with something that could block its effect, and find out who the hell's out there trying to poison the druggies. Passively to wait for new victims to arrive and then go all out and try to undo the damage already done will never put us on top of this thing. It all depends on where you place the initiative."

"I agree with your point," Benson offered as he pulled his gaze from the packet, "but is it our job to get that much into the detective work? We've got all we can do just to keep up with patient care, and to go sleuthing around like you suggest, well . . . . I can't even imagine where we would start. I guess I just don't understand what you have in mind," he admitted, palms up.

Cantrelle nodded in agreement to the need for more explanation. He was aware that Corley and Weaver were also listening intently. The others waited expectantly.

He thought it best to begin with some kind of introduction, even at the risk of being tedious. It was important they be aware of the background music if he expected them to pick up the rhythm.

"Remember years back when we had a similar kind of onslaught with LSD cases, though they usually got better, not worse. And remember how we took our guidelines from the research and teaching centers because we figured they were in a better position to work out what there was to know in dealing with LSD, and how we learned slowly and much later that, from a clinical standpoint anyway, we knew more than they did by virtue of our having tougher cases and having them much longer? Remember? Also, remember that we meekly underestimated our data and didn't even bother to publish any of our findings—and on this I stand guiltiest among the guilty—when those findings might have been quite helpful to our sister hospitals? Well, I think with this Blush thing we're being given a second chance. From the standpoint of case material alone we may be the front-runner hospital because it might be that right now we have the largest collection of these cases around, anywhere."

"We do, as far as we know," Corley confirmed. "Certainly statewide, as far as we can tell at this time," she expanded.

"See!" he pounced, "I'm sure that as this plague picks up—and it will—other hospitals will get their share and before long we'll all have more cases than we'll ever know what to do with. But for now we're in the proverbial worst and best position to do some basic work. And maybe publish it this time."

"Sounds good," Benson allowed with a skeptical arching of his eyebrows, "but specifically what? Publish what?" It was apparent that the group had appointed him foil for the occasion.

"First," Cantrelle demonstrated as he pointed to the packet on the table, "we send *that* to the state lab in Sharpsfield to separate the Blush from the heroin. Then we ask the lab to do a molecular analysis to get some idea of what it looks like. Also, animal studies could pin-point which brain structures it attacks, and we could correlate those findings with the brain tissues from autopsies if, or when, more patients die. Then we know where to look in animal studies when our pharmacologists test different agents that could conceivably block Blush's effect, hoping to find one that humans could tolerate. Generally, it would be the same investigative procedure used in tracking down an infectious process and evolving a specific treatment for it."

"Can we do that? Sounds like a hell of a lot to ask of the state lab. Isn't that part usually done in the big research centers, like Bethesda?" Benson reminded the group.

"Right," Cantrelle agreed readily, "but the point is that we're in the best position to get it started. This thing is upon us right here, right now, and we can at least do the preliminaries to get the big show going. There aren't that many cases yet, despite our personal sense of it, and it'll probably take some time before the problem reaches the size to move it up in the level of national awareness. And you all know how long it takes NIH or a teaching center to get going on any project, what with grants, reviews, recruitment of subjects—they don't have wards of Blush patients waiting to be included in research like we do, you know. Plus, they like to have it all mapped out punctiliously before anybody even touches a patient. I'm afraid we don't have time for all of that if we hope to knock this thing before it gets out of hand. What do you think?" he appealed as he rounded out his delivery.

What could they think? His call to altruistic arms was laudable in its own right, and the prospect of having Moreland take a beginning *and* a leading step in at least the preliminary work of wrestling with the Blush problem touched the fiber of everyone present.

"Suppose we do get DMH and the state lab to go along with your proposal," Weaver allowed, racing on ahead to likely eventualities, "just what would we do here as our part?"

"Pretty much what we're already doing," Cantrelle advised. "We're diagnosing them, segregating them to keep them under closer scrutiny, and testing them to record their clinical course. As you know, each one now gets a battery of lab studies which includes an admission MRI we repeat at about monthly intervals—I know that beats the hell out of our budget, but it's got to be done to follow the degenerative process along—plus before-and-after neuropsychs when it can be worked out that way. As you know, Clay is doing the before neuropsychs on selected drug rehab cases at Valley Medical Center. We select those rehab cases most likely to relapse after discharge, give them the neuropsych battery just before they are discharged, and wait for them to be admitted here should they run afoul of Blush. Gruesome to say, but the odds are all in our favor. So far we've gotten three patients who were tested pre-Blush and are now here post-Blush, and Clay has run them through the repeat neuropsychs for comparison. We expect more subjects to surface over time. So far, Clay and his psychology interns have given neuropsychs to about thirty candidates at Valley; they've been working weekends and nights to keep up with the flow. We plan to stop after about seventy-five and just let circumstances bring the repeaters to us for follow-up," he detailed.

"That's the work that you intend to publish?" Weaver asked.

"Right. It might become helpful in establishing a baseline. You see, if the state lab isolates Blush and comes up with its molecular structure—or someone else does it if the state lab can't take it that far—the pharmacologists then might be able to give us a lead as to what drugs we already have available that might ameliorate or even block Blush's action. And if we don't have anything already on hand, a new agent might be synthesized. If we have a pretty good profile on the mental status before and after the Blush effect in untreated cases, such as we will have now, we could use that profile to measure the effectiveness of those agents in the treatment of new cases. True, we wouldn't be able to take the neurochemistry part of the project very far just by ourselves, but we're in the preferred position to do the essential preliminary work and I truly believe it's more than just a matter of opportunity. It's a matter of responsibility. And I'm beginning to feel tired of this oratory," he quipped.

The storm had now spent itself, and for a moment the silence in the room was complete. Corley and Weaver leaned back in their chairs, a gesture enabling the others to adjust their positions as well. The packet in the center of the table looked like a smoking pistol, its deed done.

"Well," Corley resumed, almost cheerfully, "It seems we have our work cut out for us."

Her comment brought a few chuckles from the Council.

"I'll pass this on to the state lab," Weaver agreed. "Stan Mullen, one of their chief chemists, is an old friend. I'll explain to him what our plan is and we can send a copy of our formal research protocol later," he explained as he made a gesturing reach for the packet.

Cantrelle stretched for the packet and conveyed it to him.

"I'm sure many such packets will be showing up before long," Cantrelle advised as he did so, "and somewhere, someone may already be running it through chemical and molecular analysis, but this is the first sample I know about and right now it just may be the only captive sample available in this area. Maybe the world."

"We'll be very careful," Weaver chided as he tucked the packet into his coat pocket.

It was now clear that both Corley and Weaver were relieved to have a positive recourse in the face of the boy's sudden death. It also appeared that the Council had now come to see the incident as very likely a part of an evolving societal piece and had moved away from the tribal fear of being penitentially locked up forevermore with an accusing corpse.

"Ruth," Martha continued, "I want you to alert your people to the possibility mentioned by Dr. Cantrelle. At the sign of any distress in any Blush patients, put the patient on one-to-one coverage and have the CPR teams on alert. Dr. Weaver will notify our back-up Med-Surg hospitals and their ERs of what we might be facing. We'll also bring our physicians up to date on the matter."

"I'll have a staff meeting with them this afternoon," Weaver volunteered.

Now things were beginning to move, Cantrelle savored as he wheezed a sigh of relief.

"No matter what we do, it may not be very helpful, but doing nothing would be intolerable," Corley attested as she directed a shy smile at Cantrelle. "And that brings us to the next item of business this morning," she resumed.

In concert, several members shifted in their chairs to announce their readiness for some new and perhaps more congenial business.

"I understand the Triage Unit is coming along nicely," she observed.

"It is. They're really moving the new admissions along very well, treatment plans and all," Weaver reported.

"Too well, I'm afraid," Corley added. "The other units receiving those transfers are running out of beds, especially Blush beds. Over the past two months we've received forty-seven, as Dr. Weaver mentioned earlier, and we had to set up a special wing for them. Forty-seven beds—forty-six now—is just about maximum capacity for that wing. With no end in sight, and with the added management tasks we talked about earlier, we're at the point of having to open another wing very soon, no doubt about that. The question is whether we proceed, wing at a time, or just go ahead and plan for designating an entire one-hundred-sixty-bed building as our holding area for Blush patients? Either approach has its merits, as I'm sure you know, having gone through similar adjustments before. If we opt for an entire building then we'll probably have to open one of the buildings we closed a few years back. We'll need Sharpsfield's approval for that, plus an increase in budget. If this Blush thing continues—I don't know what else to call it—we and Sharpsfield will really have no choice in the matter. But they may not want to lay out that much money so early in the problem."

This time it was Benson's turn.

"Go for the whole building," he urged. "God damn it, we're all sick and tired of being given just barely enough, if that, to do everything the job demands of us. We spend half our time on our knees begging them to give us the goods to do the job right, which they're so damned quick to say we don't, or at least not to their satisfaction, and particularly if something unpleasant happens, like this morning! And especially if *they* think the effort costs more than it's worth. Don't you love their god-damned piety? No, I think that if we're going to take this bitch of a burden at all, we ought to do it without having to go back to them over and over again for handouts. Put it in words they'll understand," he suggested acidly, "tell them that we believe that if we're in for a pissy penny, we're in for a fucking pound." He ended with his hands flat on the table before him.

Riegel applauded while the others exchanged nods and smiles of agreement.

Corley beamed benevolently at her aroused Council and shared her pleasure with Weaver whose eyes now sparkled at the prospect of a new campaign. He reveled in riding at the head of the column in the service of his monarch to beset any dragons at hand.

Their flag unfurled, the Council awaited their leader's word. She surveyed their expectation.

"Let's go with it," Corley directed. "I'll call DMH this morning and shake their tree. They may want to send someone here to take a look for themselves before they agree to anything. If they do we may have to convene again to detail the particulars for whoever shows up. If so, I'll get back to you in enough time. For the time being each of you should start thinking about personnel shifts so that we can staff a new building, knowing that for the time being and until we can acquire new staff we'll be pretty thin in some areas, but I'll let you all decide where those areas should be. Dr. Cantrelle," she specified, "do you think any residents should be assigned to the new building to pitch in, if only just for a while in the beginning?"

He had expected the request, yet it still took him aback upon hearing it spoken. Since he had instigated much of what was now unfolding he really had no option but to follow through on his fair share of the task.

"I'll work out something so that we can chip in," he replied. "Residents are already helping out on the Triage Unit, and that cuts into their training rotations a bit, but I think we can swing something." He quickly thought ahead to combining the residents' substance abuse study block with a clinical rotation on the expanded Blush unit. Sort of natural.

"Good," she replied. "Are there any questions? If not, we'll adjourn for the time being."

"I'll take a crew over to Building Seven," Wingate announced as he snapped his penknife shut. "I think that'll be the unit that we can activate with a minimum of outlay. Size up what has to be done to put it back on line. I'll have something for you by tomorrow morning,"

"Fine, John," Corley returned. "And now let's get on with our labors," she directed to the others as she closed the folder before her.

The signal given, they all pushed away from the table and rose to leave, at first silently, but by the time they reached the door they were animatedly comparing attack plans, once again comrades in arms.

"Frank," Corley called as he was turning to leave.

"Yes, Martha?" he obliged as he checked his step.

"I want to thank you for pulling us out of the pits this morning," she offered gratefully.

"Shucks, Ma'am, 'tweren't nothin'," he twanged in his best Huckleberry Finn. "I figured that the real pits are yet to come and we gotta save some misery for them when they arrive. Best not to go wanting, I hear tell." Weaver chortled as Corley smiled indulgently at her Training Director's madcap diffidence. "But if you all need me for anything when you meet with the parents, just call." he added, dropping the fool's play. "They might want to talk to the resident who was called to pronounce their son dead. I'll tell Dr. Feldman to hold himself ready just in case."

"Thanks," Weaver nodded, "that might be helpful."

"One other thing. I want to thank both of you for not asking awkward questions I would not have been at liberty to answer about that drug packet," Cantrelle tendered, "but I can tell you that you have some very dedicated people who don't seem to mind putting themselves at risk to do a good job for you. Maybe after all is said and done in this Blush problem I'll mention some names. But in the meantime," he shifted to the cautionary, "tell the state lab to be damned careful with that packet because we're not likely to get our hands on any more for some time."

"Check," Weaver replied, "I think they'll jump at the chance to do some first line disclosure work and get a leg up on the federal people."

"Probably," Cantrelle concurred. "Well, let me trot on back to my diggings," he warbled as he turned to go. "Oh!" he hesitated briefly, "Trick or Treat!" His wry smile now in place, he left the Council room.

Once out of the building and beyond detectable range of its hosts he allowed his thoughts to regroup around the reflection that it always seemed to happen this way, that the conferences or meetings or sessions he dreaded most were the ones which subsequently turned out to be the most productive. He likened the phenomenon to a birth process and likewise the resolution, or the decision, or the agreement, to a dialectic neonate that could be delivered only through the rigors of ordeal, but once arrived, a joy swaddled in untested promise. He wondered how far they would be able to take their investigation of Blush. He knew that sooner or later, if it lasted too long, the problem would eventually reach NIH. Once there, that Olympian bureau would organize an overweening national approach for tracking down the beast. Moreland might then have no place in their grand scheme and would have to content itself, he groaned, with the satisfaction of having been among the first to see the problem coming and, laudably, among the first, if not the first, to mobilize itself for doing something about it. A small consolation, maybe, but perhaps a quite satisfying one for a state hospital removed from the mainstream of high-powered research but doing right picket duty. He preened at the thought as his steps carried him along to his office.

The day was brighter now, actually; and the trees along his path were neon golden. The wind had subsided and branches were dribbling leaves in a desultory, languid gesture of recognition that their year's work was coming to an end. The tenacious grass, shimmering green in the sunlight, held the fallen leaves ahoist, balanced on the countless blades still striving upward. His experienced eye told him that, barring a particularly bitter cold snap, the grass would need two more cuttings to put it to settled rest for the winter. Maybe this weekend he and Todd could tackle their lawn in the first of a couple of phase-down ministrations to have it looking right and ready for the first snow. He hated it when uncollected leaves and uncut grass marred the billowy veil of the first snow.

He picked up his pace as he neared the entrance to the MOB. His class was probably waiting for him, he estimated with a quick glace at his watch. Two minutes before ten. They had damned well better be waiting, he glowered. Earlier in the hazy part of summer they had begun to arrive at class in a ragged tardiness which attenuated the starting point of the sessions. One day he waited until all had arrived and then fixed them with a grim stare as silence ratcheted up the discomfort level. He then skewered them with the reminder that punctuality was the courtesy of kings. Since then the class assembled early for each session in the hope that sooner or later he would show up late and violate his own imperial assize, entitling them to call down his own words upon him in sore retribution. That's the way they were, his cleverly mischievous residents, given as one to waggish sport over any covert contradiction, rank oxymoron, infinite regress, or failed syllogism wherever detected, be it in thought, action, or feeling. His coarse and obvious malfeasances were generally discounted out of hand. It was his more elegant *non sequiturs* which the residents preferred to sniff out for starting the jolly chase. And he loved them for it. So what if an unwitting solecism of his own occasionally stumbled into their snare? Or if his actions sometimes belied his avowals? He never did offer himself as a model of faultless content, he reminded himself with a patronizing helping from his presently restored reservoir of self-approbation; it was the method, the attitude—in a word, the form—that counted, and that's the attitude he undertook to nourish in them, even if they occasionally nipped at him in their boisterous growth, much as cubs nip at the parent in challenge of their training. And so his cubs, who sometimes played a little rough, awaited him. And he would be on time. Out of courtesy, of course.

He pulled open the entrance door of the building and at a trot made his way down the hallway and into his waiting office.

"Your third year class is waiting," Mrs. Andretti mentioned to him as he entered.

"I know, and I'd better be on time," he replied, acknowledging the thoughtfulness in her reminder.

He entered his office at a gallop, picked up a text and a journal article placed together in readiness, and, relay fashion, resumed his sprint past Mrs. Andretti and up the hallway to the classroom at the far end. As he neared the door he slowed to a more stately gait. The only thing his entrance lacked was the striking of the clock, and he tried to banish that thought as just too precious to account.

They were all in their places but with something less than sunshiney faces. He was then abruptly reminded that the news of young Jordan's death was probably now making the rounds and that they had come upon it later than he and had not yet had time to adjust to the shock of it. Plus, they'd not yet had a forum in which to address the inevitable distress the death of a patient, particularly a young one, brings to a psychiatric staff, and particularly to its younger members. It had slipped his mind that he had already received his quota of crisis support from the Council meeting earlier, his lapse an oblique measure of that support's effectiveness. Now it was his turn to preside over his residents, much as Martha Corley had done over her council in helping them to come to terms with the tragedy. They had all come to know young Jordan, inclined as residents are to identify with the adolescent patients, especially college students, and a few had worked with him as a part of their clinical assignment. And now, as a group, they seemed in search of a channel of their own for expression of their woe.

"You've all heard, I guess," he observed to them, feeling a reluctance to start up the matter again and undo his own shaky closure on the gloom.

A few nodded glumly.

"Any word yet on the cause of death?" one of them queried.

"No," Cantrelle replied, adjusting his inflection to the timbre of their discomfort. "Apparently he died peacefully in his sleep," he reiterated, beginning to hear the phrase as something of a press release, "but an autopsy is planned for today or tomorrow, and we should know something by the end of the week."

That seemed to mollify some aspect of their distress, undoubtedly the part relating to their wrenching need to make some sense of the loss. Being young and new to the vicissitudes of human frailty, they manifested more openly that sense of personal failure all good doctors felt when even an unquestionably hopeless case died, for, after all, their holy duty as physician was foremost to comfort and particularly to heal, and when the patient's death overrode those efforts the sense of defeat and failure came in the form of self-reproach, a sentiment noted most keenly by the litigious, just as the Council's initial concern this morning was quick to demonstrate. Perhaps more obviously so with the Council than with others, the death had to make *sense*; it had to be made *explainable*. The grief process demanded it, and especially with any case of sudden death in a young patient under treatment. And these kindredly young residents wrote large what all others of the care-taking legion felt in a more harnessed form. Moments such as the one at hand reminded him that residents kept him in touch with the innocence and hope of the unexamined life, and did so in a less distorted way than did one's own children. He saw his residents as unblemished registrants in our collective human endeavor and having preferential first call on all the good and pure illusions necessary to that strict calling. In effect, the residents were the closest thing to being the undomesticated wild life of an altruistic humanity not often seen this side of heaven, and occasionally he would remind them of that privileged distinction. But pejoratively, of course. And this morning he could already read in their innocent, hurt faces the bruises of collision with humanity's strictest sergeant, Death. The purity of their pain suggested out of hand that they, in their heart of hearts and like everybody else, despite all reason, understanding, and learning, held Death to be either an accident or a crime, and especially so one's own, should it ever occur. The thought of Death as a cause rather than a consequence was alien to the society where the social emollient was the belief that everything could be fixed if only the right effort were made. He typically saw in the residents' reaction, even in those cases which would obviously be regarded as death by natural causes though occurring in a person who happened to be one's assigned patient, clear evidence they truly believed that every physical being was blessed with immortality, much like protozoa fortunate enough to live in a toxin-free environment, and that Death, when it arrived, was the result of some fell and wholly avoidable assault upon the promised infinity of the organism's existence. Death was not accepted by them, or probably by anyone else when you got down to it, as the ordained essential cost of metazoon complexity, no matter the perfection of the environment, despite the secret, hidden hopes of every health food devotee and every rabid environmentalist. He knew his residents understood the teachings of theoretic biology—some of it he had taught them himself—but for all their learning, it simply did not touch them where they lived as people, and particularly at times like this. Human, all too human, that German crank had said.

"The only college student among the Blush admissions and he's the one who dies," a resident observed resentfully.

The comment jolted him out of his musings. The narrowness of the remark didn't sit well, and he was unsure whether or not to address it.

"But we got another young one in last night, I hear. A twenty-two-year-old heroin addict. Our Blush unit is filling up," another resident announced, perhaps intentionally to dilute the implications of the earlier remark. He hoped so. In any event, he could now elect to pass over the remark. Moreover, he was surprised to hear that last night's lone admission Dr. Feldman alluded to in his phone call was yet another Blush patient. Perhaps the residents were adjusting to the evolving routine of it better than he.

"It was announced at the Council meeting this morning that we've had forty-seven Blush admissions thus far, and I guess the one last might will make it forty-eight when morning report is completed," he tabulated for them. "I can mention to you that tentative—*tentative*, mind you—plans are being considered for designating an entire building for Blush patients."

"That means we expect it to get worse!" a resident surmised aloud.

"Well, I certainly do, and how it will affect us in training is tops on our agenda," Cantrelle added in an effort to convey adaptive vigilance in the prospect.

"But how far can it go, our just waiting for the cases to show up at our door? I don't know of anything that's being done to stop this thing," the same resident despaired.

The mantle of blame was looking for somewhere to light, but their conjoint sense of injury was keeping it aloft, circling. In due time it would, like a homing pigeon, return to its deserving origin. He also noted that in the meantime their sense of helplessness was seeking to be galvanized into some positive action they could mount to duel with Blush face on, Cyrano-like. After all, they were there to learn just that sort of thing. And he agreed.

"I think we—us, at Moreland—will be drawing on the state's fairly extensive facilities to try to get a reading on just exactly what Blush is," Cantrelle stated. "There are no reports yet from anywhere—it's still a relatively new phenomenon—as to what its chemistry is, and we hope to get a lead on it very soon," he added carefully.

"Yeah," another resident seconded, "Now that we have a sample of it we should be able to get moving."

Damn it! It was already out! Morello, probably. Not that he didn't expect it, but he would have preferred to have been informed in advance that the word was out, and informed so by Morello—not like this! He could then have mentioned it at Council, and also have been prepared for it to come up with the residents. God damn that kid!

The residents sensed that he was upset by the admission, and their tone quickly changed to that of qualm.

He took a moment to suppress a stage-size sigh and admit to himself that, despite the method, the result was right. The residents needed to know. Coming first-hand from one of their own probably gave them some sense of group initiative in the matter, and he really couldn't find a hell of a lot wrong with that. And besides, with the sky threatening to come down upon them and upon everybody else, reliance on administrative punctilio might truly be just too petty. Yet, sometimes he was exactly so, it now appeared.

"You all seem to be commendably on top of things," he conceded with a good sport nod, "and, yes, we're rushing off a sample of what is supposed to be the stuff to the state lab for analysis. So, between the autopsy report, the histologic sections, and the chemical analysis we might get some important news soon enough,. Yes, we might have something to work with in a little while. And I'll keep you posted on what comes in."

Apparently that's what they needed to hear. Most of them now radiated smiles of approval. They could at last see some prospect of striking back at their skulking enemy. One resident leaned over and gave a comradely poke to his colleague who grinned in readiness to stand to. A female resident smoothed out her skirt over her lap and then looked up, prepared.

"I'll meet with the other residents to pass on what I just told you, though God knows it'll be old hat to them ten minutes after this class is over," he added lightly.

A ripple of laughter announced that the cloud had passed.

"Which reminds me," he proceeded, "this is a class, isn't it? At the risk of doing violence to your forward thrust I'd like to get on with today's assignment which takes us back about seventy years. O.K.?"

They submitted in a collective display of good-natured tolerance, making sure he noted their largess. It was all antic because they swore by this course and the rite of mastering its material. It demanded much of them but conferred so much more in return, though later than sooner, a condition they readily accepted; and, to the wide attest of residents long graduated, a bargain in the making. The course transcended the standard requirements of residency training and was actually a seminar in advanced readings. It was his attempt to inculcate in his residents the spirit of scholarly exegesis coupled with the discipline of research as the amalgamated foundation of medical education. They were not allowed to settle for being merely trained. Animals are trained, people are educated, he would bellow periodically when a resident dared question the value of being held to so many ranging readings not currently popular in the standard program requirements. Or, why not just go with the latest findings, the latest classification, the latest treatment techniques, work at keeping up with them and call it a day? To that he would retaliate by cautioning the resident to remember that the best training consisted in learning what the questions were, not merely the answers, because just about everybody, every article, every book held all the answers anyone could want to know. And if you didn't like one particular answer, there was no large problem in that because the array of available answers changed from year to year, month to month, and sometimes day to day. A better knowledge came of knowing the enduring questions upon which dashed the ceaseless waves of answers drawn by them. Better, that is, if you were planning to go anywhere worthwhile. They were all aware of his lofty contempt for the fads that swept though Psychiatry, too often carrying in their wake the specious and the fraudulent as tawdry assaults upon the majesty of the field's strict scholarship. And he never failed to expose to his charges any fad that was merely the updating of some hoary inanity dressed up in trendy terminology, ready for another go at the world and its current generation of the unknowing and uneducated. This course, with its solid and secure universals, was intended to be his residents' foil against such tacky particulars. It was also to be their guide for keeping better company. From time to time the question arose as to whether he was truly expecting too much of his residents, who, by and large, had precious little of a liberal education, pre-med and med school being what it was, and so were generally no more mature than their twenty-six or so protected years could permit, only two years of which were psychiatric training. On the one hand, he could quite readily agree that he was expecting too much; but on the other, he felt their callowness was the exact reason for giving them this course at this time in their professional lives, else forever leave them in peace. An occasional resident might wonder aloud as to what benefit an appreciation of the factors forcing transition from Newtonian mechanics to Einsteinian relativity in system thinking could conceivably grant to the everyday practice of Psychiatry. Actually, he knew that all of his residents wondered as much at one time or another. So, traditionally, he began the course with an explanation cast in the form of a simplistic example providentially detailed in the very first session. After pointing out to the new group that the course, by virtue of their mode of participation in it, would enable them to gain a pretty good estimate as to the future and character of their very own professional lives, he would go on to explain that just about everybody knew that electricity flowed over wires and that to have an electrical circuit for lights and appliances to work as they should a black wire was connected to a black pole and a white wire to a white pole, and that all electrical wiring followed that general principle. Moreover, he would continue, it was known that some people were very good at connecting white wires to white poles and black wires to black poles, and were also good in laying out electrical circuits and switches throughout homes, buildings, and the like to enable the electrical power to accomplish desired functions. The people who did this work were called "electricians," and the world needed a lot of them, he agreed. But, he would add, some people found themselves more interested in the design of the wires, the poles, and the circuitry, and those people tended to dwell on ideas about ohms, voltage, watts, amperes, and the formulae describing the behavior of those constructs. Through the use of such formulae, these people were able to design the wires, the poles, and the types of circuitry used by the electricians. Those people who designed the wires and switches were called "engineers," and the world needed a fair number of them. Finally, he would point out, there were people who puzzled over what electricity was in the first place and how it related to matter and time, and those people were the ones who developed the formulae used by the engineers who then designed the wires and switches the electricians connected. Those people were called "theorists," and the world needed only a few of them. In Psychiatry he would explain, there were those who were very good at connecting the right treatment to the right patient and were quite content to do just that. These psychiatrists were called "clinicians." And the world needed a lot of them. But there were some psychiatrists, he would carefully point out, who delved more into what mental disease and its treatment were all about so that good forms of treatment might be available for the clinician's use. These people, he would explain with elaborate humility, were called "teachers" and "researchers," and the world needed some of them. Finally, there were those psychiatrists who sought out the very structure and function of the human mental apparatus in the pursuit of a general psychology which defined disease and its treatment, and these people were called—he would pause for effect—"metapsychologists" or "theorists," and the world needed only a few of those. He would conclude by saying that the residents' level of participation in the course, determined pretty much by personal differences in taste and talent, would likely give them, as individuals, a good preview of where they most likely would make their best effort in the field—clinician, teacher-researcher, or theorist—and that whatever their subsequent level or locus of participation, as foretold by the course, they would perforce be better apprized and more appreciative of the other levels of endeavor necessary to keep the field a collaborative and majestic human enterprise and not have it become just a farrago of embarrassing and pernicious fads. And at the end of his Parable of the Wires, as it was called, he never failed to wonder if the homily of it was more embarrassing than anything it was intended to forfend. But he usually wrapped up that concern with an affirmation of faith in their simple idealism which he hoped to keep ever alive, ever young, and ever pure. Anyway, it appeared that the residents did understand at least that part of it.

"Let's review," he began. "It'll help us set the frame. On Monday we wrapped up the "Ego and the Id," which, as you all now so thoroughly know, is Freud's enunciation of the structural model. We've gone over the thematic reasons, driven by clinical observations, which led Freud to a re-assessment of unconscious function and also of the psychic agencies previously defined thereby. As I'm sure you will now never, ever forget, the clinical fact of guilt existing on an unconscious level where the Pleasure Principle was supposed to be king—guilt ain't pleasure—plus the evidence of conscious-type logic operating in the unconscious, where the rules of thought were supposed to be quite different, convinced him that his earlier model of the mind, the topographic, was not adequate to embrace all the facts. Remember Newton, and the unexplained advance of Mercury's precession and the apparent shift of the relative position of the stars during solar eclipse? Well, as we overstated on Monday, the situation with the Topographic Theory had become roughly similar to that of Newton's Mechanics as Freud observed clinical data which simply could not be fitted into his own existing model. Never mind that Newton's mechanics or Freud's topographics adequately accounted for ninety-nine percent of the observable world, physical or psychological, as the case was; it was what *didn't* fit which Einstein, or Freud, considered vital—vital from the standpoint of both research and learning. And that's where ordinary people like you and me differ from the creative genius. If any one of us, by some quirk, had come up with the Topographic Theory we likely would have been more than content to sit on our pontifical behinds for the rest of our lives, content to draw upon its professional dividends. Minor inconsistencies that would crop up clinically in the theory's application would probably be set aside as "Other," as we do so casually these days in our diagnostic classification schemes. We would not, I'm sure, focus on the inconsistencies at the risk of discounting the very font of our glory, and then do so in the very chancy hope of heuristically extending our reach into the unknown. No, we wouldn't, any more than it is common today for leaders in our field to dwell on the limitations of their propositions or rush to print retractions when evidence disproves their position. No, we would be merely human about it and fall right in line, I'm afraid, and devote ourselves to protecting the large benefits of our accomplishment while minimizing any of its shortcomings. And we would enlist adherents enroute. In a word, politics. But not Freud. He did not hesitate to forfeit what had given him fame, but proceeded in the hope of moving ever closer to truth—and to even larger fame, I'm sure, though he certainly could not have been guaranteed success at such when he took the daring step. But it was that step—and hear me well on this—that made it possible for us to be sitting here this morning, struggling and yet privileged in our effort to catch up with the great man because we're so much more advantaged than *any* of our counterparts of *anytime* prior to the year 1923. And he took that daring step all alone, without a learned and compassionate training director to guide his way. The Siegfried of the Psyche, would you say? It's that special courage, that dedication, that love of the truth—mixed with ability, of course—which sets creative genius apart from ordinary mankind, like us. Odd, when you think about it; he studied people to learn about life, and now we study him to learn about ourselves." He heard himself becoming rhapsodic, so he quickly adjusted himself to a more exacting demeanor, though the residents already seemed mesmerized. "Well," he continued, "to sum up, the new model—the Structural Theory—shifted the emphasis away from what the mind was storing to what the mind was doing, and the agency now credited with a large measure of the doing was proclaimed to be the Ego, part of which was now quite unconscious in its function. So you can see that the new model transformed the notion "unconscious" from a proper noun to a busy adjective, a change from location to mode; from part to process. Quite a different orientation. Now," he paused to signal his own shift, "it became necessary to rework earlier-defined concepts so that they would articulate with the new system. Some he never got around to, like Narcissism and the Dream, as we mentioned along the way, but the concept of Anxiety was so central to his model—both models, you now know—that it was inevitable his next major monograph, and his last major metapsychological work, would be on Anxiety and its revised definition in the new model. Any questions so far?" he inquired as he paused to catch his breath. He scanned the group who seemed to be wearing expressions of rapt comprehension. Their silence invited him to proceed. "O.K. Then that brings us to today's monograph, *Inhibitions, Symptoms and Anxiety.* Who presents this morning?" he asked as he scanned the group again.

"I'm up, Dr. Cantrelle," returned resident psychiatric physician Thomas Lofton, hand upraised.

"Good, Dr. Lofton," Cantrelle replied with an approving nod. "Anyone who likes William Blake can't be very far from the correct understanding of anything," he chided in his sometimes intrusive way of connecting some aspect of the resident's personality with the work at hand, "but before we get into the text of the monograph, I would like to give an overview of the main issue Freud addresses. The paper is long and tough and we might save some time if we took a few minutes right now to lay out the issue."

Dr. Lofton smiled as he nodded vigorously, grateful for the reprieve.

"In general, Freud undertakes to redefine Anxiety and its function," Cantrelle resumed. "In the earlier model, as you remember, Anxiety was seen as a break-down phenomenon, the failure to maintain repression of certain affects or ideas, usually sexual, the feeling of anxiety itself being the physiologic derivatives of those self-same, now dissociated affects or ideas. So, if someone felt anxiety—not fear, remember—it was because certain repressed and forbidden impulses, not recognizable as such because of their dissociation—with anxiety people don't know why they're frightened; with fear they do—were being lured back into consciousness. Libido, as we say, more or less correctly. But in this new model, the role and source of Anxiety has to be expanded to accommodate the new structuring of the psychic agencies—we now have an Ego, an Id, and a Superego—so that Anxiety can be understood as a signal function of either agency plus the use of psychic energy in the support of such function. Dr. Lofton will lead us in a review of the particulars which bear on this very central point. Right?"

Dr. Lofton smiled wanly.

"Not only that," Cantrelle continued mercilessly, "he'll show us how Freud comes to identify Anxiety as the subjectively recorded component of a more instinctual and unbound psychic energy which drives the psychic apparatus in the first place and serves as the underpinning of those object ties and identifications which developmentally coalesce into psychic structures, like the Ego and the Superego, plus a good part of the Id itself. In other words, the transformation of energy into structure, the little bang present in each and every one of us tiny, struggling cosmoses. You just might sense that I regard this monograph as no ordinary human effort, and you'd be most perceptive were you to do so. This monograph rounds out the most elegant, the most comprehensive model of the mind ever devised by man, and subsequent developments in the research on ego function, particularly autonomous ego function, have served to validate farther the incredible scope of Freud's model and its heuristic value. And it's been around since 1926. What has the psychiatric world been doing in the meantime? By and large, trying to catch up, and especially in the area of biologic research; research on the *brain*. Freud's glorious model is a model of the *mind*—not the *brain*. As you all know and as I've reminded you too often, Freud was a biologist, a neurologist who saw that the biology of his day, hampered by a limited and primitive technology, could not offer much in the study of human behavior, particularly clinical behavior. So, he decided to work on the mind until something better came along. This model is the result, and it's been waiting around for brain research of corresponding scope and relevance to arrive and unveil the collaborative and biologic side of human behavior, a *brain* model, so to speak, for pairing with the *mind* model. Now, technology has brought us along far enough so that we—or, more particularly, someone we'll mention in a minute—can evolve a biologic model of behavior to complement Freud's psychologic model, and to make adjustments, if necessary, so that we will have, as the exalted but not necessarily understood phrase runs, 'an integrated approach' for the understanding of human behavior. So, Freud's model may be seen as a guide for pairing up neurochemical discoveries with documented clinical and psychological phenomena, as I'm sure your current course on Panic Disorder and Phobia formation is doing, as an example. And that, in a nutshell, is what Dr. Lofton is going to do for us this morning."

Lofton was beyond smiling at this point.

"One final thing before we start," Cantrelle added. "The other paper assigned this morning—the paper by Burleson—is a remarkable effort at constructing that awaited biologic, or *brain* model of behavior, using the known neurochemical and neuroanatomic substrates as points of departure. He offers his model as a tentative beginning, much as Freud offered his earliest model way back in 1895. It's a landmark paper by one of the great thinkers of our time, and you'll see that he's superlative in his use of the Structural Theory in his endeavor. We probably won't have time to get to his paper this morning, but at least you'll know where we're headed. Who has that paper?"

"I do," answered Dr. Linda Aranzuela, the only flamenco dancer in the resident group.

Cantrelle smiled his approval. Clever, meticulous, and fun-loving, she was exactly as her Castilian ancestry demanded.

"O.K., Dr. Lofton, you're on," he signaled.

"Well," Lofton began tentatively, "as Dr. Cantrelle said, in this paper Freud needs to change the concept of Anxiety, but first he reviews his earlier ideas about it. He gives a review, and it starts out with a discussion of . . . ."

Cantrelle listened more to the collective ferment of the group than he did to young Dr. Lofton's brave effort at grappling with the monumental. He had watched and heard successive generations of residents do the same over these many years, and he hoped, fate permitting, that he would be favored to see and hear it for more years to come. Every time he met with his residents in this precious Helikon of learning he felt himself in touch with the closest thing he could believe was holy: the pursuit of Truth. And no less so this day, for all its worries and woes.

". . . and so Anxiety, if Freud now sees it as serving a signal function, would have taken its stamp, I guess we could say, from a form more prototypic than just the libidinal, and for that reason . . . ." Lofton intoned.

The words and the residents told him that, all in all, everything was happening as it should. They also told him how deeply he loved his work.

Six

The damned thing was back, and why at this particular moment he couldn't even guess. What he was doing at the instant of its arrival was something totally new, so it couldn't be that what he was about connected directly with something he had done before, or even familiar with in any way he could figure. But yet, here it was, back again in force, and right here in his hectic Moreland office. The *presque* part of it, however, was less urgent this time and the *vu* part was now the pushier element. What the hell could he be on the verge of, assuming he could believe in the validity of the feeling? This was getting to be amazing, his being called to pay attention to something and not having the foggiest notion what it was. He shifted his gaze from the wall back to the sheets of lab reports on his desk, the material he was plying when that spooky feeling of having almost done it all before came upon him but this time notably coupled with the strong and disquieting sense that he was all set to see, or feel, or do—who the hell knows?—something actually new and different. The more he puzzled over it, the more it faded, and in a few moments it was gone, leaving him to feel oddly and completely alone. The peculiar feeling of emptiness he felt on its departure gave him the sense of having had a spectral visitation of some sort but now being plopped back into the world of ordinary reality and left blinking to regain standard focus. He could understand how some of the more suggestible could swear to astral projection, clairvoyance, teleportation, spiritual contact and the like in their effort to apply a sense of purpose or meaning to the experience. But what the hell was its purpose for him? He hadn't figured it out in thirty years and he wasn't likely to figure it out this morning, he grouched as he returned to the stack of papers on his desk.

A packet of several sheets on the top of the stack included a copy of the clinical lab results on the Jordan case along with the autopsy report, plus the freshly arrived, eagerly awaited pathology report on the brain tissue sections Jess had requested. So, pre- and post-mortem studies were now available for comparison, the histology report having arrived late yesterday. In the intervening week since young Jordan's death nothing much else had happened other than that DMH approval had been secured for re-activating Building Seven, an accomplishment now making the rounds as something of an administrative stroke. The DMH had turned out to be surprisingly congenial to the Council's proposal, and Engineering and Maintenance were already well along with their hammers and nails in restoring the building to habitability. The effect was positively invigorating with the staff at Moreland energized by the spirit of mobilization. For its part, the enemy, Blush, seemed undaunted inasmuch as the hospital's admission rate climbed steadily as new cases were housed wherever possible until Building Seven was opened, which was expected to be within "ten more working days." All in all, things were moving at break-neck speed, given the system's usual glacial tempo in making even urgent adjustments.

The thicker packet of papers on his desk contained the protocols of the neuropsychological testing on those patients initially evaluated at the drug rehabilitation center when they were simple druggies but who were subsequently admitted to Moreland as Blush cases. They had been re-tested upon admission, and would be tested again six weeks farther on. There were already four such cases, yielding a rate tragically far in excess of initial expectation. Here, neuropsychological profiles pre- and post-Blush were available for comparison. So, Jordan's post-mortem neuroanatomic studies were now at hand, at least in that isolated case so far, and the pre- and post-Blush neuropsychological measurements were coming in steadily. The result was that it was now possible to demonstrate Blush's effect not only on the anatomy of the brain but also upon mental function, and maybe the interconnection between the two. That left the neurochemical part of the triad to be determined, and nothing had come back from the state lab yet in their work on that providential sample of the drug. When those results came in, Moreland would then have in its possession basic and probably singular data on the anatomy, the psychology, and the chemistry of this spreading pestilence which carried the demure name of "Blush."

He and Moyer were already well into the text of the paper they were writing. They had finished the preliminary and introductory sections, detailed the method of study, and had already laid out the format for tabulating the data. And, wonder of wonders, they had already polished up some of the sections to their satisfaction and were in the unique and enviable position of merely having to wait for the data to arrive for it to be processed, and then to access it to the text of a paper whose most difficult part had already been completed. Whatever, it was great that they, too, had garnered some of that spirit of mobilization buzzing around them. And all in less than a month! Why couldn't they have moved so resolutely with LSD twenty years earlier? Maybe that's what was behind the verge feeling this morning!

He then picked up the autopsy report with taut anticipation. It had arrived at the Admin building late yesterday after he left, and Weaver had immediately sent a copy of it over to him so that he would have it first thing in the morning. He knew Weaver was just as jubilant about the evolving paper as he and Clay were and was lubricating administrative wheels left and right to help the process along. He and Clay, in gratitude, had offered to add his name to the authorship of the paper but Weaver had demurred, contending graciously that only those who actually did the work of gathering the data and writing the text should be so designated, contrary to the practice in some centers. So he was just now seeing the autopsy report for the first time. Immediately upon arriving at work a short time earlier and finding it waiting on his desk he called Clay to break the good news and urge him to dash over so that they could take a moment to go over it together, along with some of the neuropsychologic test reports. Doing so, they could perhaps get an early start on the data tabulation which each hoped would in short order lead to formulation of the paper's conclusions, plus its wrap-up discussion section. *Voila*! Just about all done except for the chemistry report due in any day from the state lab! Clay, as joyous as he could allow himself to be seen, had said he would be over in a trice, as soon as he finished morning report on the Triage unit. So while he awaited Clay's arrival he would have the luxury of a few moments to scan the report in the quiet and splendid isolation of a short run of untrammeled time prior to the activation of his public day.

But it all depended on there being some positive findings in the autopsy, so he quickly riffled through the several pages of the report to estimate scanning time—an inveterate habit acquired in a speed reading course years earlier—and then settled down to the traditionally-cast opening paragraph: ". . . *the body is that of a twenty-one year old Caucasian male, adequately nourished and showing typical livor mortis and no external signs of trauma or of terminal angor . . . .*" He skipped over the general observations and proceeded to the gross findings. ". . . *the liver capsule was smooth and glistening and the liver itself was normal in configuration and size, weighing 1740 grams. There was no evidence of fatty infiltration, nor was there visual evidence of necrotic discoloration or cyst formation. Color was normal and there was no exaggeration of tissue architecture. The gall bladder was negative for evidence of stone, thickening, or inflammatory process, while the ductal system showed . . . .*" He leafed on and reached the gross findings on the heart. His first-line hope was that death had been caused by a hidden congenital anomaly of the heart, an anomaly which might have led to an electrical instability and ultimately to cardiac arrest. Such things were not uncommon, and probably accounted for a large portion of the unexplained sudden deaths in the young, such as those occurring in athletic exertions and the like. But the gross findings were very much normal—no irregular pattern in the coronary vasculature, no vessel atresias, no septal defect, no abnormality in valve morphology, nothing unusual in overall size and weight. Nothing. And certainly no evidence of vessel occlusion or myocardial damage. He had wondered if an undetected myopathy could have been the culprit, but that frail hope was now set aside as he passed on to the gross examination of the brain.

Here again, the opening description was that of a perfectly normal-appearing brain, and his spirits now began to sag in earnest. The cerebrospinal fluid was described as clear, and the tissue linings of the brain were ostensibly normal in texture and color. The major blood vessels were grossly normal in size, number, and distribution with no aneurysms—a distant second-line hope—or visible areas of leakage. He had even considered that maybe a small, focal hemorrhage in some vital area, such as the brain stem, might have caused the catastrophe, but here again no evidence of such was forthcoming. He scanned ahead, noting enroute that the sulci and gyri of the cortex were normal in appearance and that the cerebellum and medulla were likewise apparently unremarkable. Soon enough he reached the description of the brain slices. Here the pathologist's report showed a focusing of descriptive detail, as though he, too, were becoming concerned that no ostensible cause of death had so far been suggested by the findings, thus encouraging a most minute examination of the deeper structures of the brain as etiologic possibilities narrowed. The more frontal coronal slices again revealed nothing of significance and the deeper structures were described as free of hemorrhagic discoloration, displacement, or softening. The ventricles did not show enlargement or distortion. However, the mid-brain slices revealed what the pathologist described as dulling of the normally shiny or glistening surface, and specifically in a circumscribed area of the medial portions of the thalami. The dullness was described as a barely noticeable opaqueness distinct from the surrounding and glossier surface of the other thalamic regions and neighboring tissue. His spirits, like a rejuvenated Tinkerbell, began to rise. The dullness extended the caudal length of the medial portions of the thalami and hence continued through several coronal sections. Cantrelle could feel the pathologist's channeled attention and excitement as he read more intently the description of the cited thalamic areas which, the report continued, seemed softer to the touch than the tissue of the surrounding structures, though only barely so, The dullness was bilateral and apparently equal in extent. This immediately suggested to Cantrelle that if some pathologic process were at hand to account for the observed changes, it must be focused only in some nuclei groups of the thalamus since not all of that structure seemed similarly affected, thus far. He knew the pathologist assuredly must have thought the same and would use microscopic slides of the affected areas to trace out the altered appearance on the cellular level. That would be farther on in the report, he guessed. But at the moment his mind raced ahead excitedly at the prospect of coupling the patient's behavior with the affected thalamic nuclei groups, *if*—and such a large 'if'—*if* the tissue changes turned out to be valid evidence of an ante-mortem process with definite cellular localization, and not just some diffuse, non-specific post-mortem event that had nothing to do with a living response to Blush. He decided the former, solely by the emphasis the pathologist was placing on the finding.

Just then the office buzzer went off.

"Yes, Mrs. Andretti?" he answered, pulling himself away from the report.

"Mr. Moyer is here, Dr. Cantrelle," she replied.

"Good. Thanks," he returned.

He got up from his chair, report in hand, and made straightaway for the door in a quick loop designed to return him non-stop to the next paragraph of the report. He opened the door at the apogee of his orbit and beckoned forth Moyer who seemed ready to pick up on the tempo Cantrelle set.

"Come in, Clay," he opened with a wave of the report. "I think our pathologist is about to tell us something very important." He was already back to his chair when Moyer closed the door and followed.

He waited for Moyer to settle in and then began a re-cap of the report he had covered thus far. In doing so he filled Moyer in on some of the neuroanatomy cited inasmuch as Moyer's training did not include much in the way of such study. He reminded Moyer that the thalami—there were two of them, one for each hemisphere—were the big junction boxes of the brain where it seemed that feelings and actions, and likely even thoughts, and especially thoughts about the self, were integrated so that our behavior came off smooth, anticipatory, sentient, and emotionally balanced. It seemed to be a major area where input from "higher centers," meaning the cerebral cortex, was matched with input from "lower centers," meaning the hypothalamus and the autonomic nervous system, to produce behavior that was cognitively and emotionally blended to suit the environment, both internal as well as external. He mentioned that lesions in different areas of the thalamus produced a rich variety of behaviors ranging from comas and catatonic-like trances, to various forms of confusion and excitement, many with vivid display of autonomic dysfunction such as profuse sweating, excitement, vascular irritability, gastrointestinal stimulation, and the like. Those lesions, he emphasized tactically, tended to be diffuse, extensive, and sometimes massive in their impact, such as with infarction of large portions of the thalamic mass because of occlusion of nutrient blood vessels. The resulting clinical findings thus tended to be pervasive and even global, masking the probably discrete and punctate functions different portions of the thalami performed. Hence, it had always been difficult to correlate clinically specific portions of the thalami with their probably equally specific functions, such that the finer complexities of thalamic function still awaited the advent of enabling technology for the probing of their secrets. In fact, some investigators, guessing ahead, had registered the hunch that the thalami would someday prove to be the "self center," the organ of the brain which managed consciousness of the self and of its boundaries in relation to the non-self world. He had a few years earlier lightly mentioned that proposition in one of the A.M. Staff Conferences, but to prepare Moyer for what he suspected was forthcoming in the report he recalled aloud that the thalami were composed of several groupings of nuclei, designated by their location, such as antero-medial nuclei, or the posterior-lateral nuclei, and that there were, if his med school neuroanatomy served him right, seven or eight such clusters of these nuclei bilaterally and that each cluster likely tended to some particular task of mind-body integration as yet undisclosed to the probings of research.

"That's as far as I've gotten in the report, Clay. Now that you're here you can hold my hand as I shakily press on. Do you realize what this report might give us?" he exulted less in failure to contain his anticipation and more in declamation of the moment. "If the slides show discrete lesions in specific nuclei we might have a basis for coupling those nuclei with function. But you know," he realized as he reined himself in, "we still don't have a hint as to the cause of death. Thalamic lesions alone wouldn't do it, I don't think." Thus sobered he looked at the waiting report held in his lap as he puzzled.

"Let's see what the rest of it says, Frank. Don't let your crest fall too soon," Moyer urged sensibly, motioning in the direction of the report.

Cantrelle resumed reading as bidden.

"Let's see. Nothing else on the thalamus. Cerebellum and peduncles O.K. Anterior pons unremarkable," he checked off as he scanned the pages. "Here we go! Something else!" he announced as he straightened in his chair. "Listen to this!" he directed. ". . . '*Sections through the mid-pontine area show a localized area of similar dulling in the region of the superior portion of the reticular formation.*' Clay!" he yelped, "I think that could do it! The reticular formation is where a lot of the regulation of breathing takes place—that's what's called the respiratory center. This could total up to respiratory arrest—and the reason for his death! I bet those dull areas represent cell damage, and I bet there's a connection, I mean a functional connection, between the dulled region in the thalami and this dulled region in the reticular formation, and I bet it has to do with disruption of breathing. And one further bet, disruption of breathing during sleep . . . maybe. I'm sure someone has described a tract connecting thalamic nuclei with the reticular formation, but my med school level of neurology doesn't offer me a hint. Where the hell are the neurologists when you really need one?" he railed on jubilantly as he rapidly scanned the rest of the page to reach the part dealing with the histology of the affected cells. "Wait! Here we are!" he noted upon reaching that portion of the report. Moyer waited patiently as Cantrelle skimmed over the descriptions and interpretations of representative tissue sections from the various organs to reach those of the brain. "Now let's see," he mumbled as he drew a sharper focus on the page before him. "*This* is what we've been looking for!" he announced to Moyer through a wide smile which he sustained as he scrutinized the print before him.

"I'm all ears," Moyer reminded him after a few moments of silence.

"Right." Cantrelle returned quickly with chagrin over momentarily forgetting his friend's suspense. "Here it is," he offered as he began to read, " '. . . *sections through the region of the dorsal medial nuclei region of the thalamus show a general diminution in the number of cells, both parenchymal and glial, per visual field. The remaining cells show a disorganized configuration suggestive of a disruptive process active in the regions studied. Vacuolation, both intra- and extracellular, is extensive, revealing the progression from initial cell injury to cell death to subsequent cell resorption. Pyknosis'*—that means getting smaller and blacker, Clay—'*of nuclei in various stages of the process show random distribution in the group studied with little similar involvement in neighboring thalamic cell groups. The net effect is one of loss of cell density in the dorso-medial group with vacuolation of the cellular matrix. Glial response*'—that means tissue effort to make up the damage, like scar tissue—'*is minimal such that the affected regions show early honey-combing and extensive loss of normal cytoarchitecture.*' Clay, that would account for the dull appearance in the gross specimen and also for the slight sponginess to the touch. This pathologist is really doing his stuff," Cantrelle applauded. "Let's get over to the other area, the reticular formation at the level of distal pons, I think it was . . . . Here we are!" he noted with his finger as he projected his voice in Clay's direction. " '*Transverse sections through the brain stem at the pontine level demonstrate normal pyramidal and olivary architecture, and the regional cranial nuclei are readily identified.*'—those are standard orienting structures on that brain stem level, Clay—'*However, scrutiny of the reticular system bilaterally shows the same vacuolation as noted above in the dorsa-medial thalamic nuclei with diminution of cell density and a general disorganization of structural orientation. The same honeycombing is noted along the reticular formation adjacent to the spino-thalamic tract and is present in more rostral as well as caudal sections tracing the length of the affected region . . . .*' It goes on to give more detail regarding the loss of cells in the region, plus what he considers a high degree of localization in the pattern of cell loss. Listen to this! '*. . . in general, the pattern and character of the described lesions are in part reminiscent of and consistent with the microscopic findings seen in tissue injury to specifically-acting CNS toxins though this particular distribution and combination of such injury has not thus far been noted in the literature. In addition, the degree of vacuolation with minimal gliosis is suggestive of those lesions associated with CNS disorders suspected to be of auto-immune origin . . . .*' He goes on to list the autopsy findings and suggests that clinical correlation with the toxicology of the case is necessary for a complete diagnosis—rather!—and then suggests that '*in the absence of other possible contributors*'—I wonder what that means? Like being smothered with a pillow?—'*that death was caused by failure of the respiratory system because of cell destruction in the respiratory center.*'"

He sighed as he lowered the report to his lap. A wave of exhaustion—as well as relief—swept through him. For the moment he felt that he had urged the whole process along—pathology and all—by will power alone, and that a certain sense of fulfillment was thus merited. At such a moment it was easy to feel that if he hadn't willed it so forcefully, it would never have taken place, much less have followed the course it did. Anyway, it was now accomplished, and he needed to rest for a while, certainly to swivel his chair into position and stare at the wall a bit, the absolute ultimate in spiritual rest. He noted that Moyer was apparently feeling the same, sitting there in an absorbed weariness, lost in some distant reverie. He was resting, too.

"Drains you, doesn't it?" Cantrelle mentioned in recalling both to their mission.

"Yeah, and it makes you wonder if we can see it through," Moyer reflected.

Cantrelle knew exactly what he meant. It was an exhilarating delight to be among the first to grasp the importance of some event, and it was consummately fulfilling to be vindicated in one's hunches about the origins and meanings of such an event. But it was also overwhelming to feel the responsibilities that came of such preferment because now they were both, he and Clay, thereby designated the ones, maybe thus far the *only* ones, to shoulder the task of follow-through their unique position imposed. What had started out as a jaunty adventure had now become, through the advent of vindication, a sober responsibility which reached far beyond the earlier personal satisfactions sought.

"Yeah, I know." Cantrelle answered simply.

After a moment of chastened silence, Moyer continued.

"It looks like it all adds up, but we have no way of knowing for sure that what seems to apply in this one case will apply in all the others," he observed, ever the pragmatist.

Cantrelle thought for a minute. Moyer was right because the findings in this case could just possibly be specific for this case alone. For example, the Jordan boy might have had an idiosyncratic reaction to Blush with the result that everything described in the post-mortem findings was really in the nature of a unique, personal sensitivity to the agent. Something like the proverbial allergy to strawberries not often seen in others. If so, then the findings would be more specific for this one case's reactivity to the agent and not something characteristic of the agent itself.

"That's true, Clay," he mulled, "and since the MRI and all the lab tests we've tried don't seem to pick up the lesions beforehand—they didn't in this case—I guess we actually have little to go on just now to see how general, or specific, these findings truly are. Looks like we're back to waiting," he noted in ominous monotone as he looked at the report in his lap.

"Do you think Jess has looked at the report yet?" Moyer wondered.

"Oh, I'm sure he has," Cantrelle replied. "He was eager to have something solid to pass on to the family. He's probably already called them. In fact, we should probably check with him right away because I'm sure he's also been in touch with the DMH about the implications of the report."

He reached over to the phone and began dialing.

"Hello, This is Dr. Cantrelle. Is Dr. Weaver available? . . . Thank you." He waited the obligatory moment. "Jess? Good morning . . . O.K., and yourself? . . . Good. Jess, thanks for sending over a copy of the post-mortem . . . I just finished going over it with Clay. Looks like we'll have a paper forthcoming soon enough. Sure you don't want your name on it? . . . All right, all right." He then shifted to a back-to-business tone. "I think the three of us ought to get together this morning to go over the report and talk about its possible implications. How about ten o'clock or thereabouts?" he suggested as he arched his eyebrows in the direction of Moyer who nodded approval, "O.K. I'll call back in a few minutes to confirm it . . . Well, if you can't, we'll work out another time. See you."

The phone back in its cradle, he returned to Moyer.

"He's probably already traced out the implications just as we have, but since we three are the only ones on campus this far along in sizing up the beast we ought to grab the chance to pool our uniqueness because soon enough we may find ourselves forever lost in a sea of intense and meaningful human discourse," he observed in return to his usual cynicism.

"Yeah, sometimes it happens no matter what you do," Moyer affirmed as he got up to leave. "I m going back to the unit now. I'll meet you at Jess' at ten."

"Sure," Cantrelle agreed. "By the way, I forgot to ask you how the unit's doing. Wouldn't want you to think I'm unconcerned," he teased.

"It happens that we're doing pretty well, I'll have you know," Moyer harrumphed, "despite all manner of neglect from those who should stop by more often to share in the burden of demesne," he reproved.

"All right, I'm sorry I missed yesterday's conference. I just couldn't make it. I do have a few other things happening in my life besides Moreland and its saintly mission, you know. Not nearly as important, of course, but occasionally prevailing. And besides, I'm sure you and Berends handled the conference with refreshing deft, if I might so guess," he bantered in kind.

"But it just wasn't the same," Moyer sighed as he tilted his chin up and away.

"Get the hell out of here," Cantrelle scolded through his laughter, "but be there at ten o'clock, damn it."

Moyer rose and left in a burble of chuckles at Cantrelle's mock outrage. As the door closed, Cantrelle swivelled around in return to the wall.

He genuinely did regret missing yesterday's clinical conference on the unit. After all, he was the one who had emphasized the importance of such a conference in maintaining the overall orientation of the unit. Because of the forcefulness of his plea he had been dubbed the one most suited to the chairmanship of the conference, and had accepted such, though he usually delegated the actual performance of that duty to the several psychiatrists of the unit on a rotating basis to give them experience in the rôle. But he always attended, regardless who chaired. Yesterday, however, he had other business.

That particular business concerned Todd and his ongoing troubles in school. His teacher had requested a parent-teacher conference regarding certain trends in Todd's school performance. The teacher had noted of late a definite slackening in Todd's academic effort which had long been problematic in any event because of his desultory and uneven commitment to just about any work assigned. Yet, his effort, though checkered, was usually enough to award him with satisfactory and occasionally, when a subject struck his fancy, good grades. But over the previous month or so his motivation even for barely passing grades had been visibly enfeebled, despite the teacher's efforts to encourage him otherwise. The teacher felt that her resources were reaching the point of exhaustion and thus wanted to speak to Cantrelle and Laura to apprise them of the status of things and to search out some collaborative approach to the problem. For his part Todd characteristically disclaimed any awareness of the teacher's concern or her purpose in the proposed meeting. So the meeting was convened with neither he nor Laura fully sure of the agenda, though both were fairly certain it would be oriented along the recurrent theme of Todd's failure to repair, Laura showing decidedly the sharper readiness for joining issues. They were not disappointed, though Cantrelle was genuinely surprised to learn that Todd had been missing significantly more school and was falling behind on that account alone and not so much from minimal effort when he was suitably in attendance. Laura had probably brought it up earlier but he, Cantrelle, had somehow let it go right by him. Actually, he did vaguely remember her mentioning it a few times but he had considered the events as isolated occurrences. For her part, Laura was not surprised at the teacher's disclosure and nodded knowingly as the teacher detailed the problem. The teacher specifically inquired as to whether any particular family problems existed as contributors to Todd's faltering effort, and did so with commendable discretion and tact. He and Laura assured her of their willingness to explore that possibility though he actually was disinclined to target the family as a conveniently more visible and more accessible arena of inquiry. Laura suggested out of hand that the mounting successes of his siblings, Richard and Ellie, posed no small problem for Todd, and, in the main, automatically established him as the underachiever of the family. The teacher concurred readily, though Cantrelle privately suspected that the circumstance was really more an effect than a cause. The teacher and Laura thought otherwise, or at least saw more cause in it than he preferred. In any event, the teacher suggested that Todd's blunted, debilitating sibling rivalry was probably escalating with his movement into his late teens, competition themes and identity issues being what they were at his point on the growth curve, and that professional counseling beyond what the school offered was now definitely to be considered. In saying this she made polite deference to Cantrelle as a noted psychiatrist, but her manner also made it clear that she was speaking to him in his identity as a father, not as a physician. Cantrelle admired her professional touch but that didn't spare him the feeling of discomfort in having his duty to his own son pointed out to him.

Following the meeting he and Laura went to lunch together at one of their traditional pre-nuptial spots. The country-style inn had figured prominently in their courtship and it was where they had had their first glass of Chablis together. They had long since moved on to vintage Chardonnays and posh restaurants, but returning to the inn was always refreshing as well as tenderly nostalgic. The effect was especially welcome that morning after the teacher conference, particularly in view of the doubts the conference unavoidably raised as to the now abridged glory of their matrimonial venture. After some mutually restorative assurances helped along by the good food, Laura brought up the issue of securing a therapist for Todd. Cantrelle instinctively balked at the idea but could offer nothing more positive. Todd had previously rejected such arrangements, even when he was younger and compliantly more amenable to such undertakings. Twice before Todd had agreed to sessions with child psychiatrists, only to refuse further meetings after the initial evaluation. Cantrelle felt strongly that Todd was now even less congenial to the idea than earlier and that a too energetic pursuit of the matter would simply define another locus of conflict. Cantrelle would like to preserve as much amity as possible for later use when Todd most likely would be more compliant, as is so often seen with teenagers after they leave some of their turbulence behind. But Cantrelle understood as well as the others that the problem was right now, and hopeful anticipation of a better time was certainly no defensible stance to take at this juncture. So, reluctantly, he concurred with Laura about seeking out a prospective therapist though he knew in his heart Todd would pick up on the ambivalence surrounding the effort and use it to reinforce his own predictable resistance. Thus their luncheon went: reverence for the past, indented pride for the present, and circumscribed hope for the future, all officially sealed with a rejuvenant glass of Chablis, current vintage. And in the periphery of this survey was his promise that some day, and soon, he would just sit down and talk to that boy.

He now allowed memory of the luncheon and its homily to recede, and he sat motionless in silent witness of its departure. After barely a moment of the quiet, blessed solitude that followed, the buzzer once again jolted him forth.

"Yes, Mrs. Andretti?" he reported.

"Dr. Cantrelle, your class is waiting and you said you wanted to meet with Dr. Weaver at ten, didn't you?" she reminded.

God, he'd forgotten to ask her to check with Jess to find out if he'd be free at ten so that he and Clay would meet with him as planned. She'd undoubtedly heard him say as much as Clay was leaving and had been waiting for her instructions. He wondered how many times she had similarly covered his ass over the years.

"Oh, yes, Mrs. Andretti. Thanks," acknowledging his oversight. "Could you please call Dr. Weaver's office and see if he can meet with me and Mr. Moyer at that time? And if not, call Mr. Moyer and inform him?"

"I've already called Dr. Weaver's secretary and told her there was a likelihood you and Mr. Moyer might need to meet with him at ten and that we would confirm it once I'd talked to you further. His secretary said she was sure he would be available at ten to meet with you if you could make it," she explained matter-of-factly.

Damn it, he grumbled to himself as he bounded out of his chair and stepped into the outer office, that woman just knew much too much and thank the good Lord for it, he conceded once again as he winced in grateful recognition, which she received with the slightest twinkle of the eye. Sometimes it was nice to feel needy in her presence.

"Thanks for being on top of it," he offered briskly to deflect the chagrin of the moment. "Now let me get on to those devoted residents whom also I am tempted to forget," he stated with playful candor as he entered the hallway, closing the door, and the matter, behind him.

A few gallops later and he was again sitting before his class who sensed that he was caught up in something else beside the topic on the docket for discussion. So the class waited attentively for anything he chose to offer as lead-in, as he so often did. But today he restrained himself, preferring to meet with Jess before any public review of the autopsy report was undertaken. He would broach it with the resident group later. He thus went directly to the course material scheduled for attention, an action interpreted by the residents as signaling his determined preoccupation with some other matter.

"Good morning, everybody," he offered unconvincingly. "I guess you've all been breathing more easily now that we've covered Freud's major works and are now ready to move on to the next major players in line. With the Ego firmly established, by dint of the 1923 and 1926 papers, as the psychic agency of future study, we can see how Ego Psychology took off in the thirties and continues to this day. The papers we'll review over the next couple of months will show how we arrived step-by-step at the concept of Ego as we currently understand it. We'll start with Nunberg and work our way through Waelder, and ultimately to the biggie, Hartman, Kris, and Lowenstein, and beyond, to the more current trends in Self Psychology and Separation and Individuation themes. And that will take us to the end of the course. But before we leave Freud altogether I think we should, as I mentioned last time, spend a few sessions on the great dissidents of his day—Adler and Jung. Because Freud is so pre-eminent there's a tendency to look upon Adler and Jung as apostates of little note other than that they chose to betray their master. Forswear the thought, unless thou canst not do otherwise for that thy God is a jealous God and Sigmund be his name. Adler and Jung were not simply invidious opportunists as has sometimes been implied. No, they were good and learned men, especially in the case of Jung, but their discoveries and contributions were sometimes outside the then current mainstream of methodologic development, and for an insular and parochial movement such as the psychoanalytic school in the first decade of this century, such transgression was simply unforgivable. We'll take each man separately and see what the doctrinal issues were that forced a split from the body of orthodox analytic thought, which, as you know, at that time was the topographic model. I think you'll see that Adlerian notions in particular do not seem so dissonant with the later structural model which we just recently achieved in our discussions. But bear in mind when we go through Adler that his ideas were offered at a time when the topographic model, the Psychology of the Unconscious, was the true word. I think you'll then see the polemic a bit better. Who's up to lead us in the discussion?"

"I am, Dr. Cantrelle," Dr. Aranzuela replied with a flick of her upraised hand.

"O.K. Let me get things started and then you can take over," he advised. "First, you remember that in the topographic model Freud posited the Libido hypothesis as well as a dual instinct theory, the latter to account for essential conflict. The two classes of instincts, I'm sure you'll never forget, were the self-preservative instincts and the sexual instincts. The sexual instincts, gathered together under the libido hypothesis, accounted for the psychosexual stages of development, and hence character formation, and, not the least, symptom formation in the neuroses. Remember? Well, imagine yourself suggesting to the master and the entire following that perhaps another instinct entirely, quite different in its compass, was more likely the engine driving human behavior. Nothing less than blasphemy, one could suppose. Yet, that's about what Adler did. He suggested that the aggressive drive was—remember, Freud did not see aggression at this time as being a separate instinct, but held that aggressive behavior was merely a decay phenomenon, a result of frustration of the sexual or of the self-preservative instinctual urges—a separate instinct in its own right and that it drove behavior accordingly, whether the sexual drives were satisfied or not. It had a life of its own, he said, and accounted for certain individual as well as sociologic phenomena. You see, early on, Adler is reaching into the social sphere, and does so at a time—around 1910—when the psycho-analytic movement is focused totally upon the individual, at least in so far as the technically proper locus of behavior study was concerned. Adler moves right on to describe society from the standpoint of aggression and its communal derivatives, and he divides individuals and their collective social classes into three character groupings; four actually, but one is so lamentably rare as to be hardly worth mentioning. As I'm sure you remember from your reading of today's material, the four basic character types are *The Getting*, *The Avoiding*, and *The Ruling*. The fourth and regrettably far less common, it seems, is what he calls *The Healthy and Socially Useful Individual*. It is instructive to note that he sees the first three as pathologic for lack of social feeling, and we'll spend a few minutes on what he means by that. But first we'll work on Adler's use of the concept of the aggressive instinct, a notion Freud didn't reach as a doctrinal acquisition until 1923, as we learned just a few sessions back; and then we'll go on to the discussion of Adler's use of these four basic character types, their genesis and influence in shaping society's strivings. And by the way, 'Adler' in German means 'eagle.' Ready, Dr. Aranzuela?"

"Yes," she replied in her spicy accent. "Apparently Adler was very much impressed by Freud's *Interpretation of Dreams*, and Freud must have been very much impressed by Adler because shortly after the publication of that book he invites Adler to join his group. At the beginning, they share an interest in understanding the nature of neurosis and psychosis, but big differences as we will see in their approach soon show up. The differences, as this paper says, were based on . . . ." she carefully detailed to her fellow residents as he listened for the annual go-around on the evolution of social psychiatry and the origin of what would later become, in America, at least, Community Mental Health, supportive psychotherapy, the PTA, and a host of other approaches, procedures, and institutions Americans would prefer to believe they created in their own image as Americans but which were formulated long before by the young Adler, only to be re-invented fifty years later by American mental health thinkers who saw little value in knowing their doctrinal history, and were thus compelled to mock it. He wondered as he listened how many bright and promising pursuits of this very moment would prove truly to be the same old wine in shiny new bottles and that the phenomenon of discovery is essentially the phenomenon of growth, and for the person or persons experiencing the phenomenon it is always new and for the first time, like these residents discovering what for them is new, unique, and theirs alone, while for him it is simply history, almost thirteen years of it, cycling its new participants through established developmental steps. After all, this is a young society, this America, in attitude if no longer in age, and there were still many things we had to set ourselves to as though we alone were discovering such things wholly for the first time and properly for the entire world. It just was more fun to go at it that way. And in truth, for some things there probably was no other way, his very own lectures could tell him.

". . . so the concept of organ inferiority and the need to compensate is seen by Adler as the driving force behind . . . ."

His thinking was abruptly shunted back to Todd and his attempts at compensation, which at the moment were taking a less than laudable turn. To whom could he send Todd for therapy? Certainly no one very close personally because of the artifacts and awkwardness which would come of that closeness. On the other hand, surely someone who had acquired a good sense of such problems and whose competence was well established. Generally, the therapists who fit that ticket were the ones he knew personally. Actually, the best possible pairing was with Burleson himself, but he knew that Burleson no longer saw private patients, given the excessive demands placed on his time by the endless teaching duties—even if he were close at hand, and he wasn't. So he knew he would have to go a bit beyond his comfort and familiarity zone in seeking a therapist for his son, but from the outset he knew that to be inevitably the case in the overall. He always regarded analytic psychotherapy—psychoanalysis for sure—as a post-graduate course in one's self; an adventure in discovery in which one is both the subject as well as the observer. It was probably the highest form of investigative scrutiny to arrive upon the human scene. Therapeutic benefits accrued not so much as a primary goal in itself but as a consequence of one's enlarged awareness coupled with the depth of such insight, salutary change being a function of re-aligned development and fuller maturation. He would have been delighted to have Todd undertake that form of therapy. Yet, he knew that Todd, because of the very nature of his problem, was not capable of that kind of therapy, and would fit better, if he agreed to it at all, the approach called 'action therapy' which was given more to various training regimens in the re-shaping of behavior and thus less to the pursuit of insight and analysis of symptoms. But while Todd's limitations and symptoms seemed to point him in the direction of action therapy, his personality seemed pre-set to resist just such effort to modify his behavior.

". . . and thus, the primary intervention of the therapist, Adler says, is the use of encouragement to try some new approaches to life once the patient has the understanding of the cause of his symptoms,"

Dr. Aranzuela continued. "Adler is more concerned with the patient taking a positive action on his own behalf and progressively gaining the self-confidence he . . . ."

He hoped he'd been clear enough to Todd in offering encouragement, he mused. He knew he tried to stay on the positive side with him, gently pointing to newer and better efforts and drawing upon their shared reservoir of general good will while urging him along over the bumps. He was sure that Todd was keenly aware of the tactic, however gentle, and even appreciated the effort, particularly the faith and confidence it implied. The likelihood was that Todd, despite the poor showing imposed by his learning deficits, had basic good ability, probably equal to that of his unblighted siblings, and understood all too well the concerns those around him had for his welfare, but it was also probable that his very awareness carried in its wake a debilitating anguish in the face of anyone's attempts to assist him. The boy was excruciatingly tender-hearted despite all his efforts to escape being so, and his need to salvage his pride under such demeaning circumstances gave too large a boost to obstructionistic behavior. For the time being, anyway.

"Adler, then, is the originator of the 'holistic,' as we say, approach to treatment, and his use of the term 'life style' both as the psychodynamic as well as the sociologic concept is still much basic to our use of the term today," she detailed. "In fact, the term, very much the same as he originally defined it, is now a big part of our everyday thinking. And his premise that the drive for superiority in overcoming the primary infantile state of helplessness is what we know these days as the drive for mastery. So, all in all . . . ."

He glanced at his watch as Adler's unsung contributions to the American mental health scene were revealed. The discussion, with its inevitable and patriotic disclaimers that a foreigner could have proposed so long ago what currently seemed to be distinctly American, would follow the opening exposition now in process, and later a resident or two would depart the session at its conclusion a bit miffed that American pre-eminence in the field had been impugned, somehow, by imposed awareness of Adler's work and its remarkable prescience. His efforts over the years to point out to such residents that their very reaction was an experiential example of Adler's notion of the drive for superiority—the deployment of a compensatory truculence to offset any sense of inferiority and helplessness—usually accomplished little in extending the heuristic opportunity of the moment. And these were uniformly bright and solid-citizen residents, the "healthy and socially useful." Small wonder that any symptomatic and suffering valetudinary would have trouble with that kind of therapeutic ordeal. A valetudinary like Todd, for example. What a way to talk about one's own son, but there was too much truth in it not to.

". . . And so Adler proposes, even in his early writings but more aggressively after his trouble with Freud, I think he would agree, the establishment of child guidance clinics as the best approach to dealing with the beginnings of a neurosis and not just to wait until it reached full bloom in adulthood for analytic treatment then. So you can see that Adler supported a much more active approach for identifying such problems early, even recommending an arrangement with schools to single out the children for attention, as I understand it. Is that so, Dr. Cantrelle?" she appealed.

Her request for corroboration was purely innocent though his feelings wondered otherwise. He nodded his assent and held his tongue to allow her to move on. Sometimes this course took a distinctly downbeat turn, he gloomed.

". . . Because he emphasized the holistic view of the individual," she pursued, "his ideas on psychosis are very significant. First, he believes that organic factors play a large rôle. and so he recommends a combined biological, psychological, and social approach to the understanding of psychopathology, and to the psychosis in particular. Here we have the first words on . . . ."

Dr. Aranzuela seemed to be hitting all the major points quite nicely, he noted as he felt himself ease his attention away from the class collegium. He was having trouble restraining the anticipatory drift of his mind, intent as it was on the meeting with Jess—he glanced at his watch again—just ten impatient minutes away. He didn't want to give short shrift to his class, but Dr. Aranzuela was making it easy for him to seek an early departure. So he didn't interrupt to extend any particular point she raised and thus could allow the class to seek its own level of discourse on the topics broached. Dr. Aranzuela had set the level of discussion sufficiently high enough for him to permit the class to follow through on its own with little risk of missing additional major points.

And the class did just that as he sat benevolently by and approved. The discussion reverberated around the point that, surprisingly, Adler's name never seemed to come up in discussions elsewhere on the origins of the community mental health movement. There was a general agreement that perhaps the matter was just another example of a more pervasive "presentism" so typical of immature and imitative movements. He was pleased to hear the residents use that term unbidden and do so fairly accurately. A few minutes later, when he decided that the session and the topic had run its course, he signaled so by leaning forward and clasping his hands together before him on the table and summarizing.

"So if anyone, like board examiners, asks you about inferiority complex, life style, the drive for mastery, supportive psychotherapy, Dale Carnegie, the PTA, child guidance clinics, and the biopsychosocial approach to behavior, you can dazzle them with an insufferable display of masterful knowledge. Anyone dare to ask any questions? . . . O.K. If any arise later, bring them up at the beginning of the next session at which time we'll otherwise take a plunge ever deeper into the Unconscious as seen by Carl Jung. Your reading list has the reference material. You'll like this turnabout, going from the everyday exigences of Alfred Adler to the ageless cosmos of Carl Gustave Jung."

He hurried the class to closure and then rose from his chair, carefully avoiding any unspoken appeals from the residents to linger, trailing fashion, on some freshly unearthed point sprung from the morning's discussion. To linger so was fairly routine as he and the residents would shuffle down the hallway together in an ambulatory address to the session's reverberations. Not so today, and he vaulted ahead of the group who seemed to appreciate his need for altering the post-class agenda. Hence, they cleared a ready way for him. Smiles all around bade forgiveness for his neglectful haste, and he grinned back his intent to make it up to them at another time.

He swung past his office in lunging strides, waving to Mrs. Andretti as he did so, and then swivelled his way through the building entrance to be staggered by a blast of frigid air he had moments before decided to breast in favor of the delay retrieving his coat would impose, the trot to the administration building being less than a block away. Now he wasn't so sure about his decision, but he was already enroute. Plus, the sun was out. Also, the frigid air would be invigorating. He redoubled his resolve and moved up the drive rapidly.

In less than half a minute he reached the entrance of the administration building and, panting, pulled the door open for a quick entry as chills rattled his frame. Once inside the building's warmth he regained his steadiness and idly wondered if he was coming down with something. This would not be the time to succumb to the god-damned flu, he groaned in a quick inventory of his vital sensors. Receiving no additional signals he let the matter drop and proceeded to Weaver's office.

Moyer was already there, settled in a chair and chatting with Weaver. They acknowledged his approach as he traversed the secretary's outer office. Weaver waved him in and motioned for him to close the door behind him. That done he proceeded to settle in as he readied himself for catching up to the conversation.

"'Morning, Frank. Put the residents through their daily dozen?" Weaver inquired politely. He rarely failed to mention the residents at some point in their interchanges.

"Socked 'em with Adler this morning. They're still blinking," he replied to a freshet of snickers. "Jess, we wanted to meet with you this morning to go over the path report," he shifted. "Clay may have mentioned before I arrived that he and I reviewed it briefly a little while ago, and we felt the three of us should check our bearings so that we don't go off in separate directions. The paper is just about done, but we might want to hold this path report aside for now; it may soon make it necessary for us to write another paper, if you know what I mean," he suggested darkly. Moyer nodded sententiously at the morbid prospect.

"I know exactly what you mean, Frank. I had the same thought," Weaver agreed.

"We figured you would," Cantrelle replied. "We can get back to that later. Right now, the only thing we're waiting on before we go to press is something from the state lab on that sample. If we have the chemistry of Blush nailed down, plus all the clinical data we've already gotten, we'll have enough to put together one helluva paper as the first published word on this god-damned plague," he proclaimed as his voice rose in anticipation.

"The psychological test results alone would be enough for a basic paper," Moyer savored in restrained glee, "and at this point we just keep getting more of those 'before' and 'after' readings than we can keep up with. Shame to say, but with this particular plague we have, as Frank says, an embarrassment of riches. The only question we have now is when to call a halt to this phase—the psych phase—of data gathering."

Weaver smiled benevolently at their joint zeal as he rolled a pencil back and forth between his hands.

"That's just to bring you up on where we stand on the paper; it's not the main reason for coming here this morning," Cantrelle continued. "The reason is because of what I think you already suspect from the report. Clay and I feel . . . ."

"Before you go on I need to bring the two of you up to date on something," Weaver interrupted with delicacy. "You mentioned the state lab. I got a call from their boss chemist first thing this morning," he added hesitantly.

Cantrelle and Moyer came to alert attention. They both sensed that the way Weaver was proceeding likely boded ill. A joined silence braced them for disappointment.

"He said they took the sample as far as they could in their present set-up. They got it down to the category of a macromolecule with an iminodibenzyl radical as its probable hot spot and were ready to follow through with the analysis even though it would have taken them outside their usual operating range, and budget. But they were willing to do that. They believe they could have worked out the overall molecular structure just like we wanted, though maybe not as fast as we wanted. But word came from higher up to stop the analysis and transfer everything, sample and all, to NIH and to CDC."

"CDC! How the hell did they get into this?" Cantrelle exploded. "I guess by some stretch of the imagination we could call it a communicable disease, but to spread out the work between them and NIH is probably going to slow the whole fucking thing down to a crawl." He recalled that years ago when its address was Chamblee, Georgia, he drove by the Communicable Disease Center while enroute to his internship, all his earthly possessions stowed in the car. He recalled feeling reassured by the Center's August dimensions and also, he assumed, by its readiness to help in his sally into battle against all fell pathogens. He could never have considered then that today he would regret the Center's intrusion into his life. "And who the hell blew the whistle on the state lab? Here's a chance for the state—the *state*, mind you—to get back on the psychiatric map in a big way. The state that hasn't done a fucking thing in the field except play pathetic catch-up ever since Palmer left us to ourselves, and now some small-minded bureaucrat cocksucker who probably wants to protect his incompetent ass from stress, or more likely exposure, has taken it upon himself to decide what's best for everyone. Do you realize how long it'll take the Federal government to get moving on this? If the work has already been transferred the loss of momentum will take us just about all the way back to scratch. And the Federal government sure as hell doesn't see Blush as the problem we see it as being. The CDC has thousands, millions of cases of activist-borne venereal disease to pore over, and they're going to set all that aside to begin work on Blush, which, by their reckoning, is the scourge of a mere handful of electorally incapacitated citizens? Don't bet your ass!"

He was off and running and he would have gone through his entire repertoire on bureaucratic incompetence, the Peter Principle, Federal inability to distinguish means from end, politics as the traditional profit-sharing venture of the moral coward as well as show biz for the ugly, the talent of public servants for shrinking before your very eyes into invisibility at the hint of challenge by the unknown, and from there on to every other thread in the fabric of statutory failing—until Moyer brought him to a halt with a sobering question directed at Jess.

"Have more cases come up elsewhere?" he asked.

"Everywhere, apparently. I'm told unofficially that the decision came from the governor's office. It's not clear, but apparently someone in Washington called and set up the transfer. The DMH was informed that cases are cropping up *everywhere* in the country—and as a result it's no longer just a local or state problem, but a *national* one! Also, the sample we got and sent forward is apparently now only one of several the NIH has been able to get a hold of. But for the time being I suppose we'll just keep doing what we're doing on our level," Weaver advised.

Defeated was hardly the word for what he felt. He looked at Moyer for validation and Moyer raised his eyebrows in his characteristic gesture of resignation. But Cantrelle didn't feel ready for shrinking—that word again—just yet before anybody's eyes. If anything, he felt all the more provoked. It was all the same to him, and it was happening all over again as well. Shades of the LSD episode flashed back. Back then the study was allowed to slip right out of their hands, but moreso by personal dereliction than anything else. This time, however, there was the danger of its being willfully taken from them despite their repentant readiness to follow through, chastened, wiser, and better. To his own reckoning, the result was the same, regardless of the offending agent. As he was preparing to re-mount his diatribe he noticed that Moyer had sunk into deep thought. Over the years Cantrelle had learned that whenever Moyer pulled into himself like that it was because he was sizing up something from an alternative perspective and that one of his penetrating questions was likely on its way. Understanding such of his friend sometimes had an arresting effect on his own animus, wholly in deference to what better fare might be forthcoming. So Cantrelle held back on his own delivery and waited.

"Jess," Moyer resumed, "do you think that call from Washington to the Governor's Office came from the Attorney General's office or from the NIH itself?"

"I don't know; I didn't ask," Weaver replied with some surprise at the question. "Why do you ask, Clay?"

"Because it might make a very big difference," he pondered.

"What do you have in mind, Clay?" Cantrelle pursued.

"Nothing, really," Moyer managed in a faint attempt at deprecation. "It's just that this Blush thing might become a king-size embarrassment to the Federal administration with all its ballyhoo about its war on drugs. The Attorney General has been world-hopping for months and generating headlines daily on how well his generalship is proceeding in this drug war to end all drug wars. I was just wondering if Washington is more upset about these cases than we've given them credit for. And after our meeting this morning—and that path report—they might soon have damned good reason to be upset. Maybe they smell a rat. Or should I say louse?" he tacked on mercilessly.

After an agreed-upon chuckle Weaver responded.

"We may never know, Clay, but you might have something there," Weaver allowed. "I did find it odd that Sharpsfield could act so swiftly on making such a change in policy, because when I spoke to DMH just days ago they still seemed eager to go at the problem head on and give us the support we needed. Now they've punted in the direction of Washington, and remarkably fast, too. There might be something in what you say, Clay."

Moyer just shrugged, but Cantrelle knew better than to trust the gesture.

"Well, I guess soon enough we'll hear more about it, one way or another," Weaver added. "I do know of some people in the DMH who would be damned glad to foist the whole problem off on the Federal Government. But like you've said, Frank, there is always a noose attached to favors, especially Federal favors. But there's not much we can do about it now," he sighed. "By the way, you did want to talk about the path report, didn't you?" he reminded as he gently moved them along.

"Yeah," Cantrelle affirmed quickly, recalled to the urgency he felt earlier. "Jess, I'm sure you realize that this report, especially the histologic sections, might be telling us what the hell we're in for. If this isn't just a case of young Jordan's particular sensitivity to Blush then we can expect *all* of the users to drop dead, sooner or later. Worse, if we know it's going to happen, what's our responsibility? Do we just stand by and let them die or do we try to do something to prevent it? And if we try to prevent it, how? And if we do prevent it, then what? What's the long term prospect in that particular? A growing collection of irreversible comas on ventilators? What a prospect! Just the thought of it! And like you said, where would we put them? At the rate they're coming in—in the thousands, you now tell us—we'll be out of psychiatric and nursing home beds in six months. Does anyone realize how many heroin addicts there are out there? And what happens if the nuts who are lacing the heroin with Blush decide to do the same with cocaine, or with methamphetamine? Now we're talking about millions of people, probably. Jess, if what happened to Jordan is what's going to happen to all Blush victims, we're watching the beginning of a mass slaughter. Hundreds of thousands of people, at least!"

"We're praying, Jess," Moyer added soberly.

"So are we," Weaver replied simply. "You're right in everything you say, Frank. In fact I went through the very same scenario with Martha before you and Clay came over. She agrees. That's why it didn't much surprise me when the call came telling me the state lab had transferred the job to NIH and CDC. It occurred to me that maybe the problem was beginning to work its way up the chain and that some people in Sharpsfield were beginning to wake up to what we already knew would likely be coming our way. I also considered—please forgive me—that sometimes we under-estimate them. Maybe some real thought went into their acting so quickly."

"Maybe," Cantrelle conceded reluctantly, "but what about our rôle if another Blush patient dies? Then what? Do we wait for a third? And a fourth? Are we on our way to becoming a hospice? A charnel house? And if they're doomed to die, do we keep them here? At the rapid clip they're coming in, and if they're here until they die, sooner or later—and most likely sooner than any of us would like to think—we'll quickly run out of beds for the regular patients. And what do we do with them? Wouldn't it be a bitter irony if this hospital swells up to a five-thousand patient census like it was forty years ago in its heyday with Palmer? I wonder how the DMH would like *those* apples. God, I'm making it sound like it's their fault," he exclaimed in a vain attempt to check himself, "but I'm not so sure they appreciate what might be ahead! This thing could become a horror!"

"Settle down, Frank," Weaver soothed. "Martha is scheduled to talk to them today and bring them up to date on our concerns, and she'll point out exactly what the hospital's needs will be if what you say comes to pass."

"But Jess," Cantrelle persisted, "what do we do in the meantime, while we're waiting? Long-range planning is fine—couldn't do without it—but what do we do if this thing is upon us before everybody dots the cabinet-level i's?"

"I guess that's where Martha and I come in, Frank," Weaver replied evenly.

Cantrelle immediately backed off. He hadn't intended to back his good friend into a corner, but that's what he had done. He knew his chagrin was evident enough without having to announce it, which likely would only have compounded unnecessarily the discomfort of the moment.

There then followed a despairing silence in which all avoided looking at each other.

"Jess, have there been any other deaths reported, anywhere?" Moyer spoke up.

"Not that I know of. None reported so far," Weaver replied with evident relief.

"That's good to hear," Cantrelle offered in a tone wreathed with conciliation.

"Frank, I can assure you that your dedicated leaders are measuring the full size of the threat and not just being danced along by upper chambers," Weaver teased. "In fact, right now Martha and I are holding our breath just as fearfully as you. I realize that you and Clay, because you work on the cases day in and day out, see the urgency of things with a clarity we may not have on our level, and certainly not likely on any level farther up, but please understand that we're not unaware of what might become our collective world if everything manages to go wrong," he offered in reassurance sprinkled with forgiveness. After a smile to denote that the matter was settled he added lightly. "And speaking of everything managing to go wrong, how's the paper coming? I mean from the standpoint of sending it off for the first of its inevitable remedial reworkings as only the supercilious editorial staff of an esteemed medical journal can inflict?"

"As I mentioned," Cantrelle replied through return of laughter, "We're about ready to launch it. Our problem has been more when to call a halt to fussing over it. Clay suggested, and I agree, that we go ahead with what we've got now and limit the paper to the before and after of the Blush effect on cognitive functioning. The neuropsych results offer more than enough data to establish our report as a baseline study that others might find helpful, and also something we can add to later—if events so deem!" he added with pointed emphasis. "Right now we think it's better to get a limited paper out fast rather than wait for more definitive findings on the long-term effects. By that I mean whether the lesions on Jordan's slides are generic for Blush or not. You know. So, Mrs. Andretti willing, we'll have it ready for mailing Friday. Fast enough for you?"

Weaver smiled his satisfaction.

"I'll tell Martha this morning," he promised. "She'll want some copies to spread around in the DMH, assuming you'll permit such a desecration of your labors. I'll need a few copies myself to circulate to the Publications Committee to get their clearance, which ought to come easily enough since you two comprise twenty-five percent of its membership. Then it's ready for the mails, and I'll lick the stamps myself."

"It's a deal," Cantrelle agreed, mollified by Weaver's delight in being able to help. "But Jess," he returned to the unsettled point, "will NIH and CDC report back to the state lab? I'm curious as to how we'll find out what they come up with on Blush. I hope we don't have to wait until someone in Bethesda or Atlanta decides to put the findings together in some paper of their own for publication. That's too dicey. We derelicts never did get around to the LSD paper, remember?" he could acknowledge with kindred culpability. "If we have to wait for their paper it'll take untold months for the information to get to us. And journals just don't immediately publish what they receive. There's a lag period that can sometimes stretch out as much as a year, or beyond. If we have to wait that long to get some idea of what Blush's chemistry is—well, I can see this thing stretching out indefinitely while the cases multiply like crazy. Any leads?"

"Frank, I think they'll disseminate their findings as fast as they can," Weaver offered. "Let's give 'em the benefit of a doubt. I'm sure they'll appreciate how urgent the situation is. They'll probably publish it first in one of their in-house organs, like a quarterly review they put out on all their research. And I'm quite certain they'll put us on the mailing list," he reassured.

"I guess I'm just worried that the project will become too spread out. Even more, I don't like the idea of the chemistry being taken out of our hands and delegated elsewhere. That means we'll lose all control over keeping that part of the investigation in line with the clinical end of it right here at good ole MSH. I feel we're losing too much say-so," Cantrelle persisted.

"I think you've made that point abundantly clear, Frank," Weaver chided. "By the way, which journal will you be submitting the paper to?"

"We're going with the biggie, the *American Annals of Psychiatry*," Cantrelle announced with some pride. "Burleson is the chairman of the editorial board of that one and I'm counting on him to endorse the value and timeliness of our paper. It's certainly chancy going with the *Annals*, especially if we hope to get the paper in print as soon as possible. Everybody submits to the *Annals* and the editorial board must have hundreds of papers to sift through to make deadline. I just hope ours doesn't get lost in the shuffle. I believe that if we can get it in soon enough, and if they think the paper acceptable enough and the situation urgent enough, we'll be able to make deadline next month or so. In the journal world that would be fantastic speed, but Blush is moving along at the same clip, as I'm certain the editorial board would appreciate. The board would want, I guess, to put forth something relevant to the urgencies of the field. I feel pretty sure they'll move fast on the article, much the same as we've tried to do."

"I think that's reasonable, Frank," Weaver agreed. "Clay, are you going to send something to the Psychology journals?"

"Later," Moyer replied. "After the initial article I'll rework some of the neuropsych results and send in something that focuses more on the thalamic nuclei and the integration of cognitive function, though someone will have to help me with the neuroanatomy to get me started. The paper will be speculative in large part, but those thalamic lesions in the path report are just waiting to be written up in a paper on localization of brain function and correlative neuropsych test performance. It'll be a slight shift in emphasis from our initial paper, a shift from the psychiatry of the thing to the neuropsychology of it, but I don't think it'll be too hard to swing. Ideally it should turn out to be the companion paper of our initial article but geared more for the psychologists out there who are doing, or trying to do, the assessment on the Blush cases they're receiving but for which they don't have the benefit of pre-Blush testing as comparison, like we have. Or the help of autopsy reports to suggest localization of lesions. My hope is that the paper will give them the lead they need in focusing their testing efforts. I bet it won't be long before someone comes up with a series demonstrating the step-wise progression of the organicity in these patients. It's just a matter of selecting the most efficient and most discerning tests we now have going," he explained, clearly well along in structuring the pitch of the proposed article. "It might even spawn some new test battery," he added.

"Looks like there's no stopping you two fanatics," Weaver observed merrily.

"Jess, there's another thing," Cantrelle added, "something else that puzzles me; you might be able to give me a little help with it. The repeat MRI we did on Jordan was read as negative, though the path report shows definite structural lesions. Could you bring the path report to the attention of the radiologist and ask him to double check the shots of those planes to see if something was suggestive on the film but maybe not distinct enough to report? It could, of course, be that when we got that second MRI—I think he had been here only two weeks when we did it—the problem was then more neurochemical and less anatomic, or at least not anatomic enough to show up on the films. It was later on that things progressed to the point of possibly being anatomic enough to show up. When we got our MRI we perhaps didn't do so at a late enough date. It would help to clear up that small mystery. Might also alert the radiologist where to look on the other cases—especially if Jordan's case turns out to be typical, God forbid," Cantrelle intoned, returning to the doomsday theme of earlier.

His mention of the hovering dread recalled Weaver and Moyer from the more congenial matter of papers and publication.

"I'll do that, Frank. I'll call him and bring him up to date," Weaver promised.

"Also, Jess," Cantrelle added, "at some point someone is going to have to meet with the staffs of the Triage unit and the Blush unit to fill them in on these findings, plus the transfer of the chemistry work to NIH and CDC. The staffs feel they're part of the team helping in the research end of this problem and they're doing an inspired job in working with these patients. They're also forwarding pretty good suggestions on how to manage these patients in the best way to support the research. I can tell you they're eager to hear anything that says their efforts are paying off in taking the measure of the beast. I guess you know that they're also on tenterhooks about whether or not they can expect their other Blush patients to start dropping dead," Cantrelle advised.

"A day doesn't go by, Jess, without their asking some question about what the administration or the DMH knows about the situation," Moyer pointed out. "They tend to think that so much more is known at the top than at the bottom where they are. We tell them as much as we can, but it doesn't have the ring of authority it would have coming from you and Martha. Your shock troops would enjoy having you and Martha visit the front, I guess I'm saying."

"I know it sounds lame," Weaver began, grinning sheepishly, "but I've been trying to get over to the units since last week, but it's been one damned thing after another. It's even budget-making time, if you can believe it, and we've been hammering out one to send to Sharpsfield by tomorrow at the latest and it's got to contain provisions for expansion of our Blush unit beyond Building Seven, just in case. That's one potentially significant benefit of the state lab's demur on the Blush chemistry: Sharpsfield now knows that the problem is bigger than we all initially estimated, and so our budgets will likewise have to be bigger than we first thought."

"I knew you would find some workable benefit in that default," Cantrelle grumbled.

"Haven't you heard about ill winds, Frank?" Weaver joshed. "But seriously, I'll take it up with Martha and I'm sure one of us will meet with the unit staffs, probably in a day or so, and give them an update on where things stand. It'll also do us good to get out of this building for a while," he sighed.

The silence of closure followed, announcing that the meeting was over. All three began to shift in their chairs in preparation for rising.

"I'll get back to the two of you as soon as I can after our talk with DMH later today," Weaver added in conclusion. "I might then have something on how NIH and CDC'll forward their findings, and to whom. Right, Frank?" he assured.

"Thanks, Jess," Cantrelle sighed in obvious relief. "I know you'll do what's possible, and even more," he granted with genuine gratitude.

"Time for me to get back to the shop," Moyer interjected as he rose.

"Yeah, let's get rolling. Thanks for the time, Jess," Cantrelle offered as he rose creakily from his chair.

"Don't forget, when you're ready with those stamps, bring 'em by," Weaver urged.

"Sure thing, boss," Cantrelle assured as he and Moyer departed.

Once in the hallway, he and Moyer continued their assay as they proceeded on to the front door.

Cantrelle, feeling a heavy weariness beginning to descend upon him, sighed mightily.

"Clay, I think we're beginning to lose control of our grand project," he lamented.

"Maybe it really was too big from the very beginning. I think we probably did expect too much from the state lab. When you think about it we really didn't spend any time with those people to find out if they were truly up to what we, in effect, decided they would do for us," Moyer observed.

"Not just for us, Clay; for a lot of other people as well," Cantrelle bristled. "The sick ones."

"True," Moyer yielded, "but I think we ought to give them credit for taking it on without a word of complaint."

"I guess so," Cantrelle conceded.

"In fact, my guess is that they feel kinda bad that the project was taken out of their hands, and probably without any say-so from them," Moyer posed. "You recall they seemed eager to get in on the project and show their stuff. I think that if anything we ought to contact them and thank them for what they were able to do. And ask them at the same time for a summary of their findings, and to be sure to send the summary to us directly and not through channels. Explain that we need the summary, which they can make as detailed or as brief as they like, so that we'll have an idea where NIH and CDC stand in carrying the analysis forward. Then you might mention in turn that we'll forward directly to them copies of all future reports we get from NIH and CDC on what the analysis yields. O.K.?"

Son of a bitch! He hadn't thought of that, he realized, abashed again. And once again he was confronted with the recognition that he didn't know what the hell he would do if he didn't have this cynical monkey looking after him all the damned time.

"You're right, Clay. A good idea," he concurred in embarrassed understatement.

They reached the front door and jockeyed it open. As he stepped outside the icy air now almost staggered him to a halt. He again felt a chill race through him as he huddled his shoulders up around his neck. They stood near the entrance as they prepared to set off for their separate stations.

"Jess'll probably call me first after he hears something from Martha about her contact with DMH, and I'll call you as soon as I can," he promised.

"O.K., and I'll finish the tabulation of the test results today and bring them over for Mrs. Andretti to work up into tables. I'll have them over later this afternoon. Could you mention it to her when you get back?" Moyer suggested.

"Sure. I'll probably finish writing the discussion tonight, and tomorrow she can type up a rough draft for your review. Don't make too many changes, for Christ's sake!" Cantrelle pleaded.

As they spoke they could hear off in the distance the undulating sound of a rescue vehicle. Its approach pulled them away from their planning and they turned to watch an ALS ambulance, now in view, turn into the front gate of the hospital. It sped along the drive and roared past the administration building, its siren now dimmed as the fury of its engine echoed off the buildings along its route. When it swooshed by them enroute to the interior of the hospital grounds Weaver burst out of the door and bounded in the direction of his car to follow in pursuit.

"Code 99 in Building Seven!!" he yelled over his shoulder as he ran past them.

Cantrelle and Moyer looked at each other in stark apprehension. Code 99 meant an extreme medical emergency, which meant that someone was in severe distress, or dying, or dead. And Building Seven was the Blush unit. Weaver's car screeched away as they stood motionless in mute dread, knowing that once again it was too late.

Seven

It turned out that all of it was. First and foremost it was another Blush patient, dead. As for himself, it was the flu, as the chills had suggested. And with the paper, it was quickly off in time for an early deadline. And overall it was an almost completely wretched week.

The death of the second Blush patient confirmed their worst fears. Too, it came while the patient was asleep. Investigation had shown that this second patient had sometime earlier finished a light breakfast and was sitting quietly in a chair. He had yawned a few times and then gotten up to go to his bed. The attendants thought nothing of it and had even helped the patient to get comfortable for a short morning nap. That was all, and nothing out of the ordinary was noted. When an attendant came back half an hour later to check on him, the patient was dead. There had been no hint of his having any distress or discomfort before or during his nap. Staff were busily at hand working with patients nearby. So, again, it seemed to be a case of a quiet and easy death during slumber. The autopsy yielded pretty much the same findings as in the Jordan case. The gross sections revealed localized dull areas in the region of the thalami as well as in the reticular activating system. The microscopic slides showed the same vacuolation and honeycomb effect in those dulled areas, confirming that the tissue changes were definitely the characteristic pathophysiology of Blush and not a unique sensitivity reaction limited to the Jordan case. While the slides were being processed for the second case a third Blush patient died, just three days after the second, also in his sleep. That one also died peacefully and without a hint of advance distress. The very same day a report arrived of the first death of a Blush patient elsewhere in the state system. Pittsfield had had its first Blush death, and again as the patient slept. Since then reports of Blush deaths had come in steadily, and Moreland alone subsequently tallied seventeen almost exactly in the order of hospital admission. It was now possible to plot the time period from ingestion to death—approximately ninety days. The

Jordan case, for all its initial mystery and strangeness, had turned out to be typical and ordinary in all particulars save one: his was the only case thus far at Moreland not of hard-core heroin addiction. All the others were, and the special poignancy of the tragedy in his case was thus belatedly heightened with his being revealed a hapless and probably accidental victim pointlessly chosen to lead the macabre procession.

The only thing acceptable about the whole awful mess was that the victims died peacefully in their sleep. After the second death and because of the yawning that had occurred immediately before the nap, it was thought that perhaps signs of sleepiness signaled the impending demise. Hence patients were for a time watched carefully for just such behavior. But it turned out that weariness or sleepiness by itself was not a valid indicator inasmuch as other patients, noted to be as alert and responsive according to their usual, died right along with those less so. The length of time the patient had the disorder, roughly correlating with the degree of dementia, was the more valid indicator and predictor. Before long, staff could fairly accurately single out those most likely to expire next, and these patients were usually collected in a small ward of Building Seven for their final days. That ward had subsequently acquired in the nether argot of the hospital the tasteless title of "The Toll Booth." The lights never quite went out on that unit and bed checks were made at least every half hour, during the night especially, to note the patients' breathing. No staff member seemed eager actually to see a patient's last breath, and no such event was ever recorded, thus far. The reports always specified the occurrence in words suggesting that the patient had been noted at such and such a time to be unresponsive and without detectable respiration or heartbeat. Cantrelle and others had speculated that death was most likely to occur at the circadian nadir, that time in the middle of the night when all vital body functions are normally at their lowest ebb, the time of deepest chill for all of us.

For a while and over the ensuing weeks the question of the use of ventilators arose. As it became easier to predict who was most likely to die next, the issue of prevention surfaced. The idea of putting someone on a ventilator prophylactically and continuously for an indefinite period of time could not be countenanced except by those who hoped mightily that in some way the lethal phase of the disorder might prove to be transient, like in the polio cases of old, and that the patient, if sustained until that phase subsided in favor of a healing period thus far not enabled to come forth, might subsequently improve to the point of being able to manage his own breathing without the aid of a ventilator. Such hopefuls, a small number to be sure, even speculated that the tissue damage detailed in the histologic sections might be as much a product of the patient's death as it was a cause of it, and that if the patient were not allowed to die, much of the observed tissue damage might not occur at all. The fact that such lesions didn't occur in others dying of respiratory arrest from other causes didn't seem to dampen their arguments. The tenacious hope carried by their premise was echoed and reinforced by addicts who, remarkably, were now showing signs of collecting themselves into activist groups. Formerly shadowy, elusive figures who skirted any form of visibility or disclosure, many addicts, now led by several more or less rehabilitated ones in the professional and political ranks bent on achieving a kind of left-handed apotheosis, were stepping forth to claim their inalienable right of representation and were making large store of society's failure to preserve the life of their kind, charging that society had in effect levied a death sentence on them by backing off from the use of ventilators in sustaining the life of their stricken brothers and sisters, and, moreover, most likely regarded their death as an unspoken societal beneficence. They uniformly held that no such effort at prevention would be spared to protect the life and limb of more preferred citizens were a similarly lethal disease to occur in a more favored sector of society. The advent of political activism among a group so traditionally identified with the worst ills of society outraged citizens who were otherwise naturally sympathetic to any sufferer's plight, regardless of the character of his misfortune, and thus inclined in any event to support measures for easing his suffering. But a stance of militant entitlement, never a surprise to the mental health worker experienced in working with substance abusers, alienated citizens who were now being accused darkly of willfully permitting genocide based on an unfair and unconstitutional bias which revealed, their leaders held, the drug addict to be a doubly designated victim of a noxious society for being addicted in the first place, the withholding of ventilators being merely the final, lethal act in that victimization. One newly formed group in San Francisco, the news media reported, had petitioned the legislature for compensation of damages done to them by the state's war on drugs and had had no difficulty in securing the services of a large legal firm to guide the group's litigation.

The restraint on the use of ventilators actually had a much simpler and more mundane basis. Firstly, the patients would not cooperate. Applying a ventilator before it was actually needed—and such had been tried, though not at Moreland—was tantamount to making a patient breathe thereafter in and out of a paper bag, and was thus stoutly resisted. The only way to enforce its use by the patients who weren't yet having trouble with breathing was to tie them down in restraints. On the other hand, waiting until the patients actually needed the ventilator created a critical emergency, even when one knew well in advance that it was coming. When it arrived, it then became a dire matter of sustaining the patient's breathing until the ventilator could be applied and activated. To know exactly when and how to act was essential, and monitors, such as the kind used for tots with sleep apnea, were used for a while to signal the arrival of that moment. Though a few lives were saved, what in effect had actually been saved became problematical. The Blush patients sustained on ventilators did not show the hoped-for remission; rather, repeat MRI visualizations revealed progressive destruction of the thalamic nuclei and of the reticular activating systems as the lesions in these areas became sufficiently extensive to show up clearly on the MRI films. Also, the dementia proceeded to the point of coma and from there to the wretched problem of determining when to discontinue life-support measures. Since those initial efforts no attempt was mounted anywhere for having ventilators forestall the inevitable, and only when a family was particularly pertinacious on the point was any effort considered. And even those cases were becoming fewer and fewer as the futility of the effort was becoming too evident. Yet, the more vengeful activists among the addicts saw in that very recognition a willingness on the part of society to exploit doom in satisfaction of a covert and long-held determination to rid its world of those members tainted by drug addiction. And their tone was roundly unforgiving.

Nor was their umbrage aimed only at what they considered society's secret satisfaction in having drug addicts settle the problem by their own hand with society remaining overtly sinless. They marched on various legislative chambers—city, state, and even national—demanding that more be done to protect the innocent addict from the scourge of Blush which was flourishing because of society's sin of neglect in doing far too little in the first place. The incredible sight of openly professed drug addicts marching together as to war, chanting and singing slogans from the other side of the collective social order, and led by the more resolute in a new and open avouch, figures often from the arts and entertainment industry, the sports world, and even government, was a scene no one earlier thought possible but which now seemed commonplace, and it loudly testified not only to the pervasiveness of the drug problem in the nation but also obliquely to the desperation felt by its victims in their collective clamor which ultimately did little to dispel the individual helplessness each felt in being compelled to seek out his waiting executioner, a theme which subsequently became a popular item on talk shows. And everybody awaited the movie. Several political figures, not previously identified with an awareness of the nation's heroin problem or programs addressing it, now began to recall that all along they had had commendable concern for the unfortunate *hors de combat* in the nation's war on drugs and regretted that the various remedial efforts brought to bear had not been more balanced in addressing the needs of those targeted citizens. These advocates, too, were now seen on talk shows. And once again the American people, by dint of a gathering calamity, were being treated to a national display of the tawdry along with the true, the tragic along with the trash. And heroin addicts were dying in escalating numbers. And not only in America, for Europe had reported in and was now listed among the contributors. But America was far and away first and foremost, moving at a pace not likely ever to be matched or bettered in this sinister derby already several months in the running.

During all this he himself had had a small contest of his own. The chills that had rattled him on the morning he and Moyer met with Weaver turned out to be the harbinger of a more debilitating experience. Later in the day he developed aches, a runny nose, scratchy throat, and generalized weakness of first-run flu which was making its move earlier than usual this year. Toward the end of the day at his private practice office he developed a fever along with its toxic haze both of which he was able to subdue with blessed aspirin until he dragged home that evening after the last of his scheduled appointments. The presence of fever notified him that he was in for a few days of bedrest since ordinarily he was relatively immune to the pyretic effects of the usual viral infections. It pretty much had become standard procedure for him to remain fever-free while sharing with his family and friends the same viral assaults which ran their temperatures to sweaty heights. Thus, in the absence of fever, he was usually able to go about everyday business albeit at a throttled-back pace until convalescence freed him of the restraint. So the presence of fever was no small item for him; rather, it was a guarantee that his stint with the evolving malady would be a bit more protracted than usual and definitely beyond the general proportions of his standard viral experience. Thus resolved, he took to his bed that evening laced with the usual analgesics and decongestants, fully expecting to be able to work on the paper in the quiet of his study the following day cozily swathed in robe and slippers and sipping sympathetic tea. And so he did for the better part of the first day as the flu gathered force and targeted his sinuses and bronchi as easy prey. Moreover, he paced himself sensibly in polishing up the paper's final draft. For the first day home he felt rather pleased, all in all, that his body defenses were holding up fairly well, that the paper lacked only the tiniest dotting of a few i's to achieve final and irrevocable completion, and that surely by noon the following day that point would be surpassed, not merely reached, with the expected felicitous result that his flu-enforced days at home had merely facilitated a more expeditious completion of the paper. Now who could want more than that? So toward the end of the first day he was already plotting his return to work day after the next, anticipating sliding over a little closer to his wife on that morning before arising. Such was his usual for testing his recovery. It was quite standard for him to experience a marked compensatory rise in lustiness as he began to convalesce from illness, a trait over the years he'd worked into stock practice which he rationalized as helpfully informative: if he was again able to ravish his wife he was ready to resume his assault upon the rest of the world. And so at evening time on that first sick day home and shortly after a light dinner he took stock of his situation and found it to be fairly good. He was in the process of conveying as much to Laura, who had joined him for coffee in the living room, when he heard a pop in his left ear, his bad ear, the one with the hearing loss, the one which had had the protracted drainage after a lingering case of mastoiditis when he was a boy, the one that always clogged up with fluid during colds. But it had never popped before. He stopped talking and waited, surprised as much as concerned.

"What's wrong, Frank?" Laura asked, alerted by her husband's abrupt change in demeanor.

"My ear just popped. Distracted me. Nothing really," he reassured as the event passed.

He continued with his optimistic assay, though a bit less convincingly now. After a few more moments he took a sip of coffee and began pointing out to Laura again that the hospital had gone all out, especially Martha and Jess, in making it possible for him and Clay to pull the data together, when his ear popped once again. Perplexed, he was just beginning to wonder if accumulated fluid was starting to drain from his middle ear when the room began to swirl violently. He dropped his coffee and clutched at the arms of the chair to brace himself against the feeling of being flung along with the room's rotation. He strained to steady himself in the accelerating swirl while nausea rapidly welled up within him. As he struggled to hold himself upright in the chair he began to vomit in projectile gushes. He felt himself rocking uncontrollably with the gyrations of the room; his head and shoulders hung over the side of the chair while his frantic hands, now splattered with vomit and coffee, kept slipping on the arms of the chair as he grabbed desperately for something to steady himself. His splayed-out legs stiffened before him in an attempt to stop the spasmodic rocking. By now he had instinctively closed his eyes which were keeping a rapid pace in trying to find a fixation point in the furiously rotating room; closing them seemed to help in reducing the intensity of the room's turbulence.

"Frank! Frank! What's wrong?" Laura screamed. "Children—Ellie, Todd, hurry! Something's happened to your father!"

He tried to speak and tell her not to get upset but he couldn't do so above the sensation of reeling and falling. He continued to clutch at the arms of the chair to prevent sliding completely out of the chair on to the floor—the thought of having this continue while he was lying on the floor terrified him; he might never be able to get up! Silly thought, but maybe not. Another spate of vomiting arrived, now producing little but heaves. Over his retching he heard the frightened clamor of his family but he dared not open his eyes to look.

"Do something!" he heard Ellie shriek as she pulled at his arm to help him to a more upright position. He then felt other hands hold his other arm; probably Laura's.

"Dad, can you hear me?" came Todd's voice, steady and directly in front of him though the sound seemed to be moving rapidly and repetitively from right to left.

He tried to nod in assent, but the rocking sensation overrode what little nodding movement he could muster. He then remembered that he could speak.

"Sure," he grunted.

The sound of his voice must have carried some measure of reassurance because Laura then returned her appeal to him

"Frank, are you having a stroke?"

As though he could comment on that at a time like this, he thought as he attempted a testy grimace! He settled for a shake of his head and found that he could now do so more easily. The nausea was abating and the rotation of the room was beginning to slow down. And he was becoming convinced that as long as he kept his eyes closed he was able to maintain some control over the storm.

"I think I'm having an attack of vertigo, probably from labyrinthitis caused by this son-of-a-bitch flu," he enunciated carefully and evenly so as not to stir up any more commotion. As he talked he felt and tasted the dregs of vomit in his mouth but he didn't yet dare to let go of the chair to wipe it away. He then realized he must look a sight. "I'll be all right, everybody. I don't have any pain or anything—just dizzy and a little nauseated," he explained.

"Is there anything we can do? Shall we call Aaron?" Laura pursued urgently. Aaron Feldstein was their family internist and long-term colleague of Cantrelle since they began their private practices together some twenty years earlier.

"No, not yet. Let me settle down and then you can help me up to bed. I'll need to lie still for a while and keep my eyes closed or else the vertigo will start up again. There goes my light reading for tonight," he clowned.

Todd giggled, but no one else was amused. Laura, who was still shaking from the shock of it all, seemed determined not to permit any trivialization of the matter.

"You're sure you don't have pain somewhere? Or weakness? I don't want to put you to bed and then have you get worse. We could go to the ER now and let Aaron look you over. If the trouble is in your ear he would probably want Harry to look at you." Harry Potkin was the family ENT man and also a close colleague from the time they had adjoining offices at the start of their practices.

"Laura," he now felt bold enough to say, "I'm pretty sure this is just labyrinthitis. Looks a lot worse than it really is. And Aaron and Harry would say the same thing: stay in bed, keep your eyes closed, and stay away from French cooking for a while. Later on when I'm a little better we can contact them for any diagnostic studies they may want to run. I swear, hon."

Laura grumbled into acquiescence as he heard his family relax in partial relief that he was able to discourse in his usual way, and even mount a wait-and-see plan of action that seemed to meet the urgency of the moment.

He gave them an additional moment to let the decision sink in and then he decided to try again. This time he would try insolence.

"By the way," he resumed, eyes closed and head resting on the back of the chair, "it smells terrible in here. When a man comes home from work he expects his home to be reasonably tidy and inviting. A messy place doesn't do much for the burdened soul, and so I'd like to suggest that . . . ."

"Frank Cantrelle!" Laura exploded in laughter mixed with apoplectic sobs. "If that flu doesn't kill you, I will!"

By now Cantrelle and Todd were chortling together as Laura and Ellie fought back a vengeful exasperation at being teased for their frantic solicitude.

"I swear, Frank," continued Laura in brimming tears, "first you scare us half to death and now you make a joke of the whole thing. You could have been having a stroke, and we wouldn't have been able to do anything but stand by and watch you suffer, and maybe even watch you die. And you think it's funny. Frank, I'm very upset with you," she continued through quivering sobs as her words brought forth more than she could control.

He immediately stopped his snickering. She was right; he had abused their solicitude, and had thought only of regaining a flippant upper hand in the face of being disabled and dependent on their help. He had also wanted to reassure them, and himself, but he had gone too far in discrediting their fear, and had brought more hurt than relief.

"I'm sorry, Laura. I didn't mean to make light of your fright," he atoned, but the nausea lingering in the pit of his stomach discouraged further display of lament. The sense of rotation had now subsided to a rhythmic background swaying, much like the roll of a ship might seem to holiday passengers. "I think we would all feel better if I got cleaned up and stashed away safely in bed. Right?"

Laura, her solicitude fully restored, leaned over to stroke his brow.

"Todd and I will help you to the bathroom and I'll hose you down," she attempted in reciprocal amends. "Then we'll put you aside for the evening." Her attempt at sangfroid sounded even more lamentable than he felt.

"I'm ready. Let's go," he said, bracing himself.

Their hands under his arms, Laura and Todd helped him to a standing position. Though he kept his eyes tightly shut the swirling increased, provoked by the movement. He held on to them as he steadied himself and allowed the vertigo to subside some before moving further. Nausea tickled at his stomach. What a fucking mess, he mumbled under his breath as he braced himself for the journey upstairs. After an interminable series of starts and stops with reassuring comments from Laura and the steady, stalwart support from Todd's Herculean strength he eventually tottered into their bathroom. Now alone, Laura began to undress him tenderly as he leaned, hands spread apart, against the bathroom wall. He noticed that even in the space of the fifteen minutes or so since the vertigo began he was beginning to adapt to it such that he was feeling more steady on his feet, but not by much. As she washed his naked frame she kissed him lightly here and there as though the mere cleansing of him were not enough for her to give. With care to keep his eyes closed tightly, he nuzzled her gratefully and touched his forehead to hers in a primal marking of their mystic bond now mobilized once again to the single-minded advocacy of their devotion. He managed somehow to brush his teeth and rinse his mouth, provoking a new surge of nausea in the doing, but the sense of refreshment was worth it. She then helped him back into the bedroom, into pajamas, and into bed. She sat on the edge of his bed and stroked his forehead as he found the least contentious horizontal position his vertigo would permit.

"I'll call your secretaries in the morning to let them know that you'll be home a little longer than expected. You need rest," she pronounced.

"Yeah," he conceded. "It looks like I'll be underfoot for a while. Maybe I can call Clay tomorrow and get things settled about the final draft," he chanced.

"Who'll dial the phone for you?" she reminded him haughtily.

"Some sensible and devoted person who knows that not very long from now I'll be well enough to exact revenge where it's due," he retorted with a wry smile.

"Yes, m'lord," she chirped obediently.

She then leaned over and kissed him gently.

"I love you too much, my adorable menace. Please don't let anything ever happen to you," she whispered.

He held her for that important moment and lightly stroked her hair.

"The kids are waiting, wondering if everything is under control. If you want anything just call. I'll be back in a few minutes anyway," she soothed as she began to rise.

"I'll be O.K. I've just got to figure how to get used to this thing. My left ear feels like it's packed with cotton," he offered in casual reassurance. "But while you're down there will you please clean up that mess?" he added with mock innocence.

She gave out a gasp of total exasperation and slapped his hand with her fingertips before she stomped out of the room.

He lay there savoring his smile for a moment, but then recalled his medical school days when he learned on the ENT block that eight percent of the cases of multiple sclerosis began with an episode of labyrinthitis, fully thirty percent of acoustic neuromas began the same way, a small percentage of berry aneurysms as well, and then some miscellany. He marveled at how malicious one's memory could sometimes be, and conceded that over the next several days there would be ample occasion for his medical education to turn on its master to augment the wretchedness of his sore labor by way of meticulous detailing of all the possible neurologic complications that could enrich the course of his convalescence.

But no complications arrived, other than the wretchedness of being so completely bed-fast and obligatorily blind for a while. After a few days he was able to master getting out of bed for brief periods, though carefully with a minimum of excess motion as might stir the return of vertigo and nausea. But even when comfortably at rest, whatever his position, he was dogged by a sustained light-headedness that gave him the sense of lacking his usual mental grasp, of being less sharply in touch with his surroundings, and of being cognitively frail. He wasn't sure, but he suspected that the sense of mental waywardness would subside only gradually over the next several months along with the shakiness of his equilibrium which just now could easily be tottered by any quick movement or shift in direction or position. He also knew that the problem of motion sickness incident to driving now awaited some future point in his convalescence, and the gradual and planned approach to the restoration of his usual logistic range lay ahead as just more laborious waiting and its crouching wretchedness. And likewise, he knew that for the time being he would log in small successes here and there, such as a few hours a day in a sitting position, a gain he would be able to parlay later on into a sustained return to his study and to his desk, which he feared might not immediately welcome him back. He already felt strangely out of place in his essential lair, as though every element of its ambience still belonged to the former Frank Cantrelle and hence unable to settle for anything less, a sense he likened to the strained politeness of club members after one had failed in some way to sustain qualifying performance. So he knew visits to his study wouldn't be for long, and even then not so much for reassurance as for measuring gains in his gradual return to standards. He knew this all too well, because as a general practitioner many years ago he had treated and counseled several cases of labyrinthitis, and did so with the confidence and objectivity that came of not knowing how his patients felt. But he did now.

After the first week he did contact Aaron, and subsequently Harry, and each concurred in his diagnosis. They also concurred in his being sent to Freeman Aldridge, M.D., the renowned neurologist of textbook fame and chairman of the Neurology Department at Franklinton. Just to be safe, they said. He complied, secretly delighted in having the absolute last word in Neurology relieve him of the hovering differential diagnosis his medical school memory had inflicted upon him. Laura drove him to the appointment as evenly as she could, the most extended period of motion since the onset of his illness, and he arrived at Aldridge's office providentially symptomatic for the esteemed neurologist's assay. Again it was declared that the problem was labyrinthine and not brain, to the satisfaction of all on hand. Though he really didn't feel up to it, he took advantage of the moment to broach with Aldridge the Blush issue and the histologic sections which had been described to date. Aldridge affected a polite interest but begged off from any additional discussion by stating that he hadn't really heard much about the problem, only that the hospitals were seeing an unusual kind of untoward drug effect in heroin addicts and that their transfer to long-term care facilities seemed to be the best approach to the problem thus far. Despite his unsteadiness Cantrelle did not fail to be offended by and dismayed at Aldridge's casual dismissal of the matter, though he knew that Aldridge, like so many others out there in the elegant and elitist teaching world and acute treatment centers, had little call or occasion to focus time and resources on cases that typically belonged to Moreland, and thereunto destined. But Blush was different. It wasn't just a matter of a psychotic drug addict showing up in the ER of a university hospital for initial evaluation and the all-important transfer to a state mental hospital; Blush was a man-made assault upon a segment of the population, an undesirable segment to be sure, but a segment which then became a medical as well as a human tragedy of national proportions. He couldn't understand Aldridge's polite apathy on the matter. Thank God for their haste in getting the paper together. Perhaps it was specifically the kind of non-awareness Aldridge displayed which they unwittingly but accurately hoped to target with the paper. He was sure Clay would agree since of late Clay had begun to complain darkly that the country seemed bound and determined not to be aroused into an unpleasant awareness of Blush's presence.

The consultation ended most cordially and with generous reassurances offered all around. It would just take time, all agreed. Cantrelle complied with the platitudes of Aldridge's consultation wrap-up, but had earlier abandoned hope for a better closure of the meeting and was thinking ahead as to the function the paper should serve in protecting Blush from being banished from deserved medical awareness, as had been the case with Schizophrenia for so many years. He realized he was expecting quite a lot from their modest, tentative paper, but this brief re-entry into the medical world, and as a patient at that, had re-alerted him to the work that needed to be done even while this son-of-a-bitch vertigo was yet having its day, as the dizzying ride back home to continued convalescence merrily avouched.

When Moyer was informed of Cantrelle's distemper he called immediately and inquired of Laura what was happening to his collaborator. He visited Cantrelle on the third clinical day and sat on the edge of Cantrelle's bed as they agreed to a transfer of duties for completion and dispatch of the paper. Cantrelle, talking with only one eye open, explained to his concerned comrade what remained undone for bringing his part of the paper to completion, a task, Moyer assured, he himself could manage readily enough to keep to their deadline. In addition, Moyer promised to keep him posted on events at the hospital and to keep himself available to assist in whatever

Cantrelle needed to have done. Also he volunteered to convey reassurances and messages to Weaver and Corley, as needed. Moreover, he would keep the residents posted on each stage of resurrection being negotiated by their fallen leader at any given moment and transmit to them as bidden any transcendent verities come of his ordeal. At the conclusion of that first sickroom visit, Moyer gave Cantrelle the traditional comradely poke on the shoulder as a parting gesture and Cantrelle, touched more than he wished to acknowledge, playfully banished his friend not to return until the paper had been shipped off to the journal and to Burleson's mercies. That agreed, Cantrelle then had the most restful and contented day of illness thus far suffered.

In three days Moyer was back to report complete success in having launched their missive the previous day, and by no-nonsense overnight mail at that. With Moyer again sitting on the edge of the bed they shared a moment of satisfaction in a job finally and well done, feeling at last beyond the grasp of that gnawing dread—but no less wretched even if feeling foolish about it—that someone might scoop them for their not moving fast enough to get the work out. Childish but genuine, and glad to have it off their venue. A few moments were given to grunts and smiles of mutual congratulations, and to the shared sigh of relief which seemed to make it all the more official than anything else they separately felt. Their conversation then turned to estimates as to when the article, if accepted, would appear. They agreed upon the likelihood of a January publication date at the earliest. But even that was considered running too far behind the march of clinical events. Moyer was uncompromisingly clear on that point as he informed Cantrelle that the Blush admission rate was increasing with such linear predictability that not only could a graph be plotted by the gradient of the admission rate to show that at the current pace Moreland would end the year with approximately ninety Blush patients on the rolls but also that there would be a mortality total of approximately twenty-five by that time and likely soon to catch up with the admission rate. Hearing such grim reports ruefully reminded Cantrelle of his enforced uselessness, but he liked to think that the reports also whipped his healing processes into hot pursuit which thus far, he lamented, carried him only to his not very distant study, and then no more often than twice a day.

Such was the sum and substance of that remarkable first week of illness.

By the beginning of the second week he felt stable enough to take short, measured strolls around the lawn. The sensation of being out of doors and back again in the bright daylight was one of shaky reclamation, but the backlash was a mounting intolerance of the confinement his time indoors carried. Being able to journey outside on his own, however modest the sortie, was tantamount to crossing the rehabilitation Rubicon, and, once done, stood no undoing. It now became an agonistic joy to fetch the morning paper as weakness slowly relinquished its debilitating grip. Always previously something of an adversary, the phone now became a staunch companion in the mapping of his re-entry. After a few days of tactically placed calls to signal his approaching return and also to inventory the altered lay of his territory since his departure he began to feel once again the old functional resolve which transformed restless need into charged purpose. His work, he affirmed, was still out there waiting for him though temporarily in the keep of good people who remained loyal to the cause, which loyalty, surprisingly, had not disappeared in a puff of smoke upon his being whisked from the scene by circumstance. The fear that if ever he slipped he would be left behind forever had always stalked his consciousness. Thus, the first week of his illness baited that menace like never before. But the phone calls and their reassurances were like reinforcements shoring up a shaky battle line in preparation for resumption of a temporarily stalled offensive, and for the time being his grim stalker, the vertigo, retreated to the borders of his awareness. Toward the end of the second week he was accompanying Laura on her marketing trips and bearing up nicely under the threat of car sickness. The light-headedness and vertigo remained fast company, though. Not only the motion of their car but the motion of the traffic as he watched it kept him holding firmly to the arm rest of the door to brace himself against the sense of impending rotation. With their daily trips, usually of carefully planned sweep, he measured his convalescence by the length of time in transit before he had to close his eyes to hold his unsteadiness to a tolerable level.

As his convalescence moved into a third week the sense of being caught in an enforced abeyance likewise sharpened. With the subsidence of the vertigo, though not yet far along enough to release him from the prohibition on solo driving, he was able to reclaim his typical Sunday schedule of activities, more or less. He estimated that his return to full restitution would probably retrace the developmental sequence of his typical week, but in reverse. He was now at about the Sunday level: lolling around, doing a little puttering here and there, making a few trips on foot to and fro, maybe even taking a stroll, tackling some light reading which he was now back to doing though with pared down zest and retention, followed then by the likelihood of an afternoon nap after some minor exertion at yardwork or from tinkering with one of his cars. Lately, his red Corvette had come to mind as deserving a bit more of his attention, and so he undertook to change the spark plugs and adjust the timing, a chore he ordinarily could whip through inside an hour from beginning to end. This time, owing to weakness come of desuetude, plus a certain rubbery blunting of his manual skill, and also to frequent waves of light-headedness come of his bending over the engine or making abrupt shifts in position, the task took him most of the morning. Had it not been for the engine's grateful and immediate roar into life with just the lightest touch of ignition his physical depletion would have been a cranky burden for the rest of the day. But as it was, he contentedly savored far into the evening the throaty purr of the exuberant engine as it reaffirmed a responsive loyalty after its own griping idleness, which loyalty, both could now agree, would soon enough be shifted back into useful gear. He already knew it would be the Corvette he'd drive to work upon his return, if not the first day—caution, not taste, dictated this caveat—then certainly the second.

But one Sunday a week was enough, and here he was having Sunday day in and day out, and mostly by himself.

Saturday was the more sprightly side of the weekend: office hours in the morning, followed by local jaunts in search of some timely book, or for the myriad supplies needed in Sunday's maintenance projects; or maybe a stop at the haberdasher for a tie or shirt—never enough of those—plus the periodic visit to the liquor store, and, in the Autumn, the afternoon college football game on TV. As for the evening, anything from dinner out, to having a few friends over or visiting with them, to an evening at the theater when in season, to nothing more than a quiet settling in at home. No matter how Saturday evening began it ended with their glow time, and with rare exception. But these past few weeks had qualified as rare exception. He estimated, finger to the wind, that within the next few days he would probably be ready for a Saturday. It was beginning to feel that way again, finally. If that particularly large step went well then soon enough he would be ready for a Friday, which was usually a wind-down day, the major work of the week having already been addressed. Success therein would take him to a Thursday venue, and so forth until he had traversed a fully restored week, following which he would be ready for the real thing at cruise speed.

As his balance improved, his self-preoccupation released its grip on his attention, and gradually he restored his external world to relevance. But for the while, that world was the world of his home at all kinds of times he did not usually allot to it. He began to notice the swirl of activity Laura conducted each morning to get the family going. He had no idea she traversed the length and breadth of the house so many times each morning in readying the children for their departure. Moreover, it seemed, and especially in Todd's case, that nothing was done until the last minute and that Laura somehow was charged with the sore responsibility for its being done as condition for Todd's leaving the house. Even he himself would heave a sigh when the door finally slammed shut behind Todd as he bolted for the school bus. He had noticed as well that Todd, solicitously more cooperative about the business of school attendance when the labyrinthitis symptoms were more debilitating, had begun to resume his usual balkiness, a sure sign that at least in his own estimation his father was now well out of danger. With that settled, the confrontations with his mother returned, usually behind closed doors to keep the unpleasantness of it contained and away from unwanted paternal witness. He hadn't realized how much negotiation Laura had to go through every morning with Todd just to get him going, and their muffled interchanges, sometimes energetically intense enough to be heard by him deep within the cloistered depths of his study, or the bedroom, shamed him for his breezy neglect of the problem which Laura, by default, had pretty much long taken upon herself to manage as best she could. He wondered if she harbored a resentment toward him for his nonfeasance. If she did, it didn't show. Whatever, his neglect now seemed compounded by his enlarged awareness of the scope of the problem though he still felt too disabled to give her a hand with it. So the mornings became vexatious in the least with dread of Todd's refractoriness followed by his own self-recriminations after Todd's wrenching departure. Damn it, when he was back in form again he'd have to spend time with that boy and do some very straight talking.

Ellie, however, was a delight, thank God. She even managed to help Laura with breakfast when she herself wasn't particularly rushed, but even so she never failed to line up on the helpful side of the scrimmage line. Whenever she said good-bye to her suffering father, which was unfailing, she did so from the happy position of accredited standing. Todd usually left under a cloud of probation.

The silence that followed their departure gave him ample opportunity to take inventory of Time—how much time was left before the kids would leave home for good, as his older son Richard was well on to managing; how much of his time had been given, or squandered, in his teaching, which, against the backdrop of Laura's total family effort, seemed selfish in the utmost with the financial and, hence, family benefits therefrom being quite modest and easily matched by a fraction of that same amount of time if applied in his private practice; how much time left for him and Laura together, and especially for him now that he'd been convincingly reminded of his mortality; and, of course, how much time left for him to make up the accumulated arrears come of career and family free-wheeling in the dogged and prodigal pursuit of this thing called Truth. That was the real problem, Truth, and going at it even casually cast up one's share of messy derivatives called the Vicissitudes of Life. But go at it he must. He needed to. And the need to resume search for the Grail was yet another sign of recovery, and also of impending release.

Release came that very Friday. After the kids got off to school on that special day he proclaimed the time at hand for him to tackle the drive to Moreland. Earlier in the week he had taken the wheel for short drives around the neighborhood and, with Laura riding shotgun, had pretty well reconnoitered the leading edge of his recuperation. Doing so resulted in progressive enlargement of his range such that by the end of the week he felt he had restored his normal boundaries. Hence the decision for the Friday launch. Laura would accompany him, of course. And the idea of his first day back being on a payday sounded just the cheeky note he needed.

His planfully unannounced arrival at Moreland that morning with a blessed minimum of nausea and light-headedness in tow turned out not to be as revelrous as he had hoped. Greeted he was, and happily so by Mrs. Andretti, some residents, and various members of the staff who, lamenting his paleness, reassured him that he looked just too fit for continued abuse of sick leave in what obviously had been some kind of clandestine pleasure jaunt, and that likely it was more the recovery of his conscience, finally, that urged his return to decent work, which, if addressed adequately and soon, just might eventually result in forgiveness all around. Their cheery banter formed the bridge he sought, but which, once traversed, put him in touch with the heavy grayness pervading the air. To the man, each welcoming person followed up on the greeting with a query as to whether he had heard or kept up with what had been happening, and more particularly how many Blush patients had been admitted and how many had subsequently died. The figures varied from one well-wisher to another, but tended to collect around ninety admissions and thirty deaths. Mrs. Andretti had clipped out and pinned on the bulletin board two newspaper articles, both of back page location, reporting on the alarming increase in the admissions and deaths at the state hospital because of a deadly new street drug making the rounds. The articles went on to reassure the reader that the victims seemed to be limited to heroin addicts. He noticed that the datelines were a week past, a time when he hadn't yet resumed news reading. So the word was getting out, finally. To his knowledge, though, there still hadn't been any coverage on a national scale. The dailies had yet to turn their clichés loose on Blush for running it to editorial ground, and he hadn't yet seen anything on TV. He likened the peculiar media silence to the reluctance of any reporting source—medical, media, or governmental—to disclose problems for which some corrective had not yet been defined or could be proposed. No one enjoyed advertising inadequacy. Plus, there was always the entente whereby what happened in the drug culture was the business of its denizens alone, the boundary line between it and proper civitas to be sustained by all parties, either side.

He took a moment to settle in at his desk as he tested the seating like a rider reclaiming a trusty mount. The paperwork had accumulated in neat and unsympathetic stacks, but otherwisc all was as he had left it three weeks earlier. He then gave a quick call to Clay to announce that he was back and made faint apology for not having notified him in advance, explaining that it had all happened on impulse and also that he preferred to try it first in secret to avoid having to account for failure if he didn't manage the return brilliantly. Moyer, delighted to know that his co-author was back, teasingly acknowledged mixed feelings about not being on hand for the sight because of the unquestioned satisfaction he would feel in beholding his collaborator struggle along with revealingly mortal weaknesses. However, the gentle comfort of having his partner placidly returned to his duties adequately offset the loss of spectacle a more public return had promised.

Things hadn't changed there either.

They agreed that come Monday they would get together and take stock.

Satisfied, he then decided to walk over to the administration building and say hello to Jess, and maybe to Martha as well. He began to realize that in effect he was retracing his general itinerary this first day back as a means of taking the measure of his recovery, almost picking up just where he left off weeks earlier. He remembered the chills the last time he went to the administration building. He pronounced himself now so much sounder as he walked along hand in hand with Laura.

"When's the last time I was here?" she asked as she scanned the grounds.

"Now you know how I feel," he answered.

"It still seems so peaceful, Frank. It's hard to believe that people are dying here left and right," she added.

"No one believes it, I'm afraid," he snapped.

As they walked along he took in the familiar vista of the campus and felt rising sympathy with his wife's comment. He himself had trouble believing that young people were dying, now at the rate of one every other day or so, in the seemingly ever-quiet Building Seven just beyond the curve in the drive. He attributed his incredulity to the usual abhorrence of death but also to the sober fact that he had not actually seen a Blush patient die and so was able to forestall too keen an awareness of what no one else wanted to witness, either. Though he was much closer to Blush and its victims, he was *de facto* just as removed as the reader of those newspaper articles when it came to the grim business of witness. To know the horror of Blush you really had to see it, and even he, committed to doing battle with it, didn't want to be so close as to watch it. He could well understand that the general citizen, lay and unvetted, would have little yen to put himself close to its chill. And general citizens not only made up neighborhoods but also nations as well as their governments.

He pulled open the door of the administration building and they both trotted up the steps to the hallway. He noted that he was doing better as the morning wore on and that for some time he hadn't even noticed the hovering light-headedness which he was careful not to summon via injudiciously abrupt movement. He was learning: just keep looking straight ahead and ignore everything else. Sort of narrow, he considered, but it worked. Too very well, he rued.

As they neared Weaver's office they could hear his voice in an on-going phone conversation. Moreover it seemed serious in that there was no hint of the usual bon homie in his tone. When Jess spoke an entire paragraph without some included gesture of smiling good will it was a grave matter indeed. As they waited in the outer office and made their acknowledgments to the secretary he could hear enough of the conversation to surmise that Jess was talking to someone in officialdom about something distinctly unsettling. He didn't wish to eavesdrop, but at this point in his return to work he was literally all ears in his hectic need to catch up. He had to restore his informational milieu as soon as he could and the network of listening posts had to be re-activated. So he beamed in on Jess even while he and Laura chatted politely with the secretary whose mother-in-law had a similar case of labyrinthitis several years ago and hasn't been the same since.

After several minutes of contrived interest he was liberated from the conversation by Weaver's summons.

"Lord be praised!" he expounded. "Do I see Dr. Cantrelle standing out there? And in the protective custody of his we'll-never-know-what-she-sees-in-him wife?"

He was immediately before them, beaming broadly and with an arm around Cantrelle's shoulder. He leaned over and gave Laura a peck on the cheek and gathered her in with his other arm and herded them into his office. His exuberance bade they be silent until it had subsided, which was paired with their being settled cozily in the chairs before his desk. Then Weaver, still beaming, sat down and exhaled heavily.

"God, am I glad you're back, Frank." he sighed, but then caught himself. "You are back, aren't you?"

"Yes, Jess, I'm back," Cantrelle assured. "Looks like I'll be ready for work Monday, the way things are going today. So far, the sight of this place hasn't given me any relapse that I can tell."

"Good. The residents and Clay will be glad to see you," Weaver promised.

"I've already talked to Clay, and I bumped into some residents in the MOB a few minutes ago. Jess," he shifted, "they tell me there's been about ninety Blush admissions so far, and about thirty deaths. Is that the case?"

"Ninety-three admissions as of yesterday. Thirty-one deaths," Weaver corrected.

"Jess, that's awful! The Triage Unit must be pandemonium. And Building Seven must have the atmosphere of a morgue," Cantrelle lamented.

"Our admission rate has doubled over the past month because of the increase in the Blush patients," Weaver rued. "The Triage Unit is holding up pretty well, though, thanks to your residents. Just about all of them are putting in their elective time there to help out, and Clay has made things a little more flexible on the ITU for the junior residents there to rotate one day a week on the Triage Unit as additional backup. And not one hint of complaint from your residents. It's as though they heard the call to medical arms, and are marching bravely to the fray, as only the anointed young can do."

Cantrelle felt a surge of pride well up in him and with it a detectable increase in the light-headedness. Write it off as giddiness, he thought.

"Building Seven, on the other hand, is just about as you say," Weaver continued, "but I think it's seen more as a leper colony. People don't want to go near it, as though Blush were contagious. The rest of the hospital doesn't regard the Blush cases as valid patients but more like doomed unfortunates who should be allowed to perish elsewhere, out of view. That's the staff's gut feeling. Their public attitude is more professionally solicitous, though not to the point of encouraging many of them to volunteer for assignment to the unit. Not only that, but I think their covert feeling is shared by Sharpsfield and the DMH because," he shifted his gaze to Laura as a gentle reminder that she was herewith privy to confidential considerations, "they're talking about transferring all of the Blush patients, ours as well as those in the other commonwealth facilities, to a long-term care center designated as a Blush collection facility."

"You mean like Mountainview?" Cantrelle suggested.

"Probably. Martha attended a superintendents' meeting at the DMH last week and it turns out the state system has close to three hundred Blush patients on its rolls with about another one hundred more scattered in private institutions throughout the state," Weaver detailed. "Given the rate of increase thus far, it's expected that we'll have at any given time about seven to eight hundred of them occupying hospital beds somewhere in the state by year's end, which isn't very far off."

"Then what would we do here at Moreland? Much of anything?" Cantrelle asked as concern began to gather on the edges of his thinking.

"Just the Triage, it seems. It's only a proposal, so far," Weaver soothed, sensing Cantrelle's discomfort which not unexpectedly mirrored some of his own, "but it would provide for immediate transfer to the collection facility once the Blush patient is diagnosed. We would not get involved in the extended care of any of them."

"Then we would close Building Seven?" Cantrelle speculated.

"Probably, but it won't be any time real soon even if the plan is adopted. Frank," Weaver continued in the tone of appeal, "Blush is banishing a part of our staff. Actually, a part of our hospital. No one goes near Building Seven and the people who work that building feel like they're in some kind of macabre exile. And they complain that people, their co-workers elsewhere in the hospital, treat them like undertakers; like they're tainted in some way. The old taboos about the dying and the dead are taking over here. Wait till you're back a few days, you'll see. It's not only the DMH that would like to move the Blush patients far away, I can tell you. And it's getting harder to find people to work in Building Seven. As more patients come we have to keep enlarging the staff, but the experienced and competent people already on board elsewhere in the hospital won't volunteer to form the staff cadre the unit needs. So we hire people right off the street, no experience at all, and the unit then becomes something a lot less steady, less professional than the other units around here with the result that the building is seen as all the more alien and different. Plus, the aides who work there have a high turnover rate, and the personnel office now spends too much of its time just recruiting for Building Seven. In that way, you're right; it's like recruiting for work in a morgue. People see the whole thing as something to be shunned, avoided; not something like respectable disease to be treated, battled, and conquered. Blush touches a basic, primitive horror in people, and, because of that, very basic taboos are mobilized to address it. Here as well as at DMH."

He sat there and listened to every plaintive syllable of Weaver's *crie de coeur*. He now understood better why Weaver was so glad to see him back. He evidently needed someone to talk to in the way they had always talked.

Laura shifted slightly in her chair to indicate her willingness to be excused from the business the two men had before them, having sensed early on that she'd become an accidental participant in something more typically private in their friendship; but Jess, reading her gesture precisely, waved her back into attendance with the flat of his hand as he shifted his tone.

"Yes, my recovering friend, we have some tasks awaiting us next week," he summed. "No luck in their going away before then. Clay got the paper off to the *Annals* a few days after you took ill, as I'm sure you know, and I want to thank you—I've already inflicted my gratitude upon him—for citing me and Martha in the acknowledgements. The DMH liked your generous reference to them, too."

"They were generous in helping us get the unit going. We were only being fair," Cantrelle sniffed.

"Nevertheless, it was well received, and it's been helpful. They rarely get any credit," Weaver pointed out.

"They rarely deserve it," Cantrelle snapped.

"All right, all right," Weaver offered in placation. He could see that his friend's convalescence hadn't yet yielded a dividend of magnanimity. "Martha thanks you, too," he added.

Cantrelle nodded curtly.

A moment of loose silence followed as Cantrelle chewed on some thought. He stared at the edge of Jess' desk as he did so.

"I had hoped to buoy your spirits by reminding you how devoted we are to your worship and it seems all I've done is plunge you into worry," Weaver attempted.

"Oh," Cantrelle exclaimed, recalled to the conversation. "It's not that. Such worship is meet and agreeable, and I will endeavor to accord it just allowance, my devoted sir," Cantrelle quipped to cover his lapse. Actually he was struggling with a flash of the verge, the intensity of which he hadn't felt in some time. He was trying to puzzle out its meaning on the basis of what they had been talking about, but, as always, found himself grappling with vapors as he tried to corral the phantom and grasp its purpose. Again it felt like a visitation from something unlaid with its message still not understood. And, as before, it left him unsettled and wanting as his pursuit chased the shadow back into imperceptibility. Feeling empty-handed and chagrined, he resumed.

"I was just thinking about the long-range effect of transferring the Blush people elsewhere," he dissembled though identifying a genuine concern which had surfaced earlier in his thinking. "But that can wait. Right now I just want to get my legs again and the stroll this morning seems to be doing that just ducky."

"He would have you believe that he's been like a caged beast," Laura interjected to help return the visit to pleasant convention, "but he really began to enjoy the leisure time. It was the siren temptation of indolence that chased him back to work, really. A few more days of home comfort and he probably never would have returned, though he won't admit it."

Weaver guffawed at her indictment as she reached over and touched her husband's hand to soften such rank disclosure. Cantrelle, affecting chagrin, hung his head in elaborate deflation as he stifled a burble of disclaimer. They all needed a little banter just now.

"Well," resumed Cantrelle sportily, "now that I've been publicly exposed my formal return Monday will be less than the triumphant procession I had planned. Now, probably more like an apologetic slink. Thank you, sweet," he smiled fulsomely to Laura.

"No matter how you get back we'll all be better off," Weaver summed up in hint that it was time to get back to work.

"Oh, one final thing," Cantrelle added, "Clay and I had begun to talk about a follow-up paper correlating the brain cell lesions with the neuropsych findings described in the first paper. The state lab probably has enough material from the tissue studies to make a representative sample, wouldn't you say?" he suggested.

"I should think so. Why?" Weaver asked.

"Because we may need your help in getting those reports so that we can use them in the write-up," Cantrelle explained.

"That shouldn't be a problem. We've gotten permission for autopsy in over half of the Blush deaths, so you should have plenty enough material to work with," Weaver assured.

"Great," Cantrelle sighed, not feeling exactly at peace with such a windfall. "On that grim note I think we'll take our leave so that I may enjoy the remaining few and fading moments of derelict indolence with my refreshingly honest wife. Right, Hon?" Cantrelle teased.

"Don't let him upset you, Laura. Let me say that when he's in your presence he's a vastly better person," Weaver assured, "and I would be delighted to hear all the honesty about him you would care to offer."

With that round of chuckles Cantrelle rose and stretched.

"Christ, I'm getting old," he groaned in mid-contortion. "Twenty years ago I would have thrown this thing off in a few days," he added speaking to his unsteadiness as he stood before them.

"Sure, sure, old man. Just try to hold yourself together until Monday," Weaver ahemed in Laura's direction as they stood up to join him.

Just then Weaver's secretary leaned her head in as she held the door open.

"Dr. Weaver, there's a call for Dr. Cantrelle on line four. It's Mrs. Andretti," she explained.

"Thank you," Weaver nodded as he turned the phone toward Cantrelle.

"It's starting already," Cantrelle groused as he reached to take the call. "Yes, Mrs. Andretti?" he asked as he hefted the receiver in place. He listened for a moment and then replied, "I suppose so. I'll be over in about a minute; we're leaving now." He put the receiver back in its cradle and began his explanation.

"Morello heard that I'm back and he's waiting at my office this very minute. Sometimes that boy's energy frightens me. Anyway, he wants a minute to bring me up to date on something. Of course, with him nothing can wait. That'll be O.K., won't it, Hon? Only take a minute. Promise," he entreated sweetly.

Weaver smiled slyly as Laura nodded her approval which carried a hesitance that implied certain unspoken restrictions he was sure Cantrelle understood clearly. Weaver reflected on how much he delighted in being around these two people who seemed to know how to do marriage just right.

"So I'll see you Monday, Jess. You might pass it on to Martha if you see her," he added unnecessarily and more in the nature of planning out loud.

"Of course," Weaver agreed readily.

"Then we're off," he announced as he and Laura began to gather their coats.

Weaver walked them to the door. The get-together closed with Laura's asking to be remembered to Pam, Weaver's wife.

Cantrelle was feeling more confident as the morning progressed, and the walk back to the MOB became sprightly as he relaxed the earlier caution. The morning sally was really moving his convalescence along nicely, he observed approvingly as they sauntered up the drive. The scenery was returning to its status as routine and given.

"This thing with Morello shouldn't take more than a few minutes, whatever it is, and then we can get on back home," he promised.

"They're all so glad to see you," Laura commended, "and I feel I'm losing you to them after our weeks of exclusive time home. Right now I feel the same way I do when our vacation comes to an end and we get ready to resume our separate ways."

The regret in her words stabbed at him. He realized that he hadn't considered how she felt about his return to work. If anything he had assumed she felt pretty much as he did, eager to hasten along the convalescence and regain lost time. But there was another side to it, certainly, and he had lost sight of it in the general discomfort of the illness and in the confinement imposed by his frailty. Just now that neglected other side was becoming apparent to him on the suggestion of Laura's regret. How many times before had they said that any time they were together was good time? Just about every blessed time they came to the realization that they shared something special which was uniquely theirs forever, regardless of its valence. Even like the past three weeks. He squeezed her hand and reciprocated her saddened smile as they neared the door of the MOB. The moment had become charged, just as Laura was saying, for the MOB door had now become the portal by which they would leave behind their tender world of the past three weeks. And yet they could not *not* go through that door, for likewise they could not remain forever where they had been and now no longer really were. And at this critical instant there didn't even seem to be time to savor the poignancy of the moment which was catching them in the middle of the driveway before the very steps of the MOB. He stopped walking and held her before him. He lifted her face tenderly and looked into her moist and loving eyes. There was so much to say, but what more could he say beyond what the past three weeks of her total devotion had already said for him? He pressed her tightly to him and then kissed her deeply as everything in their world stopped for this perfect moment to be theirs alone. Their special truth thus beheld, he relaxed his embrace to look at her angelic face, now streaked with a few vagabond tears. As he did so he felt giddiness return, and he drew on his slight but noticeable swaying to make a point while he daubed her cheeks with his handkerchief.

"Hon, there's no chance of my ever being better without you. See?" he demonstrated as though balancing on a wire. He then gave her a peck on the tip of her nose and continued, "Now let's get in there and brazen it out for the people we've scandalized by our public display of vertigo blended with lechery." With that he took her hand as they pranced up the steps and into the building.

They entered his outer office where Mrs. Andretti and Morello awaited.

"Hi, Chief! You must be feeling better," his irrepressible chief resident greeted in typical excess. "Heard you were back so I thought I'd catch you before you changed your mind about staying."

He was coming on a little stronger than usual, Cantrelle noted, and it prompted him to wonder if the bluster was a cover-up for some unpleasantness needing to be addressed. Maybe that's what Morello meant about his changing his mind about being back. He cringed at the thought of being presented with something that would gnaw at the tranquillity due the sunset weekend of his happy time at home with Laura. He wasn't ready for any new trouble. Not yet.

Laura sensed his concern and before he could respond to Morello suggested that he and Morello take care of their business while she and Mrs. Andretti caught up on their news.

"Sure," Cantrelle agreed. "Please come in, Dr. Morello," he directed as he led the way in.

"First, Chief, the residents let out a cheer this morning when they heard you were back. They've felt lonely these past three weeks," Morello announced as he plopped into a chair upon Cantrelle's invitation.

"I missed you all, too; and you can tell them I'll catch up to them after a day or so back. Mr. Moyer kept me posted while I was home and he tells me you all kept things moving right along and with nary a complaint. And Dr. Weaver just confessed on all of you," he explained with nodding satisfaction. "You might mention to them that gratitude is enroute from several quarters."

"That's O.K., Chief," replied Morello, squirming in embarrassment.

"But knowing you as I do, you had something more than greetings in mind? Am I right?" Cantrelle pursued, hoping to move things along.

"Well, yes," Morello allowed with some hesitation. "It's something I meant to tell you a while ago, and I would have, but you got sick. So I thought I'd hold on to it till you got back." He then became silent and checked Cantrelle's face to estimate the safety of further disclosure.

Cantrelle waited, surveying Morello over steepled fingers.

"I think you'd better get on with it. You've gone this far," he urged.

"Well, remember that sample of Blush—or, rather the heroin with the Blush in it—we got from that patient, Frieden?" Morello resumed more resolutely. "You remember, he passed it on to Mrs. Rolf and she contacted me and I told her to take it to you . . . ."

"Yes, I remember," Cantrelle replied in calculated understatement. The very thought that he might somehow have forgotten! His light-headedness was becoming more prominent as his heart rate picked up in alarm at Morello's drift. In a flash he just knew he was going to be told that they later learned the sample was bogus, a plant, and that both had withheld that information because he had already sent the sample to the state lab as the real thing, and, after all, they were only trying to protect him but now thought he should know before the whole thing really got out of hand.

"Well, it has something to do with that sample," Morello continued with a sidelong glance.

"So I gather. What about it?" Cantrelle posed, his impatience beginning to show.

"I didn't give it all to you. I kept some of it myself," he blurted in a rush of disclosure.

Cantrelle's relief in having estimated wrong told as he exhaled through a simpering smile. He dropped his hands into his lap and gazed at Morello's incredulous face.

"I said I kept some of it," Morello repeated, perplexed. "I don't mean I kept it to use it. I mean I didn't turn all of it in. I knew I was violating the DMH rules and that I could have gotten all of us in trouble, but I did it anyway. At first Mrs. Rolf didn't want to go along with it. You're not upset?" Morello pressed.

"Mrs. Rolf conspired with you?" Cantrelle inquired more out of curiosity than annoyance.

"Well, yes, in a way. She more or less went along with it and promised not to tell you just yet," Morello explained.

Cantrelle recalled her skittishness at the time she presented the sample to him.

"I'm sure your action carries a redeeming explanation, Dr. Morello," Cantrelle continued as he worked at trying to raise a show of official displeasure which Morello seemed primed to hear.

"It does," he affirmed with gathering courage. "I needed to keep some so that I could send it off."

"WHAT?" shouted Cantrelle, his earlier relief canceled. "Send it where?"

Morello's gulp now registered the peril he had anticipated.

"I sent it to someone at NIH," he squeaked.

Cantrelle was dumbstruck.

"Of all the agencies to include in your little artifice! Like *who* at NIH?" Cantrelle fairly yelled upon regaining speech. The light-headedness was now whirring away with renewed enthusiasm, but he didn't care.

"A friend of mine who's working on his Ph.D. in macro-molecular research. He's a biochemist. An old fraternity brother," Morello offered in wide-eyed alarm. "I know how you had doubts about Sharpsfield and their ability to follow-up on the Blush analysis so I thought I'd play it safe by sending some to Jeffrey in Bethesda. He needed a topic for his dissertation," Morello detailed in self-explanatory innocence.

Safe? Jeffrey? Dissertation? In Bethesda! Cantrelle found it hard to believe what he was hearing, but he knew it was true. Every cockeyed word of it.

"Dr. Morello," Cantrelle seethed, "do you realize that you are guilty of unauthorized movement of an illegal drug across state lines? Trafficking? A federal offense! And I guess you used the U.S. mails, didn't you?"

"Federal Express," Morello gulped.

"That's enough right there—using the mails even if it hadn't been across state lines—to put you and your ass in safe storage for at least a year and a day! And to compound it by sending it to a federal agency in Washington, DC, undoubtedly qualifies you—and Mrs. Rolf—and dear Jeffrey—for very special attention from the FBI! Do you realize that? Not to mention the heat it would bring down on Moreland and all the rest of us!" Cantrelle ranted in a crescendo of outrage which he knew could be heard in the outer office. But, again, he didn't care. Son-of-a-bitch!

"But, Chief," pleaded Morello, "I thought we needed some backup on our work, and I knew I could trust Jeffrey. And I figured I could trust you."

That stung, and for a moment he wasn't sure whether to feel shame or aggravated outrage. He chose neither, but merely settled back in his chair with a sigh of exhaustion. Morello waited, hoping.

As grave as the consequences could be for Morello's lapse in judgment, he knew he himself was over-reacting. Maybe it was the pent-up frustration of his three tedious weeks of inactivity. Maybe it was the need to reaffirm his absolute authority in the face of a transgression, however well-intended. Maybe he was left a little labile by his illness—"organic" was the term—and was likely to have more such outbursts with even trivial inconveniences. Whatever, he felt his composure gradually return as he sat in his swivel chair and looked beyond Morello at the far wall for one soothing moment.

After a couple of deep breaths he returned to Morello.

"How many people know about this?" he demanded.

"Just four—you, me, Mrs. Rolf, and Jeffrey," he enumerated.

"Just four, you say. How do you know that 'Jeffrey'—whoever the hell he is—hasn't passed on the happy word to a few dozen of his very closest friends?" Cantrelle belabored while trying to maintain control. "Didn't you say he was looking for a dissertation topic? Doesn't that usually include some kind of committee review? For Christ's sake, how can you say 'only four' when it could already be a matter of public record?" he charged as he neared eruption again.

"But he hasn't submitted a dissertation proposal yet," Morello countered.

"How do you know? And besides, what about his happening to mention it to a friend or two?" Cantrelle persisted.

"Not a chance, and I'm pretty sure because I talked to him this weekend," Morello checked, now feeling himself on safer ground.

Cantrelle backed off for the moment and gathered his composure anew. He didn't want to get caught up in a counter-punching exchange with his chief resident who, he could never forget, was as selfless and idealistic a resident as ever he had. He thought it better to take a few minutes to get the full picture before proceeding to kick him in the ass, as at this moment seemed unavoidable. Also, his vertigo was now well on its way to full return along with the sickening emptiness in the pit of his stomach. He saw that the walls of the room had become a bit wavy and he was sharply taken with the dread of vomiting right in front of Morello. He settled farther back in his chair with eyes closed and took a moment to let the queasiness pass.

"You O.K., Chief?" Morello inquired urgently.

"Sure, I'm all right," he lied. "Just having too much fun too soon." He sat still in his chair which now seemed rather less acceptable because of its being a swivel. At the moment it didn't quite fit his need for strict stability, he considered, and it offered nothing in the way of steady reassurance. The thought brought him abruptly to the jolting doubt that maybe he wasn't really ready to be back at work if this was how he was reacting to the tasks awaiting him. The doubt sharpened into a fear that he just might not be up to making it in on Monday to follow up on this newly announced crisis which, now broached, sure as hell could not be casually set aside to whenever he felt equal to confronting it. Or for undertaking whatever needed to be done to resolve it. Damage control, that's what was needed! Damned sure that! And this particular onus was probably only one of several on the docket waiting for him. That canny thought, of itself, did precious little to assuage his nausea. He picked up the phone and pushed the intercom button. Almost instantly Mrs. Andretti answered.

"Mrs. Andretti, would you please track down Mr. Moyer and have him call me immediately?" he instructed. "Thank you," he bade as he replaced the receiver.

He sat for a moment leaning over his desk with his cheeks resting on the heels of his hands. Morello watched patiently.

"Chief, I really don't think you have anything to worry about with Jeffrey," Morello pleaded. "He was my roommate for awhile as an underclassman and then he was the best man in my wedding. He understands that the circumstances surrounding the Blush sample are pretty touchy and he wouldn't do anything to put us in Dutch. If anything on his end came up about having the sample in the first place he would tell them he'd put out a local search for some Blush and got it from an anonymous street source. I understand it's a lot easier to get now. In fact, a direct admission showed up two weeks ago with several packets in a shaving kit. I admitted the patient. We sent those samples on to Security just like the rules say."

The way he said it somehow alerted something in Cantrelle. Maybe because it was too generous an explanation or too eager a reassurance, but it smacked of additional confession in the offing.

"You didn't by any chance send Jeffrey some of that Blush, too, did you?" he probed wearily.

Morello hesitated, and then straightened a bit in his chair.

"Yes, I did." he said. "The patient had three packets of heroin that almost certainly contained Blush and I sent one to Jeffrey because the Blush I initially sent him was only a small amount. Not only that, Jeffrey was interested in the sample to sample consistency of the compound that was reaching the street," Morello justified with gathering confidence.

Jesus Christ! A supply network for 'Jeffrey' with Chief Resident Morello the operative! He couldn't even gasp; he was certainly beyond yelling. The weariness of having been saddled with one son of a bitch *fait accompli* was beginning to settle in.

Just then the buzzer sounded.

"Yes, Mrs. Andretti," he answered eagerly. "Good. Put him on," he directed briskly as he steadied the receiver cord with his other hand. "Clay? Yeah, I'm settling in . . . almost . . . but I need your help right now. Can you hop over here? . . . Knowing them, they'll find it in their hearts to forgive you for excusing them a few minutes early. It's pretty important . . . we'll be waiting for you . . . . Yeah, Dr. Morello . . . thanks! . . . . Well, he's on his way," he extended to Morello as he hung up. "Excuse me for a moment," he directed at Morello as he got up and opened the door. He then leaned out and announced, as much to Laura as to his secretary, "Mr. Moyer is on his way over. I need to see him for just a few minutes before we leave." Laura nodded in acceptance.

He then closed the door and returned to his chair.

"While we're waiting maybe you can bring me up to date on what's been going on with the residents over the past few weeks. There's got to be something there I would be pleased to hear," he peeved.

"Not much to say, really," Morello supplied. "The senior residents are being plied by the headhunters and some are lining up interviews here and there. You probably know which ones are looking for what."

He pretty much did. Before the illness he had already started writing the seemingly endless letters of recommendation for the soon-to-graduate, and it was sometimes startling how entitled some of the headhunting firms felt in their expectation of his help in their recruitment efforts. He uniformly steered his residents away from such firms and encouraged the residents to work directly with local medical societies and private groups in sounding out practice possibilities. Those sources didn't have the inclination to gild any lilies for which they could surely be held accountable at a later time, should the resident decide in favor of any offered opportunity. The headhunters held themselves so much less accountable.

"Any sign of their stacking arms yet?" he asked. It was typical and appropriate that senior residents began to disengage at some point down the line in their last year of training, and it was always something of a challenge to keep the training process moving along at the normal developmental pace with certain maturities yet to be cultivated onto the very end of training rather than have everything degenerate into a reactionary abandonment of scholastic rigor in a headlong rush along the goal gradient of graduation. That's why he reserved some of the headier, more global courses for the last few months of the senior year. Still, every once in a while, a resident or two tried to duck out early.

"No, not really," Morello replied. "Blush has them stepping right along because with *that* demon around there's just no rest in sight; they're pitching in just like the junior residents. It's not like it used to be."

That's for damned sure, he mumbled under his breath along with a few words of puzzlement as to how Morello could dare return to the subject which only moments earlier had provoked enough ire to urge caution in just about anyone else. As for himself, he was determined not to be carried off on another flight of righteous indignation, and so he let it pass.

"How about your Fellowship? Coming along O.K.?" he managed.

"Yeah. They got your letter and all of the others, and I have another interview—actually, a meeting with the Selection Committee—two weeks from now. They make their selections just before the holidays. After the first round of interviews they pretty much said I had the inside track," Morello preened.

"Did your experience with the Blush patients come up? I would think they had some interest in that," Cantrelle searched. The interviews had occurred while he was out ill and he was now seeking to catch up on particulars and not appear that he was thereby forfeiting his just umbrage at Morello's confessed, self-styled crusade in confederacy with best man Jeffrey. Being behind on crucial events was a debilitating pain in the ass and there was no side-stepping the rôle of suppliant in working one's way back to the front of the line.

"I mentioned it," Morello continued breezily, "but it didn't seem to interest them. They made a few polite inquiries, mostly about how we were managing all the work that came with such hopeless cases, but that was about all. I don't think they see Blush as their kind of problem. I think they see it as a state hospital problem," he suggested.

Just then they both heard the exchange of joyous greetings in the outer office. Clay had arrived and was conveying his sentiments to Laura whose spirited greeting suggested she was holding up nicely.

"Better get him in here," Cantrelle resolved as he rose and opened the door.

"There he is!" exulted Moyer upon seeing Cantrelle. "I like your shade of pallor. Makes you look Keatsian," he bashed jovially as he grabbed Cantrelle's hand in a vigorous shake. "How you feel? O.K.?" He was as exuberant as Cantrelle had ever seen him and just now Cantrelle didn't feel himself up to the mark.

"Good to see you again, Clay. Please come in," Cantrelle responded.

Moyer took his usual chair against the hallway wall of the office as Cantrelle closed the door and returned to his desk. Moyer exchanged acknowledgments with Morello as Cantrelle adjusted himself in his chair.

"What's up, Frank?" Moyer resumed with a shift to the circumspect. "I had expected you to be a little more upbeat about being back, but it seems you don't feel quite up to the luxury of it yet."

"Right, Clay," Cantrelle agreed. "I think we have a problem, or what could become one, and frankly I need you to be in on it just in case I have to be out longer than I hope and something urgent comes up about it and needs someone from Residency Training to pinch hit. Also—and this is why I wanted to talk to you right now about it—I just left Jess a little while ago and I really don't feel like going back over there to report this to him because I really want to get my ass back home and into my wheelchair for the remainder of this weekend. And I don't want this to wait until Monday when I expect to be back, God permitting. So I'm asking you to meet with Jess sometime later today to fill him in on this. He should know."

"Sure. What are you leading up to?" Moyer queried.

"Dr. Morello purloined some of that Blush sample we got and sent it to a friend at NIH, and then followed up with even *more* of it later to make sure his friend had enough for a chemical analysis!" Cantrelle disclosed as succinctly as he could and at the expense of justified editorializing. Cantrelle could feel Morello cringe in anticipation of more pain.

"Fine," Moyer announced after a moment of silent review.

Morello audibly sighed as he relaxed in his chair.

"Fine? Clay, you don't seem to understand!" pleaded Cantrelle as he squirmed to offset his dismay at Moyer's betrayal. "Dr. Morello, unauthorized, sent an illegal drug across state lines through the mails to a personal friend at NIH! NIH, mind you! The friend intends to use it for a dissertation project! I can't think of a better way to ask for trouble!" Cantrelle emphasized, determined to receive agreement.

"Yes, I understand, Frank, but I find the risk acceptable in light of the potential good it could bring," Moyer persisted.

Morello beamed in vindication.

"Maybe I'm still not with it," Cantrelle shook his head in feigned perplexity designed to cover his exasperation, "but when a resident steps out of line and does something that puts the entire Training Program in jeopardy I'm inclined to see that as a god-damned source of concern! I'm funny like that. Let's suppose NIH calls Martha or Jess and demands to know what the hell we're up to? Then what?"

"Then we'll tell 'em," Moyer explained simply.

Cantrelle just sat there, feeling the wind being taken right out of his sails. How could he get these people to appreciate the gravity of the issue?

"Frank," Moyer continued in a more conciliatory tone, "you've been out of commission for a while and so you're out of touch with the tenor of things. Things have changed a lot since you got sick."

"I'm still vaguely aware of what's going on, like rules and regulations governing the behavior of citizens, even residents," he retorted.

As he spoke, the klaxon of an ALS vehicle grew louder with its approach. They waited till it faded into the interior of the hospital grounds.

"Frank, that's some of what's been happening since you've been away," Moyer pointed out. "Those ambulances come almost daily—last week it happened twice in one day—and they come almost exclusively for Blush patients. As you know our Blush people are dying at the rate of twenty or so a month. That's bad enough, but the worst of it is that no one seems to care."

Cantrelle just sat there as he felt the cast of the interchange begin to turn around. It was no longer a matter of bringing Morello to heel; rather Moyer and Morello, clearly united in purpose, were going to take him to task for having lost touch with what they would now display as a more up-to-date reality.

"For example, so far the only word we've received from the concerned townspeople is a complaint that the noise of the ambulances is bothersome," Moyer detailed. "Once in a while wasn't a problem, they felt, but coming as often as the ambulances now do makes the neighborhood unpleasantly noisy. Our stalwart citizens even contacted their local congressman about it and he called Martha and suggested we tell the ambulance people they turn off their sirens when they drive to the hospital. That's how much the citizens whose behavior is governed by the rules and regulations you mention are concerned about the fact that every time they hear that bothersome ambulance siren it means a young person just died. Martha told that oily ward heeler to go fly a kite. You didn't know about that, I'm certain. And being flat on your back I'm sure you weren't keen about keeping up with the daily news and national trends, but if you had been you would have noticed a remarkable absence of coverage in the media about the hundreds—that's right—hundreds of Blush patients dying every day across the country. Right here in this state alone the rate is up to a minimum of three a day, according to information Jess got last week—information, I might add, he had to seek on his own initiative because Sharpsfield is disinclined to advertise death rates at its institutions, and especially when the public prefers not to be told about it in the first place."

Cantrelle felt the dawning awareness that, unknown to him, his usual working priorities, now rendered quaint and obsolete, had been unseated and that he was being led to umble pie as an overdue rite of passage to newer urgencies.

"Jess did some checking—again on his own—with a few other states," Moyer continued. "It turns out they're in the same boat as we. Their hospital systems are taking in more and more Blush patients, especially the state hospitals near the urban areas, and these patients are dying with predictable regularity, just like ours. With all that going on—across state lines as I think you phrased it—one wonders why the federal government hasn't been more vocal about the problem. Hardly a peep other than a pathetic lament that this great nation is confronted with—saddled with, might be closer to their true sentiment—so vexatious a problem. Frank, I'm not the only one who's come to believe that any official tears shed anywhere beyond the hospitals are piss-ant crocodile tears. After all, the ones dying are loathsome drug addicts. Also, they're bringing their deaths upon themselves. They've been a vile problem for too long and nothing else has ever worked in ridding society of their fetid existence. And so deep down in everybody's heart there is a sense of good riddance, plus a desire for collective silence about it."

Morello was now nodding right along and Cantrelle surmised that this very discussion must have occurred times before among the residents, perhaps with Moyer orchestrating. He wondered if Moyer had known all along about the shipment of Blush to Bethesda.

"And while we're at it, Frank—for I believe you're just dying to be brought up to date on how archaic your thinking has become during your illness—you might wonder if we've gotten any feedback from NIH on the Blush research they're supposed to be doing, which we were led to believe had begun with the original Blush sample forwarded to them. Remember?" Moyer taunted. "That was weeks ago, as you know. Of course, Blush samples now are much easier to come by and so NIH doesn't have to depend on little old us any more to provide them with specimens for their research to move the more swiftly. Right? Wrong! They haven't done a thing that we can tell. Jess tried to find out if they had taken the analysis any farther than the state lab did, and they said they hadn't because the format for the expected analysis was still in the proposal stage. Proposal stage, hell!" Moyer roared. "They're trying to bury the whole thing!"

"Yeah," Morello piped up, "Jeffrey says no one there is really interested in working on Blush. He tried to talk to someone about it and he got the impression that the people at NIH kinda resented the idea of being looked upon as just a bigger poison center for the states.

He said they didn't see Blush as being genuine research but more of a passing thing that would sooner or later run its course."

"So, Jess and I, and probably a lot others—certainly the Blush patients if they were able to think about it at all—are coming around to the idea that NIH is dragging its feet in direct response to Sharpsfield's demonstrated eagerness to pass the buck along to them. Jess says it's almost like a conspiracy of silence when he calls anyone to find out what's being done. He's the one who signs the death certificates, so he's not allowed the luxury of splendid isolation all too many others seem to be enjoying."

He didn't want to hear the last remark as personally directed anymore than he wanted to credit the grim cynicism of Moyer's ranging indictment. For years he'd been accusing Moyer of detecting contrived and clever malice where only incompetence or inadequacy existed. Moyer, he had so often charged, also tended to see everybody as inherently knowledgeable and resourceful as he was. Thus anyone's failure to perform was both motivated and planful and not just an innocent and simple matter of limitation. Truly, his sensor was set to see more cunning design and less simple laxity. Occasionally, just occasionally, Moyer was correct in his melancholy indictment of officialdom, and in his eyes that was often enough to justify his sustained, hovering distrust of conventional exculpations.

"Clay," he attempted, "don't you think you're painting it a little dark? Maybe the people at NIH are just having a little trouble getting it together and getting started. Wouldn't be the first time, especially if it's a project imposed upon them by external circumstances, as is the case here. I think we can also sympathize that they may look upon Blush as being something less than pure research and more of a social problem which they're being called upon to cure."

"And that's exactly what they're there for!" Moyer corrected unsympathetically.

"Sure, Clay," Cantrelle soothed, "but don't forget that they're scientists and their interests are typically universal, even cosmic, as I'm sure they would prefer, and whenever they feel themselves weighed down by mundane things like Blush they might grumble, and maybe even hesitate a little. And as for the townspeople complaining about the sirens, you make it sound like they have no other thought than that they're being bothered by unnecessary noise. I'm sure those people know exactly what that siren means and are inwardly upset about a death knell being so close at hand and so often. Like hearing the fluttering of the wings of the angel of death every other day or so. I bet they're scared and don't know what to do about it. I see their complaint as more in the nature of morbid dread than selfish insensitivity."

"Nevertheless, the upshot is the same," Moyer insisted. "They don't want to know about it, they don't want to hear about it, and they don't want to deal with it—not a bit unlike the three monkeys that live in every one of us at some time."

Cantrelle felt this last comment was indeed directed at him. It was beginning to seem that he'd been living in a fool's paradise these past three weeks though it would have been hard to convince him of it at the time. And yet, everything Clay said had a disturbing ring of truth to it. True, state and federal action did seem to be a bit sluggish in response to what all could agree was becoming a horrific social tragedy. Likewise, it was true that people didn't want their peace disturbed by miseries about which they could do nothing and which they dreaded might somehow come to touch them, personally. Moreover, it was also likely that just about everybody saw in this medical calamity an opportunity to rid society of one of its most embarrassing and debilitating problems. Few people could identify with the drug addict, much less sympathize with him, and the host of other social and medical ills which followed in his wake were simply abhorred by the general citizenry. The drug addict was seen as a threat to the nation's children, a drain on the country's health resources, and an incubation medium for domestic as well as international crime. The addict had become a most obdurate indictment of American society; his existence called into question the validity of the American conception of personal freedom, the role of government in regulating social intercourse, the capacity of the nation's legal system to protect society from its offenders, and now even the dutied call of the body scientific to protect those offenders from the dread consequences of their own doings. The thought that at last society might be free of such a blight by simply doing nothing to delay its departure had to be a part of everyone's thinking on some level, he agreed, but could this society's established institutions afford that posture? He was sure they couldn't, though his dear friend Clay Moyer was contending that society now thought otherwise. He decided to take open stock.

"Clay," he intoned sarcastically, "you and Dr. Morello make me realize just how very simple I am; simple beyond redemption . . . ."

"My years of effort have finally paid off," Moyer chortled.

"Damn it, you're enjoying this, aren't you?" he smiled against his will. "You're also probably right that I'm behind in my estimate of the priorities facing us. Next, you'll have me apologizing to Dr. Morello for not seeing the inherent wisdom and social responsibility of his felony. Maybe it truly is a situation of our having to run for our lives while I, in a toxic stupor come of living yet in the world of three weeks ago, rant on about obeying the speed limits. Maybe so. Maybe also everybody really wants Blush to go right on about its business and resolve the drug problem of this great nation, letting the addict arrange his own execution while everyone else stands by in humane and compassionate neglect. And maybe there is a cruel justice in that approach—even if derived from a covert policy of specific inaction, as you apparently believe. But even if such were the case, you and I and Dr. Morello and Moreland and DMH and NIH can in *no way*, I agree, merely stand by, however wisely. And the reason we can't, I again agree, is because there's no way we could do it innocently. A lot of other people out there can pretend to innocence, but we can't. True. It simply ain't in our job descriptions, as you've deftly reminded me just moments ago. Right? Right! Right to all of it! But the idea of taking the pathetic, all too human tendency to deny and avoid and then fashion it into a national policy of permissive genocide bespeaks a kind of cruel innocence on your part. You expect too much complexity of people—I've always told you that—and you endeavor to prove them capable of it it one way or another. And thus culpable. Your innocence is that you believe governments are actually responsible for how a nation is governed. The government is a *consequence* of how a nation is run, not the *cause*. I don't know where I'm going with this, but I feel I should say it, if for no other reason than to contribute my bit in identifying the god-damned priorities. And to stir up my vertigo some more, damn it! But to see the malevolent hand of government as directing national neglect of this problem is, I think, erecting a very convenient straw man. The problem is the people. Like the people offended by the ambulance sirens, not the congressman who panders to their fears. This supposed cynical neglect of Blush which has you—and Dr. Morello—all worked up is really no different from what has been society's tradition with schizophrenia since time immemorial, though we grew up with that tradition and so we're kinda used to it. Even back when one quarter of all the hospital beds in this country were occupied by schizophrenics there wasn't much in the way of social or governmental concern about it, you might remember. Those loathsome and embarrassing lunatics were conveniently out of sight—almost five thousand of them right here at Moreland only forty years ago—and no one thought there was a big ass conspiracy afoot then. I know there's a big difference between being born with a crooked gene that ends up as insanity and being the victim of a heroin mickey, but in a way that's exactly the point I want to make, if I ever get around to it. I think that rather than go off on some cynical chase about who's not doing enough and why not, we should be more concerned about stopping what already is happening too often. Like how to block the effect of Blush on the nervous system, and how to stop whoever the hell is putting it in the heroin in the first place. That's the point! And I didn't come here this morning for all this," he wheezed with a weary sigh, "and I don't want to leave here more upset than when I came, but I will," he added in self-pity.

Moyer was now raising his eyebrows in his usual gesture of futility.

"Frank," he attempted, "I don't know which of us is the more innocent, but I do know that you'll be a lot more surprised than I will be if it turns out that we're both right, which would then make me more right than you. Right?"

"I don't know what you mean!" Cantrelle puzzled.

"I mean that the government's benign neglect might not be totally independent of the spiking of the heroin," Moyer cautioned.

"Now what the hell do you mean by that?" Cantrelle exploded all over again. "That the government is behind the problem? Clay, have *you* been taking something? You're demonstrating my very point! The government is not that organized, that efficient, or even that clever, much less that monstrous, to do something so unconscionably wicked. We don't construct it to be that capable. Purposely. Also, how could it keep its actions from being known? There is no such thing as security in Washington. Remember that senator from the South who publicly boasted right in the middle of World War II that he learned that the reason our submarines were doing so well was because the Japanese were setting their depth charges too deep, which the Japanese then quickly corrected? That's the kind of people we have a lot of in Washington. And who would head up this operation? The present administration? The majority party? Who? And where would all this be done?"

"Jeffrey says they already know that the heroin comes from Southeast Asia by way of a banana republic in Central America. They've found out that much," Morello eagerly contributed.

"Good for them," Cantrelle snapped. "I'm glad to hear that it's not a cash crop spin-off from our domestic farm subsidy program. For the government to be tied to such an international enterprise as Blush it would demand a degree of competence and organization impossible to conceal among the likes of our legislators," he added acidly. "Now, Clay," he appealed, "let's be realistic, because I'm worried our residents might . . . ."

The buzzer interrupted him.

With a grunt of annoyance he reached across his desk for the phone.

"Yes, Mrs. Andretti?" he managed civilly enough. As he listened his expression changed quickly to alert expectation. "Yes, bring it in." As he hung up he turned to Moyer. "There's something from the *Annals* in the morning mail! Just arrived!"

"Jesus Christ!" Moyer moaned.

There was a faint knock on the door. Cantrelle bolted out of his chair and set a new wave of vertigo into motion. Steadying himself enroute he reached the door and opened it. Mrs. Andretti was holding the letter for his ready grasp. He took it and gestured to her and to Laura who was now sitting straight up in wide-eyed attention.

"You'll both know in a moment what it says by the character of the tumult," he quailed.

He closed the door and returned to his chair, exhausted by the exertion, the apprehension, and the dizziness.

"Here, Clay. You open it. I'm too dizzy to read," he demurred, handing it over.

They were now bursting with boyish impatience leavened by dread. Clay ripped open the envelope.

"'*Dear Contributor*,'" Clay began reading, "'*We are pleased to inform you that your article has been accepted.*' Hot Dog! We're in!" He read on rapidly in a mumble and slowed down to emphasize, "'. . . *will arrive under separate cover within a few days of receipt of this notification. If the suggested corrections and/or revisions are acceptable to you please return the copy signed and at your earliest convenience . . .'* etc., etc. And there's a personal note to you, Frank," Moyer added as he handed the letter to a wildly heaving Cantrelle who took the letter in trembling hand.

"'*Dear Dr. Cantrelle,*'" he read the handwritten lines at the bottom of the form letter. "'*Congratulations to you and to Mr. Moyer on a crisp, clear, and well-designed piece of work which I am sure will become a reference paper in this new area of investigation. With a bit of luck we might be able to make deadline for next month's issue. Warmest regards. Burleson.*'"

"God damn it!" he whooped, eyes flashing, "he probably helped convoy it through. See, goddammit! Someone else is interested in getting Blush on the front page!"

By now all three were noisily standing in readiness to pat each other on the back when a faint knock on the door came.

"Yes?" yelled Cantrelle, turning away briefly from the victory chants.

"May we come in and join the celebration?" Laura chirped as she poked her head in through the slightly ajar door.

"You bet!" he demanded as he opened the door full and swept her and Mrs. Andretti in to have them read the letter.

"Look at this, Hon," he bade as he waved the letter, "maybe it'll make next month's issue. Now that's *fast*! They must really like it! And they must also agree with the timeliness of it—and the urgency! Moreland will be back up front again! Wait till Jess and Martha hear about this!" he rattled on.

Laura scanned the letter and passed it on to Mrs. Andretti. She then applied herself to her husband's side as his arm automatically gathered her in. He continued to talk vigorously with Clay and Morello who were also talking, ascendancy in the tripartite conversation shifting from one to the other as they worked and reworked the theme of Moreland's return to the psychiatric map, the establishment of Blush as an issue of desperate proportions, and the identification of Moreland State Hospital as a leading contributor to the work so urgently needed.

Mrs. Andretti presented her sweet congratulations, and in return Cantrelle announced to all present that she had meticulously typed every blessed word of the article and had arranged the format for the tables and statistics to make the article immensely readable, and no doubt ultimately acceptable to the editorial board. An exaggerated frown then came over his face.

"Clay, I hate to mention this just now, but having this article in print obligates us to the follow-up article on the neuropathology and the neuropsych test results. The second phase paper. And I guess the third phase paper, the biochemistry of Blush, most likely will be handled by our trusted colleague, Jeffrey, at NIH," he added jovially in the direction of Morello who giggled in reply.

"Christ, you're not even a full day back to work from a sick bed and you're already mapping out our life's work for us," Moyer joshed, delighted at the prospect.

Cantrelle was gripped by a fresh wave of the staggers as he opened both arms wide in a gesture of broad noblesse, prompting Laura to reach for his arm to steady him.

"Dear," she urged, "save some of the celebration and planning for next week. I would like to take you home in approximately the same shape as you were when I brought you here just an hour ago. I want us to be able to catch up on some things over the weekend before you wear yourself out at work next week."

"Now that's a proposition if I ever heard one," Moyer cracked.

All joined in with laughter of salacious good will, the kind typical of a nuptial party. Laura blushed effusively, which encouraged the laughter all the more.

"I didn't mean it that way," she stammered in mortification.

"They'll never know how you meant it, Sweet," Cantrelle resolved gallantly as he pulled her closer to him. After a few more chortles from all in the merriment of their much-needed good news he shifted the gathering back to wind-up business. "My loving wife is right. I'm still a little unsteady; you might even say flaky from what's happened these past few minutes, and I would now like to get on back home."

They all automatically became more attentive to his change in tone.

"Clay," he continued, "would you meet with Jess and fill him in on everything that's happened. I would love to be there to see the expression on his face. I'll be home if you or he needs me for anything."

"Sure, Frank. I'll go over right after you leave," Moyer assured.

"Dr. Morello, I think I owe you an apology. You did the right and courageous thing. It just happened to be too daring for me to accept on the first hearing. Your immediate supervisor, Mr. Moyer, eased the way for my delinquent understanding, as you saw demonstrated, and I hope you will never forget the truth of what you witnessed, that sometimes teachers are the last ones to learn. And, Mrs. Andretti, we all thank you for getting that article off in jig time. Too often you stayed after quitting time to do it and I know I'm embarrassing you by mentioning it. If for any reason I'm not here when the revised manuscript arrives next week zip it over to Mr. Moyer and let him give it the final O.K.. Then, forge my signature to it—I know you can—and ship it back Federal Express, such as Dr. Morello is wont to do. Anything else?" he queried.

There were no suggestions.

"O.K. then, I'll now return to my lap robe and chicken soup. Shall we, dear?" he extended his arm in gallant invitation.

Laura hooked her arm through his and they proudly paraded out of the office and into the hallway, waving as they left. He felt particularly resplendent in the glow of triumph. Those wonderful people who labored under the indictment of being his friends—what ever would he do without them?

As they walked up the hallway to the front door he beamed broadly.

"Hon," he announced, "if I can come here and fight, we can go home and f. . ."

She immediately clapped her hand over his mouth, having sensed what was coming.

"Don't you dare say that, Frank Cantrelle! Someone could hear you! I've already been mortified enough for one day," she scolded.

They left the building with her hand over his mouth and she didn't relax the stricture until they were outside and on their way down the steps. She freed him for speech as they reached the walk, whereupon they savored a moment of their special blend of inanity as hand in hand they giggled their way to the car which they entered with the glee of two adolescents on a domino date.

He pulled out of the parking slot and headed for the main drive leading to the front gate.

"What I meant in there about catching up on some things over the weekend was our getting ready for Thanksgiving next week," Laura carefully corrected.

"Aw!" he feigned.

"And you have to help me. Everybody'll be home. Richard and Meredith, Ellie and some fellow she's dating, and, of course, Todd. And you'll be well enough to eat a full meal without vomiting. And now with the article's being published we'll just have a lot more to feel good about, and thankful," she summed up.

As they neared the junction with the campus' main drive the ALS ambulance, now proceeding silently and at a more solemn speed, slipped ahead of them. They pulled in behind the ambulance and followed it to the front gate.

EIGHT

It was the miserable time of the year, he grumbled as he sat at his desk. The room was still cold even though he had turned up the thermostat more than half an hour earlier when he pulled out of bed and dragged himself to the steaming coffee awaiting him in the kitchen. The guy who invented the programmable coffee percolator deserved a Peace Prize, he concluded for the hundredth time since he got it as a present Christmas morning, because he couldn't think of anyone else who had done so much to bring peace on earth toward men of good will or who contributed to the personal comfort of so many when they were least able to manage for themselves, such as a few minutes after arising from a deep Winter sleep.

He sipped the hot coffee devotedly as he looked off at the far wall of his study. The windows revealed that it was still black as pitch outside and an occasional rattle said that the wind was up. Why was downside February so raw and lonely? The miserable time of the year. The tune had already been humming along in his head when he got up. A silly little ditty he used to sing to the kids when they were small and trapped indoors by Winter's blasts, and especially if they were afflicted with the sniffles. For some reason the lugubrious little tune in funereal minor mode kept replaying itself in his head this morning:

The miserable time of the year
The miserable time of the year
There's nothing for you
But fever and flu
The miserable time of the year.

As he stared vacantly at the darkened far wall he contrasted the present somber stillness with the sparkling bustle of Yuletide only a handful of weeks back. The annual Christmas party for the residents, the teaching staff, and selected others filled the house with seasonal splendor. He had even met the mysterious Jeffrey of NIH who was brought along as a guest by Morello. Jeffrey proved to be a likable, wholesomely handsome and bright young fellow who had a touch of the poet about him and seemingly given to runs of adventurous whimsy. Not surprisingly, he and Ellie quickly established kindred interests, and Laura had pronounced it good, despite the six-year age difference.

Shortly afterwards, the great big tinseled wind-up produced a buoyant Christmas Day with a large fortune of presents for everybody. Laura wore her diamond tennis bracelet daily for one week running. His elegant and much too expensive pen set rejuvenated his interest in paper work for a while. Somehow Todd had managed to expect a motorcycle, though how he could have done so constituted something of a mystery, given the parental embargo recorded time and again on the matter. Ellie and Richard were, as usual, all gratitude and satisfaction.

By New Year's Eve he felt sufficiently recovered from the labyrinthitis to join in the bibulous celebration, but for a few days thereafter he was forced to resume a penitent caution in getting about. He was genuinely surprised at the devastation caused by less than half a bottle of champagne; he had credited his recovery as being more solid than that. Those losses had been adequately recouped, but it was now the down time of the year—gray, threatening, and persistently cold. Plus, he'd always thought it a coarse infelicity to hail deepest Winter as the beginning of the New Year. If anything, it was the dying gasps of the old. Springtime was the genuine beginning of the New Year, and it began naturally, not sidereally; it began with the sprouting of the first crocus, the arrival of the first robin, and with all the other stirrings that said life was beginning again. Right now things were still at a low ebb. The miserable time of the year, indeed. And he went through this baleful dirge every year at about this time and it was as much a part of the sere landscape as anything else.

But there had been a couple of post-holiday bright spots. The article did indeed make the December issue of the *Annals* which had arrived the week between Christmas and New Year's and was now only eight weeks into the open world. Almost the very day after the issue's arrival the phone began ringing—friends, well-wishers, concerned citizen groups, families of Blush victims, representatives of activist groups, and most notably program chairmen of various teaching centers already busily arranging various Spring and even Autumn symposia and conferences. One drug company had already volunteered to bankroll this year's Palmer Foundation Conference if it could do so exclusively. It was as though the article had become the missive a waiting world had been attuned to hear. And now the Word was out less than two months! He was amazed that an article in a professional journal could reach so far so fast. He had never before considered that persons other than the profession's subscribers would have much interest in what a rather stilted, dry journal might contain. But apparently there were many groups who had their watch-dog committees whose task was to be on the alert for developments—professional, social, political, economic, or whatever—as might impinge upon the group's interests. And, apparently, they didn't waste time in tracing out leads. By and large he was inclined to demur at invitations to participate in such conferences or to appear as guest lecturer at some meeting, and thus far he had held to his rather limited but preferred speaking commitments of long standing and which he had tailored over the years to suit his work as Training Director. He was content to dance with who brung him. But not so with Clay. Ever the social reformer at heart he was accepting engagements left and right in what seemed to be his moment of arrival, and he had already held forth on one occasion, a regional meeting of neuropsychologists, where he imprudently announced that a second paper on the correlation between observed tissue pathology and subsequent neuropsych test performance was in the works and soon to be in print! Any qualifications he may have added to that large promise were lost in the cheering. So now the private intent to follow through on a second paper had been transformed into a proclaimed public duty. As usual, Clay saw nothing particularly wrong with the notion. Jess cackled when he heard about it and saw it simply as just more good copy for turning admiring eyes toward Moreland—and for levering into position an attentive generosity the DMH just might not otherwise muster.

Moreover, the requests for their participation in various meetings and gatherings carried the problem of implied endorsement of the hosting body itself, an issue every popular speaker sooner or later is obliged to address. While he might see as a definite boon any opportunity to move Blush a notch or two higher up in the public awareness, the civic medium by which this opportunity now existed was potentially problematical. Appearing as guest speaker at some association to address the science and psychology of Blush was one thing; having one's presence interpreted as support of that group's political platform was another. An activist group favoring the legalization of marijuana had already made inquiry as to his availability for a rally to be held later in the summer in conjunction with a concert, and though he might have wanted to participate so as to deliver his sermon on the horrors of Blush and the need for national preventive measures he was sure his participation would be read, certainly reported by some, as his support for the legalization of marijuana and God knows what else. Here again, Clay had fewer scruples about such niceties and functioned on the premise that anything that drove home the point that not only was Blush the newest and deadliest syndrome on the socio-medical scene, but also was one of international scope specifically designed to target a particular sector of society, making it thereby a phenomenon transcending the narrow agenda of any special interest group. Thus, any notoriety was perforce a good and necessary thing. And it was precisely on that level Clay spoke his piece, unconcerned how his hosts might distort his message in support of their political agenda. Both he and Clay had already been sent feelers on the possibility of appearing on a local talk show. He had politely begged off, but Clay had indicated interest.

For all the media as well as public interest in Blush, relatively little was turning up regarding its source. It had been known for some time that the raw opium came from the traditional suppliers, the middle east and Southeast Asia. It was also known that the opium was processed into heroin before shipment for distribution in the West where the United States, just as traditionally, received the bulk of it. Backtracking on the movements of Blush revealed that the heroin probably took on the Blush additive in Central America for subsequent distribution in the North. It was also determined that while some Blush found its way to Europe and to an occasional African or Asian port, the greater part of it was apparently listed for North America and the subsidiary Caribbean. And perhaps not oddly, Blush cases from Central America were being reported with about the same increasing frequency as elsewhere.

The media had by now identified Blush as the moment's *cause célèbre*. With tabloid ferocity some leading dailies were proclaiming Blush the new holocaust whose obvious goal was to rid the world of heroin addicts by way of a "final solution" such as was applied to European Jewry a half century before. The occasional, non-addicted weekend dabbler in heroin was seen as a potential victim more innocent than most and thus specifically the one to be discouraged from replenishing the dwindling ranks of the steady users for reaching that critical crossover point where dabbling, pushed a bit too far, ceases to be a mere casual pursuit. Again, governmental response was seen as inadequate in the face of what amounted to mass murder of Americans by some foreign hand, sovereign or otherwise. There was no shortage of accusations that the net effect of Blush, horrific as it was, still wasn't seen by the current Administration as wholly incompatible with the general goals of its vaunted but largely ineffective war on drugs, all the national meetings, resolutions, multi-national task forces, and even military operations thus far staged by the Administration in collaboration with participant Central and South American governments notwithstanding, such grand show of effort consistently falling short of strategic goals with an abashing thud. There were even darker considerations that maybe the American people themselves, and ultimately the Congress, shared a reluctance to bring Blush to heel too soon and forfeit thereby a rare opportunity to scotch a social problem that perhaps had become too noxious for society, even American society, to accommodate. No one was openly admitting to it, the typical editorial ran, but it was generally the activist groups which raised the cry of failure in high places, while the vast majority of citizens, having no connection whatever to the drug sub-culture, stood by as bemused spectators wondering about the workings of Fate and perhaps—just perhaps—seeing the hand of Divine retribution finally at work. But Clay was not so uncertain. By now, and after a few speaking engagements under his belt as workouts for flexing his rhetoric, he had resolved that the government, or some nearly autonomous agency of the government, was the central power behind the Blush plague. Not only that, he had said exactly that in his last speaking engagement with a fringe group of anti-nuclear power, anti-vivisectionist, and anti-pollution advocates who had found soldierly confederation on the Blush problem. In a question and answer session after his prepared delivery on the disruption of cognitive function characteristic of the Blush effect he was asked if he saw a political strategy behind the spread of the Blush problem. In his ruthless and remorseless candor he said that he did, which energized that particular question and answer session beyond anything imaginable. Too many people now had, on the basis of

Clay's opinion, their long-held suspicions of shadow government confirmed, or at least strengthened, and their partisan alliance achieved firmer bonding in the forge of what could now be a justified militancy. Solidarity, American style. And by approbation Clay was added to their list of distinguished consultants. Worse, he loved it.

In response to the gathering storm of protest over the government's very modest stirrings the Treasury Department's international operations division was reported to be in the process of beefing up its activities. Increased surveillance of the usual portals of entry of heroin and its associated contraband was undertaken with the typical result that large caches of heroin and other contraband items were being intercepted at different transfer points along their way to America. And just as dutifully, the astronomical street value of such caches was being vigorously reported as evidence of the agency's effectiveness in stemming the pernicious tide which nevertheless seemed to reach America's shores with undiminished regularity, if sustenance of the country's drug habit served as any indicator. It was again demonstrated that while price might fluctuate in accordance with interception rates, item availability didn't, by and large. And as price varied, so did the crime rate. Moreover, Treasury efforts to track down the precise source of Blush were thus far no farther along than the standard efforts to track down the core operations of the heroin trade itself. Leads, as always, pointed to one or two Central American republics whose national economy was underwritten by the drug trade and where international drug cartels reigned while the civil governments pretended to rule. Washington's relations with those governments were delicate indeed inasmuch as those bodies, usually juntas of one shape or another, represented renegade efforts to generate an economic hegemony over their contiguous zones of influence. On the more poignant side, the squalor and poverty of those nations had been minimally assuaged over the years by local reform efforts generously funded by American aid, while the drug trade wealth, however concentrated at the top, regrettably represented the country's best effort in lifting itself above the privation of an aboriginal existence. While it would be a long time before such countries would be able to produce a good automobile or a reliable camera, they were instant, flourishing, and accomplished competitors in the international drug trade. It was now their turn to exploit regional spheres of influence, and American dollars were plentiful, just as native gold was once plentiful for the conquistadors.

The recurrent investigations mounted by task forces, subcommittees, and various blue-ribbon panels over the previous two decades had consistently identified the usual line-up of Latin republics and their respective and then current strong men as the lead players in the cocaine and marijuana trade. Sometimes the drug king pin was the republic's Sheriff; sometimes its Robin Hood. Investigations by a recent Presidential Commission on Blush's origin pointed to one republic that previously had been identified with creative social and political reform and which had been touted as the prototypic evolving economy of the Central American group. The Presidential Commission rendered a report which conveyed its disappointment that the republic which had thus far been regarded as the model effort in furthering the democratic process for social and political reform also seemed the one most likely to be funneling the tainted heroin into the United States. However, the findings of the Commission, as was so often the case, raised more questions than it answered. Though it appeared evident that the heroin was being rendered into Blush in this one Central American republic, the reason for its doing so was not. The Commission considered that perhaps the action represented an attempt to shift business away from the poppy, thus away from the Middle and Far East, and on to the cocoa leaf, and hence exclusively to Latin America. In a word, a drug war on an intercontinental scale. It was suggested that international drug interests were having the equivalent of a war of imperial conquest in which the intent was to divide the world into protected markets, thus tracing the same developmental steps as did nations one hundred fifty years earlier in the establishment of economic and trade interests along with their spheres of influence, that period of colonialism when the major industrial nations staked out their claims on the rest of the world. The Commission saw in the evolution of Blush a spoiling tactic being used to bring a "foreign" drug power, the heroin-producing interests of the East, to heel in the Western Hemisphere where local interests were united behind cocaine and marijuana, the local produce. The Commission raised the question as to whether the Eastern interests would unite in a retaliation which could quite possibly take the form of counter-tampering, cocaine being the likely vehicle. In a word, the Opium Wars all over again but in a different octave and with different players.

But even more perplexing to the Commission was the public figure suspected in being key to the Blush distribution scheme. Inigo Pontalbas, the forty-one-year-old democratically elected president and son of the immortalized dictator General Emiliano Pontalbas who, by way of extensive land reform and temporary nationalization of industry, raised his tiny country from vassal status to relative economic independence in achieving a degree of autarky rare in that portion of the hemisphere, was suspected as being the evil genius behind the region's challenge to Middle and Far Eastern encroachment. For several years, Inigo Pontalbas had been touted by Washington and by other capitols in the hemisphere as being the first in the new wave of "mature" Latin statesmen who saw their nation's destiny in stages of measured and progressive democratic reform, eschewing the violence of midnight break-in-the-door revolutionary eruptions in favor of a more patient reform rooted in enormous expenditures for education of the masses, coupled with handsome subsidies to the entrepreneurial classes for the stimulation of industry. Large social rewards had been realized and the standard of living rose as never before, right along with the national debt a fledgling industry had yet to redress. The Commission felt that the mounting burden of debt was probably the prevailing factor in establishing the Blush gamble as an acceptable risk. The Commission admitted to difficulty in seeing the motive as springing from the personal ambitions of Pontalbas himself.

Inigo Pontalbas—"Doctor" Inigo Pontalbas; he had an ivy league Ph.D.—was the current issue of a renowned aristocratic family descended from the conquistadors who claimed his country for the Old World. His father was named after Emiliano Juarez and thereby assigned at birth the counterpart duty of liberating his nation from foreign control, which he very much did by achieving through the power of his charisma a nationally rooted alliance of the country's cautious aristocracy and its politically restive peasants. The result was a relative democracy that encouraged generous amounts of foreign aid from the United States when Cuba was at its peak of activity as the Caribbean staging area for Communist expansion. It was said that to this day there were at least as many statues of Emiliano Pontalbas as there were crucifixes in that progressive little country, each statue in its own way an oblique endorsement of the son, Inigo, and his kind of Presidency.

Inigo Pontalbas, like so many of the children of the Central American aristocracy, had come to the U.S. for his schooling. And like so many of those of his social class from that part of the world, had secured favored entry into one of the prestigious American universities, in this case one of the Ivy League schools. But unlike others of his ilk he did not devote his undergraduate years to a series of parties and frolics, but had early revealed himself to be an unusually apt and serious scholar with intellectual gifts which destined him for the study of Philosophy. In time he had attached himself to Professor Walter Seymour, the world's leading social philosopher and most outspoken advocate of Keynesian economics as the vehicle and prime mover for corrective restructuring of a society's economy. After the usual stint of undergraduate work, which in his case was a stretch of genuine scholarship rather than the convertible-driven bacchanal of so many of his compatriots, he continued his studies on the graduate level as the up and coming assistant to Seymour, and possibly in time even his successor. His master's thesis, suitably adjusted, was included in Seymour's then latest book as the chapter on government-supported entrepreneurial investment as the most efficient means of enhancing international economic competition. He had just received his Ph.D. and faculty appointment as instructor when his father was assassinated in a Communist-backed coup attempt. He then left Academia and returned home to carry on his father's work, and did so with singular and ruthless skill. He was freely elected to his second term as president two years ago and had until now been seen by Washington as one of the region's most, if not the most, promising and capable figures in the emergence of Latin America as co-partner in the hemisphere's new economic alliance. Washington now wondered if, on invitation from Blush, he was reverting to type as the provincial politico so common to the region's tradition, archaic and obsolete as such now was. Or was it his particular brand of entrepreneurial crusade, now completely politicized, being played out on a global scale to secure the western hemisphere as a protected market cleansed of foreign influence? Washington concluded it was an attempt at the latter. All quite speculative, to be sure, but thus far the most feasible estimate on the basis of what was known, or so the Commission concluded.

But why couldn't these drug figures live and let live, he had asked himself probably a hundred times before and now once again this morning as he stared at the earliest hint of gray gentling the dark windows on the far wall. Certainly there were enough addicts to go around for everybody. It seemed that adolescents now took to drugs in about the same way as the kids in his day took to cigarettes, and a certain number of those adolescents, probably to number in the millions, would take the drug experience just a step or two beyond the point of easy return. It seemed to be in the nature of adolescence to be intemperate, and in a society where excess was equated with liberty as well as the heralded freedom from want, there was little likelihood that such a known and obvious danger as addiction would cause a dearth of customers for street drugs anymore than the proven lethality of cigarettes strapped the tobacco industry for new recruits to the legions of career consumers. So why the greed over who took what and from where? There was enough to go around, unfortunately, and in time some of our young might become versatile enough to be addicted to both heroin and cocaine concurrently in a typical American extension of that traditional phenomenon of adolescence called the "altruistic surrender." Then everybody would be satisfied, almost, and without having to resort to Blush as a tie breaker. It was so easy if only people would be reasonable, he saw. God, he was in a foul mood this morning.

And he didn't know exactly why. Certainly there was enough going on to keep him unsettled. The Blush death rate was rising and falling like the stock market as people kicked the heroin habit for a while, only to return again and fall victim to Blush. Public concern and reaction waxed and waned in response, never quite freeing itself of its fundamental ambivalence. He and Clay now had a second paper hanging over them, hardly begun but impatiently awaited. The initial congratulatory calls had gradually been replaced by puzzled inquiry as to why the second paper, which was certainly now all the more necessary, hadn't been gotten out yet in view of the need created by the first, etc., etc. Also, there was the matter of Clay going more activist-political than expected and thereby, Cantrelle feared, abandoning a certain scientific objectivity which had always been basic to their collaborative offering. Now Clay was helping people use that offering—their joint research, his and Clay's—as planking for various activist platforms. And then, this morning, the verge thing was pounding at him like a god-damned hangover, and, as usual, without a hint as to why. Surely he'd never been at this particular nexus of Time-Space before, or anything remotely similar to it, and perhaps that was precisely the why of the verge.

He tried to write a few lines as introduction to the new article. Those first few sentences were always the toughest and he figured it was probably because he, like most others, tried to say too much in the limited space of the opening lines. But, opening lines which didn't give something of a condensation of the paper's purpose and justification were hardly worth the bother. To hell with it! He tossed his pen down on the desk and then stood up, stretching as he tried to shake the pall of confinement that had hovered since his arising over an hour earlier.

And then there was the matter of moving the Blush patients to Mountainview, their final resting place before the grave. All arrangements had been completed and the first contingent of transfers drawn from the several state hospitals of the Commonwealth arrived at Mountainview and were settled in, discretely removed from public view. Blush patients now spent no more than a month at Moreland and so the ambulance runs had decreased markedly with Death now being triaged to Mountainview along with its bearers. In a strange and unreal way Moreland was returning to normal with Blush falling into a niche as acceptable societal attrition, much like that of auto accidents, hurricanes, military maneuvers, and other such inevitabilities with their own tally of unavoidable casualties. It was indeed strange that as the Blush death rate increased across the land, public concern mellowed. In part this was due to society's success in mobilizing resources to accommodate the problem. Procedures were now well worked out and applied, a certain satisfaction accruing from the timely identification and disposition of the cases. Acute treatment centers were no longer glutted with Blush cases, overwhelmed by the task of doing duty both as hospital as well as hospice. Diagnosis, initial management, and transfer took place with the precision of clockwork such that Blush had now been efficiently shorn of high visibility at the front end of society. It was only at the distal end, at Building Seven and the hundreds of other Building Sevens across the nation, that the horror of Blush continued to appall. It seemed that society had reclaimed the management policy long ago perfected for leprosy and had found it quite suitable for Blush, and had then applied it. There were now Blush colonies.

Another aspect of society's adjustment was the even more curious notion that the problem was seen as not at all between Blush victims and society, but between the victims and some inscrutable force now calling margin on accounts too long indemnified by a society statutorily required to be protective. It had gone without saying that most people felt that the drug abusers had for years been getting away with sheer murder in their exploitation of society's easy stance on individual freedom. Punitive action, when applied, had been directed primarily at the distributor and not at the individual consumer who had been seen as more suitably a subject for medical rather than penal attention: a victim more than a perpetrator. But since there was little that medical treatment could offer, the unremitting plenitude of recidivist addicts as well as the promise of soaring profits to dealers made merchandising of drugs a risk well worth running. Society's helplessness in the face of its ordained, self-inflicted spoliation rubbed raw the public's sympathy for the drug addict *qua* victim and saw arise in its place a steely resentment for having to pick up the hefty tab not only for the addict's wrongful self-indulgence but now even for his self-destruction. The advent of Blush relieved society of at least that part of the burden which called for right retribution to be served on the addict because, providentially, the rolls were now being relieved of such violators by the very cohorts of the violators themselves. Society could and now did feel restored in its conviction that those who flouted its natural laws, though able to skirt or exploit its statutory ones, would not escape a punishment whose authorship in this instance conveniently lay beyond the realm of public liability. The issue appeared to be between the heroin addict and some unseen power which truly seemed to be on the side of an offended society, and all the folklore of saviors and salvation rose—covertly, of course—to the support of that avenging spirit.

Hence, considering the number of citizen deaths at issue, there was remarkably little in the way of official initiative for collaring the avenging spirit. Official reaction was just exactly that, "re-action," a response to initiatives mounted elsewhere: to the sweep of Blush's assault, to the outrage of certain activist groups for the government's passivity, to the cry of impacted regions for federal assistance in caring for victims, to the demand of potential victims themselves for the expeditious erection of detox and rehab programs hoped to be preventive, and to sundry other petitions of similar ilk. Official initiative, such as it was, had thus far been focused mostly in the funding of basic research in the pathophysiology of Blush with quite limited epidemiological work in identifying the particulars of its origin. No new offensives had been mounted in sealing off its source or preventing its entry; that is, nothing above and beyond what had already been in place for interdicting the drug traffic in general.

It was curious and yet it wasn't, he mused cynically. Society had a way of managing itself above and beyond its codified rules, in ways that no social order could bear to have recorded as policy while maintaining its dedication to the noble principles of life, liberty, and the pursuit of happiness. So what the hell to do? No wonder he was caught up in that god-damned verge this morning, he grumbled to himself. Not having the vaguest idea what to do was a predicament he had awarded himself many times before. Certainly often enough to account for his familiarity with the weariness of it. But who the hell was he to do anything in the first place? An obscure training director tucked away in a suburb only recently elevated from sub-rural status? Maybe in truth he was no more excused of the devoir of sinister acquiescence than were those who officially represented the collective response which was, ultimately, of, for, and by the people, of which he was just one of the smallest divisible parts.

But he knew that Clay now saw himself and his own duty otherwise. No mere particle, subject to the ebb and flow of the social ether, but more a doughty little island unmoved by the tides and turbulence of the surrounding swell; an island from which more could be seen of the general roil. Plus, his own civic visibility was now a regional fact of life. Newspapers tended to carry accounts of his public comings and goings. His unflinching commentary made him a desirable item on the agenda of many a conference eager to increase its drawing, and the polemic quality of his commentary endorsed him as richly newsworthy. "Local Psychologist Assails etc.," or "Blush Researcher Questions etc.," were typical headings recounting gatherings at which Clay had been guest speaker. One recent account carried the headline "Moyer Indicts Federal Policy," confirming his ascent to celebrity status as well as the hardening of his public stance along with that of several groups which had adopted him as their herald. Accordingly, his evolving sense of mission saw a discernible shift in his personal investments. Previously, his work at Moreland—the training program, the research, and such general staff work as would accrue from time to time—had long been the just and preferred recipients of his devise, but they now drew less of his energy as his public quest claimed an ever larger share of his endeavor. He feared that Clay was attenuating the alliance which had served both of them so well over the years—had actually gotten them to where they now were—and he wondered if Clay, like himself, sensed the spectre of loss as their paths began to track divergent fixes. But he didn't want to think of it, not this morning anyway. If he did, he just might have to confront a measure of personal envy, and he just wasn't in the mood for something so wretched as that.

In fact, he wasn't in the mood for anything. He had thought of taking a cup of coffee to Laura, of sitting on the edge of the bed, kissing her awake, and then going at it. She would fall right in with it, but for him to do so would be more out of restlessness than true desire—restlessness trying to find its meaning as well as its relief. Love-making under that cloud, which occasionally did pass over their bedroom, never measured up to their sprightly usual and he didn't need another regret to keep him company this morning. Actually, to push the point, he would rather be alone for a while, maybe the whole day, judging by the way he felt just now, though the waiting agenda held a quite different view of things, and all of his grumpiness this morning probably was nothing more than wayward commentary on having to submit to a schedule designed more by circumstance than by himself. The examination he would give to the residents this morning was no bother at all. That rite of passage he would preside over with settled pride because he pretty much knew that they would do well. It was more the Council meeting later in the morning and then the CCAH inspection committee meeting which immediately followed. The Council meeting almost always left bruises where administrative policy collided with proper clinical practice, and all concerned shared responsibility in the burden of shaping positive compromises to salvage and sustain hospital mission. Bounden duty, plain and straight. But the CCAH inspection committee was something else. The Combined Commission for the Accreditation of Hospitals was one of those phantasmagoric bureaucratic wonders, begun simply enough and with helpfulness in mind but which quickly swelled into a driving pursuit in its own right, adding an entirely new verse to that American dirge, "The Ballad of Unintended Consequences." The task of establishing collective standards for hospitals and of providing guidelines for achievement of such was no mean undertaking in the first place when the CCAH was established some forty years earlier, as all then agreed. But few could have foreseen back then the monstrosity which would eventually evolve from an altruistic beginning which initially set itself the humble task of being just one of the means for achieving the end of elevating and standardizing the quality of care in all hospitals seeking accreditation. With the advent of federal Medicare and of private health insurance plans, hospital accreditation became the almighty imprimatur and the absolute precondition for reimbursement for any and all treatment given to "subscribers." In short order, hospital accreditation became essential to hospital solvency which in itself became, *de facto* as well as *de jure*, accreditation by the CCAH. Unable to resist such a goad to greatness, the Commission grew apace with escalating Federal effort to legislate medical care standards, and so drew into its ranks a whole new breed of medical and paramedical types, plus their administrative legions, to descend upon the newly opened vista of regulated medical accreditation. And the new breed came on with all the finesse and delicacy of The Oklahoma Land Rush. Persons and interests previously held discreetly at Medicine's borders were thus commissioned, like royally subsidized adventurers of old, to assay the now open Kingdom of Medicine and to stake out claims for a different kind of crown. Physicians and administrators previously without a discernible country now gathered together, like freebooters, in the service of accreditation to take their place in the policy-making chambers of Medicine's temples as emissaries of a New Order. That New Order then grew according to its own needs by feeding on its obligated host, and the doctor-patient dyad was now cordoned off as its mandated and exclusive preserve. Rules and regulations flowed as from a directive cornucopia, and in short order it was just a question as to whether such regulations served better the process of accreditation than they did the practice of medicine, however either was ideally intended. In time it had become apparent to almost all that accreditation had transformed itself from an enabling process into a self-aggrandizing industry with standardization of medical care having been metamorphosed from a cherished ideal into a medium of nourishment for the accreditation industry's own growth. Once again a seemingly desirable end had been swallowed up in the cauldron of means, and a witch's brew of blunted purpose bubbled forth. Why were Americans so determined to confuse means with ends? Or content with form? Was it because of an unalterable conviction that only particulars had reality? Was it a generic discomfort with the idea that universals might be *more* than the sum of their parts when nothing was ever—horror of all horrors—to be more than the sum of its *participants*, or citizens? No wonder our British cousins, and a lot of other people as well, viewed us with a bemused tolerance, and concern. Whatever. Thus he whined to himself as he kneaded this not particularly new lump of complaint: the accreditation industry, by establishing its own sustenance as prime goal and then subordinating the standardization of medical care to the status of means for doing so, had thereby lost, all now agreed, the capacity to correct itself. Any change in the system would have to come from outside the system itself, a provision not well delineated in the system's own regulatory codes, for if only *they* could accredit, then who officially could *dis*credit them?

He found the idea of another American savior turned false prophet gauche enough, but to have to erect—and contribute to—committees, task forces, surveys, and all the other obligatory scurryings about in support of the entire perverted mess was more than he could ever manage with good grace. His participation in pre-survey meetings and planning sessions often amounted to little more than his sustained rumble of dissent. But for it all he did his part, and he helped in fabrication of the procedures, policies, formats—and records—which would inevitably be the focus of an accreditation site inspection that would never be more than tangent to the actual business of patient care. That's what made the tumult of preparation so burdensome: an ordained and obligatory contrivance so disproportionate to its actual clinical utility and administrative relevance. It was a fact lost on no one that the phenomenon was cast in the very image of CCAH's actual, quite contrived relationship to the actual field of Medicine. But obeisance was *de rigueur*, and so given. And he hated the loss of time from patient care, teaching, and authentic administration the tedious accreditation drill demanded. A vile case of one man's poison being something else to men of quite different appetite.

So why couldn't he just push it all aside for a few minutes this morning and do some soothingly creative wall staring? Because he wasn't in the right mood for it, that's why, he sullenly reminded himself. That being the case, there was nothing left to do but to fix her coffee and fall in for muster. And sigh piteously.

Several dozen grumbles and a bit over an hour later he left the house as Todd was moping through breakfast under Laura's watchful and impatient eye. Any improvement in the weather would likely see an upsweep in Todd's desultory approach to school, for, after all, wasn't Springtime the traditional hooky time of the year? When he was a boy the lure of the fishing hole in early Spring too often overcame his academic summons, and, perhaps sad to say, his own fondest memories of boyhood years more often than not had the fishing hole as backdrop. In fact, to think about it, maybe that's exactly what he needed this morning to dispel the awful mood besetting him. Someone had said that when everything else failed there was still the good friendship of books. Just now, fishing might just as well be included in that comradeship.

So he left the house feeling he had a better place to go than where he was headed. He traced the familiar route to Moreland and keenly noted along the way all available signs of Winter's retreat. Not a robin around just yet, so maybe it still wasn't quite the right time to dip a hook. Perhaps in a couple of weeks because there really weren't many signs that Winter had released its chill grip or that life was once again priming for its annual bloom. The days began earlier and were lasting longer, and that made some difference, there now being more time to get things done for being right in there along with the vernal stirrings of the pineal to give that sense of swelling readiness vital to the might of Spring, when it came. The thought carried with it a breath of solace, but not enough to counter the morning's crankiness. However, just being outdoors and traveling about seemed to help. And so did the music, which, right now, at the halfway point in his drive to Moreland, happened to be Mozart's fortieth, the only not-so-happy symphony that celestial imp wrote. A cry of despair, actually, but so melodious in its torment that it was somehow reassuring. Like relief in knowing that things couldn't get any worse. But what get worse? Things for him, and especially for Clay, were actually going pretty well. Even for Moreland, now identified as a trend-setter in the acute management of Blush psychosis. So why this mood, he asked himself all over again with heightening impatience. Not a hint came, and the music seemed to seal the futility of further search. He was tempted to switch stations when a thought switched his focus instead. Chercher le dream. Look for the dream, the Master had said many years ago. It had been shown time and time again in clinical practice, particularly in intensive psychotherapy or in analysis, that when things became so abstruse, so murky, so complicated as to defy any effort at understanding what was going on, a dream often appeared to announce exactly what was happening and why. With that recommendation now renewed he quickly checked the edges of his consciousness in search of dream spoor that might hint at a trail. But he detected nothing and the music seemed to distract him with its thrown-up imagery of wretchedness no longer masked by prodigy. Where were the flowers, he grumped as he scanned the roadside; they couldn't come soon enough to please him. Tall, glowing daffodils of purest yellow. And sometime later, the roses. Right now, shriveled brown leaves lay where daffodils would soon bloom. Follow the yellow brick—brick red—road. He could certainly use a brain . . . plus a touch of heart . . . and, especially this morning, a bit courage. Thoughts of sweet lands and evil castles tumbled forth, followed by Poe and his celebrated claustrophobia. Then, with a jolt, he recalled "The Masque of the Red Death." Jesus Christ! The dream now exploded forth! And with it a flash of fury, and helplessness, and terror! He was at this ball—a masque—in this resplendently huge castle, and everything was high baroque. Louis XVI splendor. All the people were perfect and their costumes dazzling. But no one spoke. The court musicians were waiting for some signal so as to begin playing. He knew that if they didn't start playing soon everybody would wither into mummies. But only *he* knew it. He ran to the musicians, barely able to get through the milling hundreds of courtiers. He sensed that the change was already beginning to take place as he approached the musicians whom he implored to start the music. But the maestro couldn't understand what he wanted. He remembered that the music had to be requested in a certain way, like a password, but he couldn't remember how to do it. He frantically tried to recall the correct words, but the harder he tried the more futile it became. He again begged the maestro whose expression now was less that of perplexity and more that of sardonic malice. All the courtiers then turned to face him and watch his vain efforts. He looked at the countless faces which now began to show blemishes, blotches, and hollowness. The maestro smiled and turned his back on him to face the stiff and silent musicians. Terrified at the thought of becoming shriveled like the rest he tried to escape and began pushing his way through the courtiers while at the same time dreading physical contact with them. As he elbowed them aside he noted their costumes, now yellowing, to be brittle with decay as pieces fell to the floor to leave a path of tatters in his wake. He then realized that he didn't know where the exit was and he worked all the more furiously at pushing his way through the crowd which now seemed too tall for him to see over for locating an exit. The smell of decay from the withered flowers on the women began to make his breathing harder. He wasn't sure if he awakened at that point, but that's where the dream ended.

God damn it, he was trapped! Clay was trapped! They were all trapped! Among the doomed! The dream said that much about the immediate here and now which was fully enough to account for the pall of wretchedness he carried this morning. What else it meant of a time removed and more formative, was something else, like when he was five years old—he now remembered in a flash—and standing among all the quiet people at the coffin of his adoring Aunt Henrietta who used to sit him on her lap and tousle his blond hair. But she had caught pneumonia and died. At the miserable time of the year. He now recalled looking at the dark circles showing under her closed eyes despite the heavy layer of face powder and then noticing her pretty corsage but feeling that it wasn't nice to pay too much attention to it when everybody was so quiet, though he worried that the flowers would die if they didn't get water and were kept in the coffin all closed up in the dark without sunlight. They then would begin to look ugly. As his mind reeled with the recovery of this long-lost memory he wondered what color her dress was. Or the corsage. He figured he could now make a pretty good guess, and he instinctively scanned the roadside again. Not one daffodil to be seen. They were still covered up.

Yes, damn it, he assailed as he returned to his current world, they were all locked up within this thing, this updated Red Death tinted Blush, and they were all going through some kind of a dance while the tune was being called by someone thus far suspected to be one Dr. Inigo Pontalbas whose reasons no one could fathom, or would reveal. What the hell did it all mean? As long as one was caught up in the particulars of doing the daily job of looking after the victims, any small victory in measuring up to the task gave a misleading sense of gain and control. Worse, people seemed to be increasingly content with that arrangement for all the reasons he didn't care to review yet again. What really gnawed at him was the accommodating complacency, or fatalistic compliance, or just plain lack of concern underlying all the ostensibly altruistic measures taken to provide care and comfort for the victims. There still was no collective rising up against the authorship of the scourge, and there most likely wouldn't be as long as the victims were the right victims and the country could handle the cost. But actually we were all potential victims, the point Clay was carrying forth to a public more disquieted than aroused, and to the extent the larger citizenry disassociated itself from the misfortune of its few, to that extent the evil was cultivated for a yet broader application and, inevitably, for eventual delivery. Ask any German. Or any Jew.

And now here he was going to a meeting. No! Not *one* meeting, but *two* meetings! Both would carry the leitmotif that we were all doing rather well—he himself had said as much only minutes earlier—in bearing up under the weight of Blush and were due for some commendation—color that accreditation—in light of all that has been demonstrated in good patient care appropriately documented on the validating forms authorized for that purpose. He just wasn't in the mood for that sort of horse shit this morning, not with such a dream shaping his mood. He would probably end up being just as frantic in forum as he was in slumber, and to what avail? Maybe he could beg off in the name of illness. No, he couldn't do that, he rejected with a start. He didn't think it likely, but they just might believe him and conclude that his labyrinthitis had recurred, setting into motion a whole sequence of reverberations he would dread intend, not the least of which would be the worry his friends would feel. Also, damn it, he had indicted such dissemblance time and again in Todd's school phobia repertoire which, he suspected, Todd was probably tuning up right now at the breakfast table. He had pretended to be unaware of it rather than have it escalate into confrontation. The complicity that lurks in silence. So he himself wasn't beyond slipping and sliding in the purchase of appeasement. Why the hell was it never the right time for him and Todd to get down to brass tacks? It had to be soon, he knew. But in the meantime he would go to some fucking nonsense meeting, do his bounden duty, and pretend.

And the god-damned music! Now the station was playing "Marche Slav" as though that smart-ass announcer had an inkling as to what had been going on for the past few miles. He snickered at the insane thought that the radio might be working both ways, receiving as well as sending. As he listened to the lugubrious strains of the opening bars he laughed in happy relief at the recall of a comment he had made about that piece of music some years earlier to Chief Nurse Wotjek, who had just heard it at a concert, that the tune was originally taken from an old Polish wedding march.

Even the lights were now red! All of them! Or so he beheld as he saw the lineup of traffic lights that gathered the cars into congested gluts on the noisy boulevard leading to the hospital. His outrage was well on to decaying into giddiness as he stopped and started and stopped and started his way along the last several blocks to reach the hospital entrance. By the time he passed through the front gate he was giggling at the heady notion that perhaps at last he had confronted total hopelessness and had found it not to be too bad after all. Maybe even amusing.

Now that he was on the grounds, the place didn't seem so glum as feared. In fact, arriving was a lot easier than he had expected. As he drove along to the MOB he checked the flower beds enroute. He was relieved to see that there was not a daffodil in sight—might spoil the absurdity of it all if there were—and he was thus able to complete the route to his parking slot with a right-minded airiness he felt most fitting. As he parked he began whistling the theme of "Marche Slav," but in a more sprightly tempo to brighten his step to the MOB entrance. He manfully pulled the door open and traipsed up the hallway, swinging his briefcase in tune. As he turned into the office he was greeted by a puzzled Mrs. Andretti.

"Good morning, Dr. Cantrelle," she offered tentatively. "Are you feeling all right?"

"Never felt better in my life," he proclaimed with wide-spread arms. "And I hope you feel as well," he added as he swept past her and into his office. He closed the door behind him and then stood silent for a moment as he looked vacantly at the floor. As if in a convulsion he stiffened and then hurled his briefcase against the office wall where it whacked with the sharpness of a thunderclap. It seemed to hang on the wall for an instant before collapsing to the floor, spewing forth its papers. He looked at the askew briefcase for a moment, as though waiting for its reply.

Mrs. Andretti pulled open the door. "Dr. Cantrelle, are you all right?" she asked in alarm,

"Now I really do feel better, Mrs. Andretti," he assured, adding a subdued smile to denote sincere relief. "The traffic was heavier than usual this morning, that's all," he chirped as he removed his coat.

A smile crept over her face.

"Are you sure you're O.K.?" she inquired again just to be sure.

"I'm positive," he affirmed, now in a more serious tone. "I just have something on my mind and I can't get a handle on it. That's all."

She looked at him for a moment to ascertain that he really was as he said.

"The tests for the residents are all ready," she added. "They're in my desk, when you need them. And Dr. Weaver called earlier this morning to give you a message that Mr. Moyer also will be attending the council meeting this morning."

He pricked up his ears.

"Oh? Did he say why?" he asked.

"No, just that he thought you should know," she said.

"Thank you, Mrs. Andretti," he returned. "Now let me put my life back in order," he grunted as he bent down to reclaim his briefcase and its scattered contents. "I'll be out in a minute to get the tests."

She nodded and closed the door behind her.

With his briefcase recharged he carried it over to the windowsill where he stored it in its usual place. As he did so he pondered what his secretary had conveyed. Why have Clay at the Council meeting? And why would Jess be so concerned about passing it on? A warning of sorts, he was sure. At least an effort to make certain that he, Cantrelle, was alert for whatever the arrangement presaged. He then settled into his chair, the better to think. It then came to him that some kind of recognition or commendation had come forth regarding the paper. Nothing official had arrived from DMH or the Office of Public Welfare since its publication and usually an acknowledgment was sent by one or the other to state employees who had distinguished themselves in some way. It was standard policy. Once, years earlier when he had been the keynote speaker at a symposium staged by the psychiatric association of another state, he had received a congratulatory letter from the DMH, duly routed through Martha's and Jess' office. It probably was going to be some such thing this morning, a we-knew-all-the-time-you-could-do-it letter from Sharpsfield, and Martha had determined that Clay should be on hand for the round of encomiums. After all, Moreland once again was the visible and distinguished flagship of the state mental health system. Maybe of all the state hospitals in the country. Just maybe. He felt himself preen a bit in preparation. He wished he hadn't been alerted so far in advance because now he'd have to carry a squirmy smile of abashment somewhere in his visage for well over—he looked at his watch—Christ! It was already five after nine and the residents were waiting and probably suffering unspeakable tortures of anticipation! He bolted out of his chair, grabbed a journal to thumb through while the residents scribbled their answers, and made for Mrs. Andretti who, he surmised enroute, had mercifully chosen not to interrupt his brooding to remind him of the time.

"I'm ready to give the test," he announced as he stood before her desk.

The tests were already waiting for him and she handed them over with a smile in relief that he seemed back to sorts. She probably detected some of his chagrin and was attributing it to his extreme behavior earlier when actually it more derived from what he sensed was afoot with the Council meeting. Be that as it may, the status quo had been restored and it was time to proceed with the test.

"If any more messages come, especially from Dr. Weaver, pass them on to me right away. I'd prefer they not wait till after the test is over," he requested.

"Of course, Dr. Cantrelle," she guaranteed.

With that assurance he paced up the hall in the first leg of the morning's awards relay.

The residents, ready to have at whatever kind of ordeal he could inflict upon them, added to the note of high expectancy. Residents, the ones in good standing, anyway, began to feel more confident on the downside of the academic year as the gestalt of the year's academic effort began to take cohesive form within them. It was like the pieces of a jigsaw puzzle, the first few in place not revealing any discernible pattern. After a critical quantity had been pieced together, a pattern or theme arose which made the remaining pieces, yet to be placed but already apprehended in a collective sense, much more easily integrated. So at this time of the year the residents usually showed that winsome self-satisfaction of impending mastery, and today was no different. He smiled a coy good morning as he took his seat at the head of the table and then distributed the test sheets to the residents. They tackled the test—much more difficult than the earlier ones in the course and now directed at the general concept of conflict-free ego function and the neutralization of aggressive energy in the formation of psychic structure—with a confident cheeriness that reminded him of better days. One resident even hummed while penning his way through the questions, and it seemed not to bother any of the others in the least. It might even have been heard as the moment's harmony. He flipped through the journal he had brought along and furtively scanned the references at the end of a few major articles to see if their paper had been cited yet. It hadn't been, but it was still too soon for that because the articles appearing now had already been in various stages of press at the time their article was published. But, lo and behold, there was a short article on the pathophysiology of Blush, more like a preliminary communication. Fresh from NIH, or so it implied. It reviewed the general findings to date, reaffirming the thalamic nuclei, especially the dorso-medial-posterior group, and several nuclei clusters in the reticular activating system as the predominately affected structures. Sero-analysis of the breakdown tissue, the article detailed, had fairly well established the pathologic process to be auto-immune in nature, indicating that Blush, in its attack of the affected nerve tissue, initiated an auto-immune reaction that preferentially targeted the nuclei in question for its site of action. The author speculated that Blush's initial effect was to damage those very nuclei, liberating perhaps uniquely altered nuclear protein into the immune system and thereby setting up the destructive auto-immune reaction. The author reminded the reader that the process would thus be no different from what the immune system does when confronted with any altered or foreign protein, such as that with invading bacteria whose protein, alien to the infected victim, stimulates in the victim the defensive formation of antibodies which then deactivate the bacteria by breaking down its protein linkages. But with Blush patients, the article hypothesized, the offending protein had been drawn from the nuclei of the brain tissue attacked and then altered in some way by Blush's action to make the nuclei protein alien to the immune system which subsequently produced antibodies to break down that protein wherever it occurred in the tissue of the victim. In this case, the protein thus targeted was in the remaining healthy thalamic and reticular activating nuclei which then underwent progressive degeneration as the immune reaction kicked in. Very much like a finely localized Multiple Sclerosis, the article suggested. The article then speculated on the macromolecular structure of Blush itself, suggesting that it most likely contained an activating moiety, a "hot spot," affixed to a specific peptide linkage probably closely duplicative of the particular proto-encephalon found in those thalamic and reticular activating nuclei.

Well, it sounded impressive, he thought as he put the journal down to reflect for a moment. If nothing else, it testified to the canniness of those people South of the Border who supposedly were the ones behind the Blush traffic. Also the advent of the article reassuringly affirmed that at least some preliminary Blush research was being cranked out by the Feds. He had begun to wonder if anything at all was happening down at Bethesda, so little had come forth after the State lab handed over its early findings, as well as the general quest, to NIH. He picked up the journal again and scanned the references at the end of the article to see if their paper had been cited. Not a sign of it. He consoled himself with the explanation that their own article was strictly clinical and thus would have little place in the line-up of references which had to do primarily with various aspects of macro-molecular research. Still and all, he chuckled to himself through a rueful smile, a good word here or there . . . .

The residents were now leaning back in their chairs and stretching, a sure sign that a point of completion was nigh. He checked the clock on the back wall. Only a few minutes to go.

"All right, start applying periods. And don't forget to sign your tests," he announced, as always.

The residents reluctantly began to surrender their papers amid a few last minute jots here and there. He gathered them together over a canvassing smile of good will which received in return a few sighs from the residents to recruit his compassion and mercy.

"You did mean neutralization as the conflict-free prototype of sublimation, didn't you?" one resident implored anxiously, revealing no small amount of conflict-bound uncertainty.

"I sure did," he affirmed.

"Good," exhaled the resident in relief.

"No assignment for the next session," he announced. "We'll use the time to go over the test and take stock. See you."

He departed the conference room hurriedly to deposit the papers with Mrs. Andretti before hieing it over to the Admin building. He decided to take the journal along with him for Clay and also to bring it to the attention of the Council.

"Mrs. Andretti, there's a chance the council meeting might run over a bit," he instructed as he sped along, "and so you might call the CCAH committee chairman—Dr. Grant?—and tell him I might be a few minutes late."

"I'll do that," she agreed.

"I'm on my way; I cannot stay. How long we'll play, I cannot say," he sang with a carioca beat as he waved good-bye and rambled down the hallway. That absurdity again, he tittered as he reached the building's rear exit. Who needed a coat with the sun so high?

Once out on the parking lot he settled back to his usual mien of sustained preoccupation as he paced along toward the Admin building. The groundskeepers, he noted, had freshened the flower beds along the drive in preparation for Spring's arrival and, as he surveyed the beds' quiet, empty humus he had the gross thought that they could just as well be seen as the freshly turned graves of last year's flowers. For God's sake, he sighed as he shook his head to dispel the thought, he'd never had a Spring as complicated as this one was turning out to be.

He hurried his step and reached the Admin building almost in a lunge. He scampered up the steps and entered to see Moyer and Weaver standing in the hallway outside the Board Room. They trailed off their conversation in concert with his arrival. As he approached he squinted to discern their expressions.

"What's up?" he probed.

"Someone from the DMH is going to meet with us this morning, Jess says," Moyer informed him.

"Oh, we've become that important?" he ragged.

"I guess you could say so," Weaver returned with a hint of portent.

"Probably here to take our measurements for the monument," Cantrelle persisted, though marshaling a wariness on the edge of his mind.

Just then Corley stepped out of the Board Room.

"Oh, good morning, Frank. I had asked Clay and Jess to wait for you. I wanted us all to start together. Now that we're all here we can go in and get started," she motioned with her hands clasped together before her.

He wasn't used to such ceremony for a simple Council meeting. And besides, Martha was explaining herself too much, he thought. Something was up, and it no doubt had to do with that guy from the DMH.

They filed into the Board room with Corley leading and Weaver bringing up the rear. He skipped over the familiar faces girdling the table to fix on the alien one he knew would be positioned at the head of the table next to Martha's place. He looked, and saw that his expectation was seriously in error. It wasn't a guy at all; it was a doll. A very lovely, svelte doll who sat near the head of the table with the poise and comfort of someone obviously at ease with her office. She had been chatting with Charlie Riegel when they entered and she now turned to them as they approached the chairs awaiting them. He and Clay were to sit together and directly across from her. His open surprise was balanced by her pleasant and faintly triumphant smile which seemed to escort them to their seats. As they jockeyed their chairs to take their places at the table he and Clay exchanged raised eyebrows and were preparing to settle in when Martha chose to make introductions.

"Dr. Cantrelle and Mr. Moyer, I'd like you to meet Miss Alison Dieter," Corley began. "Miss Dieter is the Deputy Program Director of the Office of Public Welfare and presently on assignment to the DMH. She's here with us this morning to assist us with some issues which have come up concerning our rôle in the state's management of the Blush cases. She . . . ."

Cantrelle and Clay had begun to lower themselves into their seats when Martha began the introduction. They both automatically returned to full height when she began and now found themselves standing as though at attention as she continued. Dieter, sensing their awkwardness, interrupted.

"I'm very pleased to meet you, Dr. Cantrelle, Mr. Moyer. I trust you weren't waiting long in the hallway," She took them both in with a generously sympathetic smile suggesting closure of the introduction.

Feeling released from that arrest, they took their seats as they returned the greeting. The irksome thought occurred to him that he and Clay were performing exactly alike before her, shades of Tweedle Dee and Tweedle Dum—rising, nodding, smiling, sitting, and saying hello, all in tandem. Certainly they were both surprised that the scheming DMH's agent turns out to be a woman—no need to check with Clay on that score—but falling into identical patterns of obedience rankled their oft proclaimed separate sovereignties, as he was sure Clay would agree. He felt he had to say something.

"Much too long," he asserted in a lame stab at gallantry.

She smiled indulgently in return, being careful to direct as much to Clay.

"Miss Dieter is here," Corley continued as she tilted her delivery in their direction though ostensibly speaking to the Council at large, "as a representative of the Research and Publications section of the DMH. As you know, all research and all publications, especially publications issuing from state-supported research, have to be cleared by the DMH before being released to the public. Moreover, before any research can be undertaken in the state hospital system it first has to be reviewed and approved by the DMH. That you all know already."

Various nods around the table said as much. Cantrelle and Clay were already listening between the lines as Dieter idly rearranged some papers before her.

"You also know that Blush admissions are increasing with each passing month," Corley added. "Even though we keep them here only thirty days on the average, we've just about filled Building Seven and we've had to concentrate a disproportionate number of our personnel—medical, nursing, and clerical—in that building to take care of the patient turnover. And there's no hint of any slackening of the pace, I'm afraid."

Again she was over-explaining herself with this review and probably leading up to something she was hoping to make go down easier, he suspected.

"With that as background I would like now to turn the discussion over to Miss Dieter," she yielded.

Too carefully staged, he judged. It wasn't like Martha at all; she must have been coerced into it, he concluded. His attention took on a prowling readiness.

"Thank you, Dr. Corley," Dieter offered graciously as she turned to the waiting Council. "As Dr. Corley mentioned," she began while continuing to arrange several sheets of paper in front of her, "this facility's standard mission and management procedures necessarily remain unchanged, regardless of the burdens placed upon us by the additional work we're now called upon to do. That's what I'd like to touch on this morning."

Her manner was almost casual, as though it had been carefully coordinated with her strikingly sylphlike bearing. What the hell was she doing in Program Development? She should have been—and who knows, maybe had indeed been—a Dior or Givenchy high fashion model. He was used to the plain and dumpy types locked in eternal combat with calories. Coordinated—that was the word he decided upon as he inventoried her charms while Martha spoke. She was almost anemically fair, and her hint of make-up seemed to highlight rather than shade the convent-like whiteness of her skin. Her hair was jet black, straight, and cut short in finishing school page boy style. It actually shimmered in the light and, despite its modest length, flowed as liquid iridescence with her movement. Her eyes seemed—he could not totally capture them in a glance—equally black, and were hauntingly deep in their suggestion of discreet intimacy. Her profile was an exquisite Medici cameo. The nails were perfect, he noted as she shuffled her papers; shaped, polished, and just long enough to combine with purring. She arched her caressively slim fingers delicately as she adjusted her papers which she managed with swift precision. He guessed her height to be about five foot eight and her weight to be not an ounce over one hundred twenty-five pounds. The fluidity and style of her movement and gestures prompted him to wonder if she'd studied dance at some time, maybe even ballet, for which she was obviously too tall. Her upper half said so much, and he was sure her legs would say so much more when he got around to seeing them. With reluctance he allowed his estimation of DMH to go up, and he wondered how Clay was feeling.

"First, I'd like to extend the gratitude of the DMH to Dr. Cantrelle and Mr. Moyer for their excellent research and recent publication," she began with an approving smile directed at them. "The Office regards that piece of work as a salute to the State Hospital's effort, an effort in which all of us in the system share and to which we all contribute. The Commissioner sends his personal regards and encouragement in support of your special efforts. He also notes," she continued smoothly, "that your more privately-based activities in extension of your research have brought an additional notoriety, a much more public awareness, to the tasks faced by the State Hospital system in managing the Blush problem. The Department, as well as OPW, believes the increased public awareness of this terrible problem can only help in strengthening the legislative support we depend on."

Just as Napoleon said: success has a thousand fathers, he thought ungraciously as she spoke.

"In a recent meeting between the Secretary and the Commissioner," she continued, "it was agreed that the DMH would maximize its participation in the management of the Blush problem as well as assist in those decisions necessary at both the departmental as well as the local level for generating facilities necessary for the care of these patients."

"Do you mean *new* facilities?" Riegel specified.

"If not new, then the designation of certain existing facilities for exclusive use in accommodating those patients," she explained.

"I suppose most hospital complexes in the system have buildings that have been deactivated over the years and which could be put back on line, such as we did with our Building Seven. That might handle much of the bed problem," Riegel agreed.

"That's exactly correct, Mr. Riegel." she smiled her approval. "But beyond that," she continued, "the Secretary and the Commissioner have agreed that it would probably be overall more efficient and cost-effective to concentrate the Blush patients in certain regional facilities rather than have them distributed throughout the system as they are now. Presently," she detailed as she wafted her comments along the length of the table, "each hospital in the system holds the Blush patient for approximately one month before transfer to Mountainview, just as you do here at Moreland. In fact, your triage and disposition process has been adopted as the standard procedure for all the other facilities, and the Commissioner commends you on that point as well. We've been told in Sharpsfield that the triage notion had been yours for some time, Dr. Cantrelle, but that an enabling opportunity had not been forthcoming until the situation with Blush. That's true, isn't it?"

"Yes, it is, Miss Dieter," Martha spoke in confirmation. "Dr. Cantrelle hardly let a day go by over the past several years without warning us that the day would come when we would have to abide by his advice about setting up a triage unit."

"We all at Moreland favored a triage unit to be established at some time, but other priorities always shaped our policy, at least until Blush hit us," Cantrelle blandished.

Dieter looked at him for a moment as though to take fuller measure of his meaning and then smiled gently with a nod of acquiescence for letting him have it his way.

"In any event," she resumed smoothly, "each hospital in the system now utilizes a triage unit in the same manner as you do yours, but the new thinking is that the hospitals will no longer transfer Blush patients to the interior units of their complexes after the patient's diagnosis has been established. In other words, the Blush patient would be at Moreland, as an example, only for the ten day evaluation period on the triage unit. At the completion of that evaluation and after some initial stabilization has been achieved the patient would then be transferred to a different facility entirely, one used exclusively for the management of the remainder of his hospital course."

"You mean until he dies," Moyer clarified outright.

"Yes," she agreed evenly.

Not a hint of a flinch, Cantrelle gauged as he assayed her reply. This girl, this nymphic herald, had more to her than just beauty. Therefore, there had to be more coming, he reckoned.

"So there will be regional Blush hospitals to house all the Blush patients in the system?" Mrs. Fawcett, the Director of Nursing, queried.

"That's right," Dieter affirmed.

"How many?" Mrs. Fawcett persisted.

"Based on currently projected admission rates, three, with the possibility of a fourth, should the need arise," Dieter explained.

"That would mean taking three of the dozen hospitals in the system off line for general admissions," Riegel concluded. "I guess the remaining non-Blush hospitals would now receive those diverted general admissions to compensate for the shift in beds."

"Correct," she agreed. "Beds now being used for Blush patients in those remaining hospitals, such as here at Moreland, would be kept available for the additional general admissions come of the enlarged catchment area of each hospital."

It all sounded so neat, so efficient, and *wrong*, he thought as he tried to catch Jess' eye for any collaboration available there. He knew Jess sensed his appeal but made no overt gesture of alliance. Suppressing a sigh, he decided to open the discussion beyond the tallying of beds. But Clay spoke first.

"Where will our regional Blush hospital be?" Moyer began.

"The eastern facility will be Logantown State Hospital," she answered. "It will draw from the three state hospitals, Moreland included, in the eastern sector of the state. The general psychiatric patients at Logantown will be apportioned to the three regional hospitals, honoring distances for family convenience as best we can. In effect the three feeder hospitals—Moreland will be one of them—will be swapping their Blush patients for regional general patients."

"I can see the administrative and logistical advantages to the plan," Cantrelle began, "and certainly as they apply to the management of the Blush patient, but those very advantages are conversely the disadvantages for the general patient transferred to a more distant facility. Yet, there's no question that the urgency of the matter grants Blush patients first priority."

"Yes," she concurred as she looked at him fixedly. Thus far her manner encouraged no discussion; she was more given to inform than to inquire, it appeared. At least on this issue, he suspected.

The uneasiness present in the room from the outset was now becoming more evident to all, except to Miss Dieter who seemed determinedly impervious to it. The sense that questions should be asked and issues defined hung heavy in the air, but her manner was akin to levying a tacit injunction against inordinate inquiry, and the effect was like two weather fronts colliding above their heads to give the atmosphere that shaky imbalance typically described as threatening. A few of the council members shifted in their seats. Riegel looked about for collaboration.

Martha spoke.

"Miss Dieter, there is an initial discomfort with the notion of sending our patients to die at another facility," she began. "The tendency among the staff is to regard the patients as *our* patients, people from our own clinical neighborhood, and thus our responsibility to follow for the care they need. Moreland has always been regarded by the immediate townspeople and the people in our catchment area more as a local institution rather than just one of several state facilities, and the staff feel a reciprocal obligation to the people for that reason. So the thought of sending our Blush patients, despite all the stress that comes of their care, away to another facility for their last days seems like an abandonment, a departure from our traditional relationship to the community."

"Undoubtedly," she readily agreed, "but local preferences have to be put aside in this matter."

Her answer had the ring of fiat about it, and the silence that followed thickened the air even more.

"But if the separate state hospitals are willing and able to manage their local allotment of these cases," Mrs. Fawcett persisted with rising resistance, "why is it so important for them to be gathered in regional centers? And besides, where are the other two centers?"

Dieter's lips thinned in restrained anger. It obviously was not her wont to be taken to task. After a moment of silence to convey her displeasure with the impertinent challenge, she spoke.

"The other two centers will be Hallsburg and Mearesville hospitals," she announced, addressing the easier part first. "The answer to your other question is simply that Blush is not just a community problem, regardless how it is seen locally."

"Could it be that the DMH doesn't want the problem to be seen at all?" Moyer asked with undisguised relish. "Those three centers are as out-of-the-way as you can get in the state system."

Her flash of injured dignity was followed by a compensatory contempt at his blunt *lèse majesté*, and she answered with malicious condescension.

"Mr. Moyer, the DMH is providing a means for relieving the local hospitals of a very thankless task, and perhaps the program would best be seen in that light," she recommended, hinting at caution.

"Oh, I'm sure," he deflected, "but we all know how sensitive DMH is to public opinion, and having the local populations too aware of a DMH problem which is not being solved might translate into electoral concerns for the current administration, might it not?"

Judging by her response, it was exactly the wrong, and the right, thing to say. She angrily shuffled her papers before her so as not to look at Moyer as she worked at regaining her composure. When she spoke, she did so as much to Martha as to Moyer.

"Insinuations as to ulterior motives in the DMH will not be useful in implementing the program, and the program will be implemented, I assure you. You will be receiving directives within ten days as to the sequence of transfers, how many and when. Your task will be to identify the particular patients for transfer, beginning with those who have the longest length of stay and then work backwards. You will also finalize the administrative preparations for such transfers with individual clinical records being complete and up to date," she serialized in drum-beat fashion with no pretense of amity.

Cantrelle noted with reluctance that she was no less beautiful in her incensed arrogance, discerning in her shift to frank imperium that awful and fascinating personal entitlement so often coupled with ruthless ambition. No wonder she thrived in the power chambers of Sharpsfield. She would probably go far, what with her singular ingredients, he wagered.

"I'm sure we'll be able to meet the schedule, Miss Dieter," Corley offered in reassurance designed to mollify.

With a start he realized something. Dieter noticed his alarm.

"Yes, Dr. Cantrelle?" she solicited as though ready to see everything through, now that issues were openly joined.

"Miss Dieter, it just occurred to me that if the Blush patients are transferred after ten days we won't have them long enough for follow-through on the research we've begun," he explained. "The paper we published was only Moreland's first in our Blush research prospectus. Other members of our staff have already indicated interest in mounting studies on related topics and we were hoping to have a Symposium in the autumn on the Blush research the hospital would have completed by then," he added in hinted anguish.

"That's very commendable, Dr. Cantrelle, and the DMH supports the spirit of this hospital's efforts, but the transfer program has been accorded higher priority," she pronounced.

"But the research has to be continued because by and large we still don't understand this Blush thing. So far we're able to offer very little in the way of treatment," he implored.

"I understand that," she agreed impassively, "and I assure you that research will indeed continue."

He felt perplexed, not only by what she said about the research continuing despite the patients' being sent so quickly to the hinterlands, but also by the hint of a sly smile which now crept across her lips.

"But I don't see how we would have enough time with the patients to do the research. And to try to do it from afar after they've been transferred just wouldn't work. I guess we could go up there on our own time and . . . ." he posed.

"That won't be necessary, Dr. Cantrelle," she interrupted. "The research which DMH feels should be continued will be done."

He immediately disliked the sound of that assurance.

"How so?" Moyer asked coyly, already nodding at what he expected to hear.

"We've"—she emphasized the word—"we've undertaken an arrangement with Pittsfield University Medical School for a research unit to be set up at Hallsburg for Blush studies. They will staff the unit and conduct the research DMH and the research cadre select."

He sat stunned, hurt, defeated. He and Moyer hadn't been consulted, or even notified, and they had done the *first* published work in the field. Burleson's note came to mind and now seemed pathetic in the light of this announcement. He quickly looked at Corley and Weaver, whose equally defeated expressions revealed no prospect of hope there. He then turned back to Dieter who was now sitting comfortably erect and satisfied, clearly mounting an effort to bear up under her triumph with becoming grace. He looked at her, unbelieving.

"My congratulations to you, Miss Dieter, and to the DMH," he heard Moyer say. "The political as well as career benefits of identifying with, and in this case, assuming control of, research which promises to have national dimension and notoriety can only be seen," he pronounced carefully, "as heaven sent. And, being all too familiar with the special brand of piety popular in the DMH, I'm sure you and your people will undoubtedly be singularly devout in your worship."

She smiled at him with one eyebrow raised slightly in disdain.

"We are reminded at this time, Miss Dieter," Moyer continued as though fresh on a scent, "that early on, the DMH and OPW chose to transfer the State lab's work on Blush to NIH. I see now that the decision to do so probably had something to do with Moreland's having too much authorship and say so in the Blush research for DMH to take credit for it, or at least graciously, anyway. We had pre-empted your people, so to speak, though absolutely *no one* in your own ranks could have gotten the research going. So transferring it away, as with transferring the patients away, serves to clip our wings and give your people and probably OPW *et al* another chance at moving in on a hot item. Right? And what you've delivered this morning is your department's next move. Correct?"

She continued to smile, patiently giving him his say.

"I commend you and your people on your tactical skill," Moyer continued, "and I also commend Pittsfield University for its enterprising approach to generating faculty payroll."

Pretense ostensibly put to rest, she granted a slight nod in haughty acknowledgment.

"I'm sure in its deliberations on all of this," he proceeded, "the DMH must have anticipated that at some point Dr. Cantrelle or even I might indicate some willingness to continue our participation in the research, the inconveniences and altered ground rules notwithstanding. Understandably we would now be outsiders requesting permission for entry into what was no longer our territory. Now I ask you, Miss Dieter," he completed with syllogistic inevitability, "to *whom* would we direct our request for such permission?"

"To me," she relished.

Moyer let out a hoot of vindication. Cantrelle recoiled from Moyer's open display of inductive triumph and felt the urge to shut him up for fear that a terrible situation would, by his scornful gloating, be transformed into a hopeless one. But it wasn't necessary, for Moyer settled down quickly enough, the better for allowing the others present to soak up the revelation.

A moment passed as the other members exchanged furtive glances in validation of each other's shock at such cynical opportunism on display in the person of this coldly beautiful creature. Cantrelle felt himself pulling away from the scene, for *not* to withdraw would run risks he chose not to accept. Were he to contest the matter he would probably erupt in a violent display likely to carry his retaliatory resignation from his teaching post, something which would do only local damage and undoubtedly please the DMH as an additional windfall. But to try to reason and negotiate with her and the DMH might be seen as begging come of subjugation, and there was absolutely no way he would stoop to that.

Miss Dieter waited with the patience of the victor.

Finally, Mrs. Simpson spoke.

"I guess it will be the Social Worker's task to square it with the family about the patient's transfer to a regional center. Any helpful suggestions as to how we might approach it?" she posed.

Miss Dieter, noting a veiled scorn in the query, fixed Mrs. Simpson with a stare.

"I'm sure your department will rise to the occasion as never before," she replied with a mirthless smile.

"Suppose the family objects?" Mrs. Simpson persisted.

"Then the family will be given the option of taking the patient home and caring for him as it prefers. There is nothing that requires the state to treat these patients, and, as you know, a fair proportion of them never do make it to a hospital, but simply die on the street," she replied.

"Miss Dieter," Moyer returned, "will there be any public disclosure of the DMH plan to transfer these patients? You know, something to keep the populace abreast of the DMH's efforts?"

"There may be a brief announcement, but nothing more than is usual when the department undertakes a new procedure," she replied with contrived evenness.

"Such modesty. You'd think the department would want the world to know of its exertions in the service of the doomed. Could be so reassuring to so many," Moyer taunted.

"Yes, of course. But odd you should bring that up," she pursued, "I had intended to address later a similar point as it applied to you and Dr. Cantrelle," she gloated, "but since you've already brought it up we might as well proceed now. You are aware, I'm sure, that any survey or investigative work done under the auspices of the DMH has to be cleared first by the Department prior to public release and publication. That means all research, all reports, and anything that bears on the system's operation, patient management, or clinical procedures. Certainly any outcome studies."

This was already known to all present. Hence, her reason for bringing up the policy bespoke the advent of some new application, as all were now alerted to expect. And especially Moyer and Cantrelle, who sharpened their readiness as they now silently watched her.

"I bring this up because the Department lately has had some concern about unauthorized public statements being made by state employees about the Blush problem and the state's approach to its management," she proceeded.

"By state employees, you mean me and Dr. Cantrelle, don't you, Miss Dieter?" Moyer supplied.

"Certainly you two are included," she parried, "and we would want you to be reminded, especially you, Mr. Moyer, that the Department was generous in its support of your Blush research and also rather swift in its approval of your paper for publication at a time when no such approvals were available anywhere else."

"Let's not be too egregious in labeling a necessity as a virtue, Miss Dieter," Moyer cautioned. "For the Department not to have approved of our research proposal when the world was screaming for some help with the new plague would have been an act of consummate political stupidity the Department could never commit, even in its more misguided moments. So, clearing our paper for publication was not as selfless a gesture as you would suggest. In fact, our paper more than likely offered your people another ticket to punch on their route to preferment, as the new Blush research program you just described to us strongly suggests. Rather, you and your people may thank us and Moreland whenever you wish for pointing the way to richer pastures for all of you."

Corley blanched at Moyer's words. They were penetratingly true, as the rapt and united attention of the other council members confirmed. Moreover, the members stared directly at Dieter as he spoke. But the words were also much too incendiary. No good could be served by escalating the inherent conflict in the clinical-administrative dialectic, Corley had often said on gentler occasions over the years of her tenure in smoothing the hospital's course, and this wretched confrontation evolving just now, right in front of her, begged no less for some quick, soothing balm.

"Clay," she intervened, "Miss Dieter is perfectly within the scope of her duties to reaffirm DMH procedure and policy, and we owe her the respect of our attention as she does so. Please," she implored, "let's attend to our duty as reasonable representatives of Moreland in making ourselves available to her counsel."

Moyer and Dieter continued to look at each other as Martha spoke, listening but not heeding.

"Thank you, Dr. Corley," Dieter permitted, "I was trying to make the point that public utterances by state employees on the State's management of the Blush problem are a source of great concern to the DMH and the OPW . . . ."

"And possibly even beyond?" Moyer suggested.

". . . and especially if those utterances," she continued resolutely, "are discordant with the intent and goal of the State's public stance on the matter. Mr. Moyer," she specified, "you and Dr. Cantrelle at present are the system's most publicly visible figures in the Blush program . . . ."

"An inconvenience soon to be effaced by the Pittsfield faculty's new diggings, I'm sure," Moyer averred.

". . . and the Office would strongly encourage you to clear your public statements with Sharpsfield before you make them available to public gatherings. The Department can be most helpful in this regard, and the continuation and support of your research can be significantly enhanced by the Office's confidence in your readiness to cooperate with standard procedures. I sincerely hope that you and Dr. Cantrelle will consider our request."

Cantrelle sensed the presence of a sincere plea somewhere in her marshaled words. He wanted to speak before Clay moved the confrontation another notch along by invoking the right of free speech as he damned well knew Clay would, but Martha spoke first.

"Miss Dieter," she began in a stilted, rise-above-the-nastiness tone, "I assure you that all of us will take your recommendation under study, and we'll discuss it among ourselves to achieve a consensus which I trust will be in compliance with our standard directives."

Dieter nodded, satisfied for the moment.

"The transfer arrangements you brought up earlier I would like to pursue in more detail as long as you're here and have the time," Corley continued, "but for the moment I want to thank you, Dr. Cantrelle and Mr. Moyer, for joining with us for this part of this meeting. However, I think we can now release you to your impatient duties awaiting elsewhere."

Dieter nodded in compliance.

He didn't like being summarily dismissed, but he understood that Martha felt compelled to do so in order to defuse collision which had already progressed far beyond recall. With elaborate grace he rose, as did Moyer, and spoke.

"Yeah, Dr. Corley, I guess it is time we got on with other things," Cantrelle sighed. "Miss Dieter, I'm quite impressed by your style of embassy, and please be assured that I've found our discussion to be very informative indeed. I trust we'll speak again."

"Thank you, Dr. Cantrelle," she returned. "I'll look forward to it. What about you, Mr. Moyer?" she teased as she shifted to him.

Moyer looked at her through a half smile.

"Miss Dieter," he explained, "I think you know I derived a singular pleasure from our chat. It was real."

Closure done, he and Cantrelle then left the now silent room.

When they closed the door behind them and entered the hallway they did so with the relief of being released from a pressure cooker. The air in the hallway was cooler, lighter, fresher.

"Whew!" Cantrelle wheezed. "What a kick in the ass! Not that we ever expected a hell of a lot from them in the first place, but to pull the rug right out from under us, and from under Moreland especially! What a prick thing! Those bastards really show the difference between administrators and politicians. Charlie Riegel is an administrator. He'll use the rules and regs to move heaven and earth in helping Moreland and everybody at Moreland. Those bastards use rules, regs, Moreland, the people at Moreland, and everybody else just to help themselves! Fucking politicians, that's all they are!" he ranted as they moved down the hallway.

He knew he was overstating it, speaking totally out of bias, and otherwise smoke-stacking in search of relief from his injured pride, but at the moment it seemed the right thing to do.

When they reached the front entrance they paused for a moment before opening the door. Moyer had not said a word since they left the meeting and didn't seem particularly attentive to Cantrelle's tirade as they walked down the hallway. Upon reaching the door he turned to Cantrelle and spoke as though surfacing from some busy inner debate.

"I'm not going to do it," he said simply.

"Do what?" Cantrelle asked.

"I'm not going to shut up. I think I'm beginning to see something," he explained with a look of distant preoccupation.

"Damn it! Not you, too! Anything you care to mention just now, Clay?" Cantrelle asked with concern that his embattled friend was now also being plagued by the verge.

"No," Moyer said, shaking his head as though to clear it. "But they're not going to muzzle me," he continued with more evident resolution. "If we had to clear everything we say about Blush with DMH first, before long we'd even have to have their permission to fart. So I'm just going to keep doing what I've been doing. But now, after this morning, I'll have a lot more to talk about."

"Amen," Cantrelle proclaimed. "Christ! That reminds me! I have to get over to the CCAH meeting," he blurted as he stole a glance at his watch. "Late again! Look, Clay, I'll catch up with you later. Gotta get my ass into another harness now. The big accreditation show, you know."

"Sure, Frank. We'll get together later. I'll call you and we can then go over this morning's damages and see what's left," Moyer suggested.

"Yeah," Cantrelle grunted as he waved and took off at a half trot toward his car. Moyer turned toward his bicycle leaning against the building's facade.

Enroute to his car he decided that he must be out of his goddamned mind! It had just happened that a corrosive political opportunism invaded their academic world and had dashed to flinders their boyish dreams of the Grail. That very opportunism had also probably snuffed out Moreland's chance of return to national prominence. In doing so, DMH had enacted a feudal revanchism by converting three state hospitals into present-day leper colonies. Then, further, DMH had expropriated the freedom of inquiry Moreland needed for achieving an understanding of its daily travail. Yet, here he was, worried about being late for a goddamned accreditation meeting! There just had to be something wrong with his priorities. Or maybe it was simply that he was as native as anyone else to some implacable, primal calling; to wit, that insatiable, undeniable, and most fundamental of all social drives, the search for certification. Every human social endeavor, he had so often taught, was rooted in that remorseless search, whether it took the shape of pre-history animism, or mythology, or religion, or science. Even the science at Moreland. Every doctrine, every school of thought, every system of philosophy known to man offered, to be worth its salt, the key to right certification, often called The Truth. Certainly every religion, every cult, every guild, every society, every nation, and every race worked at granting a confirmatory certification for each and every one of its deserving members. But to become a deserving member demanded a rigid, strict performance of passage which, done well, conferred on the member a vital certification seen as arrival, membership, status, even salvation. After all, who really was anybody without the secret handshake, or the diploma, or the membership card, or the accreditation? Those were the signets, the essence of definable identity, meaning, and hence believable existence. And we all agree to it because we all need it. The accreditation industry perforce had the strongest lobby imaginable: all of us and every phantom of our aboriginal fear of alienation. So in the frenzy of compulsion we certify ourselves and each other and exult in our established meaning, as in any savage rite of purification. And that's why he was rushing to the accreditation meeting, he decided as he reached the door of his car.

"That poor Dr. Grant. I wonder if he realizes how much he means to us?" he snickered as he pulled the car door open.

NINE

The dying at Moreland had returned to normal: an occasional patient from natural causes and the less common gruesome suicide, both expectable accompaniments to any state hospital milieu. Now, instead of the frequent visits by the ALS ambulance, a weekly hospital vehicle the size of a small school bus transported freshly stabilized Blush patients to scenic Logantown State Hospital for their settled but abbreviated stay. The vehicle was specially staffed and it typically departed the hospital at 9 A.M. on Wednesdays for its two-hour trip to Logantown. Even though it was usually back at Moreland by three o'clock the same afternoon, it had come to be called the "One-Way Express" in assignment of its pitiful cargo. Anywhere from eight to twelve patients were so transported weekly, and while the first few departures of the bus cast a heavy pall of sadness over the hospital, in remarkably short order the bus' comings and goings had found their place in the hospital's standard routine which included the horror of insanity, the misery for loss of home and family, and the agony of disintegrating individuality as just typical items of address in the daily venue of patient management. In fact, it had become *too* routine, he felt. The staff, initially offended by the idea of sending patients off to their death, were now inured to the point of being once again their typically efficient selves in helping the deliveries along as though the meaning of the transfer had sunk from view leaving only the surface ripples of medical logistics needing to be managed. In fact, concern over the logistics as well as the patients' comfort and management enroute to Logantown had become pre-eminent. It was as though the need to do the job well, that ever-present drive for mastery, had more than adequately dulled the ethics of the matter so that what the deed had lost in humanity it gained in efficiency. It was certainly not the first time the human predicament had witnessed that sort of thing, he considered. He wondered if perfected paradox was just another one of those cultivated and neutralized derivatives of ambivalence. Probably.

In addition, he wondered as he stared off, if the people, *vox populi*, had also now come around to some kind of acceptance of the issue. Approximately fifteen hundred Blush victims were dying weekly across the nation, but seldom did that horrific total merit a headline. In fact, headlines on the matter took more the cast of this or that group objecting to the use of federal funds for research on a malady that didn't touch decent, law-abiding, tax-paying citizens in the first place. To spend good money to protect a group the government already spent too much money to embargo was considered to be folly beyond forgiveness, despite such punctilious renderings of constitutional law which granted all citizens equal rights and protection, even citizens in the act of committing a crime. One citizen group, accused of being anarchist in intent, saw the Blush appropriation legislation as indisputable evidence that American democracy had run its course, much like Russian communism some years before, and had crossed a line whereby governmental approach to the nation's progressively evolving challenges saw more and more reduction to the absurd, which, in the case of Blush, they held to be a Federal display of iterating inadequacy akin the use of bigger and better votive candles to turn back the Black Plague. But several social commentators regarded this group as probably composed of hold-out communists who still held a grudge, and so gave them little account.

But not everybody saw the government's paltry response as deriving from a state of founder. Rather, some of the more aroused activists assailed the notably lame Federal efforts to stop the entry of Blush into the nation's heroin conduit as evidence of a collective national complicity in allowing Blush to ply its astringent way and have it cleanse society of one of its historically more obdurate stains. Moreover, the government's guilt by omission was compounded, they charged, by the failure to fund research on Blush beyond the most basic, since no studies thus far were identified as geared toward the development of a blocking agent which would deactivate Blush to render its heroin vehicle safe for consumption, or at least no more problematic than before.

So the timbre of the talk about the whys and wherefores of the Federal response to Blush cited either feeble fadeout from administrative entropy, much like the Blush victim himself, or the creep of crafted dissemblance come of evil intent, much like the Blush purveyor himself, though in either case the government effectively upholding withal the sentence levied by Blush. And between those two poles of culpability hovered a very large and inscrutable silence.

Like an iron filing to a magnet Clay was drawn to the dissemblance pole. Egged on by a few newly acquired activist friends who attached themselves to his evolving prominence on the lecture and town forum circuit, he was becoming more deliberate and articulate in assigning tactical intent to the government's pallid management of the Blush issue. Just two weeks earlier a minor assistant to the Director of NIH, apparently tapped to respond to Clay's recent impeachment of Federal officialdom at a regional Social Psychology conference, responded by way of a press release to clarify NIH's planful and disciplined approach to the investigation of the Blush problem. The lofty, insipid statement served only to call more attention to Clay's charge. Clay was indeed not shutting up, as he had sworn he wouldn't weeks ago at the Council meeting with that visitor from DMH. Her name was Dieter; Alison Dieter, he recalled. The memory carried a flash image of her preternatural beauty. He idly wondered how she was doing these days. Making more visits, perhaps? Like his visit to the Moreland Library yesterday where all was so cheery and hopeful? He now donated a moment of wistful recall.

"Dr. Cantrelle, maybe this one will help," the voice had urged, calling him away from his thoughts of the moment.

The intrusion had caused him to break off his staring and he turned quickly to respond.

"Yes," he had blurted, "yes, Mrs. Leon."

He could still see her before him smiling eagerly and holding, display fashion, a volume entitled *Immunology*. He'd then smiled back at her plump and happy face nested in a hood of tight salt and pepper curls.

"This is our latest edition," she had explained as her eyes opened wide in girlish delight, "and it has a section on macromolecules like you're looking for."

She had opened the volume to a page marked by a slip of scrap paper with some locator notes scribbled on it. Like most librarians, Mrs. Leon saw scratch paper an indispensable tool of her trade.

"Thank you, Mrs. Leon. This might be just what I need," he'd offered in ready gratitude as he accepted the book.

"If you need anything else I'll be up front," she'd promised as she crinkled her eyes in delight over her successful retrieval before turning to leave.

"Sure thing, Mrs. Leon. Thanks again," he had assured.

That's the way it happened. Simple, sweet, kind. Yesterday. And he left happy.

The library, any library, was his sanctum, just as it was for almost everybody else, in one way or another. He went there often enough to have what he considered to be his very own chair and table in a far corner behind the stacks and not too far from the copying machine. Moreover, the wall facing the chair was without doubt the most evocative and consoling one he had yet encountered beyond the near oracular one which held vigil, like right at this very moment, just across from his desk at which he now sat in his cozy home. In fact, he had often recalled, it was in a library he had first discovered walls, or at least their videographic wonders. So often as a boy, especially on Saturday mornings at the library across from the neighborhood playground, he would look up from his reading to squint into approximate view what was spoken by the page in hope of seeing its actual image projected on the wall before him. Sometimes—actually, often—the smoky images would become animated as though the thoughts and ideas at hand were able to move and act and show intent or purpose, something he could never put into words but which he could see, or maybe almost see, for he was never sure he actually saw what he felt he was perceiving though it was as close to doing so as he believed it could be. And he always came away from the experience with the sense that he had not gotten quite close enough to the matter to see it fully and completely but had been close enough to know that there was so much more yet to be seen. So he was always left with an odd combination of the sense of communion along with a nagging, aching dissatisfaction that fulfillment had yet, somehow, been missed. As a teenager he decided that the uncanniness of the experience probably accounted for the mysticism present in all religions, and as a medical student he expanded that hunch to include the driving force behind promiscuity as well. Now, at this point in his life he saw it just as a personal pain-in-the-ass reminder that he didn't know as much as he thought he did and that he would best do something soon to set the matter right.

With a grunt he now adjusted in place before him the weighty tome so happily recommended by Mrs. Leon. As he turned the cover he felt a return of that general sense of futility he'd come to know too well of late: an enervating, heavy weariness carrying the lament that he had neither the training to comprehend, nor the time to work away at, such matters as would include the literature on auto-immune reactions and their often critical rôle in disease. A few articles had come forth about Blush's remarkable potency in generating rapidly escalating auto-immune phenomena in specific nervous structures, and Mrs. Leon had dutifully forwarded those articles to him immediately upon receipt. But he didn't need the results of those carefully controlled animal experiments to appreciate Blush's power; Blush victims were only too available to demonstrate such. The fact that Blush was a synthesized macromolecule composed of a peptide chain carrying an activating site which functioned as a neurotoxin to specific, localized brain cells and to no others, plus, in combination with the breakdown products of those cells, generated antibodies which then progressively attacked other brain cells of the same group was the phenomenon that made it all so staggering. The reaction became progressive because as more of the cells broke down, molecule by molecule, more was dumped into the immune system to generate reactive antibodies for use against the source cell themselves. In effect, the organism's self-protective system was being used to destroy its own organs. Once started, the reaction would not stop until the death of the targeted organ. But that much had already been known clinically. Nor was it unique to Blush, for it had long been suggested that several common diseases owed their pathophysiology to the same auto-immune process. It was now understood, for example, that chronic glomerulonephritis, that relentlessly devastating kidney disease, thought to be the killer of Mozart, often began with a particular form of strept throat whereby the bacterium, beta hemolytic streptococcus, gained access to the kidneys by way of the blood stream and damaged specific cells of the kidney—the glomerular cells—causing their protein to fragment into breakdown products—large peptide molecules—and enter the blood stream where they acted just like a foreign protein to activate the formation of antibodies, as did the streptococcus itself, for targeting and destroying the now offending peptide linkages of the remaining glomeruli. But those remaining glomeruli and their peptide linkages were basic to the health of the kidney. Yet they now came under attack by the system's antibodies with the result that more breakdown peptide molecules were released into the blood stream, stimulating even more antibody formation. Hence the morbidly progressive course of the disorder. Certain medications, such as steroids, in the standard treatment armamentarium for combating such reactions could often suppress the debilitating process in the naturally acquired diseases, but thus far not so with Blush, the articles generally agreed. The rapidity and the severity of the Blush reaction marked it as unique, and thus itself targeted for investigation, which, contrariwise, seemed to be progressing ever so slowly. The Blush molecule itself was found to be heat stable, specifically fat soluble and thus readily accessible to brain tissue, and minimally subject to deactivation by the liver. Hence it appeared likely that the entire dose ingested reached the targeted cells in the thalamus and the reticular activating system and that the sensitizing reaction was in all likelihood established within the first twenty-four hours of contact, thus giving little time for effective therapeutic intervention even if some form of protective treatment were available.

He ran his finger down the table of contents, noting that there were several chapters on DNA, desoxyribonucleic acid. When he was in school DNA and RNA had been known, but were merely mentioned in passing during his biochemistry course. Now, they each had entire chapters of their own, and, undoubtedly, elsewhere had entire books devoted to them. Gad, how things had moved along, he sighed; he was so hopelessly out of touch with that part of medicine.

Feeling daunted by the breadth and depth of the lore outlined on the pages before him he again wondered what he could possibly hope to accomplish by taking what at best would be a cursory glance at the mysteries of immunology as carried in this basic text. Well, it was nothing less than some understanding of the fell and unmitigated mystery of Blush, is what. That was obvious enough, he noted in redundant agreement with himself, but the purpose was driven as much by his mounting intolerance of not having the assurance that aggressive research on the pestilence was being done *anywhere*. True, Blush didn't have the pandemic proportions of a smallpox plague, or of typhoid, or of any of the other more traditional scourges that swept through society in former times. And even though Blush was man-made, and somehow thereby less pestilential, it was still a plague despite its high-tech character and its targeting of specific victims. The pathogens in this case were the people behind Blush, not some impersonal and apolitical bacterium or virus. Blush was threatening to become the first pandemic purposely perpetrated by man to attack a particular class of the world's inhabitants and nobody seemed greatly concerned about it, except those vocal groups from the ranks of the targeted victims themselves. And people like Clay. The government offered the proper assurances of serious intent, but there weren't any of the crash programs or high-level forums which ordinarily occurred, hysteria-like, when the nation perceived a mounting threat to its safety. Quite obviously few others saw the problem as a personal threat, except, of course, those people whose lives put them in close contact with the problem. Like his own presently troubled existence. Fifteen hundred people a week and all the government had thus far said was that there was increasing evidence that certain Central American interests were probably active in the marketing of Blush and that America's long-established friendly ties with several republics in the region were being used as leverage in ferreting out the particulars of the problem. The name of Inigo Pontalbas, America's heretofore most vigorous regional ally plus ready recipient of considerable American financial aid over his years in office, still continued to figure prominently in task force reports on centralized direction of Blush distribution. Yet, nothing seemed to come of such disclosure. So it was clear enough to him that the sum effect of those mounting and hovering questions was to drive him to the stacks in a kind of reprisal raid, his foray focused on a textbook whose information might serve as mandate for establishing a bill of particulars to use in searching out the Achilles' heel of this free-booting macromolecular marauder. So he and Clay really weren't greatly different in their basic intent after all; it was just that Clay directed his assault against the powers that should be doing more, while he, Dr. Frank Cantrelle, directed his assault against a stuffy book that should enlighten more. Hardly any difference at all, he snickered as he turned the page.

He then came to the chapter on the biochemistry of the immune process and stopped right there. He knew this was the realm where he would need to focus his search, though he wasn't yet sure what in particular he was looking for. Nothing new about that, because time and time again he'd approached problems from a similarly nebulous starting point only later to have the problems take more definitive form as his survey gradually generated coordinates for framing the search more precisely. "Setting the frame," he'd often observed to his residents, including the explanation that doing so consisted of nothing more than allowing established data to drape itself around a hunch or intuition to limn its more testable form. With a little luck he might pull off a minor coup this morning by way of a salutary rinse in factual waters with the hope that, similarly, some shiny particles might pan out for use in his struggle with all the harping questions now buzzing around in his head. Sounded good, he thought as he settled into the opening paragraphs of the chapter.

The first two pages of the chapter mercifully offered a review of the basics involved in the immunologic process, and he managed those particulars with a reassuring ease conferred by the surprisingly available recall of his medical school teachings. But within the short span of the next several paragraphs the cheerful reunion came to an end. His mind began to drift along in a miasmic haze as he read about tolerized B cells, helper idiotype-bearing T cells, concanavalin A suppression of B mitogen-induced polyclonal activation, auto-antigen specific suppressor T cell subsets, plus myriad other tongue-twisting titles. The arcane words rose from the page like incantations to a deity unknown to him. As his spirits sank he felt his envy of the immunologists and their confederates, the molecular biologists, soar meteorically. Obviously, over the past twenty-five years the field had not stood still as had his elementary acquaintance with it, and what then had been a congenial familiarity come of a two-week survey of the field during the second year of medical school was now a laughable inadequacy in view of the dizzying and excruciating complexity being displayed before him—and all that after only a scant few pages into the opening chapter. So very humbling to sound out of one's depth so soon, he groaned to himself as he leaned back in his chair to regain familiar precincts. He then resumed reading. It seemed that the "initial paralyzing phase," which he likened to his own immediate experience vis-a-vis the book itself, was the effect achieved when a hapten or foreign molecular configuration was substituted on a carrier moiety, rendering it discrepant. He wondered what the hell that meant immunologically. He looked across the room at the far wall in search of consolation. Nothing there except the chilling realization that even his closer, preferred world of medicine had so soon become so vast that he was now a stranger almost everywhere else in it except within the familiar and increasingly circumscribed province of his own limited work. The damned expanding universe, no doubt, he harrumphed. Who was the last man to know everything of his day? Leibniz? Certainly not

Cantrelle. He continued to toy with self-pity for a few more moments as he worked at re-inflating his sagging ego. He hoped to get it back up to a reasonable operating level before leaving the house this morning. After all, it really was too much to expect of anyone nowadays to be so broad-gauged as to move competently and comfortably from field to field. Things were too specialized. Almost separate languages for each region of inquiry. Even Burleson couldn't do it, he prayed. Having accomplished that blasphemy he felt some return of hope for his mission, which, he now reminded himself, was to try to make some sense of the bits and pieces of research available on Blush's mode of action, plus what those bits and pieces might say about the prospect of prevention.

He closed the book with a sigh of condign meekness and scanned the room as he leaned back in his chair. There had to be some way around this obstacle of his obdurate confoundment, he pondered. He stretched himself full length in his chair and rested the back of his head in his folded hands as he looked at the brightening far window. Sunny day upcoming, he noted paradoxically with a playful grin. Christ, it was already May. In less than two months the senior residents would be graduating, a new class beginning, and the new academic year off and running. And Ellie? She would be graduating, too, and in less than a month. His little girl, much too soon grown up. Christ's sake! It was all happening so fast, slipping right by him as he spent too much time fumbling with this Blush thing. What he needed was . . . he slowed down as though his thinking were going around a sharp curve . . . was someone who could help him make some sense of the molecular biology—or was it the immunology—of Blush. He now knew exactly who that person might be, though he couldn't for the life of him recall that person's name. His lovely daughter assuredly could. And certainly Morello. He felt his interest quicken as the prospect of asking Ellie about Morello's fraternity brother graduate student friend became firm determination. That young fellow—what was his name?—who took such a shine to Ellie. Seemed bright enough, too. Bright enough to clarify a few things about Blush? Just maybe. He began to hum as he bounded out of his chair to head for the kitchen and its steeping coffee pot. Empty mug in hand, he padded through the living room with its dust motes sparkling lazily in the shafts of light, through the dining room now ablaze with the morning sun, and finally into the kitchen where the fluorescent ceiling lights, still on from his earlier visit, now glared forth redundantly in their sterile glow. He flicked the wall switch off and turned to the coffee pot set up next to the sink. Enough left for both him and Laura. He then fished a mug from the cupboard and filled it along with his own, humming as he did so a nondescript tune more rhythm than melody. He checked the clock: ten after six. Not too early to wake up Laura with the proffer of coffee, he affirmed to dispel doubts about his timing. He then balanced his way along, up the stairs, and nudged the bedroom door open, toeing it shut behind him. He eased up to the bedside table where he placed her coffee, stood before her, and slowly took a sip of his coffee as he looked down at her cuddled figure draped by the blankets. An automatic smile of delight settled on his lips. What was it about this woman that never let him forget the better purpose and meaning of things? Like no one else he had ever known, her presence moved him to perceive a fuller world, like a second eye needed for depth perception. As much as he needed others to help him understand the accidences of his world, she and only she spoke the language that deciphered his destiny. Did she know how important she was? To him? To the kids? Probably. Could she ever acknowledge it? Probably not. So he acknowledged it for her and to her. Often. Just to be sure, he sat down on the edge of the bed ever so gently and leaned over to kiss her on the cheek. As he did so her heady and bewitching warmth rose to meet him, and his kiss lingered in reply.

"Is that you, Art?" she whispered with eyes closed in pretended sleep.

"Yes, Laura. It is I, Art," he moaned longingly, going along with her ruse as he gathered her in to him.

"Should we? He's so jealous," she wavered.

"He'll never know, my dear. This is ours and ours alone," he breathed into the hollow of her neck.

"Well, if you think so . . ." she relented.

He was already out of his pajama bottoms as he slid under the blankets to her side, and he quickly brought her form to the fit of his body. As he kissed her to readiness he stroked the yielding softness of her breasts, then softly bit her neck between kisses as she sighed at the mounting strength of his demand. He moved his head to her bosom where his lips found her aroused nipples. He hungered at her breasts while his hand stroked her quivering thighs apart. Their breathing sharpened as he touched her moist impatience, and his throb, pulsing against her thigh, urged him home as he pulled her beneath him. At first gently in tender search but then with thrusts he sank his length full into her as she gasped beneath his grunts. They then became silent and kissed as their bodies began the slow and blended undulation of union. Together they glided and soared as their rhythm spiraled them dizzyingly upwards, their breathing rising to circle them closer to their frenzy. They were then swept into a convulsion of ecstasy, and his sweaty, glistening muscles crushed her to him as her hands clutched at his broad back. Invisible lights exploded to their blinded eyes as their undulation broke into violent spasms of engulfment. And then it was over. They held each other as sighs of exhaustion wafted their movements now subsiding to rest. After a moment he kissed her cheek, and then her closed eyes. He held her quietly and tightly in seal of the total truth of their love. Their sacred moment done, he relaxed his embrace.

"He'll never know what he's missing," he whispered in her ear.

"Night before last he seemed pleased enough," she corrected.

"This is hardly the time to bring up your faithlessness," he whispered in mock injury. "A man likes to think that when he has a woman locked in his embrace she gives him top notice at that moment, not *compare* him with her other seekers. In fact, I've noticed that every time we're like this you have to say something approving about that husband of yours. I'm beginning to think you've got a thing for him."

"Now who's so jealous?" she teased.

"Jealousy has nothing to do with it. It's a matter of decency and good taste. When you're screwing your secret lover it's simply awful form to boast of your husband's satisfaction with you," he explained.

"My, aren't we formal! It can't be that my impetuous debaucher of a poet is in truth a stuffy formalist under his wayward exterior, now could it? Illusion is so important to the finer enjoyment of things, we really should bear in mind. I think your complaint about my granting credit where it's due could quickly become tedious, even unpoetic," she sniffed.

"Just like a husband, I gather," he sneered.

"Worse than a husband," she sighed.

"I guess I did step out of line for a moment, didn't I?" he rued.

"Rather," she agreed. "Your best place is in the mists of early morning. The nights of the workaday world belong to him, as we agreed years ago. It just doesn't do well for you to covet the conventional. It raises questions of your credibility, and what could be worse than disingenuous poetry? Advertising, I guess."

"Thanks, I needed that," he offered in mock pain.

"Now be a dear poet and hold me tight for a few minutes of real good illusion before the kids get up," she urged.

"Yes, my love," he obeyed as he withdrew slowly to avoid abrupt injury to that mystic singularity their union granted. Their grimaces of regret bespoke their sense of loss as he pulled free, and he quickly adjusted himself to her side and cradled her head on his shoulder as she snuggled into their after-glow caress. Their breathing then became peacefully rhythmic. In less than a minute he felt himself drifting into that totally restful sleep which said that all was as it should be and that their wonderful love had made it so.

"You know," he observed, "such carryings on will be the death of us one of these days—or mornings, I should say."

"Uh-huh," she agreed in contented unconcern as she snuggled a little closer.

"I wonder if there's any privacy in heaven?" he pondered playfully. Just then they heard the tinny chords of rock music, acceptably muted, coming from the region of the children's rooms. "God knows there's precious little of it here on earth," he added in pique.

"Uh-huh," she agreed again.

He thought of his contented wife in his arms, of his roisterous children, of his comfortable home, and was thus confronted with the realization that he was pretty happy in this part of his world. It was elsewhere that trouble festered. And a lot of it, true. But still it was elsewhere, and the saving grace of that arrangement lay in the happy fact that the only real trouble he knew was the trouble that existed on the distant frontier, far from his family and home. Commute to the distant frontier he would, daily; contend with its troubles he certainly would, and relentlessly; but keep the troubled frontier distant, unfailingly. There was plenty room for elitist guilt in that arrangement, but there was also a solace in knowing that the trouble on the frontier of his life space was not imposing a tariff on all of his happiness, much less on that of his family. He didn't at all regret sounding selfish and resolute on that point. But it did remind him of something.

"Hon, do you remember the name of that young fellow who came to the party with Morello? You know, the one from Washington?" he asked.

"Jeffrey Landon," she supplied readily.

"That was quick," he observed in a tone that invited explanation.

"He's called Ellie a few times, just to keep in touch, she says. I think he's smitten with your daughter and I suspect we'll see more of him over the summer. Why do you ask?" she pursued, her interest now aroused.

"I was thinking of calling him. He's working on the pharmacology of Blush. I've tried to read some of the immunology literature to get a better sense of the research that's coming out on Blush but I'm having rough going—I'm too much out of shape—and maybe he could give me some pointers in terms I can understand. It's the auto-immune reaction Blush causes that seems to be the key to the whole mess," he explained.

"Ellie mentioned that he's having some trouble in getting his research project approved. Some change in policy, she said. I can ask her. She'll know how you could contact him," she offered.

"No, that's O.K.," he declined, mindful of keeping the frontier just exactly where it was, "I'll check with Morello. I would rather do it that way," he instructed.

"Of course, sweet," she agreed readily.

Footsteps were now moving up and down the hallway as doors were opening and closing, the music waxing and waning in tow.

"I guess it's time to pack our arbor away till next time, my dear little nymph," he observed as he gave her a peck on the forehead. "One bad thing about the morning mists, we never have time for seconds," he grumped as they began to untwine.

"You can't have all your happiness at one time," she trah-lah-lahed as she stood up and pulled her robe around her.

"Why not?" he challenged, wide-eyed at the flash of her figure.

She just smiled coyly over her shoulder as she swivelled toward the bathroom.

He sat in bed for another moment to do some wrap-up thinking. A few minutes before seven, he noted on the clock at his bedside table. She'll always be youthful, and that would keep him young. But the years were moving along, and they had done so much together. Could happiness become wearisome in its own right? They were always so tired, though they never stopped. That was another thing they shared, perhaps the most fundamental of all things: their energy levels were about identical, and thus each understood the other's unquenchable drive as well as implacable fatigue. There was so much they never had to explain to each other; hence, they had that much more energy and time for better use, and ultimately for pursuit of even more fulfilling exhaustion. Could people fit together too well such that they mercilessly aided, abetted, and goaded each other rather than dampened and modulated? But even so, once into that mutual, iterative, recruitment thing—an addiction of its own kind—there was no settling for less. Living life fully could be draining. And compulsively so, he considered.

"Hon!" he shouted in the direction of her bathroom cloister, "I've changed my mind. Once is enough."

Just then she came out of the bathroom, hair combed and fluffed, a tad of makeup in place, and looking as fresh and vibrant as the morning itself.

"Well," she shrugged, "there's always the night of the workaday world."

"That settles it! I'm gonna spank your cheatin' ass!" he thundered as he sprang out of bed after her.

She giggled and sprinted for the bedroom door and was out before he could reach her as she pulled the door closed behind her defiant laughter.

He stood there for a moment in admiration of her swiftness and then beheld his ludicrous state—disheveled, unbuttoned, and bottomless. A scene to warm the cockles of any vaudevillian's heart. Low burlesque. And the troubled frontier just now seemed so very, very far away.

His grin slowly transformed itself back into a pragmatic set as he turned from the door and reviewed his plan to speak with Morello this morning about Jeffrey Landon's whereabouts. Then, probably put in a distress call to him. Also probably best to include Clay. On the other hand, he reconsidered as he entered the bathroom, Clay had become so political about the whole thing of late a pursuit of the mere immunology of Blush might be just too banal for his present likes. Yet, he hadn't shied away from the preliminary draft of their second paper which pretty much demanded an overview of the key pathophysiology subsumed, plus a discussion of those quirky, goddamned auto-immune mechanisms as well, he groused. Despite Clay's evolving gospel of evil in high places and his ministry for spreading the Word, he remained a solid supervisor of the residents, and his course work showed no cross-contamination with pulpit rhetoric. Likewise his empirical work with the patients, Blush patients as well, showed nothing of the savior mentality so typical of the activist. Rather, Clay remained Clay, clinically as well as tutorially, but he now carried a message he felt all should hear and was determined to deliver, and the message was to the effect that the Federal government knew a lot more about the Blush problem than it was letting on, and that what seemed like administrative inertia or even incompetence in combating Blush's spread was more an exploitation of the population's nether endorsement of the scourge's retributive sweep. At times he found himself agreeing with Clay in the notion that governmental as well as individual action, or inaction, involved a balancing of needs and forces, conscious as well as unconscious, in the address of any momentary or compelling stress, internal or external; but he also pointed out that to scrutinize any one piece of such behavior would also reduce it artificially into component valences, noble as well as ignoble, and likely grant the behavior a misleading prominence. He also held that whatever the government was or was not doing about Blush was no more culpable than what any individual or group of individuals did routinely in the process of everyday living. No more, no less. But Clay didn't buy that notion, which he dismissed as quaint homily. While he patronizingly allowed that the implied innocence of such a formulation might be strongly supported by one and all, much as everybody supports safe driving, a more utilitarian approach would be to see the government as having an active, programmatic hand in its accommodation of the Blush problem, and not simply regard the display of Federal impotence as merely the net effect of innate, unavoidable cross currents representative of the nation as a whole. He stopped short of calling it a huge conspiracy, for he knew that to do so would cast him into the company of untold numbers of providentially enlightened paranoids who had passed through the ITU over the years for treatment of their psychoses. So he hesitated in taking that step publicly, though privately he likely suspected just that sort of thing. Hence, he discreetly down-played the entire matter in his daily work on the unit. Yes, it would be O.K. to include Clay in the tapping of young Landon's lode of inside information. After all, it just wouldn't be meet for him, Cantrelle, senior author of their arrival paper and co-author of their now forming follow-up paper, to turn paranoid about his very own comrade in exegetic arms. It would look most odd.

That soliloquy carried him through the opening phase of his shower and he now turned to the question of guest speaker for the resident graduation ceremony. Six residents were on tap for graduation and once again he would have to go through the wrenching experience of saying good-bye to those splendid young people, now gracefully fledged, who, in the course of perhaps the four most determinative years of their professional lives, had been a part of his day-to-day thought and concern as much as and maybe even moreso than were the members of his own family. Too often he calculated that he spent more time, week for week, year for year, talking to, yelling at, threatening, rewarding, listening to, consoling, encouraging, and laughing with the residents than he did with his own family, or, for that matter, with anyone else in his life. And every year, June after June, he sent them on. And that was the way it worked when it worked best.

Burleson would be a natural as the guest speaker, but probably every other training director in the nation planning a graduation ceremony felt the same way. The man's phone had probably been ringing with invitations since January, or even before, if he knew some of those training directors. It would probably be fruitless to ask it of him, the renowned Dr. Horace Burleson, at this pathetically late date. Such luminous figures as he filled their speaking calendars well in advance, and, in truth, it wasn't until the publication of the article that he himself began to feel qualified to consider approaching Burleson for anything. Burleson's brief note of congratulations had opened a channel that earlier had not been clearly established, and it had taken a few weeks to get used to the idea of having a working tie with that great man. So, all in all, he wasn't really *that* delinquent in lodging the consideration of an invitation even though it was just seven weeks before graduation, he convinced himself. It's just that the timing was poor. Having thus absolved himself of out and out dereliction he felt emboldened at the prospect of calling Burleson and making the plea. The worst that could happen would be a polite regret, he recited to himself in shoring up his resolve. That established, he proceeded to feel downright decided on the matter. He was sure Martha and Jess would approve of the effort, though he'd have to clear it with them first, and today if possible.

Thus convoyed through his shower and almost through shaving, he neared the windup of his toilet and began to hum a snappy tune to carry him through dressing. He was now distinctly deft in manner, having got the day off to an overall good start, and he traversed the remaining rituals of preparation with a satisfaction come of having put structure to some of the day's uncertainty. As he was knotting his tie he winked at himself in the mirror in satisfaction with the way things had gone thus far this electric morning.

Ready, he trotted down the hallway past the now quiet bedrooms of his children and then downstairs to the dining room. Enroute he stopped in the kitchen to catch Laura at her station and to place a follow-through peck on her cheek, which she savored brightly.

"There! That'll learn you to talk cheating talk to me," he cudgeled.

He then carried the toast while managing to balance a few glasses of juice on to the dining room where Ellie and Todd were nearly finished setting the table. His contribution completed the task and Laura then entered with the jam tray and the rest of the juice.

All seated, they began breakfast as Cantrelle called attention to the busy several weeks awaiting all. Laura asked Ellie about the graduation program and the plans for the prom. Cantrelle chatted with Todd about the prospects of a summer job and the wisdom of making application early. Maybe the hospital would do some summer hiring, as had happened at other times in the past. He would check for Todd, who seemed only lukewarm to the idea of working that close to his father's watch. Laura made vague reference to eventual vacation plans but little came of that in view of the more immediate tasks awaiting all. Talk of a collective retreat to Arcady was not yet in order with current objectives being as urgent as they were. So the conversation bounced along with short-term goals taking the fore, each keeping pace with the recitation of planned tactic. Laura discreetly inquired of Ellie as to who would be her date for the prom, and Ellie brought the morning to full circle by announcing that it would be Jeffrey Landon.

"You remember him, don't you, Dad?" she urged.

Cantrelle allowed that he did, trading sly smiles with Laura.

"In fact, my dear," he announced, unable to resist, "I might be talking to that young man later this morning."

Alarm swept across Ellie's face.

"Why, Dad?" she quavered.

"Because I want to talk to him about his intentions. At NIH, that is," he teased.

"Daddy!" she blurted in exasperation. "He's a nice boy and we have similar opinions on things," she asserted in ready defense. "And besides, he's been upset lately because of his dissertation proposal being rejected. He had already begun the setup lab work on the basis of its tentative approval months ago, and then they reversed themselves and advised him to seek another project that they could help him with."

As he sipped his coffee and listened to Ellie he found himself thinking that the nice Jeffrey Landon probably hadn't defined his project in an operationally valid and testable fashion and was now being told to go back and try again. Moreover, he was probably lamenting loudly to Ellie, whose capacity for solicitude ran deep, especially if the wounded hero was reasonably good-looking. And Mr. Jeffrey Landon was reasonably good-looking, he allowed reluctantly. It simply couldn't be that a father's jealousy might be circling the edges of his thinking, he smirked as he held his coffee before him and watched the flowing gestures his daughter used in achieving the correct conversational emphasis. But then again . . . .

"Maybe he just needs *your* help, Ellie," Todd teased.

"He doesn't need anybody's help!" fumed Ellie, ready to focus her pique on Todd if he so volunteered. Todd felt just as protective of his sister as she did of him, and she knew it, though his manner was often left-handed.

"He'll probably be able to work something out," Cantrelle observed, a bit bothered that his anticipated information lode might not turn out to be as enriching as earlier hoped. All the more reason to question his suitability for Ellie.

"He's not sure. He's wondered about transferring," she added in certifying the sincerity of his grievance.

"Why not to Buckley?" Todd suggested off-handedly. Buckley University was where Ellie would start in September.

"Todd! You're looking for trouble and you're going to get it!" she threatened in high dudgeon.

Todd smiled in mock absorption with the piece of toast he was working on as he held it in readiness just below his nose.

"Now, Todd," reproved Laura, "that wasn't gallant. Ellie doesn't tease you about the phone calls you get from Gwenn. In fact, she helps cover your tracks."

"Right," scored Ellie, "and the next time she calls, which should be about fifteen minutes after we walk in the door this afternoon, I'll tell her that you would be happy to talk to her."

"She'd know better," Todd retorted blithely.

"Well then you and she can discuss it," Ellie settled with a flourish.

"All right, everybody. I've enjoyed as much of this domestic bliss as I can manage this morning. Please excuse me as I hie myself away to my labors where, like Hercules, I will confront the harrows of struggling mankind; namely, the rush-hour traffic." He then rose.

"Dad, say hello to Jeffrey for Ellie," Todd recommended amiably.

Ellie glowered over a suppressed snarl.

"Don't worry, Hon," he directed to Ellie in reassurance, "I'll keep it very professional if I get around to calling him. You two have a nice day in school—together."

Laura rose and walked with him to the door. Enroute he hefted his briefcase in one hand and held her hand with the other.

"She defends him like you used to defend me when I was a misunderstood and unappreciated resident. I just hope her judgment is as good as yours," he preened as they neared the door and out of earshot.

"I think so. I just hope his song is as good as yours," she stroked as she tilted her head against his shoulder for the last few steps down the vestibule.

When they reached the door he turned her toward him and held her hips to his, resting his briefcase against her behind, and continued, "Hon, we've got it pretty good, and it's all your god-damned fault. Wearing me down with fulfillment. Ain't you got no ruth?" he groaned as he embraced her for departure.

"Shucks, pal, 'tweren't nothin,'" she tossed.

"Well, marm," he picked up on the tone, "I'm off to that thar frontier," he drawled, dotting the tip of her nose with a kiss as he angled himself out of the door. He then trotted to the car.

As he drove off he tooted the horn to her as she waved, framed in the door.

He sighed, as he suspected she also was now doing, and then settled into the drive pattern that would be his companion for the next fourteen miles. Plenty of time to review his schedule for the day. Already he was hoping that the morning was over and that he was traveling instead to his afternoon private practice office where things generally went so comfortably and uneventfully as to establish it as compensation for his administratively-striped work at Moreland. His private practice was not part of the frontier, but rather another protected component of the cloister. The ideals of dyadic psychiatry still received full homage in his private office and it was always a relief, no matter the length of the appointment schedule, to arrive there and have his secretary fill him in on the particulars of the moment as he magically transformed himself into the private practitioner bound for Lyceum. Yes, that pretty much summed it up; going to Moreland had become Herculean of late and it was now only in his private office that he could hail Apollo.

The trip to Moreland went fast. Too fast. Rushed him right along, he grumped. Where were the traffic jams when you really needed them? After checking in with Mrs. Andretti he would have to alert her to the prospect of his making the call to NIH and young Mr. Landon. He would make the call from the ITU so that Morello might be on hand, if needed. Certainly Clay, too. First, a swing past Jess' office and then later back to his own for the call to Burleson. It all seemed uncomplicated enough when you said it fast. Untold possibilities for entanglements existed at any point in that simple circuit, and it was just too much to ask that successful resolution would proceed as swiftly as his drive to Moreland was going this morning. Mrs. Andretti, unbidden, would take care of getting the diplomas printed, if she hadn't already done so. No honorary certificate to be awarded this year. Nor any classes or individual preception scheduled for this morning, either. Very much a free morning for him. So why did he feel he was dragging himself along, though at break-neck speed? Very likely because he felt distinctly awkward about asking Burleson to come as guest speaker to a hospital which by fiat had now been reduced to investigative insignificance on the only issue that formerly might have enabled him to expect any receptivity at all from Burleson. If some ongoing survey or even low level research on Blush were authorized at Moreland and was now visibly in place, his call to Burleson this morning would be a lot easier to bring off. But with Blush patients by policy carried as patients for no longer than ten days before transfer, any kind of study that went beyond the mere recording of admission data was unworkable. And now that Hallsburg had been designated the private fiefdom of Academia, Moreland had been effectively removed from any future work on Blush. And he was going to ask Burleson to come anyway? Christ!

The hospital's smokestack now surfaced above the trees in the distance, somehow reminding him that even if Burleson agreed to come he would still have to get clearance from DMH for his appearance. He couldn't imagine DMH objecting, but lately you couldn't tell, they seemed so eager to downplay the existence of Blush. Maybe he should get clearance first before calling Burleson. He felt annoyance tighten his grip on the steering wheel which brought him back to a consideration of Hercules and his labors, just in time for him to turn into the main entrance of the hospital.

In a few moments he was pulling into his usual slot in front of the MOB. As he stepped out of his car the sunshine caught him full face. The weather was glorious, though he hadn't noticed it until now. He stood beside his car for a moment and took in the vista. Serenely beautiful grounds. Even the birds were in key. Why sweat it? Just do the best you can and don't ignore the . . . the what? . . . the flowers, everyone says. Another homily. He was getting so banal lately. Why? "Because DMH has reduced us to a god-damned clinical backwater, that's why!" he snarled.

He trotted up the steps, briefcase jigging in beat, and heaved open the heavy glass door. As he stomped down the hallway he was struck by the thick redolence of accumulated paper, much the same smell typical of a grammar school or a musty stationery store. Not unpleasant, but stagnant. The building's windows hadn't yet been open long enough this morning for the smell to dissipate, but it was also an infallible sign that the humidity was up and that the day would prove sweaty.

He turned into the office. Mrs. Andretti's smile was brightly in place, and adjacent to it at the front of her desk was a happy arrangement of flowers freshly clipped from her own garden. He knew he could expect a similar cluster on the windowsill in his office.

Good morning, Mrs. Andretti," he greeted. "They're lovely."

"Thank you, Dr. Cantrelle. The garden is beginning to get the hang of it. There's a message for you from Mr. Moyer to call him this morning as soon as you have a chance," she shifted. "It seemed urgent."

"I'd planned to go over there this morning anyway, so I'll hold off calling. But later I'll probably need your help in putting in a call to NIH. I'll get the number from Dr. Morello and take the call at the ITU where Mr. Moyer can be in on it. I'd like to stop off at Dr. Weaver's office first, though. By the way, does the printer have the order for the diplomas?"

"All arranged," she affirmed.

"Good. Anything else?" he pondered as he stared out of the window behind her. "I guess it's too soon to send the invitations," he mused in gentle inquiry.

"They'll go out two weeks from now," she supplied.

"O.K. I guess that's everything for now," he sighed, as he turned to enter his office. "If Mr. Moyer gets nervous and calls again before I get over there tell him I'm on my way."

He then entered his office and closed the door behind him. After adjusting his briefcase on the windowsill and scanning the paperwork awaiting him on his desk he settled into his chair and began to look at the wall. He needed a few moments of that balm before going forth into the day. Usually he saw his wall as a crystal ball in plano offering him a view of the distant and timeless horizon. But often enough it was also his vertical couch. At other times it was the confining categories of his perception. But perhaps most basically it was the screen on which the outline of what he hoped to understand was projected. And, if nothing else, it reminded him that what he saw was only what he knew, as Goethe had said. And yet there was always the feeling, or hope, that the wall held answers, and did so for reasons soon to become known to him. That was the prevailing sense of it this morning. So he settled a bit more comfortably into his chair, elbows on its arms, chin resting on his clasped hands, and looked more carefully at what he was wondering about. But the opaqueness of the wall seemed to look right back at him, unmoved. Of all the times to be balky, he grumped, annoyed as much at himself for the inanity of complaining about the uncooperativeness of a wall. So what the hell! Who wanted to make sense this morning anyway, he gibed. Still, a little apparition, or even an illusion such as Laura might recommend, would go a long way this morning for putting some definition to this nagging presentment that inscrutable forces were threatening to play hob with his life.

Now that he'd granted himself the time for a moment of quietude and was settled suitably in place at his Moreland desk, thoughts buzzed around his head like a swarm of gnats that had followed in his wake, trying to catch up with his attention as he'd hurried along. Now that he was at rest, they homed in on his concern and set their nettle into play. Why had so little been accomplished thus far in stemming the flow of Blush into this country? Understandably, the government couldn't undertake to protect the purity of the incoming heroin as though it were just like any other legitimate import. Eradicating Blush from the scene would be tantamount to eradicating heroin itself—no mean feat ever. Still it seemed that little or nothing was being accomplished in reducing its flow into the market network, or at least that portion of the flow funneled through Central America, and through the Avalonian paradise of El Presidente Dr. Inigo Pontalbas in particular. No real diplomatic or economic "initiatives" had been mounted to pressure that chimeric figure into more respectable international behavior; at least, none were being noted in the public press. And if any oblique levering was at play, its effect was not seen in a reduced availability of Blush. Things seemed so stymied, and young people continued to die. And why would someone in Avalon want to ruin the American heroin trade? And it *did* seem to target America preferentially. Perhaps to undermine the heroin market everywhere? Could it really be a modern day version of the War of the Roses but botanically cast as the poppy versus the coca leaf? Huge interests would have to be behind Pontalbas for him to be as big a player as he was thought to be. The drug lords, no doubt. They indeed were the kind of people who would be willing to sacrifice the lives of thousands of people indiscriminately in order to gain control of a world market. And the thought that the sacrificed persons were American citizens fanned a jingoistic rage in him as he figured it must in other good citizens who took the time to think about it. But did those good citizens also regard drug addicts as lesser citizens and hence expendable in a way preferred citizens weren't? In the general scheme of things, regrettably so, he feared. But it was still a crime against mankind, never mind that the victims fell far short of being the noblest representatives of the species. Also, to let it go unpunished identified everybody else as deserving and equal victims, if justice was to be served at all. Christ, he didn't want his thinking this morning to collapse into a cranky polemic when he wanted something soothing, something helpful to entice him forth. He exhaled deeply as he stared at the wall which glared right back at him.

"The hell with you," he spat as he bounded out of his chair. "No sense trying to talk to you."

He strode to the door and pulled it open resolutely. Mrs. Andretti sensed the command in his stride.

"Yes?" she ventured.

"I'm going over to see Dr. Weaver for a minute and then I'm going to be with Mr. Moyer on the ITU," he instructed.

He then marched up the hallway and out of the building in the direction of Administration. Several route cadences later he was trotting up steps to enter the tiled hallway of the Admin Building. He turned into Weaver's office where the secretary, also sensing his resolve, waved him in.

Weaver looked up from a chart he was reviewing.

"Oh, good morning, Frank. Something up?" he estimated cautiously.

"Good morning, Jess. Yeah. I want to invite Burleson to be the guest speaker at graduation and I want to clear it through you and Martha—and the DMH—before I call him," he announced.

"That would be great," Weaver seconded. "Think he'll come?"

"I don't know, but I'd like to try. It would be a lot easier to ask him if we were still doing some decent work on Blush, but he might go for it anyway—if he hasn't already promised himself to others," Cantrelle lodged, his resolve holding up nicely. "Time is getting short, and with someone like Burleson you want to give as much notice as possible, and I would like to get a reading on it as soon as we can if it turns out we have to look for someone else."

"Frank, I'm sure Martha will be delighted, so why don't you just go right ahead and contact him. We'll work on the DMH. If we wait for them it might take more time than you have to work with. If we tell them we've already made preliminary contact they would be more inclined to give a quick O.K. And besides, their authorization has always been a fairly perfunctory thing. They've never interfered in the graduation ceremony, you have to admit," he reminded.

That was true. They would send a representative now and again, and several times over the years they'd even volunteered help in recruiting a guest speaker. So he really had no reason to expect hindrance from them. Yet, ever since their high-handed manner in the relocating of Blush patients, and then funneling all state research on the disorder to the med school, his doubts about their agenda had sharpened, right along with his distrust.

"It suits me fine to go ahead without their O.K., Jess, but I don't want to create an incident for innocent others, " he winked, "or bother for myself. If you think it's all right for me to press on I would be only too happy," he assured.

"Sure, Frank, let's give it a try," Jess urged.

"Fine. Then I'm on my way to the ITU. I'll catch up with you later," he promised.

"Good. I'll let you know soon as Martha and I get the O.K.," Jess assured.

With that he turned and left, picking up his pace as though scrambling to his post. By the time he was back on the driveway he was almost trotting in anticipation of meeting with Clay. He reached his car, hit the ignition, and pulled away as though to gather speed for becoming airborne, but then settled down to the prescribed grounds speed as he made a line for the ITU. He wondered again, now that he was on the verge of finding out, what Clay wanted of him. Something about the stalled second paper, he hoped. He lamented that Clay had drifted away from their earlier zeal about the second paper—the very purpose of the planned call to NIH this morning—and had transferred much of his energy to the activist circuit where, like blind Tiresias, he spoke of deeds and devils not visible to simple sight. God, if only Clay would come off of it and get back to their local business and resume work at making his big contribution come from the lectern, not from the soap box. Like old times. But his evolving notoriety bespoke his greater value to the various activist groups and it was unlikely that Clay could now restrict himself to his earlier precincts. Another Rubicon had been crossed, likely. A mind stretched beyond its usual dimensions never returns to etc., etc.

He parked near the door of the ITU and then scaled the terraced steps to enter the lobby. He figured Clay and Morello would probably be on the third floor where the wards were, and when the balky elevator finally arrived he punched the chosen button to deliver him so. An aide with a patient in tow accompanied him aloft, and when the door opened to debouche them into the small lobby fronting the wards Morello was standing at the ready.

"Good morning, Chief. Mrs. Andretti said you were on your way," he announced in explanation of his tendance. "Mr. Moyer doesn't want you to get away without talking to you, not no how. He's in the conference room."

To be provided an escort meant that big business of some kind was afoot. As they stepped quickly along the hallway to its far end Morello seemed considerably less than jovial. Actually, he appeared concerned—something of a departure from his usual jingle. Also, Morello wasn't talking as they walked—another deviation from the standard. By the time they reached the conference room he had concluded that something definitely unpleasant was afoot. Christ's sake! He already had enough to contend with this morning, he readied himself to say to anyone who got in his way.

They entered the room to find Moyer sitting at the conference table with the second year resident group. A discussion was in process but came to a halt when he entered. He noted that there were not too many jovial faces here, either.

"Good morning, Frank," Moyer hailed. "I'm glad you're here because I just called again to find out if you could make it."

"'Morning, Clay. Yeah, I got your earlier message, but I figured I would just come right over. There's something I need to do and you should be in on it," he explained.

"Odd. I have the same feeling," Moyer replied cryptically.

Puzzled, Cantrelle was about to proceed when Moyer interrupted.

"Mine first," Moyer urged.

Cantrelle nodded in accession.

"It has to do with a new Blush admission. Dr. Aranzuela admitted the patient last night and we were discussing the case just now when you came in," Moyer proceeded.

Cantrelle gave a quick confirmatory glance at Dr. Aranzuela who sat alertly before an admission chart she held open in front of her. She returned his glance with an unsmiling show of readiness to proceed. Too somber for her usual, he thought.

"Something unusual about this case?" Cantrelle asked warily.

"We think so. The patient's on his way down now. You'll have a chance to see for yourself," Moyer tendered.

He didn't like being set up for some surprise, or coup, or check, or whatever the hell they intended this morning with their crafty play of mystery. If they didn't look so genuinely concerned he would take them to task for it.

"Some unusual symptom? Just when you think you've seen it all some new variation on the symptom complex turns up to remind you that . . . . "

He was interrupted by a knock on the door.

"That's probably the patient now," Moyer announced. "Come in," he called.

An aide entered, leading a patient by the hand. The patient covered his face with his free hand to suppress the low giggling. The sight immediately chilled the room.

Cantrelle winced in vague recognition as the patient was led to the chair at the head of the table and helped into place. The low giggling continued.

"Frank, I think you remember John Frieden," Moyer suggested.

He indeed did, and now did so with a sickening wrench. It was the patient who needed his "snow," the one who reckoned that Blush would claim him sooner or later, the one who said that his only chance was to come to them for help and had come voluntarily, the one who had contributed the first sample of Blush for science's go at it. And now it had happened to him. His doom had been consummated and he now sat before them as an indictment of their helplessness, a validation of their failure. He was more gaunt now, more dilapidated, more wrecked, and he flushed luridly as his giggle set a sardonic glee upon the sacrifice so visibly in process.

"I remember him," Cantrelle moaned above his dismay. Then, steeling himself, he leaned closer to the patient. "Mr. Frieden, can you hear me?"

The patient looked up as he lowered his hand. Through the giggling he blinked to bring Cantrelle into focus. His eyes then widened in recognition.

"Doc—heh-heh—Doc—heh. I told you so—heh-heh—I told you so—heh, heh, heh." The giggling then deepened into something closer to sobs as he lowered his head into his hands.

Cantrelle had had enough.

"I think you can take him back now," he motioned to the aide who came and gently led the patient away.

They sat in tortured silence for a few moments to let the flood of misery ebb a bit. Then, too soon, it was his turn to speak.

"He tried, but he couldn't stay away from that heroin, damn it," he groaned.

"But as far as we can tell, he did," Moyer corrected.

"How do you mean?" puzzled Cantrelle, still shaken.

"I mean as far as we can tell, he didn't get it from heroin," Moyer announced.

"What?" Cantrelle blurted.

"Frank, according to what Dr. Aranzuela was able to get from the history, he did stay away from heroin but had switched his habit to Crack months ago. It looks like he got it from Crack," Moyer stated.

He felt all eyes looking at him, waiting for him to—to what? He didn't know what to give them because he didn't know what he felt. Confusion? Panic, more likely; the panic of yet another unwitting, pleasing basic assumption being shattered. He felt like running—not from them but from *it*, this nightmare that seemed to be expanding beyond all possible comprehension. Got it from *Crack*? His head roared with the impossible ramifications. *Crack*? That had to be wrong. It had to be *heroin* because that was all his understanding could see, could accept.

"Dr. Aranzuela," he challenged in desperation, "are you sure? He could have gotten some heroin anyway, you know."

"According to the friends who brought him here last night, he did not use the heroin anymore and he tried to get his friends to stay away from it because of the danger. He used only Crack and sometimes Speed, but never heroin for the past several months. His friends swear to it. And the drug screen confirms it. Negative for the heroin," she stated, "but positive for cocaine."

Cantrelle felt himself retreating into mute acceptance of the catastrophic realization that Blush also had crossed a line.

"Frank, I think you know what this means," Moyer pressed.

"I think it means we'd better check our data damned well before we say a hell of a lot more," Cantrelle cautioned frantically, still groping.

"My guess is that our data, and probably soon enough other people's data, are going to say pretty much what we're too afraid to admit right now: that Blush is really just beginning," Moyer predicted. "All along we've joked among ourselves about what would happen if, for instance, it got into the beer. Frank, you've now got to know that whoever is putting it into heroin—and now, Crack—can sure as hell put it into anything else, depending on who's the target."

He was right, although it was abhorrent to admit it, and maybe to do so revealed that he, too, all along had covertly accepted on some conveniently obscure level in himself the fuller meaning of Blush, but only so far as it chose its victims with proper concern for the better interests of society. While he could mount a resolute *medical* assault upon Blush, the *societal* side of his being might be insidiously less opposed to its wicked existence, just like all the countless, nameless others he excoriated. Why the hell did this have to come up this morning? The call to NIH was now all the more inevitable, and not just from the narrower perspective of heroin addiction, for damned sure.

The room fell silent again as a consensus of despair took effect. Finally, Cantrelle spoke up.

"There's little more we can do at this point but to wait for additional cases. Dr. Berends will alert his people in the Triage Unit, I'm sure. But, please," he directed at the residents, "don't say too much until we're sure we know what we're talking about." The tone of dismissal thus given, he then turned back to Moyer and Morello. "I came here specifically to see you two this morning about something pretty closely related. Can we go to your office, Clay?"

"Of course," Moyer complied.

The conference room emptied and Moyer led Cantrelle and Morello up the hallway to his office. Neither spoke until Moyer manipulated the key into the lock.

"I sure hope it actually was heroin, somehow," Morello registered redundantly.

"But the way our luck's been running . . ." Cantrelle lamented in banal reply.

They entered Moyer's office and found chairs for resuming the parley.

"I want to call NIH and talk to your friend, Landon, about Blush's action. I was hoping you would have his number," Cantrelle directed at Morello. "We really should finish the second paper, Clay, and especially so after what we saw a few minutes ago with poor

Frieden. Isn't it wonderful to be the first on the scene for these catastrophes? We know that the pathophysiology of Blush is the key to any prevention program, right? Our little paper doesn't pretend to any such grand thing, but we need to know something about Blush's action in order to complete the paper which might in some way help in assessing the value of early intervention when that's possible in confirmed cases. You know, the ones prevention misses. Like the very case this morning, as a matter of fact." He liked the sound of that afterthought.

"I don't know his work number offhand, but I know the section he works in, and we can call there, I guess," Morello ventured.

"I suppose that'll do," Cantrelle agreed. "What's the section?"

"It's NIH, Molecular Biology, D-7," Morello supplied. "I think that should be enough to scramble him."

"Do you think he'll be able to explain to us what we're fooling around with? And over the phone? That stuff's pretty high power. I can't follow it even when it's in print right before my eyes," Moyer despaired.

"Me, too," Cantrelle allowed, "but maybe he can give us an overview of the way Blush works and then perhaps some leads as to where to go for the details. I wouldn't even know where to begin looking if we had to do it on our own. I tried to do some reading this morning in basic immunology," he explained as he reached for the phone, "and I got lost before I started."

He then dialed his secretary.

"No one local who could help?" Morello asked.

"No one I know of," he replied. "Oh, Mrs. Andretti? . . . . Would you please put in a call to NIH, Bethesda, Maryland. It comes under HHS, as you know. We want to talk to a Jeffrey Landon of the Molecular Biology Section, D-7," he detailed as he looked at Morello for confirmation. Morello nodded in affirmation. "Yes, and we'll be in Mr. Moyer's office at extension 1347 . . . . Right. Thanks." He then hung up.

"So where do you think things stand now, Dr. Cantrelle?" Morello broached.

"You mean about Frieden?" Cantrelle evaded.

"Yes, if it's true that he got it from Crack," Morello specified.

"I'm not sure, " Cantrelle dissembled to buy time. "If it's true, then we've been living in a fool's paradise thinking that the heroin group was the sole victim pool. I just don't know how we could *ever* handle the number of patients we would get if Blush were to spread through Crack as it has through the heroin crowd. I just don't know. The prospect is overwhelming."

"And final," Moyer added sententiously.

"How do you mean that, Clay?" Cantrelle asked through his puzzlement.

"It's something that I've . . . ."

Just then the phone rang. Cantrelle didn't hesitate.

"Dr. Cantrelle," he answered. "Thanks, Mrs. Andretti," he granted after a moment of being apprised. Then, hand over mouthpiece, he said to the others, "She got him. Let's put this on conference." He pushed the button on the receiver and lowered the phone from his ear.

"Mr. Landon is on the line, Dr. Cantrelle," her voice came through the speaker.

"Hello, Dr. Cantrelle?" Landon's voice followed.

"Good morning, Mr. Landon. This is Dr. Cantrelle. How are you?"

"Fine. And yourself, Dr. Cantrelle?"

"Fine. Thank you," he replied.

"And how's Ellie, Dr. Cantrelle?" Landon inquired brightly.

"She's fine, too. She sends her regards. She explained this morning that you plan to be in town for her graduation," Cantrelle acknowledged.

"You bet, Doctor. She's all revved up for college, as you know, and she has so many questions," he explained in redoubtable innocence.

"Of course, Mr. Landon," Cantrelle agreed in compliance. "By the way," he added, "this is a conference call and I've got your old friend, Dr. Morello, here. Also Mr. Moyer. You may remember him from the party."

The three of them smiled among themselves at the moment of awkward silence that followed from the other end.

"How you doing, old buddy?" Morello spoke in rescue. "Still up to tricks?"

"I'm doing O.K. And yourself?" Landon replied in recovery.

"Hunky-dory. I'm all revved up for graduation too, I'll have you know. Seven more weeks and I'm legitimate," Morello teased.

"Well, maybe you'll finally have a piece of paper that says so," retaliated Landon.

Cantrelle snickered at the youthful repartee. He was beginning to take to this forthright young man.

"Mr. Landon," Moyer entered, "I'm Clay Moyer. You may remember me from Dr. Cantrelle's party. Good morning."

"Good morning to you, Mr. Moyer," Landon replied. "Yes, I do remember you. You're co-author with Dr. Cantrelle of that paper on Blush. In fact, you and I talked about a follow-up paper you and Dr. Cantrelle planned to write."

"Indeed we did, Mr. Landon," Moyer acknowledged, pleased that Landon had retained the occasion.

"Mr. Moyer," Landon continued, "I hope to get an advance copy of that paper when it becomes available. I'm putting in my bid now, if you don't mind."

"We'll see to it, Mr. Landon," Moyer assured.

Cantrelle felt himself really taking to the cut of this young man's jib.

"Mr. Landon," he spoke up, "that's very close to the reason we've called you this morning. In effect, we have to know something—but it doesn't have to be very detailed—something about Blush's action in setting up the progressive degeneration seen in the affected brain structures. The few articles that have come out so far are either too technical for us to understand or too general for us to use. So we thought we'd come to you because we knew you'd started some work on pretty much the area we have in mind. We understand that the degenerative action is thought to be an auto-immune process, and the little reading I've done recently on that topic hasn't clarified my thinking, I can assure you."

"Right," Landon agreed in sympathy. "I can tell you what the thinking is and maybe you can take from it what you need. But I'm sure you all realize that in talking about this stuff it's easy to fall into technical jargon. I'll try not to do that, and, anyway, you can bring up questions as I go along. If it seems I'm just reeling this stuff off from the top of my head and you're impressed, please don't be. All I'll be doing is paraphrasing a few introductory paragraphs from my research proposal, and lately I've sure had ample occasion to recite those labored passages to all who would hear."

Cantrelle was indeed impressed, but mostly by the way this young man handled himself.

"So I've heard. Please go on, Mr. Landon," Cantrelle urged.

"First off," Landon began, "it's pretty well agreed that the Blush effect—you know, the flushing, the giggling, and the obtunding of peripheral awareness; that initial clinical reaction which brings the patient to medical attention—is the result of a direct stimulating effect on the mid-brain structures, especially the thalami and the hypothalamic areas. The sighing that goes along with the giggling comes from disruption of the normal autonomic rhythm of the respiratory center, a kind of preferential stimulation there as well. At that point in the clinical picture there is no evidence yet of an auto-immune reaction, only a stage we call the activation stage, meaning that the affected structures—the thalami, the hypothalamic areas, and the respiratory centers—are showing some exaggeration of their usual physiologic activity because of the direct stimulation by the physical presence of the Blush molecule at those receptor sites. Follow me so far?"

They all grunted affirmatively.

"O.K.," Landon acknowledged. "It seems that as the initial stimulation, or activation phase, begins to subside, like after two weeks or so, as your people see clinically when the patients' flushing and giggling begin to settle down and he becomes quieter and withdrawn, that's when the auto-immune response is beginning to kick in. In fact, the transition from the activation stage to the quieter phase when the patient begins to show withdrawal and dementia is felt to be caused by the onset of the auto-immune process itself. You can think of it as the affected brain cells no longer being merely stimulated into heightened activity but now being attacked by the auto-immune process and beginning to lose their function as a result. Now we're going from too much physiologic activity to not enough. But to understand how the auto-immune process brings that about we have to back up a little."

All three were now rapt in their attention to the words coming out of the telephone console. Cantrelle prayed that the switchboard, theirs or his, would not revert to type this morning.

"The molecular assay of Blush so far suggests that it's a macro-molecule of molecular weight in the neighborhood of 250,000, with cycling conjugated peptide chains of about 15,000. The peptide chains are probably morphologically similar to the standard cephalins of your normal brain tissue but with a linkage signature duplicating the particular peptide sequence found in those cell clusters for which it has affinity; namely the cell clusters in the thalami, the hypothalamus, and the respiratory centers. Think of those peptide sequences as one of the ingredients in the protein makeup of those cells with the Blush macromolecule being drawn specifically to them at their three cluster sites. A parallel would be something like iron being present in many different utensils, though the utensils share little in external morphology or function. Blush is then like a magnetized particle drawn to the cellular surfaces of those clusters on the basis of their common peptide configuration and receptor morphology just like a magnetized particle would be drawn to the various utensils because of their iron content. A neat trick in matching the peptide configuration of a conjugated synthetic agonist to that of a discrete and uniquely localized group of CNS structures."

"Mr. Landon," Cantrelle inquired pointedly, "when you say conjugated, do you mean that just descriptively?"

"You mean, am I implying something about its manufacture?" Landon quickly supplied.

"Yes," Cantrelle responded. This boy was really on his toes, he delighted.

"As far as can be said now, it is *synthetically* fabricated. I say that because the spacing of the haptens, plus the peptide-hapten coding itself, pretty much takes the linkage sequence out of the realm of the naturally occurring," he explained.

The water was getting noticeably deeper and each seemed to be trying to sit a little higher in his chair to keep his head above its rising surface. Landon paused for a moment to let his points come to rest before proceeding anew. Cantrelle checked the others to assess their readiness to proceed.

"Hapten coding?" Morello whispered, palms up in befuddlement.

Cantrelle wasn't sure either.

"Mr. Landon," he mewed, "before you go on could you clarify the idea of 'hapten coding'? Sounds like it's a critical element in the architecture of the peptide, so I guess we ought to be clear about it."

"Right, Dr. Cantrelle," Landon agreed readily. "As you may remember from your medical school basic course in allergy, people develop sensitivity reactions to many substances—strawberries, penicillin, pollen, and so forth. Some of these sensitivities may go on to full blown allergies whereby the person's system is so sensitive that even in minute amounts the allergen is able to incite a massive and often dangerous response such as sometimes is the case with bee stings. The particular molecule that causes the allergic response in the first place is called a hapten and may be only a small part of the overall molecule; its so-called 'hot spot.' That particular piece of the molecule, because of its unique configuration, will cause an allergic response in the host no matter what other kind of molecule it may be attached to. For example, if you took the 'hot spot' from a strawberry molecule someone had become allergic to, purified it and attached it to the basic molecule of oatmeal, that person would then be allergic to the oatmeal as well. Follow?"

"Yes, we're following," Cantrelle replied.

"The next step is this," Landon continued. "Because the host, the allergic person, reacts to the hot spot as he does, much like an inflammatory response to the invasion of pathogenic bacteria, a typical antibody response is established by the person's system. The body produces antibodies to combat, meaning deactivate, the allergen's hot spot and delimit the damage it may do to those cells sensitive to it. And now you have a full-blown allergy. That hot spot component of the offending molecule is the hapten, and the antibodies formed are specific for that hapten. O.K.?"

"We're with you," Cantrelle reported.

"Well, now it gets a little tricky," Landon cautioned. "When we begin to talk about auto-immune reactions we talk about the body's sensitivity reaction being directed at a part of itself. How that comes about is something like this. A hapten enters the body and selectively affects certain cells. The body's reaction results in the release into fluid spaces—the bloodstream and so forth—certain component parts of the affected cells, sort of like debris from the damage done. That debris is composed of molecular structures unique to those cells. The debris is also a complex protein. With that protein debris running loose in the bloodstream it itself is now regarded by the immune system as a foreign element against which antibodies are to be produced, just as though it were the protein of invading bacteria. Antibodies are thus formed against those free-running complex protein molecules. But antibodies, being as single-minded as they are, denature not only the liberated proteins but also similar protein still functionally intact in host cells thus far unaffected or only marginally damaged. Now those cells too come under assault, but this time by the system's own antibodies. So more and more cells are broken down, with more and more protein debris released to incite more and more antibody formation for more and more assault upon the remaining functioning but perhaps damaged cells."

"Runaway fashion, huh?" Cantrelle observed, more for the others than for himself. This much of the process he was already fairly familiar with.

"Very much so," Landon concurred. "Where Blush comes into the picture is that its 250,000 macromolecule is by and large merely the carrier for the special hapten that makes Blush what it is, immunologically speaking. The particular peptide sequence of this macromolecule allows for the special spacing and positioning of the Blush hapten in order for it to achieve its effect—a sensitivity reaction—by combining with the molecular configuration of the targeted cell wall protein. It's like a template had been gotten from the molecular configuration of the particular cell wall protein and a macromolecule built to fit it with the activating haptens included in just the right sequence to set off a sensitivity reaction, and in just the cells of the thalami, the hypothalamus, and the respiratory center because of the receptive configuration there. A very exquisite piece of work, I can tell you."

"So we gather," Morello agreed solemnly.

"Oh, but it gets even better, old buddy," Landon chirped. "Now that we have the hapten-macromolecule conjugate squared away we can look at the hapten itself, the thing that gets the whole grisly process going. Remember, the haptens are positioned on the macromolecule chain in such locations and in such a sequence as to have a specific and unique affinity for the cell *groups* in the thalami, the hypothalamus, and in the respiratory center, and even to specific cell *clusters* within those cell groups as in the case of the thalami. Plus, the haptens have the ability to incite those cells to some exaggerated physiologic response—the flushing, the giggling, and so forth. If that's the case—and it is—then the haptens must be coupling with some receptor site on those cells for the cells to be goaded into those responses, which ordinarily are normal human responses in the emotional repertoire. We all blush and giggle when we need to. So, apparently, these are normal receptor sites being activated; and thus the hapten, the hot spot conjugated to the carrier macromolecule, would have to be something similar to what we already know about the various molecules, or agonists, capable of combining naturally with those receptor sites. A lot of work has been done over the past twenty years in determining the number and types of different receptors, as well as their locations in the central nervous system. The mapping of these locations has been vital in understanding the physiology of CNS function, and, I might add, the biologic substrate of the symptoms of mental illness, which I'm sure you know a lot more about than I ever will."

"Don't take it for granted," Cantrelle gloomed.

"Believe him, Dr. Cantrelle; he doesn't know anywhere near as much about it as we do. You may proceed, smart ass," Morello directed.

I'll dance at your wedding, too," Landon threatened, and then after a shared guffaw, resumed. "So we're down to the molecular structure of the hapten itself. Well, according to very recent assays, like maybe week before last from what my associates here tell me, the hapten turns out to be a variation on the iminodibenzyl ring which is, as you know, the basic molecule in your various major tranquilizer, anti-psychotic medications such as the old standby, Chlorpromazine. But this particular variation has several unusual radicals added which apparently fit it to a subset of dopaminergic receptor sites significantly different from those keyed to the parent anti-psychotic medication molecule. Those targeted receptor sites, activated by these dopamine-like agents, are apparently located only in the structures attacked by Blush; namely the thalami, the hypothalamus, and the respiratory center. The chemical activity of the radicals plus the spacing and sequencing of the hapten on the macromolecular chain seem to provide the dopaminergic signature which singles out the dopamine receptor sites of those particular cells for the physiological effect we see as the symptoms of Blush. But those dopamine receptor sites have to be different from the ones previously identified elsewhere in the CNS, otherwise Blush would affect the others as well, and it doesn't. So it seems Blush has defined a previously unknown subset of dopamine receptor sites and has pretty much established their location. I understand the paper you and Mr. Moyer are presently working on will correlate that receptor site damage with clinical behavior, and especially with evolving neuro-psych findings. Right?"

"That's our hope, Mr. Landon," Cantrelle sighed, distinctly abashed by the histochemical complexity being arrayed before him.

"Your first paper sure framed the problem so that work could get started. Don't stop now or else some people might begin to think that Blush is going away if the human side of it isn't kept visible."

"Glory, glory," Morello intoned.

"We feel the same way, Mr. Landon," Cantrelle added. "Of course, that's why we called you this morning."

"Right," Landon replied, gently returned to his task. "Well, I don't have that much more to add. The new dopamine receptor site, the one that Blush hits, is being called D 8 alpha, or D8A for short. We all predict a great future for it."

"Mr. Landon," Cantrelle queried, "do you and your people think Blush was fabricated with those receptor sites in mind?"

"You mean, did someone already have knowledge of these receptor sites from some previous research and then proceed to build a macromolecule, plus the hapten, and then put them together in that coded sequence to achieve the physiologic and subsequently lethal auto-immune effect Blush brings? God, I hope not. Anyone who could do that would be so far ahead of us we would never catch up. But some people around here do fear exactly that, but they're in the minority. Most people believe that the Blush molecule probably occurred as an accidental by-product in some other research and that someone happened to notice its singular effect, perhaps through a likewise accidental ingestion. Or maybe in some animal studies as a preliminary to some drug acceptance work. I tend to go along with the latter. In any event, whoever isolated the Blush macromolecule, whether by accident or by design, knows an awful lot about molecular biology as well as histochemistry, I can assure you."

"Mr. Landon, we're all quite impressed by the complexity of the work you've described, even though you scaled it down to the fearfully simple for our benefit . . . ."

"Well . . ." Landon demurred.

"Oh, yes, and we appreciate it, because now we know enough to have a few sensible answers—and questions—in mind," Cantrelle asserted. "One question kept going through my mind while you were instructing us was who would go to such elegant trouble to poison people? And my associates here have wondered if your people there in Washington speculate about that, too."

"More to the point, Dr. Cantrelle," he pursued, "is the question who is *capable* of going to all that trouble. Blush is no basement operation, I can assure you. Conjugating the hapten to the macromolecule in just the right code sequence bespeaks a technologic capability not available just anywhere. Plus the outlay in resources. Formidable. In fact, that was exactly the question I raised at a local symposium about a month ago."

"What are the possibilities, Mr. Landon?" Moyer inquired with a seditious half smile.

"Only a few really. Germany, certainly. They're right behind us. Russia probably could, but they've been thrown pretty much out of step with the breakup of the Soviet system. Maybe they've fallen too far behind by now. England, definitely, but they're not putting much of their research budget into molecular biology these days. France and Sweden, the same. China is just beginning to get into the field. Japan is a sleeper; they have the technology as well as the skill and the money, but the small amount of work they've done so far in the field is more tentative and exploratory, as far as we know."

"What about Central America?" Moyer posed.

"God, no! As far as research in molecular biology goes, those people can hardly brew the coffee they grow," Landon yelped.

Morello snickered as Cantrelle smiled indulgently.

"Thank you, Mr. Landon," Moyer replied.

"Anything else, gentlemen? Dr. Cantrelle?" Landon offered.

Cantrelle looked at the others to see if there were any other questions in readiness. There weren't.

"Just one or two more things, Mr. Landon, and then we'll turn you loose. By the way, this is the longest conference call I've ever made without the switchboard bringing it to a violent and premature end. Anyway, in your explanation about the relationship of the hapten siting on the Blush macromolecule and its effect at the receptor site on the membrane of the affected cell, I didn't catch how the hapten, or the macromolecule, or both, caused the breakdown of components of the cell and how those breakdown products figured in the antigen reaction that followed. Does Blush cease its action after the breakdown products assume antigenic potency, the antibodies themselves carrying on the auto-immune reaction, or does Blush continue to hang around as a catalyst to keep the reaction going, sort of like a chemical gray eminence?"

"Hah!" exclaimed Landon. "Dr. Cantrelle, that was exactly my question in the research proposal I submitted! I suspect that Blush hangs around in some capacity because if it didn't and the patient's course simply followed that of the typical auto-immune disorder, such as multiple sclerosis, we'd expect to see fits and starts and remissions and exacerbations in patients' clinical course, and we don't. All we see is a relentless progression of symptoms until death occurs. Also, if it were just the typical auto-immune process not pushed along by the continued presence of the inciting agent we could dampen the process and slow down its progression with drugs like cortisone, which suppress such reactions. But we've found no way to alter the clinical course. And, of course, if it can be shown that Blush remains active in the host to hasten the process along, that would be the first step in seeking some agent that could block Blush's action, both from the standpoint of preventing new cases as well as in arresting the disorder in cases already established."

"But Ellie mentioned just this morning that your proposal hasn't been approved. How come, Mr. Landon? Sounds like a basic point to me," Cantrelle puzzled.

"It is, or so I think, Dr. Cantrelle," Landon agreed. "I'm told that the review committee was informed that all future research on Blush will be integrated through a special task force set up for that purpose. The chairman of the task force will be appointed by the Secretary himself and all government-funded research on Blush will have to be cleared by his advisory committee and integrated into the overall research strategy, if approved. They're trying to cut costs and prevent duplication. My stipend comes from the government, so I'm included in the net, so broadly cast it is."

"Think they'll work you and your project in?" Cantrelle asked, feeling the sympathy of kindred abuse.

"I don't know. So far they've been cool to the idea of grad students doing their dissertation work in the ranks of such a high-powered task force. I think they fear our presence would have a diluting effect upon the intensity of the task force mission. Of course, I think otherwise," Landon sniffed. "So, I've been put on hold, as the odious phrase runs."

"You could transfer to somewhere else, stalwart crusader friend of mine," Morello broached.

"The thought has crossed my mind, steady campaigner of good stripe," Landon returned.

Cantrelle immediately thought of Ellie and wondered what discussions she and Jeffrey Landon had had on the matter.

"I'll stick it out here for a while till I know better what's what," Landon continued, "and in the meantime I'll finish up on a few courses I need anyway."

Cantrelle regretted the relief he felt at Landon's plan to stay where he was. Mean-minded, to be sure, but for the moment he would prefer Ellie and this otherwise fine young fellow carry out their romantic explorations of each other at a discreet distance. He wasn't yet ready to donate his daughter to anyone else.

"I'm sure you'll do what you think best, Mr. Landon," Cantrelle offered disingenuously, "and we all wish you the best. If there's any way we can be of help to you, please let us know. I want to thank you for your time and your generous help in briefing us this morning. We're all quite impressed with the subject as well as your sure grasp of it."

"There is one thing, Dr. Cantrelle," Landon suggested.

"Yes?"

"Would you please tell Ellie I'll call this Thursday night?" he requested. "I'm hoping we can set up some plans."

"Sure thing," Cantrelle chuckled. This boy was really ballsy. He liked it, but he worried about it, too.

"Thank you, Dr. Cantrelle. It's been a pleasure. And you, too, Mr. Moyer. Even you, Dr. John. I'll be in touch. Bye," he flourished. All three bade him good-bye, and then the console clicked into silence, followed by the buzz tone.

They sat silently for a long moment, each estimating the size of what had been said. A shifting in the seats soon followed as they became aware of each other's absorption. Cantrelle then returned the phone to the receiver. The buzzing tone stopped and now the room was as silent as they.

"I guess you thought it better not to mention about the Crack just yet, Chief," Morello spoke up in offer of a marshaling point.

"I think it's better we keep that information local until we know it's not an isolated event. Just like we did before. And besides, we have to notify Dr. Weaver first. God, wait till he hears about this," Cantrelle sighed, his thinking a bit scattered yet and in search of some focus. He scanned the other two: Morello sat with his face wreathed in expectant perplexity while Clay slouched in his chair and nodded almost imperceptibly through a cynical half smile. Cantrelle decided to return to the hovering dread. "Of course," he began in contrived debate, "Landon could be way off base in his sizing up of the technologic infrastructure in Blush's fabrication. Someone just might have bumbled into a simple procedure for its manufacture, like the MPTP episode in San Francisco a few years back. You never can tell."

Moyer looked like he was trying to see merit in Cantrelle's assessment. His smile broadened as he gently shook his head. He then spoke.

"Frank, we all know that's not the case, attractive as it sounds. I think Landon is on target. In fact, probably too much on target for some touchy people out there; probably the people right around him who would prefer a simpler view of the issue, just as you yourself are demonstrating right now. No, I think he's right and he's being penalized for it," Moyer lowered. "They're trying to muzzle him, too, just as they tried to muzzle us."

Moyer's remark stung for its accuracy, and Cantrelle found himself nodding in agreement as the words penetrated.

"You're right, Clay. Just grasping, I suppose," Cantrelle conceded. "But who would bother to go to all the trouble of poisoning the heroin, and now the Crack, trade? And kill a lot of Americans in the process? So it's *not* a global battle between drug sovereignties, but maybe someone angling for *complete* world power in the drug trade and using this means to demonstrate a capacity for it! Is that possible? Or maybe it's more a political thing. Christ, could it be a sequel to the Cuban missile crisis with die-hard Communists now using Blush instead of nuclear warheads to twist our arm? Or Japan's entry into the Western Hemisphere, Bushido fashion? Possibly. I don't think it could be Germany. They're still too appalled by their behavior under Hitler. Maybe it . . . ."

"It's none of those, Frank," Moyer interrupted, "and you know it."

Cantrelle froze in silence, afraid to anticipate.

"Frank, we both know," Moyer continued almost gently, "it's being done by us, by the government of the United States of America. And we're all being waved off—you, me, your daughter's suitor, and anybody else whose nosiness threatens to get too close to the source of Blush and its strategists. Landon will never get his research prospectus approved by that graduate studies review committee; not if he stays where he is and if NIH has anything to do with it. He'll probably never be included in that Task Force, no matter how good his ideas are, simply because he's an honest, idealistic, and decent young fellow who would never lend himself to political murder, like those German scientists you mentioned a moment ago certainly did. I think he smells a rat, too, and like some of us, isn't put off at following the scent for fear of where it might take him."

Cantrelle sat numb. It wasn't that he had never considered what Clay said. More, it was a matter of his having worked at not thinking about it, and had fairly well succeeded in keeping it out of his awareness. Till now. He knew Clay was right but he couldn't permit himself to believe it. Yet he could think of nothing to say in objection, for to do so would only make him feel more foolish than he already did. Having caught himself in a crass self-deception, he could do little but accept the shame he deserved and which now reduced him to silence. He felt so tired and drained, and he must have looked it, too, to reckon the concern apparent in Clay's gaze. He noted that Morello also seemed distressed that he, Cantrelle, his mentor, could be diminished so before his very eyes. It was vitally necessary to say something.

"Clay, I hope you're wrong," he managed pitiably.

"I hope so, too, Frank," Moyer soothed.

"But if it is true, then we're among the few who suspect it," Morello exulted.

"There are others," Moyer tempered.

"Even so," Cantrelle continued, trying to regain himself, "if we're on the verge of something big, then what's our responsibility? God, finishing the paper now seems so trivial. Clay, I swear I hope you're wrong. I wouldn't know what the hell to do next if you're right."

"That's fitting," Moyer agreed, "because from here on in it *is* free form. You do what you think you have to do. I should tell you, Frank, that I'll probably take a step I thought I never would, but after this morning I think I have to. Sorry."

Cantrelle wasn't sure he wanted to know.

Moyer smiled at Cantrelle's grimace and continued.

"Oh, it's not really that bad," Moyer salved, "just tasteless. Because of those talks I've been giving and of which you've silently disapproved and barely tolerated I've been solicited for a couple of those daytime talk shows. I know, the low road; you don't have to say it. I've declined each time, for obvious reasons. Now, I think I have to appear and say what I think should be said to the many and mild, to the singularly weak but electorally mighty. In a word, the unwashed."

Cantrelle felt more amused than alarmed. In fact, the thought carried the ring of mischievous retaliation.

"Without clearing it through DMH first?" Cantrelle teased.

"They would shit a brick," Moyer retorted.

Morello exploded in relieved laughter, which seemed to sunder the confines of the meeting.

"Good luck, Clay," Cantrelle offered. "But for the nonce, I think we've turned ourselves inside out enough for one morning, fellow reprobates. Waddaya say we bag it and get back to our pencils? Clay, let's get the paper finished, huh?" he appealed. "I know it's more like a footnote now, but let's not be chased off. O.K.?"

"Sure, Frank," Moyer smiled.

"Right now I'm going to Administration and tell Jess about Mr. Frieden's return," Cantrelle announced glumly as he rose. "I'm also going to suggest we get ready to re-open Building Seven."

TEN

The prospect was distinctly elegiac, or so he decided as he gazed through the glass fronting of the building on to the flowing greensward of the hospital grounds. With one foot mounted on the edge of the settee positioned at the windowed wall he leaned forward, arms gathered at rest on his knee in the traditional stance of the pensive military commander envisioning the yet unjoined battle on some waiting field. Unjoined was right; battle, he wasn't so sure. But, for certain, it was going to be different.

He calculated that this was the thirteenth—what a hell of a note; thirteenth!—resident graduation since he took the job as Director. It was the thirteenth, annual, Last-Friday-In-June event to be held in the monolithic glass, concrete, and stainless steel architectural *tour de force à la* late Eisenhower, the hospital's newest addition to its plant, its Community Center, as it was called. For the event it would girdle a procession of giddy graduating residents, their bubbly families and friends, the fairly standard nuclear group of teaching staff and supervisors, a deciduous periphery of general well-wishers, and a varying sample of the merely curious. Ordinarily, the turnout totaled about a hundred—large enough to be official, but wieldy enough to be accommodated cozily in the nicely appointed lounge just off the building's lobby. This year the advance inquiries and the frank requests for invitations guaranteed an attendance at least double the usual with the result that the ceremony was now scheduled to be held in one of the building's larger conference wings called the General Purpose Room. The question had arisen as to whether or not the ceremony should be held in the auditorium, a suggestion he had scotched out of hand in open abhorrence of the notion that a solemn graduation be cast in the bandstand and show biz ambience of that six-hundred-seat cavern. No, there had to be genuine, natural light, plus blooming flowers almost close enough to touch. Since it could not be managed in the airy lounge, it was thus the windowed General Purpose Room where he now pondered in distant espy how this sort of thing comes to be.

The increase in attendance was no mystery, he could see. Burleson drew well no matter where he spoke, or about what. But there seemed to be so much more to it than that, if rumor could be believed. Of the probably representative sample of callers who had inquired about the ceremony particulars, about as many mentioned Clay as they did Burleson, Mrs. Andretti had discreetly informed him. Small wonder, though, in view of Clay's remarkable performance on that talk show. Three weeks had passed and people were still buzzing about it. Clay had certainly added to his forum credentials with that appearance, and his public visibility had perforce become a given on the basis of that ringing performance. The talk show improved its own rating as well with Clay's contribution. For the occasion the show had set aside its Freaks and Sex venue and featured Clay's interview as the main item, and in so doing struck an uncharacteristically sober and responsible note in serving the public interest. Even the show's host managed to present himself as a serious and concerned commentator/interviewer in place of his usual leering, peeping Tomism, a transition facilitated no doubt by Clay's controlled and closely reasoned commentary. And, probably, unspoken sympathies of the network's staff were also at play. The live audience, usually given to the hooting and hollering of a circus side show, shared the host's sober demeanor, and the net effect came off more as a documentary on Blush and its lethality being a fell instrument of social remedy. Clay's description of the progression of Blush's symptoms was wholly arresting to an audience which had more fear than information on the matter, and his concise and simplified review of Blush's effect on the nervous system's cells, making appropriate comparisons to multiple sclerosis and Parkinson's disease to use familiarity with those naturally occurring disorders as a bridge to understanding, carried the viewers immeasurably closer to an apprehension of Blush as a most evil agent, regardless the pedigree of its designated victims. The program's host came into his own at this point and through carefully crafted questions opened the discussion to speculations deriving of Clay's objective observations. Clay, tactically prepared for the moment, and the host, now firmly fitted to the role of responsible facilitator, engaged in a riveting disquisition of the role of powerful but unidentified interests in the fabrication and distribution of Blush. It was at this juncture Clay stated that his information pointed to the U.S. Federal government as the most likely genius behind Blush, and that some section or division of the NSA was the probable agency responsible for the overall implementation of a policy of eradication using Blush as its instrument. The grave questions which followed as to the political and social import of such a policy achieved a tone of realpolitik never before known to that particular talk show. It also was a tone which the network and the viewers both seemed eager to revisit in light of the fact that Clay was invited to return, the date not yet specified. But this time Clay was to be the moderator of a panel of experts ready to pursue speculations right along with him. Confessed child molesters and teenage prostitutes were out and social philosophy and shadow government were in.

And certainly Clay was in, after a fashion. Long regarded by most who knew him and by all who disliked him as a grousing cynic unable to see beyond his own dark view of the world and all its gloomy contents, he was now becoming a credible force in the public's hesitant approach to Blush and all its ramifications. Credible, but also disquieting. Previously it had been easy to write off his pronouncements of gloom and doom as just the quaint play of his prodigious reserves of choler. Now, Clay had some solid external reference points that resonated with his self-professed temperament, and the combination was becoming formidable. Martha, and even Jess, who had always regarded him with a parental and amused tolerance, now felt an uneasiness in his presence, as though at any moment he might decide to transcend their long-held workaday relationship and mount a personal hegemony derived from his soaring public status. He didn't, and Cantrelle knew he never would, but the fear was there. As for his part, Cantrelle sensed a slight but discernible shift in the residents' primary allegiance from him to Clay and to his gathering aura of celebrity as man of the hour. Here again, Clay would never foster such a shift, but sober events were now the declarative agents. Gone were the usual personal accords and polite customs. It was now no secret to himself that he envied Clay. Clay had shown real balls—and a keen responsibility—in doing what he did and for which he was now receiving deserved acclaim, no ifs, ands, or buts about it. However, it just happened to be those very balls and that very responsibility which he himself, Frank Cantrelle, had failed to show almost twenty years ago when he mewed at the challenge of publishing that paper on LSD—a paper that probably would have been as relevant then as their paper on Blush was right now—only to have it happen once again that, for lack of a special something, he was failing to follow through morally on the larger meaning of his very own thesis, thus allowing the task to become the responsibility of others, like Clay Moyer. Yes, he envied him, and he feared for him, too, as he would for himself, given a like amount of checkered prominence.

The volume of cars seeking parking places in the adjacent parking lot was picking up, he noted from his perch, and the rising tempo of bustle moved him on to another concern. Burleson. He should be arriving now, if he had not already done so to the waiting welcome of Martha and Jess at the Admin Building. It apparently was his standard procedure upon arrival at a speaking engagement to report first to the CEO of the receiving facility to pay his respects and probably also to size up the leadership before proceeding to the program's agenda. Quite likely by the time he appeared here at the Center, properly convoyed by Martha and Jess, he would already have a pretty good sense of the administrative flavor of Moreland and hence better prepared to give credit and acknowledgment where due. That was his guess, since Burleson had asked only the most basic information about the graduation exercise; like where, when, and how have you been. Cantrelle was astonished that Burleson's acceptance had gone so easily—just a phone call to his office after the hurried meeting with Jess about the Crack admission and being put through to him right away by his secretary, followed by his apparent delight in being asked, the date then being cleared by a quick check of his calendar, and all of it settled right on the spot by his forthright acceptance—and in the space of a two minute phone conversation. Settled, and see you then. No mention of honorarium, traveling expenses, nothing. It had happened so fast. Cantrelle remembered feeling that rather than being the instigator of the arrangements he was more the victim of them, swept along by the compelling and dynamic eminence of this remarkable man. Since the phone call, respective secretaries had been busy at coordinating arrangements for the event to occur as it should. As usual, all was accomplished with smart thoroughness.

Maybe. Clay's TV appearance had certainly added a new dimension to the graduation, a dimension which wasn't present when Burleson accepted the invitation. Would he have accepted so readily, or at all, if he had been asked *after* Clay's TV appearance? No hint had come from his office, Mrs. Andretti assured, of any misgivings or equivocation subsequent to Clay's public èclat, word of which must certainly have reached Burleson swiftly enough. His one subsequent conversation with Burleson, a brief one to confirm each other's readiness, went without reference to any change in the temper of the occasion. But, still and all, Burleson had to have some reservations now that the ceremony, thanks to Clay, had acquired in the anticipation of many the character of a looming polemic one might enter as guest speaker only with careful forethought. Maybe Burleson knew all of that only too well from the very start and simply was not in the least fazed by it, as some lesser person, like one Frank Cantrelle, would certainly be. Probably. Plus, fretting over it, as he was now doing, was just another one of those spontaneous and natural indicators revealing the narrowness of his little world as compared to the broad and unfettered horizons of someone like Burleson.

He was just reaching the sour conclusion that looking through windows was no more edifying than staring at walls when Mrs. Andretti approached.

"Dr. Cantrelle," she inserted gently, "Dr. Weaver just called and said that he, Dr. Burleson, and Dr. Corley are on their way over now."

"Thank you, Mrs Andretti," he sighed. He then reluctantly resumed the full upright and checked his watch. Five minutes before nine. Time for him to make his way to the gathering, inspect the seating arrangements at the speaker's table, count once again the ribboned diplomas lined up in readiness on the table, adjust the height of the microphone at the lectern, verify that the sound system was operational, set the volume to forbid feedback hum, scan the floral arrangements and the refreshment table goodies, and say hello to a few people. His little world, indeed.

He followed Mrs. Andretti down the short hallway to the General Purpose room. As he neared, a clamor of chatter, laughter, and rustling chairs arose as though the volume on a radio mob scene were being turned up with each step he took. He then entered the bright, semi-circular room and was momentarily overwhelmed by a wall of noise and the sheer number of people present. The room was filled to capacity, and people were still arriving. Housekeeping staff were scurrying about with extra folding chairs as people fitted themselves into corners and alcoves. Probably should have used the auditorium, he now acknowledged too late. The two front rows of seats, those for the graduating residents and their immediate families, still stood reserved for that purpose exclusively, thank God, and had not been pre-empted by desperate attendees, a fairly good sign that some order still prevailed. But the traditional select intimacy of a Moreland resident graduation was nowhere visible this swirling morning, and that realization, perhaps foreseen though not previously experienced, banished his usual and familiar command of the event. Suddenly he felt he was doing this for the first time. Usually he didn't prepare any formal delivery, or even bother to make notes, preferring to let the tenor of the moment select his commentary for the introductions he made and for the remarks to the residents he offered in conclusion. And that usually went adequately well, suited as it was to the comfortable intimacy of the occasion. Today, it would require something more programmatic, more decorous, more epic. Why hadn't he thought of this ahead of time, damn it? He felt panic rising, and undoubtedly because the attendance now definitely included his private nightmare which was that he would stand before a great multitude to speak and be struck dumb for want of having one god-damned thing to say. How many times had he been awakened from his sleep in a cold sweat by that endlessly variable but fundamentally unchanging specter? And now it was happening for real! Thank you for coming, Dr. Burleson! He had the insane thought of slipping away for a few minutes to think of something more formally official and canonical to say so that he wouldn't come off looking like some chummy, simple hayseed adrift among the elegant. But, fortunately, he could still regard that as just an insane thought. Best brazen it out, he resolved with a heavy sigh as his fortitude hesitantly volunteered for duty. He then walked to the front of the room and began puttering about.

"Boo!" came the hoot from behind, startling him.

He turned, almost in a flinch.

"Hon! Thank God!" he exclaimed in relief.

"U.S. Cavalry, at the ready, sir," Laura saluted cutely. "It's overwhelming, isn't it? Where on earth did all these Indians come from?" she continued the allusion.

"I don't know, but my scalp is crawling," he added as he leaned over to give her the most grateful public kiss of their many years. That done, he then noticed Ellie and her companion, the recurring Jeffrey Landon—tall, thin, sandy-haired, and beaming.

"Hi, Dr. Cantrelle. Wouldn't miss this for the world," he exuded as he extended his hand. He gave a firm shake and continued in tones of accounting for his presence. "Ellie told me about this graduation two weeks ago when I was here for her graduation, so we made a date for this one as well."

"How academic of you two," Cantrelle teased as Ellie blushed.

"Just think, Dad, Mr. Clay and Dr. Burleson, together, at the same ceremony," she gushed in recovery. "I wonder what they'll talk about?"

She was openly speaking what all those blood-thirsty Indians out there were thinking, he reckoned.

"Yes, they sure are quite a combo, Sweet. But I think you're in for a disappointment. Mr. Moyer isn't one of the speakers today," he explained, feeling he should say it loud enough to be heard by everyone present.

"There's a good chance he will be, Dr. Cantrelle," Landon corrected.

Cantrelle winced in alarm. He felt the temptation to let that comment go by for fear of what he would likely find out if he pursued it. He didn't need more consternation at this moment. Worse, he immediately guessed what he would probably hear from Landon, and just now he preferred not to know. But then again, he sighed, the situation was probably already hopeless, so what the hell . . . .

"Do you know something, Jeffrey?" he probed, taking care not to convey menace.

"Well, you're probably already aware, Dr. Cantrelle," Landon flustered. ". . . I mean, I can't be sure anything'll come of it . . . but John mentioned to me that . . . ."

Morello! What the hell did he do now! His eyes widened as Landon continued.

". . . that the graduating class is going to present Mr. Moyer with an award, and they're going to ask him to say a few words. He doesn't know anything about it yet."

He doesn't know anything about it yet! Corley, Weaver, Burleson, and Cantrelle don't know anything about it yet, either! That fucking Morello, Cantrelle roared in silent outrage! That kid was up to another one of his god-damned tricks!

"Dad," entered Ellie, reading the distress on her father's face. "Jeffrey thought you should know. He didn't mean to upset you."

Cantrelle regrouped his wits enough to nod in acknowledgment.

"I guess I could have mentioned it sooner, Dr. Cantrelle, but I . . . ." Landon continued in fulsome contrition.

"No," Cantrelle interrupted, "you did the right thing, Jeffrey. It was told to you in confidence, I'm sure, and I guess I'm fortunate to learn about it at all before the fact. Maybe. Anyway, I'll be better prepared for what we know all these good people came here hoping to see."

Laura, who had stood by watchfully as the two men worked out the collision, spoke up.

"Frank, maybe it's something that should happen. Or maybe nothing at all will happen today. But so much has happened already, and it all pretty much began right here at Moreland, and maybe this is where a meeting of ideas should take place, if it can. You've said that yourself time and time again. Remember? And that's the real reason all these people are here today."

"Sure," he allowed, "but not at a graduation ceremony, or with a guest speaker who has no idea of this hidden agenda."

"Right," she agreed, "that's unfair, but it's as unfair to one as to the other because Clay doesn't know anything about it either."

That was true enough, but he didn't want to be pulled, certainly not right now, into an appreciation of what Morello would probably term a display of fine impartiality in the residents' sinister manipulations. Moreover, he knew that Laura was right. Some meeting of ideas was inevitable and probably pre-ordained for this morning, whatever the vehicles, witting or unwitting. Everybody here had sensed as much and had come prepared to witness it. But somehow *he* hadn't come thus, on either account. Had events run too far ahead for him to stay abreast of their meaning? Probably. And was Laura now working hard at bringing him up to speed? Also probably. Moreover, Morello was right, in his fashion. Some initiative had been lacking somewhere for the moment to be seized and applied in the service of Destiny. He might even envy Morello, and thus he really couldn't disapprove of him or his enterprise. And besides, it had been leveled as an accusation time and time again over the years that whatever Frank Cantrelle couldn't bring himself to do at Moreland because of conscience or office, he got his residents to do for him in the guise of their youthful and irrepressible zeal. Acting out, pure and simple, with the added benefit that he, Frank Cantrelle, rarely had to account for his covert and often sincerely unconscious guidance in their various palace coups. Usually, he could nobly mount a conciliatory tone generally acceptable to the embattled parties. Thus, he could understand full well that this graduating class was probably taking the opportunity to make a parting stab at apotheosis with their sly piece of staging on this consummate day in their young professional lives, those sneaky little fuckers. Further, the people were right, too. They felt the need of and a readiness for the next step in this saga of Blush and its challenge to the collective morality. The clinical level of diagnosis and management, of death and dying, was saying little about why Blush existed in the first place, or who created it, or what it said about all of us. Of course, it was time to elevate doubt and fear to the level of priority in the forum of academic discourse, and Clay was doing exactly that for them, just as the residents similarly were doing their scheming part in the matter for all of Moreland on this lovely Last-Friday-In-June. It was axiomatic that it never rained on graduation day at Moreland and indeed he could not remember once in thirteen years that it had. Such a beneficence in itself conferred a certain grace upon the proceedings, and if grace were ever needed . . . .

He looked up at the three expectant faces that had fallen silent during his rapid inventory of doubt, fear, and duty. Their concern urged him to reply. He smiled sheepishly, and yielded.

"Everybody and everything seems to be just so right this morning. I've prayed that such a day would never come, but I think I can get used to the idea," he simpered.

Laura circled his arm with hers and lifted herself up to plant a kiss on his bowed cheek. Ellie and Jeffrey released bright smiles and he noted that their hands touched in deft closure of this shared moment. Those damned kids, he thought, himself touched more than he cared to know.

"Oh," Laura added as an after thought, "Todd said you should tell the story about the three Frenchmen and the meaning of *savior faire* when you address the residents. He couldn't come this morning. Today's his third day on the job and he just couldn't get off. He sends his love."

"I figured as much," Cantrelle grimaced, but followed up quickly with a naughty smile. He couldn't tell that story of all stories, not to this overly decent gathering. "He hasn't forgotten that story, has he?" He was secretly delighted to know that Todd hadn't. He so wished Todd had been able to make this graduation.

"He never will, I'm ashamed to say," Laura frumped playfully.

He then looked out upon the attendance milling before him. She must have been looking at him, waiting to catch his glance because as soon as he saw her their gaze locked. Alison Dieter, more radiantly beautiful even than he remembered her, sitting several rows away among all the others, yet distinctly set apart by that nimbus of complete self-containment she wore like a vestment of rank. As he beheld her, she nodded a coolly cordial smile, which he returned more broadly. She then leaned toward a foppish-looking man sitting next to her and whispered something in his ear, directing his attention to Cantrelle. The man looked up at Cantrelle and after a moment of appraisal offered a perfunctory smile of greeting. Cantrelle returned as much, annoyed that she was confiding something about him to this suspect companion. He preferred she be here alone, like the last time they met.

"Someone you know?" Laura asked alertly.

He turned from Dieter as he spoke.

"She's the one I told you about," he replied. "The one from the DMH, Alison Dieter. She and that fellow next to her are here to check up on us, no doubt. I figured they'd send someone even though they weren't in on the selection of a speaker this time. Maybe especially because of that."

Now it was Laura's turn to give an appraising look. She spoke as she did so, the two women coolly avoiding any display of cordiality.

"She's almost your type, and a bit prettier than what you're used to, but much too calculating to write a poem for," Laura judged.

Laura was so right in her assessment. Plus, he never would have put it quite that way. How was it that women could size each other up instantly and with withering accuracy? Men generally were usually inclined to give each other the benefit of a doubt, and were just as hopeless in seeing through women as women were with men. He smiled at his very wise wife as Dieter's spell began to fade.

Out of the corner of his eye he saw Clay and Helen approach, whereupon he hailed both vigorously. They all collected in a knot as handshakes and kisses were traded about. That done, Helen sighed.

"Well, Frank, another cycle completed," she nodded.

"By the grace of God, Helen, between that bomb-throwing husband of yours and this unpredictable crop of residents," he let drop in veiled warning. "A very combustible mixture, Helen. I wouldn't be surprised if the worst is yet to be. And I'm not the only one who thinks so, apparently. Don't look now, Clay, but in about the fifth row on your left our redoubtable Miss Dieter sits regally in survey, loyal Switzer at her side."

"That's no surprise," Clay brushed aside without looking. "This damned place is *packed*," he shifted. "All of a sudden we're top billing. I hope the good Dr. Burleson comes through."

"Don't be coy, my overly modest friend," Cantrelle corrected, "this crowd is here because of you as well as Burleson, a mixture they hope is equally combustible. Expect it."

Clay noted that Laura, Ellie, and Landon waited and listened intently as Cantrelle spoke. He then responded to their evident concern.

"Working with this resident group for four years I've come to expect anything of them, and from *your* dear friend in particular, Mr. Landon," Clay donated.

Landon grimaced a panicky smile as though public exposure were upon him.

"Right," Cantrelle interceded, "Clay, I'm sure the residents have something up their sleeve. Having you and Burleson in the same room on this their special day when they can do no wrong will be more of a temptation than their wicked little minds can resist. Be ready."

"He is, Frank," Helen assured. "He's been telling me all week that today is the graduating class' last chance to settle accounts with him for all the tutorial lashings he's given them over the four years, and especially this group. But he's counting on their essential fear of him to carry him through."

Everybody seemed to be more ready for this event than he was, Cantrelle lamented, and he was preparing to say so openly when he saw Martha, Jess, and Burleson enter the room from the far side.

"They're here!" he announced, directing attention to their entry.

When they entered, Jess in front and leading Martha and Burleson side by side in train, the din in the room respectfully decreased several decibels. They proceeded toward the head table as all watched. Burleson then spotted Cantrelle, still off to the side and standing with his group, and quickly said something to Jess and

Martha to excuse himself. He strode directly across the room toward the group and approached with extended hand.

"Good morning, Dr. Cantrelle. It's such a delight to be here," he greeted as his smile swept across the others. Before Cantrelle could answer, Burleson disengaged and was now shaking Clay's hand. "And to you, too, Mr. Moyer. Let's see, it's been almost a year, hasn't it? Last October symposium, wasn't it? And Mrs. Cantrelle, Mrs. Moyer, so nice to see you again."

The room had become almost totally silent in observance of what must have looked like contenders shaking hands before a bout.

The man was positively overwhelming and all on-lookers immediately came under his sway.

"Yes, Dr. Burleson, it was," Clay agreed.

"But so much has happened since then, hasn't it?" he solicited in gentle lament. The women tittered politely as his gaze settled on Ellie and Landon.

"Dr. Burleson," Cantrelle reacted on cue, "this is my daughter, Ellie, and Jeffrey Landon, visiting from NIH."

Burleson hesitated for the briefest of moments as he looked at Landon. Cantrelle thought he could hear wheels turning, and Landon might have sensed it, too.

"I'm delighted, Miss Cantrelle, Mr. Landon. Dr. Cantrelle, I can see that your accomplishments are not limited merely to the academic," he blandished. "But then, the distaff contribution is so evident."

More tittering followed.

"Speaking of accomplishments," he continued, "I want to congratulate you and Mr. Moyer on that splendid paper. It truly opened the issue to research. Just what was needed and at exactly the right time. The journal took great pride in presenting it to the field for you, and we really do look forward to more of its kind."

Cantrelle knew that Clay would hear that as the starting gun of the no-holds-barred debate everyone came prepared to hear this morning, and already he felt himself slipping into the role of their moderator. He quickly looked up to see Martha and Jess waiting patiently at the head table, their eyes, as well as all others, on Burleson and his reconnoiter of what the audience regarded as the opposing camp. It was time to get back on track!

“We’re struggling with it now, Dr. Burleson. But other duties beckon, such as inflicting this graduating class upon an unsuspecting public. And we immediately need your help in that,” Cantrelle eased.

“Oh, yes, we mustn’t keep them waiting, either of them. It’s been pleasant talking to you,” he directed to all as a sweeping embrace. “Shall we, Dr. Cantrelle?” he added as he gestured in the direction of the head table. Cantrelle fell in line and led the way to the table as Laura and the others settled into their seats. The room hushed in anticipation. As Burleson, Martha, and Jess took their seats at the table, Cantrelle walked up to the lectern on which he rested his hands as he leaned toward the microphone. He noticed that his hands had a fine tremor.

“Good morning, ladies and gentlemen,” he began as he marveled at the expanse of faces before him. “Welcome to Moreland State Hospital and to this, its fifty-seventh resident physician graduation ceremony. As you may know the formal graduation of Moreland resident physicians was begun under the leadership and direction of Dr. Palmer when he was this hospital’s superintendent as well as the nation’s and probably also the world’s leading spokesman for the art and science of what was then less well known as the field of Psychiatry. And you may also know that before Dr. Palmer’s work the field of Psychiatry was not so clearly established or scientifically defined as a valid and free-standing medical specialty of its own. His work here, and the work of his staff, plus the subsequent research generated, were instrumental in establishing the field as such. But include also—a very big ‘also’—the *teaching* efforts of those founding Pilgrims. Thus, the three dimensions of the discipline’s trivium—practice, research, teaching—were brought together here at Moreland so many years ago with the planting of that seedling, Psychiatry, such that the growth now stands tall, and, as a medical specialty, it embraces the biologic, the psychologic, and the sociologic givens of the human predicament. Today, harvest time again, we come to observe and honor preferentially one dimension of that field, the educational. This graduating class, like the fifty-six preceding it, bears testimony to this hospital’s rich heritage of tutorial duty and achievement, and it is our task this morning to send these honored graduates forth to a future which is now more theirs than ours, yet ever Moreland’s. To do so is the work of all of us here today, as it has been the work of many at this hospital these past four years for making possible the graduates’ arrival at this juncture in their journey. But on that point, there is only *one* who daily led *all* of us in that grand pursuit, and that person would best speak for herself at this time of due credit. So, ladies and gentlemen, I give you Dr. Martha Corley, Superintendent, Moreland State Hospital."

As he gestured her forth Martha rose to the accompaniment of polite applause and approached the lectern in her usual self-conscious manner which conveyed her keen awareness of the responsibility owed the heavy office she held. To her, and to all of her predecessors, it was never merely a job or an opportunity, but a noble duty shaped by revered people who went before and to whom she owed homage. He returned to his seat at the table as she adjusted herself to the microphone.

"Thank you, Dr. Cantrelle. Good morning, ladies and gentlemen, and graduates. This is one of my more pleasant duties as Superintendent of this hospital," she began, "more pleasant in large part because of what it says of our values here at Moreland and of the good product that comes of possessing and maintaining those values at a time in our history as a nation when values are too easily equated with expense. Values, if they mean anything, will always be expensive, but of necessity always different from expenses, and I'll have more to say on that in a minute. But first I'd like to identify the smaller part of this pleasant duty which today brings me before you and these graduates. That smaller part is my memory, rejuvenated on days like today, of when I, too, was a resident, altogether too many years ago, and sat, wracked alike by pride and fear, among my fellow graduates at a ceremony much like this one. And, lo, these many years later, I'm with another generation of graduates, but as the Superintendent. Yet, I'm essentially unchanged in that I'm still wracked by pride and fear."

The gathering donated a round of sympathetic laughter.

Martha then pursued the point that the more things changed the more they remained the same and saw in the exigencies of today dark parallel with the troubles Moreland knew when she herself was a beginning resident; troubles which, she recalled pointedly, were breasted professionally and humanely with the vital assistance of tenaciously held values. The troubles of today, larger and more baneful, to be sure, demanded, she held, the play of correspondingly powerful values if those troubles were to be met and not merely suffered.

Cantrelle noticed Dieter's careful attention to Martha's words as her companion jotted on a note pad at tactical points in Martha's delivery.

It was those values, she continued, values which held that learning, research, and practice existed for people as well, and not just for teachers, scientists, or practitioners—or for administrators like herself—and which now had to be reaffirmed as never before, else our better efforts become divided and blunted, or, worse yet, degenerate into bureaucratic rant. That was her fear.

Dieter's friend was now writing furiously to keep up, Cantrelle observed. Dieter sat impassively.

Martha then directed everyone's awareness to the pride she felt in having so distinguished a scientist as Dr. Burleson present as the guest speaker this morning, noting that the recent work on Blush done at Moreland must certainly be seen as collaborative with his many contributions to the field, and that any differences discerned were at best only differences in approach, and never difference in purpose or principle. She instructed the residents, another source of great personal pride to her this morning, to bear today's lesson in mind when troubles came their way, as good duty guaranteed such troubles would. In time, they, too, she suggested, would come to know that the pride and fear they may feel in themselves this morning, each contending for pre-eminence, will recur from time to time as natural accompaniment to their duty as ethical physicians and compassionate psychiatrists, and so please know it and treasure it as the right and proper expense to bear. She congratulated the graduates and then thanked everybody for their kind attention.

He wanted to jump up and applaud, but that would have been too partisan, so he settled for the swell of clapping that filled the room. They loved her but not one whit more than he did at this very moment. In less than ten minutes she had effectively defused the charged atmosphere of the gathering. Now it could not so easily be the titanic battle hungered for by the mob, a confrontation come of the inspired activist calling into question the ethics of the gifted but socially detached scientist whose great discoveries in the name of humanity were being set to sinister purpose by wicked others in injury of that humanity. Rather, now the gathering could be a colloquium on learning and the responsibility we all bore in applying it to the good of man, just like the theme of all previous Moreland graduations. As the applause continued, he noted that Dieter and her companion sat quietly unmoved. He rose and approached the lectern as he gently motioned the gathering into silence.

"Don't you love her?" he confessed for all. "Thank you, Dr. Corley," he nodded in her direction. "Now that our doings have been set aright, I would like to introduce the person, also a Moreland graduate, who enjoys the ennobling position of being Dr. Corley's assistant, a remarkable player in his own right, and also, I might add, her first line of defense when I and any others from Residency Training lay siege to the Administration building. If it's true that history is the residue of conflict, then Dr. Jesse Weaver, Assistant Superintendent of Moreland State, has got to rank right up there with Herodotus. Dr. Weaver," Cantrelle bade, gesturing him forward amid the ripple of audience laughter.

Jess rose and approached the lectern in his typically robust and congenial manner, most suitable, Cantrelle noted, to the now relaxed tone of the audience. The electric anticipation had subsided and a gentler good will now leavened the group into a collective, smiling benevolence. But he couldn't help notice that Dieter and her companion seemed determined not to comply. Laura, and especially Helen, were obviously relieved at the favorable turn, he glimpsed as he resumed his seat.

Jess adjusted the microphone to his height and then smiled to every corner of the room, missing no one.

"And about as old as Herodotus, too," he beamed.

Laughter now erupted from all.

"And I don't know about my position being so enabling, Dr. Cantrelle, because we know how severe and unyielding Dr. Corley can be when she needs to. I might also mention, Dr. Cantrelle, that it was Herodotus who said, 'This is the bitterest pain among men, to have much knowledge but no power.'"

The audience howled. This was vintage Weaver, managing to have the best and last word. Cantrelle felt additional assurance that the proceedings would wend a gracious path.

"But to my thinking, ladies and gentlemen," he continued more soberly, "that's very much the challenge we all face when we start out to do something in this world. We study, we prepare, we rehearse, as these young graduates have done so diligently, and then all too often we find that we are yet so limited, so very limited, in the good we can do. Knowing much about a disease does not in its own right confer power over it any more than knowing much about a sunrise grants us the ability to control it. The power to change a thing and thus have a commensurate measure of control over it derives from precincts other than those of knowledge itself." To Cantrelle's surprise, Jess continued in the uncharacteristic vein of society's rôle in determining the use and effectiveness of its knowledge as right duty in custody of that knowledge. Had something recently happened between him and DMH, Cantrelle wondered?

"Every scholar," Jess continued, "be he an ancient Socrates, colleague of Herodotus, I might add, or a more modern scientist in a white mantle of slightly different cut, bears the task of helping to harness society's power to its achieved knowledge for that knowledge to perform its miracles. Thus, the wielders of that power are the natural fiduciaries of the scholar, though history both recent and remote would not seem to say so, and certainly as many scholars before us would lament."

Where was he going with his, Cantrelle worried. He wasn't setting out to fan the flames of contention all over again, was he? That wouldn't be like Jess at all. Cantrelle sat and listened, his teeth decidedly more on edge, and it seemed to him that Dieter and her friend were now sitting distinctly more upright in their seats.

"Residency training," he continued, "is in part a formative exercise in that felicitous relationship. We, the teachers and administrators who wield the tutorial and supervisory power, place a certain faith in the sincerity and wholesomeness of the aspiring resident's quest for knowledge. He, for his part, learns and grows as he must. If we are successful, he exceeds us, which is our dividend in that now we may, through his learning, exceed ourselves. One can see that to blunt our residents into a compliant parity with their instructionals is to doom us all—residents, practitioners, teachers, and, I might add, administrators as well. And thus it would be elsewhere and everywhere; indeed in any enterprise that held growth to be good."

It was a salvo directed at Sharpsfield, Cantrelle concluded, and probably from Jess' standpoint long overdue in view of the Draconian directives regulating the amount of study permitted on Blush patients who once again filled Building Seven now that both heroin and Crack were the established vehicles. He knew that Jess felt strongly about the restraints, but this was still a surprising turn. At least it deflected contention from the match-up of the two people yet scheduled to speak. Rather, it banded them together as fellow scholars facing a common issue. Good going, Jess, he noted appreciatively.

Jess then softened his thesis a bit with an anecdote about himself when he was a resident and added a few previously uncirculated vignettes about Dr. Palmer's teaching methods when Jess was one of his residents. At Moreland such fare was as reliable as the flag in moving the crowd to patronymic fervor.

"As it was then," Jess added in windup, "we should endeavor to have it ever, knowing that at best we might preserve and retain only the spirit and not the particulars of that nobler time when challenges united rather than divided our efforts. But that very spirit alone will be ample, I trust, for protecting Moreland as a citadel of learning *and* of service, in equal measure, where young graduates such as those before us today display the wisdom come of a priestly and humane calling. Congratulations to you, young graduates, and please accept my deepest gratitude for what you already have given and for what you will continue to give to all of us. Thank you."

There was a moment of hushed silence as he turned to leave the lectern, and as though his physical release from it tripped a switch the gathering broke into a crescendo of applause and cheers, and more than just a few sobs. He, and probably no one else, had ever before heard Jess so eloquent and so passionate. As Jess resumed his seat at the table, applause continuing, Cantrelle noticed the sparkling moistness in his smiling eyes, shared, no doubt, by many in the audience. Behind Jess' solid, reliable, even-handed work as an administrator lay the heart and soul of the selfless and unwavering apostle of learning, never infringing Cantrelle's prerogatives and always standing to when help was needed. Now, at this very moment, that alter side was standing to for all to know and heed, and it was purely great, Cantrelle gloried. Even humbling, he noted, as he sneaked in the cynical thought that after Jess' missive, any wish for a polemic between Burleson and Clay would be nothing short of profane. Noticing that Jess' wife, Pam, was now daubing her eyes with a hankie brought him back to his duties. He rose and approached the lectern as the applause began to subside, though reluctant to cease. Even Dieter and company clapped politely.

"That's the sort of thing we have to measure up to around here, ladies and gentlemen," he summed up for all as he fitted himself back to the lectern. "It's a damned good thing he doesn't have any power."

Relief laughter abounded.

"And now, ladies and gentlemen, we move on to even more in our program. It's not often we find ourselves in the presence of a person whose name has become synonymous with his field. We hear of such people, read their works, and think of what it must be like to be who they are. But we never ever approach such identity and we content ourselves with the hope of meeting such people at some time in our lives so that the experience will sustain us in our better endeavors. You've already seen this morning what working with Dr. Palmer has done for Dr. Corley and Dr. Weaver, whose great good fortune cannot help but leave the rest of us, not at all so joyously anointed, feeling the sting of envy, as would be all too human. But be of good cheer, all the rest of us, for our moment is happily at hand. Our next speaker is the man whose name signifies what American psychiatry is today. His work has not only brought our field to the level of technical and doctrinal formulation it embraces at this time but also has provided the paradigm for the growth its destiny and this nation require, especially with the public brow contracted now as it is in such woe, as perhaps Shakespeare's Claudius might say. A listing of Dr. Burleson's credentials would extend the morning beyond our keep and prolong this introduction beyond its purpose, but I should be remiss were I not to pay tribute to the remarkable scope of his art, from Chairman of a University Department, to editor of the leading journal of our field, to Presidential Advisor on national matters of mental health. In addition, he is author of several of our seminal texts which have set the standard of the field, plus voluminous journal articles which span thirty years of progressive enrichment of our profession. Include, too, his generous and peripatetic representation of us all and our work in the literally hundreds of presentations he has given at various symposia, seminars, meetings, and lectures. At those presentations, academic as well as civic, he has always defended and extended the credo that in this era of man's existence the scientist is the bounden catalyst of a struggling world's hope for social progress and is not merely a white-frocked, as Dr. Weaver might say, ancillary tucked away in some smelly laboratory tracing sub-atomic ripples in the tide of existence. Rather, the scientists of today, like the poets of old but perhaps not so linguistically gifted, or, I should say, not given to the medium of mere language, are for this era the spokesmen of our reaching spirit, adversaries of our vaunting self-deceit, and keepers of a holier faith than ever could come of man's checkered search for a personal divinity. They are, he has so amply shown, the apostles of a gospel whose tenets call us to live by the honest sum of our abilities in coming to know our world that we may in time come to know our cosmos, so that ultimately we may come to know ourselves. And, as such, of the many gospels of Man theirs, the scientists', is the only gospel that allows for its own fallibility and thereby dedicates its followers to the acceptance of its errors and its failures as premise for keener pursuit of its perfection through the labors of learning and discovery so that ultimately it may truly conceive anew and clearly see beyond. In a word, the pursuit of truth not yet known even by its own gospel, which remains duty bound, like its followers, to the secular laws of logic from which a richer faith might be derived. This credo, their credo, offers a grace distinctly unlike that of the gospels of earlier times which drew their power from a logic based on a faith already given. The scientist, ladies and gentlemen, is the religious zealot of our time, and though he and his fellow pilgrims do not kneel or worship as one, unanimity being a virtue only in earlier dogmas and which his gospel would expressly forbid, he and his kind make up the evangelical which unquestionably is now the pre-eminent force in shaping the purpose and course of our struggling humanity. You might be surprised to know in that regard that of all the scientists who have ever lived, over ninety-five percent have lived in the past one hundred years. That's only three generations, ladies and gentlemen. Three. We could thus paraphrase John Adams and imagine an ancestral scientist of a century ago saying, 'I study physics and mathematics so that my son may study molecules and light so that his son may study cosmology and creation, so that perhaps his son may come to understand the meaning of existence.' We haven't reached a fourth generation yet, ladies and gentlemen, but we have reached that moment in our program this morning when I may introduce a man who has long foreseen the happy advent of that generation and who has done so much to prepare us for its coming. Ladies and gentlemen, Dr. Horace Burleson."

Eager and vigorous applause filled the room as people smiled and nodded to each other in satisfaction with the moment's arrival. This was what they had come for, their duty of witness to the residents' graduation notwithstanding. Cantrelle applauded along with the rest as Burleson, smiling in modest acknowledgment, rose from his chair and approached the lectern, doing so with a briskness that underscored his trim and youthful frame, that mien supported sartorially by his neat tab collar and exquisite floral print tie, all of which seemed to suit the occasion to a T. This was no gray and leaden pedagogue, this galvanic figure who seemed to glow with vitality as well as wisdom; no, not this fierce alloy of close-cropped silvery hair and steel-blue eyes. Cantrelle found it hard to believe that this sinewy man was a good thirty years his senior.

As he positioned himself at the lectern, he turned slightly and watched Cantrelle return to his seat at the table. When Cantrelle was settled he turned to the audience, scanned it briefly, and then spoke.

"If I were Dr. Corley, I wouldn't give that fellow any power either."

Delighted laughter rebounded through the room. As it subsided, he resumed.

"But I will give Dr. Cantrelle credit for being extremely generous in his praise. So generous, in fact, that I fear his introduction has greatly outdistanced my abilities so that whatever I may say or do here this morning, best effort notwithstanding, may be little more than a display of failure to live up to specs. Perhaps we should regard it all as a clever ploy in open league with Dr. Weaver's avowed strategy whereby Dr. Cantrelle herewith exceeds my scope that I may thereby be enabled to exceed myself, his stirring introduction being thus a veiled invitation to do better than what I've accepted as my own standard. No wonder your residents, having been subject to four years of such goading, go forth as conquerors after they leave here."

Cheers rose up from the graduates in the first row, followed by laughter from all.

"So, ladies and gentlemen, and particularly Drs. Corley and Weaver, and Dr. Cantrelle and his teaching staff, people of Moreland, and our graduates, whatever may be my offering this morning on this colorful occasion," he continued with a discernible shift to the earnest, "you may be mindful that I am soberly aware of my responsibility to contribute in kind and to do so in keeping with the many selfless contributions made by so many others that this noble event might occur. It is traditional on occasions such as these to honor the diligence and the skill of the graduates in achieving this mark of accomplishment in their young lives, and it is also customary to congratulate their teachers for having formed these young psychiatrists so carefully and so well that they are now ready, as of today, to pursue their independent destinies. Certainly praise is also due, and typically tendered, to the administrators, such as Drs. Corley and Weaver, whose protective and enabling guidance has kept the hospital milieu fertile for the several training programs which flourish here at Moreland, Residency Training being just one. And, of course, acknowledgments could not be complete without recognition of the graduates' families who kept a frequently lonely vigil sustaining the resident, in honor of his calling, but also in protection of his ever precious humanity as husband, or wife, or father, or mother, or son, or daughter, even brother or sister. Yes, there are so many we're used to thanking, and we do so as a matter of course. And one can only imagine how many fine words of praise and gratitude have been spoken in that duty at such similar graduation exercises over the centuries. Enough for it to sound very familiar to all of us. Yet, for all the literate skill and poetic grace I've seen displayed by so many distinguished speakers at resident graduations over the years I've often afterwards had the unsettling and irksome feeling that something important had been neglected, or forgotten, or unclaimed. I used to think that this feeling of incompleteness probably derived from the vexing unknowability of the future while the past and present were so easily and readily identified as contributors to the occasion of the graduation. Or perhaps it was merely the sense that the future, of necessity, had to be set aside as a defining agent if one were to avoid seeming visionary and fanciful, and that the past and present had to be pressed into extra duty by speakers so as to give weighty substance to their remarks. Perhaps, but the more I thought about it, the more it seemed that it was something else, a certain something else, which was missing."

As Burleson developed his point in the hushed room Cantrelle had the merry thought that the thing that was missing was notes. Burleson was giving this address without the benefit of notes; better, perhaps, for the hypnotic power of his rhetoric to have its effect, as it certainly was, with all present fixedly intent upon his every word. Not a movement visible. This man could really belt out an address. There was something about his tone, his gestures, his reach—penetrating, arresting. Whatever it was, people listened to what he said. Even Dieter and her companion, he was satisfied to see.

"Actually," he continued, "given the sense that something was indeed missing, it didn't take very much thought to discern what it was. It became merely a matter of comparing the resident's surround on the day of graduation with his typical surround the one and a half thousand days and nights he spent enroute to his graduation. Looked at that way, it was only too clear that it was the *patient* who was missing, that benighted soul who had been the resident's constant and all too often unremitting challenge in that lengthy, humbling, often discouraging, always frightening pilgrimage through the bourne of mental illness, the two of them, resident and patient, bonded together all the while by the sanctity of that most human and compassionate of ties known to brotherly keep, the doctor-patient faith. Yes, my dear residents, *your* patients. Your troubled sojourners who looked to you for miracles, scolded you for your meagerness, terrified you with your failures, and exalted you in your success. Yes, those distraught and addled sufferers were, in truth, the rightist and strictest of all your teachers—the most compelling and certainly the most forebearing. However lonely you may have been in your blackest moments of despair for not knowing what to do, your patient was there with you, his unnatural alienation now kindred to your distressed forlornness which was now not so singular by dint of his presence. Nor was your patient ever a stranger to the hurts and doubts which assailed you when the nostrums and balms honestly and sincerely taught you by your teachers failed to bring relief to those whose suffering sought out your shame. Or, my dear residents, did it ever happen that when one of your patients re-emerged sane and whole that you did not see in his joy the indelible inscription that you were most rightly *his* doctor, as your own joy agreed? Of course not. That fundamental human law which states that whatever we are, others are to us, sees no more vivid application than in the training of young doctors, and of young psychiatrists in particular. Hence the special majesty, and sometimes feared eliteness, of our field. And thus, too, the special debt we owe our patients who are never invited to these graduation ceremonies which could never take place without them. Sir William Osler, that rogue of a medical genius, summed up nicely the value of the patient in one's medical education. He said, and I paraphrase slightly: 'While clinical practice without study is like going to sea without charts, study without clinical practice is like not going to sea at all.'"

A ripple of laughter spread across the room, as much in relief from the heavy poignancy of his message as from the wit of the quote. Cantrelle managed a polite smile but was more occupied with a gnawing sense of his smallness being called to attention by Burleson's grandeur.

"Several years ago I made the suggestion to one of the graduating classes of my department that each graduating resident invite to the ceremony one or two patients the resident had worked with over the years of training. It never came to pass because the residents balked at the idea, and I suspect the patients would have as well if it had gotten that far. Well, of course, it then became a matter of our analyzing as a group the reason why such a seemingly sensible and polite gesture as all that was felt to be so unacceptable. As you can well imagine, various erudite and dynamically-couched reasons were offered, all of them crisp, erudite—and *wrong*. And we knew it. Eventually, one of the more gifted residents spoke up and said that the reason, as he saw it, was because what existed between resident and patient—all the innumerable little humanities, all the driven perils and prayers that bonded together their hopes and heartaches, all the gentle acts of faith which forgave each other's failings, all the moments of indescribable joy when success touched their efforts, all of these things—were simply too sacred and too tender to be brought to so secular and public a gathering as a graduation celebration. And I think he was right. And even by speaking of it, as I do now, I do a certain violence to this ineffable intimacy. I'm sure that at this moment there is no graduate in this front row who is not feeling a bit squirmy and exposed by what I am saying, for each and every one of them, if he or she is as good a resident as this occasion attests—and I have no reason to question Dr. Cantrelle's judgment in the matter—has experienced at some time or other in his training here at Moreland that elevating yet humbling humanity which transcends sickness and health, good and bad, high and low, to proclaim him keeper of his fellow man as well as the healer of his sufferings."

This was far more than anyone had expected, even from someone like Burleson, Cantrelle marveled as he absorbed the impact of those riveting words. The people sat transfixed, captured. One of the female graduates was daubing her eyes and Cantrelle had noticed that a few of the male graduates had already swallowed hard more than once. The silence during his reflective pauses was profound and the crammed room was perfectly still. Eerily so.

"Oh yes," he continued, "it wasn't all tenderness and pity, of course. It was you who ordered the injections, the restraints, or the periods of seclusion when such was necessary. And it was also you who disappointed his failing hopes, shored up as they were by his overweening delusions. Or soothed his desperate yearnings and frantic searches transmogrified by his baleful hallucinations. You were also the one who ordered him forth into the searing light of daily activities when his melancholy begged for dark corners. You also foiled his flights into the airiness of a guiltless mania. No, you didn't just console and commiserate, stroking his trembling hand in saintly ruth. No, you did battle; you fought him, and for him, when his illness was more himself than he was able to know, and you continued to do so as his salvaged self slowly restored its understanding of your alliance and your loyalty. And, indeed, it was work, so often drudging, occasionally fiery, and always tiring. But also, every blessed minute of it was consummately human and thus sacred to you and to him as only the two of you may say, but certainly not here and probably never to each other, but, though unsaid, known forever to the two of you alone. So it would be appropriate to feel that for all the grace and majesty of our gathering today, with all the finer and nobler sentiments marshaled in celebration of our graduates, we yet feel, I say again, that something is missing though that something for its very veneration is properly embargoed by these, the humbler doings we offer in ceremony. Perhaps we might simply say, with all due credit to those present, that the ones who offered most to the resident in that dyadic metamorphosis called Residency Training are not here today and that the more comprehensive truth as well as the fitness of that apparent lack is to be appreciated in the general affirmation that these young graduates have *already* achieved their confirmation as psychiatrists, their confirmation having been bestowed on them earlier by their patients, the ones who truly know best the skill and humanity of these young doctors. Our duty here today, then, is merely to endorse publicly what has already been recorded privately in that noble registry of human endeavor called 'Becoming a Psychiatrist.'"

Cantrelle coughed softly to keep his tears from flowing. The man was going right for the heart. A lot of people were now swallowing desperately and he could feel the restive emotion of the gathering threatening to break through the weakening controls of seemly restraint. It was as though each member of the audience feared for his neighbor's control lest someone breakdown and incite a flood of passion from all. Burleson must have sensed as much, he estimated, for the man stopped a brief moment to take a sip of water. The silence was almost unbearable.

"We are all aware," he resumed, "that a new scourge is sweeping across this land. A most deadly scourge, and, like every other predator, preying upon the weakness of its victims to do its cruel work. You may also know that public disclosure of that new scourge began right here at Moreland some eight months ago, thanks to the alertness and competence of this hospital's dedicated staff and particularly to the keen investigative spirit of two of its more prominent workers, Dr. Cantrelle who is sitting right up here at the table this morning, and Mr. Clay Moyer sitting there in the second row suitably in whispering distance of the residents to get his last instructions in."

A murmur of laughter, more like a sigh of relief, rippled across the audience.

"Other than what Moreland has already contributed," he continued, "we know little about the nature of this terrible plague. Theories abound, as they always do when pestilence mounts and remedies are slow in coming, but solid facts are hard to come by when investigating agencies are beset with the tasks of marshaling their forces in preparation for defining and then implementing a strategy for arresting the spread of the plague and its damage. The hard, detailed, and ultimately productive work of research on the scale required by the scope of this challenge will, indeed, be slow in coming as enabling initiatives such as staffing patterns, divisions of labor, procurement of research personnel, designation of research sites, and all the countless other basic requirements of a federally coordinated address to a gathering pestilence are mounted in obedience to public need. We have at other times seen this nation mobilize its resources in the face of threat, and I'm sure we'll see a like mobilization in response to Blush, as you all know this scourge is called."

Cantrelle pondered on Burleson's shift to this more official, even bureaucratic stand. His words now seemed so standard.

"Those are the steady, unadorned, and not particularly inspiring or especially reassuring practicalities of the situation, ladies and gentlemen. For a while members of that federal task force will go about their business in what may seem to be a plodding and unhurried fashion looking for all the world like they're out of touch with the urgency and critical nature of the threat. That seems unavoidably to be the way when governmental momentum is shifted along a new line of pursuit and lag time seems to stretch on endlessly before definitive accomplishment supervenes. So in the meantime, local communities such as yours right here do what they can to contain the scourge, using what resources as may be at hand. I think that's about where we are now."

Cantrelle felt himself being led down some syllogistic garden path by what sounded like a homily from out of nowhere. He suspected everybody else noted the same. The people were now relaxing from their earlier enrapture, adjusting themselves in their seats as they shifted the set of their attention. Dieter and her companion, however, seemed to sharpen their alertness as the companion readied his note pad in anticipation.

"Ladies and gentlemen," he continued after another sip of water, "it's that lag time I'd like to address for the moment, that period of time from when the existence of a problem is recognized and when the results of concerted efforts at a solution begin to yield significant results. That very period of time, that seeming interminable stretch of sustained and abject vulnerability in the face of the threat, is, I contend, often more potentially dangerous than actually the threat itself is. Now how does he mean that, you're probably wondering."

Cantrelle realized that this was now Burleson the teacher coming forth. Not the philosopher-poet-rhetorician, but the disciplined, methodical tutor armed with a clenching logic to bind his new-found students, these very people sitting before him and just moments ago enlisted by him as co-votaries, to the task of understanding and mastering a lesson meant to be kept. This was turning out to be some tour, he gulped, but it seemed that the audience was still good for the trip, judging by their shift to a more edge-of-the-seat alertness, their energy now poised and awaiting direction.

"Let me explain. I suppose," he proceeded, "we could imagine any number of infelicitous civic turns which could qualify as dangerous—dangerous, I must add, more from the political and social than from the public health standpoint. For example, frantic laws could be enacted, laws which are inherently destructive of the civil liberties of all though superficially and immediately aimed at the predators, and, yes, in this case, also their victims. Or, a polarizing regionalization of society might evolve whereby high incidence areas, such as the inner cities, would be seen as the loci of a national blight and become victims themselves because of their consequent political, social, and economic ejection from the collective national identity and then left solely to the local government to be dealt with as necessary and as possible. Certainly that sort of thing happened on an historic scale to an entire region of this nation in reaction to certain of its social ills a century and half ago. Or, a cynical apathy could be mounted as a foil to the consternation of not knowing just what to do, hoping thus to make a virtue out of an adversity and justify it on the neatly pragmatic basis that the victims, in this case self-designated, do not constitute an electorally active contingent in the socio-political line-up in the first place. I'm sure you've heard that notion whispered around. Or better yet, that the entire matter is in some unfathomable way God's hand in our nation's long overdue deliverance from one of its evils, and thus to be accepted as divine intervention for our ultimate benefit. I'm sure you could add to the list of such blandishments, and all of them would be genuine dangers in their own right, were we to adopt any of them as our means of facing this awful disease. But the danger I have in mind is one that smacks of good intention, quick fix, and social convenience."

Cantrelle's ears pricked up with those last words because of their particular juxtaposition. He immediately knew where Burleson was going with his point and a smile of settled satisfaction moved into position. This was going to be good, he savored. He nodded to Clay in the second row as though in promise of some coming delight.

"Ladies and gentlemen," Burleson continued as he leaned more into the lectern, "Blush is the leprosy of our era. Not at all contagious like the leprosy of old, not so lingering in its ruin, but much more ruthlessly lethal. So in what way is it like leprosy? Because it is a horrid social disease for which we have no cure, just as in centuries before, even decades before, when we had no cure or even treatment for leprosy. And, historically, when society has no cure for what it cannot bear witness to and also dreads contamination by, society isolates it. And shuns it. And wishes it to go away forever. Ask any leper of any time in history."

Cantrelle noted that Clay's ears were also now pricking up. A similar smile was beginning to appear.

"But, you might ask, in the strict analysis of it, what's wrong with that? After all, we have to put the welfare of the many ahead of that of the few. Standard procedure, actually, and medically sensible. We've done it with TB sufferers and typhoid carriers. Certainly similar efforts were made at other times when diseases had to be isolated to prevent epidemic spread. In fact, one could say that there's a social instinct to isolate the sick. In fact, this magnificent edifice, Moreland State Hospital, with its cloistering iron fence, might be seen as one of society's nobler expressions of that instinct. So, from the public health standpoint, such a policy is actually uncontestable.

"Then what is the basis of my fear? It's simply this: to isolate a problem is too often the first step in arranging to ignore that problem if isolation alone reduces the sense of threat."

Cantrelle almost leaped from his chair. He guessed right! Burleson was going to take a stand on local investigation of Blush.

"Ladies and gentlemen," he pressed on, "the more mean-minded of us could make a case that, in part, perhaps in large part, the reason it took so long to find an effective and arresting treatment for leprosy is because lepers by law were banished from society, removed from public view, housed in isolated colonies, and then pretty much forgotten as a social and public health problem. They numbered in the thousands, in their reasonably comfortable, federally-funded colonies carefully located far from the taxpayer. Rarely thereafter did anybody hear about those pathetic outcasts, no less shunned just fifty years ago than they were five thousand years ago; only more humanely maintained. How many of you ever heard of Carville, Louisiana? Every leper in the United States has. Eventually, but only eventually, the treatment of leprosy caught up with the advances made in the treatment of other infectious diseases which were, in a sense, the more respectable ones to have, you might say. Of course, we may note, leprosy was a slow and indolent disease, striking the relatively few, fortunately, and thereby easily set aside while medical attention was urgently focused on the more virulent diseases that swept violently across populations. No argument there, either. But once set aside, cloaked in taboo, leprosy *remained* set aside as though forsaken by the very science which owed it duty of address. It could be said that research on the cause and treatment of leprosy did indeed take place all along. That is certainly true, but the intensity and funding of any research has a way of following the flag, public interest in particular, and public interest, we need not proclaim, depends on public awareness. Thus, I think, the sufferers of leprosy suffered doubly for not being known. Certainly, they suffered longer. The public has to *see* what it is the public must do. And, likewise, young doctors, and medical students, must *see* what it is they must study. The charts *and* the voyage, Osler might say. I went through medical school without ever seeing a leper, though a large colony of them was located only fifty miles away. None of my classmates saw one, either. There could have been in my class a fellow student who might have discovered in himself a mission to fathom the mysteries of leprosy, had he but seen a case of it. But it didn't happen, not to my knowledge.

"Eight months ago two of your investigators, assisted by their staff and undoubtedly by the young graduates seated before me, took on the mission of fathoming the mysteries of this deadlier leprosy, Blush. Dr. Cantrelle and Mr. Moyer and their associates were able to *see* what they had to discern, and at that time the Blush patients were on hand to *be* seen. The result of your investigators' endeavor is that through their publication hundreds of other researchers are now able to see what before was not visible to very many because of Blush's remove. Moreover, these young graduates, for what they have seen, are now among the best, if not *the* best, informed psychiatrists in this entire land on the ravages of Blush."

Cantrelle felt himself getting worked up. There was now a crescendo flavor to Burleson's delivery as though heavy clouds were beginning to gather overhead in readiness for the Sinaitic thunderclap which was undoubtedly on its way. He thought he saw a dread fascination rising in the faces of the gathering as all recoiled inwardly from collective personal guilt in having set taboo upon lepers, regardless of when and where.

"But I understand, ladies and gentlemen, that Blush patients are no longer kept here at Moreland," he announced. "I understand they are evaluated here but transferred to another extended care facility as soon as is practicable. I also understand that the Moreland staff and its psychiatric residents, the ones who gave us our first light in this still very dark corner of American psychiatry, no longer have the opportunity to see what work needs to be done to enlarge upon their already widely appreciated contribution. I do indeed understand the probable cost-effectiveness considerations which are included in such a disposition plan, cost-effectiveness considerations which I suggest are concerned more with the short-term and with the politically sensitive than with a forthright and broad address to the reality of Blush. Earlier in this ceremony Dr. Corley reminded us that meaningful values are always expensive. Thus, ladies and gentlemen,

I fear that what has happened here at Moreland will be duplicated across this land and that Blush victims will be sequestered, removed from the squeamish, unwelcoming sight of the public, and allowed to trace their tragic course hidden from the awareness of their own people, just like the lepers of all ages. It would be a great sin to have that happen. Society should not lose sight of its unfortunates or of its human responsibility to assist. Young doctors should see and learn what Blush is, so that maybe a few will be inspired to carry forward the work of research into that scourge's fell nature. Blush is everybody's problem. It belongs to this nation and to all people and not just to a circumscribed collection of caretakers and researchers neatly set apart from the consciousness of the electorate. It belongs to every elected and appointed official who purports to serve the public good. And it belongs to the educators, as here at Moreland, so that young graduates, as these, may learn the scope of their duty as ministers to the sufferings of a collective mankind that must yet work at its own lessons in brotherly compassion. Yes, we all have our duties in the matter, duties we would probably prefer to delegate but which our inexpendable humanity forbids, and these young graduates whom we favor today stand before us as our freshest and best hope for leading us in that duty. Though the patients be missing from this gathering, they, too, join in the doing of these honors as only they can, for they are the ones who carry the strictest duty, the duty known fullest by them, but also by a clear-sighted Milton who said, '. . . they also serve who only stand and wait.' We trust, young graduates, you will not keep them waiting too long. I thank you."

Before the last syllable left his lips people were standing and applauding in a swell of freed emotion. Burleson nodded respectfully and left the lectern to return to the table. Cantrelle, Corley, and Weaver were standing and applauding along with everyone else as Burleson approached the table. As though they could not do otherwise, they clustered around Burleson to speak their praise and to touch him, properly restricted to handshaking but sufficiently representative of everyone's need to know the touch of consecration at this wonderful moment. The people remained standing as the applause sustained itself in a determined display of unwavering dedication. One of the male graduates, pushed beyond his control, was thrusting a fist into the air in tempo with his exultant cheering. Burleson again acknowledged the applause and then, at the invitation of Cantrelle, resumed his seat. Corley and Weaver followed as guide to the audience. The applause began to subside as people settled into their seats, but it continued well after everyone was seated as though to affirm its durability. Cantrelle remained standing and approached the lectern when the applause had subsided enough to permit his re-entry. As he stood before the lectern the gathering settled into a rumbling susurrus as people whispered their marvel back and forth in their return to each other's presence. Enroute they cleared their throats of stifled hurrahs and blinked their way into readiness for the next moment before them. He felt spent, too, and wondered how he might allow the glory of this unique instance to linger while moving the ceremony along to its concluding purpose. He didn't want to do anything to detract from where they all were at this splendid moment, and a disarming humility hung upon him as he looked out upon the inspired faces now dividing their attention between his return presence at the lectern and their continuing resonance with what they had just witnessed. He, too, cleared his throat.

"Thank you, Dr. Burleson," he said simply. "I would like to say so much more in gratitude of what you yourself have given to us for these many years, but most especially for your great generosity this magnificent morning. Yet, I feel that anything I might add to what has already been expressed by all of us here would only be gratuitous. So I merely say again, thank you, Dr. Burleson."

With that another round of applause arose, less violent this time and as tender as applause can say. Corley, Weaver, and Cantrelle coupled affectionate smiles with their gentle applause, a display returned amply by Burleson to all.

As the applause subsided, Cantrelle resumed.

"Ladies and gentlemen, the graduates know that at this point in the program I take advantage of my prerogative as Director of Training to have the last word with them, for immediately upon my close Dr. Corley will present them their graduation certificates whereupon never again will they ever have to listen to another tutorial word as residents. Never again. They'll listen forever after to words of instruction, words of learning, words of advice, and so forth, but never again as psychiatric residents. So, you can imagine that I cherish this perfect moment, the moment when I get in the last official resident instructional and fully in the expectation that they'll thereby remember my words best and longest. Such is my usual on this occasion. But, proud graduates, today cannot permit of such a conceit, for what has already been offered by Dr. Burleson and Dr.

Corley and Dr. Weaver is more than sufficient discount of our smaller and more selfish pursuits, be they engineered here or anywhere else"—he looked directly at Dieter and her companion—"and I would be loathe to convey to you this morning any endorsement of such narrowness by insisting upon the exercise of a prerogative now rendered irrelevant by the enlightening and elevating discourse already offered on your behalf. In a word, my dear graduates, today you have achieved, in witness of all the rest of us here, the ultimate benediction noble thoughts may confer. There can be no more fitting completion of your formal training as psychiatrists than what already has been given you this morning by these fine leaders. If there is any endorsement for me to make, it is of what already has been said to you this morning, and that is what I want you to remember longest and best."

He now looked at Laura who smiled back proudly through glistening eyes.

"So your moment has come, my nearly erstwhile students," he continued, turning to the table. "Dr. Corley, may I?" he gestured her forward, whereupon she rose and positioned herself next to him. "Dr. Corley, upon the recommendation of the teaching staff of Moreland State Hospital I present to you the following physicians for the awarding of the Certificate of Psychiatry inasmuch as they have satisfied all the requirements specified by the American Medical Association Council for Graduate Medical Education. Dr. Jonas Albright, will you please come forth?"

As the resident rose and approached, Cantrelle handed a furled, red-ribboned certificate to Corley who presented it to the resident along with a handshake. The beaming resident then returned to his seat.

"Dr. Josephine Daley," Cantrelle summoned.

Five such presentations were completed when Cantrelle shifted his mein slightly toward the curmudgeonously playful.

"Ladies and gentlemen, I should mention that the next graduate is today and has been for the entirety of this academic year the spokesman not only for his fellow graduates but for all of the residents in the Moreland roster. His title is 'Chief Resident' and he was selected for that position by the Resident Training Committee, a function it performs every year in designating for that job a senior resident who shows a particular blend of leadership, academic ability, clinical skill, administrative knack, and perhaps most important of all, the respect of his or her peers. And, indeed, it's a job being the Chief Resident, for it includes the task of representing, one to the other, our sometimes contending forces, residents as well as administration, to see to it that such contention is replaced by a more functional amity. So he is first and last a diplomat. But he is also an advisor, again to the resident group as well as to administration, and especially to the Director of Training with whom he meets weekly in review of the week's events and issues. Frequently his view is more comprehensive than that of those he advises, born as it is of his dual position of observation as both resident as well as junior staff member. As a consequence his suggestions ordinarily carry notable weight in the management of curriculum and its planning. And for all that he does above and beyond the usual training duties, he receives little recompense other than the honor of the title, the experience of the challenge, and as we shall soon witness, the privilege of speaking for his fellow graduates at this, their last opportunity, to tell us what's on their minds. This particular Chief Resident has been especially adept at that sort of thing over the past year and I would expect him to be no less so this morning. Dr. John Morello, would you please step forward?"

Morello mounted the podium and approached the lectern, wafted along by the vigorous applause offered by his fellow graduates. Cantrelle handed the certificate to Corley who conveyed it to Morello along with a handshake. Morello accepted the certificate and, true to form, leaned over and planted a kiss on Corley's cheek. Laughter helped the applause along. Cantrelle and Corley then surrendered the lectern to him.

Bristling with equal measures of anxiety and shored-up confidence he twisted the microphone into a more serviceable attitude and began.

"Thank you Dr. Cantrelle, and Dr. Corley. First, on the behalf of this graduating class I wish to thank everybody, present or otherwise, for making this day possible for us." Morello beamed. "We give particular thanks to Dr. Burleson, our distinguished guest speaker, for making this occasion one which everybody present will never, ever forget."

A spate of affirming applause rose and subsided.

"Of course we're eternally grateful to those we sometimes call the Trinity and other times call the Triumvirate depending on how compassionate or how despotic they happened to be at any given moment—the big three, no matter how you shade it, being Dr. Corley, Dr. Weaver, and Dr. Cantrelle."

Laughter bubbled up from the crowd at such playful irreverence and again it was the graduates who laughed hardest.

"Our gratitude also includes all the teaching staff members who put in four years of trench time with us, braving the shot and shell come of precepting rookies like us who had the uncanny ability of falling into every training misadventure a clinical no-man's land could offer. They saw us through all the daily dangers, and because of that they'll always be at our sides. We hope they'll always keep us with them."

A few murmurs of approbation arose from the front row.

"Then there are our families and friends whose encouragement, steadiness, and forbearance count for more of our inspiration than our vanity can admit, preferring as we do to see ourselves as authors of our own destiny. Part of our training consisted in learning to call that vanity 'narcissism,' and an even larger part of that training consisted of transforming that narcissism into a wisdom which comes, they tell us, of being able to laugh at oneself."

Morello then recounted personally revealing anecdotes involving his fellow graduates as well as himself, all tellingly visible at this remove from the time of their occurrence, and all illustrative of the fragility of vanity in the rough company of honest and unbiased objectivity. A few of the graduates writhed in chagrin as the anecdotes recalled abashing incidents in their training, and the audience chortled in sympathetic goodwill at each of Morello's confessional offerings. Cantrelle was delighted that the ceremony was now taking a lighter turn after the heavy going of the previous hour. He hoped Morello wouldn't get carried away and get too playful. He could trust him, maybe.

"So, ladies and gentlemen" he continued, "we were put through the paces in exchanging our narcissism for a tested maturity, and our teachers helped to keep us afloat as we struggled along, and we thank them all in getting us going in a task that will continue as long as we presume to treat the ills of others. But of our many teachers, one stood out above the others in his efforts to strip us of our vanities, our self-deceptions, our false courage, and of all the accompanying pieties that went hand and glove with those failings, and he did it as a colleague first and as a teacher totally."

Here it comes, Cantrelle noted as he braced himself.

"As you can well imagine, this person was easy to hate, especially whenever he put our vices to siege, but he was the first one we ran to when we needed help. He was also the one we could always count on to frame our questions and problems in a form that made them sensible, testable. Doing so encouraged our dread of failure to mutate into the duty of scientific inquiry. To this teacher in particular our confession of ignorance was identified as a significant discovery in establishing a valid line of departure for new learning. But then we had to follow through and do some *real* learning. He made it clear that if we were to be accorded the respect of the scholar, then we'd damned well better start behaving like one. And we did, as best we understood. And he approved. And there was good solace in that. But today we graduates take an additional solace in knowing that this teacher, Mr. Clay Moyer, has become publicly active in holding more than just psychiatric residents accountable for their behavior. As you know, Mr. Moyer has become spokesman for those who feel that not enough has been done at higher levels to mobilize this nation's resources in combating the spread of Blush. You also know that he has appeared with the local media in furtherance of his petition. But what you may not know—and, ladies and gentlemen, you heard it here first—is that in about six weeks Mr. Moyer will appear on "National Dateline" and be interviewed by Marilyn Fielding, the network's anchor, on his thinking about Blush."

Cantrelle froze as though thunderstruck. What the hell was this? He hadn't heard of this before! Why hadn't Clay mentioned it? Applause rose from the audience and Cantrelle instinctively looked in Dieter's direction to find that she had discernibly stiffened in her chair at this announcement while her companion sat agape, his mouth hanging open. Cantrelle estimated that for them to sit through Burleson was enough and now to hear that a state employee was embarked on a mission they regarded as gross treachery was more than they could countenance. He then quickly looked at the others at the table. Corley and Weaver were forcing smiles through their concern; Burleson seemed merely interested.

The applause subsided as the people nodded and commented busily to each other. They were getting everything they came for, and more.

"Now," continued Morello, pleased as Punch with the stir he had created, "in order to prepare him for that ordeal, we the graduates decided to extend to him the same benefit of wisdom he has instilled in us over these four years, that wisdom deriving as you know, from the forfeiture of our juvenile vanity. And since his national prominence now raises the temptation of a personal vanity to an irresistible height, we felt it was dutifully our turn to protect him from its scourge. We wondered how we might do that. Then, in a flash of humility, we understood what we had to do. Mr. Moyer, will you please come forth?"

Clay rose, blushing profusely, and made his way to the podium, visibly mumbling imprecations at Morello who seemed all the more delighted.

"Mr. Moyer," Morello resumed as he reached inside his jacket, "on behalf of the graduating class I wish to convey to you the means whereby you will be forevermore immune to the scalding sin of vanity. I hereby confer upon you this certificate appointing you *Honorary Resident*. It's good for life." He then handed the certificate to Moyer.

The audience roared with applause and laughter, led again by the front row. Even Cantrelle shook his head in deflated surrender. Corley and Weaver applauded gently and smiled to each other in relief. Burleson slapped his thighs in delight.

Morello stood erect with a triumphant glow as though posing with a prize trophy. Clay nervously unfurled the certificate and held it open before him.

"It's true," he managed in the direction of the microphone as he perused the certificate, "I'm condemned to be a resident for life, and it's signed by all six of them." The audience tittered merrily as he fumbled with the scroll.

"And now, Mr. Moyer," Morello summed up, "one of your first duties as Honorary Resident For Life is to explain yourself. So would you be so kind as to say a few words?"

"I don't know if I can think of a thing to say if I can't dip into vanity anymore," he parried as Morello retreated to his seat.

Cantrelle felt his anxiety return. The ceremony thus far had pleasantly steered clear of hard polemic. Issues identified, yes, but no gauntlets thrown. Would Clay keep it that way? He now saw that the program should have ended with the presentation of the residents' diplomas, damn it, though at this point, maybe only four or five others present would agree. He shouldn't have built up Morello so much in recognizing his Chief Resident status; it was probably heard by Morello and maybe everyone else as an introduction to, even encouragement of, what was now happening. Damn it again!

As Clay positioned himself before the microphone he didn't look up at the audience, but continued to gaze at the certificate he held spread before him on the lectern.

"The last time I received a certificate was in graduate school, and that was just a Master's degree," he reflected. "This is more distinguished. Thank you, graduates. I'll try to be as good a resident as you've been," he promised, "and then I can't possibly help being a better teacher." He then rolled up the certificate, put it aside, and looked up at the people.

"Ladies and gentlemen," he began, "the only words I can offer this morning are ones of gratitude for being a part of what this hospital means. When I came here over twenty years ago, fresh out of graduate school and just after Dr. Palmer departed, I had the sense then of a great hospital beginning its decline. Certainly with the departure of so titanic a figure as Dr. Palmer it was easy enough to believe that things here would be less good for his going. And I can assure you I wasn't the only one who thought so. It wasn't very long after he left that we began automatically to think and talk of the hospital as having two aspects—the hospital as it was when Dr. Palmer was here, and what it had become in his absence. I guess that's how eras are defined. The implication always was that things were richer, better, fuller when he was here and that since his departure we were having to make do with what we were without him. And there was a large truth to that, for with the departure of so incomparable a figure as he the emptiness left in his wake far exceeded the dimensions of anyone appointed as his successor. Thus, every Moreland superintendent since Dr. Palmer has worked in his shadow, always suffering in comparison and being held responsible for the way the hospital now was as compared to when it was richer, better, fuller. I just wonder if the time has come to take another look at that notion, perhaps especially so on this magnificent morning, to see if that view of what the hospital used to be bespeaks a steely reality or merely a golden canard."

Golden canard? . . . . Steely reality? . . . . He had never heard Clay talk like that before. Was everyone coming into his own this morning, Cantrelle puzzled? God forbid! But, at least, Clay wasn't manning the barricades.

"Let's say thirty years ago. Or even twenty," Clay continued. "Was it richer? By any comparative standard, indeed it was. Certainly as regards budget. State hospital funding in those days was a lot more generous, comparatively, than it now is, which tells us something about a change in public welfare policy as well as priority. In those days the care of the hospitalized mentally ill drew top billing or near top billing in the agenda of the Office of Public Welfare. Social programs now do. Large segments of society now define themselves as more needy and more deserving than the severely mentally ill, and they, being so much more electorally squeaky than the state hospital patient, get more of the public grease. Still and all, the hospital manages. But now a larger burden is placed on the Superintendent to stretch the administrative dollar in a way that wasn't necessary in the good old days. Let's move on. Was it fuller? Again, indeed it was. Look at the census. The hospital used to carry a daily patient census of nearly five thousand. There are barely five hundred patients here now. As we all know, this change reflects the advent and effectiveness of better forms of treatment, especially in the field of pharmacotherapy, but it also reflects a now permissible shift in emphasis from in-patient to out-patient management in the delivery of that treatment. As a consequence, those patients who remain at the hospital constitute a much sterner clinical challenge and thus, conversely, more sharply define the limit of our current treatment techniques. Still, the hospital somehow manages. Let's move on a bit farther. Better? Was the hospital actually better then? I can assure you the hospital felt better about itself back then; certainly it was regarded better by Sharpsfield back then . . . ."

Cantrelle noted Dieter's companion, his mouth now closed in a grim set, flinch at that remark and then nudge Dieter slightly to recruit witness. Dieter did not respond.

". . . But did it do its job any better?" Moyer posed. "Did the patients fare any better back then? Did the staff perform better? Or did we offer better training to our residents in those good old days? I really don't think so. I think we do an overall far better job today then we ever did back then. I agree, however, we couldn't have had a better beginning. I feel that equal tribute should be given to those who today man the helm at least as well, I so believe, as any of our distinguished forebearers might have, given the current complexity of the job those forebearers never were required to know. Blasphemy, eh what? Sort of, if our reverence forbids comparison, and perhaps that's the difference between tradition and religion: tradition can adjust itself to fact; religion must never. I trust that what we feel so strongly this morning is correctly tradition which can be adjusted to certain facts. One fact is that years ago residency training was routinely apolitical in its thrust; now it is only ideally so. Today, the resident is called upon, these graduates will attest, to manage some patients whose savage illness is a product of a political philosophy delivered from a high level in our own government . . . ."

Here it comes, Cantrelle winced as his shoulders drooped.

". . . Moreover," Moyer pursued, "political, not medical decisions, have determined this commonwealth's approach to the management of such cases, blurring once again, as politicians are wont to do, the difference between technical control, which is professional, and operational control, which is administrative. I strongly agree with Dr. Burleson that Blush patients should be treated as close to their communities as possible and not shipped off to die out of sight. That's barbarous. One wonders how Dr. Palmer would have handled a directive such as that. As well as Dr. Corley? One wonders."

For Christ's sake! He's going to start a riot, Cantrelle thought in alarm, noting that the air was picking up electricity again and that the thrum of the crowd was beginning to harden into a united militancy.

"One also wonders where such a barbarous policy had its beginnings and from where it receives its imperative," Moyer posed. "We know all too well how far it reaches, and apparently it's not just a local matter because other states seem to be following the same path, though we're perhaps farther along because of our earlier contact with Blush. It has been learned that Federal funding has been made available to the states under a rather vague provision called the 'Local Programs Enhancement Act' for use in establishing, equipping, and maintaining those Blush holding centers. The government demonstrated handsome and commendable sensitivity, we feel, in not having the money disbursed through the Indian Affairs Bureau," he snickered. "The upshot, of course, is that vastly more money is being spent to accommodate the demise of Blush victims, conveniently out of sight of the squeamish public, than is being spent on tracking down those guilty of instigating this campaign of annihilation. Also, I might add, vastly more money than is being spent on research as to how Blush's action could be blunted or even prevented. We have indeed fallen into the posture of accepting Blush and its grisly cargo much the same way as the ancients accepted leprosy, as Dr. Burleson has suggested, and we're using the traditional tactic of alienating the victims, though now, being so much more advanced, we supposedly do it more humanely with the help of generous Federal funding."

Cantrelle could sense that the audience was awash in a blend of public outrage and personal guilt. Here and there a head shook in attempted disbelief, only to return to eager attention as Clay's words totaled up to the compelling thesis that Blush was not merely some random and regrettable misadventure of the international drug trade, but a coordinated and regulated strategy emanating from some national or even international governmental agency, the United States Federal Government most particularly and the NSA or some extension of it almost certainly, with the state governments acting in fiscal compliance with the programmatic and progressive removal of an unwanted element from the fabric of American society, that unwanted element today being defined as the drug addict but being potentially *anybody* or *any* group, depending on the policy or whim of those behind the design.

Cantrelle sat fascinated, as transfixed as anyone else by the spell of Clay's missive. It was monstrous, frightening, and too believable. He tried to imagine how the audience felt, many hearing it for the first time. He had been part of Clay's progressive ascent to this point of sway and thus had enough familiarity with it to give him a sense of maneuverability even within its snare; but these people, getting it in one large, fresh, and overwhelming dosage . . . well, talk about becoming addicted, he winced inwardly at the tasteless allusion. Also, he was embarrassed by what Clay was doing, as he knew the others sitting at the table were. But there was nothing to do about it. The audience was captivated, hearing, he guessed, what they had hoped yet feared to hear. Probably not unlike a horror movie, for Christ's sake! He sighed futilely.

"Dr. Morello is right . . . *perhaps*. There *is* a tentative plan for me to appear on *National Dateline*. *Tentative*, I must emphasize. I was approached by the network several weeks ago. Dr. Morello just happened to be on hand for a preception session when I received the most recent phone call suggesting a date, and that's how he got wind of it, though he had sworn himself to secrecy. A lot of good that did!"

Several giggles arose from the audience in a trade-off with titillation. Morello smiled mischievously. Jesus Christ! Some people were taking the whole thing as a lark, Cantrelle flustered under his dismay.

"I was approached by the network, as I said, and I agreed to appear. It's still only tentative, remember. But I agreed because I think I'll have the opportunity to say what a lot of us here at Moreland, and, I'm sure, people everywhere else are thinking and wondering. I do it strictly as a private citizen and in no way as a spokesman for this hospital or the state Office of Public Welfare or any other agency. Only as a worried, private citizen, but one who has had the benefit, or misfortune, of working with an aspect of the problem which we now know was only the very beginning. Ladies and gentlemen, it is that worry which overrides any sense of good taste for bringing this up at all at this graduation ceremony, and I realize in doing so I'm contributing to the politicizing of Residency Training as I railed against just a few minutes ago. In the name of good taste I should have just accepted my certificate from Dr. Morello, said a few words about reverence for the past, pride in the present, and hope for the future, and sat down. But it wouldn't have been sincere, and we all know how unforgivable insincerity is in modern-day America," he added with eyebrows arched in uncompromising cynicism, which stirred additional giggles, especially from the graduates who were long familiar with the gesture. "Thus, Dr. Burleson's address to you, I feel, was more in keeping with the ideal we strive for—compassionate, and totally professional. Mine, regrettably, has been prowling, accusatory, and political—hardly the thing for a pleasant morning such as this. But to my way of thinking, my remarks are somehow complementary to his, though in that fond hope there may be sore presumption. I agree with Dr. Burleson as wholeheartedly as I can that the sufferings of the individual patient should never be lost sight of, but I feel obliged to add that the patient's malefactor, reciprocally, must not be allowed to continue unseen, either. In any event, I feel the difference between us, if any, is actually that come of apposition rather than opposition, but for either of which, it is true, at this moment I feel myself quite selectively mandated. How so? Because of *this*!" he waved the certificate merrily. "We all know how residents have the regrettable tendency to ask questions which put a strain on conventional answers, don't we? Well, now that I'm forever one of them, I hope to live up fully to that obnoxious calling. And absolutely because of *this*"—he waved the certificate again—"I am duly authorized to ask terrible questions, and I can do it with a good heart. I'm curious to see how it all works out. Thank you again, graduates, and thank *you*, ladies and gentlemen."

The explosive applause which followed Clay to his seat was mixed with rapid and animated talk as the audience turned to each other to press discussion of this or that point broached by Clay's manifesto. People were nodding or shaking their heads, hands were waving in emphasis, and words were swirling as in a current as the audience seemed ready to separate itself into discussion groups, work-shop fashion, and flail away hammer and tongs at the issues and implications raised by the several speakers. Cantrelle had never seen a graduation audience, or any other for that matter, worked up as this one was. And he, too, felt the contagion that was gripping them as he surveyed what he would have to bring to order in the immediate next instant. The power of the tumult awed him and he noted that Dieter was surveying the audience as well while her companion scribbled furiously on his scratch pad. At the moment of peak ripeness for action Cantrelle licked his lips, set his jaw, and took a deep breath. He then rose to approach the lectern. Upon reaching it he raised his hand to restore silence. His patience was not rewarded and he had to tap the lectern several times sharply to be heard over the din. Gradually a restless, shaky silence returned.

"Well, there you have it, ladies and gentlemen," he enunciated directly into the microphone, "a typical, run of the mill Moreland graduation exercise."

The laughter was mixed with guffaws, and chatter started to break out again.

"Ladies and gentlemen," he interceded quickly, "I wish to thank you for joining with us this morning, and I especially want to thank Dr. Burleson and our other speakers for honoring the occasion for us as they have. Their ideas have incited us to vigorous debate, obviously, and since our formal ceremony is now at an end I invite all of you to join the graduates and the speakers in the enjoyment of the refreshments arranged by Mrs. Andretti and the other ladies of our staff who now await you in the rear of this room. Thank you and good morning."

Polite applause was quickly overridden by the movement of chairs and people as all rose to seek out new precincts for gathering together to continue the debate.

He felt absolutely drained as he stood momentarily at the lectern and watched the roiling movement before him. He then turned, level smile in place, and approached the table where Burleson, Corley, and Weaver were already up and about, chatting amiably. As he neared, Burleson extended his hand.

"Congratulations, Dr. Cantrelle, on such a fine graduation exercise," Burleson beamed as he held Cantrelle's hand in both of his. "I was just telling Dr. Corley and Dr. Weaver how much I enjoyed it, seeing the people of Moreland doing what they've always done best—lead. And I was just about to say that a very large measure of credit for that should go to you and to Mr. Moyer, as this morning's ceremony so amply attests."

Cantrelle was taken aback by the man's graciousness. If anything, Burleson had reason to feel affronted by Clay's pre-emption of the ceremony's theme. But here Burleson was, seeming to delight in having been a participant, and being thankful to others for the opportunity. Maybe that's the way great people naturally managed such things, while people like himself, Frank Cantrelle, could only try.

"Please, Dr. Burleson," Cantrelle squirmed, "it was your presence that made it happen."

"You're so kind," Burleson tut-tutted as he gathered in Corley and Weaver with his smile. "Everyone here knows that Moreland is generically every psychiatrist's heritage in this great land, and visitors like myself only reflect it, not create it. I fear that all of you here are much too modest."

"Clay Moyer may soon cure us of that failing, I suspect," Weaver simpered.

"Actually," Burleson responded deftly in mock stealth, "I'm fascinated with his thesis, but hardly the sort of thing oldsters like us could pursue."

Cantrelle immediately felt excluded from the round of chuckles shared by the three mutually attesting elders. Burleson spotted the shadow of forlornness on Cantrelle's face and quickly followed up.

"Which reminds me, Dr. Cantrelle. Our paths continue to cross and we haven't yet made good our promise to get together sometime and have that talk we agreed upon long ago. Sadly, whenever we meet it's hardly the occasion for it."

"That's true, Dr. Burleson," Cantrelle replied eagerly, pleased to be included again.

"I suggest we reaffirm our intent to do so. But for the time being I think the four of us are expected momentarily by the guests," Burleson motioned in the direction of the milling people, some of whom were waiting patiently at the edge of the podium to be the first to collar him. "It cannot be avoided, I fear," he quipped to the delight of his three hosts.

"You're so right, Dr. Burleson," Martha asserted sweetly.

"May I?" he asked with a courtly nod as he offered his arm.

"Thank you, sir," Martha replied as she looped her arm in his for their recession from the podium. Cantrelle and Weaver followed in train.

They were swamped by guests as soon as they dismounted the podium. Most clustered around Burleson, though some of the approving comments came his own way as well, but with much less diffidence and awe as toward Burleson, and even Martha. He and Weaver were on about the same level of familiarity with the staff and hence with the guests as well, comparatively. He noticed that as many people were huddled around Clay as were around Burleson. In a flash he remembered to look for Dieter. She was nowhere to be seen. Instinctively he looked out of the large windows toward the parking lot and saw her and her companion walking rapidly toward their car, the companion thrashing the air in hot discourse. He watched them get into their car and drive off much too fast. He didn't like the portent of their haste. He would have preferred to have spoken with her, however briefly, before she left so as to get a sense of her thinking about all that had been said. He pondered the point until a slap on the back brought his thoughts back into the room.

"Good show, Frank," hailed the usually restrained and mannered Dr. Anthony Berends, Chief of the Triage Unit.

"That's what I'm worried about, Tony," he deferred, "a bit too much of a show. Overstated and overwrought. All of a sudden we're the goddamned epicenter of controversy, it seems."

"Yeah, I think so, too, and I'm glad. If you look around I think you'll see that everybody else is glad, too. And now we all have to ride it out, Frank. Sort of our thing to do together now, thanks to you and Clay," Berends breezed.

He looked around. The hum of discourse in the milling, eating, laughing, luxuriating crowd spoke him right. This is what they wanted, needed; and it had somehow happened as ordained, but certainly not by him. Just then he saw Burleson reach over his encircling suppliants to shake the hand of Clay, also offered over a ring of determined discussants. Each spoke to the other briefly and exaggeratedly in the lull permitted by their respective adherents, but were soon quickly reclaimed by their separate camps. Just as he was ready to shake his head in total submission to the riotous commotion sweeping along before him he spotted Laura working her way toward him.

"Excuse me, Tony," he requested.

"Sure. See you later, ole buddy," returned Berends, "and don't forget: thanks."

Cantrelle nodded a smile and then sidled his way toward Laura. She was followed by Ellie and Jeffrey. As they reached him he convoyed them over to a less impacted side of the room. Then, all in place, he stood before her.

"Tired, huh?" Laura consoled.

"Yeah, like too tired for it ever to be the same again," he sighed.

"Nah," she disclaimed, taking his hand, "Monday starts another academic year, and you, like the venerable phoenix, will have arisen once more or I don't know my hubby. And let me tell you, mister, I know my hubby."

He pulled her into a one-armed comradely hug and then looked at Ellie and Jeffrey standing by attentively.

"Well, what do you think of all this, Jeffrey?" he chipped.

"Wow!" exclaimed Jeffrey, grateful for the opportunity at last to speak his piece. "I've never seen anything like this before! You people are great! Awesome!"

This boy, Jeffrey Landon, was proving to be a pretty good kid, Cantrelle observed in satisfaction with his daughter's taste.

He then surveyed the importantly busy room, and, satisfied, turned to Laura still held tightly in his one-armed embrace.

"Let's go home, Hon," he pleaded.

"But what about the families? They usually want to meet you. And Burleson? What about seeing him off?" she reminded him responsibly.

“I’ve already settled things with Burleson—again we agreed to talk someday—and as for the proud families, today it’s Clay’s and Burleson’s show, as I was happily reminded a few minutes ago. Martha and Jess have Burleson in tow and I think it’s nice that they have such a prominent part in today’s doings. They more than deserve it, and Burleson would agree. Let’s go home.”

He took her by the hand and wove a way through the crowd, Ellie and Jeffrey following. As they worked their way along, he listened to the energized and urgent chatter that ricocheted off the walls of the room, all of it pointing toward important events long overdue and destined to occur through the enlightened leadership of those right here at Moreland. And now it was only a matter of time before such events would come, and via national hook-up, too. What had he and Clay started, he bleated, and how had it gotten out of hand? And so quickly? Talk about Destiny waiting to happen! And Clay! How could he become so focal so fast? As he reached the exit, he turned to take one last look at this morning’s *mise en scène*. He gazed at the crowd, still furiously at its work, and saw Burleson and Clay busy at marshalling separate flanks of the assembly under the sweep of their command. He decided that those were the kind of people who had what it took to make things happen. He then pushed open the exit door and held it ajar for Laura, and then for Ellie and Jeffrey. Joining them outside on the landing he took a lingering, nostalgic look at the gentle and lovely surroundings of this now restless building. The trees still seemed so peaceful and certain. Satisfied, he led the way to the parking lot.

ELEVEN

It was a perfectly clear day and the cloudless sky was just as blue at the horizon as it was overhead. Off to his right in the distance a huge Ferris wheel was turning lazy circles as though paddle-wheeling through a surrounding sea of tents, people, and cotton candy. A current of humanity flowed along the dusty paths lined by the stalls and tents in which crafts, baked goods, produce, and farm equipment were hawked as the finest of their kind. The tootling of a calliope could be heard coming from the general area of the Ferris wheel and it offered a happy cadence to the milling about of the fairgrounds crowd. More immediately on his right just fifty or so yards away a large rectangular shed with a corrugated tin roof served as the livestock judging area and he could just make out movement in some of the pens as various farm animals were herded back and forth. From the other side of the livestock shed and out of view he could hear the undulant yodeling of the hog calling contest in progress, its chords fading in and out as the breezes wafted the sound about. The same breezes stirred and whipped hundreds of pennants and streamers which laced the outlines of the various tents and stalls. Flags and patriotic bunting completed the effect. The bunting was particularly well applied to the stage where he now sat at a table with a fleshy, top-hatted and swallow-tailed official known by all to be the local Mayor. The table was flanked by several chairs in line on each side, each chair containing an official in similar attire. He was the only one on the stage in street clothes and hatless. Somewhere behind them a brass band was finishing up on "There'll Be a Hot Time in the Old Town Tonight." In front of the stage sat row upon row of silent, gaunt people, mostly men, in folding chairs set up on the grassy lawn. They stared impassively at the stage and were perfectly motionless in their plain, ill-fitting clothes which contrasted sharply with that of the officials and his as well. Their grim appearance seemed better suited to a memorial service than to any carnival event. As soon as the music stopped the mayor rose and walked up to a microphone set at the front of the stage. He smiled his full and ample girth as he began to speak.

"Ladies and gentlemen, today we have the honor of having with us Dr. Frank Cantrelle. Dr. Cantrelle, will you please come forth?" the Mayor bade as he turned to urge him along.

Cantrelle rose and approached the mayor and the microphone, feeling a rush of uncertainty as to the purpose of all this. When he arrived at the microphone he was greeted by the mayor's overdone smile, which only enlarged upon his own uncertainty. He then peered out on the motionless audience who looked back with vacant, dead eyes. He began to feel that something was terribly wrong.

"And now, ladies and gentlemen, the moment we've waited for," the mayor continued. "Dr. Cantrelle will play the old traditional, 'Turkey in the Straw.'"

He now knew for sure that something was terribly wrong.

The mayor handed him an object which he accepted tentatively, trying to smile as he did so. He then examined it, hoping to find some clue as to what he was supposed to do with it. It was a length of copper tubing about five inches long and about an inch and a half in diameter. One end had been cut lengthwise in strips about two inches long, the strips varying in width and bent outwards, sunburst fashion, to form a splayed flange. The mayor and everybody else watched in silence as they waited. He then realized that he was supposed to play this contraption by twanging the strips as he held it to his open mouth, Jew's harp fashion. Not knowing what else to do he put it to his mouth and struck the strips. But no sound came forth. He tried again, but still no sound. He saw that the mayor had by now lost his smile and was beginning to flush with anger. The people in the audience were fixing him with a widening stare from their dead eyes and he discerned malicious, evil smiles creeping across their faces. He began to blow on the contraption as he plucked the strips but the effect was only to provoke the mayor all the more as members of the audience, now smiling broadly in malevolent glee, lifted their hands in unison to point accusingly at him. He blew harder to still them because he knew that any tone from the contraption would do so. But he couldn't get it to make the slightest sound. The audience rose as they pointed with their boney fingers and began to move toward him. He blew harder and harder, and just when the enraged mayor was about to snatch the contraption from him he bolted upright, gasping for air.

"Wait! No! Wait! I can . . . Uh! Uhhh!" He clutched the contraption as the mayor grabbed at it.

"Frank, wake up! Wake up! You're dreaming," he heard Laura's voice coming from somewhere.

"No, Laura, Get back! They're coming!" he shouted.

"Frank! It's all right! It's a dream!" he heard her implore.

He blinked his eyes open wide and sat stock-still as he tried to catch his breath. His heart was thumping wildly as the mayor and the people and everything about them slowly receded from his presence. He felt her hand gripping his arm while she stroked the back of his head with the other. The worst of it was over and he was coming back into focus as the others disappeared.

"It's all right, Frank," she said again more soothingly as she switched on her light.

The others were now gone and his wits were returning. He took a deep breath and then blew it out in a huff to signal return of control. He wiped his mouth with his sleeve and spoke as he lowered his head to rest it on his forearms bridging his raised knees.

"It was that dream again," he anguished.

"That's what I figured," she consoled as she continued to stroke him.

"It's always the same and it's never the same," he groaned.

"I know," she acknowledged gently.

He lifted his head and looked at her in the faint light of her table lamp.

"You'll never guess what I was doing," he dangled, working to invite some measure of mirth to the moment. They were careful to keep a grip on fancy whenever they shared some distressing event. Kept things balanced, they agreed. "I was at a state fair and standing on a stage before hundreds of people and trying to play 'Turkey in the Straw' on a piece of copper tubing!" he shuddered.

"One of my favorites," she oohed.

His laughter completed his return to stability, and he signaled as much by taking her hand from its stroking and giving it a relieved kiss before nestling it entwined with his between their hips as they sat together in aftermath.

"And the people!" he continued. "They were so damned strange. Like they were sick, or dead. No corn-fed wholesomeness in that crop. Their staring eyes, glazed over; you know, like when someone just dies and in that split moment the eyes change to lifelessness. Ugh!" he shuddered as he recounted the effect for her.

She didn't quip at that image but just squeezed his hand in assurance.

He then turned and looked at the clock. Four forty-five. Almost time to get up anyway.

"Like always, the damned thing's telling me that I'm postponing something I really shouldn't be postponing and that I'd better get cracking," he resumed, referring to the general pitch of the dream, the basic form underlying its content which varied wildly from one time to the next. "And as far as that goes, you can have your pick. Any suggestions as to what I'm neglecting?" he continued in pique.

"Yes, I have," she offered slyly, "but it can wait until tonight, if you prefer."

"That does it! I just barely escaped with my life and you have only one thing in mind!" he remonstrated broadly. "I need some coffee, is what I need!!" Ordinarily, it was indeed the case that when they were up this early together it was in concert with a throbbing erection, but nothing could be farther removed at this moment and she knew it, but at least their conjugal raillery was now fully back on track. He gathered himself together and leaned over to give her a chaste kiss of gratitude. "You try to get some more sleep, Hon; we had a long drive yesterday. I'll be back later on with your coffee. Gotta do a little work on that stupid dream," he explained.

She slid down and back under the blanket, sighing cozily as she gathered her pillow to her. He eased himself out of bed and into his slippers and robe and then switched off her light as he scuffed out of the room into the inky quiet of the hallway. His groping steps brought him to the kitchen where the lurid green light of the percolator's timer blinked off and on like the diodic pulse of a dutiful little Martian. He found the light switch and flicked it on. The fluorescent lights stuttered into life, momentarily blinding him with their piercing glare. He blinked his eyes a few times in adjustment and then tapped the "ON" button of the percolator. There was now little to do but wait, and think. He leaned the small of his back against the counter and dug his hands deep into the pockets of his robe the better to ponder. This time the dream had been particularly menacing. Usually it was merely unpleasant, nettling, and occasionally even hilarious, such as the time he had unwittingly learned the lines of the wrong operetta but didn't realize it until opening night when it came time for his solo. Or the time when the final exam was given in a foreign language he was supposed to have learned along with the course material but somehow had forgotten to do so. But it was always his being called upon to perform some crucial task far beyond his capacity and being abruptly confronted with his stark inadequacy before God and all. Where the hell was that coffee, he grumbled as he stole a glance at the percolator. Another god-damned watched pot, he concluded. He shut his eyes to undo the delay and resumed the pondering. Also, when he would waken from the dream there was usually close at hand a lurking sense of relief that not only was it just a dream but that any real, living problem currently threatening him with angst could not, in comparison, hope to be as dismantling as the dream was, so there! But there was little of such smug relief this morning, so far. He needed to go at the damned thing, and he audibly sighed at the prospect. The manifest part seemed evident enough at first glance; it was the cast of terror that puzzled him.

The aromatic pungency of the perking coffee finally arrived and he opened his eyes in relief. The kitchen's harsh whiteness was still present, but now its brightness afforded him clear view of the percolator's emergent dripping. He watched the brackish stream trickle into the carafe and he was not surprised that it brought the Ferris wheel to mind. That damned Ferris wheel! The Wheel of Life. Or a prayer wheel? Certainly the eternal workings of existence. Galactic. His awe of Ferris wheels when he was a little boy. Still today, he admitted. They looked so airy and flimsy. He now remembered that the time he got lost when a little boy he was drawn to the Ferris wheel as the most visible and orienting structure in the carnival. Plus, there was a security guard standing nearby. He had earlier stood before it with his family and dreaded that his father would want to take him aloft on it. It may have been mentioned, but it didn't happen. Thus it was one of the most prominent if not the most prominent place he had been to at the carnival with his parents before he got lost. He was certainly lost on that stage with that piece of copper tubing. Tubing. Sitting under the house and holding a wrench for his father who was fixing a pipe. Age three? His mother calling to them that his father was wanted on the phone and his father's expletive, or what surely must have been one. The man in the top hat. The mayor. The same authoritarian type who could just as well hand him a wrench, a wrench a three-year-old would hardly be able to use. His recurring discomfort with closed-in spaces, not to mention his abiding horror of being buried alive. He took a deep breath at the thought of it to offset the automatic sense of suffocation the thought brought. The deep breath sent him right back to huffing and puffing at the copper pipe, now a failing conduit of life-giving air. The people in the audience, their eyes already dead, waiting for him to make that pipe—pied piper?—restore them to life, or lead them away from the grave. "Turkey in the Straw?" His terror at the anesthesia when he was six and underwent ear surgery, begging the anesthetist simply to let him fall asleep as he promised he would if they didn't put that mask over his face, and then struggling as they held him and clamped it over his nose and mouth. He again breathed deeply at the memory of the suffocation he felt as he tried not to inhale the ether, and then remembering reeling and falling down a swirling vortex—Wizard of Oz? Wizard! Fraud!—and seeing a turkey and watching its neck stretch as it gobbled, frightened. It was Thanksgiving time when he went into the hospital. He felt his heart pounding in tempo with the memory of the experience. Serenade the Blush patients with "Turkey in the Straw?" What a cynical song of sympathy! But he couldn't play it. Was he rejecting them? What were they doing at a state fair where livestock judging was going on? State Fair! Hey! State Hospital! Livestock! It was so obvious now that he saw the connection. Was it veterinary psychiatry for them as they became mute as beasts with the progression of the disease? Why had he been put up there—or had put himself up there—before them? To look as pathetic and inadequate as he felt? Questions that could just as easily be declarations had he the courage to admit what he felt? Or was what he felt becoming too obvious? That he didn't want to go back to the evil blight of Blush which had damaged his world of teaching beyond any hope of restitution? The rolling fields behind the hospital, farmed by the state until recently, were no longer clean and wholesome. And he himself was no longer particularly clean and wholesome—just hopeless? The coffee was almost ready, thank God, and he fished his mug out of the cabinet to have it at hand when the dripping stopped. Not a moment to lose. He thought he felt a caffeine headache beginning to compound his self-pity. He didn't need it to go that far. Others saw the situation at Moreland as an institutional renaissance—dangerous, inspiring, and even destructive in a daringly syncretic way. And he felt left out of it, just as he did at the graduation ceremony. Clay was now the ascendant figure, and justly so. Being on vacation for two weeks had relieved him of the demeaning feeling that he was now little more than a caretaker Director of Training while Clay fought on Moreland's frontiers for its new manifest destiny. As he poured the overdue coffee he came as close as he would that morning to seeing himself, thanks to that damned dream, as a trapped yet alienated clownish figure whose meagerness nourished the craven thought that the sooner all of the Blush patients were dead and gone the sooner things could get back to normal so that he could go to work with a good and innocent heart, like before. He blew on the coffee before taking a sip, and, that done, he smiled grimly as he stared beyond the cup. If only his residents could know how noble and magnanimous their director was, deep in his heart of hearts. It was now time to go to the wall.

He balanced his full cup as he worked his way through the darker regions of the house, the kitchen light shading into umbral murk as he neared his study. He opened the door to be greeted by the mustiness that had accumulated over the past two weeks and which now seemed heavier in the dark than it was yesterday when they got home. He felt his way to his desk and switched on the lamp which yielded its pale, yellowish glow of chosen low intensity. His study, like his office, was suffered only subdued lighting. Gloomy lighting, some thought. Meditative lighting, he insisted.

As he nestled up to his desk, carefully setting his coffee in its appointed place, he sized up the distant wall still fogged in the sooty shroud of night. The windows were not yet silhouetted against the dawn and their blackness quenched the feeble light his desk lamp ventured in that direction. All in all, the conditions were pretty good for some restorative wall staring woefully in arrears for the two weeks he had been in a cabin which used walls as much for hanging things on as for keeping out the wind and rain and for holding up the roof. He then hunched over his desk and rested his arms in place before him, overlapping them at the wrists as he settled into a distant gaze. At first nothing came, other than the immediacy of being back in his study this first morning in over a fortnight. That awareness reminded him that the new crop of residents, undoubtedly awaiting his return this very morning, had all shown up for duty, brushed and scrubbed, on reporting day July first. God, that was already over a month ago. He had seen them through orientation, and, once they were settled in the custody of their supervisors and preceptors, had taken off for the waters. All pretty standard. Several of the teaching staff were just starting their vacation, having opted for the traditional month of August, a choice which suited him fine. To have had too many out at start-up time, July first, would have brought training to a standstill. As it was, July was given over to the settling-in process for the new arrivals as well as for the senior residents who were shifting to new assignments for the beginning year. Some residents also were on vacation, the schedule worked out far in advance to sustain adequate coverage. So the teaching, but not the clinical or administrative assignments, were kept light for the July-August transition time as the curriculum jogged in place to warm up for the full chase which began when a faculty quorum was achieved in late August. By Labor Day, symbolically and factually, all would be in motion for the full-tilt, non-stop gallop to next June thirtieth, except for the brief Christmas detour. Clay was still out there, bicycling through the flinty wilds of New England, in his annual exertion he proclaimed to be vacation. He would be home later this week, probably this coming Sunday, and be back on the job Monday. That god-damned TV appearance apparently was indeed going to happen and specifically on the Sunday after his return, a scheduling which prompted Clay to move up a few weeks the usual late August slot he preferred for his cycling exertions. This had resulted in some overlap of his and Clay's time away from the residents, not the best arrangement but one which was managed uneventfully if he could trust the check-in calls he made last week to the meticulous and circumspect Dr. Berends who lately seemed all too eager to help Clay along in accommodating his teaching duties to his public appearances. Clay's indictment of the NSA in his graduation address had earned a news story in the local papers, and before he left on vacation he had made a couple more appearances—one in Washington, DC—in which he reiterated his theme that Blush was a federally directed assault upon social undesirables and that the executive branch had to accept direct accountability for the crime. It was as though his appearances thus far were calculated increments in the intensification of confrontation, with his forthcoming interview on *National Dateline* to serve as climactic formalization of his impeachment of the government as Blush's silent executor. Thus, all his earlier utterances would be offered as premise for the long overdue arousal of public outrage. Certainly the people at Moreland had been talking about it that way, and a wait-till-the-rest-of-the-country-hears-about-this expectancy had charged the air. And now everybody was awaiting his return. Despite Clay's efforts to keep the matter his private business and his individual effort, Moreland had become identified as the source of his transmissions, much as in those cartoon renderings of a radio tower sending off waves from its topmost point in ever-widening concentric circles. It had become almost obligatory to endorse Clay's contention, for to oppose or question it, as some certainly did, was seen as a breach of faith in the duty of sustaining such a worthy crusade, which, even if wrong in its specific allegations, could only result in the focusing of much-needed public attention where it would assuredly do some good. But by and large a lot of people thought he was probably right in his particulars. Also, his conviction in the power of emerging truth seemed to bind his followers one to another as well as to him. But what did he, Frank Cantrelle, putting envy and self interest aside, think of Clay's annunciation? He had always known Clay to be a solid performer, incredibly knowledgeable and informed, but also one who tended to read more conscious intent in a person's shortcomings, particularly if those shortcomings added burden to his, Clay's, efforts. But even if they didn't add to his burden, he tended to regard such shortcomings as the measure of the possessor's limited grasp of the duty ethic. Mere capacity was not seen as explanatory enough, and oftentimes this led to problematic discourse in assessing resident performance. His notion of accountability was a keenly honed one and one which he applied with an unnegotiable pragmatism which discomforted those willing to cut their fellow man, and themselves, a little more slack. So what did he himself think of Clay's thesis? He really wasn't sure—or clear. He agreed that the government was lax and dawdling about the whole thing, but in being so was probably no better or worse than the population as a whole in wishing not to have to bother with the loathsome problem at all. True, there were genuine questions, such as what were the government's efforts to track down and eradicate Blush's source? Or why the restriction of funding of Blush research to just those federally endorsed and administered projects, which, in truth, seemed to discourage the participation of many potential contributors. The eager Jeffrey Landon, for one. Also, the Surgeon General had been unaccountably quiet on the entire issue, raising questions as to whether there was a lack of federal unanimity on the matter in the first place, the silence perhaps bespeaking failure at achieving any forthright policy. But what about

Clay's specific surmise? Did it click? Apparently for many others it did. But what about him—even-handed, fair-minded, reasonably unbiased Frank Cantrelle? He had to say it lacked something. It was too broad a leap to take. It seemed over-wrought, even pat, maybe just too generic what with all the scandals seeping forth from government chambers over the past several years. It certainly was trendy, though, and perhaps in part it owed its swelling ranks just to that. But he couldn't say any of this to anyone, except Laura and perhaps Jess, but not to Ellie now that she seemed aligned with Jeffrey Landon's interests, for to do so would surely invite the charge of disloyalty at best and small-minded envy at worst. And there would be some truth in it, either way. So, summing up, he really had to disqualify himself for lack of conviction, and because of a reluctance to cheer without passion he perforce removed himself from the ranks of the ready. Two weeks vacation and all the more alienated, damn it, and not just because of simple time away from the job. He hoped Clay would never ask him to stand up and be counted. He knew that Clay sensed his reservations and thus carefully avoided any breaching of their unspoken entente. And for his own part he had done the same. But it was that very truce which put him peripheral to what everybody at Moreland now considered to be the real action. So there he was: obligated to irrelevance, profound in his doubt. As he rolled that particular summation over in his head the old feeling of being on the verge began to sweep over him. The first time in weeks. It had been lurking at the corners of his thinking for the past several minutes and he knew better than to try to beam awareness at it for fear of chasing it away entirely. It had now sprung forth and was upon him, somehow coaxed into reach by his grazing thoughts. The mayor in the top hat was washed back into view along with the usual wordless feeling, and again he felt himself right there on the verge of the "something." He closed his eyes to look inwardly at what he felt he was ready to see. He even held his breath. But the expectation, indistinguishable from his recognition of achieved readiness, interposed a disjunction, like a shifting in depth caused by a tidal bore, and he felt the readiness begin to recede. He tried to dampen his sense of expectation, but the effort only aggravated the decay. He then saw himself, copper tubing in hand, standing before the crowd which awaited his address. That somehow settled it. In short order the moment was completely gone. He sighed and opened his eyes. The room now seemed a little less distinct but more familiar. What the hell was this thing he could almost see? He then noticed, as though bidden to do so, that the far windows were beginning to hint at grayness. He idly picked up his coffee mug as he surveyed the windows and took a sip. Even the coffee had gone cold. God, he felt so disconnected, so disjointed, and about as cranky as that good old bear with hemorrhoids. The ass end of that last thought brought a trace of a smile which he levered into an initiative for getting up from his chair, cup in hand.

He returned to the kitchen's overbearing white glare and poured himself another cup of coffee. The first cup was approaching full effect as he felt his body replace sleep's torpor with a more serviceable birr now beginning to make itself felt. Another cup would bring him up to speed and fix the pace for the rest of the morning. As he added the cream he raised his eyebrows at the irony that most likely the same country that yielded this coffee also delivered the ubiquitous Blush. He had even read last week that Inigo Pontalbas planned to meet with the Secretary of State on the latter's forthcoming good will tour of Central America and had accepted an invitation to visit Washington in turn sometime in the near future "for definitive discussions on matters of trade and kindred interests." Undoubtedly the government was feeling its way along in search of the best portal of entry for grappling with the flow of Blush into this country. It was a positive and hopeful sign. It also must be, he sympathized, tricky business meeting with a head of state to go over plans with him for putting him out of business, as would surely be understood out of hand to be the purpose of those discussions. It all seemed so arcane, so other-worldly, this craft of realpolitik and the practice of power, though it also seemed to come naturally enough to those who brokered in its commerce. He wondered if Clay was discovering a knack for it. If so, he knew Clay wouldn't be long for sleepy, prosaic Moreland, residency training, and quaint friendship. That thought prompted another sip of coffee, whose bite elicited a squint as it went down.

He checked the wall clock. Twenty after six. Time to take some coffee to Laura who about now would begin to feel the tug of the day and could use some bracing. He selected a cup, filled it, going light on the cream as she preferred, and balanced his way back to the bedroom which was still insulated in darkness. As soon as he entered she groaned in recognition and shifted her lie to free the edge of the bed for his sitting beside her in their long-observed ritual for starting the day. He placed her coffee on the bedside table and then sat down gently beside her. He took a moment to smell her heady, bewitching musk, concentrated by a night under blankets—Nooky Number Four, he had named it on their honeymoon—and then cleared his throat with another sip from his cup. She groaned again to signal consciousness.

"Shall there be light?" he asked.

"I guess so," she mumbled as she gathered herself into a sitting position, propping her pillow against the headboard. "How are you feeling? I mean the dream."

"Oh, I'm coming around," he breezed as he switched on the lamp to its dim setting. He then delivered the cup to her waiting hands.

Why was it her hair never looked messed up but only in different shapings of coziness, he marveled as he watched her curls shift as she sipped her coffee.

"I'll give you a minute to return to life and then I want to ask you something, Sweet," he warned.

"Go ahead. From your tone I think I'd rather be half dead when I hear what's on your mind," she quipped into her cup as she dove in for another sip. "It's about what the dream means, isn't it?" she posed solicitously as she resurfaced.

"Yeah," he mumbled.

"You know, it could be just a dream," she offered in generous simplicity, her protective instincts already in gear.

"I would like to believe that, but it says too much," he rued. "Hon," he continued, "am I displaying my smallness by thinking that Clay is becoming crazy paranoid like those flakey cult leaders you hear about? Or is he seeing what I'm too limited to see? One of us is out of it, and my dream points the finger at me, literally, and particularly at my impotence on this Blush thing."

She looked at him with concern framing her face. She then lowered her eyes as she spoke.

"I was talking to Helen the other day and she said she too was worried that Clay's sermons and all the hoop-la would put a strain on your friendship," she confided, "and she admitted that at times she also has trouble when she tries to talk to him. Apparently a lot of people, some of them pretty odd, are flocking around him and egging him on beyond what she believes he really intends, but he's touchy about being told so by her or by anybody else. Oh, he listens, she says, but that's about all. And if she shows too much concern he just dismisses it as nagging. So, if you're out of it, Frank, you have company."

"That's exactly what I'm worried about; that it's the company *I* keep that might bespeak a kind of default on my part," he sighed. "I don't know where I belong, and that's the main point. I don't even know what the hell I'm supposed to be going back to this morning." He hated the thought of sounding like a peevish, whining pain in the ass but he knew that if he didn't air his ruminations here with her right now he would sure as hell lather his work with them later on this morning, and no one awaiting him elsewhere deserved that. His loving wife didn't either, but she was his first and foremost line of hope. And besides, he reasoned flippantly, her smell made him do it. Thus exculpated he resumed. "Sweet, what do you think about this . . . this whole mess?" he implored with a wave of the arm. "I haven't asked you much about it. Not directly, anyway."

She looked at him pensively for a moment and saw that for him the vacation was really over. She had hoped they might linger a day or two in the reverie of the two playful weeks which had enabled him to put all the worries at some distance, or so it had seemed. He had barely mentioned anything of the "mess" while they were away and she had hoped that they would thus be vouchsafed a more gradual re-entry into what he now had waiting. But she could see that it was already fully upon him, delivered intact and in its entirety by that dream. Thus, her work was resuming also, just as abruptly, and now her own harness was waiting.

"Frank," she said measuredly as she looked down at her coffee, "you have to be careful in a way he doesn't have to be. He really can elect to speak for himself, but you can't and also continue your work at Moreland. You're responsible for too many people, and *to* them as well. For you to do what Clay is doing you would have to forfeit your position as Director. So, as I see it, my tortured husband, this Monday Morning Moment of Truth comes out sounding like a choice between default and forfeiture."

"Yeah," he blurted in a burst of liberated urgency, "even if I really believed in what the hell he's selling! Do *you* believe in it, Hon? You gotta tell me."

She knew that sooner or later his grappling with the question would force him to search out her thoughts on the matter, though she really didn't credit her thoughts about any part of it as being very considered or particularly well-founded, and mostly because of her distance from it all. She also knew that he would depend on just that, her distance from it all, to give her a less indentured position of observation and thus perhaps a more sensible view. Whenever he got mired in an issue or problem he would usually reach up to her to pull him out by way of some penetrating, clarifying, even simplifying suggestion or opinion, and that's what he was hoping for now.

"Well," she began off-handedly. "I feel about the same as you do about it. I don't believe that the accusations he's making are really justified. But on the other hand, I don't like my disbelief. I think that if what he's saying is right, then *someone* in the government would surely by now have come forth in his defense, or at least in support of his urgings. Also, if the government is really behind Blush I think it would have leaked out long ago; some elected official or someone close to federal workings would have stepped forth by now to sound an alarm. You know, like Watergate. But no one has, and it's hard to believe that every blessed person in and around the government is in on the conspiracy and flawlessly keeping the silence. Washington isn't made like that. Everybody is always trying to be holier than everybody else and no one would let the chance slip by to become the holiest of the holy by exposing the government's hand in Blush. Not to mention the media. And yet I agree with Clay and every one of his followers that something has to be done and that the government should be the one to do it. And I suspect that the silent majority as well as the squeaky minority pretty much agree on that special point and probably support Clay in much the same way I do. I think the people hear him saying that if the government is not behind Blush as he thinks it is, then the government had better come up with who is."

She looked mostly at her cup as she spoke but would turn to him from time to time to offer a furrowed brow in underscoring the sincerity or importance of some point or comment she wanted him to note. As he listened he watched the almost honeyed and uncritical—or was it his touchiness looking for cause?—play of gestures and intonations that carried her words, and he well knew she was being careful not to indict even obliquely his draft-exempt status in the evolving siege of Washington by cheering on too lustily the girded and bannered militia being led by Clay.

"So you don't think I'm a wimp hiding behind doubt?" he heard himself pose.

She smiled at her cup as she answered.

"I don't, but Art surely does."

"I knew I could count on that son-of-a-bitch to turn an advantage in this," he bellowed, his assertiveness now reclaimed by way of indignation.

"But you have to understand," she soothed, "Art is like Clay, free to speak for himself without imposing unfair jeopardy on others. Plus, he just happens to be exceptionally good at it; like Clay."

"And irresistible?" he accused.

"Well . . . yes," she confessed, "but there's also something to be said for the unique satisfaction that comes of listening to 'A Barnyard Concerto for Copper Tube.'"

"I'll copper tube you, you vixen," he erupted as he snatched her cup from her hands, placed it out of peril, and threw himself on top of her as he manhandled her across the bed. As he subdued her laughing, squirming body he clutched a handful of curls to bring her lips to his. They kissed deeply. He then rested his cheek on hers.

"I feel better," he murmured, "and I'm ready to feel a lot better, but it's . . . ." He looked at the clock on the table. "Christ! Five before seven! What happened to the time? I have a class at eight thirty! No concerto this morning, Sweet," he groused as he lifted himself to his knees. God, she was beautiful, he sighed as he looked at her lying before him in just the right attitude of supine disarray. He leaned forward and gave her a quick promissory kiss. "Tonight, sweet, or my name ain't Elmer. I swear by my reaper," he twanged as he dismounted the bed and headed toward the bathroom. "I don't have time for breakfast, Sweet, and besides the kids will probably sleep in this morning," he advised enroute. He then closed the door behind him.

Laura resumed her sitting position in bed, knees now under her chin, and stared at the door separating them. He stares at walls and I stare at doors, she mused; he sees prospects and I see portals, and we're both hopeless visionaries. Good, she concluded with a smart tap on the mattress. She then swung herself out of bed and into her robe. He could use a glass of juice on his way out, she decided, already up and on her way to the kitchen.

The shower was pelting him forward into the morning as he pondered his arrival at the office. Mrs. Andretti would have the mail, the forms, the memos, the reports, the invoices, and God knows every other form paper could possibly take arranged in neat stacks on his desk such that hardly a sliver of desk surface would be free. There would be the usual backlog of problems and misadventures incident to the beginning of a new training year. And then, perhaps most irksome of all, there was the dismal and smarting metamorphosis from the gay liberty of vacation to the dutied cadence of teaching and of practice. The first day back was invariably a long one and it never felt like anything other than a ritualistic ordeal for the address of arrears which had to be made good before anything resembling reconciliation could proceed. But usually by the end of that first today he could feel some satisfaction in redemption done, which would then cast the savor of vacation even farther back in memory. And it would be so today, he pronounced in various octaves as he worked his way through his shaving.

By the time he was fully dressed he sensed the return of some of the familiar tattoo of preparation that had paced him to work countless hundreds of times before and which by day after tomorrow would be fully back in the daily line-up of automatic functions that carried him through his duties. Vestment done, he took a last look at himself in the mirror before heading out to the kitchen. Half the fun of going to work, he thought slyly as he checked himself, was dressing well, and this morning he would have to weigh in convincingly. Hence, the particularly impressive floral print tie defiantly reminiscent of vacation.

He then trotted down to the kitchen where Laura had set up a glass of orange juice and a slice of marmaladed toast in easy reach of his transit to the coffeepot for one last gulp before leaving.

"You've been having breakfast for the past two weeks and if you don't have something this morning you'll begin to drag in a little while and we wouldn't want you to feel any more wimpy than you already do, now would we?" she explained when he entered the kitchen. "And besides," she added as she sized him up quickly, "that tie deserves a strong supporting cast; otherwise, it'll look like it's wearing you."

He grunted a chuckle through a mouthful of the toast he was already addressing. After a sip of the juice he was able to speak.

"Yes, ma belle dame. There's a chance I'll be able to zip by at lunch time on my way to the office," he suggested, meaning his private practice office, "and maybe we can have a bite together just like in the fast-receding past two weeks. What do you say?"

"You know I would love that," she gushed, but she also knew not to count on it.

"O.K.," he snorted through another glump of toast," we'll shoot for it." With that he brushed his hands together and then took a swig of juice. After daubing his mouth with the napkin he leaned over and planted a peck on her lips. "If I can't make it I'll call. Ta-Ta."

He picked up his briefcase and trotted out of the house past the stationwagon which, he noted upon approach, needed a good washing to remove the dappling of shattered interstate insects which covered every leading surface. Maybe on the way to his practice office, he considered, if Laura didn't get to the washing by then. Settling in behind the wheel of his commute car he fired the engine, pronounced it sound, and then backed out onto the road. As he pulled away from the house he waved to Laura who was now standing in the doorway to see him off. A stab of regret went through him as their vacation officially slammed shut behind them to remand them once again to their separate tasks. He had left the house on a run in part to avoid a wrenching farewell at the front door, and the suggestion of lunch was in part a ploy to defer the finality of their vacation's completion. He made the same suggestion every year and Laura went along with it dutifully. It seldom ever happened that lunch together actually followed.

As he cruised along he felt the return of his route's familiarity. The lawns were now noticeably dryer and the trees had taken on that dark and heavy green which said that estivation was well along. The trees looked like they were in a languor, and especially so this morning without a hint of a breeze to stir them. The ocean breezes never let things get this torpid, he observed critically. And things here seemed so dusty in comparison to the bright, crisp cleanliness of the shore. He fought back the feeling of parole having been revoked and his being returned to custody for having been too indecorous in his delight at being away, much like Russian diplomats during Soviet times who were speedily sent home for re-education if it became apparent that they were inordinately enjoying their foreign assignment.

Too quickly he reached the iron gate which amply reinforced the notion of return to stir. Mercifully, the grounds, though slightly desiccated, were just as brushed and combed as when he left, signifying that once again the grounds crew had come out ahead in the annual tussle with the riotous side of nature's exuberance. The fellows on the tractors and mowers could probably begin to ease off a bit and slip into a more garrison mode now that the battle had been fought. Naturally, that thought brought the dream back to view and along with it all the rich feelings that go with one's behaving like an ass in public. A bolt of fear shot through him at the thought that just about anything could be awaiting him when he walked into his office, and the feel of it was exactly the same as when he stood on that stage with a piece of copper tubing in hand. Just as he began to shudder in earnest he reached the front of the MOB in what seemed a perfect piece of malicious timing. Pearly shore, where are you, he bleated to himself as he pulled into his slot and brought the car to a halt. He then took a deep breath. The scene of himself quaking and whimpering at the prospect of entering his very own and very prosaic office stung him into an eruption of derisive laughter, and as he switched off the ignition he felt a dawning relief at having met the menace of the dream and having prevailed. He then had the giddy thought of riding a tractor across the hospital lawn in a victory sweep. Apparently, he mused as he stepped out of the car, vacation had enhanced his sanity not at all.

Though dread still stalked him as he walked up to the building he now felt more in the company of mature expectancy. God, coming back was such an ordeal, he agreed as he pulled opened the glass door. He entered the hallway to be met again by the cloying mustiness of accumulated paper. Probably from the paper on his desk, he sighed. That thought brought him to his office door and he entered to see Mrs. Andretti brightly in place and with an extra touch of chic about her. A vase of flowers on the corner of her desk balanced the cameo. He was so relieved to see her thus. It boded well.

"Welcome back," she beamed as she looked up at him. "I can see that you didn't have very much rain. Was it nice?"

"Very," he returned, "but in a few days I'll be free of the torturous memory of it, and the Moreland pallor will soon restore me to full institutional fitness, I'm sure."

"Dr. Cantrelle, I think you give up too easily," she teased. "Protect the vacation spirit for a few more days, maybe even for the week! There's nothing urgent going on. The new residents are settling in very well. In fact this year it's been easier getting things going than ever I remember. It's probably the graduation. Everybody's still talking about it and I think it's made everybody a little more helpful and cooperative—and lots more proud of the place.

And the residents think they're at the only place worth being at. So I don't think anybody would mind if you worried a little less and took it easy for the next few days. Honest. After all, they do credit you with the way the graduation turned out."

He felt the anxiety drain from him as she spoke, bless her. He hadn't much considered that things would be perfectly fine in his absence. By his reckoning, the odds simply could not support such a hope. When he left, it was more with the sense that issues were joined and awaiting thunderous resolution. But now, as she spoke, it appeared that maybe he was the only one who felt that way. He knew better, but he did wonder if maybe he had overworked the scene and had fashioned mere problems into total afflictions. Her words came as sweet reminder that it could perhaps be so. She probably reflected reasonably well what most others felt, and the amity she conveyed returned him to the peace of homecomings he had enjoyed on all previous years and had generally taken for granted. To reconcile the sense of dread lingering within him despite the glow of bright expectancy now pleasingly alloyed to his return was a more manageable matter by far than what he feared actually was his lot for this pointed morning. And his unease remained, for he knew he would be getting off much too easily for it all to be so simple. When he left, he did so in the echo of an opening shot having been fired with opposing forces lined up and ready for certain battle. Now she was assuring him that harmony was still at hand, and she was probably right, but most likely only for the immediate scene. Her assessment was local and short-term. But it was a good thing to hear, and most pleasant to feel. And for many that was probably enough. Like a thrilling parade before a bloody battle that was sure to come. He had looked ahead at the likely terminus of the parade route and had positioned himself there some two weeks ago in dread readiness. There was certainly welcomed solace in seeing on this first morning back that the parade was still passing by. It gave him time to position himself for the next shot. He doubted that all of his worries would turn out to be foolishly chimeric because Clay and Burleson had placed far too many indictments, subsequently trumpeted in the press, for there not to be some counteraction. The manner of Dieter's departure from the graduation pretty well guaranteed such, for it was most unlikely that the DMH would not feel the need to defend and reaffirm its Blush policy, and then do so in a way to discourage further defections. He feared that Martha and Jess had already been darkly reprimanded for permitting so political and so partisan an event to occur on state property. He would check in with them later this morning for he was sure they too would be looking well beyond the parade if their attention had not already been directed so by a vengeful DMH.

"Any calls or messages from Dr. Corley or Dr. Weaver?" he chanced.

"No. Dr. Corley was away last week and today is her first day back, too. Dr. Weaver would like you to stop by this morning if you can, but he didn't say there was any urgency," she supplied evenly.

That sounded pretty good, and safe, he guessed.

"When you have a moment call Dr. Weaver's office and tell him I'll zip over and show him my tan after I finish up here this morning," he quipped. With that said he entered his office.

Again, that stale, musty smell, and despite the open window and the flowers on the bookshelf. It was probably present all the time, only that he got used to it after a few days, he suspected. And getting used to mustiness so as to be unaware of it, was, of course, the entire issue in the recent uproar whose fallout he dreaded facing this morning. But so far it was only paper mustiness, he delighted. Even the stacks of paper didn't look so high on his desk as he had anticipated. He picked up a reaf of letters, their envelopes neatly stapled to the back, and began to scan them one at a time before returning them to the desk. He reached one which carried an elaborate, showy letterhead in color which listed so many phone numbers, fax numbers, regional offices, and the names of so many corporate personnel listed down the left of the page that hardly any room remained for text. It was from *Watchfire*, a television program that was the high tech answer to the tabloid. He never watched it, except by accident, but a lot of people apparently did, and certainly everybody knew of the program. Anything controversial was its métier, and good taste had absolutely nothing whatever to do with it. In fact, it was largely believed, the more offensive the material the more energetic the programming. He read: ". . . *so pleased to note that the attention you and your institution have brought to bear on the terrible health problem facing the people of this nation has seen a responsible rise in the public outcry for action. We at Watchfire support your efforts and the efforts of all others who endeavor to inform the public on matters of vital interest, local or national, as may influence the quality of life in our land. Our efforts, we submit, have always been in the service of the public interest . . . .*"

"So I hear," he harrumphed, as he smirked at the piety rising up from the page.

"*. . . and we now hope to extend our reach in that mission by devoting an edition of our television series to the menace of Blush and the status of American medicine's response to the problem. Your work in the field identifies you as a knowledgeable and concerned figure and we would hope to have you join with us in such an edition, which is planned for a late September, early October airing. Your appearance on the program as guest speaker and roundtable discussant would carry a personal remuneration to be specified in future discussions of a more contractual nature . . . .*"

"I wonder how much," he cast idly as he flipped to the second page.

"*. . . when we would hope to comply with your preferences in any matters favoring the high quality presentation we intend. We stand immediately available to pursue any interest you may have in assisting us in this contribution to the public awareness and . . . .*" etc., etc.

The expansive signature of the CEO and Executive Director for Programming seemed historic in size and easily suitable for a charter or declaration. I guess that's the way one has to be in that business, he sighed. As he folded the letter back into its envelope the thought of his being on *Watchfire* as part of their usual venue of freaks and perverts gave him the right rollicking attitude to get the morning's work going.

"Mrs. Andretti," he bellowed through the open door, "how come you didn't tell me right off that *Watchfire* wants to pay me a bundle for being sensational? Just think, I could help them oodles in their ongoing ratings battle with *National Dateline*, and they in turn could give me some oodles all for myself. Might even pay for the vacation. What shall I wear? How about my lime sherbet leisure suit and gold necklace? Or should I go casual?"

He could hear her giggling as he toyed aloud with the outrageous in framing the scene.

"Just think," he continued, "Me, the *Watchfire* answer to *National Dateline* and Clay Moyer. Each of us trying to out-exposé the other in a national hook-up with the attentive NSA and DMH swelling the network ratings. I wonder how much *National Dateline* is going to pay Clay. I'll have to ask him when he gets back," he continued in his foolery, "because I wouldn't want to go in under the rate. Maybe I should get an agent, but he would only advise me to hold out until market pressure forces *Watchfire* to capitulate to my price which he himself would set. Say, I already feel corrupt and I'm not even famous yet." With that fillip, he tucked the letter into the breast pocket of his jacket. "Oh, my God," he then blurted in abrupt shift. "Be right back. I forgot something!" he announced as he raced out of the office.

He went directly to his car and opened the trunk. The several gifts for various secretaries and clerks were neatly in order just as he had placed them the night before. He and Laura made it a point, like everybody else, to return with peace offerings for hosts of friends and employees as the right means for returning to responsible status in the community. The sharing of vacation's largess by way of gifts was as clear a statement as any that duty had not been totally forsworn during those playful weeks of relative abandon. He located her present and then slammed the trunk shut. As he trotted back to his office he thought of his annual pre-departure threat to bring her back a lobster ashtray, of course never perpetrated, and knew she was probably thinking the same at the very moment. He then re-entered the office.

"Here," her proffered in an outstretched hand, "clear evidence that you never left my mind once."

"Oh, Doctor Cantrelle," she oohed with coy delight as she accepted the right-off-the-shelf boxed gift.

"I think it'll match the others. Got it at the dustiest antique shop this side of Hudson's Bay," he explained as she pried open the box.

"Oh, it's perfect," she exulted as she held it up before her.

"Nicks and all," he added.

Years earlier he began giving her assorted pieces of old crystal, all of the same Victorian pattern, and by now she had accumulated close to a score or so pieces as birthdays, Christmases, and vacations had tolled the years of her working with him and as various antique shops and shows had accommodated.

Her eyes sparkled as she turned the nappy this way and that to savor its gleaming facets, the little finger of each hand delicately arched as she angled the piece in the light.

"You shouldn't have!" she gushed in appreciation.

"Anything to bribe myself back into your good graces," he tossed.

"Tsk," she pursed, putting the nappy carefully back into its box.

"And now to the stack of paper," he announced as he turned to enter his office. "I'll meet with the class in a minute."

He returned to his desk and sat down in a heap. He watched the door creak slowly shut as he sat. He thanked it for that. He then sighed as he accounted his sense of fatigue. This thing of re-entry was work, he grumped as he slumped a little lower in his chair. Going from full-time private pleasure to full-time public duty—well, almost full-time—demanded no small exercise in tractability, a maneuver he still managed poorly. He looked at the wall fronting his desk and wondered drolly if congressmen and senators felt the same disjunction upon return home to their constituencies after so many weeks and even months away at the capitol, living a vastly different life from what their home districts offered. Probably not as much as one might think. Perhaps that's what enabled them to be what they were and do what they did. It probably was basic to the breed to be able to identify self-interest with the common weal, and vice-versa, and thereby rise above the ordinary dualities of daily labor. That notion brought him back to Dieter, the beautiful Miss Dieter, whose cold loveliness had been more on his mind than he wished to admit. Maybe it was more her nimbus of veiled menace and its implicit invitation of challenge. Maybe all such women who were so comfortably aware of the power of their beauty carried that shade of menace. Laura, he quickly and loyally affirmed, was certainly comfortable with that awareness in her own right but there clearly was no menace afoot there. No, he considered, it had to be something else with Dieter. But, in any event, here he was, the first hour back and juggling irreconcilable dualities. Why couldn't he be a politician and look upon the matter as being truly to his and to everyone else's benefit? With that he slammed his hands down on the desk as a combined gesture of defeat as well as of launching himself into the day's labor. When everything else fails, he sang as he prepared to rise, there is always the consoling futility of the classroom. He rose, stretched, and then marched out of the office, past Mrs. Andretti who was again looking happily at the nappy nestled in the open box before her. He thought better of chiding her for her delight, and, as alternative, chose to announce what she already knew. As it was, she seemed sheepish enough at being caught in display of how much she delighted in his gift. She must have missed him, he thought.

"I'll be meeting with the third year at the end of the hallway classroom. Gotta get the faith going again."

"They're waiting for you. I'll hold any calls till you get back," she assured as she put the box cover in place to consign the nappy to future attention.

He ambled up the hallway and waved greetings enroute to a couple of staff psychiatrists at their desks in their offices whose doors stood open for morning ventilation. In a few moments he reached the end of the hallway and grasped the knob of the classroom door. As he did so, the chatter inside came to an abrupt halt. Maybe they missed him, too, he wondered. He wasn't used to the idea of being missed, or even considering himself being missed, but this year's return had somehow put him in touch with the notion, which thus far seemed to gain validity as the morning moved on. A wave of unwonted self-consciousness swept over him as he opened the door and entered the classroom to the bright reception of seven upraised, smiling faces. He smiled back expansively in display of being equal to the moment despite the hidden impulse to shrink humbly away. All the way back to vacation.

"Good morning, everybody," he called to all.

Assorted greetings came back in return.

He looked at the waiting group in brief survey and then sighed.

"I don't know that I'm ready for all this flat-out thirst for knowledge I see before me," he blandished.

He was lying; he felt the turbine hum of zeal gaining speed within him as he stood before these magnificent young people seated around the table with texts and notebooks arrayed before them. The scene was absolutely unfailing in its power to mobilize him to tutorial fervor; it always did, and most likely always would. He could not understand the nature of the transformation that occurred within him when he stood before a class or conference, but he knew he had little say-so about it. It just happened, and words, ideas, themes, even entire lectures seemed then to come forth unbidden, usually thematically appropriate to the occasion, and he would serve them up effortlessly to usually enraptured residents in what must have seemed a flourish of virtuosity. Yet, he felt he had little at all to do with it; it simply just happened. Quotes, references, dates, everything. And he rarely had the need for notes. He likened his lectern behavior to that of a lumbering, lugubrious hound dog, unprepossessing in the extreme, catching a scent and being transformed as though by a thunderbolt into a streaking pursuer hell bent on closing the distance between itself and some quarry, all the right moves and sounds of pursuit automatically coming forth fully formed and complete. As he savored the punctual quickening of his senses he was suddenly taken awash by a swoop of the verge, that inveterate visitor, and along with it the consternation that prior to this morning he hadn't experienced it for the preceding several weeks, maybe even a full month, and now *twice* in one morning? And that dream? Maybe that was the start of it. Sweeping through him just now as though making up its own arrears the visitation distracted him from the muster of pedagogic return and he reflexively looked at the far wall to set his bearings for the eeriness to peak as it usually did in flash-flood fashion. And he tried once again, enchanted, to "see" in this sharp instant what he felt was being dangled before him just beyond his focus. As he listened, and felt, and tried to see, he was aware that the residents were watching him expectantly and unwittingly contributing to his concentration by sitting motionless. Sooner or later some resident was going to diagnose him as having petit mal, he rued within his awareness of them.

It quickly subsided.

"A vision of vacation past just flashed before me, bidding a final farewell," he quipped tactically. At such a time style was so much more important than truth could ever be.

The residents twittered in pleasant reply and adjusted themselves in their seats to denote their readiness.

He scanned their expectant faces.

"You remember the course we had some time ago in the hazy past, fully four weeks back? You might even remember that it had something to do with Psychosomatic Medicine."

Assorted snickers came in return.

"Well, not really," he corrected. "We used the field of Psychosomatic Medicine as a vehicle for discussing something even more basic. We discussed ways and means of defining and cherishing questions, and how to challenge and distrust answers. Remember? I see the spectre of stark recognition on the faces of several of you. Good. Couple that memory with what you've heard about this course and you'll have the proper mind-set for absorbing what this course can do to you and for you. Firstly, I should say that the title of this course is 'Metapsychology' which, loosely translated, means the conceptual development of dynamic psychiatry from 1895 to the present. To trace that arduous line of development we will use the Standard Edition which the library has available in the reference section. Beware of other translations you might find on the kiosks of the local drug stores. Even if there were no significant thematic differences in other translations the pagination wouldn't match up and that alone could confound our efforts at collaborative discourse enough to convert our merely difficult task into a hopeless one. So stick with the Standard Edition and we need not fear Babel. We'll start off with *Studies on Hysteria*, the most underrated book in the annals of psychiatry. And most underread too. For Wednesday be prepared to discuss the first section, 'Preliminary Communication.' Decide among yourselves who is to present. To open the discussion I'll give some background pointers about the book itself and how it came about, at least from the standpoint of the noble collaboration mounted by Breuer and Freud; its heritage, its import, and its legacy, all of it pretty well subtended in the book itself though perhaps not readily visible on the first reading. You will see the coming together, the collaboration, and the subsequent divergence of two entirely different systems of thought borne in the persons of the authors, and in that difference you will come to see yourselves correspondingly as new and evolving acolytes of the field . . . . or else. And with luck you will come to understand something of why psychiatry is what it is today. And then you will better know the meaning of your own work in the field, the grand intent of all this being to make you a more knowledgeable and more mature therapist. Sounds so lofty, doesn't it? Well, now that you've been emancipated from the rigors of the ITU where you spent the year grappling with the rather unadorned basics, you've earned the privilege of entry into the work and world of the out-patient. This course is the Michelin Guide to that world, and beyond. You will certainly come to understand your recent in-patient experience better as we move our discussion along in the coming year, but your out-patients will rise to preferred reference in your thinking as your work in this course puts you in closer touch with their psychic innards. But all that in good time. For the moment, like today, I want you to touch a toe to the waiting waters by joining with me in reconstructing the prevailing

'Weltanschauung' of Victorian Europe in 1895 when *Studies on Hysteria* was published. What was it like then? More specifically, what was it like then in Vienna? We will use the term *fin-de-siècle* in describing the ambience of that era, and particularly in regard to Vienna which was at that time the artistic, social, and scientific hub of a Europe preparing to enter upon its period of decay. Scientifically, what was the spirit of the times? The scientific philosophy? Ever hear of Newtonian mechanics? Or of Whitehead? I know you've heard of Einstein. But what does that have to do with *Studies on Hysteria*? Just everything, because *Studies on Hysteria* is Psychiatry's chronicle of its transition from one causal frame of reference to another, and—hear this—to the then startling notion that the observer is constituent to the event observed. I think we'll see that such a notion continues to be startling even today, at least wherever the capacity for self-observation and self-correction is not well featured, shall we say? But to you—psychiatrists with the weighty duty of understanding yourself that you may better know the self of others—the notion becomes merely vital. So let's talk about *fin-de-siècle* Vienna and a few of its inhabitants as a means of supplying our own introduction to . . . ."

He listened to himself as he spoke. Wistful query flitted in and out of his mind as to how many times he'd said these very words to the many successive classes on the annual first day of class to the proud survivors of the second year of training. At least a dozen times before. Again, time alone did not seem to be an adequate measure of his feeling of oneness with the scene. Counting the years seemed as empty as estimating the number of breaths or heartbeats in a lifetime. One breath or one heartbeat seemed so much like the other that it was hardly worth enumerating their separateness, or their sum. Better to lump them all together as just the cadence of being alive. Somehow that thought reminded him of the *Watchfire* letter in his coat pocket, and of Clay, and of the Blush patients. Did Blush move this very instruction a little closer to quaint irrelevance, like teaching Classics in an air raid shelter?

". . . such that we see at this time the beginnings of Da-Daism in the field of Art whereby the process of perception of the world is itself being portrayed rather than the fixed object of perception in a static world viewed through a pre-supposed and traditional perspective. The viewer's, or observer's, perception is featured in relation to the object itself, whatever it may essentially be. Picasso, of course, is a major player in this movement and not at all different in spirit from his progressive contemporaries in the scientific and political communities. Decidedly more visual, though. In fact, it may be that . . . ."

It may be that they don't have the vaguest idea what he's talking about, he considered as he looked at their uniformly blank expressions, polite with expectation. But that's as it should be at this initial point of the journey, he reminded himself, and it truly was a matter of the course's slowly explaining itself as it unfolded to them and through them. There really was no way he could tell them in advance, like now, what they would eventually come to apprehend in their own separate and unique styles. So therefore, he once again decided in a bold leap of logic, this course must never be allowed to become irrelevant, or, like shelved Victorian crystal, precious only to the narrow and specialized interest of the knowledgeable collector. The turbine hum was now ascendant and its pitch near shrill enough to whip his words into a voluntary of pulpit rhetoric. The sense of mission was returning to him as he spoke, and it felt wholesome, strong, and good. A satisfied smile lightened his lips as he spoke.

". . . with the result that the near mystical concept of action at a distance, such as gravitational force acting over intervening miles of space though completely undetectable at any point in those miles of space and known only by the behavior of the distant bodies affected, was now replaced by a focus on the nature of space immediate to a given body and how that space was affected by the mass of the body, thus to account for the behavior of that body and of nearby bodies. Not force at a distance, but change in the local field relative to the body. So what does that have to do with *Studies on Hysteria*? You'll see that this book chronicles almost naively the shift from the mechanical to the relativistic frame of reference in the observation, clarification, and interpretation of human behavior, though only certain pathologic behaviors are addressed in the text. But the shift in perspective is the main point for us, not the particulars of Hysteria as it was understood in those days. A shift in form, and not so much the inclusion of new or different content. This is not to say that we won't include clinical methods in our work for this course; not to do so would be inimitable with the philosophy of the course itself. And dangerous, too. Remember Burleson's comment about Osler and what he said about charts and going to sea? Well, those words apply in spades in this room. In the course of our discussions you will see that Freud never strayed far from the hard data of clinical observation. He always held the observable clinical fact as the arbiter of the generalization. Indeed, that's the very foundation of his position in this text. But more about that later. For our purposes we will make very ample use of our clinical cases in tracing out the meaning and application of the metapsychological concepts defined in the course, so keep good notes on your out-patient cases.

"But for today I'd like to take a few minutes to review briefly the history of that era, 1875 through 1910, and particularly European history. Once we've set the historical frame of reference we might have a better handle on the Victorian mind and the prevailing dualities of the day. It's always dualities, doesn't it seem? You might well review your Hegel, I should add. Anyway, the industrial revolution was in full swing and the success of Newtonian mechanics seemed to promise that society was well on its way to the long-sought mastery of existence. The Franco-Prussian war had established Germany as the dominant continental power, now a federated republic under Bismarck as opposed to the loose collection of principalities it had been before. The shift of political and industrial power to middle Europe strengthened Vienna's claim as the cultural capital of the continent and it was commonly agreed at the time that anything of note happening in the Western World happened in Vienna first, like we say of California today. It was also commonly agreed that Vienna was the place to be if you felt you had something to give. So that's where you went to study, or to compose, even to paint, though Paris still held strong claim to ascendancy in those pursuits. But for our purposes, Vienna is where you went to practice. Now, Freud, as you know, wasn't a psychiatrist. He was an obscure neurologist who started out studying the nervous system of fishes. You probably don't know that at one point in his early work he barely missed out on being the first to introduce the use of cocaine as a local anesthetic. Yes, cocaine. Josef Breuer, a bit older and well-positioned, was a prominent neuro-physiologist who had already made brilliant contributions in the field of physiology and certainly didn't need to tackle the enigma of Hysteria to establish himself in the exalted chambers of the scientific world. But the problem of Hysteria was a clinical feature of the Victorian landscape, though rare it is to us today. Also, it confounded the therapeutic armentarium of the day—Charcot and Janet specifically, the leading representatives of the French school—and it thus threw into question the premises as well as the serviceability of the theories of psychopathology then in vogue. In effect, Hysteria flourished as a symptom of the flaws and contradictions of the Victorian Great Society and therefore stood in indictment of its vaunt very much as drug addiction and probably the various Character Disorders stand today vis-a-vis our Great American Society. Societal diseases, so to speak, and inscribed on individuals specifically vulnerable as well as embarrassingly representative of the whole. So it was certainly the undertaking of the day to offer a new and different understanding, as well as treatment, of that bugaboo, Hysteria, and it took no small amount of audacity to impose this new offering on a scientific world which would rather have remained more conventional about the problem than bestirred by some new, crampy analysis, a point which pertained more to Freud's premise than to Breuer's, as we shall see."

By now the residents sat in a dazed immobility, the happy expectation long gone from their faces. They made no pretense of assimilating what he was saying, their not having any prepared framework for accessing his comments into comfortable and convenient modems of reference. He had noticed over the years that with each successive class the residents knew less of history, less of the classics, less of the philosophy of science—certainly less of the arts—and more and more about calculators, circuitry, computers, and printouts. He knew that correspondingly he sounded to them—and keenly felt on this first day back from vacation—distinctly antique in their world of high impact plastic and walkman self-absorption. Yet, he could say that as the course moved along, something characteristic would happen. The residents would move from grappling with the course material as though it were a foreign language to reveling in the enlightenment come of having achieved a new perspective. It was as though the residents would discover a long-lost inheritance, which in truth it was, to lift them above dependence upon work-a-day details and short-term imperatives. Reassuring as that prospect was, he still regretted getting so caught up in this initial lecture which was intended to be a casual, airy overview ringing of welcome, and not a heavy missive bonding them to vacant silence. Hound Dog was right. Once started he couldn't stop himself. Almost.

"Any questions so far?" he asked, more to curtail himself than to re-engage the residents. Of course, there were none. "What I'd like to do, then, is to stop here for today and pick it up on

Wednesday," he elected. "I'll finish up the background history with just a few more comments or so—promise—and then we'll dive into the 'Preliminary Communication.' The style of writing will at first seem odd, different to you—and immensely more literate than you're used to managing in any current-day textbook—but you'll get the hang of it soon enough and then it will flow more easily. We'll go slowly in the beginning until you make that shift, and then we'll move along more at your usual pace. Anything else we should mention this morning other than that it's good to be back and ready for business?" he asked as he scanned the faces now returning to focus. The residents began to resume their smiles in delight of being released from this initial soaking and agreed by way of scattered, irrelevant mumbling that the morning's work had achieved closure with nothing more needing to be said.

"O.K.," he concurred, "see you all Wednesday."

He sat for a fleeting moment to look at the residents gathering their materials for moving away from the table. He was, to say the least, right pleased to be back. He had missed them, and he had missed the turbine's thrum, now resolutely back in tune as accompaniment to the scene. Granting himself a smiling nod he rose from his chair and led the way out of the room, the residents trailing in chatty clusters. He felt the satisfaction of a solid lecture done, though perhaps in excess of what he had intended. Yet the overall effect was, judging by the way he now felt, good and full, all very much as God intended. He veered off from the group as he neared his office and entered to find his secretary jotting on a small notepad. She completed the notation upon his reaching her desk and tore the small sheet from the pad and handed it to him.

"Dr. Burleson just called to welcome you back from vacation and to convey again his pleasure in having been a part of the graduation ceremony," she explained as she handed him the note. "He said he was just then leaving his office for an overnight trip but that he would be back tomorrow afternoon and perhaps you might return his call then if you had a chance."

Might? *If* he had a chance? Holy Christ! He'd call back at three in the morning if Burleson asked, he exulted as he took the note! Burleson calling *him*! He must want to follow up on the graduation in some way. Maybe invite him, Frank A. Cantrelle, to participate in some conference, like years ago, but now as a colleague come of age and ready to be included by intent, not by accident, as back then. Or maybe it was just for the two of them to get together and have that talk they'd promised each other since their first meeting. There were so many possibilities and they all seemed splendid, he beamed as he nodded approval in Mrs. Andretti's direction for such fine delivery service. Now there was all the more reason to drop in on Jess this morning.

"I'm going over to the Admin Building to see Dr. Weaver for a minute. If Dr. Burleson calls back, please transfer his call over there," he pursed with eyebrows arched over half-closed eyes for the correct measure of insufferable conceit.

"Maybe I'll just tell him that you're not receiving any more calls today," she sniffed, picking up on the tone.

"Rather," he added loftily. "Can't have this office become pedestrian, now can we?"

They broke into giggles as he left, feeling commandingly in step for managing the training helm in such invigorating currents.

He hurried over to the Admin Building with his attention locked in on the prospects stirred by the phone call. Maybe there was even the possibility of some joint research on Blush. After all, Burleson had come out so strongly in favor of keeping the patients close to their communities, and hence longer here at Moreland. He so obviously wanted the general citizenry to be keenly aware of Blush and its ravages. Research here would be a natural follow-up if that could be accomplished. Or maybe he had in mind some joint petition to the DMH for Moreland to be included in the research format as an additional center for Blush study with Burleson's group pitching in on some clinical project. There were just so many nice possibilities, he totted up as he reached the entrance door which he swung open with a flourish. He then bounded up the hall steps and, breathless, swooped into Weaver's outer office where the secretary, initially startled by his huffing entrance, once again smilingly waved him on to Weaver's sanctum. As he approached he could see Weaver bent over a reaf of papers presently dominating the business of his desk. Cantrelle stood in the doorway for a moment to catch his breath.

"Lafayette, voilá ici!" he announced.

Weaver abruptly looked up from the papers, blinked, and then broke into a huge smile as he rose from his chair while extending his hand in greeting.

"Come on in, Frank. How was vacation?" he urged, hand waiting.

"Jess, I've come to tell you that . . . ." Cantrelle reached into his coat pocket as he remained in the doorway to achieve the right effect for his entrance, ". . . that I've decided to go on stage. See!" He then pulled the envelope out of his pocket and strode up to Weaver, taking his extended hand in a brisk, comradely shake, while offering the letter with the other. Weaver, uncertain as to what he was being pulled into, accepted the letter dubiously. "*This* is what Moreland needs!" Cantrelle continued broadly as Weaver unfolded the letter. "A window to the viewing world so that our message can be heard, or should I say seen, or whatever, and in keeping with the finest traditions of this hospital's noble heritage."

Weaver listened with one ear while he read, and his initial puzzlement quickly yielded to the return of the welcoming smile. By the time he reached the end of the letter he was burbling out loud.

"Think we ought to clear it with DMH first?" Cantrelle continued merrily.

"God, you really know how to come back from vacation full tilt, don't you? Fully rested? Family enjoy themselves?" Weaver canvassed as he motioned Cantrelle to take a chair, subsiding into his own as he did so.

"Everything went well," Cantrelle pronounced. "Weather was pretty good. The kids completed their summer tans. Laura and I frolicked like honeymooners, and I basked in the warmth of reflected glory, meaning the epic you, Martha, Clay, and Burleson mounted at graduation. Odd, but being away so soon after the event gave me a chance to see it better. At first I was a little worried about it and what we had stirred up, but while I was sunning myself on those rocks I began to see it as exactly the thing needed here and probably elsewhere, too. Even began to regret not having gotten up and spoken my piece, or some piece, to add to the whole. Laura assured me that not having done so did not brand me a wimp. Mrs. Andretti has also donated some reassurances along that line," Cantrelle recounted, knowing that he was fishing, and regretted doing it.

"You needn't worry on that score, Frank. Everybody knows where you stand. They see the graduation as your thing, I can tell you. A master stroke. Certainly *Watchfire* knows where you stand," Weaver guffawed as he waved the letter in Cantrelle's direction.

"Yeah, how about that, Jess," Cantrelle smiled in satisfaction. "Can you imagine me sitting up there with a panel composed of an ex-transvestite turned drug pusher, an ex-nun turned drug pusher, an ex-abortionist turned drug pusher, and an ex-drug pusher turned missionary to discuss the impact of Blush on toilet training in the Modern American family.

"If you could promise that format, *I* would watch it," Weaver sputtered through red-faced laughter as he leaned back in his chair.

After that moment of shared jocularity they were back to cases.

"How have things been? Anything happen while I was away?" Cantrelle queried. "I mean anything big and bad."

"No, not really. Good comments keep coming in about the graduation. Several agencies and a few training programs have asked to be notified when we mount any new programs or conferences so that they can attend. One teaching center has been particularly solicitous of closer ties for sharing the burdens of residency training, but you're used to that," Weaver recounted.

"I mean anything from DMH?" Cantrelle specified. "I can add a note to the good tidings—and I will in a minute—but anything from DMH? As I said before I left I was worried about the way Dieter and her chum frumped away from the graduation—not a civil word to anybody—and wondered if they tried to push the point in another way. Like this upcoming thing with Clay. By the way, that's in a couple of weeks, isn't it?" Cantrelle rattled on, seriatim.

"No, not a word from DMH," Weaver reported. "As far as the graduation goes, I figure it was too well received by everybody else for them to stand opposed to it. And, anyway, it's now mercifully over. Wouldn't yield them any gain. And as far as Clay's concerned, that's pretty much a *fait accomplí*. They couldn't stop it even if they set out to do so. To make a public effort to do so now would amount to some kind of public confession. Plus, suppression of free speech and that sort of thing. No, I think they feel it's better to keep quiet and just clench their teeth till it's all over. Clay's due back from vacation next Monday. Yep, the following Sunday is his big night. Gives him a whole week to get ready. I do worry that Clay has become something of a lightning rod for any civic or political turbulence, bringing down upon Moreland more thunderbolts than we could ever need, as though we ever needed *any*. Martha is worried about it, too, but like always she's not complaining," Weaver brooded.

"Nothing Federal either?" Cantrelle chanced.

"Nothing we know of, and, anyway, that would probably be transmitted through DMH rather than to us directly," Weaver suggested.

Cantrelle sat in absorbed silence for a moment.

"Burleson called," he then announced.

"Yes, we know," Weaver returned evenly.

"You know?" Cantrelle countered, surprised.

"Well, we figured he would call you," Weaver replied. "He called us last week to thank us for having him as a guest and to assure us that he was looking forward to our next conference. He mentioned that he intended to call you when you got back. He didn't wait long, did he? I think he's volunteering to strengthen our ranks. Maybe that's another reason DMH is keeping quiet; our flanks are too well protected, someone like you might say," he teased.

"Well, damn it, they never shrank from blind-siding us before," snapped Cantrelle, the right nerve having been struck.

"All right, all right," Weaver retracted, his arms raised in surrender, "but, Frank, I don't think they're as prowling and predatory as you think. I think they're just a little miffed that so much is going on over which they have little or no say—like Clay's stardom and this hospital's leadership noises—but for which they'll be held accountable, regardless. I can well understand their exasperation with being held so much more accountable than their actual participation justifies. You've got to understand that, Frank," Weaver solicited. "Their responsibility extends to the whole state system, not just to our little world here at Moreland."

"O.K., O.K.," Cantrelle acknowledged fretfully, preferring to dismiss any consideration that might yield undeserved largesse, "but to get back to Burleson, do you think he might want to join up with us for some Blush research? He's got a hot-shot team at his shop, but no patients, and he's not included in the DMH-Pittsfield research axis. Think he wants to check us out first to see how we feel about some joint venture before dropping it on DMH?"

"That's what we're wondering," Weaver allowed. "Martha's concerned that if it is something like that, would a tie-in with him and his group, however splendid from a clinical and academic stand-point, just alienate us all the more as disloyal competitors with DMH and their research arrangements elsewhere. Yet, it would be hard for them to say no to such a proposal. Could be a real problem, but likely nothing more than a variation on the age-old problem: the

Content—us—stretching to change the shape of the Form; and the Form—the DMH—working at keeping us fully corralled in its keep."

"Just a pain in the ass, if you ask me," Cantrelle bellowed, his patience noticeably strained. "When doing the right and good thing by any sensible reckoning upsets administrative punctilio you've got to wonder what the hell purpose administration is serving."

"May I suggest you give yourself a moment to recover from the umbrage of returning to administrative abuse before calling Burleson. We wouldn't want him to think that beneath a veneer of collegial amity our people chafe from executive tyranny, although it is good to see that you're wholesomely back in characteristic form to guide your residents to tempered wisdom," Weaver chided with relish.

Cantrelle harrumphed at the jibe.

"I know I'm back when I find myself joining in laughter at my own abuse," he added in riposte. "I'll call Burleson tomorrow; he's out of town today, anyway," he continued. "And that reminds me, how are the Blush admissions? Up?"

"Way up," Weaver glummed. "We've filled up Building Seven again even though we're shipping them off less than two weeks after we get them. Now, as many come down with it from Crack as from heroin. More females, too. The DMH is opening units left and right throughout the system to handle the numbers. And they're hiring like mad. It's ransacking the budget, but Federal relief funds are holding the system together, thank God. The patients have to be in the hundreds of thousands across the nation. You would think by now it's ruining the drug trade. But I guess not, because they keep coming in."

"Any estimate on the number of deaths so far?" Cantrelle asked.

"About eighty thousand, but you would never suspect it because they die so quietly, and the families still are not very eager to let on that one of its members died of Blush. It's too incriminating, I guess," Jess sighed.

Cantrelle was shocked by the number and he now realized how thoroughly he had been away and how completely he had shoved aside the horrid reality of Blush and its wastage. He had covertly forsworn thinking about it while he was with his hale and happy family, sunning himself on those solid and eternally steadfast rocks. He didn't want to think about it even now, back at work where it was his rightful concern. No wonder they died quietly; no one wanted to know or think about it. If he, Frank Cantrelle, a worker in the field and something of a contributor to the literature on the subject, had trouble keeping the loathsome entity in mind when it was not immediately before him he could imagine and understand the problem the average citizen had in awarding Blush priority in the roster of daily concerns.

"I didn't realize it had gotten that bad," he groaned in self-reproach.

"Oh, yeah, the past couple of weeks have been really busy, everywhere. I guess when you step out of it for a while, like being on vacation as you've been, it's easy to regain a view of the world before Blush. Simpler and nicer, I vaguely recall," Weaver teased.

"You don't have to rub it in," Cantrelle grouched. But he knew Jess was right. There was a need, a natural avoidance, *something* which chased Blush from mind all too readily if it were not forcibly kept at hand. Conceding thus, he realized that Jess and Martha probably had the added burden of holding the reality of Blush before assorted others, like local legislators and community leaders, to prevent its being forgotten where it wasn't obdurately visible. In that particular, Jess and Martha probably even held common cause with DMH in its efforts to keep the state budget office suitably mindful of Blush's cost. Nothing was simple, he was reluctantly allowing himself to avouch. Thank God for people like Clay who were not likely to let the world succumb to the blandishments of lotus, the natural antidote to Blush's harsh astringency. Lotus an antidote to Blush? How much irony could this world offer?

"Well," Cantrelle concluded as he clapped his hands to his knees, "my sense of discouragement is back up to operational level to convoy me through the remainder of this first day of Paradise Lost. I guess I'll trot over to my station and send a polite note of demur to *Watchfire*. I wonder how much they would have paid? I'll probably take off a little early this morning, Jess; going to have lunch with Laura who probably feels as disjointed as I do about being back. One last lunch before succumbing to the looming surround. Woe, woe! By tomorrow I'll be fully transfigured back into my civil service form, prince-to-toad fashion, all dressed up in my job description. Anything you or Martha need from me today?" he queried as he levered himself from his chair.

"Nothing that can't wait a day or so," Weaver waived. "Though you may see it as ruinous to your bliss, we're glad to have you back," he chortled, returning the *Watchfire* letter.

"I bet you say that to all the toads," Cantrelle returned coyly. "Check with you tomorrow."

"O.K., Frank. My regards to Laura," Weaver tossed as he returned to his reaf of papers.

"Will do," he agreed, pocketing the letter as he left.

He entered the hallway feeling relieved that he had now formally reported for duty, crossing that imaginary but strict line separating vacation from duty status. He was back, and thus far there were no reprisals for his having been away. A foolish annual fear, but one he could never shake, no matter how blameless he felt upon departure for his standard, authorized, necessary, commonplace two-week jaunt into self-indulgence. Later in the day he would have to thread his way through a raft of afternoon appointments in his private office where his patients would indeed hold him accountable in one way or another for his two weeks of demonstrated self-interest. That, too, was standard procedure upon return. Abandonment was not to go unpunished, he would be reminded. Their censure of him might in time be a workable, analyzable issue important to the management of the case, but not on the first day back when their hurt, come of felt neglect, reached out for revenge, not interpretation. But playing the hand he was dealt was what he got paid for. Too bad his own hoard of guilt resonated so readily with his patients' reproaches. His personal analysis had at least cut it down to tolerable size, but he still believed in his heart of hearts that leaving his patients, however well or far in advance he prepared them for it, unavoidably hurt them and did truly inflict a psychic pain for which he was responsible, *and*, moreover, that however inevitable such vicissitudes were in the realities of every life, or however much it came of balancing his clinical responsibilities with the many other responsibilities in his life, he still was fundamentally guilty as charged. There was no way around it. It was just a matter of apportioning his guilt in the most just and workable manner. Such was the job description closest to his heart.

He ambled up the drive to the MOB and was soon savoring again the rank mustiness of the hallway. A few residents were standing about, chatting in carryover from the morning's offering. He smiled his way past them and entered his office. After dictating a letter of gracious regret to *Watchfire* he settled down to his own reaf of papers, finding that as he worked his way through the heap his memory of vacation receded with each sheet browsed, much as though he were papering over his happy times with layer after layer of printed inconsequentia. And more of the same awaited him at his other office this afternoon. The day offered only one hope of gay revanchism, and that was lunch with Laura. He clicked his pen to the At Ease position and returned it to Stand By in his jacket pocket. He then decided to take a minute or two—no more—to catch up with the waiting wall before hieing himself off to Laura's care, and maybe beyond. He settled back into his chair, took a deep breath, and began to look at what he could not yet see was before him.

Twelve

The moonless night was about as black as it could be, and the headlights of his car stabbed their way ahead on the nearly empty road. The street lights, stretching off in the distance, looked like the spacing of celestial bodies such as seen in those time photos of the midnight sun dipping near but not touching the horizon, each light's glow overlapping the next in the sharp clarity of the air. A front had moved through earlier in the afternoon, dumping rain in tropical-size drops, and the air was now freshened and cleansed. The temperature was to go low enough overnight, it was predicted, to qualify as a cool snap, harbinger of Autumn to come now that August was beginning to run through its store of days. Soon, the slant rays of Autumn, he thought with relish.

He had closed the office just a few minutes earlier after having seen the last patient on his way and then gotten through the remainder of the calls which had accumulated over the two weeks. With most of the calls their original purpose had long faded as time alone had brought some resolution to the inciting issue, and in some cases, if not many, the call was merely a disguised maneuver to have him check in upon return to verify his continued existence and restored availability. Some patients needed stark, convincing evidence of such, and regularly. Actually, the day's load of patients hadn't been all that bad, he conceded. In terms of presentation, they had collected themselves into two general groups: those who smiled broadly upon seeing him back, and those who pouted in display of their hurt for having been abandoned two weeks earlier. Regardless of group membership, all managed at some time during the session to reassure him their lives worsened appreciably upon his departure though he could have scant concern for such at the time, they understood, what with his obligation to trace all mortal pleasures with his family and with any such fortunate companions he might have chosen to take along with him. Just as in *Richard III*, on this day wounds bled anew in the presence of their perpetrator. Yet, characteristically, by the end of each session arrears were somehow made up and all was forgiven for the session to end on a high note of cheery satisfaction with things now being back to normal in this joint business of therapy. The period of neglect had come to an end.

He grimaced as he reviewed this obligatory ritual of return. So precisely articulated, it seemed. Each one seemed to know his individual part. He then recalled being with Laura for lunch. It had turned out to be more requiem than jubilee. They both had hoped to carry forth the airy buoyancy of their two-week frolic by way of a defiantly merry snack. They made all the right sounds and moves, but there was no escaping the waiting encroachment of urgent ordinaries. They found themselves ruefully toasting to the departure of blitheness, now on its annual migration to elsewhere, but certainly to return again next year. So lunch ended on a note of wise and solemn acceptance, much as at a funereal meal.

And now he was hurrying home, the burden of return on this first day back just about done. He and Laura would commiserate on the wearying business of re-adjusting to an abruptly altered ambience since it happened to be the primary and prevailing one of their existence. The pull and pleasure of carnal regression had been so lusty this vacation, and small wonder, he asseverated, in view of the troubles being left behind in the keep of Jess and Martha. And in Clay's keep, too, for that matter, though Clay had followed one week later for his own two weeks of vigorous disport somewhere off in the crispy green of the New England outback.

He took his standard route home from the office and again noted the thinness of the traffic which earlier in the day had been so oppressive. Maybe everybody was in agreement that summer was just about at a close and that it was time to start relocating indoors. The Labor Day weekend just a couple of weeks off would seal that shift. Furnaces, fireplaces, storm windows and the like would soon thereafter assume their place in the queue of chores which, phoenix-like, arose from the dying flames of summer. And this year there was to boot the added odyssey of taking Ellie off to her freshman year to that right little college in that right little college town which providentially happened to be within reasonable commuting distance to Jeffrey Landon's current place of graduate labor. When Richard went off to pre-med three years ago it was just a matter of helping him load up his jalopy, supplying him with a checkbook, and reminding him to call. With Ellie it would involve plants, steamers of wardrobe, untold quantities of beauty aids, a nearly complete kitchen, *plus* the checkbook. Trailer rental would be *de rigueur*, and the entire family, save Richard off on his own migration, would be retainers and handlers. But, in truth, he wouldn't have it any other way, for the idea of his daughter being left in need to the helpfulness of unknown others was totally unconscionable. So he would be foremost in helping to stevedore Ellie's transit to college, and Todd would be there right alongside him with the proper quips to lighten the load. There was enough to the prospect to offer a settled and patriarchal satisfaction, but for the moment, this deepening night, it all seemed so wearisome.

He was now also aware of being tired of driving. He had driven several hundred miles yesterday, not slept particularly well last night, thanks to that unsettling dream, had scurried about today in traffic he had become unused to, and now was winding up the day in the final leg of a pace which indeed seemed to be dedicated to the combustion of gasoline. Even though his office was no more than three miles from home this last lap now felt gargantuan in sweep, made worse by the peculiar sense of newness super-imposed on its long-standing familiarity, like meeting a friend not seen in a while. Being awash in other scenery for two weeks seemed to loosen the tie of easy familiarity with streets he'd traveled for over twenty years, and the streets now seemed different in some imperceptible way. Had the grass and trees grown a bit? Or looked seedier with the passage of summer? Did the sharp edges that were usually softened by a glossing familiarity now stand out more? It would take several days before the streets, yards, buildings, trees, and even people returned to their usual accommodated and habitual fit.

He turned on to the side street that led to the house. One more mile, almost precisely, he noted as he stared hard ahead to offset any slacking of vigilance this close to safe port. He wasn't sure if he was hungry; probably, but it was weariness that ruled. Could it be that his appetite was weary, too, he joshed, nibbling at a bit of giddiness. He decided that he was just too tired to make sense. The light of his driveway then hove into view to relieve him of any additional disquisition on that point. He swung into the driveway and coasted to a halt short of the garage where he decided without hesitation to let the car seek its rest for the evening. There was no threat of rain to mar its happy sheen and he was hardly up to jockeying it into the garage and all that went with sliding garage doors back and forth and maneuvering the car between power mowers, barbecue grills, and lawn furniture, all hurriedly stored therein preparatory to the vacation. The Jaguar was still in the shop for long overdue maintenance and so its garage bay was relatively free. All of the reclamatory undoing could wait for another time. He popped open the car door and creakily pulled himself out into the night air. It was perfectly quiet, except for the cracking of the engine as it cooled. Not even a cricket. No music from the house, either. Good. The air was cool, already moist with the dew it would apply liberally by morning time, and he took in a large gulp of it and held it full-chested as he looked at the restless stars. Exhaling heavily he waved an imaginary fist at the heavens and silently railed that those stars could blink on much as they damned well pleased but he was going to turn in probably within the hour and sleep the sleep of the shriven. So there, he added with brazen flippancy, which he well understood to mean he was near the edge of lunacy come of being work-drunk. Too quick a transition from total abstinence to a day-long binge.

He stepped up the walk to the front door.

"A turn to the right . . . a little white light," he hummed jauntily as he moved into the arc of the entrance light which Laura always kept burning in wait of his arrival home in the evenings, just as in any unabashedly wonderful, idyllic husband and wife arrangement. Corny, perhaps, but it did keep him from stumbling around in his staggering exhaustion after a tough day. Like today. ". . . my blue heaven," he concluded as he turned the knob and opened the door. "I'm home, Hon," he reported loudly to the general interior of the house.

"I'm a-coming, though my head is bending low," she sang back from somewhere in the region of Ellie's room.

It always struck him odd and even a little mystical how often and independently they struck the same chord, in this case literally. He hums to himself on the way in, she answers him in song, similar in mood and in medium. He often wondered if one had anything to do with the other, like telepathic waves reaching out to each other to keep the sending and the receiving in sync, a sort of mutual psychic automatic frequency control; or whether it was just the recurring statistical congruence of behaviors in two very similar people. He had often brought it up earlier in their marriage but Laura just as often wrote it off as simply "the fit" they shared. In fact, she saw it as hardly worth mentioning since it was merely the way things were supposed to be between husband and wife. To him, it was always uncanny.

He plopped his briefcase down on the vestibule bench to retrieve it later when he made the rounds of his study. He then moved along the vestibule and pulled himself up the three steps to the hallway, leaning wearily on the banister intended to be more decorative than functional. He wondered if he was really as tired as he was making out to be to himself and to the several others he secretly hoped would notice. Yes, actually, he was, despite the covert expectation of sympathy carried by his behavior. It wasn't the work, or its quantity—today was even somewhat less than standard for the quantity part of it—it was the matter of doing it against the grain, not feeling ready to resume doing it, not wanting yet to do it, fighting it in the doing while putting on a good face—*that's* what was tiring. Tomorrow he would resist it a little less, and the next day less yet, and by the end of the week he would again feel at one with it. And next week he would proclaim it to be the only valid way to proceed in life. He figured a yawn would be right just about now in this self-pitying soliloquy.

As he reached the level of the hallway Laura appeared from one of the bedrooms and made for him, a ruthful smile carrying her along.

"Frank," she consoled with outstretched arms as she approached, "you look as though gravity has it in for you."

"Being weightless in orbit for two weeks, I suppose so," he agreed.

She gave him his usual homecoming recharge hug along with a quick kiss and then entwined an arm in his and directed him to the kitchen.

"How about a cup of tea while I warm up your dinner?" she urged.

"Sure, Sweet," he agreed as they entered the kitchen which, as in the morning, glared in contrast to the darkness he'd just traversed enroute home. Actually, he would have preferred a beer, but this close to bedtime the alcohol would pillage his sleep of any sound restfulness.

"Anything at the office?" she inquired as she busied herself with the tea bag and mug.

"Pretty standard fare. Like I say, I'm always surprised that things seem to hold together so well in my absence," he observed to her. “Makes me feel that my worries while we’re away are the fluff of a precious conceit. Nothing new in that, but I’m always surprised when I’m reminded of it. How was your day, Sweet?” he shifted.

“I’ve had my squabbles with gravity too,” she submitted. “Unpacking is so discouraging. And Ellie is already preparing to pack up again. Noah wasn’t nearly as planful. She seems to think she’ll never return.”

That was the right and the wrong thing to say; right because it was so accurate, wrong because it was so true. The thought of Ellie’s leaving recruited a renewed heaviness which he had begun to think was lessening now that he was back home. In fact, he had wondered vaguely earlier in the evening if a lot of his weariness wasn’t really a blunted moroseness about her packing herself off to her destiny. Like Noah, she was embarking upon a journey from which there was no return. Her new world awaited and she—his darling little girl with the big blue eyes and quick mouth—was not likely ever to return to being as she was when she was his. Right now he needed that tea to wash down a lump that was forming high up in his throat. When Richard left it was different; for himself if not for Laura. In Richard he saw himself, this time better prepared, going off to do victorious battle in a needy world. And Richard echoed that feeling by viewing his departure similarly. There was sadness, but there was also glowing pride. With Ellie it was more the end of something too important to be without. And yet, she must go. Plants, kitchen utensils, and everything.

“I dread her leaving,” he said simply to Laura.

“I do, too,” Laura said softly as she pored fixedly over her putterings at the stove, her lips tightened bravely at the prospects of the loss of her dearest companion.

“This won’t do,” Cantrelle announced to Laura as he turned her toward him for a hug, “the two of us standing here lamenting our splendid handiwork as though our success is also our loss. I think we agreed a long time ago not to have all our happiness at one time. Could lead to a bad case of sniffles, I’m told,” he bantered as he looked into Laura’s glistening eyes.

“You’re terrible,” she laughed through a sob as she threw her arms around him. They hugged for a moment of shared recognition of their own and each other’s part in this thing called Their Life and of the critical rôle each of their children played in that drama. But to feel it most keenly only upon their children's departure was an irony of the worst sort, they agreed without having to say so.

"I don't know that I'm up to such robust sentimentality this late in the day," he quipped in disclaimer as he reached for a merrier note.

"Tea coming up," she answered cheerfully as she disengaged and turned toward the steeping mug next to the stove. "And the phone's been ringing all day long," she continued lightly, "with Ellie and her friends calling each other to compare travel plans and packing lists. And one call from Jeffrey Landon. All in all, dear husband, I think we can truly say it's totally out of our hands." She then handed him his tea.

He took a careful sip and then closed his eyes to savor the blessed comfort it brought.

"I guess that's exactly the point," he resumed pensively. "This being swept along on the first day back by a pace so quickly alien to us when we're out of it—doesn't that make you wonder why we live this way in the first place?" In one form or another he posed this question every year upon their return from vacation. "Don't you feel that in a way we're like the fish that thinks his swimming around is what causes the river to flow?"

"I like that. The fish causing the river to flow," she observed as she opened the microwave and retrieved his dinner. "Every year you attack that imponderable question from a different angle, but tonight you really seem to have penetrated to the core of it," she cheered.

"Good," he preened, "but why do you think so?"

"Because today I dipped into our near-depleted checking account and splurged. Got something special for dinner. Here's what happened to that presumptuous fish of yours: swordfish steaks!," she displayed as she carried his dinner to his place at the dining room table. He followed, snickering at her pert pragmatism.

He sat down to the savory aroma of his dinner, eyed it eagerly, and then looked up at Laura as she settled into her usual chair.

"I suppose this meal carries a moral mixed in with the bay leaf, huh?" he wondered in her direction.

"Yes, and please don't choke on it. The moral, I mean," she instructed matter-of-factly.

"Spicy!" he mumbled through a now full mouth. "The moral, I mean." The first mouthful convinced him that he was indeed hungry and he proceeded through his meal with prowling absorption. Their conversation now settled down to a more casual spacing of interchanges between bites. He felt himself being restored, as much by the conjugal repartee as by the food, and already he was anticipating a brisker management of the morrow's chores. He was beginning to settle into harness.

"By the way, how are the kids managing being back?" he extended.

"Well, you can imagine that Ellie pretty much hit the ground running. She doesn't have time to reflect on the meaning of our flight from Eden, bound as she is for fully accredited coeducational Avalon. Todd's busy re-inserting himself into his peer group; eager, I guess, to reclaim his place in their pecking order. In fact, he hasn't come home yet. He and his friends went to a rock concert tonight," Laura added with perceptible concern.

That's why there was no music saturating the property when he drove up, he realized.

"The kids just don't seem to have any trouble shifting from one world to another. I guess to them it's really all the same thing; stopovers on a driven itinerary. But for geezers like us, it's a point of arrival, a place to stay," he philosophized, the food beginning to cloak him in a blanket of contentment.

"Driven is right," Laura affirmed with a sigh. "I don't think they feel they have the time to talk about the creaks and groans of change. Might throw them out of step," she added as she looked across the table as though studying some distant scene.

"Ellie has no problem in talking about her part in Sturm and Drang. Even Richard has held forth on the topic, as I recall," he added in understated reference to his older son's knack for ringing rhetoric when it came to complaining about the system.

"That's true, I suppose," she allowed, "but it's Todd I worry about. He keeps everything to himself, almost never openly complains, and if you try to talk to him about something you know is bothering him he stonewalls you and there you are, reduced to the status of a failed counsel."

He looked sidelong at her as he chewed. She was really back to task. Her worry about Todd seemed to relax only when they were all on vacation together, away in a more forgiving clime where the simpler chore of primal living convoyed all to the happy congeniality of holiday play, and equally. Maybe she had arrears to make up, too.

Also, with Ellie's leaving she would probably focus even more concern on Todd in the coming months. Maybe Todd sensed as much and was shoring up his insulation in anticipation of just that. And for her part, Laura may already have detected as much in Todd. She was surely alert enough to reckon it. He suspected that a certain jockeying of position *vis-a-vis* each other had likely already begun.

"You know he tends to pull back all the more if he knows he's being watched," he offered in gentle warning. They had been over the point many times before and it hardly needed mentioning, but doing so was more in keep with agreeing upon certain basic facts before proceeding with the discussion.

"I know," she agreed, as she had every previous time, "and how to reach him without making him feel he's being examined is the problem, just as we've so often said. But I feel we have to make the effort all the more now with Ellie on her way. He'll be the only one in the house with us now, and for him to continue his arm's-length posture in the family—I guess now with just the two of us—would make for a kind of awkward stand-down family life style for all three of us. We would have to be careful about everything we said. We would never be able to count on his joining with us in anything. In effect, he would be gone, too, though he would still be sharing the same roof with us, and he's too young to feel he has to make his own way."

"Laura," he attempted to correct as well as soothe, "he doesn't keep us at arm's length. He's just not as exuberant as the other two. He's more measured, more careful because of his larger store of self-consciousness. I think we would all be a bit more uncertain of ourselves if we had his problem with that damned dyslexia, which I feel we can say is resolving nicely if we can believe the teachers' reports. But to him, he'll always be tainted, different; and for us to expect him to behave as though he didn't see himself that way, rightly or wrongly, is like asking him to behave as someone else. I can tell you he is some touchy on that score, as though we wanted him to forego being his real self and to become our preference. Now that's when the arm's length thing might get into the picture, if it does. But in our effort to make him more sharing, it's his sensing an implied dissatisfaction with him as he is that steels him, and hurts him, I'm sure."

"Frank," Laura replied in alarm at the thought of Todd's feeling hurt by their—or her—efforts, "he's got to know that we're not displeased with him, our son, but only with the distance he keeps us at. He's got to see," she continued with returning conviction, "that our point is for all of us to have more of life together as a *family* than it is for him to have less of it for being himself; or even less recognition by us of who he really is. Why does that keep coming up," she shook her head disconsolately, "this notion of parents depriving their teenage children of identity? You can't deprive someone of identity any more than you can deprive someone of feelings. Maybe in keeping with some trendy notion of enlightened parenthood we give them too many options, thinking it to be in their best interests to do so; options that probably should be earned rather than merely given. Maybe going at it that way deprives them of basic accomplishments which they should have that could enable them to know themselves a lot better. But of course, making your kids earn their opportunities and advantages is very un-American. The good, successful American parent provides full and plenty such that the kids unquestionably have it better than the parents had it when the parents might already have had it plenty good enough when *they* were coming up. How good do you have to have it to satisfy the entitlement our system encourages? Frank, do you realize that the children of royalty, now as well as years ago, have more daily responsibility and duties than the average American teenager? It's the old, envy-driven peasant notion of equating wealth with indolence, or success with freedom from responsibility, that shapes our sense of duty to our children. So when we talk of giving Todd more space I wonder if what . . . ."

She rattled off her drumbeat dialectic on the folly of rearing children according to precept, an offering she made from time to time when she felt her husband was straying from some principle or practice which needed to be re-affirmed on some particular issue of child care, her avowed area of unchallenged and unnegotiable dominance. Going at it astride her very own high horse set him on notice that he could not put her aside with impunity. He knew it wiser to hear her out, which he did while he finished his meal, paying suitable attention to her missive as he tidied up and settled back into his chair to display an enhanced receptivity.

". . . so I don't think we ought to tiptoe around here as though to do otherwise would disrupt some delicate psychological timetable. Maybe a more direct approach with Todd is long overdue," she summed up.

Ouch, he quickly reflected, trying to digest his meal while his wife suggested not so obliquely that he stop trying to be a non-directive therapist to their son and become more of an active father. Maybe in her heart of hearts she did see him as a wimp. Now that would be something hard to digest. In any event, it all sounded like his cue. He decided to go with his usual: respond to her implied question with a direct question of his own.

"Sweet, why does this come up tonight, our first day back?" he moaned.

She shifted in her chair, obviously discomfited by his query. She looked aside briefly in apparent effort to decide how to proceed. He saw in her behavior the all too familiar sign that she had something fairly specific on her mind but was uncertain how to bring it forth.

"Got something to tell me, haven't you?" he urged, feeling pleased he had regained the initiative.

She then looked at him carefully before continuing.

"I mentioned that Todd went to a rock concert tonight," she cited.

"Yes," he replied expectantly.

"But I didn't mention he went with a group of friends that included that fellow Eddie Shanks," she added with distaste.

"But the rest of the group were his usual friends?" he salved.

"That's not the point," she persisted. "Eddie Shanks is nineteen years old and he's now out of school. What's he doing hanging around with a group of sixteen and seventeen year olds still in school? What can he have in common with them? Or more precisely, what can Todd feel he has in common with Eddie Shanks?" she listed.

"We don't know that Todd feels he does, other than a common interest in having transportation without needing to depend on us for it," he suggested in mild deprecation.

"Frank, it's more than that and you know it. You don't want to think that your handsome son might see something kindred in that seedy character just about everybody regards as disreputable. There aren't many parents I know who would be pleased to have their son run around with him," she leveled with indicting clarity.

For the second time this evening he felt taken to task by her. Why was he resisting her obviously valid concerns, pettifogging her efforts to sharpen his awareness of applications needed right here at home? Was she now seeing in him the same veiled defiance she was trying to have him address in Todd? He didn't know what to tell her.

Sensing that he needed more time to think she proceeded.

"And today when I was unpacking I found something," she intoned with grim conclusiveness. "I was emptying his backpack when I came across a small plastic bag with greenish, ground-up leaves in it. I'm sure it was marijuana even though I've never seen it before."

"Why were you going through his backpack?" he automatically paltered, immediately blushing in shame at the sound of his words.

She saw no need to add to his discomfort by scoring his defensiveness.

"He often leaves dirty socks and handkerchiefs in it," she replied mildly. "But, Frank," she continued with resumed urgency, "I think he and perhaps others in his group are at least dabbling in marijuana and that Eddie Shanks is supplying it. We can't just sit by and let it happen as though we're too busy to be aware of it. We've got to talk to him about it."

She was so unalterably right, and just now he felt so unequal to the moment. Why couldn't he face the tough challenges of his own home? Why did he have to bob and weave so much? He made a good living helping others face their challenges, but he couldn't seem to live privately what he taught and practiced publicly. The corny thought of finally coming to see himself face to face and finding himself and his nostrums to resemble a button-down Eddie Shanks flitted across his mind. Corny, but not so corny as to leave no tracks at all. Sure, Todd is smoking marijuana. The damaged, the awkward, the unblessed, in their pathetic vulnerability were particularly liable to marijuana's vaporous charm, and so why wouldn't his blemished son be included in its corrosive and mordant thrall? He couldn't even claim to be greatly surprised at the disclosure, for certainly he had wondered and worried about such a thing even in the case of Richard, much less Ellie, though neither had given him any cause whatever to be concerned for their judgment. However, Todd never freed him, or Laura, of the need to be mindful of the misfortunes that could befall the less wary and less happy. He stared at his empty plate for a moment, partly to avoid Laura's gaze which he felt resting heavily upon him. He then looked up.

"Do you have it?" he asked.

"I took a small amount but left the bag and most of it in his backpack. Here's what I took," she explained as she handed him a folded sandwich bag.

"I guess this time he didn't have any dirty socks or handkerchiefs in his backpack," he guessed weakly as he reached for the bag.

"Yes, he did," she corrected.

God, he wondered in alarm, was Todd trying to be found out? She read the look of surprise on his face with penetrating accuracy.

"I wondered the same thing," she added. "Did he want me to find it? He had to expect me to check his backpack, like always!"

"Did you . . . . " he began tentatively.

"Remove his dirty handkerchiefs and socks? Yes, I did," she completed with a hint of defiance. She knew exactly what was racing through his mind. He had momentarily felt the tug of hope that she had left his backpack to look untouched so that Todd would not know they knew. He smarted at his own dodge, which he knew Laura would not hesitate to bring to open attention if he tried to insinuate that he did not indeed feel tempted, if only for the instant, to agree to a pact of mutual dissemblance with Todd, each knowing and each knowing the other knew but agreeing to pretend not knowing, thereby each granting covert approval of the other's cravenness meant to appear as craftiness. He and she were too aware that at times before and on lesser issues he had barely skirted that arrangement with Todd, never quite feeling that he had crossed the line which would make him Todd's co-conspirator against Laura, against the teachers, or against whomever Todd may have been resisting at the time, though now he felt he had no slack at all to draw upon in the name of prudence or patience. And to do nothing in the face of this turn of events would at its very best be an appeasement. He opened the sandwich bag and peered in.

"I've only seen marijuana once before, and that was twenty years ago, but this looks like the stuff," he said in disheartened weariness as he re-folded the bag and returned it to Laura.

"I'll throw this away," she announced. "What do you think we ought to do with what's left in his backpack?" she pursued.

He was now mindful of appearing cowardly at every turn and he dreaded that even sensible and defensible prudence coming from his discredited lips would be shouted down as just more cravenness.

But he couldn't bring himself to damn the torpedoes, either. He took a breath and took a chance.

"Let's leave it there," he said to Laura face on. "I'll talk to him when he comes home tonight. I want him to have the option either to yield it up to us himself, or throw it away, *or* hide it better. It's his move, his decision, and he has to make it one way or another. I'm afraid our taking the stuff away from him will also be taking away his opportunity to decide on his own to shun it. Also, I don't want to get caught up in the game of finding where the grass is hidden. You know how wretched that could get."

Laura looked at him as though sifting his words to isolate any impurities that might alloy indecisiveness to their address of the problem. She then nodded and reached over to stroke his cheek.

"I think that's best. I wouldn't have thought of that because I guess I'm too upset. I probably would have made it worse, ending up shouting, and God knows what else,"

He wasn't sure if he was feeling patronized, but he did feel that his approach was sensible, especially so now that Laura concurred with it.

"I think we have to treat him as we would like him to be," he offered more confidently. He then listened to the ring of his words for any unintended piety. There was some there. He wondered if he would best just shut up for now. Also, he'd damned well better not sound pious with Todd later.

"Do you think he's been smoking it long?" Laura searched.

"Actually, we don't know if he's smoked it at all," he reached. "Sometimes these kids carry it around as a badge of membership, as though the mere possession of it suffices, and never ever smoke the stuff. Sort of like being altruistic suppliers to their friends. But if he has smoked it I've seen no signs of it, though it's true I haven't kept an eye out for it," he explained, palms up.

"I haven't seen anything either," Laura added, "but now in retrospect I wonder about his hiking excursions by himself while we were on vacation."

"Yeah, finding that stuff puts everything under the pall of suspicion," he concurred. "Can't help it, I guess. Now, if he takes a little too long in the bathroom we'll both start sniffing at the door."

She slapped his hand as she giggled.

"This is no time for silliness. You're incorrigible."

Humor to the rescue, he chortled to himself. Fool speed ahead.

"You're right," he agreed as he stifled a smile. "Eyes out and chin front," he snapped martially. The food was restoring him noticeably, and while he regretted the prospect of confronting Todd latter in the evening he did feel an odd lightening of spirit and freeing up of means. The discussion with Laura, or rather Laura's forthright, not-to-be-denied testimony on the matter, had perhaps stripped him of Loöcoan coils in readiness for the task ahead. Refreshed so, he pushed away from the table after a last gulp of his tea and then stood up to gather the plates and flatware for their return to the kitchen, his inveterate gesture of gratitude for the effort and devotion conveyed in the serving of his dinner, one of those daily givens into which he read volumes of earthly meaning. Laura had long since given up trying to keep him seated during family dinner while she set up for dessert and coffee, though in the presence of company he would usually bow to decorum and to the helpfulness of the other ladies present.

"Any coffee?" she asked as she led the way into the kitchen.

"Not tonight, sweet. I'm already trembly enough," he quipped as he placed his plate on the counter. "I think I'll check in with Ellie. She doesn't know about the marijuana, does she?"

"Not about what I found," Laura sighed, "but maybe she knows more than we do."

"Yeah, maybe so," he agreed uneasily. Maybe he and Laura were the last ones to learn about it, he wondered. What a kick in the ass that would be, he groaned silently. If so, then they were the blind among the seeing. Then how do you now look the problem straight in the eye? Better not to see it at all, maybe. He was glad Laura couldn't hear that tacky run of thought. There would be no explaining it. "I'll trot up and say hello," he beamed, faking simplicity.

He made down the hallway, glad to be liberated from the rigors of concerted resolve. He would have to think more about this whole thing with Todd, and alone, he mused as he plodded up the several steps to the upstairs hallway. As he neared Ellie's door he could hear her bustling about within. He stood before the door and knocked softly.

"Yes?" came the muffled return from within.

"It's me. Dad. May I come in and supervise?" he retorted.

"Sure," Ellie announced as she opened the door and leaned forward to give him his daily peck on the cheek. "Looks promising, doesn't it?" she suggested as she gestured towards the expanse of the room.

To him it looked like a mess. Open suitcases, open drawers, books, shoes, and stacks and racks of clothes everywhere. All the clothes seemed freshly laundered, especially the recent vacation clothes now in a neat pile off to the side. Also, every light in her room was on—overhead light, wall lights, lamps, and even the desk light.

"Settling something once and for all?" he chided.

"In a way," she proceeded undaunted. "I'm breaking everything down into immediately needed, soon to be needed, and eventually to be needed. What's left over will be on my back. When I pack for the first run it'll be the immediately needed and that should hold me for registration, orientation, and the first week or so of class."

First run? The prospect of several "runs" was news to him. He had assumed there would be only one major assault, complete enough to establish and sustain a firm beachhead with the subsequent offensives supplied and supported by a comfortable and reasonably steady liaison with the home base.

"Ellie, my love," he tendered gently, "a measure of uncertainty is perfectly permissible when plunging headlong into the future, maybe even desirable and wisely not to be diminished by having immediately at hand the answer to every conceivable need, which obviously you intend to provide for, but could you possibly leave a few things behind just to humor chance, and your parents?" He knew it would be just as pointless to appeal to her on this matter of over-packing as it was when he brought it up to Laura in her preparations for any of their embarkations, such as vacation.

"Sure, Dad, and that's why I'm taking only the most essential things," she explained, confirming his estimate of futility.

He sighed in submission as he cleared a spot on the edge of the bed and sat down.

"How's it feel with the big change coming up, Sweet? Only two weeks to go," he posed with a hint of the wistful.

"Twelve days. It's all that I've had on my mind, even before vacation. I'll never get it all done," she summed up handily, finger to chin as she looked from item to item in an on-going inventory of her effects. "I think I'll need at least two more footlockers," she announced as she tapped the air decisively with her finger.

He thought for a moment. Here he was, seeking the channel for some give and take about feelings in the face of the new era bearing down upon them in their father-daughter world, and foremost in her mind—and appropriately so—was the doing of those things to put herself a leg up on the new era even before its arrival. But maybe for her the new era was already here. And was here for him, too, though he couldn't see it, his vision being what it was lately. Feelings versus actions. Or feelings without enough action, hence his sense so often of being pulled along by others and their deeds. How could he presume to talk to Todd? Ellie had her mother's strength and decisiveness, thank God.

"How many runs do you think it'll take?" he asked.

"Probably only two," she estimated. "The rest of what I need I can probably take in the car."

"You do intend to come home from time to time?" he registered.

"Oh, sure, Pops. When the holidays come I'll be ready for some peace and quiet," she chirped.

Peace and quiet. She probably didn't know. So much the better for that, he acknowledged in calculated relief. He felt himself working hard to sustain his precipitously fading world, and wasn't doing it very well.

"I guess Jeffrey will be around to help out if you need something," he probed deftly.

"Probably," she answered evenly, "but he'll be so tied up with his new research project—something to do with temporal lobe malformations and schizophrenia—that I'll most likely be the one to help *him*."

Spoken like a true daughter of Laura Watson Cantrelle, he smirked in grudging amazement at how much the two were alike.

"He keeps trying to get in on the Blush research NIH is doing," she continued, "but they keep telling him he doesn't have enough training or enough experience. So he's going with this temporal lobe study in hopes that he can chalk up some credits fast. They've already approved his proposal for that study."

Where they can keep him out of the way, he grumped as he listened. That boy was showing some tenacity. He and Ellie did appear to strike the same note which it seemed was soon enough going to be the major chord in their young lyric.

"I guess you'll do his statistics for him," he suggested coyly.

"We've already talked about that," Ellie acknowledged in the closest thing to embarrassment her preoccupation with inventory would permit.

"Looks like we're all pushing hard to catch up from vacation," he breezed in shifting the subject.

"If I stick with it I might—just might—get it all ready," she asserted, shaking a finger at her array as though to scold everything into obedience.

"Well, that sounds like a definite dismissal, my sedulous daughter, so I'll steal away to where indolence still has good standing—my study," he teased, hoping he didn't sound peevish.

"Don't go too far because I might need you to lift something," she teased back.

He got up, tousled her hair, and gave her a peck on her proudly pert nose.

"Check with you later, Sweet," he tossed over his shoulder as he left.

He made for the study and shouted his intent to Laura still in the kitchen as he passed in the vicinity. He took the three steps down to the lower hallway in one leaping stride and opened the folding doors to his sanctum. As he closed the doors behind him he sighed to draw in more of the safe and indulgent congeniality he found there as nowhere else, and especially today. He attributed the spiritual kindness of the room to the four or five hundred books standing at serried attention in the full-length bookshelves along the inner wall. He could look across from his desk, and often did, to be reminded of their patient loyalty, each laying some claim to his equally loyal friendship. Some of them were hopelessly outdated, but he could no more put them aside than he could do so with human friends who may also have had their day. No, once he had a book, he always had it, like the old libraries before the advent of technologic shelf-cleaning. Hence, a sum of several hundred, going as far back as his teen-age Civil War tomes, and each as protected as he liked to feel he was when among them.

He approached his desk, grateful of its readiness. Ever since this morning when the dream threw him out of his routine he anticipated getting back to his chair and settling in to some consoling wall work, and he envisioned his desk chair quietly settled at the ready, awaiting his return. And now, after an unusually lengthy day, he could at last ease into his chair and into that other dimension it offered and survey the play of truths upon the deep and timeless wall bounded by the now dark and empty windows guarding its flanks. He pulled out the chair with a certain care and deliberateness, positioned himself just so at the desk, and then moved the chair back into position beneath him as he sat down. The approach had acquired a ceremonial rigor about it to guarantee the most direct path to that other dimension where, at its most basic, edges were not as sharp, the ether softly suffused with gentle light, and all its contents in a collision-free continuum of possibility. But it was so much more than that, and yet words alone could not call it forth any more than word sentences could capture a tune. He had long ago ceased feeling any awkwardness or secret shame over the quirkiness of this esoteric rite though he faithfully was startled as though caught at something forbidden when anyone happened upon him during such a sitting. Laura was thoroughly aware of the unwritten rules and would slowly ease herself into view whenever it was necessary to interrupt. He now looked at the wall and beyond in a recap of the day in order to get the images forming. The heaviness of the overly-green trees came to mind, and immediately, as though in a current upon him, he felt the dolorous haze of the summer's heat just as it was the week before when they were on vacation. Ellie and her suntan lotion; Todd and his hiking shoes; Laura and her hair which took on a reddish tint in the sun. But he himself felt so gray. Like a thick, tightly-clothed Victorian, mustachioed to the gills. He saw Freud, glowering at him in warning, cigar in hand—the photograph in Volume Eighteen. No need to offer a warning. It was a shame Alison Dieter was so beautiful. Or it was a shame beautiful Alison Dieter was doing what she was doing? Did her hair turn reddish in the sun? A small Greek island would be her place—sun, silence, and black hair. So why the hell was the Parthenon coming into focus? Should be the temple of Aphrodite. Maybe his soul knew something he himself didn't know—as it always seemed. He felt himself drifting, and the heavy linearity of Parliament Building marched before his view, followed by Mary Poppins being wafted along by her parasol. That current took him back to the sun, to pince-nez Chompollion, Rosetta, and black basalt. The sense of the verge was gathering, flitting in and out of the edges of his awareness. As always, he dare not try to look at it directly. Look at the wall and you'll almost see what's behind you. Stay with the wall; don't turn around, it would be too bright and you wouldn't see anything. A cartouche—a royal cartouche—approached and centered itself in the black. Maybe he could copy it and figure it out later. He looked at it harder but it didn't get any clearer. He would only be guessing at its lines. Yet, it would at least be something. He felt he almost knew what that "something" was. He could almost see it. This was as strong as it had ever been, but that was always the way it felt when it got going. A tinkling momentarily sharpened the cartouche's lines, and then he heard Ellie's distant shout that she would get it. "It" was the phone. He blinked his eyes a few times to gather in the now re-formed room. The cartouche was gone. With a heavy wheeze he lifted his chin from his palms, lowered his elbows to the arms of his chair, and sat back. He then closed his eyes in hope of re-storing the image of the cartouche, if he could. His breathing was again beginning to pick up when he heard a gentle knock on the study door.

"Yes," he sighed.

It was Laura. She opened the door softly, knowing she was disrupting his congress, and stepped just enough inside to guarantee his attention.

"Ellie says it's for you. It's Jess," she stated with tentative concern.

"Jess?" he looked up in surprise. "That's unusual. He never calls," he offered to Laura in support of the look of uncertainty on her face. She waited as he picked up the phone.

"That you, Jess? Yeah . . . Oh, that's O.K. What's up?" he asked smartly. As he listened, his half-smile of greeting abruptly faded and his eyes squinted under quickly tightened brows. He straightened up to his full height in the chair. He swallowed hard as he listened.

"What's wrong?" Laura beseeched as she approached him quickly. He lifted his hand to wave her into silence as he continued listening.

"Jess, I hate to question what you say, but are you sure?" he interrupted. ". . . She was the one who called . . . ." he enunciated as he nodded in acceptance of what he was being told. ". . . No one saw it . . . ?" He looked at Laura's eyes widening in fearful speculation. He wanted to spare her additional delay in knowing, but he needed to hear Jess. "Do you have her number . . . ?" he asked with mounting urgency. “Wait . . . .” He fished for a pencil on the desk. “O.K. . . .” He wrote it down and repeated it to Weaver for corroboration. “. . . You’ve spoken to her when . . . half an hour ago? . . . we’ll call her right now. Jesus Christ Almighty! . . . all right . . . good . . . I’ll call you back as soon as we decide on something. ’Night, Jess. And, Jess, thanks for calling . . . ’night.”

He put down the phone slowly and put his head in his hands. He then looked up at Laura who was standing at the edge of his desk frozen in dread of what she might hear. He tried to soften his words as he spoke.

“Clay is dead,” he said.

Laura took a half step back as she brought her fingertips to her mouth.

“Dead?” she gasped.

“Killed. A hit and run while he was biking,” he explained through a gathering numbness. He got up to comfort Laura who reached for him as he approached.

“When?” she pressed through her horror.

“Jess said it happened late this afternoon. Probably at the same time we had that heavy rain,” he stammered as he put an arm around her shoulder.

“The same time we were complaining about being back from vacation,” she blurted as she burst into tears and buried her face in his chest.

“Yeah, I guess so,” he agreed.

“What about Helen? And the kids?” Laura asked abruptly as she pulled away in alarm at the thought.

“Jess said Helen was the one who called him. About a half-hour ago. He said she sounded all right. Apparently they didn’t find Clay until a little while ago,” he explained in the flatness of descending grief.

At that moment Ellie leaned into the study.

“Anything wrong? I thought I heard crying,” she inquired anxiously.

“Yes, sweet, something’s wrong,” he replied. “Dr. Weaver called to tell us Mr. Moyer was killed earlier today in an accident.”

“Oh, no!” Ellie gasped as her eyes widened in horror. She ran to Laura who stretched out an arm to receive her.

As the three of them stood there wrestling with their dismay, he noted that it didn't sound right saying that Clay was killed in an accident. Killed? No, *died* in an accident. That was kinder to all.

"What about Mrs. Moyer? She and the kids are up there all by themselves. Who'll look after them?" Ellie posed through urgent tears.

"We will," Laura assured her.

He knew exactly what the plan would be, and he smiled at Laura in grateful relief that again their conjoint vibes would come through in a pinch without their having to agree upon their duty or action.

"I have her number," he reminded Laura, probably unnecessarily. "We can arrange for whatever help she might need."

"I feel so ashamed being stupidly caught up in shoes and curtains and cutesy college junk while those poor people, our friends, are suffering so much," Ellie sobbed in another wave of grief. "This makes things different now."

He leaned over and kissed her on the top of her head and then stroked her hair.

"Yeah, Sweet, I'm afraid it'll make a lot of things different," he consoled. He then turned to Laura. "I'll call Helen and then you can get on the line and talk to her and work things out."

Laura nodded in agreement as she stroked Ellie to soothe her wounded world.

He stepped over to the phone and dialed the number Jess had given him. As it rang he wondered how he would begin, what he would say.

Laura waited and Ellie suppressed her sobbing.

"Helen? . . . We just heard . . . ." His eyes searched back and forth as he listened to Helen's painful and sobbing account of the previous several hour's nightmare. ". . . No details or indications as to how it happened? . . . Dark blue? . . . They'll probably come up with something. If it was around five o'clock there must have been other traffic on the road, or someone who noticed a dark blue vehicle . . . We can imagine. Look, how are the kids? . . . And yourself? . . . I'm sure . . . Helen, that's one thing you don't have to worry about. Jess and all the rest of us are right here . . . . You might get a call from Martha if she hasn't called already . . . . Helen, Laura's been standing here listening and she wants to talk to you. All right? . . . Sure."

He silently handed the phone to Laura.

"Oh, Helen!" Laura groaned, returning to tears immediately as she spoke.

As his wife sobbed he imagined that Helen on the other end had broken into tears as well upon hearing Laura's voice. He tried not to listen as Laura and Helen spoke their pain. He sidled up to Ellie and gathered her hurt to him. He whispered quiet reassurances to her as she daubed at her eyes. While he held her he looked away in groping surmise of what was now upon them. The wall immediately came into view, itself now quiet in deference to the moment, but waiting as he waited.

". . . But, Helen, it would take an extra day for them to get there and I could be there tomorrow morning . . . ." Laura explained.

He stared at the wall in acknowledgment of agreement to rendezvous at a later moment.

". . . Well, then it's settled. I'll be there tomorrow morning. You can pick me up at the terminal . . . Helen, how could you bother with such a thought! It's no problem for me, and besides, it's the least we . . . ."

A dark blue vehicle at around five o'clock, he mused. And while he was on his way back to their cabin. He and his bike thrown into a gully. He tried to piece Laura's words into an explanatory coherence as she spoke but was nagged by the feeling of violating the sanctity of the moment's grief by trying to grasp something beyond it. Yet, somehow, the misery of the moment was just not enough. There was something else. He stroked Ellie's quiet head and held to his gaze.

". . . So if you feel like calling during the night, don't hesitate, Helen. We'll probably feel like calling you to check on things but wouldn't want to wake you . . . but you should try to get some . . . ."

He led Ellie to the settee in front of the fireplace and both sat down tautly at its edge to await completion of the phone arrangements. Unaccountably, he thought of Ellie's over-illuminated room and how insensitive and rude it now seemed. She was right. She wouldn't do any more sorting tonight.

"Good-bye, Helen, and kiss the kids for me. I'll see you in the morning."

She put the receiver back into its cradle and looked at it as she sighed deeply. He and Ellie stood up to receive her report.

"Her sister is in Hawaii with her own family, so she would have real problems in getting back soon to help. And his mother and her mother are widows—she didn't say that, but I remember. So, as you heard, I'll catch the earliest flight I can in the morning and help her get things ready for the trip back. I'll drive their van back with the kids. She'll stay until the coroner releases the body, which will probably be day after tomorrow, she thinks, and then she'll fly back with Clay." Her lips quivered as she spoke, tears welling up again. She quickly braced herself and continued. "I should be back by late tomorrow, but I'll spend the night at their home with the kids if either of the grandmothers hasn't arrived by then."

"I'll come with you and help, Mom," Ellie volunteered.

"When we all get back they'll be just on the other side of town, so we can run back and forth if we need to," Laura reassured. "The kids will be glad to see you, Ellie, I'm sure."

It seemed she and Helen had settled it all so swiftly, he marveled. He figured there probably was so much they didn't have to say to each other. The eternal feminine—Helen, Laura, Ellie, and all of the rest. Women—so steadfastly wise and capable when it was important to be so.

"I'll drive you to the terminal in the morning and stop off at their house on the way back to check on things. I know where Clay keeps an extra key in the garage. I'll notify their neighbor; they're good friends," he listed as his part.

"I'll pass that on to Helen. Will you pick up a gallon of milk before you stop off and throw out any milk that's now in the fridge? Helen may have done that already before they left, but just in case," Laura instructed.

"Sure," he nodded. They think of everything, he sighed. Also, he felt that this phase of the ordeal had already slipped from his grasp in rightful transfer to those in the best position to bring the now empty house back to life.

Those details settled, Laura shifted to the grim recounting of particulars as were told her and as she knew he needed to know. She sat down as she began to speak.

"Apparently Clay went for his daily afternoon five mile ride. Laura said he figured he would be back before the rain was expected to begin. When he wasn't back by the time the rain started she assumed he'd stopped somewhere to wait for it to let up. When he wasn't back at nightfall and long after the rain had stopped she called the local police. They checked his route several times and saw nothing. No sign of any accident, and no word from any hospital or anything. I'm sure by this time Helen must have been frantic. The police later found him and his bike down in a deep gully in the underbrush. He had been hit from behind and thrown clear of the road. There was dark blue paint on his bike."

"No fresh skid marks to alert them to the site of the accident? That's the first thing I would have looked for. Helen was waiting all that time?" he protested, his anger now gathering force within him.

"She said they didn't expect any skid marks because the rain would have caused the car or truck to slide," Laura explained.

He felt his anger go blunt at the explanation. Still, they took a damned long time, he lamented. He also bristled at the thought of Clay's body, soaked and broken, lying by the roadside and fouled with grime and blood. He remembered as an intern working the emergency room how defiled the bodies of motorcyclists and bikers looked when they were brought in.

"The police are looking for a dark blue vehicle with damage to the right front fender. She didn't have any other information," Laura explained.

"The kids must be devastated," Ellie moaned.

"Well, they're twelve and fourteen now. We still tend to think of them as helpless tykes. Helen says they're handling it very bravely, especially Jonathan," Laura offered, her lip again betraying a tremble.

"They're good kids, and Helen won't let her grief distance her from them," he resolved for all of them.

"Well," Laura groaned as she rose, "I'll go up and call the airline and start re-packing."

"I'll be up in a little while," he said, returning her tortured smile as she rose to leave, "I want to think a few things over."

"Sure," Laura agreed sympathetically. "We'll leave you alone. I guess we all have to do some thinking about this," she added as she reached for Ellie's hand.

Just then the sound of a car pulling into the driveway claimed their attention.

"Must be Todd," Ellie observed.

"Don't leave yet," Cantrelle suggested. "We'll tell him together."

They waited as the door opened, almost with furtive slowness. At the sound of its being closed Cantrelle summoned in a voice pitched to carry.

"Todd, we're in here. We need to talk to you."

They waited until he came, all facing the doorway.

After a moment which seemed stretched by hesitance Todd entered the study to see his family standing and looking directly at him. Fear flashed across his face.

"Is something wrong?" he begged through a swallow.

"Yes, Todd, there is. We just received word that Mr. Moyer was killed in an accident this afternoon. Your mother is going to fly up tomorrow to help Mrs. Moyer make arrangements for returning. We're all pretty upset," Cantrelle explained in man-to-man directness.

"That's awful! What kind of accident?" he pursued, his consternation now resolved in favor of mobilized solicitude and readiness.

"A bike accident. Hit and run. We'll take care of things until your mother gets back," Cantrelle supplied.

"Sure, Ma, we'll look after things. Sure you don't want me to go with you and help?" he offered readily.

That was a possibility to consider, Cantrelle thought. Todd probably could be helpful manhandling the vacation equipment and minding the kids. Laura was considering it, too, he judged by her deliberative silence.

"That's sweet of you, Todd, but I think I'd better go alone. We'll manage O.K. I worry that Mrs. Moyer might think we're descending upon her and taking over. This has to be done her way," Laura explained simply.

"Sure, Ma, I understand," Todd agreed.

"C'mon, Ellie, you can help me pack," Laura motioned in Ellie's direction as she moved toward the door. She figured Todd would get the particulars and be brought up to date in a father-to-son breasting of the tragedy much the same as she and Ellie would pursue mother-to-daughter as she packed. Ellie followed her out of the study.

"It's one hell of a mess, son. His poor wife and family!" Cantrelle restated.

"He was just about your best friend, wasn't he, Dad?" Todd observed gently.

"Yeah, I guess so," Cantrelle realized. He didn't sort his associates into designations of "best friend" or otherwise, but more on the basis of how much they and he accomplished together. Yet, it was true that he was probably closest to Clay; they had done so very much together over the years. Anguish swept through him in recognition of the accuracy of Todd's remark.

"You'll carry on the work, won't you, Dad?" he urged.

This boy Todd. He really knew his way to the heart of things. The question was like touching a lighted match to vapors seeking ignition. His smoldering anger now burst forth.

"You're fucking right I will, son. This won't stop us," he growled. It felt good having anger pull at his sinews. "Just because some stupid, drunken son-of-a-bitch runs Clay Moyer down doesn't mean that our work is done, you can bet your ass. But first," he softened his voice as he began to rein himself in, "we'll take care of some other things."

"I want to help, Dad. Remember, a long time ago one Sunday you and Mom had Mr. and Mrs. Moyer and their kids over for Army hamburgers and he showed me how to ride my brand new two wheel bike?" Todd pointed out in memorium.

Army hamburgers. That inside culinary joke the family brandished about. "Army hamburgers" were just about any hamburgers he grilled, their reckless seasoning blamed on the traumatic residues of a dyspeptic military experience. But Clay liked them. He did remember the occasion, now that Todd mentioned it, though it wasn't so long ago; only eight years, but, forgivably, a very a long time indeed to Todd since it was fully half his lifetime ago.

"Yes, Todd, I do. Mr. Moyer really knew bikes," he affirmed as he recalled the day, now consigned to the treasury of shared innocence. He also knew how to use bikes safely, he thought sharply as he spoke.

"Will we look after Mrs. Moyer?" Todd posed, as much to his father as to himself.

Cantrelle was touched by his son's open and ready concern for Clay's family, speaking the mind of everybody in his own family. Todd was like that—all feeling, and often too much of it for easy management. But always the right feeling.

He approached his son to give an affectionate tousle of the hair and realized that he now had to reach up to do it. Todd was now just about as tall as he. Already. He accomplished the tousling while

Todd smiled receptively. He then rested a hand on Todd's shoulder as he spoke.

"Sure, Todd. We'll all pitch in to help her along. Her own family will help most, but we, and the people at the hospital, like Dr. Weaver and Dr. Corley and their families, will be right there to help when needed," he assured.

But how much could one really help, he questioned in his own mind in challenge of the hopeful words drawn from him by the moment. The Moyers were truly alone in their misery, try as others might to make it seem otherwise.

"Later, when it's all over," Todd suggested in as delicate a reference as he could manage, "I'll call Mrs. Moyer and ask if she needs any help with the yard."

Cantrelle smiled approval as he returned his hand to his side.

"That would be good, Todd," he concurred.

That agreed, Todd began to shift with unease as they stood there almost toe to toe, the right resolves having been registered with apparent little else to add.

"Anything else we should think of, Dad?" he asked.

Cantrelle looked at his handsome, winsome, and vulnerably young son.

"Well, yes, Todd," he recalled. "There is something I need to talk to you about," he groped with restrained distaste.

"Yeah, Dad?" Todd searched, concern returning to his face.

He looked into his son's innocent, compassionate, pathetically kind eyes, now widened again in threat and too angelically blue for their own good. Just like his mother's, only more so. He lowered his gaze just enough to free Todd from tether, and then exhaled softly.

"I guess it can wait. After we've gotten through this mess you and I can sit down together," he promised with ambivalent relief. "Now run off to bed because we'll all have to get up pretty early tomorrow morning."

"Sure, Dad" Todd returned in a discernible sigh of relief.

He tousled Todd's hair one more time as he was turning to leave. He then watched his so quickly grown son stride to the door.

"Oh, I forgot, Todd," he directed after him. "How was the concert?"

"Great, Dad," Todd declared as he stood half-way out of the door. "Only problem was that the stadium seats were still soggy from the rain." He then turned, bent over, and impishly pointed to the wet seat of his pants, prompting a giggle from each. He then left.

Cantrelle grinned at his son's departure, amused as always by the nimbus of jolly ineptitude that seemed to follow at Todd's heels. He and Todd could talk later, and Laura would certainly understand.

He again felt exhausted. Gravity was beginning to return, he presumed. And how the hell was he going to manage without Clay? There was the teaching schedule alone, not to mention the conferences and supervision. He would have to meet with the residents in the morning. Berends would probably do the same with the Triage staff. Jess had probably already notified Berends and other key personnel. There was just so much you could anticipate, and the rest you simply had to let come as it might.

His thoughts carried him back to his desk and he sat down in a heap, planting his chin in his palms as he positioned his elbows just so. The wall had been quietly patient through all of this, and now it was time to bring forth his store of nettles for the wall's tally. No matter how well all concerned might manage this god-damned mess it was still so utterly and totally wrong from the get go. Wait till *National Dateline* hears about this! He then wondered how the DMH would receive the news! They would probably never have a finer opportunity to display disingenuous regrets. That nagging, unsettled something inside him was beginning to sharpen into anger as he thought of anyone feeling gain in Clay's death. He wondered if someone from DMH would show up at the funeral. Clay in a fucking coffin—and all his impossible questions being buried right along with him. He then saw taking shape on the wall's foggy reach a composite of his early days with Clay at the A.M. Staff Conference: his dread of Clay's impending and inevitable questions in the case discussions, the resolute respect each had for the other despite transitory and even recurrent disagreements, the shared sense of failure in not moving on the LSD study, the happy diversion in the birth of their children for upping the volume of their separate family musical scores, their fixed bond in the belief that truth was never to be weighed against convenience or convention—and just about all of it never spoken openly to each other though completely shared in understanding. Now, they wouldn't be able to laugh about it all as old men pleased with their work in the world they had traversed together. He felt the tears ease down into his palms as he acknowledged farewell to what would never be. The wall shimmered and receded as he tried to stare his way beyond the anguished moment. The road was wet, too, his misty vision reminded him, and maybe Clay had had the same trouble seeing in the rain. Certainly that fucking driver wasn't seeing too well. Clay should have known not to ride in a driving rain, that hard-headed . . . . In a flash, the wall jolted him into wide-eyed awareness! He knew something was wrong about this whole thing all along and the wall, or something, was rushing at him right now to tell him exactly what it was! Clay would never ride in a driving rain! Never! He knew this to be certain because several times over the years Clay had said that he had an abiding fear of slipping on a wet road and mangling a knee or especially an ankle, because he already had a weak ankle from a jeep accident when he was in the Army. He wasn't riding in the rain at all! He had gone out earlier to avoid it, as Helen said. Nor was it raining when he was hit, Cantrelle now understood in a rush! Plus, it wasn't because it was raining that there were no skid marks! The rain hadn't even started yet! There were no skid marks because there had been no attempt to avoid hitting him! The wall was now sharp, and clear, and firm, and he knew he was right. Clay was hit on purpose! He was murdered! They would never find that dark blue vehicle because it was no where near New England by now!

He didn't need his palms to prop him up any more and so he sat back in his chair to absorb the full scope of his awareness. How could he have been so stupid as to believe it had been an accident? Because it was easier, that's why! Easier for him as well as for everybody else, some others in particular. Those motherfuckers! He knew he had to get back at them, and he would! But at whom? He squinted ahead and clenched his teeth as he nodded to the wall. He now saw that there was work to be done, but he and the wall would have to keep it between themselves for the time being. Right? He saw that the wall had no need to reply. He nodded again, this time slowly. He then rose to go to bed. There was a lot of work ahead.

Thirteen

He carefully held his position in line as he followed at the mournful, measured speed which carried the lengthy cortege forth exempt of the rules imposed by the route's stop signs and traffic lights. The Funeral Director led in the first car. Theirs was sixth in line, as had been arranged by the Director in accordance with the protocol demanded by a burial motor procession. The fact that he was a pallbearer had nothing to do with their placing—that was a protocol unto itself, he had come to understand once again—or even that he had been one of those to speak—offer "expressions"—at the memorial service. The designation of the first several cars after those of the immediate family was made by the survivors with the helpful guidance of the Funeral Director and was based solely upon their estimate of how the deceased himself would have lined up his following. The number of cars in the procession stretched out over several city blocks as they moved along in hushed obeisance with headlights on and engines respectfully throttled down. As he drove along he caught brief glimpses of the hearse and the black limousines ahead as corners were turned and hills crested, and from time to time he was reminded of his relief—today only—that their family sedan so close to the front of the procession was a sedate charcoal gray and not some trendy suburban hue that seemed perennially enroute to sun and sand. But for all that, its color could have been canary yellow for the brilliant sunshine and cloudless sky which seemed garishly out of tune with the emotional tenor of the occasion. A leaden, overcast sky with a baroque drizzle would have been more in keeping. It certainly would have enlisted the sidewalk lookers-on and passing motorists into a more dolefully resonant espy of the procession. Aside from a measure of curiosity, the onlookers all seemed to regard the procession with the discomfort they would a guest who showed up for a light lunch in formal attire. Moreover, having the car suitable in color did not protect him from the self-consciousness and its discomfort come of onlookers' stares, as though validating signs of grief were being sought by them in satisfaction of the scene's theme.

For his part, he felt more inclined toward a show of defiance. That sense of it reminded him of his dissatisfaction with his words at the memorial service just minutes earlier. The two other speakers, Martha and Jess, had spoken of grief, loss, forever-rich memories, and the gratitude of all for what he had given. They did tender eulogy to reach all in general and to comfort family in particular. In his address he had made some gestures in that direction, primarily to Clay's mother, the only surviving relative Clay had other than Helen and the kids, and had held Helen and the two kids apart in the safe knowledge that any public statements of condolence to them would have been gratuitous, even egregious. Rather, his comments had been less about loss and more about shame—shame that this could happen; shame that the hopes of learning and truth could be so affronted; shame that Clay could ever have been allowed to feel that he stood alone while he stood among us, his friends; and shame if we didn't redouble our efforts in his name to complete the work he began and which we justly inherited in dutied mandate. As he recalled the tone and some of his words he blinked to focus his concern that it all may have sounded less a note of dole and more a cry for revenge, more a knell for blood oath to be taken and less a call for communion of the bereaved. But in truth, that was exactly the way he felt, determined to set matters right, to make those responsible pay. It was one thing to annihilate impersonal thousands as a matter of social or even political policy, horrible enough as that was, but to single out an opponent for murder! That took it beyond the play of contending philosophies and made it so much the viler—and viciously personal. Or maybe it was just that the agony of Blush had now come immeasurably closer to home and that he, Frank Cantrelle, was beginning to feel something akin to what the family of Blush victims had known all along. But, no, he insisted, Clay had been targeted, stalked, and killed as a distinct and important figure specifically because of his growing prominence in the movement to coerce the federal government into conceding responsibility *and* accountability for Blush as a programmatic, coordinated assault upon a segment of the population marked for annihilation, only to fall victim himself to the self-same malevolence. No, Clay's situation was a bit different, and his murder escalated confrontation far beyond the level of public debate. And, oh yes, it was murder. He just knew it. Not any one thing told him so, but he just knew it and he knew he was right. The mere idea of considering it otherwise did violence to his sense of moral outrage as well as to his freshly galvanized loyalty to Clay. That was one of the reasons he hadn't yet mentioned his surmise to others who probably already sensed in his demeanor more covert resolve than collaborative grief. Not that he hadn't had his tears; he had, and he would continue to know their searing return when memories would leap unexpectedly into awareness, memories activated by the ordinary and routine events of his day which now no longer included Clay as a living participant but which keenly called him forth, though now in grim lament. Those tears as well he kept to himself, and he even felt embarrassment that Clay, in memoried form, might witness those tears, as though he were crying in Clay's presence for missing him so much. In truth, he didn't feel that Clay was really gone, but merely transformed by a vile blow which now separated him from his mission with the result that he, Frank Cantrelle, had become the champion ascendant since he could no more turn his back on that mission than he could on the orphaned child of a dear friend. And for the while he would keep that notion to himself as well. In fact, he had the odd but deeply gratifying sense that he was a participant in this funeral not so much as a mourner but as a co-conspirator along with the enduring Clay in their continuing but now modified collaboration for blowing this Blush evil wide open. And he wondered if his "expression" had inadvertently conveyed as much.

"How did my comments sound?" he asked. "Not too bitter, I hope," he added disingenuously, hoping that they were heard, if not as a burning grief than as a deep wounding and nothing more.

"Hurt and angry—and determined not to let grief get you down," Laura answered as she looked straight ahead, her handkerchief clutched at the ready in her lap. Ellie and Todd sat discreetly silent in the back.

"I didn't . . . well, wave the bloody shirt, did I?" he posed tentatively.

"Oh, no. It was nothing like that," Laura assured as she reached over and touched his hand on the wheel. "You just said what everybody felt but couldn't say because of their . . . their . . . ."

"Their sense of decency?" he volunteered in readiness for the worst.

"No," she corrected in even tones, "because of their confusion about all that's happened. And also because of the grief, which is just getting us all down. It's just so sad . . . and so wrong," she added as she carefully daubed her eyes with the handkerchief.

"Yeah, I know," he sighed, sounding more pointed than he intended. "It's going to be terrible for Helen and the kids tonight when it's all over," he shifted. "Think we should call some time later this evening?"

"I'll call just before dinner to ask if they need anything, but I don't think they should be disturbed tonight. After all this, and all these people, they'll need time for themselves as a family to settle into their private mourning. I'll stay in touch with Helen over the next couple of days; keep an eye on them," she explained.

She had her end of it all worked out, he thought, and he reached over and squeezed her hand in proud appreciation.

"We can help with the kids, if you want us to. Take them to the mall shopping, if they would like," Ellie offered.

"Maybe in a few days when they're eager to get out and about again," Laura considered. "We might work it out with a visit. I could spend a little while with Mrs. Moyer while you two take the kids shopping or something. Jonathan really takes to you, Todd."

"Yeah," Todd agreed in sad commiseration.

"And Samantha thinks you're Miss America, Ellie," Laura continued.

The conversation was becoming too tortured. Speaking of the children's simple and innocent affections was too wounding to be continued.

"They're good kids and they'll make it okay," Cantrelle affirmed.

In one way or another they had covered the same ground many times over during the past several days, and the traverse always proceeded in the same fashion. First, there would be a joint acknowledgment of just how awful and cruel the situation was. Then there would be a specification of the woe relative to the prime sufferers. The discussion would then recoil in prudent retreat for having ventured too close to the agony of the matter and be followed by the registration of some platitude or general assurance that those concerned undoubtedly would be equal to the rigors of the moment, particularly in view of the understanding and support available to them by the likes of those in attendance. Because of his evolving private agenda he registered the tracings of a cool cynicism skirting the edges of his public lament, directing a segment of his attention beyond the immediate needs of the moment and toward strategies impatiently awaiting his use.

As it was, the past five days had whooshed by in a frenetic, hazy swirl with very little of anything standing out with any degree of clarity. Yet, all the parts performed precisely. Laura made an early flight Tuesday morning to meet with Helen and drive the kids home the next day. He and Ellie and Todd had been on hand for their arrival to help with getting Helen's house back into operation. Helen returned with Clay's body the next day and set about the initial arrangements for the funeral service and then resumed as best she could her other family duties. Laura returned home that evening and did the same with her own charges. Helen's sister and her family arrived from Hawaii the following day and pitched in mightily while pretty much all of Moreland stood at the ready to help in any way asked. Jess had dropped over at Helen's briefly that evening in follow up on Martha's solicitous phone call earlier in the day to declare himself and Moreland at her disposal. Everybody was standing to, and smartly. And for a while it seemed that everybody was just too busy to be aggrieved.

But last night was the night of the viewing. The protection of sheer and pressing business was now over and the sepulchral quiet of the funeral home urged forth a swell of accumulated and delayed grief as hundreds of friends and acquaintances filed past the bier to make acknowledgment and to offer right condolence. Helen and the kids bravely presided and touchingly offered reassurance to the mourners who groped for means of saying what they felt and wanted her to know. He and Laura, and Jess and his wife, stayed most of the evening but left discreetly a short time before the viewing was over to allow Clay's mother, Helen, and her sister and their families their moment of private grief at the coffin on the last night.

Earlier in the evening the aggregate of mourners in attendance testified to Clay's prominence. The array included various family and friends, a sprinkling of the merely curious, the entire Resident and Teaching Staff, members of the hospital's general staff, and even officials from several of the sister state hospitals, as was a representative from the Dean's office of Clay's alma mater. They were careful to make their tenders to Helen in the kindest and most solicitous manner; likewise the Deputy Commissioner of the Department of Mental Health who lamented to Helen the great loss the mental health system of the Commonwealth as well as that of the entire country would suffer with Clay's passing. He'd watched the Deputy Commissioner carefully, perhaps too carefully, for after the latter had offered his condolences, said his piece to Helen and was turning to leave, the man noticed that he was being scrutinized. He managed only a curt nod through his obvious discomfort at being singled out. Cantrelle returned the nod, and with a certain relish, for he intended to see more of this Deputy Commissioner before very long. One of the notables from *National Dateline* arrived to convey deepest sympathy and to lament the loss of what he was certain had promised to be a most creative association with Clay and one which would undoubtedly have been of historic significance to the country, if Providence had been kinder. He assured Helen that Clay's passing only strengthened the network's resolve to pursue the questions raised by him.

He recalled that he'd been holding Laura's hand and was musing on how the constituent elements of the evening's entire reality were being focused by Clay's coffin when the turning of heads announced to him without his having to see or to be told that Burleson had arrived. He turned to confirm his surmise and saw that Burleson was being urged to proceed ahead of those standing in line. Burleson had demurred with gestures that he was quite content to wait his turn democratically but was now allowing himself to be offered forward toward the coffin and to Helen. Helen eased his way along by smiling graciously and extending her hand to greet him. He took her hand as he reached her, greeted her gently, and then spoke a few words of kind recognition to the children. He then resumed speaking to Helen as everybody watched. He spoke soothingly as he held her hand, and Helen, her head lowered, nodded a few times in acknowledgment of his words. When he had finished Helen looked at him gratefully and then leaned forward and gave him a kiss on the cheek. He then shook her hand with both of his and moved on to the children and briefly repeated his attentions. As he watched, Cantrelle estimated it was in the mind of most present that the scene before them offered a fateful contrast to the one of a mere six weeks ago when Clay and Burleson had spoken from the same podium as contending yet conjoined forces in that epic meeting of manifestoes which allied their missions, though swift misadventure had now disordered the hopes so joyously raised then. He was just beginning to perceive that his task of rectifying the wrong of Clay's death would most likely place him in some altered relationship even with

Burleson, probably moving him in closer reach of working with the man, when Burleson, in seeming confirmation of the prospect, his duties to Clay's family now done, walked up to pay his regards. As usual, after greeting Cantrelle he warmly acknowledged Laura, appealing gently to her grief and then to their joint distress at so great a loss. He nodded in the direction of the children, lingering in his glance at Richard and Meredith long enough to receive a brief introduction since he'd never met them before, and then reminisced for all of them that the happy occasion of several weeks earlier was now made all the more precious for its imposed poignancy and thus all the more edifying to all of them in the richness it knew and offered, now never to be duplicated, but never to be forgotten. Cantrelle, sensing that Burleson was more affected by the event than he wished to convey, felt ready in comradely turn to offer the man a measure of commiseration. Burleson then recalled that he should also pay his respects to Jess and his family who were seen to arrive at that moment, but mentioned to Cantrelle as he was disengaging that it seemed there was now even greater reason for him and Cantrelle to get together in the near future to catch up with their converging interests. Seemingly it had become their standard way of parting, no less applicable on this occasion than on any other. And then, with a courtly nod to all, he left and approached Jess and Pam on his way out. The evening ended some time later when the principals and their respective families took their leave of Helen and her family to gain the relief of their homes and to prepare for the morrow.

And now it was the morrow, and a Friday morning, very much like any Friday morning when all would be in various states of readiness for the A.M. Conference. But that conference was now in abeyance these vacation weeks of the training year, though it might have been so in any event, what with Clay's rise to prominence and the demand such prominence made on his being elsewhere. Indeed, just two days from today, this now final day, Clay would have been vibrantly before the world on national TV. The world! But more than that, Clay himself had changed; and along with it, something had changed between the two of them. Clay had actually moved on to the next phase of his life—what an irony!—while he, Frank Cantrelle, ever the late bloomer, was still tooling around in the precincts he and Clay had shared for the past many years. So, in a way, Clay had moved on ahead and had done so well in advance of the accident. Accident? What the hell kind of talk was that? This requiem business was making him downright biddable. Yes, Clay had gone out of their joint life, so to speak, long weeks before, and his death seemed now to be the swift and determinate culmination of that shift. He saw himself left so far behind, and not simply within the context of grief. Clay had seized upon something and it had thrust him forward to a premature doom. But how could doom be premature, he peeved. To hell with it! Clay was too close to something and couldn't be permitted to lay it out on national TV, and that was the long and the short of it! Clay was going to finger the Federal government, probably the NSA or some kindred agency, that much he knew; but how much else Clay knew, or had concluded, or was going to say, he didn't know. But obviously someone else knew, or suspected, or feared. And now here we all were, lined up in funereal subjection to someone's idea of maintaining security on an enterprise held to be more important than the lives of mere individuals. And his was dutiful car number six taking its cues from those ahead on their way to an appointment with finality. Finality? In a large pig's ass! It wasn't over for him, god damn it!

"You okay, Frank?" Laura asked.

"Oh . . .yeah . . .sure!" he retorted. She must have heard him draw in deeply as he worked himself up to the expletives. "We must be getting near the cemetery; we've been driving forever," he dissembled.

He wasn't familiar with this township and so couldn't gauge their distance from the cemetery.

"I think it's just ahead a short ways," Laura estimated. She'd visited with Helen often over the years, knew the township better, and thus had a general idea of their likely route for today.

He let the matter drop and returned to his brooding. It didn't necessarily follow, he continued, that the group Clay was going to accuse were the ones responsible for his death. Any group sufficiently bothered by Clay's snooping and his readiness to go public about it could have done it. He didn't want to lock himself into Clay's suspicions as the only channel for proceeding against the perpetrators. It was quite possible that one faction undertook the act in the full expectation that suspicion would fall, if it did at all, on the faction or factions Clay intended to designate during his TV interview. Exploiting the opportunity, so to speak. In fact, given the kind of operatives Clay held to be behind this, that opportunity just might have been irresistible. Or was he himself just being paranoid, and convolutedly so in order to defend a fundamentally false premise, the premise that to believe this was an accident was to strain credulity beyond reasonable limits? Possibly. Plus, there was the significant point, nourishing the prowling and nettling doubt which nibbled at his conspiracy construction, that no one else seemed to question that it was all nothing more than just a very tragic accident. He couldn't believe that some others out there didn't harbor some suspicion, but so far no one else had breathed a word of such. Did they find the idea too offensive to own up to? Or just that it would be too cruel to convey? Or just too crazy? Whatever, the upshot was that he felt vastly alone in his torment, and he wondered if that very feeling was the benchmark of all good paranoids before they abandoned the fraternal and trusting world of consensual validation. He felt particularly suspicious of his stout reluctance to share his thoughts with Laura. He even wondered—feared, more accurately—that his messianic outrage was essentially nothing more than an inability to accept a hateful blow which all others were managing more realistically in the service of healthy mourning, but that he, unable to accept even natural infringement of his preferred design, was doing nothing more than erecting an imaginary opponent to best in a contest of conflicting omnipotences. It wouldn't be the first time he reacted to calamitous disappointment with sweeping, immediate, and automatic counter-punching, only later to be chagrined by so graceless a display of angst. Hence, for the time being the wisdom of cautious silence; no need to add to the store of potential future regrets. And maybe—the very thought of it grated—just maybe it would all blow over in a few days. Maybe when the wave of pain and dismay—and the hateful sense of helplessness carried in their wake—subsided, and, given a couple of days or so for return to routine, he would settle into ordinary acceptance like everybody else and the entire spectre of malevolence and murder would retreat to those nether regions whence it came. Maybe, but he didn't think so, because he knew that every time he saw a Blush patient he would be reminded of what needed to be done. There was no getting away from it. Or from this god-damned burial, he reminded himself as he returned his attention to the painfully deliberate creep of the car ahead.

"It was nice of Jeffrey to make the trip for the funeral," Laura observed in the direction of Ellie. He had driven up the night before to pay his respects at the viewing and in doing so had acquired an additional attachment to the family and its fortunes. He and Ellie seemed agreed upon some yet unspoken agenda which saw to its own arrangements. Morello had driven in as well, as did several other former residents, and Landon was taken in along with them for lodging by the local network of Moreland graduates. The bonds of shared scholarship were indeed eternal if readiness to provide bed and board were any measure of such.

"Yeah, he's right in there with Morello and several of the old gang," Cantrelle teased lightly, grateful to get away from the weighty fatalism of his thoughts.

"Frank, who was that man last night from the Department of Mental Health?" Laura inquired belatedly. "You know, the one you commented to Jess about."

"Bartley. Allan Bartley. The Deputy Commissioner. He's their Mr. Nice Guy. As far as I can tell in all my dealings with him—and Clay would agree—he's basically a really good sort—reasonable, honest—and we often wondered how he fit in with the rest of them in that hotbed of cynicism. I guess even the DMH believes it takes all kinds," he snickered in immediate return to darker business.

"Dad," Ellie saw fit to mention, "Jeffrey said that Dr. Morello wondered if residency training would ever be the same again because you and Mr. Moyer were such a team in the way you two went at teaching. He said it was like a double-barreled Socrates, but that your questions were usually gentler than Mr. Moyer's."

"Less penetrating, you mean? Yeah," Cantrelle chuckled in proud satisfaction, "he was full choke, I was modified; and between the two no one escaped our tutorial blast."

They all smiled hesitantly at the irreverence taken. It was too true that residency training would never be the same—certainly not for him, nor for the residents, nor for Moreland, and, as Morello insinuated, nor even for those graduates who had known the better time. Moreover, he didn't want to be reminded of that just yet; the present gloom was enough to keep him sufficiently morose. But Ellie was just trying to help with the conversation on this impossibly long procession.

The cars ahead began to slow down even more as he noticed on his right the beginning of an iron fence whose serried pikes were not greatly different from those surrounding Moreland. But here, the gathered tenants were already settled into death, and linear rows of gravestones trailed off into the distance over the slow roll of the cemetery's field. It seemed that no two gravestones were alike, as though effort were at hand to protect the individuality of these departed souls from the all-blanketing abyss of death. The cars now came to a momentary halt as the lead vehicles began to negotiate the entrance to the cemetery, a pause long enough to prompt him to wonder if someone up ahead was collecting tolls. The cars then resumed their slow passage as he and probably all others in line shifted into an aroused dread of the rite now so close at hand.

"I wonder why they never plant any trees in a cemetery? Would look less barren and more natural. And restful," he complained as he drew up near the gate. He wasn't going to enter that gate without uttering some protest. "And it wouldn't look so much like a ghetto for the dead," he snapped as their car traversed the entrance and turned to follow the others down the roadway toward the interior of the cemetery. Floral arrangements freshened graves here and there, and a few people, all elderly, were seen about, tending to particular plots, or just visiting. The engine noise now seemed too noticeable as well as alien and invasive. The silence within the car accordingly took on a hushed note.

After a series of labyrinthine turns the lead vehicles came to a halt. Cantrelle followed suit and waited for those ahead to step out of their cars before opening his door as signal to those behind to do likewise.

"O.K.," he said. "Let's form up on your side, Laura, and go as a group when Richard and Meredith join up with us. As soon as we reach the grave you and the family take your positions near Helen and the kids because I'll probably have to line up with the pallbearers at the hearse."

With that they stepped out on to the roadway. Richard and Meredith walked up readily, and, all gathered, they proceeded forward as quietly as they could. Other than a few bird chirps and the grinding of gravel under foot all that could be heard was the urgent mumblings of the Funeral Director and his assistants as they marshaled people into position near the dirty, gaping hole in the ground flanked by two gravediggers standing near their respective heaps of dirt. Strips of artificial turf were laid over the bare heaps to soften their brute readiness. As they neared the grave they heard sobbing which came from Helen's sister who was being consoled jointly by her husband as well as by Helen herself. Clay's elderly mother was nearest the Minister who was standing at her side, resolutely awaiting his moment, and she kept a comforting eye on the children as the other adults tended to the moment's needs. Jonathan held his sister's hand. Laura instinctively placed herself behind the children and Clay's mother upon approach, and Todd, Ellie, Richard, and Meredith deployed themselves on her flanks. That done, Cantrelle slipped off to the side and proceeded toward the hearse where one of the assistants was waiting to supervise the pallbearing. When he reached the hearse he nodded to the assistant as present and ready, and then looked down the roadway along the line of halted cars to see at least a hundred people in groups and clusters walking forward. Most of them he recognized, such as Martha and Jess and their spouses, but many he didn't—those from the side of Clay's life he'd never known. For a moment he puzzled over the thought that this man whom he knew so well, perhaps better than any other among his friends, could have a side to him, complete with friends, to which he, Frank Cantrelle, had never been party and of which he knew nothing. He was just beginning to feel the numbing effect of humility leaven his grief when he noticed far down the road a solitary figure walking forth along with the others at a measuredly unobtrusive pace. He squinted to be sure, but he immediately knew who it was and his pulse quickened at the meaning of her presence. His first thought was that the DMH probably didn't know she was here, and his second thought was the question as to why she was. He watched her intently as she neared, occluded from moment to moment by those in front of her, but he discerned her clearly withal. She was dressed in black, which, he suspected, made her more distinctive than she perhaps had wished, and a large-brimmed black hat gave her suitably bowed head a measure of concealment he knew she wisely intended. He hadn't seen her at the viewing, but maybe she'd been there, too, he wondered. But probably not, at least not officially or she would have been with Bartley. So what the hell did this mean? He looked around quickly and saw that no one else seemed to be noticing her or his interest in her. Helen's brother-in-law was just now checking in with the assistant for his positioning as pallbearer, and the Director was observing the gathering crowd to estimate the moment to begin the interment. That noted, he watched her as she approached the main body of people encircling the grave site, and as she stepped off the roadway she looked up at him in silent greeting. He saw best her red lips behind the gauzy, black veil covering her face and enough of her dark eyes to convey to her at a glance his pleasure, his surprise, and his concern at her being among these present. He felt she read him correctly as she discreetly lowered her head and proceeded to the graveside. He then watched her as she faded into the group. No matter what, he affirmed again, Alison Dieter was a blindingly beautiful woman, an acknowledgment he ought not to be making under the present circumstances, he hurriedly added in self-reproach. He then shifted his gaze back to the assistant.

At that moment the assistants received their signal from the Director and turned to assemble the pallbearers. As they did so Jess walked up to assume his position which was opposite Cantrelle's. They nodded to each other without saying a word; it seemed that together they had been officiating non-stop in these proceedings for days and were well past the need to greet each other. He then braced himself, as did the others, to offer the appropriate stalwart readiness. The assistant opened the hearse door and began to roll the coffin out to the waiting pallbearers who found their positions at the carrying rails. Then, upon the signal from the assistants, the pallbearers shuffled along in lock-step toward the waiting grave. The assistants led the way directing the path and pace and soon the coffin was lowered on to the several temporary beams straddling the surface of the grave. There it rested as the Minister, alone at the head of the grave, called the gathering to prayer as he opened his book of psalms.

"As the Lord giveth, the Lord taketh," he began, holding his right hand forth in blessing.

Cantrelle furtively scanned the gathering without knowing why. All heads were bowed. What did he expect to see? Someone who was too guilty to show reverence? He didn't know why, but it seemed right that he be vigilant. He looked at the coffin and found it hard to believe that his buddy, Clay Moyer, was in it. Yet, that's why everybody was here, he reminded himself in mock discourse. His thinking began to tinker with gross denial of it all.

". . . Let us not only see what we have lost," the Minister continued, "but let us know now and ever what we have gained in having had our moments with Clay Moyer. His family, his friends, and those who knew him are the richest recipients of what he intended for all, and though his time was called much too soon in advance of our understanding and acceptance, we must know that in the ways of our Savior we are received as we are ready."

Sobs here and there punctuated the Minister's homily. Cantrelle glanced over to check his own family. Todd, burly solid, was standing between his mother and Ellie with a comforting arm around each. Richard and Meredith stood sedately behind them in joined reverence. They made such a pleasant, proper couple, he observed once again.

"... And perhaps we can find our answer in the parable of the traveler journeying to a distant land. Along his arduous route he asked many questions as to the best way for travel as well as to the location and distance of the land he sought. And he received many answers. But soon he came to understand that the answers he received were from fellow travelers who were also seeking that distant land, and no wiser as to its whereabouts than he. He then knew that his path would become the path of many to follow and that in his lonely seeking he was leading the many ...."

Tears welled up in his eyes as he thought of Clay's feeling of isolation in his last days. Inspired isolation, yes, but isolation nonetheless, and cruelly obliged by the timidity of so many of his friends, one in particular. More sobs were heard, and a few may have been his own.

"... Such that the path he has shown us may seem lonely and empty, but only because just now he is no longer with us to comfort us as we follow. But we must know that the loneliness and the uncertainty we now feel as our loss are also our bounden legacy, for they were companion to the path he found for the betterment of us all. Thus, our grief is our guide, and ...."

You bet your ass, he resounded to himself as styptic to the flow of anguish threatening to dilute his talion resolve. Those things the Minister was saying needed to be said, he figured, but not as an end in themselves. No way, he resolved with private emphasis.

"... And so let us pray: Our Father, who art in heaven ...."

The susurrus of prayer saturated the air with acceptance of the inevitable which he estimated now to be at hand. As the last syllables of the supplication faded he looked up to see the Minister signaling the Director to proceed. The Director then motioned Helen and her family forward and positioned them near the Minister. They all awaited the Minister's signal, and, that given, he and the other pallbearers lifted the coffin by straps that had been placed along the length of the beams. When the coffin had been lifted free of the beams the gravediggers quickly gathered them for removal. The Minister now opened his book and began reading as the Director bade the pallbearers to lower the coffin slowly.

"And though I walk in the valley of the shadow of Death I will have no fear . . . ."

How many times had he heard those words spoken over friends or relatives? A lot, and with escalating frequency, it seemed. How many families of Blush victims were obliged to hear them as well? Death really was the great irony as well as the great leveler, he felt driven to observe for want of some more novel reflection. And it was so common, this thing Death, so universal, though it seemed ever unique in its every moment of arrival, he puzzled as the coffin descended into the grave. He and the other pallbearers had quickly found a smooth unison in paying out the straps, and that in itself told him that everybody had a stake in death and dying, ready to be activated at any moment and for which they were resignedly and silently prepared. Each one of us carried his own death along with him to some future reckoning date, he decided just as the coffin settled on the bottom of the grave. He and the other pallbearers were then bidden to release the straps and rejoin their families.

". . . As it was in the beginning, is now, and ever shall be . . . ." the Minister intoned in summation as the Director and his assistants passed silently among the crowd distributing single roses for the final farewell. He accepted one, but passed it on to Laura for there was no way he was going to throw a farewell rose on Clay Moyer's coffin; he and Clay still had business together! The assistant sensed not to offer him another. The Minister's recitations were now concluding. He closed his book as he reminded all of the ultimate simplicity of existence awaiting us in the timelessness of ashes and dust. He then approached Helen, hugged her, and then stroked the children's heads. Her arm in his, he led Helen to the grave. She bravely dropped her rose in, the children following suit at her side. Heavy sobs from the gathering resurfaced and threatened to break free of control but subsided as the Minister led her and the children away toward the waiting car.

Some son-of-a-bitch was going to pay for this fucking crime, Cantrelle anguished as he watched. He instinctively put his arm around Laura who was biting her lip as tears trickled down her cheeks. Ellie was holding her mother's arm for mutual comfort; Todd stood next to his brother and Meredith at plaintive attention. Richard stood erect and wise. Checking his family for readiness after Helen, Clay's mother, the children, and the Minister had gone a certain distance, and after Helen's sister and her family had proceeded past the grave, he took a signal from the Director to follow in the procession as guide to the rest of the gathering. They filed past the grave and dropped their roses in but he refused to look down at the coffin as he conducted Laura along. In short order the gravesite was behind them and they were walking along the path to the roadway. Grass and sky and distant telephone poles now came back into view. The spell was ending, and he felt he was exiting from some black and wretched chamber as he spotted their shiny sedan waiting in line to whisk them away to where they belonged. He noted that Helen and the kids were getting into the limousine for their transit home, what was left of it.

"Yeah," he spoke, "they'll need a little time for themselves today. You can check in on them with a call tonight."

Laura nodded in agreement.

Silence returned as they proceeded toward their car, Richard and Meredith veering off in the direction of their own. He strained to hear even one bird call, but there was none to be had. With a start he remembered Dieter. He decided to wait until they got to the car to look back and see if she was still alone. His perplexity about her attendance was returning. He saw Helen's limousine pull away and then that of the sister's family. He watched them move along the roadway to retrace the route to the cemetery gate. Their departure seemed to free him up for conversation.

"I wonder who's looking after the patients? Everyone at Moreland seems to be here," he grumped in an oblique reproof of the whole business.

"Dad," Todd asked, "were some of the patients allowed to come?"

The words cut right through him. Of course no patients were allowed to attend, he realized in a blast of shame; they were out-of-hand unfit, unworthy, and unwanted. Patients were not permitted the tender expressions of the graceful sane. No matter that Clay had worked with some of them for years or that they may have felt closer to him than to any other person in their tortured existence, the fact that they were patients exempted them of the duties and callings of humanity. The law, civil and tribal, said so. And he was as guilty as anyone else in that regard because it had not occurred to him in the least that a patient might have wanted to add his bit to the doing of loyal requiem. Just as they couldn't attend graduation.

"No, Todd, not today," he replied morosely. "There will probably be a memorial service held some time later at the hospital and those who'll want to attend will be able to do so." He wasn't sure that would be the case at all, but it seemed to be the right thing to say just now. He would have to talk to Jess about it later.

They had now reached the car. As they waited for the others of the gathering to return to their places in the waiting line of vehicles he scanned the dispersing group as it fanned out toward the roadway. He looked for only one person and he spotted her at the far edge of the group walking toward some distant point down the line of cars. He resumed puzzling over why she had come. Was it just simple sentiment? No such feeling had been betrayed at any time earlier in their contacts, and certainly nothing of the sort had issued from her office in the preceding months. He would probably never know, but the mystery of it was compelling.

"Would you all like to wait in the car until we're ready to go?" he suggested. Also, their doing thus would serve as a signal to the others now reaching their cars. Laura nodded, and he opened the door and then closed it behind her. Todd and Ellie returned to their places in the back seat. He knew they felt relieved to be back in the insulated comfort of the family car. He continued his vigilance as he moved around to his door where he positioned himself so that he could be at the ready when it seemed the right time to get in and take his turn in the departure. He stood and looked over the forming queue as people reached their cars. The assistants were now making their way forward to join the Director at one of the lead vehicles. It wouldn't be long now, he sighed in relief. He noticed someone moving ahead of the assistants and seemingly pointed directly for him. The figure approached and while still a distance away caught Cantrelle's eye to certify his destination. Now what, he wondered.

"Dr. Cantrelle?" the figure asked as he reached the car.

"Yes?" he answered, uncertain.

Stoutish, mid-fortyish, and dressed in blue serge, a white Windsor collar contrasting with striped shirt, the figure extended his hand.

"Dr. Cantrelle, may I extend my deepest sympathy," he offered along with a gentle handshake. "I'm Jerry Rosten. We've never met."

"Thank you, Mr. Rosten," he replied, holding a quizzical tilt to his gaze. The name seemed familiar, but where? He was sure he'd never seen this man before. Had he heard the name? Or read it? Read it? Yes! That was it! The florid signature! Recognition spread across his face.

"I see you remember my letter, Dr. Cantrelle," Rosten smiled in acknowledgment of Cantrelle's flash of recall. "I received your reply day before yesterday. I noted that the letter was sent the day this happened, perhaps written before you had learned of the terrible tragedy. But I'm afraid I might be assuming too much."

"No, Mr. Rosten, you're right," Cantrelle admitted, feeling himself drawn into a need to set the record straight. He had totally forgotten about the proposal, "the feeler," and to be reminded of it now so unexpectedly set his mind scrambling to gather details for orienting his recall.

"Mrs. Moyer and her children seem to be a very fine family. The boy strikes me as having a lot of his father's courage. But who am I to say since I've never had the pleasure of meeting them," he observed contritely.

"They're all quite courageous," Cantrelle retorted testily, again feeling pulled into more interchange than he preferred. He peevishly registered that Rosten's sympathy was being subsidized by a presumption of intimacy the mere exchange of business correspondence could not support. And the briefest of exchanges to wit. Savoring that, he was becoming resentfully wary of what purpose this proffer of sympathy might harbor.

"Of course," Rosten conceded readily. A slight pause signaled a forthcoming shift in topic. "Dr. Cantrelle, I know this is positively the wrong time and place to bring this up, but I was disappointed when I received your reply, as you can imagine. When I found out about Mr. Moyer's death I knew I had to ask you to reconsider, because with Mr. Moyer's death your joint work lost its spokesman, and the country lost its chance to hear what needs to be said."

As he listened he wrestled with the problem of hearing more truth than he wanted to bother with just now. Moreover, this man Rosten had a way of getting to issues fast, as probably befitted his line of work, he grudgingly allowed.

"And in all honesty, that's one of the reasons why I'm here today," Rosten continued, "so that I could say this to you at this particular moment. The other reason is that I happen to believe in what Clay Moyer was trying to accomplish. I have a nephew out

West who right now is dying of Blush poisoning, and my kid sister's grief at the loss of her only child is something I feel entitled to draw upon for speaking to you this way at this awful moment, Dr. Cantrelle."

All of a sudden Jerry Rosten wasn't so unacceptable, Cantrelle mused as he listened. There was no question about giving the man credit for having balls, he totaled up, and it was even beginning to appear that Rosten might have some principle mixed in with his pushy manner. He could have misinterpreted the signature. And besides, things were different now.

"And, Dr. Cantrelle, I'm going to say something that may offend you beyond your wish ever to pardon," Rosten added in a more ominous tone, "but I have to because you're the one who has to hear it and this may be the only chance I'll ever have to say it to you."

Cantrelle braced himself for what he immediately sensed was coming. He looked Rosten in the eye, carefully and expectantly.

"Dr. Cantrelle," he said with simple directness, "there are some people, and I'm one of them, who doubt that Mr. Moyer's death was an accident. And every one of us would like to know how you feel about that."

He wanted to hug Jerry Rosten for the relief he felt along with the return of conviction in his sanity. So he was *not* the only one; he *wasn't* alone! He should have had more faith in his convictions, he should have trusted his intuition, he should have done all kinds of things, he scolded himself in relief which, he estimated, was so visible across his face that it reciprocated an easement in the stiffness of Rosten's erect stance. An important point had been negotiated, it all seemed to say.

"I'm not offended in the least, Mr. Rosten," he replied as evenly as he could, "and I agree it's an issue to be addressed," he added, knowing he sounded a bit stilted and carefully suggestive. Just then he heard the engine of one of the lead vehicles start, and then another. Engines up and down the line now began to turn over and catch. "I'll be in touch with you, Mr. Rosten. Thank you for coming," he said as he grasped Rosten's hand in a firm shake.

"Thank you, Dr. Cantrelle," Rosten replied as Cantrelle bent his way into the driver's seat.

When the line of cars lurched forward Laura turned to him.

"Who was that man, Frank? A friend of Clay's?" she queried.

"In a way. We had some dealings recently but they were put aside for the moment. He wanted me to know that he hoped we could continue to work together despite this setback," he generalized.

"Is he at the hospital?" she asked.

"No, he works in communications; publicity. Getting the word to the people, so to speak," he limned broadly. He chose to avoid specifics for the time being.

"I'll be glad to get home," she relented, "and get busy at something. I don't want to do any more thinking for a while."

Nor did he, but the prospect of achieving a restful amentia was most unlikely. Yet, he sure needed a few minutes at the wall. On the other hand, he considered, he was spending more and more time of late staring at that damned wall, plus the wall at Moreland, and even the wall at his practice office. Why not just become a holy man in some Himalayan cave and get it over with? Because he owed too many bills, that's why. It was just that simple, he grinned cynically as he paused at the cemetery gate before swinging out into the daily traffic where everything seemed as before. They were now on their way home and he was so glad Helen had decided against a post-interment totem feast. It was so much better this way; allow everybody to seek the dimension and fit of his own mourning without some kick-off brunch to celebrate a common starting point.

The mid-morning traffic had picked up and in due time he found his way back to familiar precincts as he approached their township. As he drove along, the silence in the car became more clearly the family's statement of contained expectation of arrival home where their lives could resume as before, just like the traffic in which they now swam. Well, almost like before. He was becoming aware with the increasing distance from the cemetery of a gathering sense of selfish relief that his family remained whole, solid, intact, and that no major adjustments in their hopes were mandated by this morning's business. New work for him, yes, what with the advent of one Jerry Rosten providentially at hand. The resources Rosten could bring to their collaboration, if one could be mounted, were indeed estimable far beyond anything he otherwise could have known but which now just might be within his reach. The prospect was heady, and he began to wonder if Clay had felt something of the same in his planning with *National Dateline*. He suspected so. He even decided that he could imagine how it had proceeded with Clay, that initially his collaboration with others had been couched in caution and circumspection with dutiful concern for over-extending himself along uncharted and unfamiliar paths, holding fear of exploitation foremost as the most serviceable beacon for safe passage, only to have involvement beget more and more of itself with caution sooner or later being subordinated to the frenzy of all-out pursuit, caution now acquiescing to the heady dictum that if one was in for a penny, then certainly one was in for a pound, as Benson had said at that meeting which now seemed so long ago. But he would keep a cannier—no, best not use comparatives—a canny eye open so that things wouldn't get out of hand, if they got going at all.

They were now safely back in their neighborhood, and the liberty of conversation could once again be observed.

"I think I'll have to go to the food store this afternoon if we expect to have anything for dinner tonight," Laura observed, implicitly delegating the issue of lunch to whatever one's individual taste dictated as suitable and sufficient for the remainder of the day. Moreover, it was Friday and lunch typically was celebrated by each at different and separate pursuits, exempt of any attendance requirement for an organized family meal. Even mentioning shopping suggested the need to mount an overriding initiative for carrying her beyond the restraints as might linger from this morning's business. For a while, things wouldn't be so spontaneous as before, and certainly not so taken for granted as had been their collective wont. Such was the work of mourning, he figured.

They were now on their street and almost home. From the rearview mirror he could see Richard and Meredith a short distance behind.

"Dad, do you think it would be O.K. if I went out with Jeffrey tonight?" Ellie broached carefully.

The fact that she would ask him rather than discuss it with her mother informed him that she considered the request to be an issue bearing on family policy during the grief period. He also knew that she and Jeffrey had their own thoughts and feelings to review on all that had happened.

"I don't see why not, Hon," he returned. He knew that Todd would hear the sanction as extending to him as well. "But not too late, O.K.? You understand, I'm sure."

"Right," she agreed.

He turned into their driveway and brought the car to a sighing halt before the garage. He remained still for a moment to savor with his family the unspoken relief at being home and again free. Now to get inside and on to kinder things, he resolved as he got out and walked to the side door. He opened it and entered the mud room that led to the kitchen. All seemed in order just as they had left it, as though he feared a lurking power might work some change in their absence, like elves doing their unseen rinky-dinks.

"I'll put on some coffee," Laura tendered as they filed through the kitchen.

"Great. Let's open some windows. It's stuffy and close in here," he advised as he proceeded through the dining room toward the hallway, opening windows enroute. The fresh breeze wafted him along, ultimately placing him in his study where he completed his window sweep. He then assumed his chair at the desk, reached over and switched on the desk lamp, and slid into a slouch as he rested his elbows on the arms of the chair and his chin on his clasped hands. Now where to start, he wondered as his metabolism subsided into a repose setting.

He took up the wall and stared at it fixedly and beyond until the peculiar drifting sensation arrived whereupon he relaxed into a sort of glide with no fixed course or destination. Just drifting. His breathing slowed as his eyes ignored the readily visible to avoid confinement by the already seen, and he searched for that indescribable sense of being on the verge to know the line of departure for new knowing, new seeing. As he waited and hovered he imagined flying over the recent course of events cartographically laid out below like a landscape, displaying the continuity of their effects, one upon the other, like the rolling flow of a region's topography. Highs, lows, quiet stretches of level ordering, abrupt and chasmal shifts, and bounded by indistinct horizons. Pretty, in a way. A cartographic survey of his present existence. Was he himself also included in the dark surveillance that undoubtedly had been leveled at Clay? If so, certainly not with the same priority. And just where was Dr. Inigo Pontalbas when everybody's innocence hit the fan? Receiving our Secretary of State on the latter's goodwill tour of the central republics, of course. Pussy cat, pussy cat, what does he there? Frighten some Blushers from under a chair? Political pressure back home, albeit rising much too slowly, probably forced the visit. Gives the appearance of something being done. Something in addition to murdering embarrassing dissidents back home. How did they get the stuff into the country? Fly it in on midnight sorties to abandoned cotton fields? Or ship it surface in hollowed-out bananas? When he carried bananas on the riverfront for summer work during his medical school years bananas were just bananas. So simple back then. That smell of muddy river water and wharf creosote. Bracing. So was Rosten's parallel goodwill sweep. Maybe he had some ideas about the present use of bananas. The question was when to call him. What would Clay say? Probably wouldn't sit here admiring the problem, but would simply go forth and solve it. And get himself killed all over again. Instead of reaching the verge he was merely becoming giddy. It was something that couldn't be forced. It came when it wanted, not when summoned. How could something a part of him be so contrary to his preference and need? The enemy within. How could something in the government, maybe not even the Federal government, be so inimical to the sensitivities of those governed, to those who elected that government in the first place to perform at the pleasure of the electorate? Was there a government within the government? No new thought there. Did evil have its lobby, too? A lot of evil did get transacted by lobbies, and the government seemed congenially responsive to it. But those were people, not "the government"; they were the lines, not the triangle. So where was the evil? It was on that rainy road in New England. It was on the wards of Moreland. It was in the hollowed-out interior of bananas. That's where it was. He would call Rosten tomorrow after Clay had had a good night's rest.

"Here's your coffee, Frank," Laura said as he noticed her standing beside him with the steaming cup. She carried her own cup as well, informing him that she needed a moment with him.

"Oh, thanks, Sweet," he returned with gratitude as he accepted the cup. "Kinda hard to get back into stride, isn't it?" he offered in return, giving her the opening he sensed she wanted.

"Yeah," she agreed as they both took a sip. "That's what I was going to mention to you. But what I really was going to say was that Clay's death leaves you pretty much alone in your research on Blush. Ellie told me that Jeffrey said that a lot of people are wondering if you'll be able to continue what you and Clay started. Apparently NIH is not all that interested in Blush because he said that other research budgets were recently raised but the Blush budget was going to stay as it was until the new fiscal year, or so he heard."

"Blush is this nation's shame and the government isn't going to spend a lot of money to advertise it. It's not a decent disease, like

MS or muscular dystrophy; it's our flaw as a society, so for damned sure let's not own up to it," he gritted as he felt the play of anger licking at his words, assigning all the more reason for him to contact Rosten.

"I know," she agreed quietly. "It's just that I worry about your feeling that everybody might now expect you to leap tall buildings in a single bound to keep things moving. Or worse, that you might feel that you really have to do it in order to keep their faith."

Christ, if she only knew, he mulled. But maybe she did know, he considered; maybe she, too, suspected something about Clay's death and this was just her way of saying that she feared for her husband as well, especially if he took Clay's place on the ramparts. But if such was her purpose she was likely navigating on sheer boding alone, not given as he was to defining noisome presentiments in terms of impending collision of bearing forces. That was his particular tilt.

"I guess we're all wondering a bit about what happens next," he deflected. "Plus, the burial makes us feel a resolve we just might not sustain in the face of things when all is back to normal, I suspect. So if you sense that I'm frantically looking for a phone booth so that I can . . . ."

At that precise moment the phone rang, prompting both of them to break into a burst of surprised laughter.

"I'll get it," Ellie shouted.

That much was solidly back to normal, they agreed with sympathetic shakes of the head as their laughter pulled them a measure closer to their usual frolics. Soon enough they would be tripping along together in merry tune, just as before, despite the work ahead, he was relieved to think.

"Dad, it's for you," Ellie announced as she leaned into the study. "It's the answering service."

"A cancellation, I hope," he pleaded as he reached for the phone. With a little luck he might be home early this evening from his practice.

"This is Dr. Cantrelle," he answered.

"Dr. Cantrelle, this is your answering service. I have a call from a patient of yours who wants you to call her as soon as you can. She preferred not to leave her name and said you would understand," the operator explained.

"Oh, she did, did she?" he retorted, already annoyed enough at the untimeliness of the imposition.

"Yes," the operator continued. "She said she was at a toll station and wished to talk to you as soon as you could return her call."

"O.K., operator, What's the number?" he submitted, beginning to write as she transmitted. "Thank you, operator," he sighed as he hung up.

"Another housewife about ready to run away from home and needs a call right away. I hope it's not one of my manics; I don't need that kind of hullabaloo just now," he groused to Laura as he dialed the number.

It was answered on the first ring.

"Dr. Cantrelle?" came the quick voice.

He knew immediately who it was, and his abrupt shift to alertness carried over to Laura who tightened her gaze.

"Yes, this is Dr. Cantrelle," he replied as his eyes searched the air for explanation.

"This is Alison Dieter. Please forgive me for intruding upon your privacy at a time like this, Dr. Cantrelle, but I'm calling to ask if I could have a moment of your time. I'd like to talk to you if we could arrange it. And if you could allow me the opportunity," she requested in controlled entreaty.

"I think we can work something out," he suggested cautiously, perplexed as to the meaning and direction of the prospect. "When did you have in mind?" he queried as he slipped his arm around Laura's waist as she stood next to him. He directed a quick smile at her in reassurance that he was managing the intrusion adequately.

"Right now, if at all possible," came the reply.

He looked at his watch quickly before responding, as much to give Laura dumb show account of the request being made of him as to gauge the time available.

"Where are you now?" he asked. The question of distance was already translating itself into the amount of time it would take. His first patient was due less than two hours from now, but this could turn out to be pretty important, given even the sparest implications of her seeking a private audience with him. Laura watched attentively as he waited.

"I'm at the intersection of Foster Avenue and Valley Road," she replied.

"I'm familiar with that area," he nodded. It was about fifteen minutes away, he estimated, on the far side of his township toward Moreland. She obviously had selected the site tactically.

"There's a coffee shop, *L'Éléphant*, in the shopping center at the corner. Could you meet me there?" she requested, her voice resuming a hint of the directive.

"Yes. Give me fifteen minutes," he agreed.

"Thank you, Dr. Cantrelle," she replied simply as she hung up.

As he hung up he squinted in puzzlement as to what this meant. The possibilities were too legion. Was she really doing this on her own, as it seemed? Or was this a non-official contact from the DMH attempting to deal with some consequence of Clay's death. Did they know something, or fear something? The options were lining up hurriedly for his review when Laura intervened.

"Gotta go, huh?" she asked sympathetically.

"Yeah. Gotta talk someone down from the precipice," he fudged. "It won't take long and I'll come back here before going to the office." He'd somehow decided not to give specifics to Laura; not just yet, anyway.

"It doesn't have anything to do with a phone booth, does it?" Laura quipped anxiously as she fought back her discomfort with his reticence, a task she'd more or less gotten used to over the years, especially as it related to questionably clinical matters which she suspected was the case just now. But she wouldn't push it; he had enough to contend with already.

"No!" he lied, "my everyday me will do well enough for this job. And besides, Sweet—and I hate to say this—it'll give me something to do until I go to the office. Otherwise I would probably just sit here and stew in my woe. Which reminds me," he added as he rose from his chair, "will you be back from shopping before I go to the office? I would like us to finish off the morning together before the day pushes on."

"I won't go shopping till this afternoon. The house needs attention first," she complied.

"O.K., Sweet. Now be a good Brunhilde and send me forth on my quest," he breezed as he rose from his chair, managing a final sip of coffee on his way up.

"I'll show you to your steed," she agreed and hooked her arm through his.

Arm in arm and juggling cups they walked back to the kitchen. At the kitchen door he handed over his cup and gave her a parting peck.

"Don't worry, Sweet; it's nothing very important," he assured as he turned to leave.

She smiled in acceptance, but knew otherwise, and returned his flick of a farewell wave.

He pulled his everyday car out of the garage after a tempting look at his Corvette. It would be a few weeks before he felt right about returning to that particular display of abandon. He then headed for *L'Éléphant*. Why name a coffee shop so? The trunk? Why would she choose such a place? So incongruent. Dieter was a panther; fearful symmetry, claws and all, though she certainly sounded a bit tamer on the phone, just as he knew himself a bit too giddy at the thought of her waiting for him. Maybe she wasn't as steely as he'd originally guessed. But then again, he considered more soberly, this could be nothing more than a shielded move on the part of DMH to bury the hatchet. But calling for a meeting on this particular morning would be the most tasteless way to make that gesture. They would have to think about it first, and then they wouldn't send her alone to do it; they usually operated in pairs for such delicate maneuvers, the better to keep each other in line. No, he would accept it at face value, that she wanted to say something on her own. He knew that she was aware of his wild fascination with her beauty, but this morning would certainly not be the time to convey any reciprocal pleasure with that. Yes, maybe she wasn't so ruthless after all. In fact, maybe she wanted to confess on someone. Maybe even on herself. Damn it—he hadn't considered it seriously before—but maybe the DMH had something to do with Clay's death! Not the NSA or the big Fed, but something as local and provincial as the DMH pushed beyond its tolerance and now involved well over its head with one Alison Dieter preparing to bail out. Now that would fit with what he'd come to know of her thus far. She could be recruiting him, Frank Cantrelle, as a future and sympathetic witness to vouch for her disaffection with and innocence of the department's recent excesses, so to speak. That particular notion gathered in more of the pieces, he estimated with a cautious sense of satisfaction.

He was now on Foster Avenue and only a few minutes away. The morning continued beautiful, and already it was getting hard to believe that just an hour or so ago he'd helped lower Clay Moyer into a grave. It was as if the exponential part of it was well on to passing while the consequential part of it was now coming into force, this meeting with Alison Dieter probably being the first of untold meetings he would have with others before this thing was over. "This thing"? As soon as he thought it he wondered what it was he specifically had in mind. Revenge, exposure, retribution, truth, justice, loyalty, self-satisfaction, personal triumph, guilt, ambition? Probably a bouillabaisse of them all, but mostly the god-damned injustice part; of that he was certain. The thought that someone or someones could flaunt the rules so lethally and expect to get away with it burned within him, and even if it had not been directed at a close friend it would still demand some form of retributive address. So maybe "this thing" was being an avenger, but with a white hat, of course. And maybe not much beyond that.

The shopping center at the intersection was now in view ahead on the right and he began to scan the store fronts in search of *L'Éléphant* as he began the turn into the entrance to the parking area. He spotted the shop near the center of the store fronts, next to the theater. Sure enough, the shop sign featured the name flanked by two dancing elephants. He wondered about the proprietress' jolly dimensions. He then thought about the panther within, who would not be merry.

He found a parking place nearby and walked quickly to the shop. He felt electric anticipation rise within him along with the uncertainty of how and what to prepare for in this—yes, cryptic—encounter. He then pulled open the shop door and stepped in.

The interior of the shop was done up in lavender and pinks, giving it more the ambience of an ice cream parlor than a coffee shop which he had always associated more with darker, brooding colors. Serious business, coffee. Also, elephants decorated the walls here and there to add a cartoonish note, some even holding balloons in their curled trunks. A coffee shop for children, he wondered? Yet, probably the perfect place for spies to transfer contraband documents, he snickered as he scanned the booths. He caught sight of her, the back of her head, actually, as she sat in a rear booth. Her totally black hair shimmered in the sunlight angling toward the back of the shop, and a momentary movement of her head sent a liquid ripple down her hair's ebony drape which reached almost to her shoulders. He already felt himself at a disadvantage and not a single word had yet been spoken. He walked resolutely up to the booth and stood before her.

"Good morning, Dr. Cantrelle," she said calmly through a cordial smile as she looked up at him. "Thank you for coming. Their coffee is weak," she indicated in the direction of the cup before her, "but I think it'll serve the purpose. May I order you a cup?"

"No, thanks, Miss Dieter. I had a cup in my hand when you called," he demurred as he took his seat on the other side of the booth, waving off the approaching waitress. He felt that his words sounded frail, coming as they did on the heels of his being surprised at her having changed clothes. The statuesque black dress, black hat and veil were now gone. In its place she wore a mauve suit cut for business, and jewelry to go. A different kind of panther now. He quickly concluded that she had driven in the night before to make the funeral this morning, and had returned to her room afterwards and changed. Maybe she had been to the viewing the night before after all, but he doubted it. All of this smacked of Sneaky Pete, and he figured that just as she didn't want to be seen with him right now she didn't want to be seen at the viewing, certainly not other than officially with Bartley. And since she wasn't with him . . . .

"I'm sorry for intruding upon your private moments with your family, but my reason for doing so is of some personal importance to me and I trust it will also be of some importance to you, Dr. Cantrelle," she began by way of explanation.

He nodded in anticipation.

"I suspected as much, Miss Dieter," he replied.

"Yes," she continued. "But first, let me speak to the questions I know you must have. Might save us some time. I'm here strictly on my own and only you will know about it. If at some later time you attempt to use this meeting to secure some preference from me or from the DMH I'll deny that it ever occurred, and I'll manage to cast your motive in a vindictive, sexual light."

The way she said it suggested that it wouldn't be the first time. It also sent something of a chill through him for there was just enough carnality in him when he was near this splendid creature to give punch to her threat. Now he wished he'd told Laura about the meeting. He nodded again, this time trying to appear unthreatened.

"I'm on my way to Pineview State Hospital where I have a Plans and Operations meeting at two o'clock, so I have to speak my piece to you in less than half an hour if I expect to be on time and not give rise to any questions as to my whereabouts, especially on this morning."

So she had conveniently coupled her attendance of the burial with a scheduled afternoon visit to Pineview. The major throughway from Sharpsfield to Pineview took her nearly to Moreland's front gate on its route. She was covering herself nicely. He couldn't help but admire this woman's skill in managing things her way. She was almost too clever, too competent. And maybe too deadly as well.

"Dr. Cantrelle, I wanted to meet with you to set something straight between us," she announced.

God, what a way to begin, he thought with a start.

"Mr. Moyer's death has made it more important that I do so, and today is probably the only day I'll ever feel so strongly about doing it as I now feel. So, in a way, it's now or never. Dr. Cantrelle, I know that you see me as the standard cold and calculating manipulator of the system for my own personal gain," she observed as she fingered the rim of her cup.

"That's just the company you keep," he returned, continuing to show himself equal to her candor. He also contrived not to dwell on her exquisite hands as she attended to her cup.

"You needn't be gallant," she smiled in return. "I'm actually very much as you suspect, and unlikely to change. It works for me, and for the time being I'll continue to go with it."

Did she have to be so damned tough all the time, he grumbled to himself.

"But the reason I asked you to meet with me is not just to confirm your worst suspicions about me, but to tell you something you don't know," she moved on. "You see, Dr. Cantrelle, in a way I've been to this funeral twice before. Once, about twenty years ago, when I was a little girl, and a second time about ten years ago when I was a big girl." She now looked abstractedly at her cup as she spoke. "And each time I attend it, it gets a little worse, because the people I bury are people who should not have died, but were forced to." She now looked up and away from him as she swallowed hard. He saw her eyes glisten. In a moment she returned to her cup. "I think you know. Dr. Cantrelle, that despite our differences and the troubles we've had, I've respected you, what you've done as an educator and as a researcher, and what you and Mr. Moyer have contributed to better the care of the mentally ill, but I've especially respected your troublesome and unsettling work on Blush."

He now felt his credulity being put to a test, so he listened a bit more keenly.

"Sounds like a rank blandishment, doesn't it?" she allowed, apparently sensing his skepticism. "And I guess you have a right to scoff at what I'm saying. Go ahead, if you need to, but it won't change anything with me. You're allowed, don't you see?"

She actually looked a little hurt that he might doubt her sincerity, he noted. Or was it guilt? Maybe he was right. Maybe she was trying to bail out and he was going to be her parachute. Actually, he'd be hard put *not* to want to rescue her. At this precise moment he wanted to touch her hand, reassure her, protect her.

"I once had a brother, Dr. Cantrelle," she began wistfully. "A wonderful, handsome older brother. He was every little girl's big brother Jack. Actually, his name was William—my big brother Bill. He was twelve years older; I was something of an add-on in the family. Bill was also everybody's All-American boy—honor student, star athlete; even sang in the choir. I worshiped the ground he walked on, literally; and he doted on me, his kid sister. Needless to say, I was ferociously jealous of any attention he showed any other girl, and, as you can imagine, I was given little respite from that endless ordeal. And then he went to war. He stood high in his college class, to be sure; but, as it turned out, he stood equally high in the draft. His country called, and he answered, willingly, bravely, and proudly. He said that the rightness of his country's action was more than he, a twenty-one-year-old college senior, could determine, but that as a citizen it was his duty to serve his country as nobly as he could. Within six months he was a shiny new second lieutenant leading an infantry platoon in the central highlands of Viet Nam. And he was heroic, as everyone who knew him expected, and as we, his family, feared."

She was again looking off away from him and her words were now coming less easily. He knew where they were going and he felt himself pulling away from their inevitable destination.

"He dutifully sent home all the medals he won, charmingly dismissing them as mere trinkets which he thought we might add to the Christmas tree decorations as his contribution since he wouldn't make it home for Christmas that year. The year came and went, my brother Bill on the far frontier implementing his country's foreign policy while a certain number of his fellow American colleagues were in safe, suitably neutral countries such as Canada, Sweden, and

England defending their personal liberty and their smoking habits. And then, three weeks before he was to complete his tour, he was killed."

She stopped for a moment and again turned away. He saw her lip quiver as it struggled to break from her control. She held her diverted gaze while a tear trickled down her flushed cheek to nestle at the corner of her lips, seeming to quench their turmoil as it did so. The tear sparkled in the silence as they both waited. He knew she wouldn't wipe it.

"One of his fellow officers wrote to us and explained that Bill's platoon had been caught in an artillery barrage of, oddly enough, 'friendly fire,'" she continued as she resumed looking at her cup. "This fellow officer, whose motives we came to sympathize with, thought we should know that the barrage had come from an artillery unit which had had more than the typical array of disciplinary problems, and had been known for its notably high consumption of the local drugs. It seems that the misplaced barrage had occurred because, quote, 'someone had gotten the wrong coordinates,' unquote, as the phrase ran. And so we had a funeral, very much like the one today, on a lovely spring morning, almost twenty years ago."

She again paused and he imagined her re-visiting the scene in changeless memory. Her being at the funeral this morning was more than simple tribute, he now saw. His respect for this remarkable woman was quickly catching up with his appreciation of her beauty.

"My parents were devastated. My mother cried for months. She even retrieved a pair of his baby shoes from the attic and placed them on her dresser next to his picture. My father felt as much guilt as he did grief, for he, too, had been a very young lieutenant once, but that was in World War II, and he, too, had won medals, but he had come home a hero to have a son and to teach him right from wrong. We tried to find out more about Bill's death, but the Army, and the government, said that there was no more to offer. Their official position was that the source of the artillery fire remained 'undetermined.' We did learn that seven other members of my brother's platoon were killed in the same incident."

"Didn't the Army have some kind of investigation?" Cantrelle pressed, his sense of injustice now at full muster.

"If so, the results were buried along with the incident. We suspect there was, and that's what my father tried to find out," she explained in passing. "At first, it nearly destroyed my father, a war hero of another era, but he held us together and then dug deeper into his work. Would you like to know what his work was? He was a planning engineer for the state highway department. He designed the throughway I will be driving on fifteen minutes from now on my way to Pineview. You see, after the war, his war, he went to school, studied, married, and went to work for a state government which then honored its heroes. And he rose quickly, and laudably. But after my brother's death he became bitter and his bitterness took the stamp of a political activism which sought to ferret out government corruption in any form, anywhere, on the premise that the American government had become a betrayal of the people's mandate. He even got himself elected to a position in a national libertarian organization. Needless to say, the presence of such a vengeful spirit in the state's highway department rankled more than a few, one in particular being our then governor who you remember was so keen on a Federal cabinet appointment. My father was soon quite unwelcome at his own job, which was progressively downscaled into near insignificance. He was even transferred to a more distant office location which required he travel eighty-five miles daily each way to and from work. But he was tenacious and not to be cowed, not this hero with a touch of hypertension. And for years he took it all as it came while we worried about his health, my mother still asteep in her protracted grief, and me an uncertain college freshman watching from a distant campus. And then one day he didn't come home from work. They found him that evening dead of a heart attack at the wheel of his car on the shoulder of the road. Yes, another road he had helped design. He, too, had had only a short ways to go to reach home. He was fifty-nine years old. So we had a second funeral. Mercifully, that time it rained. Ironies at every turn, wouldn't you say? Both died among their ideals, but essentially alone; both died doing what they knew to be right; and both died with a helping hand from others." She was now fully composed, and for the first time this morning she looked at him directly as she spoke. Her dark eyes were cold with hate. "So you see, Dr. Cantrelle, Mr. Moyer's funeral is an old acquaintance of mine," she continued, "and I couldn't very well let it go by without paying my respects."

No way, he amended to himself as he began to grasp the meaning of this woman's enmity.

"And, Dr. Cantrelle," she continued, cutting his thoughts short, "I trust that you've considered that Mr. Moyer also received a helping hand—an official helping hand—in meeting his death, haven't you?"

He felt startled by her question, though he wasn't sure why. Maybe it was because, despite Rosten, he didn't yet feel prepared to take the notion beyond the stage of private suspicion. But here it was, time for the open discussion stage, and, as usual, he didn't feel ready. He was excruciatingly aware of her waiting for his reply. Oh what the hell, he yielded, why not shoot the works and maybe set her back on her heels for once?

"I have, Miss Dieter," he breasted, "and as a matter of fact I suspect the helping hand came from your people at the DMH."

It was now his turn to await her reply.

It was swift in coming, and, like everything else about her, it cooly blunted his expectations.

"No, Dr. Cantrelle, it didn't come from the DMH," she replied evenly. "There was some talk about transferring him to another facility, and maybe even forcing a reorganization of your teaching staff at Moreland to separate the two of you. There was even talk of transferring your training program to a more cooperative facility."

"Without me?" he blurted.

"Without you, Dr. Cantrelle," she smiled coolly, "but there never was any talk or intent of an arranged accident."

He felt like a schoolboy being patiently and carefully corrected, and also being informed of a disciplinary measure he'd been spared.

"How can you be so sure?" he retaliated peevishly.

"You forget, Dr. Cantrelle, that *I'm* in charge of Planning and Operations," she reminded him.

He felt more archness in her reply than actually was present. It was his turn to stare at the cup he now wished he had; it would have given him something to hold on to. He stared at its empty place for a moment. That done, he looked up, ready to admit being chastened.

"I see," he conceded, though he secretly reserved the right not to believe her. He didn't give up so easily either, he'd like her to know.

"And to get to my point in all of this, I suspect that you, too, will probably look for some redress of this wrong, Dr. Cantrelle, and I'd like to suggest . . . ." she continued.

"But what about you, Miss Dieter," he interrupted, "since you seem to have reason enough to go to the trouble of putting yourself at risk in meeting with me this morning? Where do you stand in all this? I trust not still at some distant campus." He knew it was a cruel thing to say; she had not intended any cruelty with him, and he had now used a shared intimacy to wound her. He blanched in shame at what he had done. "I'm sorry, Miss Dieter. I shouldn't have said that."

"Quite all right, Dr. Cantrelle. I think it's an appropriate question, since I presume to tell you that I have so much more experience in this business of wrongful funerals than you do. Quite simply, my stake in all this, as you say, is two-fold. Firstly, I have my own agenda for helping to correct the ills of this suffering nation, and it doesn't involve a frontal assault upon the evil citadel of perverted government. I'm not my brother and I'm not my father."

He puzzled at her statement. Alison Dieter, a closet reformer?

"May I ask how?" he pursued, not really expecting an answer.

A smile of bright and innocent confession lit up her face.

"Dr. Cantrelle, I intend to sleep in the White House!" she said with open simplicity.

He smiled in marvel of her resolve.

"Any room in particular?" he asked in like innocence.

"The master bedroom, preferably," she clarified.

His smile fled as his mind made a quick connection. The state's junior senator! The state's junior *bachelor* senator! Of course! That bright new star of the Washington scene! Annapolis graduate. Nuclear sub service. A rush of jealousy welled up within him only to be deflated by the realization that the arrangement was probably already a done deal, and had been all along, and that his own dark and proscribed fantasies with and about her were nothing more than the road markers of yet another one of his side trips to a Fool's Paradise.

"Good luck," he said in his best sporting manner.

"Thank you, Dr. Cantrelle," she returned in mock appreciation of his blessing.

He couldn't bring himself to say another word about the matter, and his silence conveyed that he considered her prospects to be allowably feasible. In fact, a reasonably good bet. Somehow it suited what he had come to know of her. He began to wonder if the unlabeled fascination he long had with her and her manner was in truth the rudimentary beginnings of what might later become a humble respect for this nation's First Lady. On further thought, it was a very good bet indeed.

He noticed that she stole a glance at her watch.

"I should be getting back on the road," she mentioned as she brought her purse on to the table and opened it. "Please bear with me while I powder my nose, Dr. Cantrelle." He watched as she checked herself out with the assistance of a silver compact.

"And secondly? Your purpose was two-fold, you said," he pursued, recalling her to her agenda.

"The second part concerns you," she added as she touched her cheeks with a dainty powder puff. She then snapped the compact shut and returned it to her purse. "Your well being," she continued. "I can assure you that you're in no danger from the DMH. In fact, because of Mr. Moyer's death they'll now do whatever they can to deliver you from *all* evil. Mr. Moyer's death rattled them badly, a few because of the tragic loss to us and to the system—Bartley was sincerely affected, and that's why he was the one who came to the viewing—and some of the others more programmatically so because they knew the DMH would be suspected of an assassination. So right now you could probably get anything you want from them. For the moment it's very important to them do keep you happy and healthy. But since they didn't kill Mr. Moyer in the first place *you're* really not a lot better off than you were before, for all their good will."

"You think I'm at risk, Miss Dieter?" he asked hoping not to sound too theatrical.

She closed her purse and then positioned herself to rise from her seat.

"Dr. Cantrelle, I've told you all this to show you how important it is to me not to have to attend a fourth funeral," she stated archly. "Now the least you can do is show some responsibility in doing your part."

She began to rise, motioning him to remain seated as she did so.

"I prefer to leave unescorted, if you don't mind, Dr. Cantrelle," she requested. "I know it offends your gallantry, but, for the moment, business is business. I've enjoyed talking to you this morning and again I must thank you for meeting with me. You've been patient. And now I'm asking you to be most careful about your comings and goings, if for no other reason than out of consideration for those who see you as too important to be without." She then slid out of the booth and stood up.

"Any suggestions?" he asked, in part to delay her departure. He felt it extremely unlikely they would ever meet again, except perhaps very, very officially and not otherwise.

"For starters, I wouldn't ride any bicycles if I were you," she suggested brightly. "I've taken care of the bill. Good-bye, Dr. Cantrelle," she added with a curt nod. She turned, walked to the front door, and out.

His eyes followed her out of the store and some distance into the parking lot before she disappeared.

His head now swirled with more thoughts than he could manage. The lavender elephant on the opposite wall balancing on a striped ball seemed to be mocking him. So maybe he wasn't as graceful as he could be in fielding what was coming at him lately. It's not every day that you're told by two different people in almost the same hour that your best friend's death was murder. Nor is it everyday that your secret desire tells you that she wants to be the President's wife so that she can set the country straight. And with our esteemed junior senator! He couldn't be sure that's what she was up to, but it seemed a natural. In fact, she was a natural for anybody with the highest political ambitions. All of a sudden she was forever out of his league and the odd sense of abandonment he now felt rang just too awkwardly familiar. Wasn't it exactly the same he felt when he was a fourteen year old freshman and infatuated with that darling cheerleader who used to smile at him a lot but who later chose to put herself brazenly at the side of the captain of the football team? Almost as bad, for sure. At least Rosten offered himself as an ally. It had taken some time to get used to the idea of someone's wanting to kill Clay and now it was hard not to credit the thought, pushed by Dieter, that the same someone might—probably would—have lethal designs on him, Frank Cantrelle, as well. But no one disliked him that much, ever. Yet, it apparently had nothing to do with liking or disliking; it probably was more a matter of policy, for if anybody qualified as the culprit on the basis of mere malice, the DMH would have been the single-most candidate, and she had exonerated them. But could he believe her? Yes, because she wouldn't have warned him if doing so could inadvertently bring his avenging pursuits directly to her own door; no, not with the nuptial plans she harbored. Yes, he believed her. Worse, he now began to miss her. Never again would they speak to each other as they just did. Maybe if he blew this thing wide open, hero-like as her family style required of the men in her life, she would see him as a big time player and not just some offended citizen whose naive pursuit of justice was likely to get him hurt. He then looked up and around to seek some semblance of dominion over his thoughts as they skirted the edges of puerility and he now noted the repeat sequence of elephants, balloons and balls on the walls surrounding him. Maybe he was thinking like a boy scout with hurt feelings because he had put himself in a god-damned romper room that happened to serve coffee. Some murky bistro somewhere would be a lot more elevating, but any proper bistro likely to truck in intrigue was closed at—he checked his watch—five of twelve in the morning. He was beginning to feel foolish sitting there swaddled in his offended boyhood and so he decided it was now permissible for him to leave since by now she was safely well along her way. Also, this so-called gallantry of his was beginning to feel more and more like solicitous obedience. Time to go home, he resolved; home to the cheerleader who would never abandon him. He then worked his way out of the booth stiffly, stretched as he stood up, and marched with impressive bravado to the front door and out into what he was now charged to regard as an exclusive, custom-fitted no-man's land. But fashioned by whom? If not the DMH, then who? Back to the big, bad Fed? That's what Clay had said all along. As he walked through the parking lot he noted that the day was beginning to heat up. The sun had begun to dazzle in earnest and objects in the distance were already slipping into their shimmer. It was now just about high noon and he was no farther along in this mess than he was days before. For certain he'd call Rosten tomorrow. He reached his car, opened it, and quickly entered its protective shade.

Fourteen

"I can't believe you're really going to go through with this," Weaver groaned as he held the top of his head in cupped hands and searched the top of his desk for the reasonable explanation he knew would not be forthcoming from his friend standing before him.

"Please, Jess," Cantrelle pleaded, "we go over it every time I come here now. Y'know, you just might make me stop showing up regularly to brighten your day, and if I'm then forced to use the dawdling inter-office memo system to get your approving signature on my requests I just may never get around to catapulting us into the glory of national prominence."

Weaver shook his head in mock consternation. He could not hide his delight in Cantrelle's droll playfulness with the outrageous, but having television crews skulking around the campus for "theme shots" as background reference to be used in the up-coming TV documentary was something he had trouble with, even though Moreland's totally partisan Frank Cantrelle happened to be one of the documentary's chief programmers. And the DMH was going along with it without a murmur of complaint! He couldn't understand it. And all he could get from his ever-perplexing friend, who was even more confounding over the past few weeks, he might add, was a whimsical insouciance intended to serve as an overriding explanation, a kind of "because it's there." And how he had gotten to be so chummy with the TV moguls responsible for *Watchfire* was more boggling than he could manage. Frank Cantrelle had held such people and their huckstering as below contempt, and now here he was helping to program one of their specials—"really, Jess, a cut above their usual"—on Blush and the evil genius behind it, or so the advance notices seemed to promise. It was fully enough that he was doing this in the shadow of Clay's death, and in truth it was largely assumed that Clay's death had been the igniting spark that fired Frank Cantrelle to undertake this venture as a kind of follow-through in tribute to his colleague and to the *National Dateline* TV appearance that had never come to pass. But to use a talk show of such proven tabloid tawdriness to redress the crushing loss truly defied all understanding, or so Weaver held. The less charitable saw it simply as Frank Cantrelle's tasteless exploitation of his friend's death as a means of re-establishing his prominence now that the authentic head-liner, Clay Moyer, was gone. The more concerned, among whom Jess counted himself, wondered if Frank Cantrelle had simply jumped the traces of sane restraint and was galloping wildly off in pursuit of some avenging chimera. Jess dreaded the almost certain accuracy of the latter.

"Jess, just sign the thing and let me get on my way. I promise not to turn over any more rocks," Cantrelle teased as he urged Weaver to perform his office.

Weaver looked up and sighed.

"Frank, you know you really don't need this from me now," Weaver insisted. "Mrs. Andretti could take care of it just as she routinely does for everyone else. It's just a simple leave request which you know I would okay without question."

"I know, Jess, but I'd feel better if your approval was official," Cantrelle persisted.

"Okay, Frank, even though there really is no rush about this since you assure me that the Special won't be aired for at least another week," Weaver continued in balky hesitance. "In fact, you don't even need this from me; just don't show up for work on the day of the Special and have someone call in for you. You've got more accrued leave time than you'll ever use."

"I know, Jess, but I feel better doing it this way," Cantrelle held.

That was another thing, Weaver noted. Lately everything had to be documented, and immediately. He seemed to be keeping records of everything—where he was going, when, meeting whom, and what. Could it be that Clay's death had made Frank Cantrelle too conscious of the impermanence of life and its fundamental fragility? Seemed so, Weaver mused as he once again felt himself being urged along by his frenetic friend's puzzling haste. He really had no objection to signing an undated leave slip for him; it was the unnegotiable urgency he objected to and hoped to stymie on the outside chance that additional time offered by any delay might give Frank Cantrelle that much more of an opportunity to come back to his senses.

"Okay, here you go," Weaver relented as he signed the slip and handed it over to him. "Now be sure to leave the carbon copy with my secretary. Got to do this exactly right, don't you know, god-damn it," he directed with heavy sarcasm.

"You always were a stickler," Cantrelle returned with shameless effrontery.

Weaver smiled and turned his head away so as not to give Cantrelle the satisfaction of seeing the merry extent of his *lèse majesté*. This character not only jerks you around but he makes you like it, Weaver snickered to himself as he put his pen back in his jacket pocket.

"Now that whatever you do with the time, whenever, is duly authorized, is there anything else of an official nature I can help you with today?" Weaver chided through an egregious grin.

"Not at the moment, Major, but you might mention to her Colonelship that her indulgence of this video extravaganza can only redound to the glory of her command. The troops are delighted, I'm sure you've noticed," Cantrelle ragged.

"Oh, I've noticed," Weaver agreed readily. "The women, staff and patients alike, are a lot more attentive to their make-up these past few days, thanks to the prowling presence of that TV crew. And the men are walking more erect. Chins a bit higher. No slouching staff around here."

"I think it's good for all of us," Cantrelle summed up with some show of pride. "No doubt everybody feels a little more important, a little more acknowledged, thanks to that TV camera and its all-seeing eye. It's like the world is finally paying them some long overdue attention. And the crew's been here only two days."

"I know, but it's all you hear about. Everybody who comes to this office mentions it or asks where the camera will be today, and so forth. It's easy to see how a TV camera can start street riots," Weaver groused.

"C'mon, Jess. The crew's been pretty good about it," Cantrelle insisted. "They haven't really disrupted anything, at least not intentionally, and they don't do a thing without checking with you or Martha first. I think they're going about their job pretty well; impressively professional."

He didn't feel it at all odd to stand before Jess' desk and defend the comings and goings of a television crew on the hospital's campus. The more action afoot in that regard, the more the sense of mobilization for carrying this project along. It had been three weeks since Clay's funeral and he was determined that the crusading resolve he and a few others felt earlier would not be allowed to wither along with the grave flowers in their passage to pale memory. No siree! He had called Rosten, met several times already, agreed upon a general format for the TV interview whose advent would constitute a marked departure from the program's usual genre, and had conveyed Rosten's request for filming privileges through Moreland's front office as well as through the DMH. And it all went so easily; clear evidence, he said to himself and to any others bold enough to ask, that it was an idea whose time had come and thus there was no stopping etc., etc. More privately he felt it was as much a matter of his oath forswearing any and all interference in the performance of his mission. Plus it was also possible that one Alison Dieter had had something to do with its swift, unfettered launch. Hard to say. But he also allowed, just as privately, that the glitzy show biz beat the project had inevitably acquired delighted him as well as bothered him; delighting him because it was a refreshing change of pace inviting a certain license, even abandon, in the service of free expression; and bothering him for exactly the same reason, plus the adulterating effect it might have upon the sober and ominous portent of the program's intended message. It was something he watched carefully. He knew that Jerry Rosten shared that concern as well, partly in fear of not pulling off the program as planned and hoped, but also that the entire production might be suffered as a pathetic attempt to capitalize on the setback of its rival, *National Dateline.* Rosten clearly wanted to do the thing well, for personal reasons as well as corporate, and he openly acknowledged him, Frank Cantrelle, as his best bet for pulling it off just so. But Rosten also seemed to fear that if it were done well, what would he do as an encore? Show biz was like that; if you gave a good performance, even once, you were forevermore held to that standard and judged accordingly. Could he then ever go back to romping about with the bathos of human folly after the accredited gravity and importance of Blush, or after so sober a collaboration with one Dr. Frank Cantrelle and the honored late Clay Moyer? Not likely. So, probably for Rosten, too, it was likewise a matter of crossing a line and getting on with something he felt he had to do, if he could. Thus a kindred sense of dedicated venture had evolved between himself and his votary, the good Doctor Frank Cantrelle.

Plus, there was the consideration, so far reflected only by the mysteriously beautiful Alison Dieter, that he himself, the good Doctor Frank Cantrelle, might also be the object of someone's yethhounds. The astringent effect of that thought relieved him of the duty of nicety he ordinarily observed in so many of his doings. After all, military courtesy was sensibly relaxed on the front lines, he reasoned. No matter that he might now seem to be more impatient than usual, even abrupt, or that his priorities had shifted away from many of the congenial pursuits he formerly shared readily with staff and friends, the exigencies of deliverance bade he brook no delay in bringing forth the Word all must needs hear. The sense of mission was gaining force within him, and he liked it. He suspected that Clay had experienced the same kind of thing.

"It's just that you don't know what kind of a story line will end up on the film footage, and I guess I fear being surprised," Weaver worried.

"Jess, I've told you, they're not after Moreland, or the state system; they're after Blush and the fact that Moreland and the state system have been put in a hopeless position in a losing battle now getting too big for everybody to ignore. That's all. No local exposé intended. I can vouch for them," Cantrelle insisted.

"I sure want to believe that, Frank, and believe it just as solidly as you do, but the media is the media. I can't help but remind myself that when push comes to shove the profit motive is their true and only church," Weaver remonstrated with eyebrows arched in punctuation of that verity.

"Do you think that once, just once, a network might act in the public's behalf on some issue far too important for the pursuit of narrow self-interest?" Cantrelle posed sarcastically, miffed at Weaver's veiled concern that Moreland might not be the only entity at risk for being duped into naive confederacy.

"Oh, I suppose so," Weaver allowed in amelioration, "but if the network did, wouldn't it strike you as a bit disingenuous, sort of like an old-time Labor Day celebration with the management hosting a sumptuous annual picnic for the hungry laborers who made possible the huge profits the management enjoyed every blessed day? The people and what's happening to them should be the featured news, not what the networks contrive as profitably programmable, and I guess the presence of that TV crew on the grounds makes me wonder all over again what's the means and what's the end."

"Want the proletariats of the world to unite?" Cantrelle snapped uncharitably. "Or have we already been through that one?"

It wasn't very long ago he could and often would join with Weaver in comradely commiseration on what they agreed was the sterile and nationally embarrassing path the American media seemed compelled to follow, but now he found himself with adjusted allegiances defining paths he himself could not tactically avoid if he hoped to get to where he wanted to go.

"Yeah," Weaver smiled futilely, "where's the revolution when you really need one? I guess it's just like they say, that as soon as a revolution decides to become respectable it has to get rid of its revolutionaries, making it inevitable that the more things change the more they remain the same."

"You know, Jess, as a philosopher you're one veritable pain in the ass," Cantrelle flashed. The thought that he, newly inspired Frank Cantrelle, was merely re-enacting some droll, repetitive little chapter in the human comedy was not miscible with the heady genius he felt griping his soul. After all, he had Clay Moyer's ghost as warranty of purpose in the follow-through on their continued work together which now, like war, was diplomacy of a different sort. So maybe a TV special wasn't the same as a textbook or journal article. So what? It was better than some anemic symposium tucked away somewhere, timidly and deferentially raising the question as to the multiple determinants potentially operant in the epidemiology of Blush, the symposium being just as shamefully dilatory in arrival as it was impotent. No, he'd go with Jerry Rosten, he reaffirmed to himself the umpteenth time, knowing he would have to avow so over and over again until the documentary was a completed, aired deed. This one time of all times he wasn't going to let doubt or hesitance nibble away at his purpose, however wise or prudent additional counsel and review might seem.

Weaver smiled at Cantrelle's pique. He knew his friend too well not to know that an inner driving effort to protect purity of mission was in force, and, as with all zealots of all times, critical review was expressly forbidden since faith, like the most primitive nerve impulse, works only and ever in accordance with the all or none principle.

"Actually, Frank, whatever my reservations, I think what you're doing is good for us," Weaver allowed. "I guess you might be right that the only way to get the people—the unblemished ones, anyway; by latest count they still outnumber the Blush patients—to own up to the national scope of the problem is to slip it into their fantasy time. I bet few people out there realize that the number of deaths from Blush is now about equal to the combined battle deaths of the Korean and Viet Nam wars, and in only about one year's time, yet those wars together took fully a dozen years," Weaver lamented as he shook his head in nettled disbelief.

"That'll be one of the big points made by the special," Cantrelle seized. "Just because the deaths aren't recorded as KIA's they don't seem to count in the national mind. But sure as hell someone out there is ambushing those poor druggies, and the killing ground is the length and breadth of this great nation. That's what the people don't want to know. And the stuff's coming in from a foreign power, too. If that doesn't constitute some kind of an invasion I don't know what the hell does."

His pulse was beginning to quicken as he spoke, and he was tempted to proclaim right then and there that Clay's death was murder and, as such, stood as indictment of the government's complicity in and probable authorship of the whole incredible Blush mess. But he couldn't yet yield to that goad; not right now, anyway. That would be carefully and subtly managed by the coming documentary. Indeed so much hung on the successful advent of that documentary that he found himself dreading that the police investigating "the accident" just might come up with a credible suspect; some alcoholic driver of a dark blue pick-up truck and known to the townspeople as a ne'er-do-well, often in scrapes with the law, and long known to be destined for prison. Even if he were the true culprit and not just some convenient arrest to clear the desk sergeant's blotter, he didn't want it to happen. It was now most important to have Clay's murder go unsolved. It was crucially important that his murder be connected with the Blush cartel so that a higher justice be loosed to bring the Blush problem and its perpetrators to book. He had now become the champion who needed Clay's death to be a widely incriminating murder justifying what needed to be done that so many others could be saved. There was no question in his mind that now he could not and would not recognize Clay's death as being a simple accident, even if evidence and confessions abounded, because too much would be lost thereby; lost to him, lost to thousands, and even lost to Clay. No, he had resolved, he would not be deterred by some small fact at the sacrifice of a larger truth, and he would bear the weight of that knouty onus as best he could, just like every saint, every tyrant, and every madman the world has ever known.

"Oh, by the way," Weaver injected to lighten the interchange, "your friend is in town."

"Who's that?" Cantrelle wondered in relief at being pulled away from his churnings.

"Burleson. He's in town for some meeting. I read it in the paper," Weaver explained.

"Some symposium? I didn't hear of any. Did you?" Cantrelle puzzled.

"No. It was a small news story in the paper. There's a meeting of some academic group today and tomorrow. Mentioned him as the presiding chairman. Where is that article?" Weaver mumbled as he fumbled for the newspaper on the credenza behind his desk. "Here. You can read it. Right there," he pointed as he handed the newspaper to Cantrelle.

Cantrelle moved around to the side of Jess' desk as he accepted the newspaper. He quickly found the article under area news and proceeded to scan the several brief paragraphs allotted. Why bother to mention it at all if they bury the article near the Lost and Found, he grumped as he read about the exclusive gathering of a select few blue ribbon scholars who several years ago formed themselves into a kind of think tank called the Committee for Advanced Studies and who met quarterly at different sites in the country to address towering issues such as the societal effects of ozone depletion or the impact of technology on the structuring of the American work force, two previous topics studied by the Committee. Their white papers, he read on, were usually directed to cabinet-level government for additional review. He had heard vaguely of that group a year or so ago, but hadn't connected Burleson with it. That fellow really got around, he chuckled to himself as he neared the end of the article which noted that the Committee would conclude its session tomorrow evening at which time it would host a dinner to be attended by various civic, government, and academic leaders for discussion of its findings.

"I'm surprised you didn't know anything about it, Frank, because I was sure you, the TV personality you've come to be, would be among the invited," Weaver chortled merrily. He didn't often have a chance to rag his restless friend, but even less often did he let such an opportunity go by unused.

Cantrelle smiled appreciatively at the jibe. Jess' quips were always good fun; they tickled more than stung.

"I haven't made my debut yet, that's why I'm not invited. Highly regrettable oversight, they would agree if they knew what was coming up on *Watchfire*," Cantrelle retaliated as though wagging a finger. He had just begun to savor a furtive satisfaction at the thought of a notoriety which surely would earn more than just a brief paragraph in the area news when he was abruptly brought up short by the thought of how Burleson might regard the crusade in video. Probably would mention it most graciously if they ever met again though he sensed that by taking the sensationalistic path he had now chosen it was highly unlikely that he and Burleson would continue their quaint coquetry of so much common ground impatiently awaiting exploration. He feared Burleson would simply distance himself from the hoopla that was sure to follow in the wake of the TV appearance. Such a parting would also be highly regrettable, he mused with the savor of cynicism, but there was nothing else for it if that was the way it had to be. The gains to come of his intended course would more than offset the losses because, after all was said and done, some things were never meant to be in the first place. So there. That inner rhetoric done, he returned to Jess. "I can imagine Burleson feeling scandalized when he finds out about the special," he rounded off as he handed the newspaper back to Jess.

"You never can tell, Frank. Burleson's already identified with our troubles and it wouldn't surprise me if he showed up later on some national format like *Meet the People* doing something like what you're up to. His approach is different, but he pretty much ties in with our thinking about Blush and government responsibility. By the way, did you notice in the announcement," Weaver posed as he hefted the newspaper in reference, "that two of the members of the committee are Nobel prize winners? God, I'd be afraid to open my mouth if I sat in on that meeting."

"Not our world, Jess," Cantrelle sighed. "Too lofty, Olympian. No smudges up there. But maybe they couldn't do what needs to be done way down here in the dregs we call gritty reality. They don't deal with budgets and death certificates. By the way, how have they been coming along?" he queried in irresistible follow-up on the theme of death and dying. Before all this he never thought of the assistant superintendent position as the signer of death certificates, but it had always been one of Jess' duties, though previously a much lesser one.

"I guess you mean the death certificates. Not very many here lately because we send those people on to Logantown or to one of the other . . . ."

"Charnel houses," Cantrelle supplied.

". . . receiving facilities," Weaver continued resolutely "as soon as we confirm the diagnosis. They're not here long enough to die. I guess we should be thankful for that."

"Any happy returns?" Cantrelle taunted, persistent in his tone of justified reproach.

"You mean?" Weaver groped.

"I mean, anyone come back, failing to die as expected?" Cantrelle chided.

"Yes, as a matter of fact. Two," Weaver announced brightly. "But both undoubtedly were cases of mistaken diagnosis and shouldn't have been sent in the first place."

"Those two patients must have rattled the hell out of the staff at the 'receiving facility,' as you say, sitting around long beyond their allotted time, persisting in tastelessly going on living. The staff probably didn't know how on earth to deal with them, those two living and breathing creatures who just didn't get the hang of the SOP," Cantrelle jeered. He was primed to condemn at the slightest hint anything to suggest that the staff at Logantown or at any of the other receiving facilities had lost their horror of the work and had begun to warm to its routine, like executioners throughout time with smartness in performance becoming the means of achieving victory over disgust in having to do the job at all, a device not at all unlike what the staff at Buchenwald and other such similar receiving facilities probably had had to mount, for to do so yielded the basest and most perverse form of an unconscionable end being shadowed over by pursuit of laudable efficiency in means. The true hope for the staff, and for everybody else, lay in their *never* becoming good at what they were now being called upon to do. Hopefully, he reminded himself, there would inevitably be that pesky problem of unit morale. Any staff at odds with its own work would sooner or later drive home that point by way of the group commodity known as "bad morale," the blight feared up and down the ranks of dutiful supervisors as the caustic so reliably corrosive of the administrative gloss coveted by superiors, especially those incapable of skirting the curse of accountability. No matter that such "bad morale" might attest to the worker's offended humanity and moral outrage at the job being asked, a truly inspired administrative intervention could effect an "operational consensus" in support of the root pragmatism of the job simply by proclaiming an exclusivity of purpose, polemicizing the rôles of the parties, demonizing opponents, redefining esprit, and promising victory of transporting sweep to come of tightening the ranks—all proven mobilization measures vital to the craft of successful diplomacy, or, should that fail, to the efficient performance of any conquering army. Or political party. No, he would stick with the inefficiency and disarray sown by "bad morale," certain that in this case it meant that at least the worker's moral sense was still in good shape. He then chuckled to himself at the vagrant thought that such was probably the reason why Mussolini couldn't get his soldiers to do anything but surrender.

"Why are you laughing?" Weaver asked.

"Oh," Cantrelle exclaimed in mild surprise. "I didn't know that I was—out loud, anyway. I was thinking about Mussolini."

Weaver looked at him, not certain how to respond.

"Frank, are you sure you're not pushing yourself a little too hard?" he chanced.

"Of course I'm pushing myself too hard, amigo, but what the heaven is a hell for?" he quipped. Such concern as Jess', with its assigned rights of inquiry, was traditionally and exclusively Laura's province, but over the past week or so several people had trespassed by asking similar questions, and he was quickly getting used to chasing them off by firing a few warning flippancies over their bow.

"Well then why don't you take a few days off. Take a drive up in the mountains, or something," Weaver urged, undaunted by Cantrelle's attempt to wave him off.

"I'm okay, Jess, really," Cantrelle submitted. "I'm just a little preoccupied, that's all; and that always looks worse than it is."

"A little?" Weaver exclaimed. "You probably don't realize it but everybody feels that they're interrupting something when they talk to you. We all miss Clay and we'll probably never get over it, but this thing with you always being somewhere else is getting out of hand," he registered, diffidence now set aside. "I think it's that TV spectacular you and those people are cooking up. What the hell is it supposed to be? The way you've been so cozy and sly about it you would think that it's going to reveal the missing link," he ranted.

"Even some of the residents have come to me saying that your mind doesn't seem to be on your conferences any more; that you seem to be withholding something, something you lament they don't know and you're unable to reveal. Some teacher, huh? Frank, you sure you're not off on some wild goose chase with the entertainment industry. You know, they seek sensationalism where it's least warranted. I think they call it programming. There, I've said it!" he announced, adjusting himself full upright in his chair to meet the rejoinder.

But the reply was gentle.

"Jess," Cantrelle began, "everything you say is probably valid,, though I know you don't need me to confirm it. Also, I'm kinda pleased that the residents are reading me so well. Perceptive. They're coming along okay, don't you think, despite their feelings of neglect? As far as sensationalizing our troubles here at Moreland and dancing on Clay's grave to boot, I assure you that's not what it's all about. Those 'programmers'"—he gestured the quotes—"and I won't do anything to offend Moreland or Clay Moyer, I can promise you that." He could barely contain the urge to make full breast of the matter, relieve Jess of his worries, and enlist him among the trusted to help see the thing through. But he knew better. "It's just that in the preparatory stages it's pretty much all their show in the fullest sense, I guess; but the basic purpose is unchanged, I can guarantee." He hated talking in insinuation like this and he forbade an accompanying patronizing grimace that would only have extended it.

"Just what is the purpose, Frank, other than expanding public awareness?" Weaver leveled with a glower he rarely wore.

"Jess," Cantrelle returned mildly, "we're going to pick up where Clay left off, follow through on what he began and intended, and I'll be sitting in for him. That much I trust you already know. We hope to be able to take the message about Blush and its workings a little bit beyond where Clay would have been able to take it," he explained, the insinuation hardly noticeable, "and try to give a continuity to the pursuit of answers pushed by Clay himself. In fact, Jess, I think that somewhere he's smiling in approval of what I'm telling you."

Weaver nodded in acquiescence, daunted by the notion of Cantrelle's astral alliance. He looked down at his desk, pursed his lips, and then returned to Cantrelle.

"Frank," he asked, "you don't have to answer this if you don't want to, but is the DMH behind this? They agreed so readily to all the filming that's going on."

Cantrelle was delighted with the question. It revealed how wide of the mark Jess' suspicions really were, and his suspicions were probably representative of most. Being so, it afforded the opportunity for planting an additional bit of disinformation.

"All I can say on that score, Jess, is that they sure as hell weren't opposed to it," he snickered, withholding the wink.

"I thought so!" Weaver pronounced sententiously. "Oh, well, I guess you'll fill in us *incognicenti* at some later point, but for the time being we'll have to indulge your authorized preferment as best we can and hope it all works out," he sighed in capitulation.

Cantrelle winced inwardly at the deception being perpetrated on his friend, but for right now it was helpful to have Jess mollified. Later on, everything would be sorted out.

"That's the spirit, ole buddy. Now give me your blessing so that I can slip away early today for my rehabilitative drive, not to the mountains as you suggest but to the concrete canyons of downtown America where I, Dr. Faustus, will bargain with the Mephistopheles of the Nielsen ratings in a cabal devised to doom us all to the curse of enlightenment," he managed in one breath and with a concluding flourish of a courtier curtsying to his regent.

"Do me a favor, Dr. Faustus," Jess retorted, "and go a little easier on yourself so that *you* can keep body and soul together at least until I retire."

Cantrelle smiled broadly at the oblique solicitude carried by the riposte, and he automatically compared it to Alison Dieter's more certified and comprehensive entreaty. Two different worlds and somehow he was party to both by dint of the same message. Holding them to the letter of it sounded like "Don't let anything happen to you until I've achieved my future" though he knew that their framing it so was in disguise of a kinder intent. Or was it? Or maybe what the people were saying was right; that he had changed. Maybe what they were seeing was not preoccupation, as he'd said, but a neoblastic self-centeredness which obliged him to hear kindly remarks as driven by a reciprocal self-centeredness. Yes, maybe all this skulduggery and dissimulation was indeed making him mean-minded. Just then De Quincey's admonition flashed across his mind: *"If once a man indulges himself in murder, very soon he comes to think little of robbing; and from robbing he comes next to drinking and Sabbath-breaking, and from that to incivility and procrastination.*" He could plead innocent to the middle stages but there was no question of his guilt in leaping precociously ahead to the latter two, especially procrastination as he now came to suspect of his extended dalliance before Jess' desk.

"Well, thank you for this, my liege," he switched as he waved the leave request slip aloft, assuming as he did so the resolve of one ready to blunt the inroads of procrastination at every turn. "If you need me for anything I'll be in my private office from about one o'clock on. See you later." He then turned to leave.

"By the way, Frank," Weaver hurriedly directed at his departing friend, "when is this thing coming off? Soon, maybe?"

"Not this Friday, but next. Ten days from now. The announcements will be aired this week, they say, on this Friday's program," he explained over his shoulder as he approached the door.

"What am I supposed to do in the meantime? Bite my nails?" Weaver groaned.

"Why don't you take a drive to the mountains, Jess," Cantrelle ragged in a chortling farewell.

He then stepped out into the hallway and, once there, looked at his watch. Nine fifteen. He would have just enough time, barring interruptions, to make it to the network office for a chat with Rosten and then to his private office for the day's case load. The meeting with Rosten, now on to becoming a twice-a-week thing, not to mention almost daily telephone parleys, was a necessary measure to keep the project headed in the direction agreed upon at the outset, Jess would be relieved to know. Television people, he could now confirm, were like fish in that they were vulnerable to the shiniest lure, and they went at the particulars of a story or issue in just that way, hoping the viewer would be similarly hooked. As with the most telling lures, substance was decidedly less important than immediate appeal, much as a real but ordinary gnat might be passed over in favor of a colorful, tufted, silken-tied Royal Coachman pitifully barren of any nutritive value. But the TV people saw allure as paramount and excused their bias with the exculpating, egalitarian contention that, after all, they swam the very same waters as everybody else and were just as subject as anybody else to the common currents. Only the more vindictive could accuse a few of the busier fish of being responsible for the drift of some of those currents. Thus it was important for him to support Rosten's better motives and good taste in wrestling with the importunities of his staff who saw almost irresistible opportunity at every turn for glitzing up the story to guarantee irresistibility. He marched down the hallway to the front doors, and he was soon stepping along the drive toward the MOB. He had to tidy up his desk a bit before leaving for Center City.

It was Wednesday but it seemed like Tuesday. That was because Monday had been Labor Day; not a real Monday, but a second Sunday. And it was used like a Sunday, too. The drive to proper little Buckley College with Ellie and a fair amount of her earthly possessions had been epochal in that it had gone without a hitch. All of a sudden it seemed that she was flying away, too easily and too quickly for his comfort. A little delay or a glitch here or there—some item forgotten, or too much to carry in one trip, or some form not completed, or *something*—might have drawn out the separation a bit more acceptably for the reluctant release of his only daughter. Oddly, as much as it bothered him, it seemed to bother Todd more. As much as Todd complained over the years of his big sister always being on his back for one thing or another, that's how much he cherished her and her caring, though he could never bring himself to acknowledge it openly. Ellie, however, made no secret of her affection for him, or of her displeasure with his failure to fall to when she thought he should. Their loyalty to each other was unbreachable and unquestioned. So on Sunday he joined with Todd in lamenting that Ellie had planned everything so thoroughly and so efficiently that all that was required of them was to muscle her belongings up two flights of stairs and into place in the dormitory room that would be her bower for the next several years. Providentially and not unexpectedly Jeffrey Landon happened to be on hand at their arrival at Buckley to assist in the hauling and to add to the sense of Ellie's transfer to an extra-familial dimension. On that point, too, there was a shared poignancy, but there was also some compensation in their knowing that Ellie had a pretty acceptable champion out there available to snatch her from the shark-infested social waters, should it come to that. Those currents, you know. Moreover, it gave him a chance later at eventide with all the toting and settling-in done to chat with Jeffrey over a family commemorative dinner about the temper of the times at NIH. For his part Jeffrey, kept fully abreast by Ellie of the coming TV appearance, was bound and determined the program arouse public awareness and general ire sufficiently to pressure NIH to expand its work on Blush and perhaps even open its doors to his research energies cresting for an outlet. The climate at NIH had not changed, he lamented; if anything, he feared another layer of complacency had begun to settle upon the entire project, and he provided details to substantiate his contention. There were, he acidly pointed out, fewer reports on the research in progress, fewer conferences being called for public updating of the status and direction of the on-going research, continuing failure to separate Blush research funds from the general departmental budget, and on and on. Cantrelle took mental notes as Jeffrey celebrated his personal outrage at the government's failure to address its responsibility. Ellie sat dutifully at the side of her hero good and aspirant as he threw gauntlet after gauntlet at the feet of the entire NIH edifice. He hoped the TV appearance might shake somebody up, and he of course stood available to help in any way he could. By the time the dinner was over it had become more of a rally than a requiem and, later, when everybody said good-bye and went their separate ways all did so reaffirmed of an enduring union which could now balance the sense of loss brought by the change in the daily roster at home. All in all, it had gone well enough though Laura recounted, through a spate of sniffles on the way home, that it was so much harder than seeing Richard off had been. No one had a sharper eye for sales than Ellie; now, how was she, Laura, going to keep the family larder economically full without the help of consumerdom's finest scout and her dearest companion? But grow we must, she resolved as she assured her husband that she would endeavor to meet all future sales with a show of bold resolve. Cantrelle allowed for that reason alone he would feel Ellie's loss dearly. By the time they arrived back home that evening they were jovially planning a return trip for Parent's Day a month off, Todd definitely included.

Yes, it had gone pretty well as such things go, and already it seemed long past though only two days done. Time was indeed the thief of life's treasures, he mused as he skipped up the steps of the MOB. He snatched open the door just as a lurking pang of sorrow stabbed at him, and he quickly stepped inside to shift to a dimension where the vicissitudes of family life, and loss, held lesser sway. He escaped up the hallway and entered his outer office where Mrs. Andretti awaited him, message in hand.

"Mrs. Cantrelle called a few minutes ago and asked that you call her before you left for Center City," she informed him.

"Thank you, Mrs. Andretti," he returned over a plaintive smile that sealed his failed escape attempt.

He entered his office and then sank heavily into his chair. As he sneaked a glance at the wall he allowed that the call was probably about something important which had come up, but deciding so did little to soften his resistance to picking up the phone to add to the baggage already weighing him down despite his efforts to make trim for his trip to Rosten's office. With a wheezing sigh of resignation he reached for the phone and dialed. She answered on the first ring.

"Hi, Hon, what's up?" he lilted hopefully.

"I'm annoyed, that's what," Laura replied forthrightly, "because it's starting up again. The school called and said that Todd was absent and they wanted to verify that we were aware. Today's only the second day of school and already he's skipping, Frank. Toward the end of last semester he started skipping a day every couple of weeks or so and I didn't tell you because I talked to him about it more than once and he said he would do better this year. Here it is the second day of school and he's back at it, and I want to tell you about it while I'm still good and mad. And when he comes home I'm going to tell him I told you, and then it'll be between you and him. Okay?"

He saw that his retreat was now a shambles, but it could have been worse, because, after all, he reminded himself, when a boy he himself had skipped school too many times to tell yet without doing irreparable damage to his studies. It was a little different with Todd, of course, but he could understand Todd's need to register some token defiance about the dictum of school attendance, especially if all along he was in conflict with school work and its rules by dint of his learning disability, which actually was beginning to show genuine signs of lessening its grip upon his school performance. His grades last semester had improved despite the skipping. That was probably the main reason why Laura tried to work it out alone with him then, though now her sense of betrayal and her righteous indignation were clamoring for satisfaction.

"Okay, Sweet," he soothed, "you've done more than your share. I'll pick up on my part when I get home tonight. All right?" He didn't want to sound as though he were brushing it off—she was irked enough as it was—but nor did he want to mire himself just now in an extended lamentation of his son's academic nonfeasance.

"What time do you think you'll be home?" she asked in acceptance.

"If nothing unforeseen comes up, probably around eight. The usual," he predicted.

"I'll tell him to be home by then because he and his friends usually get together after dinner and roam the malls for a while," she explained.

"Okay, Love, I'll see you then," he mewed as he leaned forward for returning the phone to its cradle.

"Be careful driving into the city," she cautioned, concern and worry now resuming priority.

"You bet, Hon. Bye," he pledged as he hung up.

He indulged himself another heavy sigh, not the least because he'd again averted open recrimination for not having followed up on the issue of Todd's pot smoking. He had meant to, but so many things had happened since that night when Laura confronted him with her discovery. Also there had been no further occurrence of anything to push the matter which by now had become a cold, possibly dead issue. But, still and all, he'd lived in fear of some new incident arising to highlight his neglect of taking it up with Todd in full parental vigor. Laura would never throw it up to him, and he certainly didn't want either of them, himself or Laura, to be alerted anew to the hanging, unsettled duty awaiting his hand. Of course he would talk to Todd about it, but one thing at a time, and tonight it would be about his truancy. He would talk to him about the pot matter at a later time, probably after all this with Jerry Rosten, *Watchfire*, and the sounding of national alarms was done with and safely behind him. Probably would give his words more punch, too, his achieving TV status first. Kids credited TV more than they credited mere parents.

Feeling that he had achieved resolve as well as a point of closure on the matter he tapped the arms of his chair smartly and sat fully upright to sign his way through a neat stack of papers on his desk. As he scribbled his signature he scanned the sheets to ascertain that he was endorsing nothing particularly important other than the routine administrative flow. He finished the stack, satisfied that there had been nothing there to disconcert or divert him, and felt some relief that at least there was paper compliance with this morning's tight schedule. He then gathered the stack together for its return to Mrs. Andretti on his way out. As he rose from his chair he sneaked another look at the wall, feeling remiss even in that most fundamental of all his devotionals; he simply didn't have the time as before. And besides he didn't feel as much need lately with his course seeming so clear. Who needed a wall when there was genuine doing to be done? The thought had a ring of liberation to it and he parlayed it into a sprightly escape from his chair. He gathered his briefcase from the window sill, collected the stack of signed papers with his other hand, and balanced his way out of the door to deposit the stack on Mrs. Andretti's desk.

"I think you have Mr. Rosten's number if anyone needs me," he remarked.

She nodded in confirmation.

"Any word yet as to when the program will be shown? I hear that the TV crew will probably finish their shooting around here by tomorrow," she mentioned.

That was news to him, but, then again, she knew everything.

"I just told Dr. Weaver the big secret. Probably Friday after next. That's the plan, anyway. They'll announce it this Friday," he explained.

"How does Mrs. Moyer feel about it, or does she say?" she dropped.

He suddenly realized that he didn't know. Could it be that Helen hadn't been made privy to the thinking and planning about the program? He assumed that Rosten had kept in some contact with her, simply out of courtesy. Or had he? Now he couldn't be sure. He was now assailed by a rush of doubts and questions as to how much should he divulge to Helen. To prepare her. Even ask her permission. From his standpoint the program was more about Clay's death than it was about Blush, and he now realized, thanks to Mrs. Andretti's penetrating question, that Helen had pretty much been excluded from all consideration as though it were really none of her concern. He shuddered at the thought that Helen might oppose the whole thing out of a need to protect her family and her memories. He had kept in helpful touch with her, generally in concert with Laura, but had said little about the program and nothing about its reference to Clay's death, much less its contention that his death was a perpetrated, intentional act. He now saw the full measure of his neglect—and deception—in keeping Helen uninformed. The covert underpinnings of his dealings with Rosten—secrets and stealth, damn it—had led so naturally to deceit and injury! That howling realization now coursed through his mind like a storm certain to blow away his straw house of resolve. What actually was his responsibility to Helen in this special case? In truth, his duty included *thousands* of people, not just Helen, or even Clay. But where should he stand? With his friend's widow, or with the nameless thousands? Why hadn't Rosten brought this up? Surely he'd dealt with such matters of family consent and advisement before. Was it a tactical omission? For the second time in the space of a few minutes this morning his strivings seemed to be in shambles. Whatever may have been the planned agenda this morning with Rosten, this matter of Helen's consent was going to be item number one, and just now that was the only thing he was certain about. And the whole thing might collapse on this one point. And why did Mrs. Andretti bring this up? Did she smell some kind of a rat? All of a sudden he felt less like the bold avenger and more like the skulking transgressor.

"I can't be sure," he evaded, "but I think I'll know soon enough."

As he thought of leaving he was almost brought up short by a numbing tug of reluctance, a tug he recognized as the urgent need to return to his chair and search his wall. But he knew it was out of the question just now and he stabbed a look at his watch to verify as much.

"Got to get going," he announced, abruptly bringing the interchange to an end.

Mrs. Andretti nodded her understanding.

He hastened out the door and up the hallway toward the building's entrance as he attempted to marshal his thoughts about this newest of his dilemmas, grousing enroute that all of these damned dilemmas seemed to sprout like mushrooms in the darkness of non-awareness to emerge full grown in the sunlight of notice. He pushed his way through the front doors to be greeted by the liberating openness of campus greensward. Slant light played on the trees' darkened verdure, now as deep into estivation as they could be, and some of the leaves had begun to show that dull gloss which identified their readiness for the color change. As he walked to his car he wondered how so much could have happened in just one year. In a few weeks it would be just about exactly a year ago that the four of them went to that symposium, had had that lusty lunch at which he received the call from Morello, and had then seen that second case of Blush. Just one year ago. A bolt of grief tore through him at the memory of that lost world, his lost friend, their lost innocence. There seemed so much more to look back at than forward to. *Forward to*, he repeated to himself as he opened his car door; the very thought emphasized the contrast between what had been added to life and what had been lost. Forward to a television producer's office in Center City to meet with people one year ago he could never imagine having anything in common with. Now he was co-producer with those people in a tribute to his lost world of stirring symposia and festive lunches, as four innocently happy people then lived it. As he drove out of the front gate he returned to Helen and to his startling neglect of consideration for her. Best he use the next minutes of travel time to take stock so that when he spoke with Rosten about it he would have it all clear in his own head. He had long learned to distrust the initial surge of guilt he experienced upon recognition of any oversight or blunder.

In a moment the campus was behind him and he was momentarily relieved to be moving in the traffic flow toward the main artery that would take him to Center City. The traffic was past its morning peak and was beginning to show that diurnal increase in silver-haired drivers which manned the byways in the midday off-hours. And more ploddingly, too. Their cars tended to be the larger domestic ones, and his ready impatience inclined him to blame the manufacturers for building lumbering, cumbersome cars that seemed designed to slow traffic nearly to the point of coagulation. But it was actually the older folks, the ones who now felt more brittle, more vulnerable, more mortal, and more needy of a secure surround who set the market for the fortress auto. Thus the perversity of his own surround on this morning when he should have been working at his desk rather than struggling his way to Center City.

As he neared the main artery the traffic began to quicken in pace. With his sense of confinement subsiding, he returned his thoughts to Helen. He recalled that he had indeed told her about the coming program. He had done so about two weeks ago, as he remembered. Of course he didn't make a big point of it in the telling, but he had said to her there was a good chance he would appear on a TV panel discussion to carry Clay's message forth. He didn't say any more than that, admittedly, and Helen heard his announcement more as a tribute to her husband and to the devotion others felt for his work. He was sure she didn't hear it as forewarning of a coming missive that would identify her husband's death as part of a high crime being perpetrated on select citizenry. Absolutely she did not hear it that way because he had been careful not to suggest anything of the sort. She had received his disclosure with a wan smile of gratitude, about as much as her searing grief could permit. Perhaps it was the sanctity of that grief—Clay had been dead only a bit more than a week—that veered him from saying more, then or later. Probably, but there was no getting around the fact that he had purposely withheld from her—by kindly intent then and by convenient oversight later—a fuller disclosure of what the program's theme would be and the rôle her husband's death would play in it. True, Rosten and a member of his staff had met with Helen a week or so later to pay their respects, inform her of the planned program, and to request her sanction of the reference the program would make to Clay and his work. Helen readily agreed, but again without the knowledge, as far as he knew, of how Clay's death would be portrayed. Maybe Rosten had said something to her about the possible implications of Clay's death. Right now that was the great big hope, though in his two contacts with Helen over the past three weeks no hint was given by her of any such thinking. Plus, Laura, who had had almost daily dealings with Helen since the funeral, reported no such intimations. And Laura! In his duplicity with Helen he had inadvertently pressed Laura into co-conspiracy! That fresh line of self-recrimination now announced itself ready for his prayerful attention. Christ, the more he thought about it the worse it got. Rosten damned well better have mentioned something to Helen about their real purpose in going on the air, or else he, Frank Cantrelle, wasn't at all sure he could go through with it. And now the god-damned traffic was moving faster than his teetering resolve could endorse. He needed more time, not more speed. Just the thought of Laura's being led into perfidy amidst her solicitude for Helen was enough for some very heavy wall time. And worse, he hadn't breathed a word of demur about it even to himself! Laura certainly would not have lent herself to such use if he had told her more of his thinking about Clay's death. So, in effect she was as much deceived as she was suborned. Oh, jolly! Such a saving in that! To his relief he saw a school bus pull out in front, several cars ahead. Good. That would certainly slow down the flow of this headlong rush into informed culpability. He then tried to anticipate how he might broach these damning concerns with Rosten. Needily, because he could sure as hell use a little reassurance just now. But would Rosten see it his way at all? He knew that now, as ever, he worried foolishly and too much about just everything; saw things as being complex far beyond anything practicality could warrant, and therefore identified guilt in every decision and in every act undertaken. But even so, never so much before as what he was fitfully about now. Worse, the guardian school bus had just turned down a side street, freeing him for speedier approach to a face off with the bruising truths of this worsening mess. And whether he liked it or not, the entrance to the throughway was immediately ahead, and that meant that he was now only fifteen or so minutes away from Rosten's buoyant greeting.

He entered the throughway determined to survey the scenery as he paid heedful attention to the radio and its comforts. Agreeable, soothing, indulgent Boccherini happened to be going at it just now, seeming to fit his need, when he was reminded that he had long suspected Boccherini of playing a double game with the Spanish court in that he wrote what that insular gathering, an anachronism even for its own archaic time, wanted, and had palmed it off to them as the dulcet melody of royal gentility, while he himself knew that in the real and larger world his music would be regarded as comedic mewing of the baroque. Almost parody. Maybe hucksters were hucksters no matter the era, or their talent. Why didn't they put on something by Beethoven who was not only more muscular but decidedly more inclined to tell everybody to kiss his ass? Solid stuff, that Ludwig. Solid like the cliffs that lined the right shoulder of the highway which snaked along parallel to the river on the left and far below. No small feat of muscular engineering here, as a matter of fact. He wondered if Dieter's father had had something to do with this highway as well. And how was she doing, his very own Dark Lady? Did all tragic figures have a Dark Lady somewhere in their destiny? Did his memory serve him right in reminding him that Petrarch had a Laura, too? But they never connected, as he recalled. Well, lately he and his own Laura weren't connecting anywhere near as much as they used to. Rather seldom these days, as a matter of fact. All his own doing, too. Mood was everything, and since this damned mess started he'd had precious few thoughts of silken thigh, and when he did, it was exclusively in the morning, never at bedtime. Nowadays, evening time found him shriven of all tingle for fleshy mischief, and in its place a bone weariness plunged him deep into slumber as relief from the demands of responsible worry. Would he and Laura ever reclaim their conjugal, romper-room antics? Right now, it seemed pitiably like trying to go back home. Maybe when this was all over—and sooner or later this mess had to come to an end—he and Laura could . . . could what? Pretend that things were like they used to be? Sure, why not? The Spanish court did it for a couple of hundred years, with the help of a good huckster. Always did like that Boccherini.

From the corner of his eye he caught sight of leaves beginning to turn yellow. Was it just a dying shrub, or was it the first sign of Autumn? This was the time of the year—early September—that he began to scour the foliage in search of valid signs of Autumn's imminence. It was a private game, to find that solitary, unique leaf chosen to be the first messenger of the coming season. He hadn't yet found it as he imagined it should be—one faintly yellowing leaf set against its deep green family. Whenever he came close to discerning that special leaf, it was usually included in the company of others bearing kindred shading. Nevertheless, year after year at about this time he'd pick up the search for that First Leaf of Autumn, undaunted by the suspicion that his quarry probably was just as imaginary as the Last Rose of Summer and perhaps even the bidden reciprocal of it.

The big green sign announcing his exit as the very next one came up ahead. He sighed as he clicked on the blinker for merging into the exit lane and then began the glide off the highway to the stop light at the base of the exit. Upon his arrival it turned green and he chuckled to himself that the god-damned color green seemed determined to get him to Rosten's office in jig time, his own preferences be damned. He then wended his way through the maze of streets, finally achieving the parking lot he'd used each time before when he met with Rosten. He pulled in, surrendered his car to the attendant and fell in line with the flow of pedestrians eddying along the sidewalks. Within two minutes he swirled through the revolving door of the building's entrance, eschewing the large, upscale doors on either flank. Revolving doors reminded him of the annual clothing store visit with his father to get outfitted for the school year. Later, when he reached high school age he was allowed to go on his own, like now. He entered the marble lobby which reverberated its din in high octave, and moved to the bank of almost completely concealed elevators, supposedly a positive point in modern decor and design. In due time an elevator shuddered into bay and he entered it along with several fellow travelers, all mutely reporting their destinations to the button panel and then mounting their silent and self-conscious vigil. His floor arrived before he had completed his inventory of the clinical types he guessed his fellow passengers might be, such as which among them might be a closet claustrophobe, oxymoronic as that might sound; or which might be the polite and canny paranoid; or which the occasional recreational druggie soon to be introduced to Blush. The door opened before any ballots were cast and he stepped out into the hallway that led to an expansive glass fronting of a large office complex occupying an entire section of this wing of the building. The first time he came here he expected cameras and klieg lights to be cluttering up the place, but it was no such thing. This was corporate headquarters, all phones and faxes with the show biz fixtures at a studio in a separate building located at the base of a dizzyingly tall antenna on the fringe of the city limits conveniently closer to the receiving suburbs. Decisions and strategies were made here at headquarters; maneuvers and missions were carried out at the studio which he might well get to see soon enough.

He pulled open the massive glass door of the executive complex and entered the palmettoed, muraled, aromatic reception area to approach the chic, exquisitely coiffed, impeccably painted receptionist who in her spare time had to be a starlet awaiting discovery. In fact, she, the Caribbean colors of the office decor, the Museum of Modern Art furnishings, and the exotic foliage qualified the scene as a living commercial for *Watchfire* and its proven ability to sell any news. He was staggered the first time he saw it. It was no place he belonged, and he was sure the whole project would likely have to be called off if in any way its staging depended on his participation. But after he spoke with Rosten on that disconcerting first visit he left reassured that despite his stagey milieu Rosten himself was for real and fully capable of delivering a program suited to the taste and bearing the message deserved. So he had returned for two more parleys a week later, and also the week following. And now again today. He was getting used to the decor but not quite to the receptionist who always greeted him as though her delight in serving him was perilously close to breaking free of the restraints of normal business propriety. And he gleefully played along with it.

"Good morning, Dr. Cantrelle. It's so good to see you again. I'll tell Mr. Rosten that you're here. Would you like some coffee while you're waiting? I just made a fresh pot, just in case you might have to wait a minute or two," she cooed.

"Good morning, Miss Parsons. I'd love a cup, if you swear that you made it yourself," he returned gallantly. He also knew that she greeted the chance to get up and dance before him, and a trip to the coffee pot could be worked into acceptable stop-gap choreography.

"You know I wouldn't let anybody else make your coffee," she assured through eyelashes fluttering a semaphore of coquetry. She then rose and flowed toward an alcove that served as the on-board coffee canteen. Her firm, fluid figure and the way she walked, very definite strong points in her presentation, convinced him that she was a dancer, perhaps a chorine at some earlier time, and probably was now holding out the hope of being seen as a more serious talent. It had even occurred to him that maybe she too was expecting more of *Watchfire* than its glitzy trappings could deliver. As she approached with the coffee held in both hands, oriental deference fashion, he was awaft in notice of the sheer of her legs as they played within the drape of her skirt. Her smile of satisfaction confirmed recognition of his notice. This was coffee as it should be, he savored with a roguish smile. She then leaned over closely to place the coffee mug in his waiting hands.

"Thank you, Miss Parsons," he nodded in broad understatement.

"Oh, you're so welcome, Dr. Cantrelle," she replied similarly and swished back to her desk. She then announced to the intercom that he had arrived for his appointment and was for now comfortably assigned to the pleasures of his coffee.

He sat and sipped and watched her at her duties. He wanted to pick up the dalliance, partly to show her that he wasn't some suburban hayseed adequately satisfied by a cup of coffee while in the presence of sheer art. He then framed a comment to be offered at the first opportunity about the sheen of her chestnut hair, but a vigilant imperative scolded him back into unwavering loyalty to Laura's blonde curls. The upshot was a lament that connubial fidelity could be a humorless warden indeed. He consoled himself with another sip of coffee. From that point on his attention to Miss Parsons amounted to little more than tasty peeps, which seemed to be about right for the office traffic, but hardly sufficient return for such delicious coffee. The awkward air of blunted promise was beginning to settle in when Rosten burst out of a side office.

“Good morning, Dr. Cantrelle,” he hailed, hand already extended as he approached. Cantrelle was relieved that Rosten didn’t greet him by first name as he had done on a previous visit in the typically presumptuous and egregious American friendliness. His frosty rejection of a first name basis must have registered with Rosten.

“Good morning, Mr. Rosten. I envy you the culinary skills your staff puts at one’s disposal,” he returned as he rose, toasting his cup in Miss Parsons’ direction.

“Oh, yes,” he accepted, “Marilyn has a way with a coffee pot, but she’s even better with pastry. So help me,” he insisted.

Miss Parsons actually blushed. Could it be that beneath all that glamour and allure Marilyn Parsons was actually a wholesome, old-fashioned girl temporarily distracted by the bright lights, just as cinematic tradition required? He wondered.

“Please come in,” Rosten motioned in the direction of his office, “and bring your coffee with you. Mine’s waiting for me on my desk.”

Couldn’t keep his coffee waiting, Cantrelle snipped peevishly under his breath as he followed Rosten who stopped at his office entrance to allow Cantrelle to enter first. Cordiality was holding up, he noted as he contrasted his inner doubts with the ambient tone of consensual purpose, and he entered Rosten’s office to settle into the chair he had by now adopted as his proper station while in conference. He felt automatically defensive in this setting, and especially so today what with his concerns about Helen swimming around in his head. He also feared being petty and supercilious as a means of maintaining his guard. It really wouldn’t be fair to Rosten who certainly was making an all out effort to be above board with him, but nor could he be grand and prodigal in service of their joint effort, for that would be just as tasteless. It was hard to strike the right balance, and the blown-up print of a Modigliani nude on the side wall did little to help the effort.

Rosten picked up his coffee from his desk and came over to the hospitality cove of the office and settled into the couch under the Modigliani print. Only on the very first meeting did he sit at his desk, which was billiard-table size and suited to the making of the most cosmic decisions. Intimidating, too. Since then it was this cozier nook set off against the side wall. Rosten took a sip of his coffee.

"Haley couldn't make it this morning but he wants to meet with you at least one more time before the airing," Rosten opened.

Julian Haley was the anchor man, the host of the show. He interviewed, commented, provoked, and summarized. In a word, he ran the show.

"He wants to go over the script guidelines with you, Doctor. You'll get a flow sheet of the questions he'll ask you and it'll indicate about how much time your responses should take. You can line up your thoughts ahead of time to pace yourself right along with the program flow. Also, you can get a sense of the totaling up effect leading to the punch line the show will deliver," Rosten reviewed.

Cantrelle nodded as he listened. They had gone over it often enough before in general outline. Now it was down to prompter notes, apparently.

"The shooting at the hospital is coming along just fine. That place is so scenic, so picturesque it's hard to get a bad shot, my crew tells me. And of course, your staff out there are all fired up to make a debut. Haley says the information you supplied is plenty enough to feed a squad of script writers," Rosten reported.

Cantrelle thought so, too, as he recalled that grueling intake meeting when he recounted the whole story from beginning to end while Rosten, Haley, a team of script writers and a secretary with a court reporter shorthand transcriber took in his every word. That session went a long way in convincing him that he was getting himself too deeply into something he couldn't control. The script writers, three of them, seemed more interested in his manner of delivery and in the emotional toning of his words and ideas than they were in the actual content. He figured they would work such givens into the general pitch of the script. He kinda liked the idea at the time. What with the questions, the clarification of terminology, the detailed development of specific events and points, plus a mini-course in psycho-pharmacology, that session had taken almost two and a half hours and three cups of Miss Parsons' coffee. That's when she and he achieved their entente. It was also when he and Haley had achieved a meeting of minds about how much less of a scandal carnival and how much more of a White Paper documentary the program would be. He felt himself on thin ice in that confrontation for, after all, it was their studio, and who the hell was he to tell them how to sell their fast food and detergents—and news. But Rosten had backed him up, as promised, and Haley had been trying to muster a good grace ever since, his absence from today's meeting notwithstanding. In truth he felt a shared sympathy with Haley because each of them was moving into unfamiliar precincts, and fatefully doing it together; he into the world of predatory showmanship, and Haley into the world of mature and responsible commentary. A different sort of entente, there.

"So I thought we might keep today's meeting just ours, the two of us. We might want to go over some things we would rather keep between ourselves," Rosten proposed.

Cantrelle looked at him before speaking. The suggestion was thoughtful and would probably be useful, especially in view of the misgivings he brought along with him this morning. Could Rosten have divined as much?

"Good idea," he managed.

"Sometimes we get so caught up in production we lose touch with the meaning of what we're doing," Rosten observed as he examined his cup in preparation for another sip.

Automatically Cantrelle raised his eyebrows in amused surprise and then quickly regretted the display of covert arrogance, but Rosten caught it all in a glance.

"Oh, yes, Dr. Cantrelle, television producers do sometimes think about such things," he continued. "Maybe not often enough, but we do. And maybe more so with me lately. Another reason for our private tète-a-tète this morning," he continued, "is that I wanted to meet with you to set some dates before I leave town for a few days. I would like to get on with publicizing the date of the program. Announce it tonight on the evening news. Begin the spots and the lead-ins. Then again in earnest this Friday on our regular program. By this time next week the word should well be out and the world waiting. And I should be back then."

Cantrelle noticed that as he spoke it wasn't with his usual flourish. In fact, he seemed tired.

"I guess it does get to be wearying, pulling everything together for something as spectacular as this. Probably good to get away for a few days. I would like to get away from some of my troubles for just a few hours, too. I envy you," Cantrelle patronized in anticipation of bringing up his own concerns.

"I don't think you do, Dr. Cantrelle," Rosten said gently. "You see, I got word last night my nephew in California died. The one I told you about. I'm flying out this afternoon to help my sister.

It so happens that my brother-in-law is a drunk and probably on the bottle right now. My sister will need some help in managing a decent funeral for her son. But I'll be back by the end of the week. I thought you should be aware that I would be away."

He flushed with shame. He should have noted right away the subdued tone in Rosten's manner. And bumbling into this man's grief in his flippant, haughty, and, yes, insolent way was as mortifying as it was unforgivable. So stupid!

"I'm so sorry," Cantrelle stammered. "I spoke foolishly."

"Please. There's nothing good anyone could say about it," Rosten dismissed. "But what we tell the world Friday evening after next will be the best thing to come out of all this trouble, don't you think? That Friday would be okay with you, I trust? The studio sees that date as the crest date, as they call it."

"Friday after next will be fine," Cantrelle accepted meekly. There was no doing otherwise. He felt his concerns for Helen slipping away into the repository of narrow selfishness.

"Then that Friday it shall be," Rosten settled. "Also, I spoke to Haley again about the necessity of keeping the tenor of the program on the sober side. He understands quite well—he's an intelligent guy—but I think he feels he might come off unconvincing if he shifts tintypes too much. He's happy being the TV personality benchmarked as the most ruthless and unprincipled interrogator of the compromised, and especially if the guest is suitably over-matched. That wouldn't be the case with you, of course. In fact, I'm sure he feels he's the one being over-matched by setting the program format so much in your favor. He's automatically adversarial, and the TV interview is his metier, and he's good at it; maybe the best. I used to kid him that the only difference between his interview style and TV wrestling was that he and his guest were fully clothed. I mention all this, Dr. Cantrelle, to give you a better view of Julian Haley. He's just as determined about this program as we are. He sees it as a singular professional challenge while you and I see it more as a moral duty, and I don't want that difference to translate into a regrettable display of coarse wrestling between you and him. Nor do I want people to say that even when *Watchfire* tries to take the high road it's still a fool's romp."

He had never heard Rosten talk like this before. He felt that he was being put on notice to make a better effort in keeping his eye on the purpose and less on the personal. And Rosten was doing it with a distinct edge to his words. Cantrelle wondered if his nephew's death had tipped a certain balance in this man's manner. Best to deal with it head on, he decided.

"I very much agree. You take care of him and I'll take care of myself," Cantrelle leveled as matter of factly as he could to blunt the sting. He didn't like being put on notice by anyone, though Rosten was doing it for the very best of reasons. And he had to be fair by directing it at both of his players equally. It was just the sensible thing to do.

"Good. I was sure you would help. Now I would like to get on with format," Rosten proceeded. "As we now have it worked out the program will start out with what we call the frame: spelling out the size of Blush, the numbers, the targeted group, and the absolute fatality of the thing. Something of the history of its onset will be given and that's when Haley will bring you on camera. Since you're one of the earliest workers on Blush your investigation and discoveries—essentially a lay rendering of your research—will then be featured first, interview fashion. Then you'll be asked to give a brief discussion of the work you and Mr. Moyer did together. It's at this point we establish his central position in your joint effort to encourage governmental awareness and assistance in combating the epidemic. You'll see all that in the script outline which, incidentally, Marilyn will give you on your way out. You should look it over and bring up any points or details you think important at our next meeting after I get back. But right now I just want to go over the broader points and the steps we take to make them. It's important that we develop two prevailing themes; one, the failure of government to mobilize an effective prevention program in the face of an escalating epidemic of maximum lethality, and two, Mr. Moyer's rise to prominence as a leader in bringing the problem before the national awareness. It's important the viewer see his effort as the product of a determined and outraged decency laboring to inform our nation of the danger, and, in doing so, indicting the government for not shouldering its responsibility in protecting the people. Or something to that general effect. It's important to show that as his message became more penetrating and farther reaching, the more the government stood culpable. Mr. Moyer's specific charge that government failure to address Blush betrays the essential high-level engineering of the entire matter will be featured in conjunction with the particulars of his death. You can understand, Dr. Cantrelle, that we can't come right out and accuse the United States government of premeditated murder of one of its finer citizens, but we can sure set the issues in such a way to encourage that conclusion."

"Clay would like that," Cantrelle mumbled in veiled deprecation. He was getting caught up in a rising resentment at hearing Clay's courageous and selfless pursuit of truth in the service of his fellow being undergo a mercantile re-packaging for its best impact upon the consumer. Nor did he relish the mounting awareness that Rosten was well into enlisting Clay's death to the service of his own stake in personal vengeance. At least that was the way it was beginning to sound to him. Maybe it was just the way Rosten was talking this morning in view of the trip awaiting him, and maybe it was as much the way he himself was hearing it because of his concerns for Helen and her kids. In any event, Rosten was different this morning. Grief, probably. Certainly not the exuberant, colorful entrepreneur he was at the earlier meetings. At those sessions he seemed ever trying to keep his zeal and zest under proper control. But maybe he never really was like that. Even so, right now he was steady, steel-tipped, and aimed. That wasn't what he had expected to confront this morning for broaching his concerns about responsibility to Clay's family. As he listened to this different kind of Rosten he wondered if it really was true, as Jess had raffishly once said, that Blush was like golf: once it touched you, you were never the same. The thought of Jess brought him back to more familiar stock, and with it, the problem of warning Helen of what was coming.

". . . and I think the best way to portray Mr. Moyer's compassion and determination is to run some on-the-spot interviews we held with your resident doctors. They worked closely with him, and their youthfulness, plus their sense of personal as well as academic loss will . . . ." Rosten detailed as Cantrelle reached a decision. He then looked directly at Rosten.

"I have to interrupt you, Mr. Rosten, because there's something I have to bring up," he blurted.

"Yes?" Rosten tendered after a slight pause.

"I figured it'd be best to deal with it now so that I wouldn't . . . wouldn't be uncertain about our plans," Cantrelle hedged.

"Uncertain, Dr. Cantrelle?" Rosten repeated not quite archly.

"It's about notifying Helen Moyer in advance about what we're going to say," Cantrelle began in a rush. "I don't know how much you've told her—I know *I* certainly haven't said much to her—and I dread the thought of her hearing for the first time while watching a TV program that in all likelihood her husband's death was murder," he explained. "She's a dear, close friend, always has been, and especially so now. And I don't think I could be party to anything that would heap additional misery upon her grief. So I have to talk to you about what can be done to protect her if we intend to proceed as planned." The words tumbled out unguarded and he knew there was no sense trying to stop them because something else in him had now taken over. He looked away from Rosten as he continued. "I had forgotten all about her with all the meetings and preparations going on. My need to get the message out, the need to get the crime punished, placed her and *her* needs in the background. And today, on the way here—I guess because it's getting close to the time—I realized that I was looking only to my—to our—purposes. I would never be able to face her again, and she would be right in thinking that I'd betrayed her, and, irony of ironies, that I'd betrayed what was closest to Clay Moyer. So that's why I bring it up. And that's why I'm telling you I've got some big misgivings about going through with it. I've even wondered if a lot of your guest participants feel queasy like this just before show time but feel they're much too far into it to bring up their doubts or to back out, and so they go before the camera more as captives than as contributors, as they so often seem to be."

"Most of them, Dr. Cantrelle," Rosten agreed readily. "Most of them do feel that way. But it's only happened once that a participant backed out at the last minute," he added pointedly. "And that's the other large reason I wanted to meet with you today—to resolve any last minute doubts; something you and I might best do alone. In answer to your first question as to how much Mrs. Moyer has been told about the program's punch line, not enough to put your concerns to rest, I fear. When I spoke to her I stated that the program dealt aggressively with the Blush problem and featured her husband's work in his effort to have the government accept more responsibility in facing the problem. We also told her that the program would just as aggressively pursue the implications of his death. That was all. She didn't ask any questions," Rosten explained evenly.

"So maybe she's prepared for something or maybe she isn't," Cantrelle posed.

"In truth, Dr. Cantrelle, I suspect that if she's prepared for an aggressive treatment of her personal tragedy, she's probably also prepared to make a personal concession for the common good. But, frankly, I don't think she expects to hear that we think her husband was murdered," Rosten rendered matter-of-factly.

"Then I don't see how we can proceed. It would devastate her. And the kids! Can you imagine their going to school Monday and the stares they would receive? Mr. Rosten, we've got to take another look at this," Cantrelle urged, resolute in his objection.

Rosten looked at Cantrelle with a peruse that was searching, yet patient. Cantrelle felt rising discomfort at being surveyed in preparation for response. As he avoided Rosten's stare he had the odd realization that he was noting Rosten's suit. A dark gray pinstripe. Not the beige Miami single breasted or the pale blue glen plaid he'd worn at the previous meetings as though determined not to relinquish Summer. No, today's funereally dark suit revealed a grimmer side of Jerry Rosten.

"Dr. Cantrelle, before we start talking about what we will and will not do I'd like to make a few things clear," Rosten began. "Firstly, your disquiet over things being too far along to permit any great changes is a correct reading. So, one way or another, we're going to see this program through, as planned. It's scheduled for a full half hour and that's a long time to show a test pattern and play technical difficulty music. And with the announcement and spots already on their way, as of today, it's not likely we would be able to slip in some re-run for show time simply because we've achieved some second thoughts about the whole thing. No, Dr. Cantrelle, we're going to have a program on Blush, as planned and as promised."

Despite Rosten's palpable intent to be steadying and reassuring in his explanation Cantrelle could feel the hard resolve his words carried. But he returned Rosten's steady gaze, uncowed.

"And there's another point, and I run the risk of sounding pontifical even in mentioning it," Rosten continued. "Your concern for Mrs. Moyer's welfare, and the children's, is commendable, and I don't mean to come off sounding patronizing or condescending. I truly mean it, but I have to point out another aspect of this thing. I might even run the risk of sounding priggishly philosophical in saying this though I'm sure some real philosopher along the way has already said it and so much better. Probably many philosophers, in one way or another. But in the day to day, rude, inelegant, not particularly majestic business of bringing home the news, we know that every fact, every discovery, every revelation has its respondent line up of winners and losers. Every one. You discover penicillin and some otherwise doomed people win, but then you've created social problems which, earlier, less effectively treated venereal disease never allowed to evolve, and lots of people lose. You declare a war on an alien foe, and win, while domestic evils are allowed to flourish in the name of a united war effort. The victors thus spoil the very fruits of their foreign effort and later wonder if they'd been fighting the wrong foe all along. And again, lots of people lose. Or—and this is the one we're concerned about here—we reveal the truth about Blush and it seems like a victory for decency and honesty, but the very people who've mandated us to divulge the discovery, the ones who helped to establish the very truth we will speak, are the ones who will bear the hurt of what we do. Dr. Cantrelle, please allow me to point out something I'm sure you already know and, because of your line of work, probably know far better than I ever will: all truth is destructive and painful in like degree that it is creative and edifying. It all depends on which side of the street you work. Ignorance is gracious and accommodating; it indulgently allows any partial or personal preference to hold sway, along with all its evil. But knowledge is a tyrant, and rules according to its own perfections. I'm sure you've seen too often how steadfastly your patients resist a disordering insight in preference to a stable ignorance. Please forgive me for reciting Philosophy 101 to you but I needed to make that point in order to make the next."

Cantrelle knew what was coming. He was also grimly fascinated by the march of Rosten's dialectic. Obviously, he had underestimated this man, had presumptuously written him off as just another clown of electronic hucksterism. He might be that when it was needed, but he indeed had another side and it was now in ascendance. Cantrelle quickly wondered if Rosten was at this very moment a working example of exactly what he was saying: Blush did seem to change everything it touched.

"And my next point is this," Rosten continued. "Though your urge to protect Mrs. Moyer is commendable, as I've said, it is also presumptuous. Presumptuous in the extreme, if it prompts you to consider backing out of the program. The lesser presumption is that you hold your solicitude for Mrs. Moyer to be more accountable than my solicitude for my sister. After all, we'll also be telling her that her son was murdered. Moreover, your concern for Mrs. Moyer, the wife of your dearest friend, is held to be prevailing, more valid than my concern for my sister. Mr. Moyer was your dearest friend, yes, but my nephew was my flesh and blood, flawed and weak as he was. In the hope of avoiding damage to Mrs. Moyer and her children you might ultimately decide to excuse yourself from the ordeal of delivering a painful truth. But, in deciding so, you might cause a greater damage, far greater than even a compassion-driven, imposed selfishness could justify. The simple fact of all this, Dr. Cantrelle, is that you are the possessor of an important truth and the only question now is where you think it would be most moral for it to do its damage."

Cantrelle heard the words like drumbeats calling him to muster, but for what good purpose he wondered since he now felt thoroughly disarmed. He looked at Rosten who sat patiently expectant and motionless in his chair. He could almost feel Rosten's consoling embrace along with the handshake for a game well played, but now over, lost and won.

"We'll have a program, Mr. Rosten," Cantrelle said with a weak smile to confirm himself as a sensible, good sport.

"Thank you, Dr. Cantrelle. I think it'll be even a better program now," he returned, adjusting himself in his chair to signal that the point had been turned.

Cantrelle wanted to rid the air of the lingering tautness imposed by the sharply drawn lines of debate. Since they were now agreed to proceed as planned something more conciliatory would be in order. Continued stiffness, especially on his part, might make him seem unconvinced, and that wasn't the case. Rosten was right in everything he said.

"How did you get into this business, Mr. Rosten?" he asked, signifying his amended impression of the man.

Rosten read the question correctly and smiled amiably.

"Your question makes me feel like the decent, warm-hearted prostitute being asked how she got into the business. Dr. Cantrelle, I had the great misfortune of inheriting a successful advertising agency. Twenty years ago I branched out into TV and became even more successful. So why a misfortune?" he submitted over a wry smile. "Because, Dr. Cantrelle—and you'll think this just too hokey to believe, but it's the God's truth—I wanted with all my heart and soul to be a Philosophy teacher in some sweet little college in the wildwood. But it didn't work out that way and I left graduate school to take over the business."

"I believe it," Cantrelle acknowledged respectfully.

Rosten accepted Cantrelle's gesture with an appreciative nod.

"I've often wondered if we accomplish so much more by not becoming what we most intend," he observed playfully.

Cantrelle broke into a broad grin. The rupture was well on its way to healing.

"Spoken like an enlightened guidance counselor," Cantrelle chortled.

Rosten guffawed, the octaves of his other self coming back into play.

"Well, Dr. Cantrelle, I think we've done enough damage this morning, and we'll have at least one more meeting before dress rehearsal," he summed up as he prepared to rise from his chair.

"Sure," Cantrelle agreed. "I suppose I'll hear from you as to when that'll be." He didn't want to make reference to Rosten's return from the nephew's funeral.

"Right. Should be toward the end of this week. I want to thank you for coming this morning. If anything special comes up while I'm away you can pass it on to Haley. Okay?" he directed in the form of practical suggestion.

Cantrelle imagined he was referring to anything particularly problematic arising from the issue about Helen.

They rose and shook hands, the gesture allowing Cantrelle a moment to gather a response.

"I think something should be said to Mrs. Moyer," Cantrelle affirmed.

"I agree, Dr. Cantrelle, just as something should be said to my sister as to what's behind her son's death. We each have our separate work, haven't we?" he shared as he released the handshake and put his hand on Cantrelle's shoulder to walk him to the door.

Cantrelle felt the hand on his shoulder as a dubbing for thrusting him forth to a hateful duty. By the time they reached the door he'd decided that he needed to think about it a lot more.

"Talk to you when I get back," Rosten assured as he opened the door.

"Sure thing, Mr. Rosten," Cantrelle returned, sounding more resolute than he felt.

He than stepped into the large waiting area as Rosten's door closed quietly behind him. Miss Parsons alertly caught his attention as he re-entered the world of everyday business. The sounds of the secretaries and their equipment dowsed him as in a splash-down and Miss Parsons was moving swiftly to lift him aboard the rescue vessel.

"Here's the script Mr. Rosten said you should have. I also have some fresh coffee in the pot if you'd like a sip before you go," she recommended as she conveyed the manila package with both hands again poised in coy tender.

"Thank you, Miss Parsons," he smiled, referring more to the relief he felt at her charm than to the receipt of the script. "I'll pass on the coffee for now, but I promise I'll be back for you to ply me with some more."

"If you promise to come back I'll forgive you for declining it now," she teased.

"Honest injun," he swore, palm flat and hand upraised in the How position.

"All right," she purred. "But don't take too long."

"Later this week, probably," he assured as he turned to leave.

"I'll be waiting," she promised as she began to wave at his retreat through the door.

As he stepped up the hallway toward the elevators he began to wonder if he had figured her wrong, too; that maybe it wasn't all coquettish horse play, but that she really meant it; that she was actually throwing herself at him and that he was discrediting it in the same way as he had sold Rosten short. Christ, more to think about, he groused as he approached the elevators. He pushed the button and then checked his watch. Good. He had over an hour before the first patient at his office. Plenty of time, barring some traffic tie-up on the throughway. The muffled rumblings in the elevator shaft told him its car was enroute. He desperately needed a moment to sit at his desk and consult his wall. There was just so much to worry about. He had to come up with some good way to talk to Helen, that was certain, but first with Todd tonight. So he really needed some time at the wall. He hoped his case schedule wouldn't be tiresomely heavy today.

Fifteen

He leaned back in his chair and cradled the nape of his neck in his folded hands as he took a deep breath. He then exhaled slowly in general savor of the day's work. The last patient had just left. That patient initially had been scheduled to be the second to last, but a kindly regret had come earlier in the afternoon by way of a phone call from Tampa informing him that a flight delay would keep the actual last-scheduled patient from making his seven o'clock appointment. So with that cancellation he was now free. Seven P.M.! A definite lift because it felt almost like having the afternoon off, just that one extra hour of free time! Plus, the afternoon had gone pretty well. The patients had worked productively in their sessions, there hadn't been too many distracting calls, and he was able to put Blush, Helen, and TV inevitabilities aside for a while as he busily got into his clinical work. It was a good several hours. He could always count on his private practice to restore his bearings after some period of deflection and disorientation come of contact with the fitful storms of his other world. Plus, the office offered benefit of refuge. But it was time to get back to thinking about Helen. An earlier stint at the wall before the first patient's arrival yielded a decision to proceed in such a way as to avoid any detours urged by her grief; rather, he'd speak to her gently but face-on about what he and several others suspected about Clay's death, explaining to her that they felt there was no option left to them but to follow through on what humanity and justice demanded, knowing that in doing so they were inciting a cruel intensification of her grief and possibly depriving her and her children of a gentler acceptance of their loss. It sounded okay in his thoughts, but how would it go in the telling? He harbored a hope, very likely a vain one, that his explication would be greeted by an endorsement borne of her own private suspicions which she had felt helpless to pursue. She always was a sensible and pretty astute girl and it just might be that he and she were closer on this point than he now knew. If so, she might greet his disclosure with a show of relief and vindication. That would be the best outcome, but not the most likely, for even if she did have her own suspicions she had probably labored to remove them from her awareness, the better to protect her grief. In any event he now had a little extra time to mull it all over, thank God. It then occurred to him that as he now sat and thought of talking to Helen, Rosten was arriving in California and would soon be talking similarly to his sister. So he wasn't completely alone in all this.

He then leaned forward and placed his elbows on the desk at their appointed stations and rested his chin on the heels of his cupped hands. A few blinks to adjust his gaze for the infinite and he was ready. The wall responded with a surge of resonance racing through his stream of thought. The sensation was surprisingly swift in its arrival and its intensity was even greater than those rare and violent eruptions which occurred unexpectedly while casually mulling some seemingly neutral point. This time it was hitting him head on, not side-swiping him from some region on the periphery of his mind as always before. Also, the rapidity of its onset seemed to suggest that his recent preoccupations were somehow linked directly to it, hence eliciting it with a readiness that had never before been the case. He realized that this was the first time his conscious intent to conjure the experience had actually resulted in its full appearance. Previously, even his most concentrated efforts had resulted in little more than a keener memory of the experience, not so much the experience itself. So whatever it was, he was getting damned close to it, and the thought of telling Helen the truth seemed to be a definite lead-in to discovering how to get the genie out of the bottle. He now felt immensely pleased with himself, along with the resurrected conviction that in the overall he was headed in the cosmically correct direction. In addition he noted that the expansive, transporting verve of the experience was not fading immediately upon its registration, starburst fashion as usual; it was lingering, its intensity upon him like an extended fanfare about to reveal its feature attraction. He quietly waited, open to the thoughts that would assuredly now come. But so far the only thoughts he could claim were thoughts about what he was experiencing. He was beginning to wonder what to do with this thing that seemed to be asking him to know something he truly should when he noticed that the green light on his private line was blinking.

"Jesus Christ!" he exhaled heavily as he closed his eyes. "Of all the god-damned times!" He didn't even consider checking to feel if the verge was enduring; he knew it was gone. Nothing could prevail in the face of a determined phone. He reached across his desk and picked up the receiver.

"This is Dr. Cantrelle," he identified to the caller.

"Dr. Cantrelle, this is your answering service. I have a doctor on your office line," the operator explained, "and he says he would like to speak to you, if possible. A Dr. Horace Burleson. Shall I tell him you'll call him back if he leaves his number?"

Burleson! The name startled him into full alertness. Calling now? That's right, he quickly recalled; Jess had pointed out that he was in town for a meeting with some committee, whatever its name was. He tried to visualize the name in the newspaper article. But why call now, though for sure it was exactly the kind of pick-me-up he needed to remind him of his better reach, just like his office practice did. In fact, it was exactly what he needed to give his mind a rest from Helen and Rosten.

"No, operator, I'll take the call now, thank you," he hurriedly instructed. He then switched to the other line.

"Dr. Burleson? So kind of you to call," Cantrelle greeted eagerly.

"Good evening, Dr. Cantrelle. Please forgive me for calling you during therapy hours. I hope I'm not interrupting you," Burleson greeted.

"Oh, not at all," Cantrelle hastened to reassure, "my last patient left a short while ago and I was just sitting here going over a few things. Your call came at a good time."

"Very kind of you to say so, Dr. Cantrelle. I know how distracting phone calls can be when we're intent on keeping to a schedule, as I'm sure your practice demands," he commiserated. "Are you sure I'm not taking you away from something you would best attend to?"

"I'm certain, Dr. Burleson. In fact, I'm delighted to hear from you. I noticed in the paper this morning that you would be in town for a few days with your committee, and that, of course, reminded me of our last meeting," Cantrelle explained, recalling once again the somber and grim gathering at Clay's viewing. Burleson's attendance and his consoling words to Helen and the children were remembered as uplifting to all present in addition to being a gracious tribute to Clay's courage.

"Oh, yes. I trust Mrs. Moyer is beginning to recover from her grief and that the children are managing reasonably well. Friends are so important at such a time and I hope to pay her a call in the near future when the time is suitable," he conveyed.

"She would like that, Dr. Burleson," Cantrelle seconded.

"That brings me to the purpose of my calling you at this awkward hour. I wondered if we could afford ourselves the opportunity to get together for that long-promised chat we've never been able to work out during the busier hours. It may be that if we await a moment of convenience we might never discharge our debt to each other," Burleson posed.

"Well, I'm free now, as I said," Cantrelle leaped. The thought of getting away from everything for an hour or so over a few drinks with Horace Burleson was irresistible in the extreme, and he had little hesitance in pushing the suggestion.

"Dr. Cantrelle, that's exactly what I hoped you'd suggest," Burleson exulted. "These back and forth promises have gone on much too long, don't you think?"

"I agree totally, Dr. Burleson," Cantrelle returned, warming up to a comradely banter.

"I still have a few items to clear up with my committee meeting—I'm calling you during a recess—but that should be finished within half an hour or so," Burleson explained.

"Fine. Tell me where we might meet and it'll probably take about that much time for me to get there. The traffic is pretty light this time of day and I should be there just as you're finishing up at your end," Cantrelle clicked off in a show of efficient readiness. If this overdue meeting of the two didn't come off this time it wouldn't be his doing, though in truth it did seem like an impulsive, last minute effort at a truly inconvenient time. A planned dinner engagement would have been better.

"Why not here at the College of Scientists? There's a splendid lounge in the private wing, and the bar is rather well stocked, I can avouch," Burleson suggested.

"Fine. I always suspected there was a lot more to that place than met the public eye," Cantrelle ragged.

"Good! It's settled! I'll meet you here in about half an hour. Just come in through the front entrance and I'll meet you in the main hallway near the statue of Edison," Burleson instructed.

"Right. See you then. Good bye," Cantrelle snapped as a verbal salute.

"Good bye, Dr. Cantrelle," Burleson returned.

As he hung up he recalled that statue of Edison standing in the middle of the ground floor foyer, towering upward as though to ascend into the dome of the rotunda. Grave, beetle-browed Edison. The several times he'd been to that building for conferences he felt that the coffee-break gaiety which flowed from the auditorium to mill around at the base of the statue during intermissions violated the dour pedagogy Edison's glower clearly advised. A good example of overwrought Victorian, he'd concluded. And here again, tonight, there was the prospect of something less than sober scholarship using the outraged statue as a collecting point for shameless retreat from the duties of one's day. He loved the idea. He needed just this kind of release, especially so because of its unexpectedness. Like a windfall amidst the day's debris.

He set about tidying up his desk in preparation for leaving. Mercifully, there were no return phone calls he had to make other than to call Laura to tell her that he would be home later because of what had come up. The thought of her setting aside his dinner came to mind. She disliked doing that though he didn't mind his food being dried out a bit. After all, it was his doing. Laura merely saw it as being coerced into serving something unacceptable to her standards. And in truth right now he wouldn't mind something, no matter how desiccated. Burleson hadn't mentioned anything about dinner. Maybe there would be snacks on hand to tide him over till he got back home. He wondered if Burleson ever did such creature things as eat. Or worse. He smiled at his irreverence as he reached for the phone; he suspected Burleson managed a temporal cocktail or two on occasion, and the thought of having one with him on an empty stomach added to the headiness of the rendezvous. As he dialed home he wondered why Burleson hadn't called sooner. If he could call now, why didn't he call a couple of weeks ago to ask how things were going in the aftermath of Clay's death? He seemed so genuinely concerned at the viewing that it nourished an expectation he would follow up on the expression of interest within the subsequent week or thereabouts, or so one Frank Cantrelle thought. But that hadn't happened, and then this call tonight, summoning a deflected impatience. Christ, the man is kind enough to call and in no time at all he's remiss for not having called sooner. He finished dialing with a snicker directed at himself for being so picky. He waited for the ring. Busy. Must be Laura and Ellie. When Ellie called, it was usually at about this time. These first few weeks at school bore some recounting to the home office, apparently. He would call again upon his arrival at the College of Scientists. And he would call from that private lounge few ordinary people knew anything about, he wagged his head in mocking vaunt. He then sprang from his chair and picked up his briefcase stationed at the side of his desk as he made for the door, flipping off the light switch as he went by. He then traversed the outer office, tracing that imaginary boundary line between the secretarial and the waiting areas, and approached the front door. As he opened it he turned off the lights to note through the expanse of windows on the far wall that it was still dusky outside, though likely not for very much longer. He stepped out onto the landing of the front steps, locked the door, and inhaled a large portion of the restful gloaming laid out before him. The sense of release, coupled with the prospect of his meeting with Burleson, urged upon him the tingle of a second beginning of this day. The dusk held the same chiaroscuro as dawn, sort of, though from the other side, and shadows that fell left then were now falling right, and so forth. And this was the best time of the year, and harvest was almost nigh. He looked across the lawn fronting his office and the Purkinje shift was at its peak with the grass for these fleeting moments preternaturally green. It was so good to know this life. Satisfied, he exhaled, trotted down the steps and proceeded to his car in the parking area. When he reached his car he stood for a moment at its side and took another scanning glance at his office building, the shrubbery, the trimmed lawn, the shade trees, the simple peace. His office had once been a private home and he had converted it for his practice. But moments like this reminded him that it was still spiritually a home, and ever would be as long as it stood. The architect had done his work well, and no amount of asphalt, sound proofing, or electronic equipment would alter the essence of its design. And his patients liked it as much as he did. Often it became their home away from home, too. He nodded good night to this haven which was also his spiritual preserve.

He then got into his car, settled himself into position, and started up the engine. It, too, seemed eager. For a moment he wished he had the Corvette for the return run to the city; would make it seem less repetitious. As it was he was being remarkably congenial to the idea of making a second trip to the city in one day in the same car. Ordinarily he'd be bitching to high heaven, but this trip was so special, so long awaited, that it stood apart from everything else of the day. Even so, the Corvette would have added something. A festive note, maybe; a daring touch certainly. The thought of a red Corvette parked in the stately courtyard of the College of Scientists. General Motors, get your camera. Rather, Frank Cantrelle, get a grip on yourself; this was to be a scholarly meeting, not a fraternity frolic, he chided himself as he pulled out of the parking area and made for the back route out of town.

In a few minutes he was clicking off the white posts of pasture fencing as they zipped by. The back route was all idyll with farmsteads, tree stands, cornfields, and dairy cows. The livestock were now in their pens and the fields were empty except for an occasional crow. The crows seemed to be the last of the daytime birds to tuck in before the nighthawks, swifts, and owls took over to bring the day to its close. It was now appreciably darker as he drove along, not the least because he was proceeding East. Within a few miles, porch lights began to come on. Off in the distance he could make out the eerie pinkish-yellow of the sodium lights at the entrance to the throughway just starting up for their nocturnal stint. Shadows looked so artificial and pale in their light, lacking the distinct, old-fashioned skulk that came of more traditional lighting, such as candles and wood fires. In a moment he was swinging around the curved entranceway under the lights' canopied arch and setting sight for the straight run into the city.

The traffic on the throughway was as thin as predicted and he settled in for an unhampered sprint for the exit that was just a short distance beyond the one he used this morning to meet with Rosten. Already that seemed so far away in time just as Rosten was now so far away in miles. But Helen wasn't. He had planned to review that matter a bit more tonight before calling her tomorrow, but now he would have to set those thoughts aside for a while. Maybe later tonight when he got back home, though he knew in his heart he would be a lot less inclined to do so after this special evening than he would be otherwise. In fact, beginning right now, he noted. Time for music, anyway. He turned up the volume to be greeted by a work he'd never heard before. Was it Saint-Saens? Seemed to have his distinctive combination of sweep and clarity of theme. As he listened he was reminded of the convoluted loopiness of Bach's *Musical*

Offering; no matter where you started or how far along it seemed to take you, you always ended up in the same place. This present work had something about it that did the same, but more subtly, it seemed. And then, most odd, he had the sense of the verge skirting the edges of his consciousness. Christ, he tittered, it's even coming with music now! But he couldn't listen to the music and simultaneously heed the verge feeling. Better to go with the music for now, he decided, as he focused on the inventions used by the composer to iterate the theme in a ranging but closed and continuous network of treatments, or so it seemed to him. How could composers accomplish such things? Were there such things as logical reductions and contradictions in sound as well? Certainly there seemed to be infinite regresses, as this piece in its own way amply suggested. Was there a special syntax, logic, and semantics of sound which only the musically gifted understood or could speak, and that the rest of us, musically mute but enamored of the sounds, were no more cognizant of what we were hearing than the chimpanzee was of Elizabethan English being used to satisfy his simple need for praise and affection. The chimpanzee got the general idea from the feeling tone, but the exquisite richness of the language was lost to him. We, too, smiled loudly and clapped broadly at the sweet sounds of a composition, little more mindful of what we were enjoying than was the chimpanzee to whom a Shakespeare
sonnet was sweetly intoned. No wonder composers were so often impatient with us. It was a wonder more of them weren't insufferable pricks, such as the likes of Mozart and Wagner. Probably the fact that they were just about universally so piss poor at quadratic equations which the rest of us managed adequately well was what kept a check on their hubris. Still and all, you wonder what went through a composer's mind when an audience listened to his composition and he knew that the larger, more elegant part of his work was not being heard. He then recalled Beethoven's unforgiving scowl. The whole problem, he snickered, is that we're simply not good enough for each other. Hey, you gods, that's your cue, he chortled.

He was making good time, though, and he worried that he might arrive before Burleson was finished with his meeting. He couldn't imagine Burleson being the equivalent of a monkey when it came to music and he chuckled at the naughty blasphemy of the thought. The man probably played a wicked oboe, or something. He then wondered if Burleson maintained any kind of a practice. Probably not, in view of his frequent travels to various meetings and gatherings. Was his university chair enough to provide him with a suitable income? Probably, what with the honoraria he received for his frequent appearances. He then wondered if Burleson, like a composer, had similar sentiments about the better part of his work not being heard or understood though loudly acclaimed by so many people who had only small ken of it. Certainly even he himself, lowly Frank Cantrelle, often enough felt reproachful that he was not being seen truly for what went into his accomplishments, lank as they were. Someone like Burleson, with infinitely more to his credit, had to have some gripe somewhere in his being for the larger measure of his art going unheard. But maybe not. Such perhaps was the difference between the common and the great.

With a smirk he abruptly resolved that it was just not politic to recite the arguments confirming his meagerness as he neared the moment of joining an esteemed and exalted colleague for a chatty evening of comradeship. Rather, seek a venue where differences weren't so stark. But maybe Burleson had his own agenda for this evening. It was just possible, he wondered brightly, that Burleson might invite him to participate in some conference or symposium being planned for this Autumn. A repeat, of sorts, of what had happened years ago when he and Burleson appeared on the same panel, though this time it wouldn't be by happenstance. In fact, the more he thought of it the more it seemed likely that such was indeed the reason for Burleson's meeting with him tonight right after his committee meeting. The committee was probably working on the format of just some such symposium and Burleson had probably nominated him as a possible participant and now wanted to sound him out before the committee adjourned tomorrow. It seemed more and more obvious, though as he thought more about it he dutifully remembered to be wary of any notions that jump-started his self-satisfaction so easily. But it did seem likely, he mused.

The music was now well into a rousing *allegro con brio* as though it openly sided with his speculation. In any event he would find out soon enough, he noted along with the sign pointing to the exit he took to Rosten's office this morning. Just a quarter mile beyond that and he would be only a few blocks from the College. He sped by the familiar exit and quickly closed on another sign announcing the one he sought. It even had a smaller sign underneath specifically designating the College of Scientists as the special advantage of this particular exit. Just exactly what he sought. He eased into the exit lane and was soon on the curving off-ramp to the traffic light at its base. This time he caught it red and accepted the obligatory delay while the music traced a merry galliard to keep him prancing in place. It occurred to him that it had become fully dark and that the traffic light facing him was now the brightest element in view. Storefront lights were not very prominent in this more residential section of the city, and street lights were more widely spaced and modest. The traffic light then changed and he swung left to note that the traffic, still modest, was predominately in the opposite direction and headed for the interior of the city where, he found it too easy to remember just now, the culinary loci were clustered. He proceeded along with the reduced flow of cars going in his direction for the several blocks to the boulevard on which he had to turn to reach the college. He caught that intersection green and made the correct turn to take him along a tree-lined broadway that had a dividing neutral ground with shrubbery and trees spaced among the ranks of street lights arching over the roadway like watchful flamingos. The trees on the neutral ground along with those lining the sidewalk draped shadows along the stately course of the boulevard both day and night, and large brownstones and set-back manor houses shaped the monied decor of the neighborhood of which this was the main thoroughfare. Despite the traffic the neighborhood seemed quiet. Maybe it was the trees, or the expanse of free space between the buildings. The net effect of the neighborhood was that of detachment from the rest of the city when actually it was just on the fringe of the commercial area. As he began to settle into the gentler ambience of the scene he spied the wrought iron fence fronting the college's grounds. He had hoped the music would reach its last bar before he made the front gate so that he could learn the name and composer, but it didn't seem likely to happen that way inasmuch as the music was still moving along with tireless brio as he was beginning to slow down for entering the gate. Two large globular lights, one on each flanking column, marked the college's entrance, and he turned in to track a circular driveway around the splashing fountain at the base of a bronze Apollo, talaria and all. Situated as it was among the building's surrounding gardens the statue was now waggishly regarded as a monument to the patron saint of floral delivery, and at this moment the music seemed to be throbbing away to generate enough current under those winged feet to get him aloft and on his way. He drove past the fountain, past the building's portico, and headed for the parking area on the left where there were about a half dozen cars parked. One, oddly, was a stretch limousine. He parked a short distance from the others and listened one more lingering moment to the music which seemed uninterested in the accomplished fact of his arrival. He then switched off the ignition with the promise to call the radio station tomorrow to find out what the piece was. He had done so before and the station personnel were always eager to be helpful. He suspected that radio people, like all missionaries, liked to be informed that some of the people out there were actually listening.

He then stepped out of his car to be surprised that there was a nip in the air. A genuine Autumn nip. A cool front must had passed through earlier in the afternoon. He hadn't noticed the drop in temperature when he left the office, maybe because it was still light and the day hadn't yet had a chance to cool off. But the coolness was now in place and he felt a certain zing accompany him as he walked to the building's entrance. For obvious enough reason he was reminded of the evening ward work in his medical school days: the cool nights early in the semester, his venturing into the unknown, and feeling a bit alone in the doing. After all, he often had one entire ward all to himself in working up new admissions and doing the basic lab work. And he felt he was in over his head there, too. He then reached the portico and walked up the spread of steps to the entrance landing, doing so with discernible hesitation. As he dwelt on the thought of being much too junior and unaccomplished to be a credible confrere with Horace Burleson the silly dream about the state fair and the copper tubing popped back into mind. He couldn't restrain the grimace which accompanied that abashing memory. Yet, however much the dream rattled him at the time, it left him with the consoling assessment that if he could breast that horrifying chimera he could handle anything in the real world. He now drew upon the inverse affirmation his recall of the dream offered and huffily pronounced himself ready for Burleson. In fact, he felt quite ready to be invited to participate in any forthcoming symposium, what with his media fame soon to be ratcheted up several hundred notches or so. Plus, it would be so much more becoming to greet the invitation with a show of polite equanimity. No gushing gratitude tonight, please.

He stood before the heavy double doors for an instant to put a period to his thoughts; he didn't want any vagaries trailing in the wake of his thinking when he stepped inside. Clay's cynical smirk flashed on the door as though on a projection screen. "Right, ole buddy," he greeted, "if you were here you would have me in the right skeptical frame of mind about all this. In fact, departed but unforgettable friend, if you were still here I probably wouldn't be standing here at all. *You* would be the one they would be sounding out, most likely." Those respects paid, he opened the door and stepped into the familiar lobby. Seeing it empty, and for the first time so, it now looked even grander than he remembered it. The large checkerboard black and white tiles of the floor seemed to stretch it out inordinately. The Edison fountain was turned off and the circular pool at the statue's base was dry, he noted as he approached it. He tried to muffle his footsteps in obedience to the silence. The broad central staircase at the rear of the lobby yawned upward and divided left and right to reverse itself along the side walls to open upon a second floor gallery which circled the lobby. Thank God he'd been here several times before; otherwise, he would be much too intimidated to remain, he chided himself. He razzed his restive awe a bit more by asking himself if he should genuflect when Burleson appeared. That notion provoked the right note of breezy irreverence as he looked up at Edison's scowl.

"Good evening, Dr. Cantrelle," came the familiar voice from the left rear of the lobby. Quick footsteps brought Burleson rapidly into handshaking reach.

"Good evening, Dr. Burleson," Cantrelle returned, a diffident smile automatically in place despite his resolve to be suitably underwhelmed.

"Thank you so much for coming. But first let me apologize for the abrupt and tardy notice. I had thought of contacting you sooner but I wasn't certain that I'd be able to arrange the time, even if your schedule permitted and you were in the mood for a chat; it wasn't until later today that something seemed possible. The committee work took a turn that freed up this time," Burleson detailed in explanation as he continued to hold Cantrelle in handshake, the other hand on his shoulder.

"I'm just delighted that we could work out the time, Dr. Burleson. I'm sure we've always suspected that when this get-together eventually occurred it would happen unplanned, sort of while we weren't looking," Cantrelle suggested merrily.

"So right, Dr. Cantrelle. That's exactly the way it seems, doesn't it?" Burleson eagerly agreed. He then released the handshake, their wavelength now jointly established and open. Burleson then backed off a half pace and shifted his demeanor to a beseeching concern. "But I must mention something before we go any farther, Dr. Cantrelle. I may have misled you. In asking you to meet with me tonight I must have implied that our meeting would involve just the two of us. Actually, I had something else in mind and I should have said so to you when we spoke earlier."

Cantrelle grinned in vindication. He was right about the symposium invitation, or something like it.

"What I would like, Dr. Cantrelle, if it's agreeable to you, is to introduce you to the other members of the committee," Burleson proposed. "They are familiar with your work and I've spoken to them often about our several attempts over the years to have a collegial get-together over a drink or two. At this point they would feel neglected if they weren't included."

He nodded in gracious agreement. It would simply be unthinkable not to include the others, especially if they were of a mind to extend him a certain invitation upon condition of his interest. My, oh, my, how briskly one's fortunes were moving along these days, he sighed to himself in mock hauteur.

"Of course, Dr. Burleson. I'd be delighted to meet your committee," he seconded readily.

"Splendid. I wouldn't have known what to say to them if you hadn't agreed, but fortunately I'm now spared that distress. They'll be so pleased," he promised. "But we shouldn't keep them waiting; I told them I'd let them know immediately." He then turned to lead Cantrelle to the left rear of the lobby whence he'd emerged. He sustained a chatty discourse as accompaniment to their transit of the lobby.

"As you can well imagine, Dr. Cantrelle, our meetings as a committee are hectically busy affairs inasmuch as we meet as a group only four times a year with an occasional extra meeting thrown in if the work piles up too rapidly. We occasionally run into each other at other functions, but we conduct no committee business on such occasions because our duties then are the duties of a guest participant or whatever, and, of course, such chance encounters of two or three of us would not constitute a quorum, anyway. So when we have a scheduled meeting our agenda is quite full," Burleson explained as they walked along.

"I can well imagine," Cantrelle politely concurred. It was becoming more evident that the invitation to meet with the committee was less social and more business. He was definitely part of the agenda if time was indeed so precious to them. "I trust it was a unanimous vote to take a break for a few minutes of social greeting this evening. It would be awkward meeting a divided group," Cantrelle joshed, feeling bolder about his place in the event.

Burleson smiled generously.

"Actually, Dr. Cantrelle, the vote *was* unanimous. We never undertake a joint action except by unanimous vote. Hence, we often do not reach a resolution on the matters which come before us, but I must say that of late the unanimous vote has happened more frequently," Burleson replied candidly.

They were now walking down a hallway which led to a rear wing of the building. It was the kind of hallway that usually led to kitchens, pantries, and the like, but obviously such would not be the case tonight.

"Also," he continued less officially, "we've just about concluded our scheduled business, and meeting you will help us all round out the evening. Unanimously."

"I'm reassured," Cantrelle retorted in playful relief. "How many are there on the committee, may I ask?" he then queried in shift to a more ready demeanor. They were approaching a double door at the end of the hallway. He figured it to be the entrance of their probable destination.

"Counting myself, there are seven members of the committee," Burleson returned. "Here we are," he added as he grasped the knob to open the door.

Upon hearing there were seven members Cantrelle experienced his standard wonderment at the frequency the numbers seven and three turned up in human configurations. Both numbers were certainly externalizations of something fundamental to all of us and yet each was proof to any convincing explanation thus far. And here it was again. Either number conferred a mystical, magical property to its referent, whatever the item. Three was so much more determinative than four, and so forth.

His woolgathering ended abruptly as Burleson opened the door and gestured him in. When he entered, the low mumble of relaxed conversation within stopped abruptly. All present looked at him, several having to turn around to do so. All were seated and distributed among three divans arranged in an exploded 'U' open to a greystone fireplace. The room was large, made to seem even cavernous by the raised paneling of the walls which had set-in bookshelves spaced strategically along their expanse. Oriental carpets covered enough of the wooden parquet floor to soften the tread, and various tables and lamps filled the open spaces between the larger pieces of furniture. An exquisite Chippendale desk waited in a corner across the room and catter to the hearth. Old, mellow oil paintings were hung judiciously so as not to compete with the warming effect of the wall paneling. A few bronzes and ivories were about, and a large oriental bowl with an arrangement of fresh flowers sat in the center of a low, oversized square table that rested within the enclosure of the divans and in front of the fireplace. Several side chairs were here and there against the walls, and a burgundy leather wingback chair was set off to the right of the near divan, adjacent the fireplace. Without doubt, it was the perfect library, the kind contrived for illustration in design magazines. But this one was real, with real people in it. In fact, he noted, there were seven people in it, not counting Burleson and himself. Shouldn't there be only six? The discrepancy rattled his shaky composure. He was already having enough to do not to cave in from awe, much less being blindsided by confusion. He quickly scanned the seven to ferret out the odd one, assuming that Burleson had been on the level with him about the number of committee members he was to expect. Was there another guest, such as himself? Apparently. Was someone else being considered as a possible participant in the symposium? He had assumed he would be the only one, tonight anyway. All of a sudden things were bothersomely uncertain.

"Gentlemen, I'd like you to meet Dr. Frank Cantrelle," he heard Burleson beside him say as he wrestled with the disquiet he feared was now broadly etched on his face. He then felt a stiff smile emerge which he offered to the seven unknowns as Burleson continued. "Come, Dr. Cantrelle, allow me to introduce you," Burleson urged as he placed a hand on Cantrelle's shoulder to guide him forth.

The others began to rise, their congenial smiles beckoning him forward.

Burleson and Cantrelle reached the fringe of enclosure formed by the divans while the members stood in place before their seats in wait of being introduced.

"Dr. Cantrelle, this is the committee of which I spoke, plus an additional guest visiting with us tonight, and I'll explain that in a minute," Burleson began, "but first let's go through the introductions. So important to know each other better. Gentlemen, I'll just point you out as I name you. Fair enough?"

Smiles all around plus a few approving comments endorsed the easy congeniality of that approach.

"First, Dr. Cantrelle, I'd like you to meet Dr. Avery Foster, Chairman of the Department of History at Hamilton University," Burleson gestured.

Jesus Christ, he thought with a start! This was the Avery Foster who was a consultant to the UN as well as to the World Health Organization! His writings on history as a formative force in shaping the character and content of global warfare were almost biblical in their reach. They certainly received almost as much devotion.

"How do you do, Dr. Cantrelle," Foster greeted amiably as he took a step closer and extended his hand.

Cantrelle looked at the tall, angular figure crowned with great shocks of wavy gray hair. His pale blue eyes sparkled with a searching energy and Cantrelle felt himself slipping into a flaccid compliance as he shook Foster's hand.

"I'm very pleased to meet you, Dr. Foster," Cantrelle answered simply.

"And this is Dr. Edwin Malloy, Chief of the Mathematics Division of the Rhenquist Institute."

Cantrelle suppressed a gasp. Edwin Malloy needed no introduction. He remembered him from that Symposium a year ago. After his work on the probability sets of the National Health Plan he won the Nobel prize for his work on indeterminate quantities. That was two years ago. He remembered that as well, because Ellie had gone on so much about it and how his work had restored Topology, her interest, to its former pre-eminence in the field of system theory.

"Pleased to meet you, Dr. Malloy. My daughter speaks of you often," Cantrelle offered lamely. His handshake was gentler than Foster's. Also, Malloy's face was positively elfin, and coupled with his modest height, gave him the touch of the magically wise leprechaun. His reddish hair called for a long-stemmed pipe to complete the image. He immediately liked Malloy. He knew that Ellie would, too.

"My pleasure, Dr. Cantrelle," Malloy echoed and then stepped aside.

"On your right, Dr. Cantrelle, is Dr. Paul Weinroth, Chairman of the Department of Biologic Studies at Columbia Tech," Burleson indicated with an encouraging crook of the finger in the man's direction. Weinroth approached.

Paul Weinroth himself! The father of gene-mapping! He also remembered him from the Symposium. He had since included a few of Weinroth's lesser, more easily understood papers in the residents' reading list for the course on diagnostic nomenclature and basic nosology in example of the future direction of psychiatric diagnosis, and, now, here he was actually shaking hands with the man whose elegant research was likely to change the topography of the entire diagnostic system of Psychiatry, not to mention the entire field of Genetics! He, too, was a Nobel laureate.

"I've enjoyed discussing several of your papers with my residents. Dr. Weinroth," Cantrelle attempted as a display of composure equal to the moment. For his part, Weinroth seemed shy, Cantrelle noted, and shook hands tentatively while appearing to pull into himself in the effort.

"I'm glad to hear that someone has the fortitude to read them," Weinroth deprecated with a self-conscious smile. His small, black-rimmed glasses made him look all the more fragile.

Cantrelle was now beginning to feel a giddy recklessness at what he was coming to regard as a game to see if he had a requisite awareness of the place and stature of the people to whom he was being introduced. So far so good. What if the next one was someone he knew absolutely nothing about and had never even heard of before? Would that disqualify him? Would the pleasing modesty of his position in being at least familiar with the names of the people who created the world in which he lived and worked be vitiated by discovery of a defaulting ignorance, like a sinner not even knowing the names of the saints to whom he prayed? He hoped not, and there was only one way to find out, he saw.

"And over here we have someone I think you may have met before," Burleson continued as he directed Cantrelle's attention to the person approaching from the other side of the seating area. "At last year's symposium when I met your wife and Mr. and Mrs. Moyer I may have introduced Dr. Markman. If not, Dr. Cantrelle this is Dr. Jeremy Markman, Chairman of the Department of Philosophy at Pacific University."

Now he remembered. Markman was the one on the panel who had spoken about the relationship of knowledge to ethics. Burleson had left the symposium with Markman, but there had been no introduction. Markman reached over to offer a handshake to Cantrelle.

"No, we weren't introduced, Dr. Burleson, because I commandeered too much of the time talking about something or other. In fact, I kept Dr. Markman waiting. Please forgive me for that, Dr. Markman. It's a pleasure to meet you," Cantrelle assured as he took Markman's handshake.

"I'm glad we can make up arrears, Dr. Cantrelle. Welcome," Markman offered pleasantly. The warmth of his smile contrasted with the wiry, restless manner Cantrelle recalled vividly from that symposium. Markman had then seemed eager to get on to something else. His tweedy, russet and brown presentation now bespoke a settled composure. Who knows, Cantrelle wondered, maybe the man just didn't like audiences. Only think tanks.

"And this rather dapper gentleman," Burleson suggested as he moved on, "is Mr. Peter Alberti, current President of the Arts Foundation of America. He keeps our taste in line, don't you, Peter?"

Alberti chuckled as he reached for Cantrelle's hand. He was, indeed, dapper, Cantrelle acknowledged as he blinked in awe of meeting this legendary figure. For years he had been director of the nation's most renowned opera, had written several operas of his own as America's finest entries in that universal genre, and had composed innumerable orchestral pieces to achieve the status as the world's foremost musical interpreter of the modern predicament. Moreover, he was a gifted poet and his contributions there had greatly upgraded America's usual pedestrian representation in the world's treasury of that commodity. He had listened to Alberti's music too many times to count and had found it bewitching, but also complex beyond his grasp. It assumed too much of the average, present day listener, he had concluded. And now here he was on the verge of shaking hands with this titan who, rumors held, originally studied in the field of sonic physics some fifty years ago. Maybe that's why he, an artist, was included among these others, even though he obviously cut a different kind of figure in his double-breasted dark blue suit, natty handkerchief in the breast pocket, colorful silk foulard tie, and French cuffs.

"How do you do, Dr. Cantrelle," Alberti intoned as he shook Cantrelle's hand.

"I'm very pleased to meet you," Cantrelle returned meekly. He felt fixed by Alberti's dark eyes which somehow reminded him of Picasso's intentness. But Alberti had a full head of hair which carried only a modest amount of gray streaking, despite his age. Cantrelle dared to wonder if Alberti touched it up a bit. Keeping the scenery fresh, sort of. That dash of secret irreverence was helpful in keeping abject servility at a manageable remove. He was so hopelessly in over his head, and everybody present knew it, but there was no sense in parading it about, minstrel show fashion. He would hold to a vague flippancy, there being no imaginable protocol to cover this sort of situation. Still and all, a composer among these people? "I love your music," he gushed to Alberti, who smiled tolerantly.

"And the other member of our committee is Dr. Roger Horlick. Dr. Horlick is the Chairman of the National Synod of Churches as well as the Regent of Midland Seminary," Burleson directed with the slightest of shifts to the deferential.

Cantrelle hadn't noticed earlier that the man wore a clerical collar, but he quickly excused himself of the lapse in observation for there being too much to absorb in these brief moments of introduction. He noted that he was by now surprisingly unsurprised to find a Doctor of Divinity in this group since just about every other aspect of life seemed to be represented. This member he knew practically nothing about, and if it hadn't been for a patient's—a minister, in fact—bringing it up in the course of therapy, he wouldn't have known at all that Horlick had written several controversial books on the religious experience as being the substrate for all societal integration of human striving and that government, no matter its effort to separate itself from church, merely represented schismatic efforts to escape the religious in all of us by giving it another name. The patient said the work was too brilliant and too unsettling to be endorsed except by a maverick few. The thought of all secular government as fundamentally being just errant strivings of apostate religion was not an idea that could receive much legislative welcome. Certainly not in America, anyway.

"I am delighted to know you, Dr. Cantrelle," Horlick said gently as he took Cantrelle's hand.

"The pleasure is mine, Dr. Horlick," Cantrelle returned uneasily. He never quite knew how to talk to clergy.

Burleson then urged Cantrelle back to group bon homie.

"Now that you've met the committee, you should meet your fellow guest, and that should take care of the introductions. Then we can all sit down and chat," he suggested.

Cantrelle looked at the remaining unintroduced person. He was considerably younger than the others, perhaps even a couple of years younger than Cantrelle himself. The man's comfortable demeanor suggested that he was well on to becoming familiar with the committee, perhaps for having spent some time with it earlier this evening. The man looked at Cantrelle with dark eyes that seemed more sympathetic than searching. Maybe a kindred apprenticeship offered something fraternal. A fresh tan suggested he'd just come back from a sunny vacation.

"Dr. Cantrelle, I'd like to introduce Dr. Inigo Pontalbas," Burleson gestured.

At first he didn't think he heard it. But he did hear it. Everything about him and in him heard it, for his heart was now pounding violently to keep a feathery feeling from swallowing him up in faint. He knew he was standing agape but could do nothing about it. His eyes went wide with shock and confusion as a wave of fear and horrid realization swirled in his mind. He was beginning to see, but his understanding was revulsed at what was beginning to form in his thinking. Anger began to flicker amid his confusion, fed by the meaning of what was gathered before him and finally coming together in his understanding. The searing recognition of his having been a pathetic fool began to assume sway in his trembling awareness. A blind fool. A joke in a vicious game of blind man's buff! He felt the power of voluntary action return and he now looked sharply at Burleson, and then swept all the others present with an accusatory stare, his wide eyes speaking his painful, awful confusion. Burleson returned his glare with a show of patient solicitude. Several of the others looked away in embarrassed discomfort. Pontalbas sustained the offer of sympathy, but now he felt offended by the man's gesture. The boiling up within him approached the level of speech and he formed words with enough force to rise above the pounding in his chest.

"What is this? Why is *he* here?" he pointed to Pontalbas angrily. "What are you people doing?" He already feared and suspected the answers, but a wounded decency demanded he speak the questions. Yet, he felt spent by just those few words and he lowered his head as he stroked at his temple in an effort to soothe its unrest. He felt slack as the numbness of defeat settled upon him.

"Please, Dr. Cantrelle, let's sit down so we can talk," Burleson urged gently.

Mute, he allowed himself to be led forth as the others cleared the way for him. They watched silently as Burleson guided him to the divan facing the fireplace. Cantrelle lowered himself into its receiving comfort as he furrowed his brow in an effort to master the rush of words and thoughts which now jockeyed for place to form some new scheme of comprehension. He leaned forward in his seat and reflexively, elbows on knees, folded his hands under his chin and stared at the low table in front of him. He needed a moment to catch up to where these people were, or at least to put himself within interrogative reach of their meaning; otherwise, he would never get beyond the paralysis of his dismay in any parley with them. And parley he must.

"Would you like something to drink, Dr. Cantrelle?" he heard Burleson offer. The sound of Burleson's voice distracted him enough to notice that the others were silently finding their seats around the table, pulling in additional chairs when necessary and placing themselves in a general semi-circle before him. He sat alone in the center of the middle divan. "I think we can provide you with your preference," he added gently.

The unintentional irony of the remark bristled and he couldn't help suspect Burleson of covert gloating, though he knew such could not be the case. It was just that he felt so wounded, so damaged, that any approach would be suspect.

"No, thank you, Dr. Burleson," he managed. His reply seemed to restore their channel and he felt a mounting sense of dread threaten return to join with his umbrage as he considered the prospect of proceeding with the ordeal ahead, as he knew it would be. He didn't want to see or hear anymore, but he knew it was too late not to. Also, it was time to pull himself together; there was no point in being more pathetic than he already was. Also, he was ready to resolve, no matter how high and mighty these people were, *they* invited him here and now *they* had some fucking explaining to do. He felt his strength returning, and he took a deep breath in welcome of it. He then turned to Pontalbas who was sitting patiently on the fringe of the group.

"How do you do, El Presidente Pontalbas?" he offered, with steely cordiality. No offer of a handshake was even suggested.

"I'm very pleased to meet you, Dr. Cantrelle," Pontalbas returned affably in an accent reminiscent of Castillian nobility.

He had become well acquainted with that accent back in the sixties when Cuban physicians, as part of the wave of political defection of that country's upper class, applied to his training program to be recycled, American style. Several remained for a while as members of his teaching staff, generally those who had been on the faculty of the medical school in Havana.

"Do you get to visit very often, Señor Presidente?" he inquired acidly.

"As often as my duties permit—and require, Dr. Cantrelle," Pontalbas parried with guileless noblesse spoiled slightly by the hint of an amused smile.

"Dr. Cantrelle," Burleson intervened, "since I cannot offer you any refreshment I suggest we get on with what I—rather, we—had hoped to talk to you about this evening."

"Yes, Dr. Burleson, our long-awaited chat," Cantrelle mocked. His fear was well on to becoming harnessed to the pugnacity he mounted whenever he felt liberties were being taken at his expense, and his high horse was already prancing impatiently in anticipation of a wild gallop.

"Yes, Dr. Cantrelle, our long-awaited chat, as I—we—hope you will come to see," Burleson returned gravely.

So now they were going to dare him to be reasonable, were they? Well, we would just have to see about that, he smirked to himself. He shot a cool glance at Pontalbas to echo his defiance.

"Dr. Cantrelle, we would have had our meeting, sooner or later, and probably in a setting very much as this, but not with the urgency current circumstances impose. I would want you to know such at the outset," Burleson urged. "So I, and the rest of the committee, regret that this first meeting with you will not be as purely collegial as we would prefer. Hence, we will of necessity be obliged to address matters of special importance to the committee and its purpose. In a word, we would have preferred, Dr. Cantrelle, that your introduction not be indented by business concerns. But, regrettably, that is the case. Moreover, I'm sorry you feel misled in coming here, but I think you'll see, I trust, that there was hardly any prudent way to prepare you for the work your presence here tonight warrants. Again, we would have preferred for you a less problematic introduction to the group, as is our usual procedure, but present circumstances declare otherwise."

Cantrelle listened critically as he spoke. So, he was to believe, he would have been invited to stop by anyway one of these fine days but problems had forced the issue and now had made his perhaps premature meeting with the committee less an academic surprise party and more a counseling session. He bridled at the implied condescension but, in favor of moving on, decided not to challenge Burleson's construction of the moment. Was this venerable, noble figure starting to become a bit tiresome?

"What circumstances?" Cantrelle leveled curtly.

"Your coming television appearance, Dr. Cantrelle," Burleson replied.

Cantrelle noticed that the others looked at him as one in fixed expectation. There wasn't a hint of movement. Therefore, it seemed, these people had discussed this point thoroughly, and, whatever Burleson was leading up to, it was obviously of unanimous concern to all present. And what indeed was Burleson leading up to anyway, he puzzled? Had he, credulous Frank Cantrelle, already disqualified himself from the stately ranks of the academic chosen—namely, the exalting recognition granted by this August committee—by agreeing to appear on Jerry Rosten's scandal cavalcade? Maybe. But then why was Pontalbas here, who was something of a scandal in his own right, and of international proportions to boot? He figured he would have to plead ignorance to learn more about the case these people were making for bringing him here, and, of all god-damned things, presuming to set him straight about certain matters so very important to *them*.

"And what's your concern about that, Dr. Burleson?" Cantrelle challenged as he assumed a more erect posture. This was no time to slouch; he would be at least as erect as the others who waited, as did he, for Burleson's answer.

"Our concern, Dr. Cantrelle, is that your appearance on television—Friday after next, I understand—might, if mismanaged, initiate a series of events that could significantly complicate certain undertakings for which this committee bears responsibility," Burleson advised.

The thought that his appearance on TV was scooping some announcement they had planned to make about Blush flashed to mind. That was probably it! And probably that was the reason for Pontalbas' presence. They were likely planning their own special exposé, and now he, Frank Cantrelle, comes along in his irate innocence and threatens to squirrel up their fully accredited, comprehensively international white paper on the true story behind Blush. Wouldn't that be a kick in the ass! Little Frank Cantrelle jumping the expository gun before they had a chance to conscript him into the ranks of the more collaboratively disciplined? They should have invited Jerry Rosten here tonight, too, Cantrelle chortled inwardly with malicious glee at feeling himself restored to advantage. But how did Burleson know the program was next week? Had Rosten put the announcement out earlier today? The announcement was scheduled for later this evening, supposedly. Also, these people must have gotten on it right away, once they heard it. Maybe they were working on the format of their own planned announcement when they got word today of the program next week. That must have caused no small eruption of pandemonium. It would explain the hurried call from Burleson and this equally hurried meeting tonight. He felt his posture relax as he settled more comfortably in his seat. He also felt a tug of sympathy for these people's position. Maybe he had over-reacted earlier, and maybe he owed Pontalbas an apology. A gentler glance in his direction implied as much.

"Dr. Burleson, I can assure you the TV presentation will not be mismanaged, as you say. The producer is going to some pains to make the program a serious and mature discussion of the Blush problem. True, that will require a significant departure from the show's usual style, but that's what's intended. The program will reach a lot of people, we expect, and it's going to open quite a few eyes about Blush and the machinery we suspect is behind it," Cantrelle assured.

"That's exactly our concern, Dr. Cantrelle," Weinroth interjected. "You see, Dr. Cantrelle, while it *is* in our interests that the public know a great deal about the effect of alpha amino iminodibenzyl encephalase, or 'Blush,' as everybody seems to call it, it is presently not at all in our interests to have attention directed to its origins, correct or otherwise. We don't feel the time is yet suitable."

Cantrelle was taken aback by the implication that the committee—if Weinroth's opinion were indeed representative—saw itself as arbiter as what the public should know about Blush and when. Were they simply being protective of their own planned announcement? And for their own benefit, he puzzled in mounting dismay? How could they presume so?

"Dr. Weinroth, who's to say when the time is suitable to reveal to the public the pedigree of a killer that's already claimed over eighty thousand of its members as victims?" Cantrelle retorted testily. "Delay gets translated into additional deaths, I'm sure you're aware."

"Quite so, Dr. Cantrelle, quite so," Weinroth concurred as he dropped his gaze with a sigh of frustration.

"Dr. Cantrelle," Markman inserted quickly, "this involves far more than numbers. It goes infinitely beyond the individuals Blush may afflict. We're talking about purpose and policy that cannot be measured or judged by selected pluses and minuses, such as the rise and fall of gruesome body counts, something we perhaps heeded too narrowly as a warring nation not too very long ago, I'm sure you remember."

"Well, Dr. Markman," Cantrelle snapped impatiently, "I'm not sure I see the benefit of minimizing death. To most people it *is* rather ultimate, and multiplying it eighty thousand times makes it worthy of notice even to the general public, I suspect. And what's even more worthy of notice, Dr. Markman, is who's behind it all. This TV program will not be gongs and bells sensationalism. This program will raise some serious questions as to why Blush is going unchecked. If the program happens to clash with some report or other that you and this committee had scheduled for release at some future time I can only say that what we're doing is in no way intended to be impedimental or pre-emptive. I would suggest that you look upon our efforts as being more humanitarian than that and see our contribution as something helpfully additional to what you intend." He was beginning to enjoy taking them to task for their arrogance.

"We understand all that, Dr. Cantrelle," Foster entered with an avuncular nod of his head. "The problem, as we see it, is that you don't understand sufficiently the implications of your intended action."

His first impulse was to tell him to go fuck himself, but he savored the cool advantage he presently felt and so allowed his anger to soften into sarcasm.

"And I'm sure you stand available, Dr. Foster, to apprise me of such," he hissed.

“As a matter of fact, Dr. Cantrelle, we all do,” he returned evenly.

“Dr. Cantrelle,” Burleson interceded, “we didn’t ask you here tonight to have a confrontation, so I suggest we not lose ourselves in competitive debate. Your time, our time, and the problem at hand cannot afford such a luxury. Our purpose in meeting with you . . . .”

“Yes, Dr. Burleson,” Cantrelle interrupted, “just what *is* your purpose in meeting with me? I’m having a little trouble figuring it out.” He directed a glare at Pontalbas in emphasis of his point.

“Dr. Cantrelle, you have every right to feel deceived and offended, as I said and as we all agree, but let’s not forget that our joint concerns would be so much better served by not making too large an effort in celebrating our sensitivities, wouldn’t you agree?” Burleson registered.

The remark stung him to the quick. He *had* been grandstanding it a bit, and now he was being called on it. He felt his advantage slipping.

“I agree, Dr. Burleson,” he submitted, “but let’s not mistake the messenger for the message. I think I deserve an explanation no matter how I request it,” he retaliated quickly.

“And you shall have one, Dr. Cantrelle,” Burleson sighed. He then scanned the members of the committee as though to pool opinion that a certain moment had arrived. Satisfied with the consensus, he returned to Cantrelle. “Doctor, we invited you here tonight to request that you re-consider your television appearance.”

“I’ve already concluded as much, Dr. Burleson. My question is why you, your committee, and your other guest would want me to do that, and on what basis,” Cantrelle snapped impatiently.

Burleson thought for a moment before answering.

“Because, Dr. Cantrelle—and please hear me carefully—alpha amino iminodibenzyl encephalase, or Blush, is solely our project,” Burleson stated in a tone of simple finality.

“It’s everybody’s project, Dr. Burleson,” Cantrelle corrected. “Just because you’ve scheduled some splendid announcement about Blush doesn’t mean you have a patent on it.”

“But that’s just it, Dr. Cantrelle. We *do* have a patent on it,” Burleson advised.

Cantrelle looked at him across the chasm of silence that followed. He then looked at the other members, and also at

Pontalbas. No one stirred. A tremor in his hands told him he was scared. He tightened his fists to control it.

"How do you mean that?" he urged in a near whisper of alarm.

"I'm afraid in its most concrete way, Dr. Cantrelle. We invented Blush—synthesized it, actually—and we are responsible for its distribution," Burleson explained. "That's the *only* announcement *we* have in mind; only for tonight, and only for you."

He didn't bother to look at the others. He knew it was true. He slowly hunched forward in his seat and began to rub his chin on the thumbs of his clenched hands as he stared vacantly at the table. After a moment he permitted his comprehension to resume its earlier track. He now saw that his initial suspicion—and fear—was correct, though he had rejected it then as too insane. His snap conclusion upon being introduced to Pontalbas was right—these people were somehow in cahoots—but he could not permit himself to see it then. *Now* there was no escape; all reasonable channels of flight had been tried, and had failed. His head throbbed with the rush of stark, blunt awareness, and he instinctively yearned for the peace of some dark corner. Despairing of that, he looked up at Burleson.

"But why?" he pleaded.

"That's what we hope to explain to you, Dr. Cantrelle; and it's what we hope you can understand," Burleson replied. "That's what the committee discussed earlier tonight before I called you. The vote was unanimous that I do so in hope that we might meet with you and make the better effort to sort this matter out."

Sort this matter out? He held no sympathy for so precious an understatement but he felt too enfeebled to be offended by it. The weariness now at work in him declared there were no battles left to fight. Now, he could only ask.

"Gentlemen, forgive me for being upset," he began carefully as he stared at the table and over a deep breath to steady himself, "but I need a couple of minutes to work my way up to what you're telling me. You see, it's as much a matter of being confirmed in my worst fears—the fears I initially recognized upon being introduced to President Pontalbas—as it is now having to hear something I suspect I'll never accept, no matter how thorough this so-called understanding." He paused for a moment and then turned to Burleson who, along with the others, waited silently. "Dr. Burleson," he continued, "you say 'sort this matter out.' I think I grasp the sensible and polite intent of your phrase, but I keep thinking of 'this matter' as being something in the order of eighty thousand deaths. Eighty thousand!" he emphasized.

"It's considerably more than that, Dr. Cantrelle. It's two hundred ninety million people in this country alone, plus the millions in President Pontalbas' country," Burleson extended grimly.

Not understanding what Burleson meant made his distress seem all the more futile. He just wanted to get away from them, as they, too, probably wanted to get away from him in their mounting futility at trying to make him 'understand' something he couldn't and wouldn't.

"Dr. Burleson, we might even go one better than that," he sneered, "if you and these others here actually are the pushers of Blush, then I'd say that this is an issue for the whole god-damned world."

"Actually, it is," Burleson agreed out of hand, "but we have ruled that our application be limited to just our local, national interests, and to the interests of President Pontalbas' country. There is good reason for that."

These people were unbelievable, he blinked to himself. He had always lived in secret terror of being in an actual situation that far exceeded his scope and comprehension and which yet remorselessly called upon him to perform some critical act or function, hence his recurring "examination dreams" and thus ever his cautious approach to opportunity. But this moment, this very real occurrence with these incredibly unreal people, exceeded anything he had ever conjured in his signature nightmare. At least that was something he could always wake up from when the time came. Right now he was hoping that what was happening to him was just that, only a dream; and if it wasn't, then something he could escape from by just closing his eyes and keeping them shut. And how often had he abjured just that in students, colleagues, officials, or anybody else who happened to fall afoul his preachment that there was no such thing as useless knowledge, no matter how burdensome. Now he wasn't so sure.

"Dr. Cantrelle," Alberti began in the mellifluous tone for which he'd become universally known, "I find myself wrestling with disappointment as I sit here and behold my colleagues' efforts to inform you of certain matters any knowledgeable person would regard as being of vast importance, efforts you curtly turn away as unacceptable. Dr. Burleson earlier this evening had assured us that your work identified and endorsed you as the kind of person who placed learning well above convenience, personal or political, and one who could be counted on to hear the meaning of what was being said, not just the sound. I'm sure we're all wondering at this point if Dr. Burleson has made a grave mistake."

He wondered if Alberti were actually reading his mind—he was almost ready to expect anything at this point—but what the man said was true and so fitting. He now felt himself being disarmed even of his outrage as he looked into Alberti's expectant eyes. Bluster, categorical rejection, contempt—all precious stratagems of the weak and foolish—were clattering to the floor at his feet. He then looked at each member of the group in turn, now doing so in gentler survey of what was before him.

"Mr. Alberti, you're right," he began quietly. "If Dr. Burleson has made a mistake, then I, too, have made a larger mistake about myself. It's true I've been overworking moral outrage and expecting you to abide it as though you owed it to me, and I guess I should feel more ashamed about it than I do. Maybe in time I will be, but for the moment I'm just too damned appalled by what Dr. Burleson has said to me about what you and this committee claim responsibility for. For example, I said eighty thousand people, didn't I? Well, the only real meaning that number has for me comes of the few dozens of patients I've had personal contact with at Moreland, some of whom I remember quite vividly, and now each one dead. But do you know what other meaning it has to me? It means Clay Moyer and his dying—being killed, in fact. As I listened to what was being said I wondered right along with my streaking outrage whether you people, if you're telling me the truth about this, had anything to do with Clay Moyer's death. Anyone who would consign eighty thousand persons to their Maker wouldn't flinch at removing one more, especially one who was pushing hard and quite threateningly at some closed doors, just as I'm doing. So I wonder if this committee which has graciously extended me an invitation for an evening of scholarly discourse is also the committee that killed my best friend . . . ."

"Mr. Moyer's death was not of our ruling," Horlick injected firmly.

Cantrelle raised his hand to stay any additional remonstrance.

". . . and could decide to remove me as well if I were as intractable," he continued, "though the difficulty posed by two accidents, back to back, striking down co-authors on a controversial subject might prove vexing if the public is to regard the occurrence as just one of those unfortunate coincidences. Better to bring the second one in and talk to him. That's what accompanied my outrage, Mr. Alberti. Unreasonable?"

"Not at all, Dr. Cantrelle, if, indeed, we had assassinated Mr. Moyer," Malloy interceded. "You're quite right that it would certainly be, as you say, problematic to remove you in a similar fashion. But don't you think that if we really wanted to dispatch you from the scene we'd be able to find a way that wouldn't smack of felonious repetition. Please, give us credit for having some ingenuity."

His comment forced a few chuckles and Cantrelle was tempted to add a snicker of his own to the general acknowledgment. After all, these men were renowned as being among the most ingenious on earth.

"Of course, Dr. Malloy, and maybe because I do we haven't yet seen the end of this," Cantrelle suggested instead.

This time only Malloy chuckled; the others held their silence.

"Dr. Cantrelle, we didn't ask you here tonight to give you one last chance to save your life, as you seem to believe," Burleson announced directly. "You were asked here tonight in the hope that you would help us in our efforts to save a lot more."

"Please listen to what this committee wants to tell you, Dr. Cantrelle. I beg you," Pontalbas beseeched.

He seemed really to mean it. Pontalbas was actually pleading with him. The anguish in his plea was stark enough, he noted with some surprise. Apparently, this was no corrupt, sleazy, Latin American generalissimo. This man had compassion, he was sure. Yet, he was obviously party to the murder of thousands. What the hell was going on? He looked at Pontalbas who waited rapt, his eyes full of entreaty. There had to be some explanation for all this. Some damned good explanation. He then looked at the others. They shared Pontalbas' plea, but with a lesser show of passion. He then returned his stare to the table for a moment to settle something in himself. That done he looked up at them.

"All right, gentlemen, we'll do it your way," he agreed almost obligingly.

"Thank you, Dr. Cantrelle," Burleson returned with a hint of relief. Pontalbas and the others audibly relaxed as they settled more comfortably in their seats. Item number one of the evening's agenda seemed to be settled, finally. "Firstly, Dr. Cantrelle, it is important that you be aware of certain facts we consider basic to your understanding of our purpose and our work," he continued.

Cantrelle withheld a flip retort as he adjusted himself in his seat.

"Few people—very few people—know of this committee as such," Burleson began. "Many people know us as the Committee for Advanced Studies, an advisory group to the academic, the social, the industrial, and the governmental sectors of our society. You might include the religious sector as well since that sector isn't beyond generating problems of its own," he nodded to Horlick. "But such is generally the lesser, more public part of our function, and our preferred way of being regarded by the populace. Our actual purpose is something else and requires of us the anonymity which you experienced as deceitful misrepresentation in asking you here tonight," he continued in explanation. "Our primary purpose, Dr. Cantrelle, is to address those critically important issues and problems which exceed the scope of those four, occasionally five, basic sectors of society either because the issue or problem is of such a complexity as to confound the best efforts of a particular sector's approach, or, as is more usually the case, because the sector is conceived and constructed in such a way as to cast some of its own issues or problems beyond its own corrective reach."

Cantrelle knitted his brow in search of an example. The idea seemed agreeable enough but he had trouble imagining consulting work on the scale Burleson was suggesting. And in any event, what the hell did that have to do with drug pushing? His impatience was gathering anew.

"Please bear with me, Dr. Cantrelle," Burleson urged, sensing Cantrelle's returning disquiet. "When a problem or issue achieves dimension enough for it to come before this committee, we convene, as we are doing this evening, and dissect it into its component parts. We then agree, if we can, upon some corrective measure and proceed to implement it. Or at least propose it."

Nothing new or special to that. Everybody did that all day long, Cantrelle disprized. It was how this justified killing thousands of people, he wanted to know. His faint sigh of strained tedium said as much for him.

"When I say sector, I don't mean some particular, discretely located or defined undertaking by a given few; I mean the overall, the essential—not the denominate—of that particular sector," Burleson detailed.

Cantrelle wasn't sure what that meant, his perplexity all too evident.

"To say it another way," Burleson offered, "we're constituted to address form, not content; not particulars. Content is of importance to us only to the extent that it elaborates the character of the form."

The more customary, scholarly Burleson was beginning to reappear. Moreover, Cantrelle felt more than casually familiar with what was being offered inasmuch as he had belabored generations of residents with the same exhortations—remember the questions, not necessarily today's answers, he'd bellowed—and his efforts had long taken on more the ring of the pulpit as he demonstrated the clinical relevance of the form and its denominative impact on that living and breathing particular called the patient. He was beginning to feel more in his element as Burleson proceeded.

"Our task, Dr. Cantrelle, then becomes a matter of facilitating certain corrective adjustments in the form, or if such is not possible, then to go beyond the accepted form and make other adjustments as necessary," Burleson summed.

Nothing particularly new here either, Cantrelle mused. Certainly the parade of psychiatric diagnostic classifications would amply prove the point. It seemed that every five or ten years there was a new diagnostic manual offered to lead the way to the nosologic Promised Land, and in short order each missive would be shown to be another false prophet. It was an open secret in the field that psychiatric nomenclature was often little more than a reiterant frolic of synonyms at best and a busy rearrangement of the deck chairs at worst. But no one seemed to be able to do anything about it except to stay within the same system with the same elements and seek the Holy Grail of an ultimate and perfect classification. So Burleson's point was well taken, though hardly momentous, he observed wanly. And besides, he was weary of being reminded of the name-calling that went on in his field.

"Dr. Burleson, what you're saying is fairly evident fare, so I'm sure you see a larger reference than I do. In fact, its reference to drug running and Blush deaths still escapes me," Cantrelle suggested tartly.

"I hope to bring the points together, Dr. Cantrelle," Burleson replied undaunted, "and you must forgive me if I underestimate your learning, but since this meeting with you is as new to us as it is to you, we may at times fall into a regrettable redundancy until we are surer of our bearings."

"I suppose so, Dr. Burleson," Cantrelle sighed, "but I think it would help me to get a better sense of it if you could mention who appoints you all to this committee and whom you answer to." He felt he was being slyly incisive by broaching that point. Identifying one's respondents and referents was his usual shortcut for stripping distortion from substance and putting things in their proper frame. Follow the money, they say.

"The committee appoints us individually, and we are therefore responsible to the committee as a whole. The committee is responsible only to itself but recognizes its essential duty to serve the common good," Burleson explained.

Cantrelle cocked his head to the side as though to correct what he had probably misheard.

"You mean to say that you all appoint each other . . . ." he began.

"Recognize each other would be more accurate, Dr. Cantrelle," Markman offered.

". . . recognize each other," Cantrelle amended with a show of annoyance at Markman's unexpected entry. "And so you're responsible only to each other?"

"Responsible to the committee, Dr. Cantrelle," Markman corrected. "The committee constitutes an entity neither of us separately can subtend."

"Okay," Cantrelle conceded in pique, "say it your way, but as I hear it, each of you is responsible only to the committee and the committee is responsible to no one else." He ended his accounting on a note of strained credulity.

"In an administrative sense, that is so," Burleson confirmed.

Cantrelle looked sharply left and right before speaking. He almost licked his lips in anticipation of the deductive coup he felt now ready to levy on these self-appointed overseers.

"If you and your committee are so autonomous, where do you get your resources to do what you say you do, like synthesizing drugs and then conveying those drugs to the victims you intend? That takes a lot of paper clips, gentlemen," he pronounced.

"That's quite true, Dr. Cantrelle," Burleson agreed. "Please accept our word that this committee has at its disposal all the resources it needs to perform its function."

"Well, then, you must get it from the NSA, or the State Department; and if you do, *they* call the tune. You don't make your own resources, I'm sure," Cantrelle construed.

"Dr. Cantrelle, I assure you that's not the way it is," Burleson demurred.

"Well, then, how about the CIA, or one of those other closet groups on Capitol Hill?" Cantrelle persisted.

Burleson shook his lowered head, not so much in denial as in lament. He then faced Cantrelle and advised.

"Trying to put the responsibility and the authority on any one agency or branch of the government is missing the point, Dr. Cantrelle, much like trying to find out which color is responsible for the rainbow. No color is; light itself is responsible, inasmuch as it is the source and is itself seen only by what it illuminates. Please forgive the quaint allusion, but it is distinctly apt in conveying the more correct sense of it," Burleson tendered.

He resented being talked to like a schoolboy. Straining his credulity was one thing; patronizing him was another. If they couldn't reveal the source of their authority, then they could say so and not stretch it out to imply that the matter was as ineffable as it was undisclosable.

"Well, let me try something just as quaint, Dr. Burleson," he tested. "Since this committee's doings carry the national imprimatur in some way hard to put into words, does the President of the United States know about you? Better yet, does he have any say so in what you claim you do?" As soon as he said it he knew he had violated some convention of accommodation. Moreover, he sensed that merely broaching the point posed an insuperable complexity. The hesitance in the air mounted as he waited.

"Dr. Cantrelle," Foster finally ventured, "I think perhaps you ask more of us than we can address. Your question is a most telling one, of course, and points perhaps as much to your incisiveness as it does to our scruples. The best we can say to you, Dr. Cantrelle, is that the President knows and he doesn't know. Or should I say that we're fairly certain that he's reasonably aware of what he would best not dwell on? More than that we cannot tell you."

"Well," Cantrelle persisted, "does he have veto power over you? Certainly he could step in and dissolve this committee, couldn't he?"

"We have never, ever known that to be the case," Burleson affirmed.

Cantrelle turned over the reply a few times in his mind and decided it was probably as much as he would be able to get from them on this critical point. Also, as he considered the question, his thoughts automatically arrayed these seven men, giants of their respective worlds, against what the nation's Presidency had more recently become, and the comparison left the Oval Office roundly burlesque. He instinctively objected to the crass mismatch for he loyally insisted upon seeing the Presidency as the nation's executive function consummate, though, admittedly, it was no easy task just now to credit such veneration what with some incumbent that might be little more than an oily panderer out for the cheers of millions even if the national electorate had to be seduced into the mold of adolescent revolt against continence and decency. But it was unfair to the archetype to equate the office with such gaucherie. Or was it, really? Who could say these days?

"I gather, then, Dr. Burleson, that no President has opposed any recommendation this committee has made. Right?" Cantrelle pressed.

"We call them 'rulings,' not 'recommendations,' to be more precise. No, Dr. Cantrelle; no President has ever opposed us or what we direct," he avouched. "To do so would not be in keeping with the discretion of his office."

Now he was really confused—and annoyed—and he intended to show it.

"You mean to tell me—as I hear you—that it would not be appropriate for the President of the United States of America to concern himself with what you do to this country?" he charged.

"Not on this point, Dr. Cantrelle," Burleson replied. "But again, to be more precise, he is obliged only to concern himself with the *consequences* of what we do—after all, his office requires that he assist the legislature and the judiciary in performing their functions for meeting the people's needs—but it is not his place to question our rulings."

He couldn't fathom it. Not the President's place to question their 'rulings'? What had happened? If these people were telling the truth, and they sure as hell seemed to believe in the truth of what they were saying, he had been living in an alter world, maybe even a virtual world, without realizing it. An ultimate fool's paradise if ever there was one and assuredly if his present dismay were any measure of it.

"Dr. Burleson," he mustered, "how long have you and your committee been doing this, giving 'rulings,' as you say?"

Burleson polled the committee with a canvassing glance.

"I guess you could say we've always stood available, either ourselves or our predecessors, but it's only more recently that our work has become more interventional," he assessed as he solicited the others who nodded in concurrence.

It seemed that no matter what or how much they admitted or explained, he came up with more questions than answers, and those questions kept crowding in on his mind, each clamoring for priority and satisfaction like a mob of frantic brokers each shouting to register first bid on the transaction board. He labored at bringing order to the tumult in his head, biting his lip in focus of the effort. After a moment he looked again at Burleson.

"Well, then, Dr. Burleson, it seems to me that if this committee does what you say it does, the Presidency is merely a proprietary position, and you can't mean that, I'm sure," he directed as though to display the folly of the entire prospect. "The Presidency is constituted and mandated to be executive in its essence, but what you're describing is something a lot less, more like a plant manager with all of you being the board of directors."

"To say merely proprietary is to do injustice to the complexity of the President's work, Dr. Cantrelle," Burleson cautioned. "We are quite firm in acknowledging his ascendancy in almost all of the matters of daily government. But from time to time problems and issues arise which transcend the constituted capacity of his office, indeed the capacity of the entire governmental structure itself, and that's where we see our intervention. To see the President as merely proprietary like a plant manager is not consonant with our purpose, but I wonder if your doing so might betray more *your* regard for that office."

"Well, maybe," Cantrelle allowed through a guilty smirk, "but that's not the point," he insisted. But maybe it was. He had brayed it far and wide over the years that the Presidential electoral process had become so vile as to seem like an anachronism. In the age of technology, with man's reach verily at the approaches of the sublime and infinite, the mysteries of life and its universe thus nearly open to his vision, the American electoral process, supposedly substantive to that ennobling reach, still shaped itself along the lines of a vulgar, coarse, frontier side show with circus antics galore and plenty of hoopla for all, being as such every bit the scene of conventioneers whooping it up as they cheated on their spouses respectably back home tending to the very civic decency the convention purported to protect. And, most appalling, the candidate who wore such tinsel best was almost invariably the one who was elected Commander and Chief. Populism, the common touch, or whatever; apologists routinely proclaimed the brawling scene as basic, refreshing, and American democratic, though usually omitting mention that other democracies of the world, particularly the northern European democracies, managed such elections without needing to detour so widely from the seemly. This hoary gripe from his tedious repertoire took him directly to his frequent query as to why Europeans seemed to know at birth what it took Americans so long to learn, if they ever did. Lack of savvy and grace in the realpolitik loomed as a disquieting first in that inequity such that sometimes the embarrassingly narrow gauge of an American President in comparison to the seasoned breadth of a foreign counterparts, particularly European ones, was accepted out of hand as the major source of anxiety felt round the world when America broke out the horns and whistles of its presidential electoral process. But who could gainsay *whatever* the very rich country cousin did? No doubt about it, while America was the most idealistic, the most forgiving, the most generous of nations, it was also the most simplistic and immature world ruler history had ever known. And those superlatives, in an international forum cynical beyond the palliatives of mere goodwill, could predictably cast long shadows when the world's challenges needed substantially more than a pious display of human compassion. Then, at such times, America was to be the Arsenal of Democracy. And just now there was no one left powerful enough to argue the point. What was it Stalin supposedly had said when asked what the Pope might think in response to a planned Soviet usurpation: how many divisions did the Pope have? It was still the same thing, approximately, though the prevailing agonist of today wore a white Stetson and whistled Country Western. Despite the treachery this notion did to his earlier righteous indignation with the committee, he was now enroute to donating a few of his own paragraphs to its mandate vis-a-vis the government's recurrent need for a helping hand. Within this rush of thoughts he heard Burleson call his name.

"Dr. Cantrelle . . . I fear we have confused you. I hadn't intended my comment regarding your personal feelings about the Presidency to distract you from our understanding. I had hoped for very much the contrary," Burleson explained.

"Not at all, Dr. Burleson," Cantrelle assured. "Excuse me for getting distracted; just a few thoughts of my own." He decided to keep them to himself. They were intemperate, narrow, and gaudy—just like the system they assailed. He began to wonder, sitting before these people, if there was anything he could say that wasn't just as indicting of himself as it was intended to be of any issue raised. As much as he might try to see himself otherwise and as much as he credited himself the impassioned critic of his societal surround, he still had the dark and troubling awareness of his being just as party to that very surround as those openly in cahoots with it, himself contributing pre-determined particulars right along with the others, though perhaps more in the obverse, yielding nevertheless an overall effect which sustained a fairly well equilibrated phenomenon called the human predicament, American style. Sitting before these people was sharpening his awareness of such, though they seemed not specifically to be urging it. The curiosity as to what Clay would think about all this snapped into mind. He suspected that Clay would be more fascinated than perplexed. Where the hell was that son-of-a-bitch when you really needed him? If Clay were here with his pain-in-the-ass questions, this meeting probably would be taking a very different turn, and these people probably wouldn't be so much at peace with being so high and mighty. It was becoming just too clear the advantages Clay's death offered this committee, and it was also becoming harder to resist the conviction that these people had arranged the 'accident.' He would keep that thought to himself as well, but he decided to work the point by asking the kinds of questions he imagined Clay might ask, were he on hand. That way, these fucking murderers wouldn't be so exempt of their crime. He liked the idea. His faltering umbrage straightened up.

"Well, Dr. Burleson," he resumed, "if you and this committee see yourselves above constituted authority and accountability, as you apparently do, how is it determined when to intervene, as you say, and what form that intervention should take? Do you all just take it upon yourselves to pass such judgments, Olympus-like?" He wondered if he was being too flip.

"Not at all, Dr. Cantrelle," Burleson replied. "Society tells us when to convene and what to review."

Cantrelle gestured with his hands to the effect that he was amenable to hearing more on the point.

"Dr. Cantrelle," Foster spoke up, "society—this society, yours and ours—tells us when it's in distress, the signals being the usual ones of crime, corruption, decay of public services, mounting social unrest, and the like. We then gather and explore the signal in some depth to decide whether the problem is suitably our concern or not."

"And what determines that, Dr. Foster?" Cantrelle returned.

"Our estimate as to whether this society has within itself the capacity to solve on its own the problem it has generated and which is yielding that particular distress signal," Foster explained.

"So you all decide whether and when society is or is not capable of taking care of itself, right?" Cantrelle seized.

"In effect, yes," Foster submitted.

Cantrelle surveyed the group fronting him, allowing his half playful, half derisive smile to fall equally upon each member.

"You all genuinely consider yourselves capable of deciding what is and what isn't good for the people of this nation? Is that so?" Cantrelle forced with restrained incredulity.

"In its simplest, yes, Dr. Cantrelle," Foster stated evenly.

"And you believe this because you're Nobel laureates, teachers, artists, and whatever else?" Cantrelle bristled.

"If not us, then who else, Dr. Cantrelle?" Markman posed.

"Why *anybody*?" Cantrelle lashed back. "Why can't the people decide what's best for themselves, and let it go at that, like our Constitution—our *legal* instrument of government—says? Or have you all decided—forgive me—made a *ruling* to supersede the Constitution?" he railed, though in doing so he detected a faintly hollow ring in his own words. How many times had he wondered if the Constitution itself had not been part and parcel kin to the very anachronism he saw played out in the electoral process, and hence an anachronism itself. In fact, the most fundamental one. Had the Constitution long passed the point of parliamentary relevance and was now well along the road to iconic reverence, like holy writ which no longer saw clear or even sensible application to the realities of the present-day world but which certainly could not be disobeyed, much less repealed. It would be like repealing The Ten Commandments! The very idea!

"Because the people and their government can only do what they permit of their understanding, Dr. Cantrelle, that's why," Horlick interjected.

The words cut through him like daggers. They were the same words he had offered time and time again to his patients caught up in self-defeating, self-destructive patterns which heaped ruin upon their owner's potential as productive, successful citizens seemingly too intelligent to be guilty of their own undoing, though they were. The comment seemed even more penetrating for having come from Horlick, a theologian, whose genre was traditionally more inclined to assist people in accepting their grievous lot. This theologian on this committee was apparently something else, though. And what was he himself, the psychiatrist, to say in response to this man's telling words? Horlick's pronouncement carried too much weight in his own and in every other psychiatrist's clinical experience for the point to be quibbled.

"I'm surprised to hear that come from you, Dr. Horlick," Cantrelle observed mildly and at the risk of sounding irrelevant. "I would have expected something more consoling."

Horlick smiled gently at the oblique concession—praise by faint damn.

"I understand, Dr. Cantrelle, but allow me to mention something I'm sure you already understand. The practice of religion is nowhere near the all of religion, any more than the American practice of democracy is the all of democracy. I hope that doesn't sound too pat," Horlick soothed.

"Not at all, Dr. Horlick," Cantrelle returned cordially. He liked Horlick; he was obviously a man whose personal depth ennobled his faith beyond the petty fervor of sectarianism. "I guess I could add that the practice of Psychiatry is nowhere near the all of Psychiatry, my practice in particular, but that wouldn't come as a revelation to anyone, I fear," Cantrelle snipped, "nor would it help anyone to understand why I do what I do. That would require more, I think, *if* it were important to me that others understand," he added as he looked toward the others. He knew he was being bitchy, but at this point, what difference did it make? Any alternative seemed to smack of submission, and unlike some of his lovely female patients, he wasn't quite ready to be overwhelmed. No way.

"I think you're aware that it *is* important to us that you understand, Dr. Cantrelle," Malloy replied to the accompaniment of his indefatigable twinkle. "I think you're also aware that we're extending ourselves to have that understanding occur," he added hopefully, "though it seems you're more inclined to dispute whatever it is we offer in explanation. Perhaps were you a bit less captious, the understanding would arrive more readily." He concluded with an impish tilt of the head and eyebrows raised in anticipation.

The man was right, he conceded, abashed. It was true that if he would stop trying to deny everything he was hearing he would have a hell of a lot less trouble getting up to speed in dealing with these people. But did he really want to deal with these people in the first place? Not really. He just wanted to get away; get away from these sweetly patronizing, self-appointed guardians of their lesser brethren; away from their lofty, practiced apologetics. And, just as much, he wanted to get away from any discourse that might credit their entitlement to see themselves as they did. But being coy and prissy about it was not the most edifying way to go, either. They really were being patient and tolerant, so much so that he wondered if they'd done this before to acquire the ease they seemed to display. Pontalbas? The name leaped to the front of his mind. Of course! They probably had gone through the same "explanation" with him at some former time. And probably with others, too. That's why Pontalbas looked so sympathetic; he'd gone through this himself and so he really did understand. Suddenly he felt existentially kindred to this man who sat patiently among the others, his dark eyes now seeming to encourage as well as to soothe. He sensed that Pontalbas, though he sat with them, was more like himself, struggling Frank Cantrelle, and more given to wrestling with the consequences of these 'rulings' than in any way author of them. Suddenly he was less alone. He glanced at Pontalbas to seal the achieved kinship. Emboldened, he invested in turn each of the others in a sweeping assize. And then, for the first time, he addressed them precisely as a group.

"Gentlemen, Dr. Malloy is right. I've not made it any easier for either of us this evening, but I suspect you know why, and some of you may be more appreciative of the point than others." He noted a smile of recognition sneak across Pontalbas' face. "I feel it's completely in order to thank you for your patience. But I think it's equally in order to assure you that the righteous indignation I've perhaps overstated and the frantic objections I've hurled at your ideas are very much exactly what you could expect from any citizen who is told that his life and his nation are being ruled by powers he never knew existed. In fact, compared to some others I might even be considered tractable." He liked talking to them this way, more the negotiable colleague than the overwhelmed ingenue. It also hinted at putting them on notice that he was recovering from his offended ignorance and was ready to talk business. He parenthetically recalled something he had said to a resident once in supervision of a case—a wealthy schizoid—that in a land of material plenty, ignorance was an affordable luxury. He knew then, but even more so tonight, that such was true only up to a point. Moreover, working up to their level and searching their wavelength suggested a reach for parity and, hence, smacked less of submission, or his fretful denial of it.

"I think we do understand your position, Dr. Cantrelle," Pontalbas replied in tones of welcome, "and I'm sure the gentlemen of this committee do not underestimate your basically rational and accessible nature. I, for one, do not think Dr. Burleson made a mistake, and I'm sure the members of the committee concur."

Cantrelle was touched more than he wished visible. He swallowed and lowered his head for a moment. It was a decent and ballsy thing for Pontalbas to say, deserved or not, and he realized that if this man could stand up and be counted before this committee on an outsider's account, then, in turn, he, Frank Cantrelle, must surely be in the right company, as far as Inigo Pontalbas went.

"Thank you, Mr. President," he managed.

Several of the others nodded their agreement as he restored himself to readiness.

"Yes, Dr. Cantrelle, we are no more arbitrary in our assessment of you than we are in arriving at a ruling," Alberti summed up, "and each carries a distinct mandate we as a committee cannot forego or relax."

He felt a bit puzzled by the remark, meant to be reassuring, though to him unsettling in equal degree. A mandate to assess his suitability. Suitability for what? To hear what they had to say? To be approached to throw the fight next week? He looked at the stylish, impeccably appointed Alberti and squinted in concentration.

"At this point, Mr. Alberti, I see my being here as evidence of this committee's interest in protecting its own function, that goal perhaps being foremost in its current thinking, for all I know," Cantrelle returned, unbowed.

"That's exactly the point, Dr. Cantrelle. Just as you said: for all you know," Alberti seconded. "The scope of your understanding is our vital concern. You see, Dr. Cantrelle, the people we invite here, as with you tonight, represent our tie to society, the respondent humanity to whom our rulings are gauged and directed. Without you and others like you, our rulings could not translate into the measures necessary for an effect. President Pontalbas, as I'm sure you're now aware, is such a participant," he explained.

How on earth did he know he was now aware of that, Cantrelle wondered? Must have read his face a few moments ago, he decided.

"We proceed," Alberti continued, "on the conviction that the better informed you are, the more skillful your application, and—a critical point—the more your application will be in consonance with the general good."

Who could argue that, he considered inwardly. But still the idea was a long way removed from Blush and eighty thousand deaths, he reminded himself.

"It's the general good as this committee sees it that gives me a problem, Mr. Alberti," Cantrelle insisted.

"As we knew it would, and as I'm sure other members stand available to discuss with you. But for my part, Dr. Cantrelle, I would prefer just now to suggest to you an auspicious way of regarding your relationship to this committee since we seem now to agree that your being only adversarial is not sufficient to our better purpose."

He liked the way Alberti phrased it. It even hinted at the melodious. And somewhere in the turn of phrase there was a wry smile. He felt it. And he felt ready for more.

"We, as a committee, can only make decisions," Alberti continued. "Actually, the decisions amount to little more than reaffirmation of basic precepts which adumbrate a needed application. Affirming the basics precepts is rather easy, in truth, but translating such into specific application, and particularly application intended to be creatively remedial, is truly the bulk of the task. We go as far as we can and then it's time for others to take over."

“Others like performing artists?” Cantrelle staked. He had locked in on Alberti’s metaphor: the creative artist, like this committee itself, wrote the score and thereafter stood in need of good performers to stage it for the public! He now felt encouraged to pursue the point.

“Very much so, Dr. Cantrelle. Allow me to commend you on your aptness,” Alberti granted over a broad smile. “Yes, performing artists,” he repeated as though to savor the clarification. “And I needn’t say how immensely important they are. They make all the difference, don’t they? The more they know about the composer and what he intended, the more everybody benefits, the general public in particular. Yes, Dr. Cantrelle, a very apt comparison.”

It wasn’t that good, but it apparently played right into Alberti’s tactic, he gathered.

“I hope it’s helpful,” Cantrelle blandished, “though I’ve got to say at the outset, Mr. Alberti, I’ve never been very good at singing a siren song, and that’s something you would best know about me right now.”

“Oh, but you are, Dr. Cantrelle, or so I’ve heard, and I fear you’re much too modest about it,” Alberti insisted. “People believe in you. They do reckon what you say, even though you may often be a bit unsure of your own footing.”

Christ, that was true, and it was a never-ending source of anguish that, withal, he might be misleading the people who gave their belief to his song: his residents, his staff, his friends—and, God forbid, even his own family. As always, the thought shook him, and now his verve retreated once again.

Alberti noted the shift.

“Yes, Dr. Cantrelle, having a certain talent for reaching people can be a daunting responsibility; that is, if one sees in it any duty to the people it reaches. We are all aware that many people thus talented manifestly see it as a personal advantage and exercise it that way, but we here see you as one of those who wears the talent with a civic reserve along with a regrettable uncertainty as to its proper place in your life.”

He felt the roil of panic licking at the edges of his mind. How could they know so much about him? Even his secret confusion, much less his secret fears! Where did these people come from?

"The artist, Dr. Cantrelle," Alberti counseled, "has the unenviable task of portraying his society's relationship to its reality. We think you share some responsibility in that task."

"Is that why you're on this committee?" Cantrelle countered in a drab effort to shift some of the burden.

"Of course. In fact, Dr. Cantrelle, I'm probably the member of this committee closest to the people in their roles as everyday individuals. I can say that because, of the three prodigies recognized as such, only music is so readily accessible to the average citizen. Almost like speech, the fourth and probably primary prodigy, though rarely counted as such. People can, and do, easily go about their business whistling Mozart; but few, for example, can lighten their daily chores by reciting Maxwell's equations. Plus, the artist must, of course, have some conception of the reality which molds the relationship he is to portray. My fellow committee members are most helpful in that regard."

He had never reckoned himself an artist, his complete devotion to music notwithstanding. His peculiar and, granted, recognized ability to touch the heartstrings of those around him when occasion required he attributed to his experience as a therapist, though in truth he had often wondered if actually it was the other way around, for even as a child he wrote quaint little stories for holiday occasions and occasionally still composed dreamy ballads with suitably poetic lyrics in celebration of those exquisite moments come of discovery of any new dimension in romance. He did sketch fairly well in his early years, mostly cartoon characters, but not with ease or grace. In short, his artistic efforts were commendable, but hardly good. And now this man was telling him he had weighty duties as an artist? It would be far more exacting to say, in keeping with what he knew to be the case, that he had duties enough, but little art to apply in their service, just like most other persons. So Alberti certainly had to mean it in a symbolic sense, this thing about the responsibilities of the artist, the artist that existed in *each* of us. And perhaps it was exactly on that account he now felt somehow closer to this man than to any other of the committee, even Burleson. Even Pontalbas. Maybe it was because he did whistle Mozart, as Alberti would suggest was the explanation, for it surely couldn't be based on a more personal familiarity with Alberti himself. Yet, he felt he could talk to Alberti more readily, more easily, despite the galaxy-size difference in their artistic skills. Maybe it was because the difference was all the more discernible and, hence, familiar in consequence of his daily submersion in music, a kind of diurnal baptism which kept that particular channel open for its traffic. And thus also open for people like Alberti whom he was used to hearing even from their great but uniquely transversable distance. It was just exactly such, he'd always felt, which was the duty of the artist: to take the rest of mankind on tours of existence, visits people would never be able to make on their own. Sort of like travel agents of the belvederean cosmos. And here was Alberti emphasizing that relationship and the responsibility that went along with it.

"I guess you're leading up to the TV program next week, aren't you, Mr. Alberti?" Cantrelle surmised reluctantly.

"As a very specific application of my thesis, yes, Dr. Cantrelle," Alberti agreed.

"But just what is it you want me to do? Cancel it? I can't do that!" Cantrelle directed to the full committee, palms upraised and fingers spread to inscribe the size of the problem. "You say responsibility. Well, there's a side to responsibility that includes a personal commitment to the television station which has gone to no small length to have the program aired. Indeed, very responsible behavior on the part of the producer himself . . . ."

"We're aware of that, Dr. Cantrelle," Alberti acknowledged readily.

". . . plus the general responsibility to inform the people that there's more to this Blush trade than mere monetary greed. Not to do so would be just too irresponsible, wouldn't you say? Or would you?"

The question brought forth a shaky silence. After a moment, Burleson spoke.

"That's exactly the point where our approaches—yours and this committee's—converge, Dr. Cantrelle," Burleson cited. "Our meeting tonight with you is for the purpose of tracing a resultant course to serve both of us from this moment forward, as I'm sure you've concluded by now."

"More or less," Cantrelle estimated. The way Burleson said it prompted the curious notion as to who was to bargain with whom. He had thus far considered them commandingly unnegotiable, and now he began to wonder if, after all, he did have a few cards to play. His spirits perked up a bit.

"As we said earlier, Dr. Cantrelle," Burleson continued, "our basic purpose tonight is to make you aware of certain considerations we feel you should have at your disposal in deciding what is your most serviceable, your most comprehensive, and your most responsible approach to the Blush matter in general and to the scheduled television program in particular. That's putting it simply, though we're no less mindful than you of the treachery that lurks in simple statements."

That admonition spoke his mind precisely, and he nodded gravely in assent.

"And it appears that to fulfill our purpose we need to unfold ourselves, as Francisco would say, to you even more so that you may see us as companions to your watch, rather than as some unholy spectre bent on evil," Burleson suggested as he surveyed his fellow members with a scanning glance.

"Exactly! So if you people are really behind Blush, as you say, then why are you doing it? Why are you killing all those people? I can't fathom it" Cantrelle exclaimed, glad to speak boldly in the comfort of being back on familiar grounds, thanks to Francisco. In his classes he had often likened the opening lines of Hamlet to the beginning of a typical analytic hour. "If you're not an unholy spectre, as you insist, what could be the good of wiping out thousands of innocent people? You've got to be coming from somewhere I've never been." As he hurled the words, a shudder of apprehension rose within him. It wasn't only that a dawning awareness deep within him now paled his words and gave them a dissimulate caste—he had been resisting for the past several minutes the advent of a vague realization as to where this entire discourse was going, hence giving oblique recognition to what he suspected, but could not accept, was coming—it was also the unexpected arrival of an overpowering surge of the verge. He really had never, ever, felt it quite this powerful before, and the shudder it brought gave credence to the fear that this time he was truly and precipitously on the verge of the uncanny. He shifted in his chair to adjust and align his shaky borders and gave an uncomfortable cough as he glanced at the room's ceiling.

"Are you all right, Dr. Cantrelle?" Burleson solicited.

"Oh, yes. Just a tickle in my throat," he lied.

"Would you like a glass of water?" Burleson offered.

"No. No thanks. I'm all right," he returned. He actually was beginning to feel somewhat better. Speaking out loud consistently worked to dispel that furtive, eerie, verge sensation, although always before he would endeavor to sustain it in hope of grasping it more fully. This was the first time he truly wished it gone.

"If you're all right perhaps we can proceed," Burleson suggested.

"I'm all right, Dr. Burleson," he assured. The verge sensation lingered on the borders of his awareness like a dull throb. Plus, his boldness was on the retreat once again, and a vigilant dread was back at its rampart in the careful company of Francisco, he reflected in a wan attempt at whimsy. Any sally into courage would not likely last very long, he observed in lament, what with some ominous feeling prowling the perimeter of his consciousness like a stalking predator.

"As I said earlier, Dr. Cantrelle," Burleson resumed, "we as a committee have been meeting periodically for some years now. Of late it has become necessary to expand our committee work in order to address the issues which come before us."

"But where do those issues come from?" Cantrelle persisted. "Does someone notify you of what's to be done, or considered? Who's responsible for bringing this committee to bear on any matter, much less Blush?" The questions tumbled out in search of familiar guideposts.

Burleson considered for a moment as he looked at Cantrelle's pained expression. He then leaned forward slightly as though to give his words more reach.

"Dr. Cantrelle, as was indicated earlier, our nation advises us as to our purpose and our tasks," he said. "All of the people of this country speak to us in the collective voice of national need, and that voice guides us in our work as guardian of this land's health."

"But, Dr. Burleson," he quickly retorted, "that's what our *government* is for." He couldn't resist the temptation to carp. "The people go to some trouble to elect presidents and legislators who, in turn, appoint a judiciary to see that the presidents and legislators do their work within the guidelines the people themselves supply and approve." But again he felt his words ring of dissimulation. He now had a pretty good idea of what Burleson meant, yet he could not simply allow that awareness to reach ascendancy in his mind without its first undergoing a purifying transduction through the sieve of proper Socratic arraignment.

"That's exactly the point, Dr. Cantrelle. Our legally constituted government does what it can on matters falling within its scope, and those matters which exceed its scope come before us. Indeed, that's why those matters come to us at all. And that's why we exist as a committee," Burleson enumerated simply.

At first he said nothing in reply but slowly lowered his head in acceptance of hearing what he knew could not avoid being said. Of course, as with earlier points, the thought was not entirely new to him. How many times had he railed against the government's bald and programmatic ineffectiveness on crucial issues at critical times? In fact, how many times had he applied a similar criticism to its handling of the Blush problem? However, on that particular point, he now knew his complaint to have been sorely inept and naive. Yet, in a larger sense the complaint still applied, though now in a higher octave. The government, at least in the case of Blush, was not just a sneaky miscreant draped in the slink of some covert agency; it now stood accused of being much worse. It now stood accused of being the craven and compliant beneficiary of a cruel levy. In effect, it stood accused of being no better or worse than any of its Blush-free citizens. The government itself was part of the problem. It was hard for him to see it any other way.

"I guess you have good reason for what you just said" Cantrelle sighed as he returned his gaze to Burleson. He felt so tired, spent; and he posed the query as much out of a sense of obligation to the moment as out of interest in what else Burleson had to say. As for the latter, he was already well on to imagining what was most likely to come, comparing it to notions he himself had held at one time or another but usually to the tune of some then current exasperation, not as standing policy. He sensed that what he was likely to hear just now would, indeed, carry the weight of policy—policy such as it was formed by this fearsome, uncanny committee.

"Dr. Cantrelle," Foster intervened, leaning forward, elbows on thighs and folding his hands together prayer-like between his knees, "there are certain basic points which must be considered for appreciating not only the purpose of this committee but also its necessity. We suspect that you probably share some, if not many, of the same notions we abide by. For example, I think you would agree with us that this country has been the most productive and overall most successful democracy the world has ever known. Blessed with a virgin continent of unrivaled richness and fertility, this nation has brought together in united purpose scions of all the peoples of this world and has done so on a scale of human accomplishment never before seen by man. So much so that America is unquestionably acknowledged as the protector of the rest of the world. America truly presides over the better hopes and dreams of all the other nations of this planet, singly and collectively. Every nation would wish to have America's material success; and every nation's security, even that of its adversaries, resides in this nation's commitment to fundamental decency and humanity—a decency and humanity which drives this nation's policies more totally than ever did its national might. Very few other nations of this world, if any at all, could be trusted with the capacity and potential this country knows. The people of America are fundamentally the people of this entire world, and if the citizens of this nation prove unable to forge in this blessed and anointed land a communal entity by which all other nations of the world may be measured, and guided, then clearly the world will have no hope of ever becoming one world. And that's unconscionable. So, as the rest of the world watches and hopes, we Americans go forth, blazing a completely new trail for collective and united humanity, displaying our successes along with our failures, sharing our victories while absorbing our defeats, seeking a wisdom in the confession of our ignorance, and praying apace that the discovered good of it all will someday become truly universal."

He felt a lump of patriotism form in his throat as he listened to Foster. It was so poignantly true. America really was the world's hope, and as often as he had heard it said by good and bad alike, as overworked and as abused as the phrase had become, and as ridiculed as the idea had been at different times by cynics, foreign as well as domestic, it was ineluctably true for the simple reason that no one—*no one*—could conceive of a modern world existing without an America in it somewhere. And somehow, tonight, listening to Foster, he knew it better than he ever did before.

"And it's just because of its success as a popular democracy that this nation is in grave danger," Weinroth added in a tone that eased the lump along.

"Just how do you mean that, Dr. Weinroth? From widespread drug abuse?" Cantrelle ventured. He knew that for Weinroth, or this committee, to pronounce a danger at hand carried a very specific reference, for these people were not likely to do so otherwise. They weren't like him, or like other ordinary Americans, given to shout that the national sky was falling whenever disquieted by something of a Federal nature. If these people said the sky was falling, one would best run for the nearest shelter.

"Drug abuse is only a small consequence of what we're concerned about, Dr. Cantrelle," he replied as he adjusted himself in his chair. "We're talking about the consequence of industrial, social, economic, and now technological success on a scale never before seen by man—and the grave danger such success brings. The question arises as to whether we've been too successful, given our mandate as a nation."

He heard distant bells ringing as Weinroth spoke and he surmised that the words were finding resonance within him somewhere, though yet too far beyond his conscious awareness to signal why. The feeling of being stalked by the verge was back again and its eeriness seemed to pace itself in rhythm with the cadence of an approaching, final recognition. The overall feeling was fast becoming much like that of a powerful dream on the verge of translating itself into wakeful reality.

"What we're talking about is something much more pervasive. Actually, something essential to our system, and hence potentially and perhaps inevitably destructive of it, Dr. Cantrelle," Weinroth continued.

"I'm having a little trouble," Cantrelle murmured through a grimace of stunted comprehension.

"Understandably, Dr. Cantrelle, because it's not an easy point to approach," consoled Weinroth. "Perhaps we can proceed this way," he offered. "Let's consider Australia. On that removed continent various forms of life flourish readily. By the standards of this hemisphere, strange forms of life indeed: kangaroos, wallabies, koala bears, duck-bill platypuses, and the like. Primal and essentially unchanged for eons. And delicate, too. Then how is it that they've managed to endure so long? Because there are no predators to speak of in their ecosystem. Koala bears and platypuses continue to thrive because there is little other than the accidents of the system, such as weather change and altered food supply, to keep them from thriving. If these creatures eventually undergo progressive specie failure, it will have to be because of some flaw inherent to their germ plasm, barring the impact of man on the ecosystem. However, introduce a few predators to the system and an entirely new definition of fitness is proclaimed, and in all likelihood those various life forms would quickly disappear, the newly defined unfit. So in a sense, Australia at this time continues to be an example of a very successful life-sustaining ecosystem, though somewhat untested by other standards. In a parallel sense, Dr. Cantrelle, America is a societal Australia. All kinds of lifestyles flourish here, lifestyles that could not possibly survive anywhere else or certainly would not endure even here if predators such as war or famine were introduced. There has never been a famine in this bountiful land, and, except for those recent acts of terror, war hasn't visited the homeland soil in almost a century and a half, and virtually only twice before that. But were such straits to occur, the aberrant, irrelevant, inappropriate lifestyles vulnerable to such predators would disappear rapidly. So from the standpoint of social coherence, what on the surface may sometimes seem to be chaotic, dissipated, and even downright bizarre approaches to life actually reflect the success of this nation as a social democracy that such lifestyles may exist at all. Perhaps the truest test of a democracy lies in how disparate it can permit its constituent elements to become, even to the point of dissolving the collective whole, and maybe even essentially to that exact point."

He had never regarded some of those weirdo cults in California as hallmarks of national success, but he understood clearly what Foster was saying, for in minor ways he'd had to concern himself annually with just such an issue in the selection and the evaluation process essential to his training program, not to mention the biases of HHS, the Justice Department, and the respondent accrediting bodies. Also, he now felt he had a better idea where Weinroth was heading.

"To be more precise on the point, Dr. Cantrelle," Weinroth continued, "if the government sets itself up as protector of the people—the people, mind you, not the crown, or the church, or the realm, but the people—then it must protect those people—of, by, and for whom it is constituted—from all predators that could do those people ill. And, most important, it will endeavor never to have itself become in any way a predator of its very own people."

Cantrelle reflected for a moment. Weinroth's remarks sharpened his awareness of something he had till now felt more than thought. It was true that this was a government whose vested interest was first, last, and always the people, despite how much the self-serving professional politicians in Washington had more recently suborned that idea to the enlargement of their own personal as well as partisan benefit. Yet, those first, last, and always politicians, whether professional or non-profit, still remained answerable to the people as electoral wrath had refreshingly shown on several occasions over the past few administrations. The fact that wrath could be electoral in its reach is likely the only thing that kept the government from becoming a good, old-fashioned oligarchy destined to breed revolutions. Yes, despite all its imperfections, America worked; a true social democracy with a capitalist racing stripe that some other nations found a bit garish. Many of our elitist politicians, too. Suddenly his mood darkened as a thought moved into focus.

"And I guess Blush is the predator you feel is needed?" he ventured.

"In a manner of speaking, yes, Dr. Cantrelle," Weinroth allowed. "It bespeaks an action the government itself could never take, could not permit of itself, could never ask of the people. And that's why it befalls us to shoulder the task."

"But, Dr. Weinroth, your reasoning as to why the government could never undertake something like Blush is all well and good. Absolutely unassailable. But that's not the point as I see it," Cantrelle countered, his aroused patriotism ready for serious field duty. "Merely to point out why our government is incapable of perpetrating something as horrific as Blush doesn't quite cover the matter adequately. It might speak to the issue of *who*, but it's the god-damned *why* of it all that screams out to me and to a lot of wholly innocent people out there. Don't you see? People just like the ones a moment ago you proclaimed as vital to what this country is."

"We didn't exactly say vital, Dr. Cantrelle," Weinroth corrected. "Basic, yes; but not necessarily vital. However, you're quite right that Blush is our version of the missing natural predator. But it's also much more than that. It's our attempt to insert a correction factor in the social equation which more and more structures this country's energies and allocates its resources. In effect, Dr. Cantrelle, it's our effort to protect the social, economic, and, oddly, even the political health of this nation. So to see us as an arcane committee of inhuman monsters bent on wholesale murder doesn't quite cover the matter adequately, either."

The rebuke was unmistakable. He sensed that the committee was becoming less patient with him. He guessed that he was expected by now to show some sign of committed engagement without recurrent retreat into moral outrage whenever additional explication was brought before him. If that was the way they felt, he could understand; there was nothing worse than a resident who thought he already knew it all and knew it better than anyone else and who used everything taught him to confirm his pre-conceptions and to affirm his teacher's limitations. Such residents were, by and large, uneducable simply because they had closed themselves to learning anything they didn't already know, and usually he endeavored to teach them what he hoped they would hold as a lasting lesson: threatened expulsion from the program regardless of how good their clinical grades were on the standard examinations. Unfair, maybe, but right. And he had no qualms about it, as was charged on several distinct occasions by the ACLU, the state Civil Rights Commission, a few local politicians, and even one member of the DMH. The hospital administration, usually at some political expense to themselves, stood behind him each time. And, likewise, the activist storm was weathered each time. Moreover, on each of those occasions he made it operationally, not just rhetorically, clear to all of them that as long as he was Director of Training the study and practice of Psychiatry was not to be a pro forma exercise adequately satisfied by someone's narrow ability to fill in the standard blanks. No, it was a matter of attitude; it was vitally a matter of attitude, and specifically the attitude toward the unknown: everybody's unknown in general and the residents' unknown in particular. Not a very affirmatively democratic standard, perhaps, but the right one as he saw it, and the one he held, oddly enough, as being consummately and apolitically American. And now, here he was, probably being regarded by this committee with the same forbearance he himself would have to labor at sustaining when dealing with a closed-minded resident, anticipating as he did so the happy moment when he would see the last of that blighted being. The thought was sobering.

"I'm listening, Dr. Weinroth," he conceded. He sensed that with a more amenable and more responsible attention promised them, the members of the committee could now ease into a more relaxed stance. A few smiled consanguine approval to each other that an important point had somehow been settled. For his part he felt he had yielded dangerously much, and had done so unwillingly, but necessarily out of stern reckoning.

"Thank you, Dr. Cantrelle," Weinroth nodded, "but at the moment I think you would be even better advised to listen to Dr. Markman. I think he has a few points to make before I have all my say," he suggested.

"Suits me," Cantrelle agreed cheerily in a display of follow-through openness.

Markman nodded acknowledgment of the introduction to Weinroth and then began.

"Dr. Cantrelle, what I'm going to say to you, at least in the outset, may seem unrelated to our urgent business here tonight, but I ask that you bear with us as I try to show its importance to the matter which brings you here," he opened. "I'm not sure how familiar you are with the metaphor I must use, but my guess is that your experience as well as the format of your own work will key you in to the essential points I hope to cover."

Cantrelle grimaced a gesture to suggest that such was perhaps possible.

"I suspect you're aware," Markman proceeded "that every proposition defines a set. And by proposition—call it statement, standard, principle, credo, or even ideal—I mean anything that posits a condition of alleged or assumed fact. Also, every proposition carries within itself a collection of derivative possibilities, actually more like inevitabilities, which we might say stand available to be called forth for operational application. In a word, a set. In addition, an infinite number of other possibilities are excluded because of their incompatibility with the basic proposition. You've probably heard of this sort of thing before; so-called Evolutionary Determinism and variable-driven sets. It bears somewhat on our meeting with you tonight."

"Yes, Dr. Markman, I've heard of it," he acknowledged in a manner tentative enough to register the thinness of his familiarity with the concept.

"I was sure you had. The typical example used to demonstrate the idea is that of the concept of the 'point'—the plain old 'point' we all learned about in high school geometry," Markman offered just for good measure as he proceeded. "I'm sure you didn't think much about it at the time when your textbook said that there was such a thing as a point—no one thinks much about it since it seems so self evident—but that basic postulation, or proposition, carries within it all the subsequent theorems which we then had to derive as well as learn to live with if we wanted them to do good work for us. You see, by postulating the existence of a point—one single point—you also postulate the existence of some other point, some 'otherness,' something other than the point itself in order for the point to have distinct existence, because it is inconceivable to have only one point. Such a singularity would be imponderable. One point located in what? So one point contains in its set every other point in existence and their relationship to each other. So actually, in positing one infinitely small entity called 'a point' you are conversely positing an infinitely huge system which contains every possible other point. In other words, the universe. I'm sure you're familiar with this notion."

"Sort of," Cantrelle replied. "I'm just more used to hearing the example of the postulation that the world is round carries in it all the laws of gravitation, planetary motion, and even ultimately the hypothesis of the expanding universe."

"Yes, that's a good one. A little handier than the concept of a point. Good, you know precisely what I mean," Markman exulted.

Cantrelle wasn't sure he was all that precise in his understanding but appreciated the vote of confidence.

"So now we can continue, Dr. Cantrelle, and move on to see how that idea applies to our business here tonight," Markman delighted. "This nation's Constitution is, as I'm sure you know, essentially the same kind of postulation, in a sense. As a document it has a majesty and humanity few other instruments of governance can equal, if any can at all. But it is still fundamentally a proposition or postulation subject to the same inexorable laws of logic as any other proposition. Reductionism applies as much to the Constitution as to any other proposition; it can never in any way be exempt of the causal laws of existence in which it itself constitutes an entity. Right?"

"Right," Cantrelle echoed.

"Or any part of it as well," Markman added.

"Right," he repeated.

"I suggest we take one of those parts, a very basic part, and look at it a bit more carefully from the perspective of inevitable extension into its derivatives, the reductionism of which I speak," Markman urged.

"Which point?" Cantrelle asked.

"The part that proposes that all men are created equal," Markman selected.

He figured it would be something like that, something that had to do with the character of the constituency of this nation's people. He decided to let Markman proceed without interruption; he wasn't yet sure what to ask him anyway, or, more specifically, just what Markman had in mind about that particular proposition. Actually, he himself felt a bit uncomfortable with the idea of looking more carefully at that proposition. It was so easy to misconstrue its intent, as everybody knew.

"Dr. Cantrelle, it's commonly agreed that the founding fathers intended that proposition—that all men are created equal—to mean equal *politically*, not equal *essentially* or *socially*," Markman detailed. "Only *politically*—the right to vote, to hold office, and to receive protection under the law as it applied equally to all citizens. They did not mean that the government saw all its citizens as being equally tall, equally intelligent, equally productive, or equally needy. That would be nonsense."

He felt there was no need to corroborate that. Too obvious.

"But then we have the problem of determining the particulars of political equality. As I'm sure you've noted, the government has over the past several decades taken the concept of political equality beyond the particulars of mere enfranchisement and the right to hold office and has expanded the concept of equal protection under the law to include, in extension, the goals of equal education, equal work status, and, to the extent it is now possible, even equitable economic status. The idea of equal opportunity is key to this general trend. In fact, *more* than equal opportunity has been ruled appropriate for certain sectors of this society as a means of offsetting certain established disadvantages in those sectors, a regrettable instance of the government's adapting as policy the notion that two wrongs will somehow make a penitential right. Of course, every one knows better, but no one has yet come up with a more serviceable idea as to how to deal with those disadvantaged sectors without making the national situation even worse. So everybody pretty much goes along with the policy, though most do so reluctantly. But it's that very reluctance and its underlying cynicism which are important to note. In effect, the majority of people in this nation are daily confronting and reacting to exactly what the government is incapable of recognizing officially. The people perceive that governmental policy is now being shaped by such interpretative extension as will inevitably generate laws likely to violate most people's sense of fair play, equal responsibility, and even common sense—admittedly in a compensatory effort to elevate the status of the naturally disadvantaged sectors because, we need not be reminded, those naturally disadvantaged define a *set* with an attendant destiny *all of its own*. Hence, the government's effort to redress those imbalances. But, then, is it now a government of the people and so forth? Or is it a government of the people as some branch of government has determined the people should and must be? If the latter, it is a government of the people in name only and thus a contradiction of itself—and doomed. But if it is truly in its current actions a government of the people with its policies actually deriving from the consent and preference of those governed, then the people's cynicism and their dissatisfaction with the consequences of this government's social legislation bespeaks a failure in the government's responsibility to address realistically and fairly the problem of inequality in such forms constituting the natural makeup of this society. We of this committee believe that the government, despite its tendency toward misplaced concreteness, or its habit of mobilizing exuberant and fiscal energy in pursuit of silly slogans, or its regrettable pull into the decay of self-service, still and all is the voice of the people. We do not feel that the government has achieved or probably ever will achieve a determinative autonomy beyond the intent of its citizenry. We feel, rather, that the government, for better or for worse, still speaks the collective mind of its citizens, and that the citizens, through the medium of their dissatisfaction with the government's social legislation, are really telling themselves, obliquely, something they truly would prefer not at all to hear: that their government as it is presently constituted and understood is fundamentally incapable of solving the problems generated by the extended reality of the nation's general constituency. In that regard the inevitable consequence is that the people's hopes for a preferred and just society are likewise doomed."

Again, the idea was not entirely new to him—he and Clay had talked about like notions many times before, and usually over beer. But he had never heard it all laid out with such syllogistic precision. Nor had he ever heard it stated in such a way as to hold no one particularly blameworthy; it was simply the way it was with each participant part—the Constitution, the government, the people—playing its obligatory role, locked in the same propositional set and unable to escape the merciless march of its dialectic. He heard himself exhale slowly as he weathered the impact of Markman's words. He felt he was losing something, that the words were somehow displacing something he would rather hold on to, but his sigh seemed to signal the departure of that special something, and perhaps forever, too. Deflated? Disenchanted? More like discredited, and by his own foolish hopes.

"But all social contracts are compromises of a sort," he felt obliged to object. "No rule can hold hard or fast in all instances. That's why we have amendments. Twenty-four by last count, I think, Dr. Markman." He hoped to lighten the interchange by assigning a breezy lilt to his uncertainty.

"That's quite true, Dr. Cantrelle," Markman agreed. "Compromise is the means of fitting the principle to the practice, and vice versa. It's also a programmatic way of holding on to a principle as long as possible when signs begin to appear that the principle's set is evolving into an application quite at variance with what had been anticipated and preferred. The dreaded *unintended consequence* we all try to avoid. In other words, Dr. Cantrelle, a need for different consequence but not yet so urgent to justify the expense of establishing an entirely new principle along with its own yet unrealized set. You see, people—all of us—cannot know that the principle, and its set, which we establish today will be right and suitable for that which cannot be known until tomorrow. Those unintended consequences, don't we know? In that sense, every proclaimed principle is a kind of measured prognostication about the unknown. But you can't hope to know the unknown unless you have a principle—or hypothesis—to enable you to get there in the first place. Let me say it this way. This country could not possibly be the wondrously successful social democracy it is today if not for the defining propositions embraced by its Constitution. However, those very propositions, in their recorded success, now confront us with problems generated of that success but which lie beyond the scope of the propositions themselves, at least from the standpoint of extended self-approbation. Those founding propositions, so to speak, have taken us to another reality, a transmuted and more determinative reality which now exceeds the practical utility of the originating propositions themselves. In effect, they have served their purpose in defining a new set of problems now beyond the corrective reach of the propositions themselves, and have done it very well. They have taken us as far as they can, what with the evolved reality ordained by their set quite adequately achieved, and perhaps it is now time for the next level of proposition, or hypothesis, or Constitution to be enacted for address of the new problems defined. It's all a very endless and perhaps impossibly progressive enterprise, but it is pretty inevitable that we try our best at it," Markman concluded, now taking his turn at exhaling.

The Ptolemaic system flashed to mind. That common sense, obvious, eminently simple notion that took the earth to be the fixed and unmoving center of the firmament. The so-called Geocentric Theory. Convenient up to a point, and indeed generative of a disciplined and scientific approach to the study of the heavens for over a thousand years, but ultimately requiring the use of endless, convoluted successions of epicycles applied to the delineation of planetary orbits to account for the apparent and occasional retrograde motion of the planets in their courses since the planets at times do seem to move backwards, at least as viewed from earth. Over the years so many epicycles had been added to each planetary orbit the primary orbits shrank almost into insignificance with the "deviations,"—those periodic retrograde motions of the planets—consuming more and more of the science's craft and effort in accommodating those "deviations" to the fundamentally flawed theory. Sort of like amendments to the initial proposition of Geocentricity. And then Copernicus came along, changed the basic percept into what we know as the Heliocentric Theory, and all the epicycles disappeared overnight. They had become adventitious, null, even embarrassing. And subsequent even to that, Relativity corrected planetary "deviations" unexplained by the science of the Heliocentric Theory. Damn the thought!

"But you make it sound like it's all decided and that everybody is just too stupid or too cowardly to face the facts of the situation," he chaffed.

"No. I hope I haven't sounded so critical, Dr. Cantrelle. I had intended to point out that people—all of us—cannot know their future unless they have the means of achieving it. I fear I have made a muddle of it, though," Markman rued. "We all can't be so optimistically clairvoyant as our esteemed Chairman, I regret," he added with a hint of the sly.

"And what do you mean by that?" Cantrelle snapped at the gentle reproof. He looked at Burleson for explanation.

"He means, Dr. Cantrelle," Burleson began in conciliation, "that I'm the one responsible for the agenda of this committee. The members never fail to chide me as being the in-house prophet since it is my job to decide what the specific direction of this committee should be, or at least the items to be addressed. I try to tell them that it's simply my job to try to look ahead; however, they accuse me of simply subordinating them to my very own set. A kind of inside joke, if you will. Nothing more."

He allowed himself to feel mollified. After all, he, too, was an item on this agenda, allegedly selected by Burleson himself, and hence entitled to feel a bit touchy when Burleson's rôle was being twitted. And besides, he didn't like this guy Markman; he said unsettling things much too easily, just like, as a matter of fact, Clay could and did and which he remembered he initially resented in Clay years ago when their relationship was just beginning. Back then he judged Clay to be coldly insensitive, even irresponsible. It was something of an irony that precisely because of what Clay had come to mean to him he was sitting here tonight, listening to the likes of Markman.

"Having a grip on the philosophical underpinnings of the government's built-in limitations is all well and good," Cantrelle directed with an unbowed forthrightness he didn't sincerely feel, "but ultimately it's what the people of this nation choose as their way and elect as their lot that really counts, not the dilemma or the contradiction imposed by some infelicitous proposition. Things go on regardless of what their meaning may come to be."

"True," Markman allowed through a sigh as he straightened in his chair, "But it's a matter of *how* they go on. I had hoped to show that it's not merely the case of a people being tripped up by a contradiction or, as you say, some infelicity in their founding principle, but a matter of the overall organizing format having run its course, having achieved the transmuting generative potential of its set, and now, in accordance with the loopy nature of everything in this universe, has returned to a point of origin, the previous solutions offered by the set now called its derivatives and lately formed into a more comprehensive problem requiring a more comprehensive proposition. In a word, Dr. Cantrelle, the seemingly unsolvable economic as well as social problems this nation is wrestling with today are symptoms, as you might say, which indicate that the way this nation conceives of itself is now unequal to its own evolved reality and the derivative problems, and that every program, law, or initiative undertaken by our government to cure this nation of those problems is little more than a temporary palliative because the very effort at correction is itself part and parcel a product of that fundamentally flawed, or as you say, infelicitous founding proposition. Thus, the government's corrective efforts, however well intended, have themselves now become a *larger* part of the problem, and, hence, are most unlikely to be a part of the needed solution. Epicycles, so to speak. The consequence is that we are witnessing a breakdown of national identity. Certainly the nation will go on in some fashion or other, but *how* it does so is exactly the concern and business of this committee."

He was tempted to discount Markman's notions altogether as just another one of those doomsday predictions that had become so commonplace lately even in the face of bustling national perseverance, but something told him that these words were different, that maybe these words were the particulars of the overall formal and essential truth of the matter and that all the doomsday pronouncements floating around were merely distorted and inelegant pretenders to Markman's more solid analysis. Plus, his mention of epicycles! Also, he saw painfully large personal application of what Markman was saying. Maybe many others would, too. He knitted his brow, conceding that he would have to give the idea more thought. For the moment he hoped that Foster, ever the historian, wouldn't pipe up to remind him that things did seem to repeat themselves, that cycles did seem to run their course, and that basic issues generally did not change, only the level of complexity in their actualization. But to do so would just be rubbing it in; hence, unnecessary. It then occurred to him that if a collective change in attitude and approach were needed, then it most certainly would be a reluctant change just as he at this very moment felt it to be so within himself, parallel and kindred. But surely if he could do it, get to be a little less fixed in his attitudes and a little smarter about the real world he lived in, then why couldn't the rest of the country do the same? Of course! Why not? He smiled as he prepared to address Markman.

"Things needn't be as grim as you make them out to be. Dr. Markman. After all, change is possible, isn't it? Your system does allow for change, doesn't it?" he taunted.

"Oh, indeed it does, Dr. Cantrelle," Markman smiled. "Change is certainly possible. But, actually, it's worse than that; change is inevitable. And as I'm sure you can imagine, that's precisely where the new set begins and where the elements of the old set are redefined. In other words, Dr. Cantrelle, that's where the job—this committee's and also that of our nation—gets an awful lot trickier. We're all better advised to look upon change much the way we look upon aging; it brings solutions to the problems of immaturity but sure as hell brings problems of its own, and less sportive ones at that."

A twitter of laughter circulated around the older members of the committee. He, however, was not in the mood for levity just now.

"Sure," he returned curtly, "for if change is what's going to happen anyway, things will eventually settle out. Somehow they always do. Maybe some old approaches and attitudes—and definitions—will have to change in order for things to settle out, but they will. You'll see," Cantrelle wagered.

"Oh, I'm sure you're right, Dr. Cantrelle. It's just that our concern has to do with the cost of that 'settling out,' as you say. An inevitable cost, to be sure, and also a very dear one to this nation's preferred concept of itself," Markman added in easy parenthesis.

He had a pretty good sense of what Markman was alluding to, at least in a clinical way, for it was a commonplace with him that so many of his patients came to him in crisis because of an urgent conflict between their idealized, extolable self and their actual self which reality was now obliging them to recognize. Here, too, change was inevitable and it took the form of everything from suicide to transcendent wisdom, either one a form of resolution in itself, but each with a quite different valence as well as cost. Also, he was beginning to sense that whatever this committee had to say to him from the abstract world of doctrinal remand, he already knew most particularly in the world of the clinically applied, a not insignificant point. So maybe these people weren't that removed after all.

"I may be oversimplifying, Dr. Markman, but I think I hear you saying that if the collective nation doesn't redefine itself in some more progressive—may I use that term?—way, then the national identity and function will undergo decay. And by decay I can only imagine that you mean the individual states will more and more tend to go their own separate ways, very much like disenchanted citizens right now grouse about doing so individually. Right?" he proposed.

"By and large and as a first step, yes, Dr. Cantrelle, but we prefer to use the term evolutionary rather than progressive," Markman suggested. "The latter has too many archaic connotations."

Progressive too archaic? His smile of startled disbelief spoke for him.

Markman picked up on it immediately.

"Yes, Dr. Cantrelle, archaic. Over the centuries the term progressive has always meant a crusading pursuit of some new ideal. As far as we know it has never meant—horror of all horrors!—an included capacity for, much less the duty of, challenging its own basic assumptions. Only the scientific attitude lists that notion as proposition Number One. Our feeling, and here I myself may be oversimplifying, is that this country, more than any other country on the face of the globe, has *progressed*"—he emphasized the word—"to the point of exhausting the traditional legislative mold available to its set, and, now, having completed its existential loop, it has to do once again what it did back in 1776: bring forth a new constellation to the globe's firmament; one to define the course of world history for another segment of the future. I'm sure the others present," he scanned the committee, "would agree that animistic and religious forms of government have pretty well run their course. Also, I'm sure you know quite well what I mean: governments based on national spirits of one form or another, such as Aryan or Bushido. Or on partisan deities such as the regional gods—Christian, Islamic, and so forth. This country tried to separate government from those heritages over two hundred years ago, but couldn't do it actually, for even today the President of the United States cannot and will not assume his duties without taking the pledge of office right hand raised and left hand on the Bible so as to guarantee to all that he knows who the real boss is. And I assure you, Dr. Cantrelle, the observance is not a mere formality."

He knew it wasn't. In fact, oddly enough, he annually pointed out in one of his courses exactly the same phenomenon. He didn't know how these people were managing it but their commentary wasn't missing any of his private biases. He automatically checked the group and saw that several were nodding their assent, even Horlick. Yet, even though he himself taught several of the same canons, he felt he couldn't agree with where he sensed all this was leading. Something in him just wouldn't give, and he felt little choice but to stand fast.

"Again I say, Dr. Markman, that's all well and good. I've even taught some of the same notions myself," he admitted with some largess, "but no matter how you derive it, Blush remains Blush and I'm afraid I just can't see it any other way. I'm sorry, but eighty thousand deaths make it wrong, at least in my simple way of thinking."

"As it would seem to anybody else," Markman conceded, "including us."

Cantrelle was openly surprised to hear this. He took a moment to consider.

"If you all believe it's wrong, then why the hell do you do it?" he retorted testily.

"Because our personal morality cannot override our duty to the committee, Dr. Cantrelle. That's why," Markman explained. "And I might add that in much the same way *your* personal preferences and values cannot override your professional duty to your patients. As individuals you and we may know and feel one thing, but in our work we tend to aspire to something better, something bigger than we know ourselves to be. That's the reservoir of anyone's hopes. In that regard, we of this committee are basically no different from anybody else, but as a joined committee we most assuredly are, just as you as a member of your profession are a different kind of person from what you otherwise might be."

God, how many times had he said exactly the same thing to his residents whenever he felt obliged to mount his ethical high horse, and, moreover, had said that the more they understood the distinction the better they would be at their professional ideals? He saw that it was becoming senseless trying to see himself as morally different from or better than these people before him.

"O.K., Dr. Markman, you've made your point," he sighed. He then looked at the floor for a moment and pursed his lips in thought. That done, he looked at Markman again, and, through a weak smile of resigned receptivity, asked, "Dr. Markman, do you think you and this committee can explain to me why those people had to die? At this point I have a feeling it's equally important to both of us for me to understand why some other way couldn't be found for whatever it is you all have in mind for this country."

"I've pretty much spoken my piece, Dr. Cantrelle. I think some of the other members probably could pick up on the point, though," Markman advised.

"But why poison them with a street drug?" Cantrelle persisted.

"Because history tells us that more coercive ways do not work, Dr. Cantrelle," Foster interceded.

"More coercive ways? What do you mean?" Cantrelle flustered.

"I mean pogroms, mass gassings, putting to the sword, imposed starvation, forced migrations, and the like. History clearly shows that such direct methods have carried a pyrrhic penalty for the perpetrator," Foster explained.

"You mean that this committee is directing an extermination program?" he exclaimed. Actually, he had concluded as much when he was introduced to Pontalbas, but its moment of open recognition had been apprehensively set aside. That moment had now arrived and he addressed it as newly perceived; it now could no longer be allowed to pass in cautious default.

"In effect, yes, Dr. Cantrelle," Foster agreed. "However, it's important to note that those designated for removal have the choice not to comply with the ruling."

"What? The *ruling*? Is that *really* what it is? You mean a *death sentence*, don't you?" His outrage was welling up all over again, though now adulterated by a familiarity with what he knew he was likely to hear. Still and all, his outrage was right, he registered, albeit becoming only more formally so.

"A death choice, actually," corrected Foster. "No one forces those people to take Blush. They take it of their own free will. Agreed, their free will is rather compromised by their predilection for street drugs. But still and all, the choice is theirs. In effect, Dr. Cantrelle, they can elect not to become victims of Blush, if they have within themselves the capacity to direct themselves otherwise. If not, they are indeed victims in the fullest and truest sense, wouldn't you say, with Blush being only the immediate catalytic agent in bringing that truth to bear?"

That truth? Bringing it to bear? He shuddered. Foster's contained, matter-of-fact manner in delivering such horrendous accounting was offensive enough in its own right, the accounting itself notwithstanding, but now his outrage was beginning to totter from the weariness of overdraught; he could no longer freely disburse it, nor could he any longer credit it as hard tender. His understanding of what was before him, unfolding in the sweep of a ruthless logic, was reducing his outrage to the whine of offended ignorance.

"I think I see better how Blush is your customized predator," he said, attempting a corrective rebuke. These people were inhuman, he continued to himself. No one seemed to be bothered in the least by what Foster was saying, with the possible exception of Pontalbas who appeared to be worried about how he, Cantrelle, was managing all this. The others didn't seem to care all that much, as though they already knew the outcome. He would best be forthright, he decided; these people were not likely to be greatly bothered by the intrusive cast of his inflamed indignation. "And just how does this committee go about identifying these people who might volunteer as its victims?" he asked acidly.

"They identify themselves in concert with the accidences of the times. They always have, throughout history, though our work as a formed committee is fairly new to the scene," Foster replied to Cantrelle's unconvinced stare. "Let me explain," he continued. "These people—the victims, as you say; we call them the adventitious—are the ones who profit least by every major human accomplishment. I'm sure you're aware, Dr Cantrelle, that every major advance in human development has its preferred class of beneficiaries. It also has its disaffected class of outliers. Its victims, you might say. Any significant change in the human predicament redefines the general constituency in some fashion or other, some to become beneficiaries of that change and others to become adventitious to it. Thus, the capacity of any segment of the constituency to benefit from any given change will determine which group that segment will fall into; or, in other words, be defined as being either a beneficiary or an ancillary. The animal world abounds with examples of this principle, loosely called the principle of survival of the fittest, which, incidentally, presupposes a completely fair, objective, and serenely dispassionate world as backdrop for the ruthless principle to play itself out according to precept. But, of course, it's not really that simple when applied to the human scene. Yet, general patterns do obtain, especially when the significant change is actually a *human* product, something imposed by human development itself and not like the animal world where significant change usually comes from without, such as drought, blight, disease, climate change, and so forth. Those nature-driven changes apply to humans as well, but over the past fifty thousand years or so, probably longer, the major changes, or challenges, confronting the human constituency have been generated by the humans themselves, as though they had managed to rise above the challenges still occupying the animal world. The first of these changes we humans inflicted upon ourselves came of the gift of speech. That step shook out the human constituency into those who had the capacity for it and those who didn't, the probable essential difference between Neanderthal, who didn't make it, and Cro-Magnon, who did. And those who had such ability zoomed on, putting a greater distance between themselves and their less capable brethren. The next big shake-out came with the transmutation of speech into written language. Again, those who gained the art of writing zoomed ahead of their brethren who didn't, the result being cities, not just tribal gatherings; recorded history, not just oral legends; and culture, not just campfire huddling. And those whose best effort was to borrow the phonetic concept from others to bring writing to their own language began what we know today as the numerical layering of the worlds—first, second, third—into those who write the books of civilization, those who study the books of civilization, and those who are just now learning to read them. I'm sure you're familiar with these particulars," Foster presumed.

He was and he wasn't. He was, as far as it was the enduring record of human woe; he wasn't as far as it was ruthlessly elitist, and hence properly un-American.

Satisfied by Cantrelle's sustained attention, Foster continued.

"And right here in our own country we can see the same discriminatory forces at play over just the past two hundred or so years. Two centuries ago when our government was founded, we were very much an agrarian society with little to distinguish one farmer from another. Each scratched out a living from the soil, and one did it very much like another with little to discriminate this one from that one. True, one might be more proficient than another and would get more reliable and more bountiful yield, but the overall difference in application was small; they still had so much more in common than otherwise. The clash with the culture of the nomadic American Indian was still limited. But the human scene then saw the advent of the Industrial Revolution, a distinctly man-made addition—and challenge. And with it came the discriminatory identification of those who profited by it and those who suffered from it. Now machinery replaced those who picked the cotton or tilled the fields. Railroads scored the Indian's plains. So what became of those people, the cotton pickers, the hewers of wood, the aboriginal hunters? Those of them who could be recruited to the tread of the new industry were absorbed; those who couldn't became adventitious and began their steady decline into desuetude and eventual disappearance. Our country was young then, more primitive, certainly less socially responsible such that so ruthless a consequence of development could be permitted. For a while, anyway. Soon, corrections in social attitude, translated into law, were attempted in an effort to ease the national angst, and a great war was fought when the intensity of political conflict exceeded the boundaries of majority rule. Yet, the nation persevered, and in the healing of its wounds the nation nourished the hope and dream that all, given fair access, would profit equitably from every great good. And so this nation labored, for itself as well as for other nations of the world; often clumsily, often naively, but always generously in keeping with the belief that opportunity, given a chance, would translate differences into affirmative communality. But, as we all know, major ethnic, cultural, and racial differences did not retreat very much. If anything, opportunity seemed to underscore such differences all the more. And then, some thirty years ago, came the Technologic Revolution. Whatever had been the societal settling-out effect of the Industrial Revolution was now magnified many times over by this stupendous advance. Now, it wasn't just the pickers of cotton and hewers of wood who became the adventitious; it was entire industries, our smokestack industry in particular, because as we were moving into the high tech era and away from a ferrous economy. Second World nations were now achieving their own belated industrial revolutions and thus set about developing a smokestack industry all of their own, at the notable expense of our foreign as well as domestic markets. So what has happened to the steelworkers and coalminers of this nation? I think you know, Dr. Cantrelle, because I understand you practice in a community that used to have a steel mill. I think you noticed those steelworkers—many of them, anyway—gathering on street corners daily to greet each other, loitering around the dusty union hall, and attempting to secure what work they could until social security picked up their case—a recurring image in the newer industrial scene. Those steel-workers who could make the transition to other work did so; those who couldn't, gathered together as you saw them: obsolete, or as we say, adventitious. A small example, to be sure, but one with which you likely have some personal experience."

He was right. When the steel mill closed some years ago the workers gathered just as he was saying, and they did so by the hundreds. Now, years later, that gathering is reduced to less than a few score, mostly the older and less healthy, and the simple. The others simply passed on or found their way into other work, some of it high tech. He even saw several of them in treatment of the emotional fall-out. Foster was painfully right.

"The sons and daughters of many of those adventitious people will find their way to some niche in the new world of high tech, but many will not, and they'll drift downward in the social scale to join with the less apt descendants of those made adventitious by the earlier Industrial Revolution so many years ago, already a substantially large segment of this society. These days that segment even has a name. It's called the Underclass, I think you know," Foster posed.

He knew. An he often wondered how large it could become before it crippled the nation beyond all hope of sustaining a leadership role in this relentlessly competitive world.

"My point is this, Dr. Cantrelle," Foster announced with palms upturned. "Every major human accomplishment dooms as well as it redeems, and the responsibility befalling those it redeems is to credit the process with the best possible grace. The responsibility of those it dooms is to accept the process, also with the best possible grace. Significant failure either way is the concern of this committee."

Now, for the first time, he understood the purpose of his presence before this group. He was being afforded the chance to avoid being a "significant failure." He presumed that he was not yet to be included among the so-called doomed, if at all, though just now the subjective sense of that designation seemed well enough upon him. He took a deep breath, leaned back in his chair, and stretched. The others merely waited. He looked around the room self-consciously in search of ventilation for his thoughts now also stretching to seek more space than his mind seemed capable of providing. Those thoughts needed more range, like lusty children who had outgrown their familiar backyard. The dark windows seemed to reflect his confinement, and the room's paneling now reminded him of the sides of a box—a furnished, exquisitely fashioned box. Little comfort in that notion. He returned his attention to the group, leaned forward, and spoke as he allowed his hands to droop over the front of his knees.

"Gentlemen, if I understand Dr. Foster correctly," he posed wearily, "you intend 'significant failures' to mean non-adaptive behavior on the part of some respondent group, and specifically behavior that is potentially dangerous to the common weal of this nation. Right?"

"By and large, yes, Dr. Cantrelle," Burleson confirmed. "Moreover, maladaptive behavior which fundamentally falls beyond the scope of the government's capacity to correct. Yes. But it need not be limited to groups. Occasionally it is seen in individuals, and our work then is adjusted accordingly."

The words sent a chill through him, and fear startled him into electric readiness. He blinked in wild survey of the thoughts which were unleashed by Burleson's clarification.

"Like my being here tonight?" he breasted.

"Yes," Burleson confirmed.

"And an accident last month?" he pressed provocatively.

"That was not our ruling, Dr. Cantrelle," Malloy reiterated officially.

"Not *your* 'ruling'? Then whose was it? Someone's!" he charged. "And as for the others, why kill them? Murder is murder!" He wondered how many ruinous exposés, accidents, heart attacks, or suicides these people had arranged for those who were unreachable by the given law but were in significant violation of the ethics of the system driving this committee. Had they attempted talking to Clay, maybe even to the point of having him sit on this very same sofa some months earlier only to be spurned by him because he saw their effort as confirmation of his mission to expose shadow government in all its forms? Possibly. If he knew Clay, he would have been rather conversant with these people, more so than he himself was proving to be, and especially on the harder issues of dealing with the discrepants thrown up by the system's modus operandi. Even so, Clay would not have conceded their larger purpose. Clay never, ever, abandoned a detail if he thought it was a telling one, and he tended to treat larger concepts, the constructs, rather rudely. He had always seen that as a flaw in Clay's otherwise divinely impartial gospel.

"You will call it murder, won't you?" Malloy returned with a suggestion of impatience. "We do not kill anybody, Dr. Cantrelle. We provide conditions for the behavior of the adventitious to remove themselves from the system. We do not *make* anybody behave in any self-destructive way; we merely allow matters to take their elected course by providing means which circumvent a society's infelicitous blunting of the laws of natural selection. As you know, in the natural state the behavior of the species is determinative of its survival. Our work is to allow the wisdom of that principle to apply within the context of an enlightened social organization which *must* pay more attention to the contribution it inadvertently makes to the threat to its own survival. Behavior of any group, or individual, which is *not* inherently destructive of its parental and sustaining society will not threaten that society's evolutionary promise. But destructive behavior, if not curtailed, *will*, and degeneracy results. Our task, then, is to allow that destructive behavior to be more specifically destructive of itself. We simply try to redirect the path of the damage."

"But annihilation? That's so final. What about training? Treatment? Something other than obliteration? We're talking about thousands of people," Cantrelle pleaded. "There's got to be another way!"

"I suppose it's my turn now. I said earlier I'd have more to say," Weinroth announced, "and I guess the moment to do so is now at hand. Dr. Cantrelle, the reason this committee doesn't recommend any of the measures you just mentioned is two-fold. First, they haven't worked. This nation, more than an other on the face of this earth, has spent untold billions in various crusading efforts to have all the remedial approaches you just named bring its variously disadvantaged citizens up to social, economic, and educational par with the more successful majority. The results have been dismal in comparison to the outlay of wealth committed. A certain percentage of the disadvantaged do benefit from such programs and do find their way into the more successful mainstream. Often they proceed to the point of sustaining themselves, but these successful ones make up a regrettably small number. The ones who do not evolve as hoped become custodial and continue to receive benefit from such programs in the form of improved sustenance, mandated health care, and overall social guidance and support. But, just like the displaced steelworkers who don't find their way into new work, they remain dependent on the programs and follow a progressive decline into debilitating helplessness—a helplessness felt by themselves, by the implementers of the programs, and ultimately by the nation. That sense of helplessness and fundamental futility among the adventitious is probably the major source of violent crime in this nation, given the scope of personal freedom guaranteed to all, plus the nation's resultant inability to prevent such crime. Thus, the crime rate is a valid measure of the government's kindred helplessness in the matter.

The second reason this committee doesn't recommend the measures you suggest is because they *cannot* work, no matter how much money and how much effort may be applied."

He was startled by the statement, even personally offended. Being told that what he and his country historically was best at and world-renowned for was, in fact, not working very well was one thing, but being told that it could *never* work was yet another. He had to respond, even though forebodings deep within himself made him question his own animus. His country had taken millions of the world's underprivileged and nourished them and their descendants into the strongest nation and most productive society this world had ever seen, hadn't it? And now this man was saying that the nation's track record didn't count! He feared the answer he would likely get.

"The system has worked for an awful lot of people, Dr. Weinroth, and those very programs are themselves a natural outgrowth of that success," he carefully reminded him.

"That's exactly the point, Dr. Cantrelle," Weinroth seized. "The system has worked, and wondrously well for those with the capacity profitably to move about in it, just like those steelworkers who were adaptable enough either to make a lateral move or to move up into the world of high tech. Another clear sign that the system is still functioning quite successfully is the observation that the more recently arrived immigrants, many fully underprivileged by any standard, are accomplishing in the span of only one generation what took our forbearers two or even three generations. So, actually, the system has *improved*. But the Underclass and the adventitious remain, and undoubtedly will, no matter how successful the system may be, because it is the system's very success which identifies the adventitious as such, and which sustains them as a failed presence."

Cantrelle thought for a moment, and then nodded slowly.

"I think I know just what the hell you're getting at, Dr. Weinroth," he said cheerlessly and with heightened contempt.

"Of course you do, Dr. Cantrelle. After all, this is a gene-mapper going on like this," Weinroth tossed, "and I'm quite mindful that just about anything a gene-mapper says is likely to offend in some way or other the American sense of social and democratic decency. The public sense of it, anyway. When it comes to our children, though, we're quite eager to pray in favor of the genes rather than of society. I think we can agree, Dr. Cantrelle, that American society tends to look upon gene research, at least the social and political aspects of it, in much the same way it does the legal profession in that, as it is practiced, it tends to bring out the worst in us. There is a general sense that as long as gene research carefully restricts itself to established, traditional, apolitical diseases such as diabetes and high blood pressure, then the discoveries, solely clinical, are all very well and good. It's when gene research goes beyond the simplistic and conventional that the American public, and certainly the government, becomes uneasy, as perhaps you yourself may now feel at this very moment since the awkward subject has entered our discussion."

"Not at all, Dr. Weinroth," he corrected quickly. "I've been the one complaining about behavior-based nosology in my particular field. I've pushed loudly for a geneto-chemical basis as reference in clinical diagnostics. However . . . ." he added with an emphatically raised finger, "only up to a point, and I would . . . ."

"That's all to your credit, Dr. Cantrelle, and we're quite aware of it," Weinroth applauded gently in interruption, "but that's still primarily a clinical application and, as such, relatively inoffensive to the average citizen. Polemics which might arise from such a pursuit would tend to be intramural among members of your field as to the implications regarding disease etiology, treatment techniques, and the like—the doctrines of your craft. Very much the laudable discourse that comes of any new approach and its methods. What I have reference to is gene research as it applies to individual and group capacities, traits, and behaviors; particularly social behaviors."

"I already know what you're referring to," he asserted in readiness to contest the point.

"Maybe you do and maybe you don't, Dr. Cantrelle," Weinroth persisted. "I'm talking about valid, impartial, and inevitable scientific research that will undoubtedly vitiate the founding proposition basic to the bulk of social legislation enacted in this country over the past one hundred fifty years, certainly over the past forty."

"As I said, Dr. Weinroth, I think I know what you're referring to," he repeated coolly. "You're referring to the genetic basis of developmental capacity, social as well as intellectual. Right? And you're talking about the Gaussian clustering of those capacities along inheritable lines, meaning race as well as ethnic group. Right? Maybe even along social class lines. True?"

"That's part of it, Dr. Cantrelle. It appears you've given some thought to the notion," Weinroth conceded.

"Everybody has, and perhaps more than some others think," he snipped.

"Actually, no one wants to think about it, Dr. Cantrelle," Weinroth allowed, "but it can't be helped when certain behaviors show themselves to be focused undeniably along racial, ethnic, or even class lines. The average citizen tries, or at least knows he's supposed to try, to see such behavior only in the individual context. That's the American preference and certainly the nation's doctrinal obligation. But when individuals demonstrating a specific behavior, whether it be socially contributory or destructively maladaptive, concentrate themselves obviously into racial, ethnic, or class groupings, the observing citizen cannot escape considering that perhaps the behavior has less an individual distinctiveness and is more a product of collective racial, ethnic, and class influences, and hence more possibly genetic in its origin with at least a respondent proclivity innately in place and awaiting certain social conditions for activation. Regrettably, even if the consideration is only a question and not a conclusion, the citizen is forsworn thinking in such a fashion with the threat that he stands subject to the accusation of being the cause of the phenomenon if he admits to being aware of it. His very awareness of some other possible cause of the problem or issue, or at least a cause alternative to the doctrinally correct one or ones, is then cited as carrying the bias that gives rise to the problem in the first place. In effect, the citizen is civically and morally obligated to deny what his responsible concern and his good common sense are bringing to his attention. A most regrettable situation. Are you aware, Dr. Cantrelle, that the Federal government will not fund any studies, no matter how well conceived or formulated, which undertake to explore possible genetic influences in the distribution of certain politically sensitive behaviors, such as criminality, for fear that the results might confirm a racial or ethnic predominance otherwise unexplainable on an individual, political, or economic basis? Even studies which would hope to extend our understanding of a group's, any group's, distribution and pattern of intellectual functioning are carefully monitored from the funding standpoint to insure that no racial determinants are identified. I'm not talking about studies contrived to prove an already preconceived, arbitrary conclusion; I'm talking about studies which undertake merely to ascertain if certain questions are at all valid. The very questions themselves cannot be raised, much less funded and pursued, and the citizen who wonders about what his daily observations insinuate is pro forma required to feel himself an offender of the nation's moral code, and, indeed, to consider himself, by virtue of his very awareness, the cause of the problem itself, for if he didn't think as he did the problem wouldn't exist in the first place, or so it is charged. Dr. Cantrelle, I think you can provide a parallel from your own field. Schizophrenia and the schizophrenogenic mother, as I recall."

He preferred not to remember that dismal display of a consequence being labeled as cause simply because the cause itself could not be seen while the consequence readily volunteered for guilt-consigning service. But it was the best the thinkers of the day, or rather some of them, could offer. It was also so painfully wrong-headed. Yet, it offered a slim hope that could not be ignored, what with other approaches being so bald of benefit in the treatment of that grim disease. In this hypothesis, every schizophrenic was by definition a victim. Not only that, he was a victim of his mother's malevolent nurturance. No matter that she herself may have consciously felt only love and maternal solicitude for her child, somewhere in her a psychologically lethal attitude—secret resentment, ambivalence, or even unholy adoration—had to be at play to work its damage on the child's developing psyche eventually to cause what we know as clinical schizophrenia. Elegant and persuasive arguments, bolstered by a wealth of social and even political thinking, nourished the hypothesis which was readily endorsed by the disordered patients themselves and then served up to a receptive nation. For decades the hypothesis offered a kind of hope because America knew so well how to come to the aid of victims—social, political, economic, you name it—and for the most part the indicted mothers were generally much more accessible than the patients themselves. Also, they held themselves available to credit the hypothesis even though they were designated the guilty, causative pathogens, if in the balance accepting such blame offered their child some hope. Rather than the etiology of schizophrenia, the hypothesis revealed more the extreme to which mothers would go in their desperation to help their damaged child, even to the point of allowing themselves to be punished as the cause of the damage they didn't do if in any way accepting the blame helped their child. Plus, it revealed how a social and political milieu could shade the nobler purposes of science, given the appropriately wrong basic assumption. And it continued until definitive adoption studies were undertaken, and in another country at that. The studies showed that it was basically all in the genes, and the schizophrenogenic mother quickly faded into professional embarrassment. No, he'd rather not remember, though he dare not forget.

"We corrected that misconception," he sighed.

"Yes, you did," Weinroth agreed, "but it took considerable realignment of cause and effect relationships in your field, didn't it?"

It did, he concurred silently, and there were still quite a few diehards here and there who would not accept the new learning. It occurred to him that even in his own field there might be adventitious people lingering around the dusty union hall.

"True," he said simply.

"Dr. Cantrelle," Weinroth pleaded, "I hope you don't think we're trying to show the government to be some evil monster perpetrating grief on its citizens. It's nothing like that, of course. The average citizen, being held guilty for perceiving realities he's forbidden, by injunction, to acknowledge—even though he does so silently within himself—may indeed come to look upon the government as dishonest and fraudulent, and there may truly be a collective sense of futility in the citizenry as a consequence of that view, though the individual probably attributes his own malaise more to the contagion of a general social distress. No, the government is not a purposively evil monster; it is merely doing what it is doctrinally programmed to do, though often less congenially than it might because of the partisan efforts of certain ambitious factions. Just now it's an awkward time for all of us, singly and collectively. And it's an abashing time, too. Remember back in the fifties and sixties in Soviet Russia when Lysenko ruled over Soviet science and how we in the West hooted and hollered wherever we got wind of one of his directives forbidding such and such research because the discoveries might clash with Communist doctrine? Remember that we marveled at how an entire nation of people could fall in line with the nonsense Lysenko pushed on them as the true proletariat science, predicting as we smugly did the inevitable collapse of the whole Soviet structure? Well, we're just about as far along in the inevitabilities of our ideology as they were in theirs at the time, and thus we're now quite vigilant in shaping our science to function in strict keeping with our preferred conception of Democracy. And it's only because our system and its ordained inviolability is now, like theirs then, approaching desperate extremes. Our government, as it is still constituted, is under threat simply for being as successful, in a manner of speaking, to have come so very far that maturity and understanding now demand a searching look at our own evolved state. But our current political principles specifically forbid just that. Plus, the narrow partisan loyalties of our political enactors, regardless of camp, tend to discount any profit as would come of such self-assessment. Party loyalty and policy aggrandizement carry a higher priority for them. Thus, we have just about completed our cycle and it's now time to look at ourselves from another perspective. But the government itself cannot yet undertake such a task; it can only be what it is constituted to be, and for the time being its duty will consist mainly of regulating the allocation of resources and services to the citizenry since our governing principles as they are currently applied have just about exhausted their hermeneutic and generative value. In effect, Dr. Cantrelle, this nation's constituted government, like a dutiful, hard-programmed robot with its encrypted flaws now coming home to roost, is doing the best it can with what it has to offer, though the nation's consequential plight calls for so much more."

So quaintly and simply put, he mused as Weinroth's words, despite their playful mix of metaphor, found a keen resonance deep within his being. He himself had never put it together so tellingly. He had been content to allow his own limited familiarity with what Weinroth was disclosing remain on the level of ordinary voter dissatisfaction with government performance. He now saw that notion as being a vain luxury; the government was probably now doing the best it ever would with an overall problem that exceeded its executive and legislative scope, and perhaps especially so now with so large a collection of horn-blowing politicians retained by the people in a desperate effort to make obsolete formats grant a yield of comfortable solutions. Christ, was the whole nation a steelworker loitering on the street corner? Of course not, but the nation's approach to governing itself might be, he wondered.

"And I suppose Blush is your way of taking matters into your own hands?" Cantrelle accused.

"It represents several things, Dr. Cantrelle," Weinroth replied. "The drug problem sweeping this country is symptomatic of a national forfeiture in the face of social problems the government cannot, of its own construction, solve. An intervention from outside the government's doctrinal gridlock is imperative, at least for now as a transitional measure. This committee is a product of that need, and for the moment, is limiting its address just to the drug problem. In that sense our work with the drug problem is a sally port for eventual address of larger national needs," he detailed.

"Meaning?" Cantrelle queried with rising alarm.

"Meaning that what we learn through Blush and its impact on the drug problem will give us valuable information in devising a procedure to address larger, more pervasive national ills," Weinroth added.

"Are you suggesting something like those social problems you talked about when you mentioned racial and ethnic genetics?" Cantrelle anguished.

"Partially, but not specifically, Dr. Cantrelle," Weinroth allowed. "We're not interested in a particular group as much as we're interested in a process. Certainly we're not given to targeting a group for removal, despite how our deployment of Blush may appear to you. We're interested—actually, it's our fundamental task—in devising a means whereby an individual's or a group's behavior may once again be determinative of that individual's or that group's viability. In other words, to free up the applicability of natural selection law from distortions imposed by a flawed social contract, at least until such time that a better social contract is formed. With this country's present system, unproductive and even socially destructive behavior is protected as part of an overall civil code which is reluctant to discriminate, even fairly, the good from the bad when it comes to the behavior of the electorate. Our task, as a committee, is to devise interventions which allow destructive behaviors to remove themselves. We do not devise extermination programs; we hope to initiate means whereby the people will again have their survival destiny in their own hands, an ultimate responsibility which is inherently theirs and from which they should never be shielded by a deleteriously naive social solicitude. Or missionary government. In large part that's why we want the Blush victims to remain among the populace, wholly visible and not sequestered out of sight to shield the populace from the coarse reality of the nation's drug problem and its collective plight. We want the people to be keenly aware of Blush so that those who can eschew drug usage may be allowed to do so, while those who cannot, despite full awareness of the inevitable consequence, may identify themselves so flawed, and hence adventitious. We would hope thereby to minimize stray and accidental Blush contact among the naive and hapless, such as was the regrettable circumstance in the first Blush case you encountered, Dr. Cantrelle. We hope that Blush's high visibility will steer the young and impressionable toward safer practices as it undermines the siren call of the drug experience. Of course, those who cannot resist that call in any wise will keep some measure of the drug trade operant but they will also target themselves for ultimate removal. Thus Blush will define the current drug culture as to those who can move on to more acceptable and accepting precincts and those who cannot. Those who cannot will be the adventitious, like your loitering steel workers. But for this to happen as we think it should, the *origins* of Blush would best be kept obscure, preferably as the . . . ."

Again he felt himself rising up in revolt at what he was hearing. The logic was ruthless, inhuman. And while he agreed with so many of the premises, he could not agree, much less think of complying, with the merciless conclusions which awaited. He wondered if he himself, just like his government, were in over his head and incapable of doing anything more than what had already been done so many times over, and that he was now reacting to an overdue and looming inevitability in much the same way his government and his fellow citizens were reacting: he was struggling to avoid a painfully enlightened future.

"No one would go along with it, except the inveterate, intractable drug users who couldn't do anything else," he lashed back. "It's asking too much of the people. I work with people all day long and I can tell you it would be too horrid a step for them to take."

"It won't be when they get close enough to see the alternative," Pontalbas announced. He had been sitting quietly and almost motionless on the unobtrusive fringe of the gathering ever since his earlier comments, his presence almost forgotten. Apparently, he had been patiently awaiting his moment. Several of the members looked at him as he spoke, and Cantrelle, his vision now better accommodated to the scene, recognized Pontalbas as being possibly even younger than he earlier estimated. "Dr. Cantrelle," he continued earnestly, "your people could not accept the penalty they would pay for doing nothing about what confronts them."

"Your country seems to be prospering with what confronts it," Cantrelle returned. The unkindness of the remark stood stark against the sincere urgency of Pontalbas' plea.

"To hear the newspapers tell it, yes, Dr. Cantrelle. Some people, it is true, are becoming quite rich, but my country is dying as they do so," Pontalbas pronounced. "My people have long known the hand of the conquistador, but not the destruction of their national treasury. And that is what's at terrible risk now, Dr. Cantrelle, but perhaps in a way you may not easily understand."

"President Pontalbas, I know your meeting with this committee tonight goes beyond the usefulness of your presence in its business with me," Cantrelle yielded. "I'm sure your concerns and the problems Blush is causing your country were preemptive items on the evening's agenda—and that I can understand—but . . . ."

"Dr Cantrelle, please let me correct a point," Pontalbas interrupted with index finger raised. "Blush is not a problem for my country; Blush is my country's only hope."

The gentle remonstrance displayed how much at variance his view was with that of Pontalbas'. Clearly, he just didn't understand, as Pontalbas was suggesting. He squinted as he searched Pontalbas' face.

"Dr. Cantrelle," Pontalbas began in response," my country is small and its people are simple, even primitive by your standards. Before the Spanish came, their cultural achievements were modest. There was yet no art of writing, and their religion saw worship of the spirits of nature. But there was art, as well as indications of early attempts at writing, as well as at a polytheistic religion. Oddly, astronomical computations were being developed, too. It is estimated that in another few thousand years, my people would have evolved a significant civilization distinctly their own. But five hundred years ago the conquistadors came, from whom part of my family is descended, and they brought the art of writing, monotheism, and the technology of the day. The simpler civilization of my people, and many of the people themselves, perished in that collision of worlds, but those who survived leapt forward thousands of years to be the bearers of a cultural blend that would enable them to know a much larger world. The social and political struggles of my country for the past four hundred years have been for the most part the legacy of that imposed massive and rapid cultural advance. A prominent parallel exists with the European settlement of North America and the subsequent introduction of slaves which, fortunately, my country was spared but only for the sinister reason that my people were themselves the slaves so that there was no need to import additional ones. Our political and social efforts over the past four hundred years have indeed been faltering and inconsistent as my people have wrestled with the demands of a modern civilization forcibly imposed on their occluded, hybrid, and still fundamentally primitive culture. But our efforts have always been progressive in intent, despite the succession of juntas, dictators, generalissimos, and even bandit leaders who have occupied the presidential palace at one time or another. Despite their grievous faults, most of these governments made some effort at land reform, or industrialization, or at least early forms of social legislation. Education was furthered and civic stability was generally the rule. But the discovery of a lucrative drug market in North America has changed all that. Now my country is divided into feudal regions by drug lords who rule the infrastructure of society. Governmental efforts at social reform have been undermined by the furiously dominant drug trade. Now, farmers mostly grow cocaine. Young people leave school early to find their place in the drug trade, the new frontier of endeavor. Our society in general has retreated from the pursuit of cultural advancement and is in danger of sinking into the darkness of international criminality. Wholesale violence and murder are now common in my country. Judges, police, even government figures are readily assassinated because of their opposition to the drug lords, as was my father when he proved too successful in mobilizing the people against the drug underworld. Violent crime is now a daily event in the lives of my people, and for all the wealth of the drug lords, my country is sinking into the squalor of social chaos. Automatic weapons and even aircraft are used by the drug criminals, and in terms of the destructiveness to my country's social structure the effect is the same as what the western world fears would be the consequence of nuclear weapons falling into the hands of Middle Eastern or even Far Eastern countries. My people are returning to an atavistic jungle mentality with a sweep of savagery never before possible. They are yet a simple, native people and have very far to go to reach the cultural and social sophistication and maturity of First World nations, but with the weapons of today available to them they can, and will, destroy their own society as the conquistadors never could. They are now fully capable of and are seemingly intent upon destroying four hundred years of social struggle because of their greed for the huge profits of the drug trade. And as long as the drug trade flourishes, my simple people will look to the quick and, they think, long overdue profit.

But if the drug trade diminishes, the better hopes, and work, of my people will return. And that's where Blush becomes our salvation, and very likely the salvation of your country as well, Dr. Cantrelle, because your underclass has the same comparative position, and simplicity, in your nation as my country has in this hemisphere of nations. Their vulnerabilities are the same, and so is the tenuousness of their grasp of an adoptive European civilization alien to their progenitors and separated by many millennia of cultural evolution. Yes, Dr. Cantrelle, I agreed to the Blush project. I offered my country as its base of operations. There is a certain justice that my country, the hub of the cocaine trade, become the destroyer of cocaine's international market. And the heroin market as well, we intend. Very soon it will become apparent to every person tempted to use drugs that he runs a large risk of dying in the doing. Most drug users, those who can, anyway, will abandon the practice in favor of some other pursuit probably more socially tolerable, and those who can't will progressively remove themselves from society, as Dr. Weinroth explained. These latter ones, Dr. Cantrelle, will have defined themselves as the unfortunate possessors of an uncontrollable, and, as you say, intractable vulnerability, and thus likely to be congenitally and unalterably susceptible to that kind of chemical addiction. In a word, adaptively flawed, and so much so that they cannot avoid the prospect of liquidating themselves. In your terms, untreatable; in the terms of this committee, adventitious. Yes, Dr. Cantrelle, Blush is my country's last hope, and possibly your country's as well."

"The drug people won't go along with it, I can tell you," he countered, not knowing or wishing to know why he derived a wry satisfaction in saying so.

"Of that we're sure, Dr. Cantrelle," Pontalbas agreed amiably. "For my part, I fully expect that some day I, too, like my father, will be assassinated. There have been two attempts thus far, and for all I know there may be at this very moment an assassin skulking around with a telescopic rifle near the presidential hunting lodge in the central highlands of my country where officially I'm supposed to be with your visiting Secretary of State. But one learns to live with that sort of thing, as I'm sure the members of this committee would agree since they, too, share the very same risk."

The same risk? He gasped at the thought. The members of *this* committee? These learned, magnificent men! The true leaders of this nation? At *risk*? He couldn't fathom such a crazy idea! These people were national treasures! The thought of being without them was totally inconceivable. Someone *kill* them? Absolutely unconscionable! The thought infuriated him. These noblest of Americans at risk, and by the putrid evil of a drug lord at that! He wanted to see the slimy son-of-a-bitch who would try to lay a hand on any of these men! He squirmed in his chair as he wrestled with his aroused truculence. And his fear. He wanted to gather the committee in with a sweep of protective guardianship but feared that his outrage was already too evident in the flush crossing his face.

"It's an upsetting thought, isn't it? One that Americans aren't used to," Pontalbas offered sympathetically.

Cantrelle looked at him. This man, young as he was, had dignity, even majesty about him. He felt ashamed of his own smallness on display before the calm and graceful courage of this patrician nobleman. No wonder Seymour wanted to keep him as member of his faculty.

"It must have been very difficult for you to lose your father as you did," Cantrelle offered respectfully, even contritely, as he wrestled with his outrage at the thought that this wondrous gathering of noble scholars, this consummate committee, was itself in danger, and, moreover, from the vilest of criminals! No way! Absolutely no way!

"For me, a personal and private loss; for my country and my people, a great tragedy. But he would now perhaps be hopeful in view of what has come in the wake of his death," Pontalbas assured.

For a moment Cantrelle had the distinct sense that he was being consoled not only over the death of Pontalbas' father, but over his now grasped recognition of the committee's mortal vulnerability. This young man's sense of noblesse was colossal. Maybe that's what made him initially seem older than he was. The contrast with what he saw in the typical American of similar age, those young adults of driven mercantile and materialist mentality, was compelling, not to mention how even our seasoned leaders compared. He assumed it was the difference between mature and immature concepts of freedom, as he had for years so often wailed. At this moment the difference was being arrayed before him, and he now recognized himself also to be among the failed. He nodded almost imperceptibly as he looked into Pontalbas' calm face. He knew everything Pontalbas said was heartfelt, genuine, and true. He then slowly scanned the quietly attentive committee, taking in each member as though checking off a mental roster. He did it soberly as he wondered if he would ever see these men again as he was seeing them tonight. Soon he and they would return to their separate worlds, they to re-convene sometime again, somewhere else. But what about him? It was too lonely to consider.

"President Pontalbas, I want to thank you for what you've said to me. It's helped me see some things," he managed through his preoccupation.

"Dr. Cantrelle, I assure you the pleasure has been mine," he smiled in return. With that he glanced at his watch and announced, "I really must be off, and with your permission, gentlemen," he gestured to Cantrelle and to the committee, Burleson nodding in acknowledgment, "I have to catch a plane, as you Americans say to justify your haste," he added merrily as he rose. Words of farewell were murmured among the committee members in turn.

"President Pontalbas," Cantrelle called above the tightness in his throat.

"Yes, Dr. Cantrelle?" he replied as he looked back to Cantrelle, who had risen.

"Good luck, Mr. President," he wished.

"Thank you, Dr. Cantrelle," Pontalbas accepted with the hint of a quick bow. He then turned, approached Burleson, who also rose, shook hands cordially, and left.

He waited until Pontalbas' footsteps faded and then resumed his seat. Silence accumulated as several adjusted themselves in their chairs. Markman stretched. Burleson, back in his chair, quickly checked a note pad. A car engine started up in the distance and then faded. After a moment, as though at a signal, they all returned their attention to his presence.

"Well, gentlemen, where do we go from here?" he invited, awkwardly.

"Actually, Dr. Cantrelle, *we* can't go any farther at all. We've told you everything we think you should know, and certainly you've surmised certain things as well. So it's come to the point you must decide where *you* go from here," Burleson returned. "Also, we cannot presume to tell you how to proceed beyond this point in your own thinking. That's yours and yours alone."

So he was right. He *was* alone. Quite alone. And soon to be much moreso, he suspected.

"I had estimated that you—this committee, I mean—would have some concern about that TV special scheduled next week, but in view of what you've explained to me tonight it might be better if we all . . . ." he began.

"Dr. Cantrelle," Burleson interrupted, "of course we have concern about how you'll manage that responsibility, but we thought it best first to have you see the fuller dimensions of that responsibility. Hence this meeting tonight. How you proceed from here will have to be a product of your best understanding, and not the result of threat or coercion from others. That also was our ruling and one which was quite easy to make since it follows so logically from the very premise of the committee's purpose. You see, it's now all in your hands."

He did see. They were giving him the same choice, so to speak, as was being given to the drug addicts, and he, like they, could decide as he was capable, and fit. He lowered his eyes in a vacant gaze and spoke.

"I think I'm going to need a little time," he mumbled, though he already knew what he had to do. How to do it was the problem.

"Of course, Dr. Cantrelle. But for the moment if there's anything else you wish to know, please say so and we'll answer your questions as best we can," Burleson assured.

"No, thank you, gentlemen. You've been more helpful than I can ever say. But I *will* ask that you forgive my rudeness earlier this evening. I truly did not know any better," he beseeched contritely.

He heard the moment of ensuing silence as mute recognizance of his regret.

"Tush, Dr. Cantrelle," Burleson resumed lightly, "we enjoyed having you. I fear that our long-awaited chat rather evolved into more than either of us had anticipated. I hope you're not too tired for your trip back home," he solicited graciously as he rose from his chair.

"Not at all, Dr. Burleson. The night air is bracing, especially this time of year," he returned, picking up on the exchange of amenities as he rose.

"Thank you so much for coming," Markman offered as he reached over for a parting handshake.

"Same here," Foster echoed. Then Weinroth, and so on through Alberti, Malloy, and Horlick.

He tried to reply to all but his acknowledgment soon became collective as the handshakes followed in rapid succession. Burleson waited to be last, and then took Cantrelle's hand in his.

"I think this was good for all of us, Dr. Cantrelle, and we thank you for your forbearance. Yes, it will take time, and luck be with you," he said warmly. He then shifted and, with the twinkle back in his eye, suggested, "I'm sure you can find your way out as you manage to forgive me for not showing you to the door. I have to sit right down and scribble some minutes, you know."

"The scourge of committee life," Cantrelle offered in step. "Good night, gentlemen," he replied.

The members, all standing, echoed the farewell as he walked away from the group toward the door. He would never forget this room, but he didn't want to savor its flavor openly while they watched him leave. He opened the door and stepped out into the long corridor that led to the lobby. As he walked toward the lobby he felt himself leave one world and re-enter another. Already the trailing world was beginning to fall back into a distancing haze and he quickened his pace to carry as much as he could of its contents forward into the world he was re-entering, much like one quickly recites a dream upon waking in an effort to fix its contents in the conscious state. The sharp report of his footsteps on the parquet floor of the lobby echoed the airy emptiness of this wing of the building and he almost raced to the front door which would open upon the prospect of a darker though more familiar world. He pulled open the massive door and stepped out on the landing. Dusk had deepened into night and the street lights pierced the darkness as kindly beacons. The air was decidedly cooler than earlier, the weather front having moved through just as suspected. He inhaled a deep draught as he moved down the walk toward the parking area. In his approach he noted that the stretch limousine was gone. Pontalbas, he surmised. As he neared his car the scene of the library rushed back to mind and with it once again the feeling of respectful, even reverent awe that had descended upon him as each of those magnificent people in turn added to the understanding he only grudgingly allowed. He envied Pontalbas' confederate status with the committee and marveled that so young a Head of State had gone so far so quickly in such perilous times. Vision and ability, without doubt, he acknowledged sportingly as he reached to open his car door. He then settled himself into the familiar seat behind the familiar steering wheel. He switched on the engine, snapped on the lights, and then declared himself sufficiently on familiar turf to begin thinking about what he should do. He knew he could never feel happy with any decision he made under someone else's sway; it had to come to him only when and where he was absolutely sure of his place, and often enough that was in one of his cars. As he pulled out of the parking area and drove off the grounds to enter the boulevard he felt a huge tug of regret over leaving the committee behind in that sacred library. After all, they were the occasion of his elevation, for that moment anyway, to the rarest world in man's ken, the world of transcendent understanding. Yet, those gifted men, their vast learning, and their glorious committee he now knew to be in genuine danger, a danger perhaps akin to that attendant upon all glory. He meant to hold on to as much of his memory of the committee as he could, like keeping postcards of the Sphinx or the Parthenon, though, similarly, there was no conceivable way of ever forgetting the living experience, or what it spoke to him. As he drove along the familiar streets toward the entrance of the throughway he checked street signs, buildings, and trees to remind himself where he was. His mind was still reeling from where it had been and from what had happened, which seemed all the more uncanny, counterposed as it was to all these standard, daily particulars of his existence. They had not changed, these streets, trees, and buildings; but yet they were now somehow different. He could not perceive them, not tonight anyway, as he had before, and there was likely more of that to come, he was sure. How was he now to approach the TV special, for precise example? The traffic was noticeably lighter, seemingly to give him more range for thought, and that minor observation prompted him to look at the clock on the dashboard. He was back to telling time. A good sign. It was nine-fifteen. Less than two hours. It had all taken place in less than two hours of compacted, pure Time! He had never known that kind of time before—complete, total, pure. His time was always blended, ragged, restless, and he now felt its ordinary urgency beginning to return. Best to soothe the urgency with some music, Time's tonal structuring. He switched on the radio just as he entered the ramp to the throughway.

When he reached cruising speed on the throughway the sense of being again free to think became distinct, as though he had broken free of a numbing paralysis. The car's speed somehow brought him back to perspective. He had discovered—no, learned—so much, and he couldn't tell anybody. What had he learned? Nothing more than the means and method of changing history, or, as Foster might say, regaining the purpose of history. Hundreds of thousands of people to perish in the process. It was monstrous, and it was magnificent. He felt weighed down by the burden of its meaning, and yet he felt elevated, even giddy, at having touched what he knew would be the closest he would ever come to meeting with the divine, at least the divine here on earth. Everything else now seemed so paltry. His work, his life, everything he had known and treasured had now been rendered irrevocably simple and small. How did Burleson manage the ordinaries of life with such a show of zest while knowing the larger truths of it all? The stuff of rulers, probably. How was he himself going to manage Rosten and being on TV next week? How would Burleson handle it? How did Burleson handle the graduation? Now there was a clue! Certainly he couldn't proceed as though he were blowing the lid off some vile federal crime and subsequent coverup. No, he now knew too much for such simple heroics. Odd that the more one knew the less room there was for opinion. Could he ever again have an opinion, an essentially personal and independent one? He knew he could never do anything that might put Pontalbas, Burleson, and the committee at greater risk. He would defend them in any way he could. That was a kind of opinion. He would have to downplay the exposé aspect of the TV Special and speak more to the efforts of people, sometimes tragic efforts, to address the ills of society and the resulting cross-purposes which so often occurred to cancel out our better efforts. Like Clay. How do you like being considered a cancellation, ole buddy, he grinned. He knew Clay would have gloried in the opportunity to meet with the committee, and would not have felt so abashed as he, meek Frank Cantrelle, did. God, he wished Clay were here so he could tell him about it. But, then, would he have been *able* to tell him? More to the point, would he have met with the committee at all if Clay were still alive? Probably not; Clay's death had been his ticket in. He noticed the music: Mahler's Symphony Number One—the "Titan." The boys at the studio were right on: enlightening freedom, exuberance, bright hope. His exit was just ahead, the road sign said, and he found himself confronted with the question of whether to go straight home or not. He didn't feel ready to re-enter his family, for to do so would bring final closure to the evening's epic. He would go to the quiet remove of his office for a few minutes to give more of his thoughts a chance to fall into place. As it was, everything seemed so obvious now and becoming more so by the minute: the ready availability of federal funding for setting up state hospices for the Blush patients, the rigid control over Blush research, the narrow and limited official reaction to the problem, and so forth. He was now on the exit ramp bearing down on the road that would take him past his home and to his office. As he turned on to his road he thought of all the people who labored and worried and suffered, unaware of how ordained it all was and how their rôles could never be more than what they presently were. He noted that the ripening cornfields to the left and right were now more like coarse, dark blankets covering the land for sleep. He, too, felt tired. Everybody was tired. Everybody worked so hard, and things never changed. He thought of Jess and Martha. They might never know how futile it would all remain. It had already been decided that their efforts would fail, though they could not stop trying. He felt so sorry for them, and so guilty because he couldn't help. And Helen. And Landon. Even Dieter. They all had to keep trying, though it was all completely decided. There had been a ruling, he now knew.

The homes and storefronts told him he was back in his element. The intersection for a left turn on to his home was the next stoplight ahead. He caught it green and proceeded straight on to his office. And to his wall. This time of all times the wall was truly vital. He suspected that such had probably been behind his thinking all along when he went through the motion of deliberating about whether or not to go directly home. He had to know what the wall would say about all this. He hoped something about how he was now coming to regard Clay's death. It had become apparent to him that since leaving the committee he thought of Clay's death less as an unpunished crime and more as a determinative event, regardless of the who and how of its perpetration, and Clay had somehow returned in his old rôle as an enabling force, not so much as a tragic hero laid to rest. He wondered how Clay would feel about this change in attitude. He figured he'd find out in short order as he noted his darkened office straight ahead.

He turned into the parking area and stopped near the walk to the front door. When he stepped out of the car he stood for a moment and listened to the stillness. It was only a little over two hours ago he had left this peacefulness, though at the time he didn't accord it so. Now he understood just how simple was the peacefulness he'd left behind. But now, for knowing it, it wasn't so peacefully his as it had been. Also, he was now partly somewhere else. Hence, there was nothing left to do but shrug, and he did so with wistful resignation, sort of like when visiting the ole college campus.

He walked quickly to the building, up the front steps, and opened the outer storm door, fishing in his pocket for the keys to the main door as he did so. He jiggled a key into the lock more by feel than by sight and creaked the door open. A vague fear swept though him as he stepped into the inky waiting room, though he assured himself that nothing would be hiding in the dark to accost him. Not any longer, anyway. He switched on the lights and his fear evaporated. He was wholesomely alone. The quiet of the office felt good. It was a reflective kind of quiet, and always seemed so after the day's work was done. Often he would savor a restful moment of it in silent, unbestirred solitude before leaving for home. He crossed the waiting room and walked up the hallway to his inner office, opened the door, and switched on the light. Everything was honestly as he left it. His chair was slighted rotated away from his desk as though it had been awaiting his return. The desk was clear, and even the ring calendar had been turned for tomorrow's date. He didn't remember doing that, but he knew he followed an automatic routine in leaving his office. He felt the impulse to explain to his office, as though it were a mute, loyal, companion, that he wasn't there actually to begin tomorrow's work. He then dropped into his chair and positioned himself, elbows on desk, chin on folded hands, and readied himself for the wall. He awaited the familiar shift in sensibility, that hint of swirling change of perspective, that particular something. But it didn't come. There wasn't even the faint flicker of approach. This time the wall did not change into that amorphous depth which consistently took him almost to knowing what he felt, or almost saw. The wall now seemed just a wall. It, too, had changed. Something wasn't there any longer. His disappointment was now verging on alarm, and he considered that, despite his readiness for some urgent wall gazing, simply too much had gone on tonight. And the sum of it was interfering with the channel. That might be it, and the problem was probably just temporary. Or was it?

"What do you think about that, Clay?" he heard himself say aloud. "Just when I need the god-damned thing to help me sort out what to do with Rosten—and even you—it goes on the blink. I guess I have to free-form it for a while. You see, old buddy, it comes down to this. I can't go on the air like a fire-brand reformer bent on avenging your death and destroying the evil of Blush. Not now, anyway. I think I can come up with something that might be acceptable to Rosten, even have it seem that his program is the main venue taking the bold initiative as it enables me, the junior participant, to consider things my meager and provincial world is now only daring to hear, and doing so only with great reluctance and mostly out of loyalty to your unfinished work. Rosten would probably like that. But you're the problem because I wouldn't want to do anything either of us could come to regret. Waddaya say?"

He heard nothing.

"Helen and your kids could also be a problem because they might think I faded in the stretch when I had led them to expect something better. Laura and my kids, too. Your status as a hero would increase as I took on more the appearance of a goat. How would you like that?"

Still nothing from the wall.

"You never were easy to please, Clay, and your being dead hasn't helped your disposition any. It probably would suit you if . . . ."

He was interrupted by the green flasher on the phone. Someone was calling him on his private line! A jolt of dread pierced him along with the realization that he had forgotten to call Laura when he arrived at the meeting! He just knew it was she calling!

"Dr. Cantrelle," he answered anxiously.

"Frank? Where have you been? I've been trying everywhere to get you!" Laura's frenzied words burst forth.

"I got an unexpected call about . . . about the TV program and I had to meet with someone about it. I called before I left but the line was busy. I meant to call again, but it slipped my mind," he accounted, quickly bringing himself to full upright. "What's wrong?"

"It's Todd. He's sick and I don't know what to do, Frank," she implored.

"Todd? Sick? What do you mean?" he lurched.

"He's flushed. I think he has a fever. He's in his room and he won't let me come near him, He keeps his head under the covers, laughing. Frank, I'm scared," she pleaded.

"How long has he been like that? How long, Laura?" he demanded in rising terror.

"I don't know! His friends brought him home about half and hour ago. They wouldn't tell me anything! I hadn't seen him all evening because when he came home in the afternoon we had an argument about his skipping school. I told him that I'd told you about his skipping and that you were going to talk to him tonight. He stormed out of the house and I didn't see him again until they brought him home! Frank, it's not what I think, is it? Please, Frank!" she begged.

"I'll be right home, Laura!" he said firmly, and hung up.

He sat stunned, not breathing as he stared at what he knew awaited him. He silently pleaded with the wall. But the wall remained distantly mute. Then, in a convulsion of sobs, he threw his face into his hands. He tried to speak to himself but the sobs tore at his lungs. The tears ran through his fingers as he thought of how often he had promised to talk to Todd—Todd, his little boy lost—only to learn tonight, *this* night, he and his son, like the empty wall, now had nothing at all to say to each other. He sobbed until the spasm passed, and then, between gasps, returned to the wall.

"Well, Clay, I guess you heard," he managed in words broken by choking tears. "Now be a good buddy and stick with me for awhile, please. I'll need to talk to someone about this . . . someone I don't have to explain things to . . . things like auto-immune reactions, big and small . . . things like why we do what we do . . . and things like knowing there's a special providence in the fall of a sparrow . . . . Remember? Remember who said that, ole pal? Another poor fool who knew more than he could ever understand . . . . Please keep in touch, ole buddy. Gotta go now," he anguished as he stood up, taking one last look at the silent wall as he stood before it. He then switched off the light and left the room to enter the empty, hushed waiting area of the outer office. He sensed a sympathy hovering in the air now that the waiting room was so much closer to his own need. He stood at the front door and looked around for a moment at the chairs, the tables, the magazines. They were so kind, so patient. And then, bracing himself against his sobs, opened the door, switched off the lights, and stepped out into the darkness.